Kirby's Lessons for Falling (in Love)

LAURA GAO

An Imprint of HarperCollinsPublishers

HarperAlley is an imprint of HarperCollins Publishers.

Kirby's Lessons for Falling (in Love)
Copyright © 2025 by Laura Gao
All rights reserved. Manufactured in Johor, Malaysia.
No part of this book may be used or reproduced in any manner whatsoever without written permission except in the case of brief quotations embodied in critical articles and reviews.
For information address HarperCollins Children's Books, a division of HarperCollins Publishers, 195 Broadway, New York, NY 10007.
www.harperalley.com

Library of Congress Control Number: 2024943820
ISBN 978-0-06-306779-0 (pbk) — ISBN 978-0-06-306780-6

Typography by Catherine Lee

24 25 26 27 28 COS 10 9 8 7 6 5 4 3 2 1
First Edition

Everyone's first step is a spectacle.

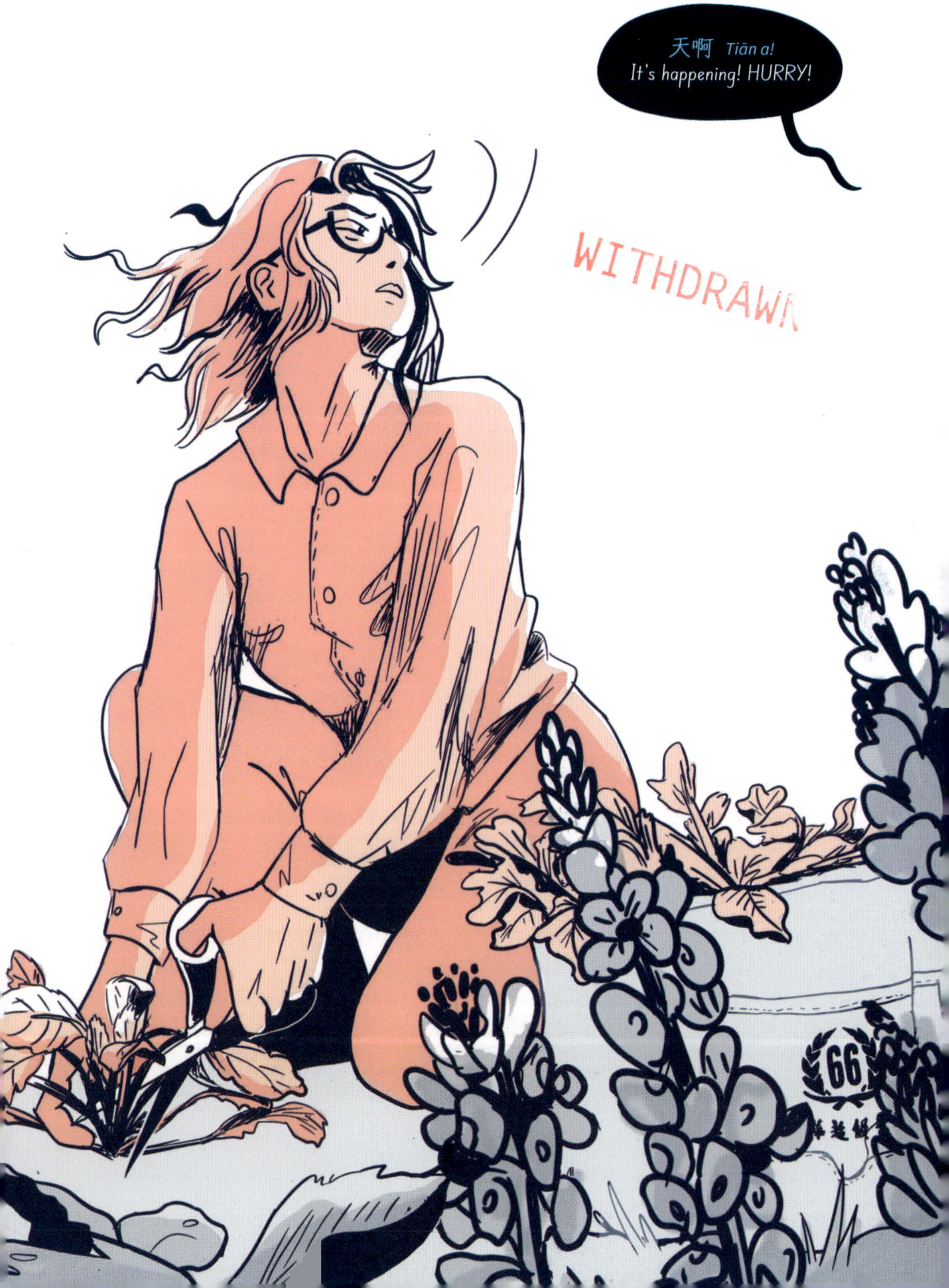

天啊 Tiān a!
It's happening! HURRY!
66

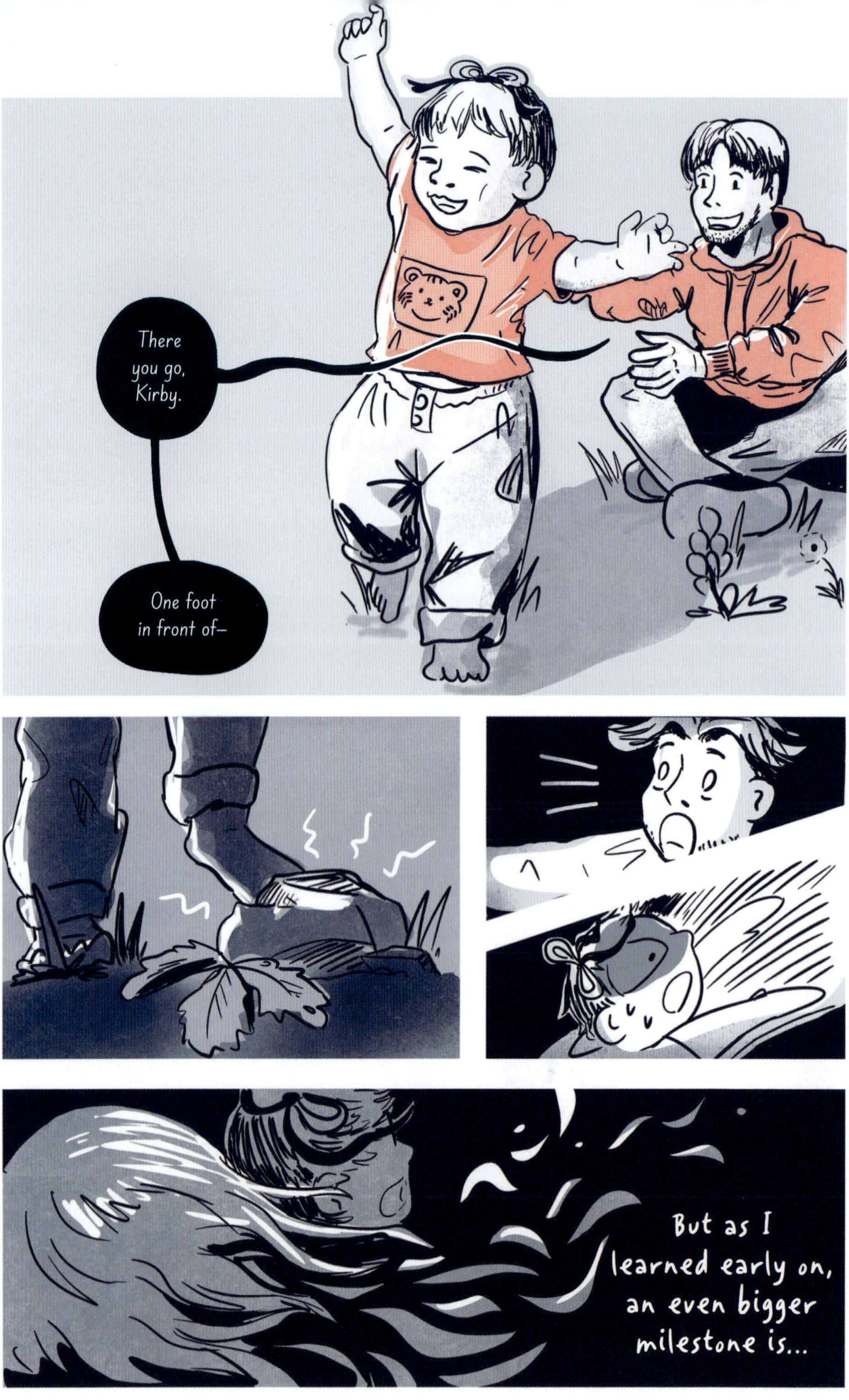
There you go, Kirby.
One foot in front of–
But as I learned early on, an even bigger milestone is...

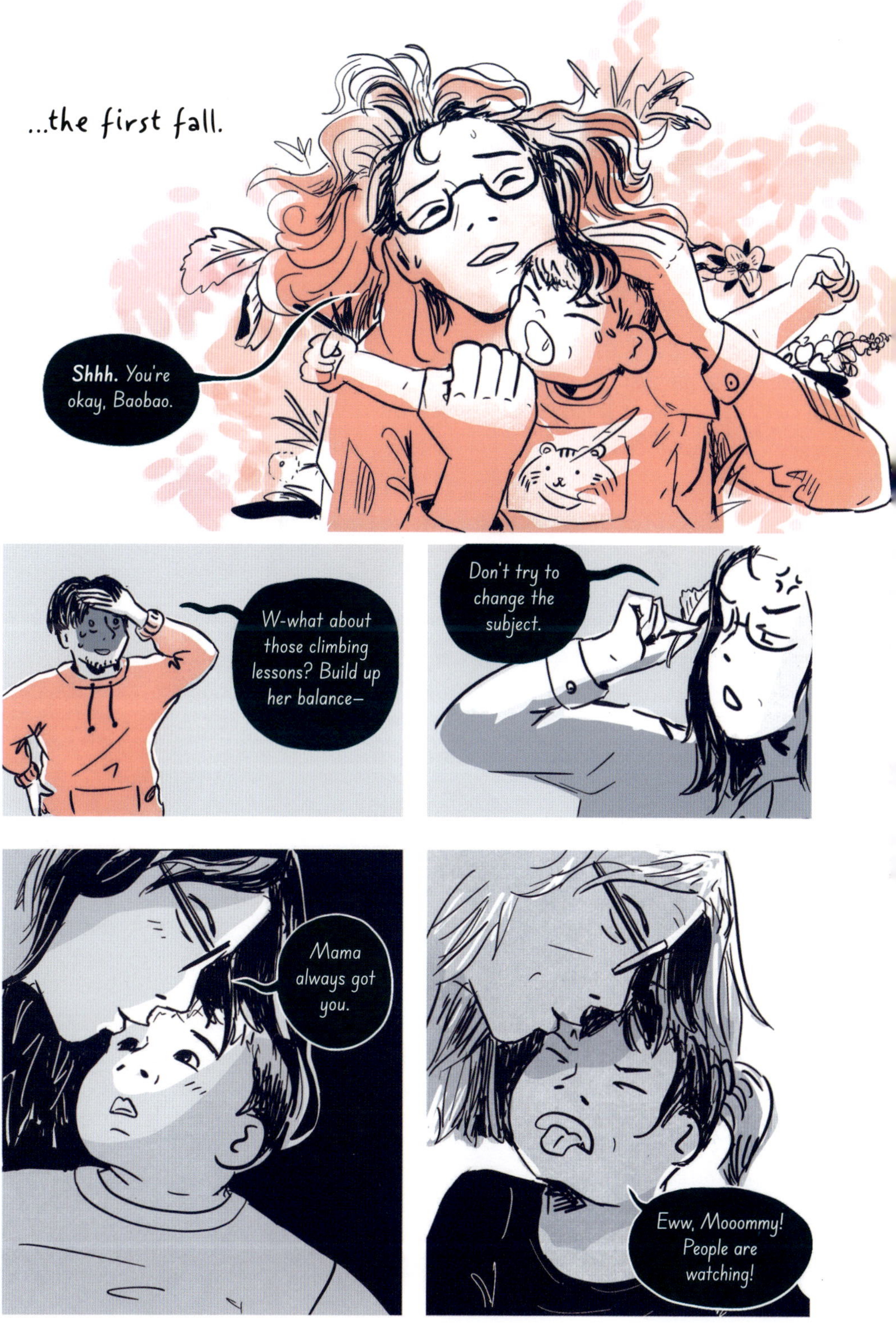
...the first fall.
Shhh. You're okay, Baobao.
W-what about those climbing lessons? Build up her balance—
Don't try to change the subject.
Mama always got you.
Eww, Mooommy! People are watching!

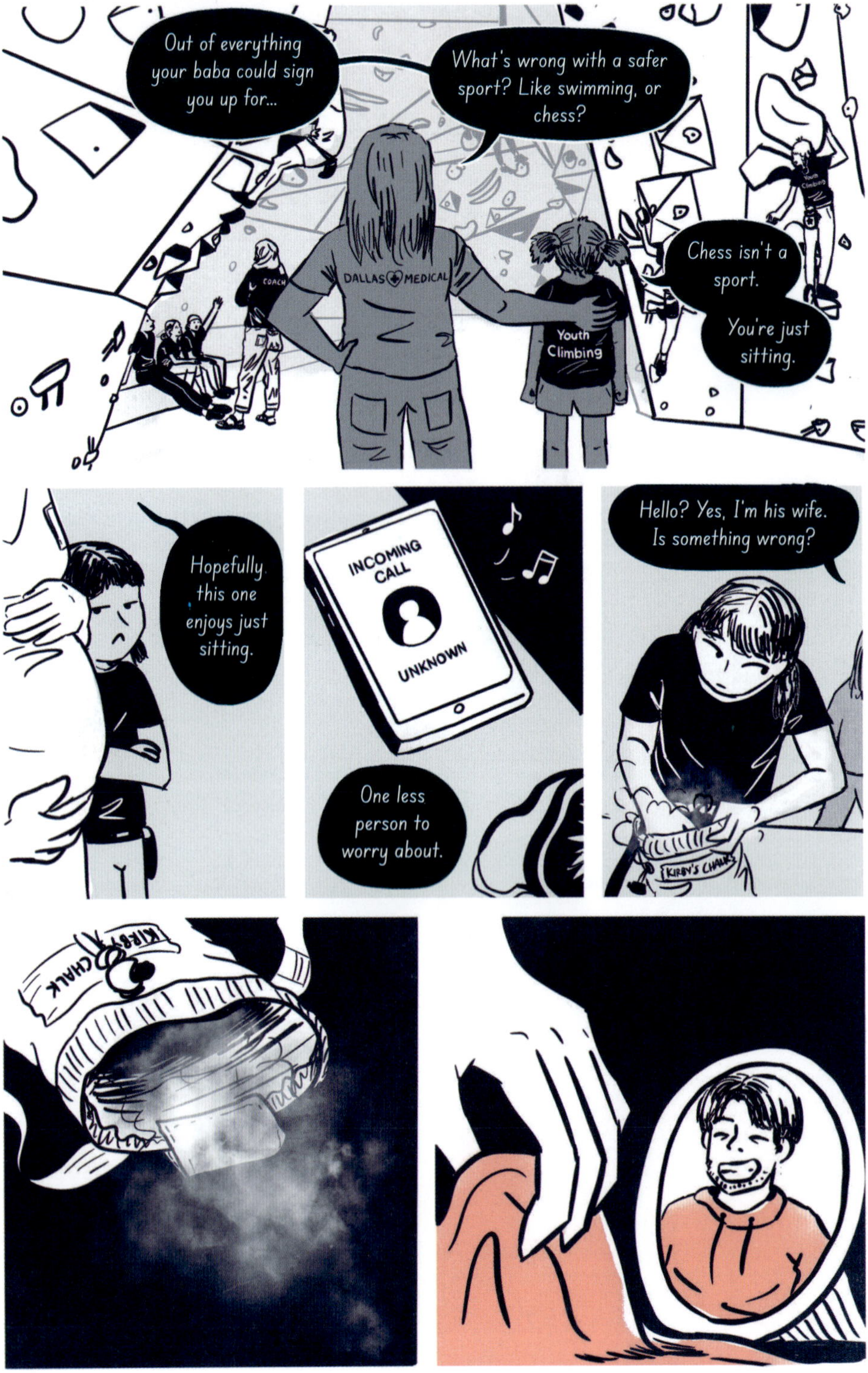
Out of everything your baba could sign you up for...
What's wrong with a safer sport? Like swimming, or chess?
DALLAS MEDICAL
COACH
Youth Climbing
Chess isn't a sport.
You're just sitting.
Hopefully this one enjoys just sitting.
INCOMING CALL
UNKNOWN
One less person to worry about.
Hello? Yes, I'm his wife. Is something wrong?
KIRBY'S CHALK
KIRBY CHALK

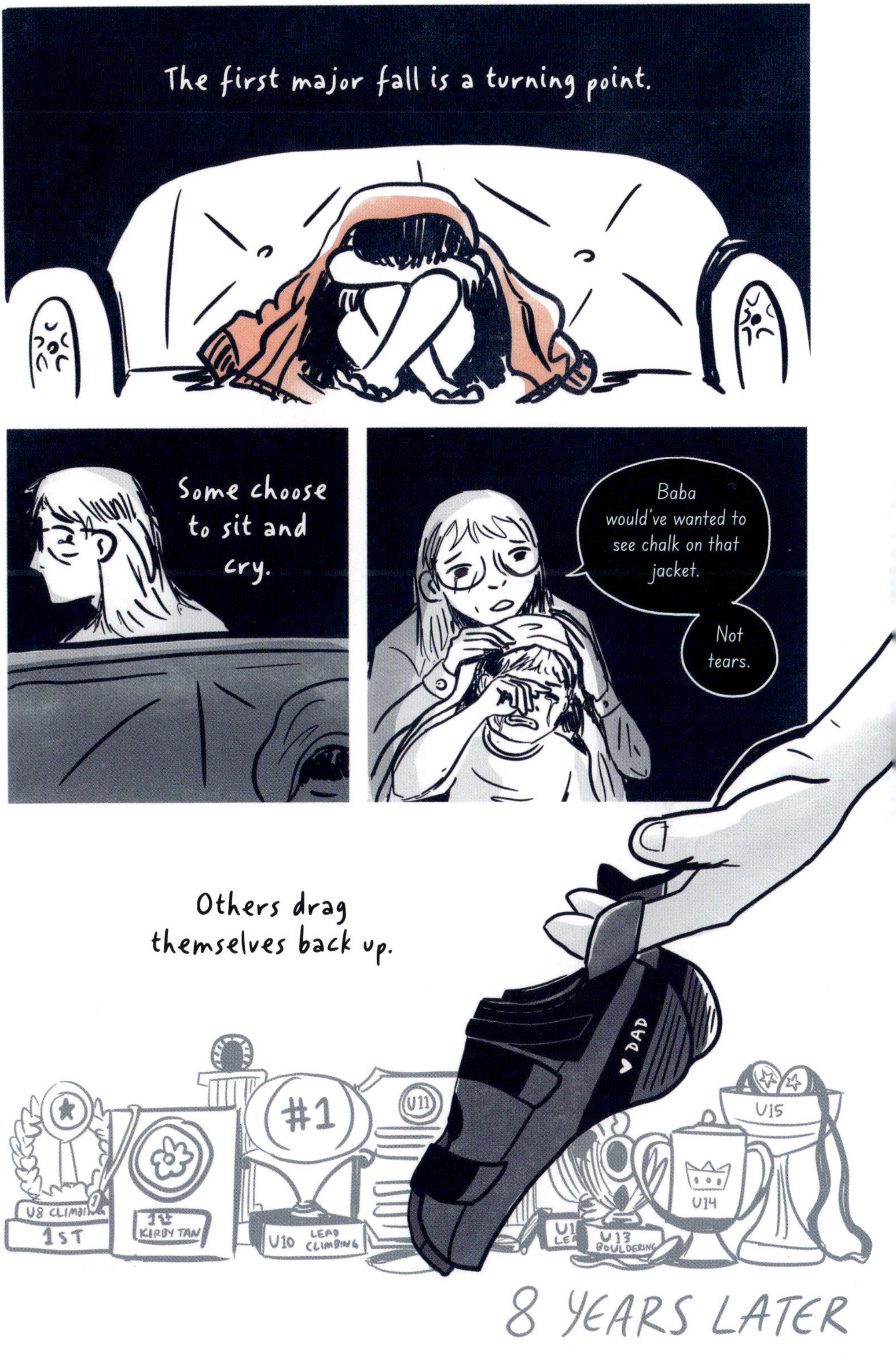
The first major fall is a turning point.
Some choose to sit and cry.
Baba would've wanted to see chalk on that jacket.
Not tears.
Others drag themselves back up.
#1
1ST
KIRBY TAN
U10 LEAD CLIMBING
U11
DAD
U13 BOULDERING
U14
U15
8 YEARS LATER

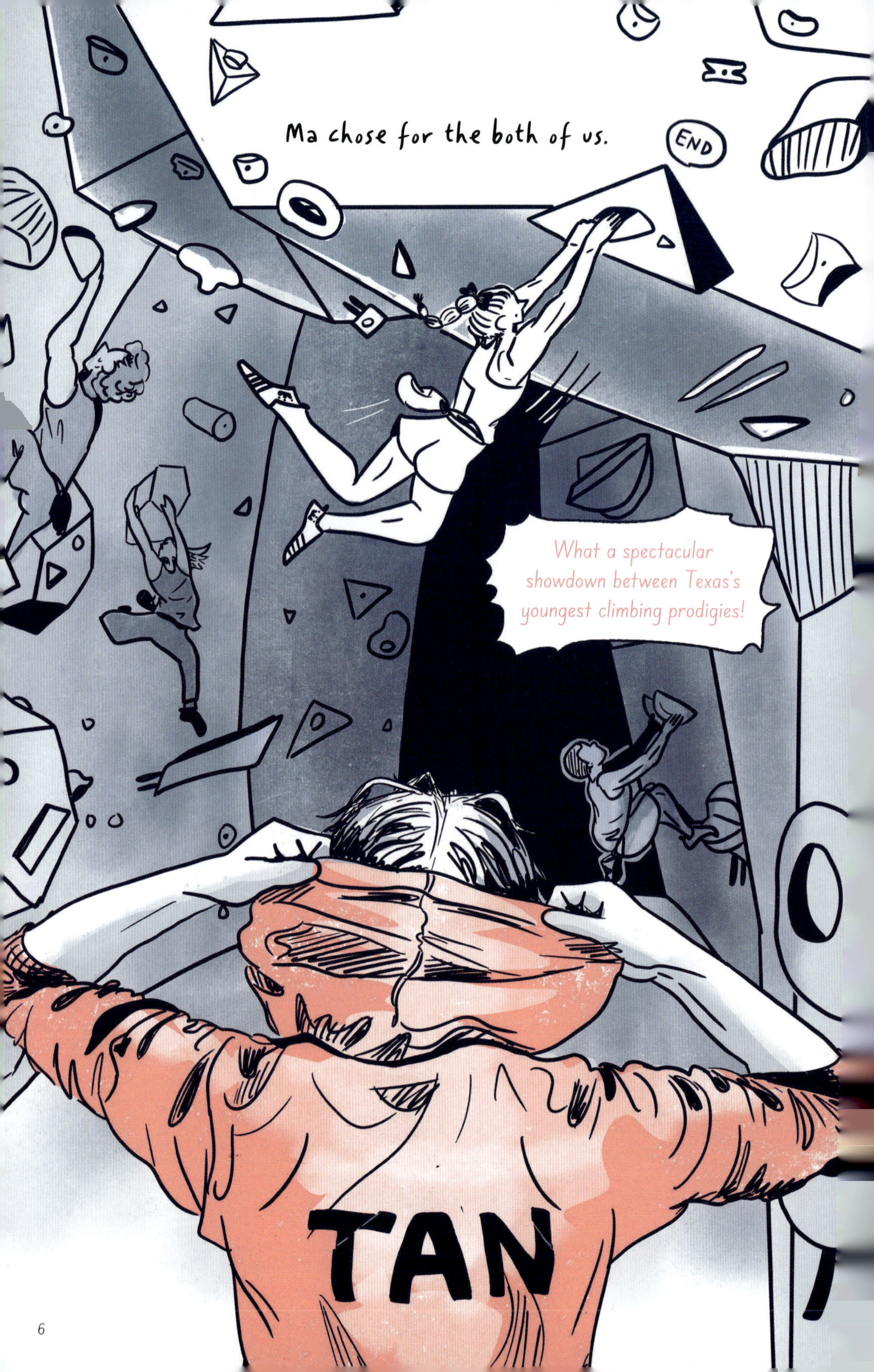
Ma chose for the both of us.
END
What a spectacular showdown between Texas's youngest climbing prodigies!
TAN

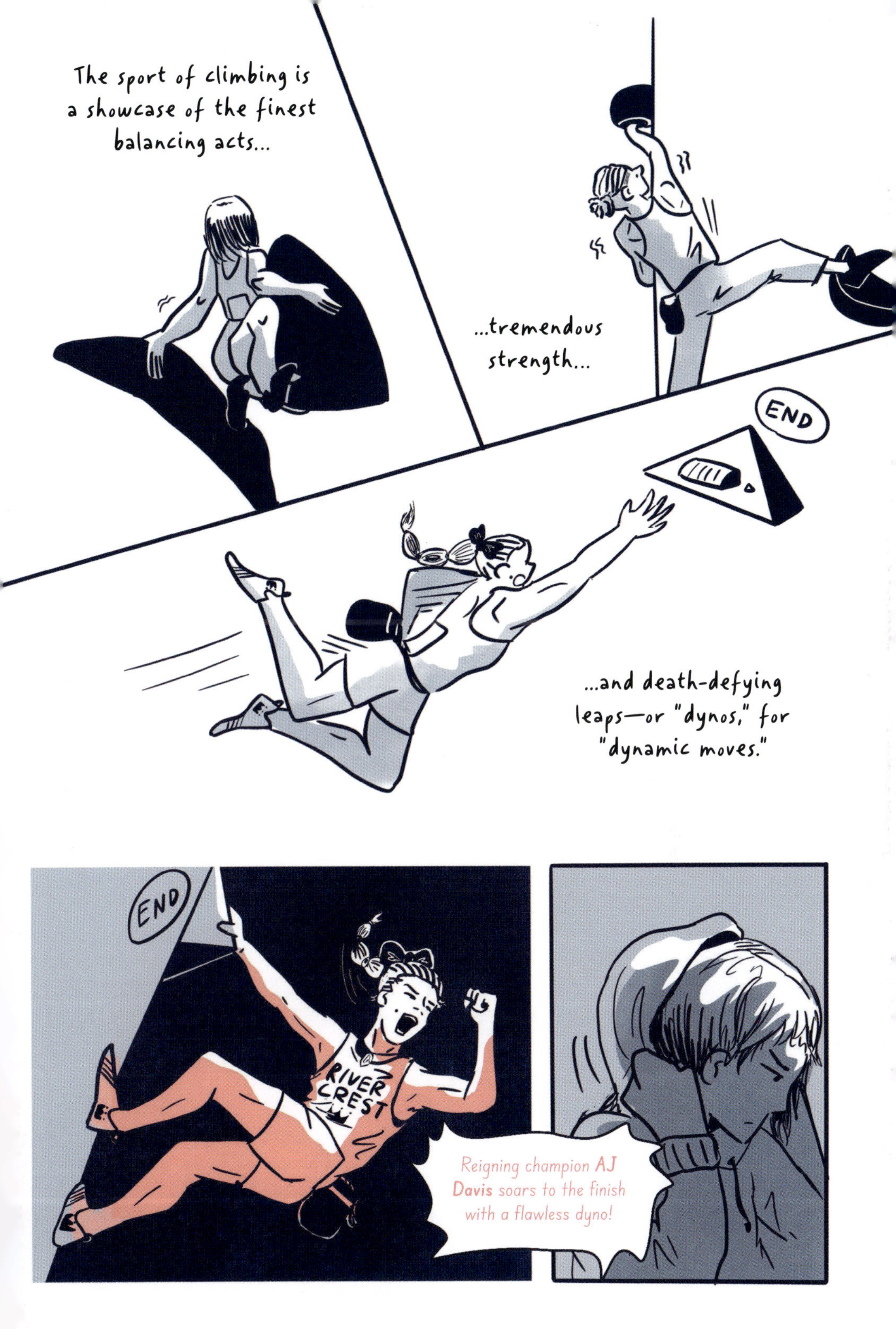
The sport of climbing is a showcase of the finest balancing acts...
...tremendous strength...
END
...and death-defying leaps—or "dynos," for "dynamic moves."
END
RIVER CREST
Reigning champion **AJ Davis** soars to the finish with a flawless dyno!

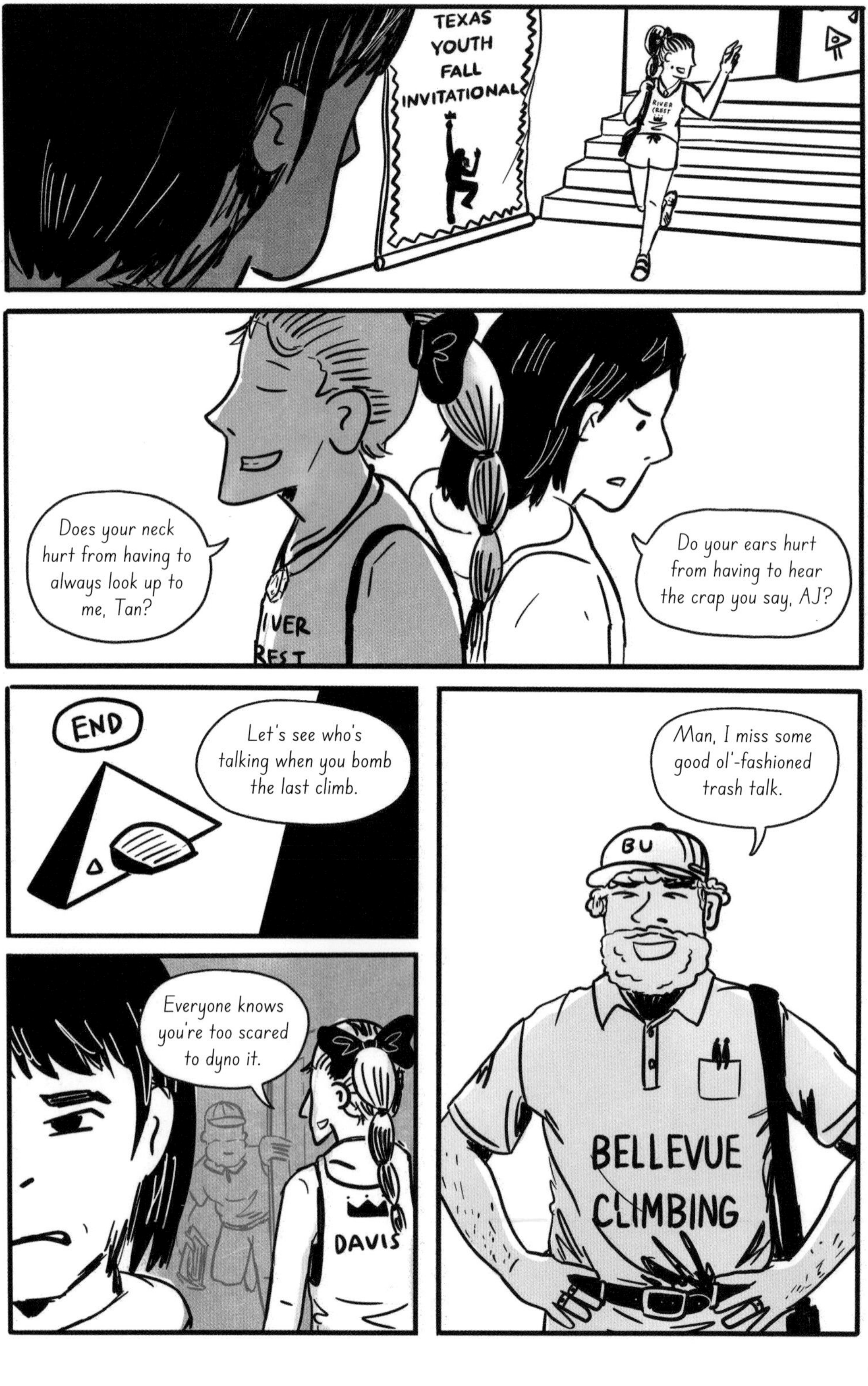
TEXAS YOUTH FALL INVITATIONAL
RIVER CREST
Does your neck hurt from having to always look up to me, Tan?
Do your ears hurt from having to hear the crap you say, AJ?
IVER REST
END
Let's see who's talking when you bomb the last climb.
Everyone knows you're too scared to dyno it.
DAVIS
Man, I miss some good ol'-fashioned trash talk.
BU
BELLEVUE CLIMBING

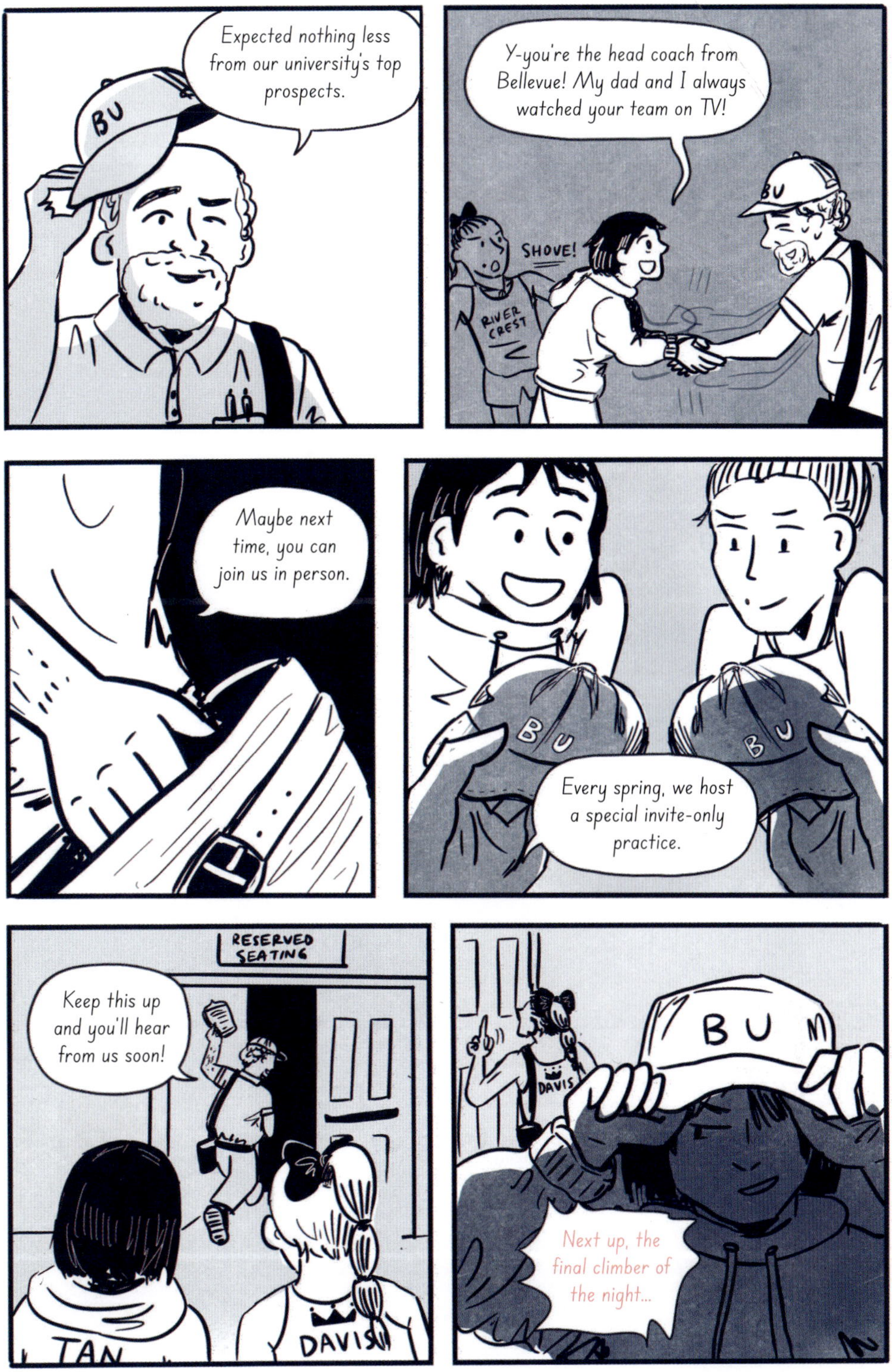
Expected nothing less from our university's top prospects.
BU
Y-you're the head coach from Bellevue! My dad and I always watched your team on TV!
BU
SHOVE!
RIVER CREST
Maybe next time, you can join us in person.
BU
BU
Every spring, we host a special invite-only practice.
RESERVED SEATING
Keep this up and you'll hear from us soon!
TAN
DAVIS
BU
DAVIS
Next up, the final climber of the night...

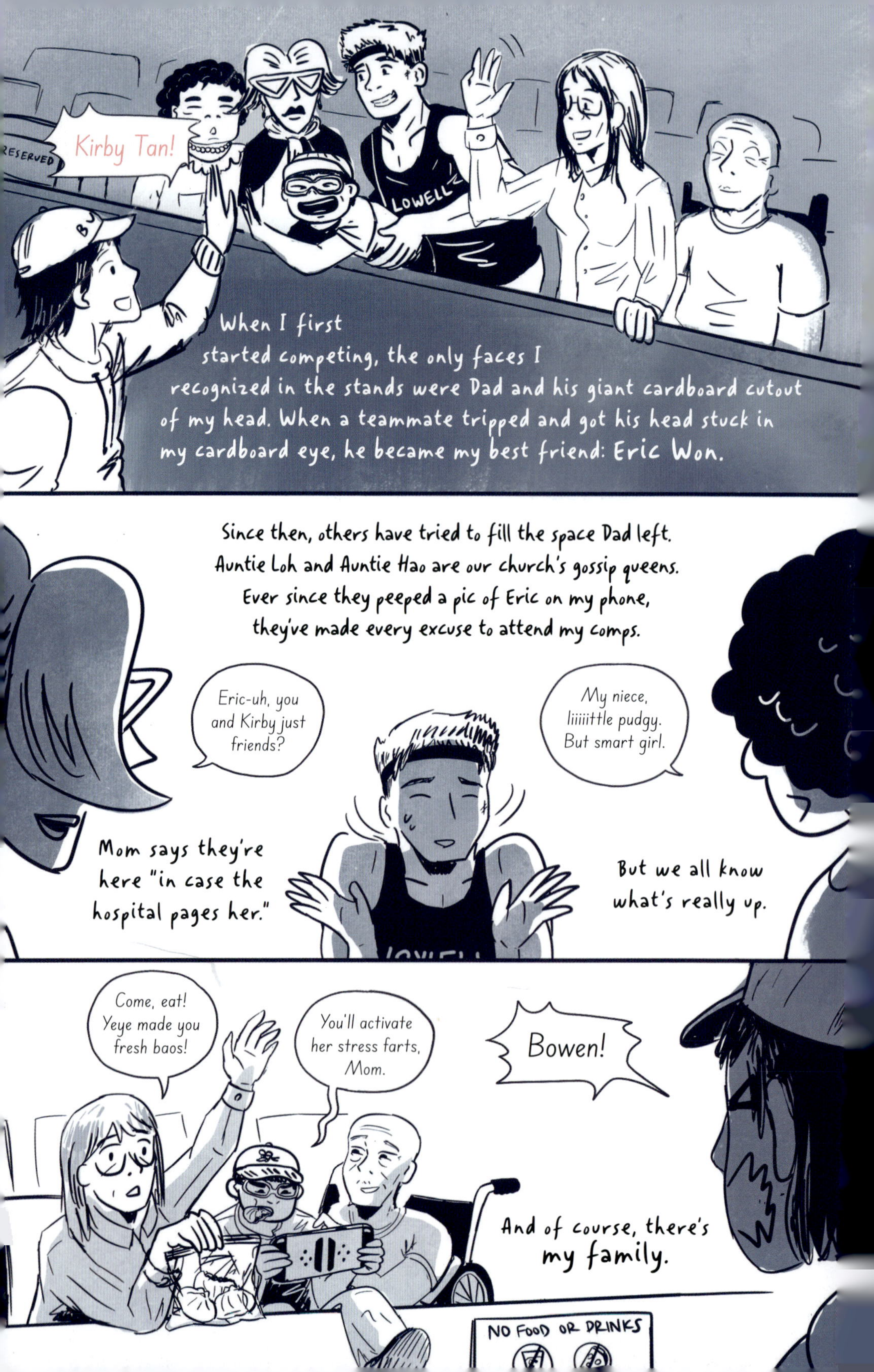

RESERVED
Kirby Tan!
BJ
LOWELL
When I first started competing, the only faces I recognized in the stands were Dad and his giant cardboard cutout of my head. When a teammate tripped and got his head stuck in my cardboard eye, he became my best friend: Eric Won.
Since then, others have tried to fill the space Dad left. Auntie Loh and Auntie Hao are our church's gossip queens. Ever since they peeped a pic of Eric on my phone, they've made every excuse to attend my comps.
Eric-uh, you and Kirby just friends?
My niece, liiiiittle pudgy. But smart girl.
Mom says they're here "in case the hospital pages her."
But we all know what's really up.
Come, eat! Yeye made you fresh baos!
You'll activate her stress farts, Mom.
Bowen!
And of course, there's my family.
NO FOOD OR DRINKS

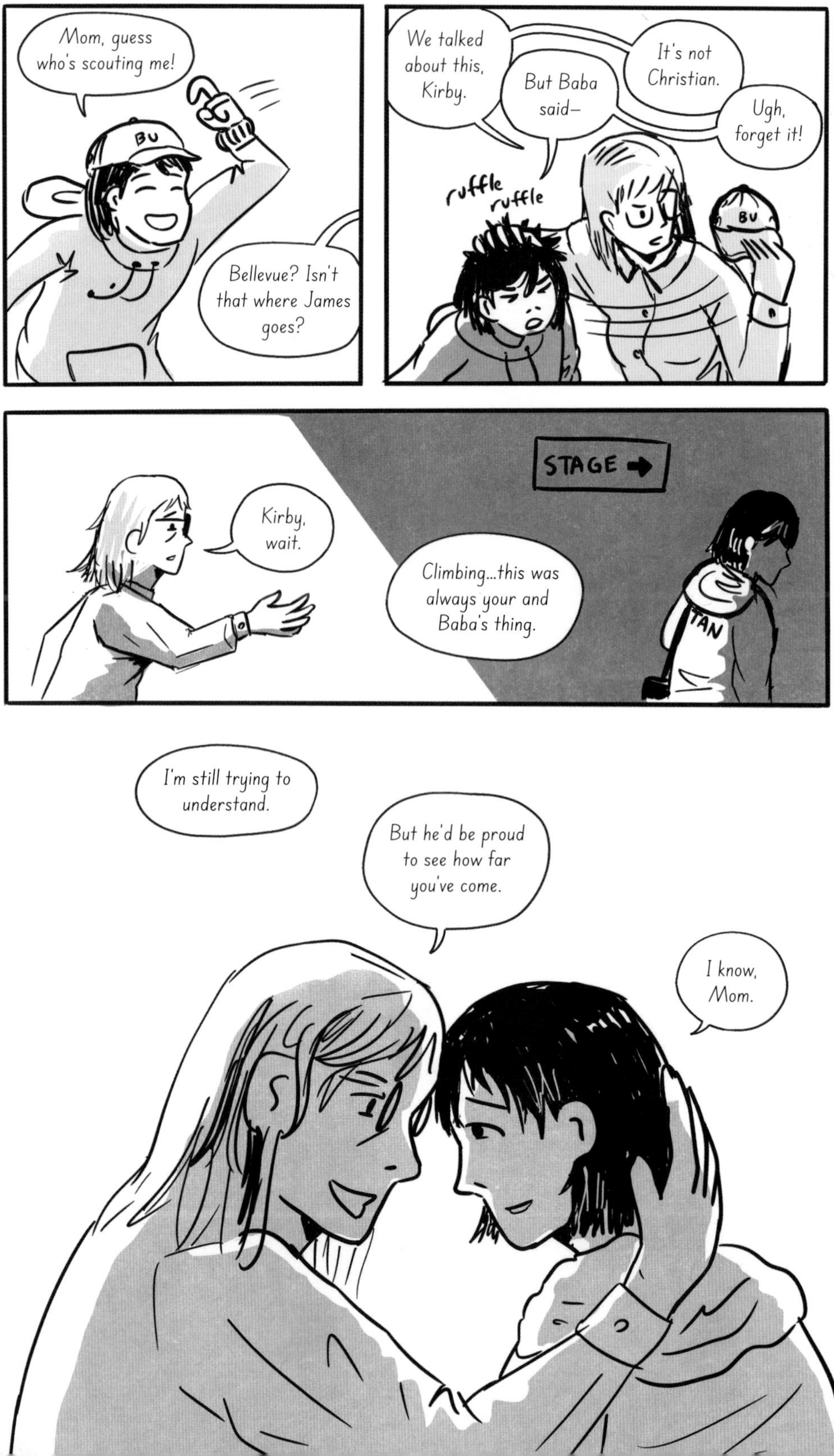
Mom, guess who's scouting me!
Bellevue? Isn't that where James goes?
We talked about this, Kirby.
But Baba said—
It's not Christian.
Ugh, forget it!
ruffle ruffle
BU
STAGE
Kirby, wait.
Climbing...this was always your and Baba's thing.
TAN
I'm still trying to understand.
But he'd be proud to see how far you've come.
I know, Mom.

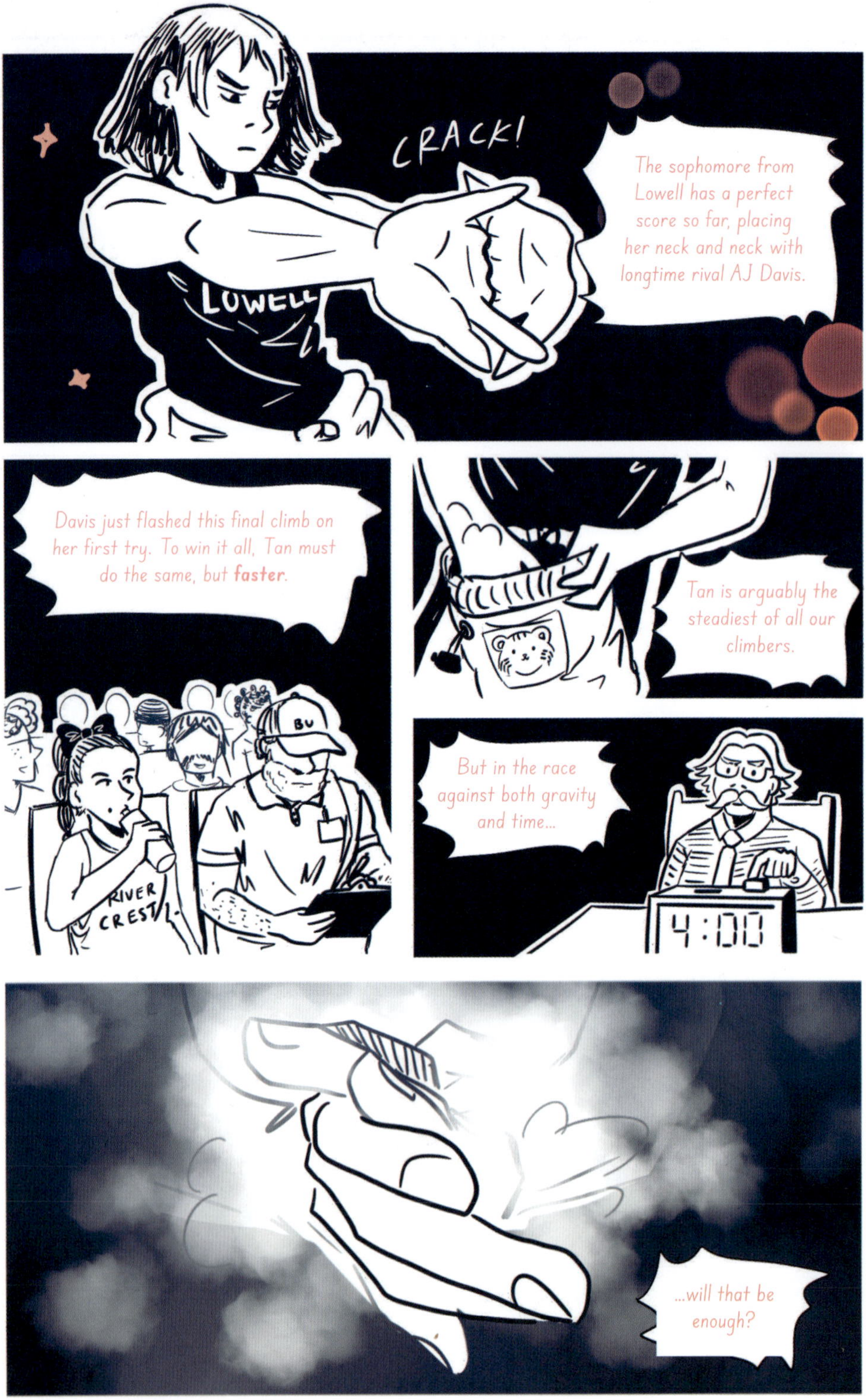
CRACK!
LOWELL
The sophomore from Lowell has a perfect score so far, placing her neck and neck with longtime rival AJ Davis.
Davis just flashed this final climb on her first try. To win it all, Tan must do the same, but **faster**.
Tan is arguably the steadiest of all our climbers.
RIVER CREST
BU
But in the race against both gravity and time...
4:00
...will that be enough?

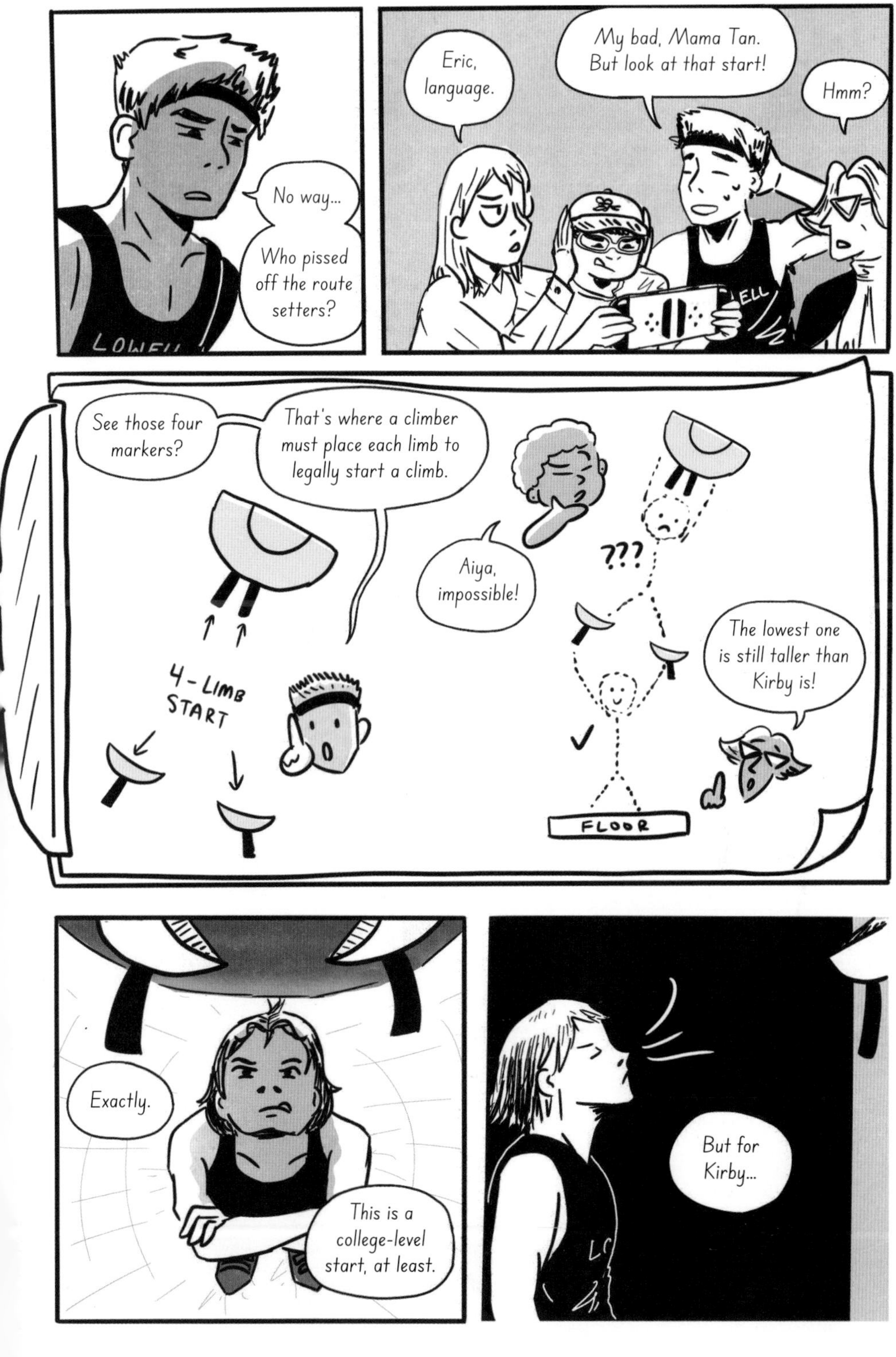
No way...
Who pissed off the route setters?
Eric, language.
My bad, Mama Tan. But look at that start!
Hmm?
See those four markers?
That's where a climber must place each limb to legally start a climb.
4-LIMB START
Aiya, impossible!
???
The lowest one is still taller than Kirby is!
FLOOR
Exactly.
This is a college-level start, at least.
But for Kirby...

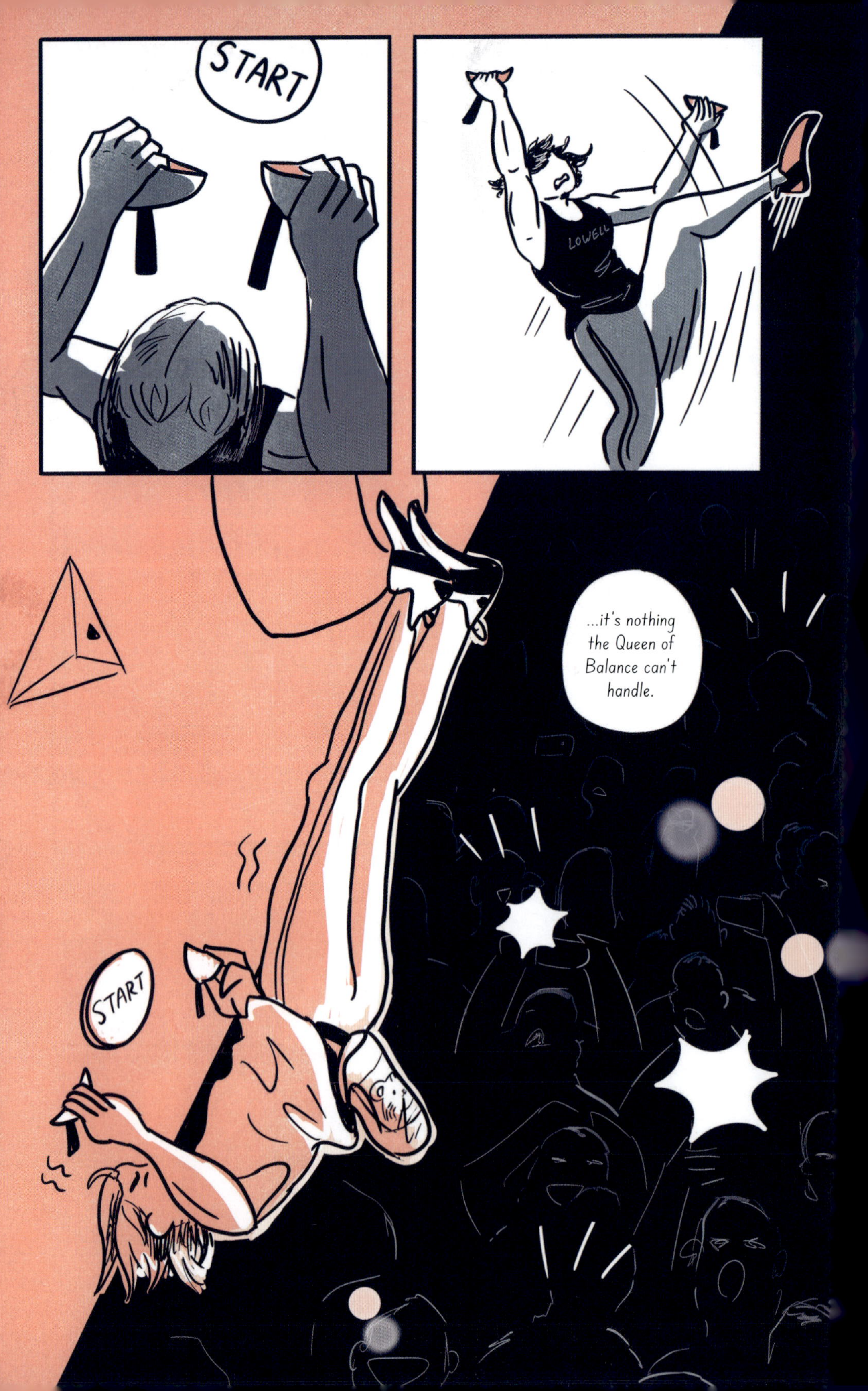
START
LOWELL
...it's nothing the Queen of Balance can't handle.
START

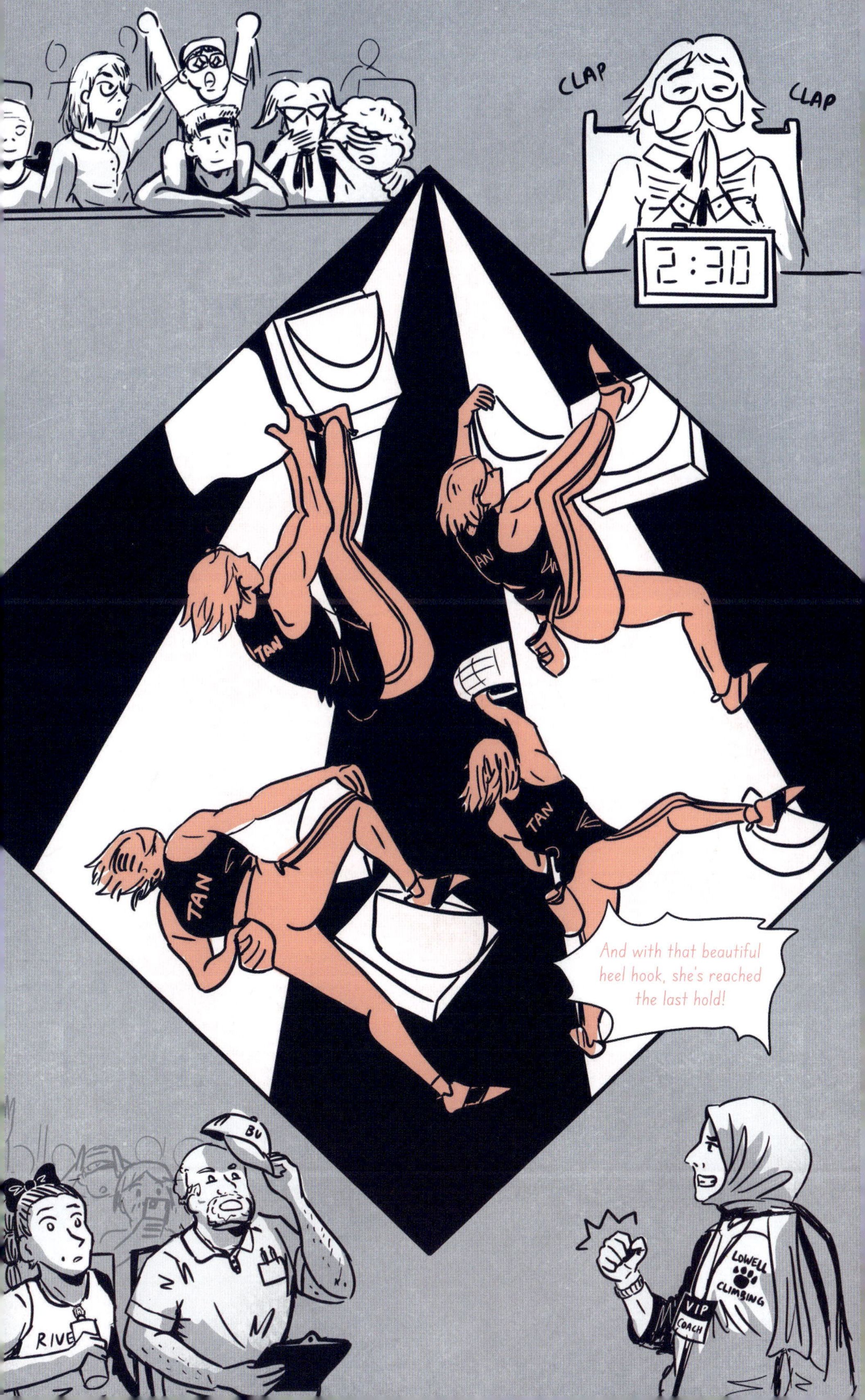
CLAP
CLAP
2:30
TAN
TAN
TAN
TAN
And with that beautiful heel hook, she's reached the last hold!
BU
RIVE
LOWELL CLIMBING
VIP COACH

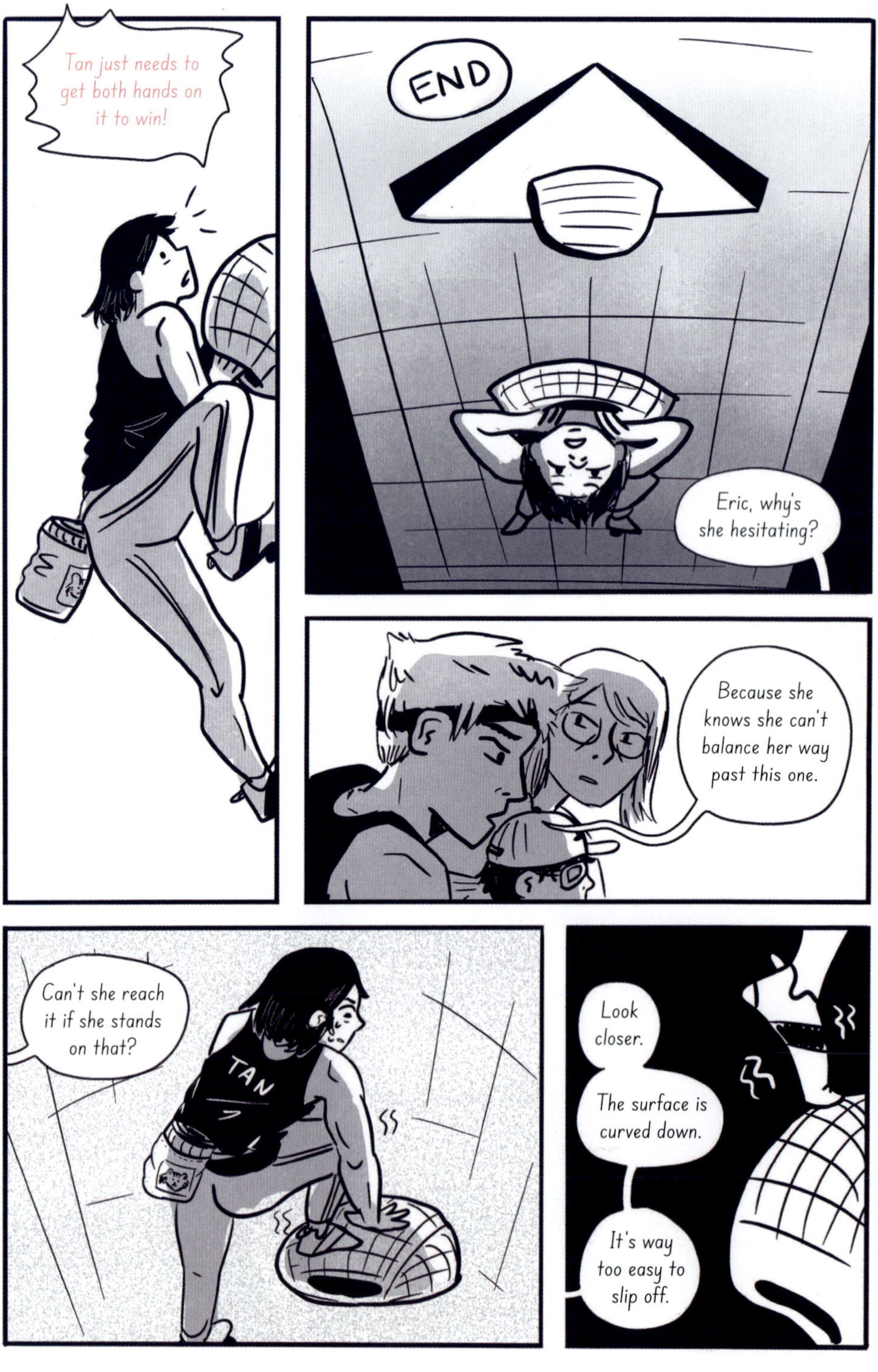

Tan just needs to get both hands on it to win!
END
Eric, why's she hesitating?
Because she knows she can't balance her way past this one.
Can't she reach it if she stands on that?
TAN
Look closer.
The surface is curved down.
It's way too easy to slip off.

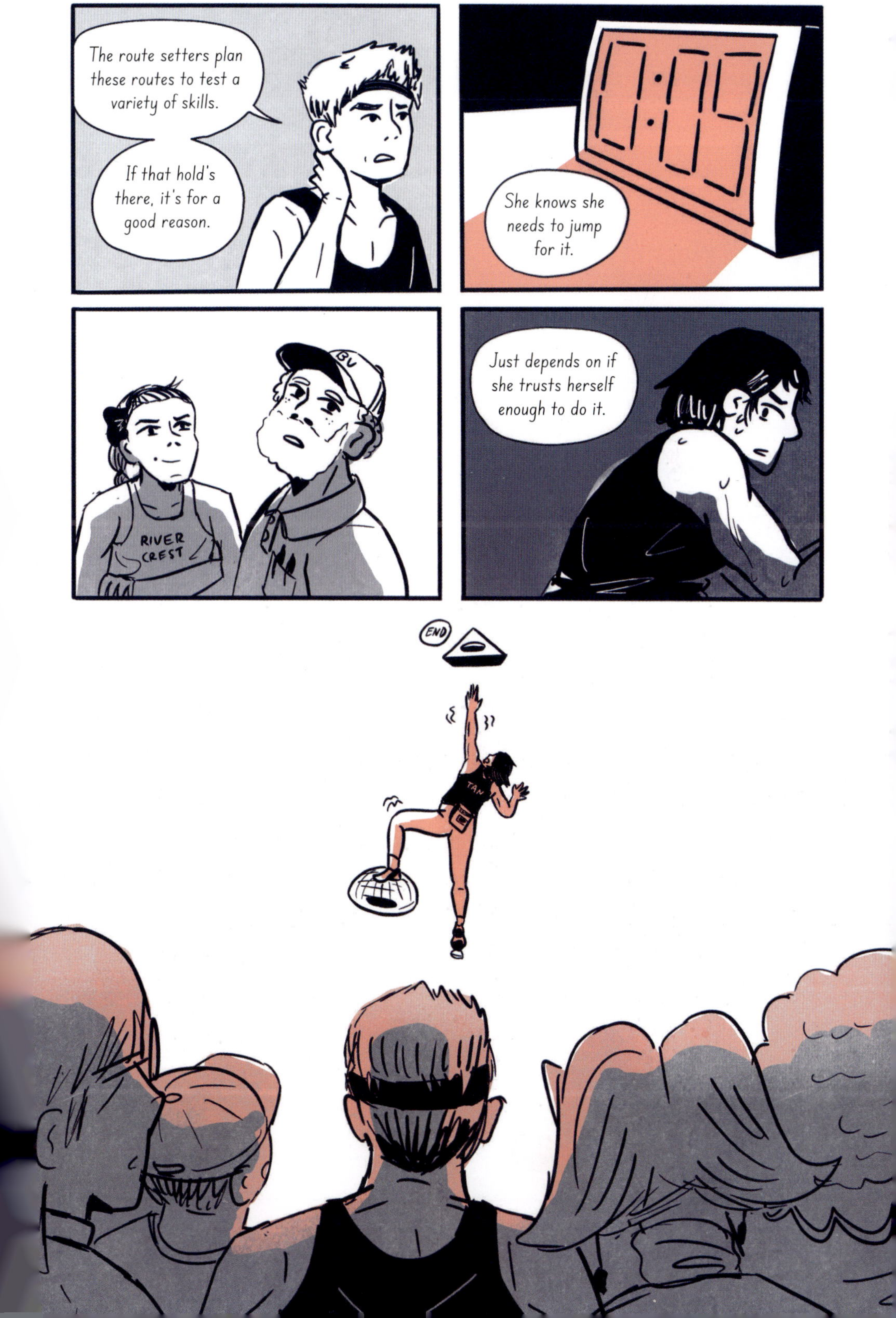
The route setters plan these routes to test a variety of skills.
If that hold's there, it's for a good reason.
She knows she needs to jump for it.
RIVER CREST
Just depends on if she trusts herself enough to do it.
END
TAN

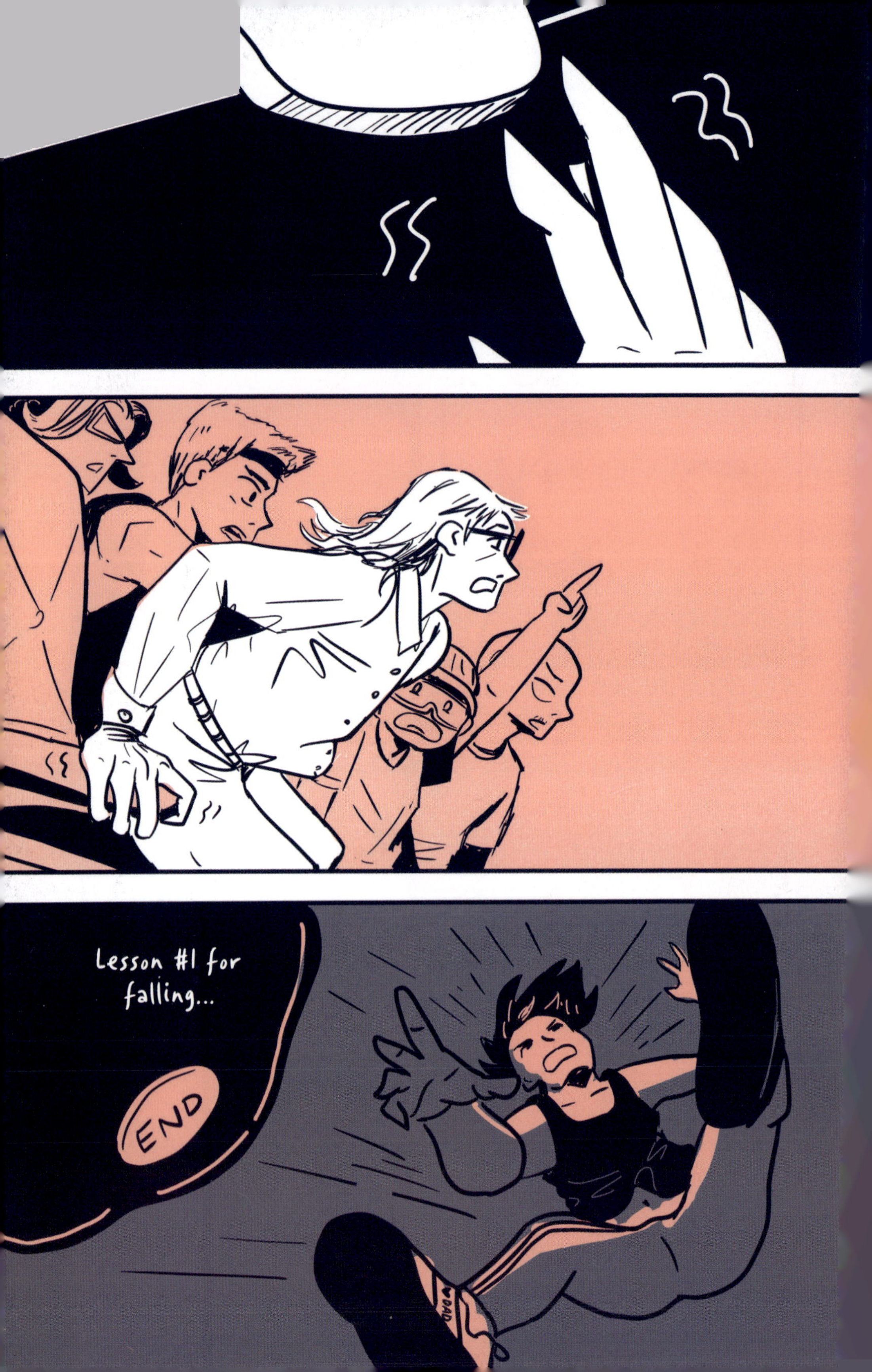
Lesson #1 for falling...
END
DAD

PART 1

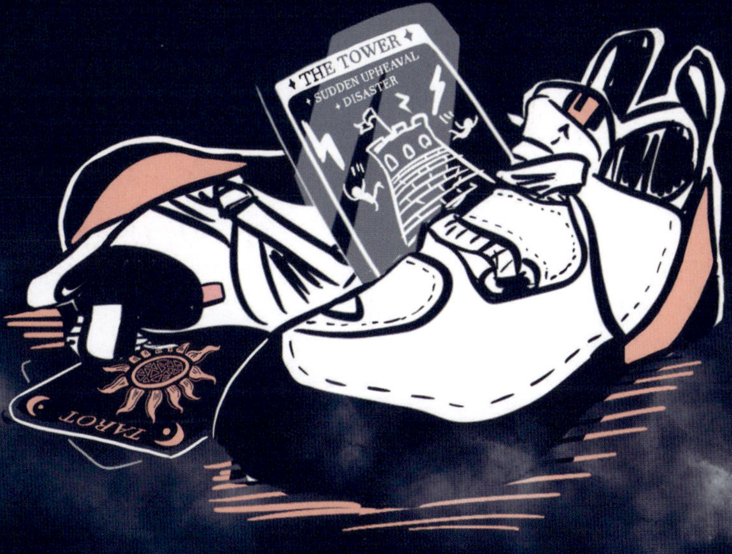
THE TOWER
SUDDEN UPHEAVAL
DISASTER
TAROT

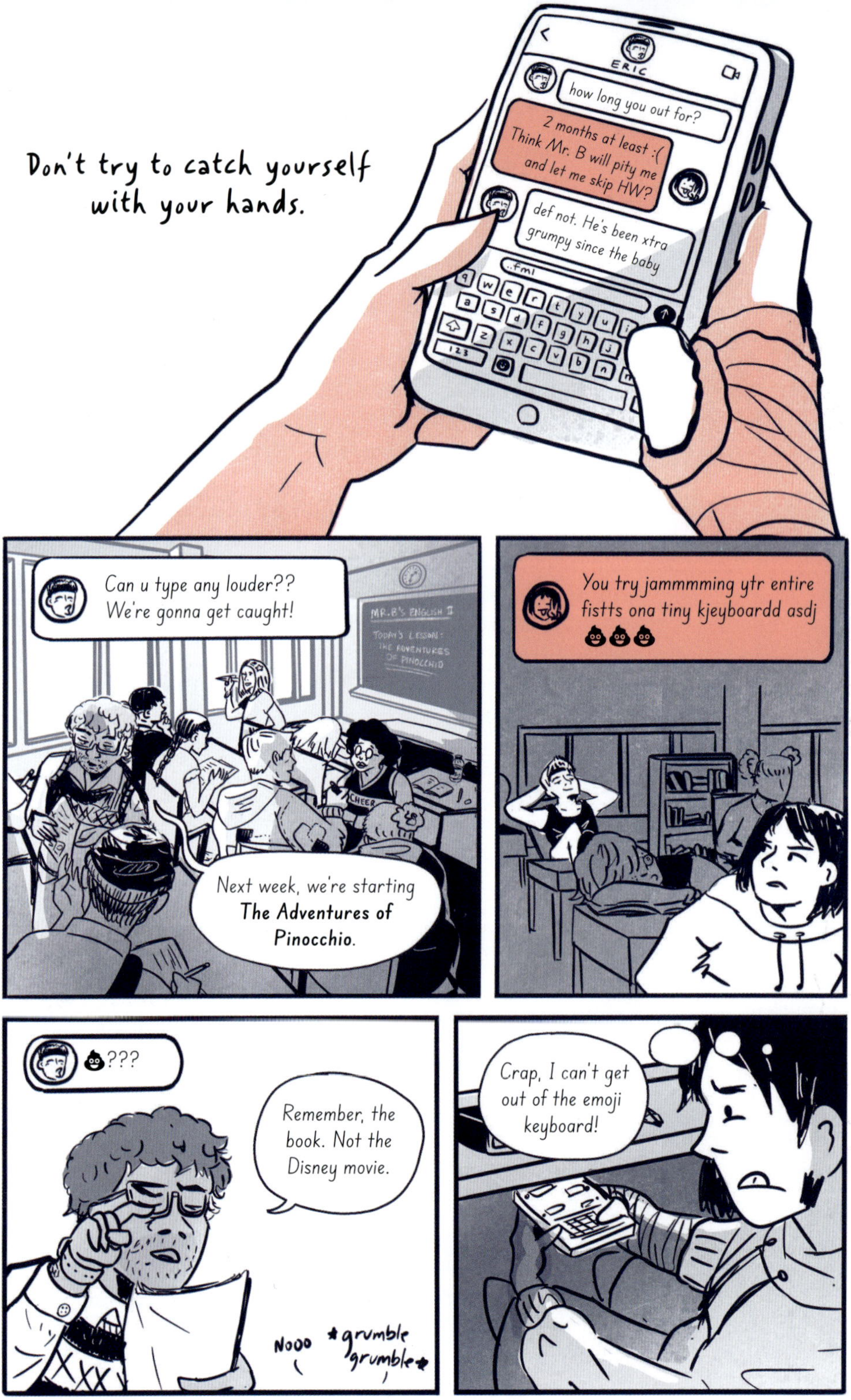
Don't try to catch yourself with your hands.
ERIC
how long you out for?
2 months at least :(Think Mr. B will pity me and let me skip HW?
def not. He's been xtra grumpy since the baby
..fml
Can u type any louder?? We're gonna get caught!
MR. B's ENGLISH II
TODAY'S LESSON: THE ADVENTURES OF PINOCCHIO
CHEER
Next week, we're starting The Adventures of Pinocchio.
You try jammmming ytr entire fistts ona tiny kjeyboardd asdj 💩💩💩
💩???
Remember, the book. Not the Disney movie.
NOOO
grumble grumble
Crap, I can't get out of the emoji keyboard!

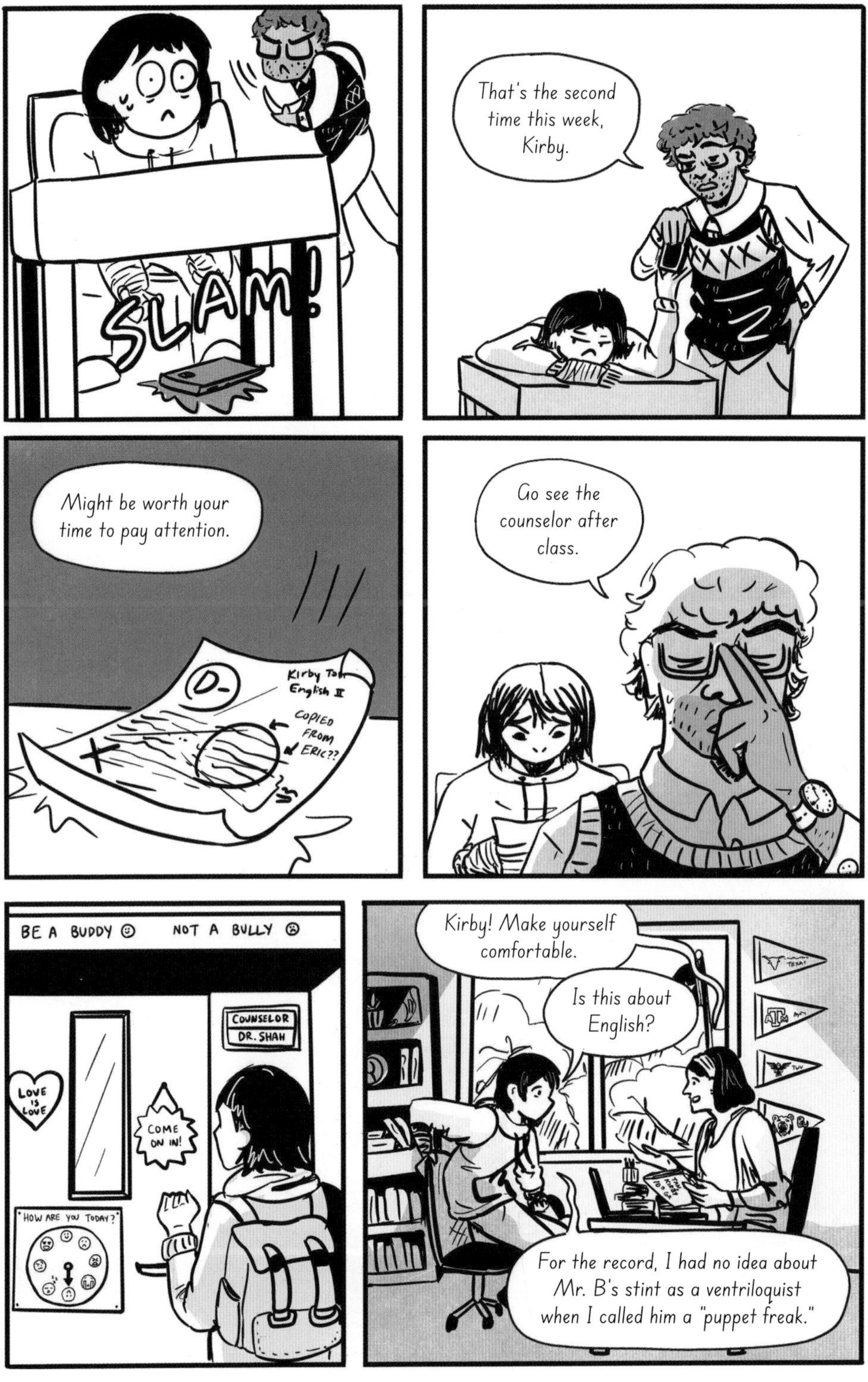
SLAM!
That's the second time this week, Kirby.
Might be worth your time to pay attention.
D-
Kirby Tan English II
COPIED FROM ERIC??
Go see the counselor after class.
BE A BUDDY ☺ NOT A BULLY ☹
COUNSELOR DR. SHAH
LOVE IS LOVE
COME ON IN!
HOW ARE YOU TODAY?
Kirby! Make yourself comfortable.
Is this about English?
For the record, I had no idea about Mr. B's stint as a ventriloquist when I called him a "puppet freak."

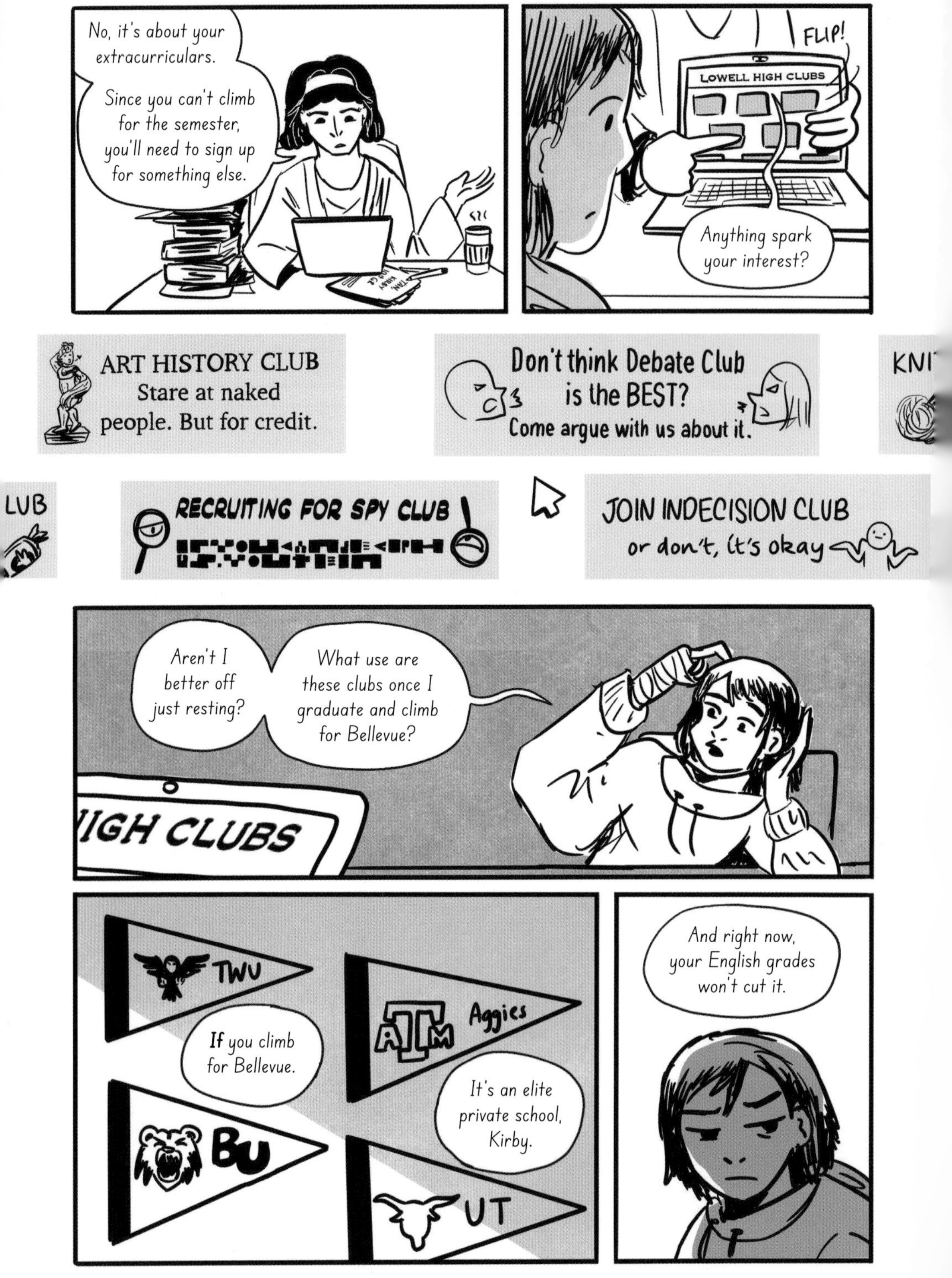

No, it's about your extracurriculars.
Since you can't climb for the semester, you'll need to sign up for something else.
FLIP!
LOWELL HIGH CLUBS
Anything spark your interest?
ART HISTORY CLUB
Stare at naked people. But for credit.
Don't think Debate Club is the BEST?
Come argue with us about it.
RECRUITING FOR SPY CLUB
JOIN INDECISION CLUB
or don't, it's okay
Aren't I better off just resting?
What use are these clubs once I graduate and climb for Bellevue?
IGH CLUBS
TWU
If you climb for Bellevue.
Aggies
It's an elite private school, Kirby.
BU
UT
And right now, your English grades won't cut it.

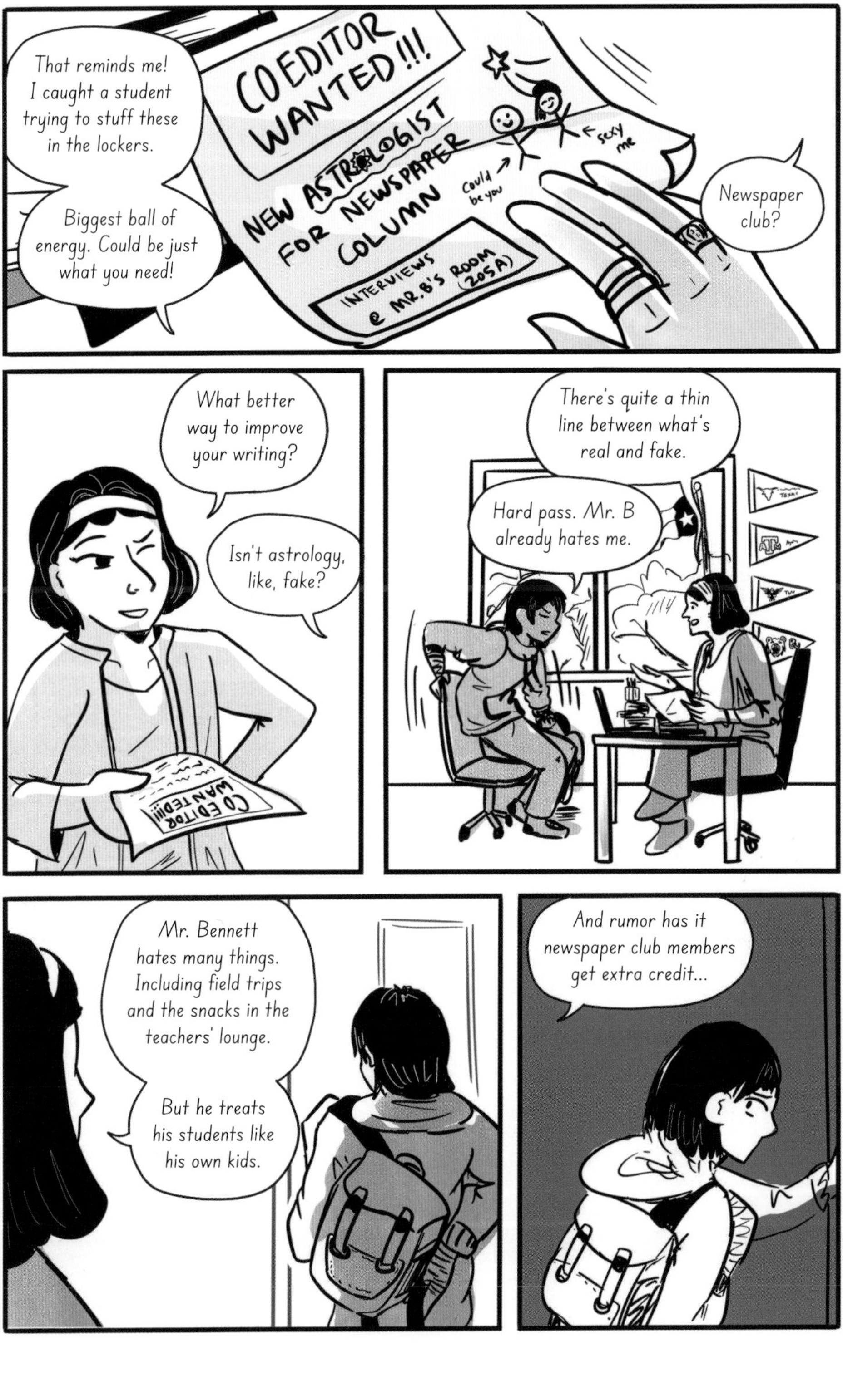

That reminds me! I caught a student trying to stuff these in the lockers.
Biggest ball of energy. Could be just what you need!
COEDITOR WANTED!!!
NEW ASTROLOGIST FOR NEWSPAPER COLUMN
Could be you
sexy me
INTERVIEWS @ MR.B'S ROOM (205A)
Newspaper club?
What better way to improve your writing?
Isn't astrology, like, fake?
There's quite a thin line between what's real and fake.
Hard pass. Mr. B already hates me.
Mr. Bennett hates many things. Including field trips and the snacks in the teachers' lounge.
But he treats his students like his own kids.
And rumor has it newspaper club members get extra credit...

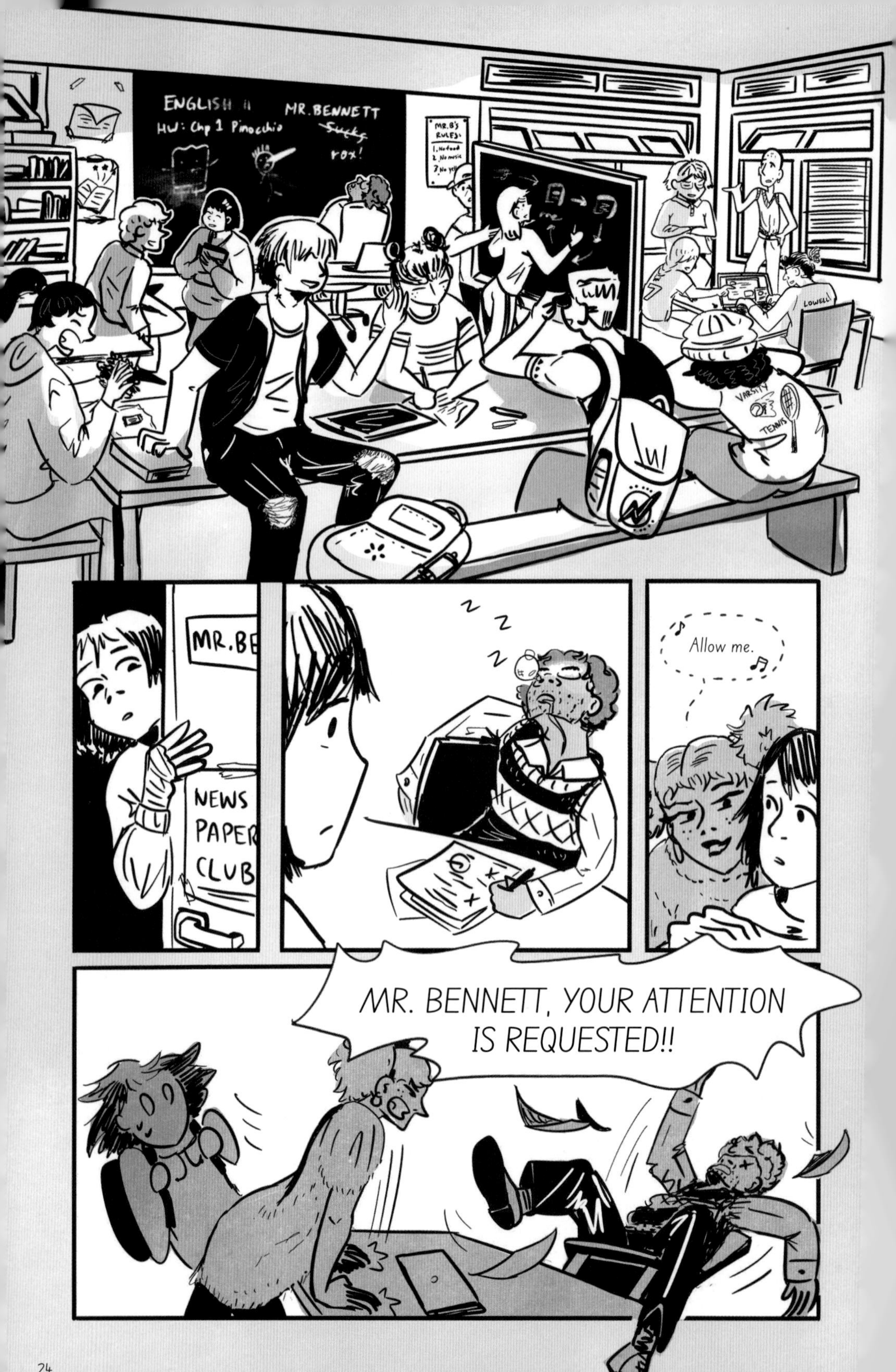

ENGLISH II
MR. BENNETT
HW: Chp 1 Pinocchio
~~Sucks~~ rox!
MR. B's RULES:
1. No food
2. No music
3. No yell
LOWELL
VARSITY TENNIS
MR. BE
NEWS PAPER CLUB
Allow me.
MR. BENNETT, YOUR ATTENTION IS REQUESTED!!

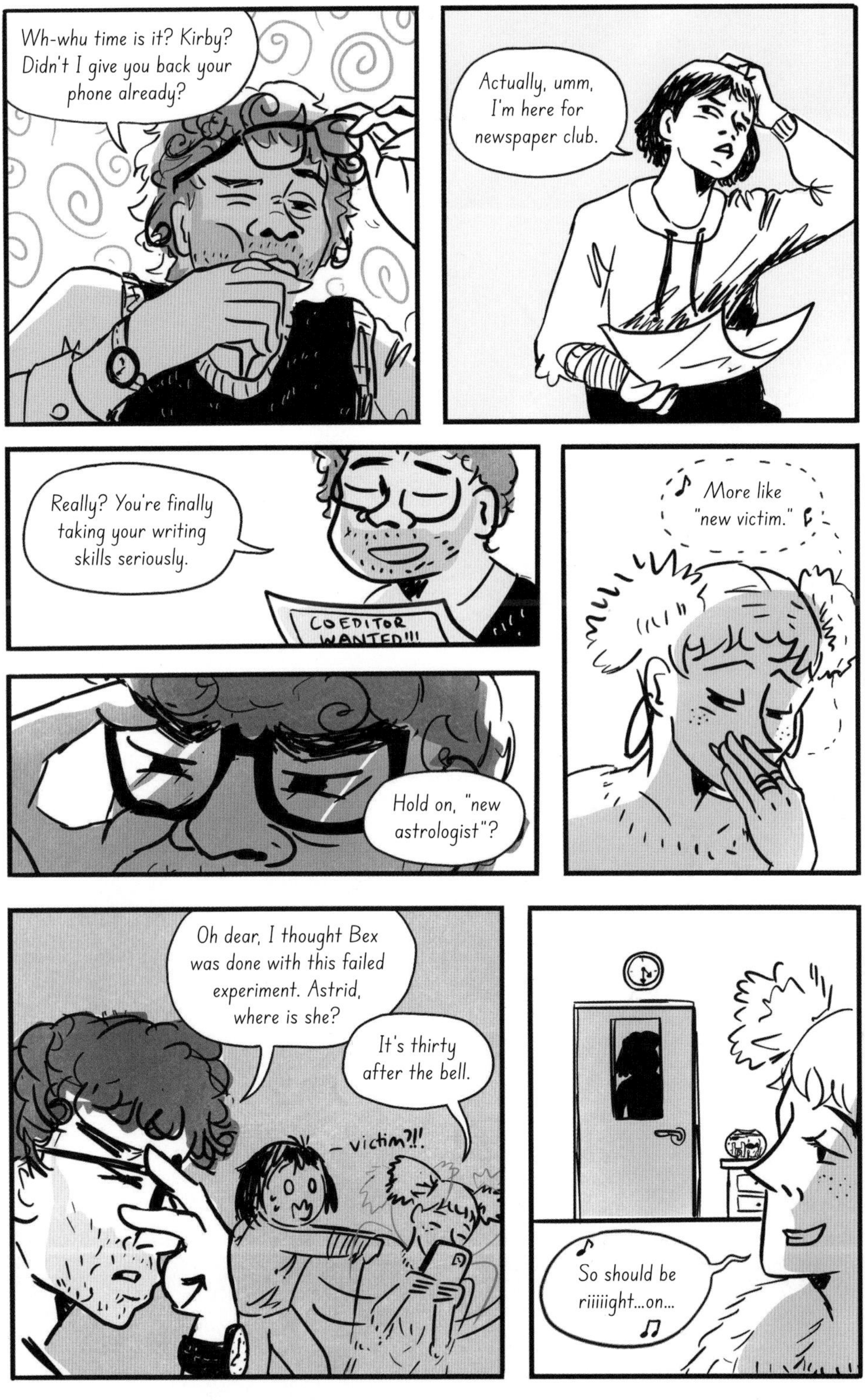
Wh-whu time is it? Kirby? Didn't I give you back your phone already?
Actually, umm, I'm here for newspaper club.
Really? You're finally taking your writing skills seriously.
COEDITOR WANTED!!!
More like "new victim."
Hold on, "new astrologist"?
Oh dear, I thought Bex was done with this failed experiment. Astrid, where is she?
It's thirty after the bell.
—victim?!!
So should be riiiight...on...

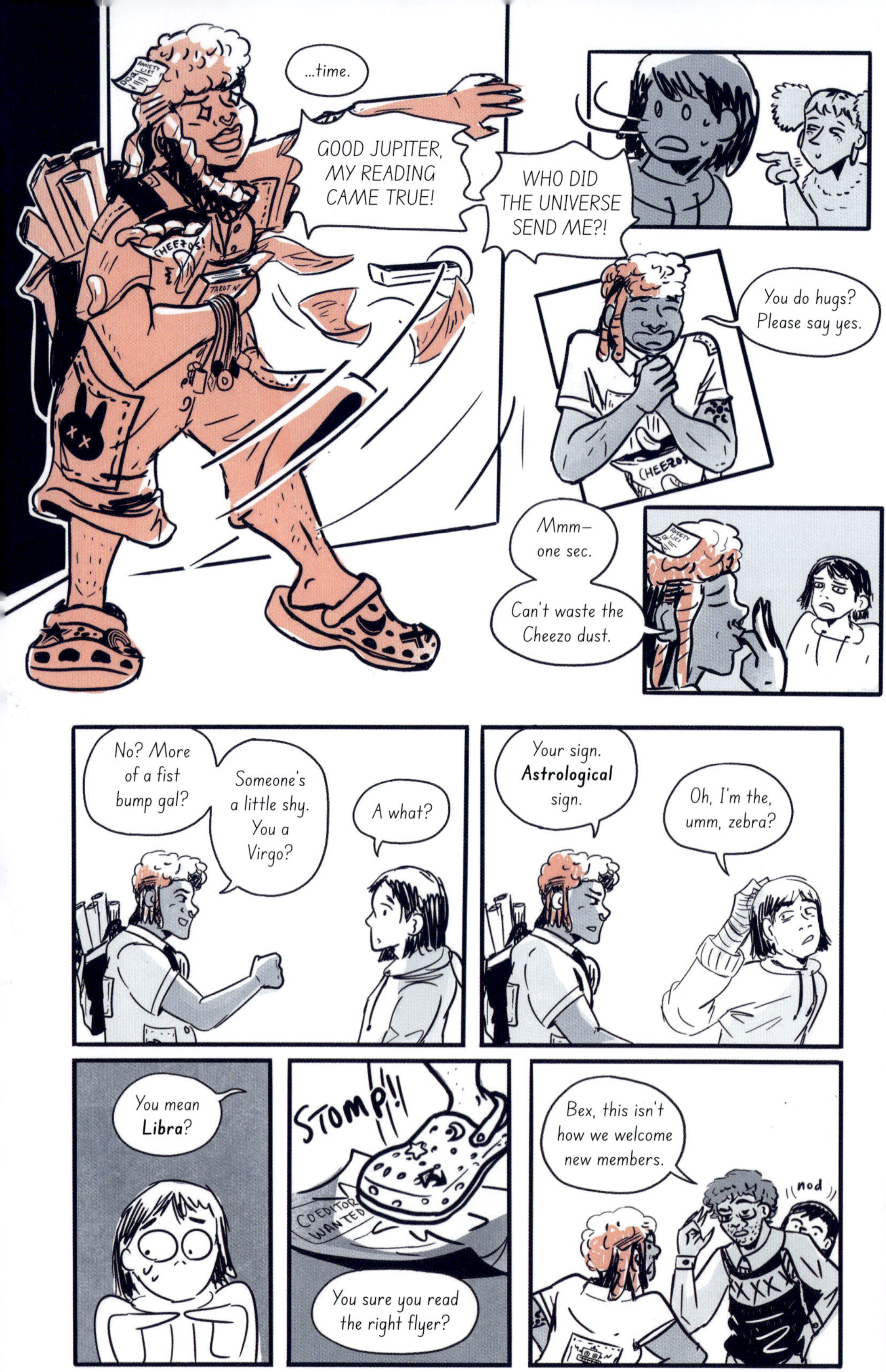
...time.
GOOD JUPITER, MY READING CAME TRUE!
WHO DID THE UNIVERSE SEND ME?!
You do hugs? Please say yes.
Mmm— one sec.
Can't waste the Cheezo dust.
No? More of a fist bump gal?
Someone's a little shy. You a Virgo?
A what?
Your sign. **Astrological** sign.
Oh, I'm the, umm, zebra?
You mean **Libra**?
STOMP!!
COEDITOR WANTED
You sure you read the right flyer?
Bex, this isn't how we welcome new members.
nod

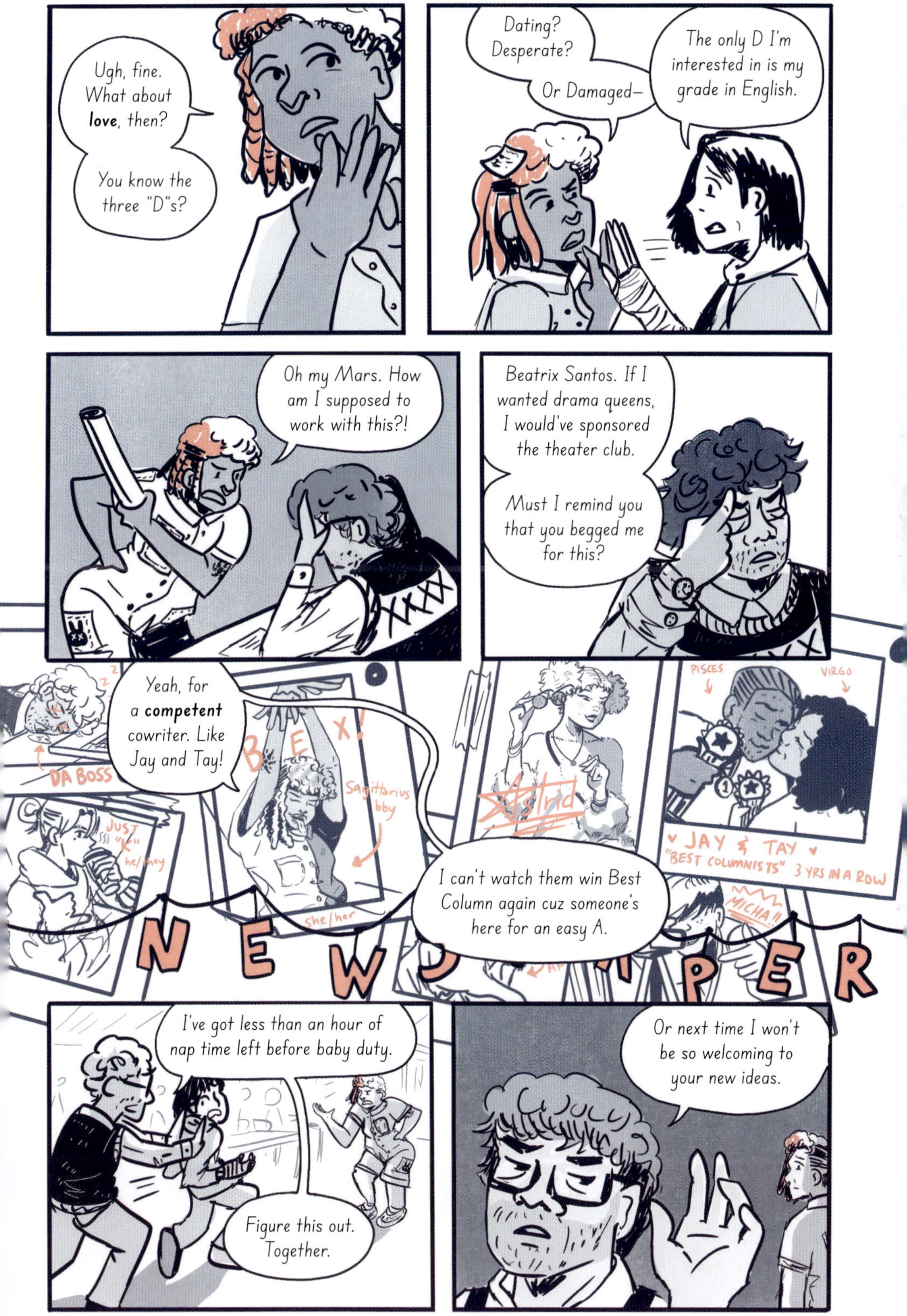

Ugh, fine. What about **love**, then?
You know the three "D"s?
Dating? Desperate?
Or Damaged—
The only D I'm interested in is my grade in English.
Oh my Mars. How am I supposed to work with this?!
Beatrix Santos. If I wanted drama queens, I would've sponsored the theater club.
Must I remind you that you begged me for this?
Yeah, for a **competent** cowriter. Like Jay and Tay!
DA BOSS
BEX!
Sagittarius bby
she/her
JUST "K" he/they
Astrid
PISCES
VIRGO
JAY & TAY
"BEST COLUMNISTS" 3 YRS IN A ROW
MICHA!!
I can't watch them win Best Column again cuz someone's here for an easy A.
I've got less than an hour of nap time left before baby duty.
Figure this out. Together.
Or next time I won't be so welcoming to your new ideas.

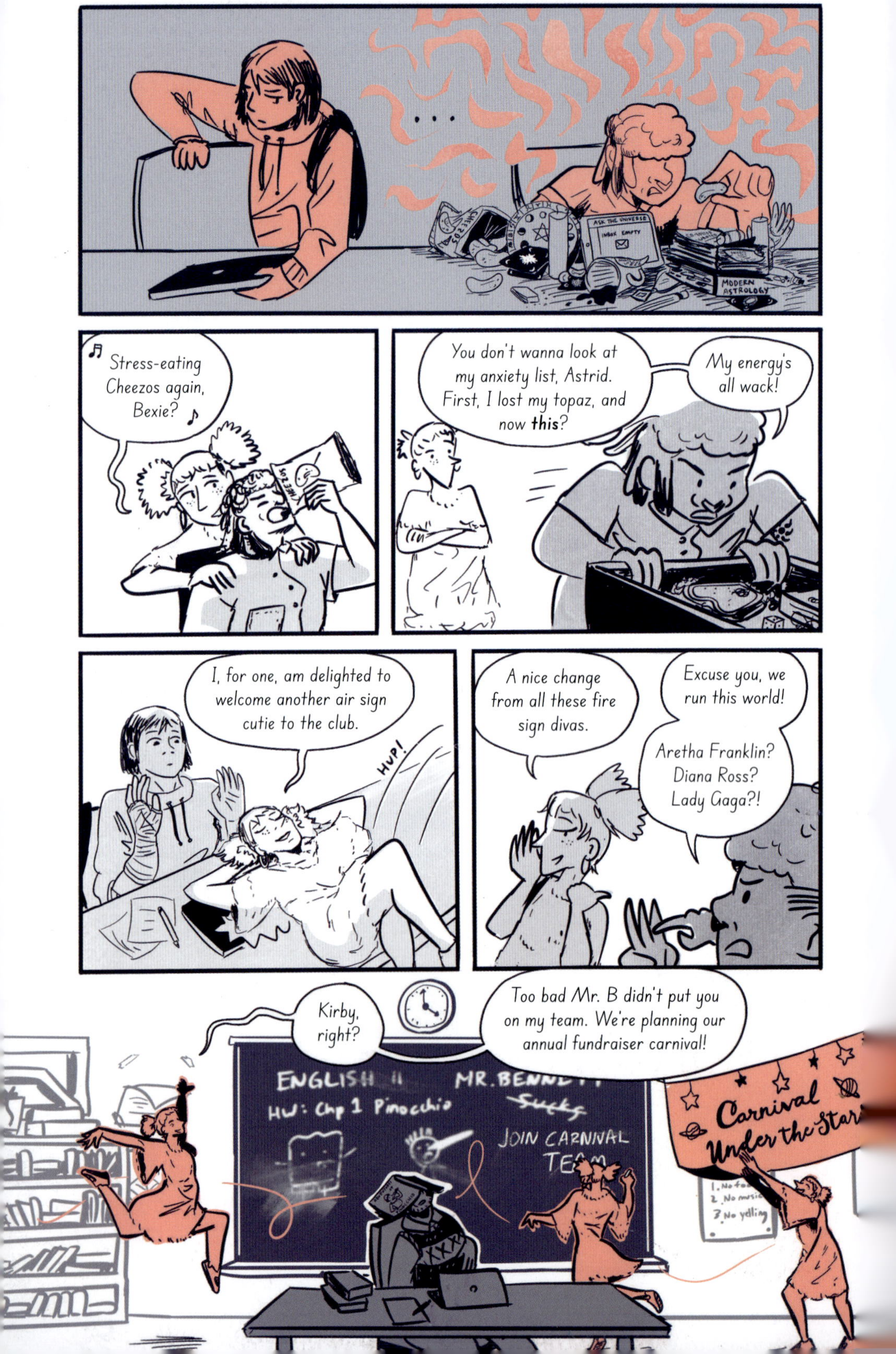
...
CHEEZOS
ASK THE UNIVERSE
INBOX EMPTY
MODERN ASTROLOGY
Stress-eating Cheezos again, Bexie?
You don't wanna look at my anxiety list, Astrid. First, I lost my topaz, and now **this**?
My energy's all wack!
I, for one, am delighted to welcome another air sign cutie to the club.
HUP!
A nice change from all these fire sign divas.
Excuse you, we run this world!
Aretha Franklin? Diana Ross? Lady Gaga?!
Kirby, right?
Too bad Mr. B didn't put you on my team. We're planning our annual fundraiser carnival!
ENGLISH II MR. BENNETT
HW: Chp 1 Pinocchio
~~Sucks~~
JOIN CARNIVAL TEAM
Carnival Under the Stars
1. No food
2. No music
3. No yelling

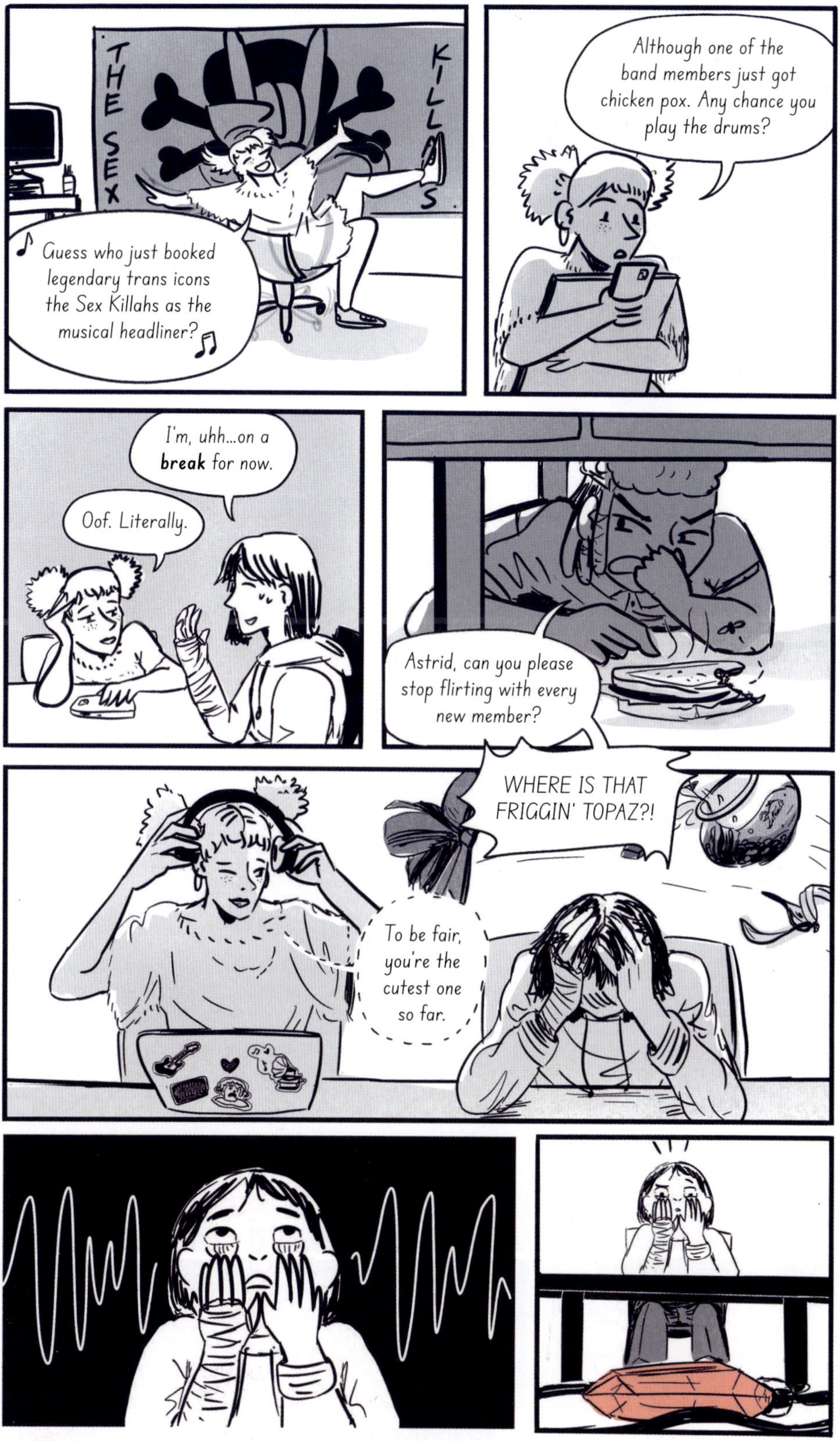
THE SEX KILLAHS
Guess who just booked legendary trans icons the Sex Killahs as the musical headliner?
Although one of the band members just got chicken pox. Any chance you play the drums?
I'm, uhh...on a **break** for now.
Oof. Literally.
Astrid, can you please stop flirting with every new member?
WHERE IS THAT FRIGGIN' TOPAZ?!
To be fair, you're the cutest one so far.

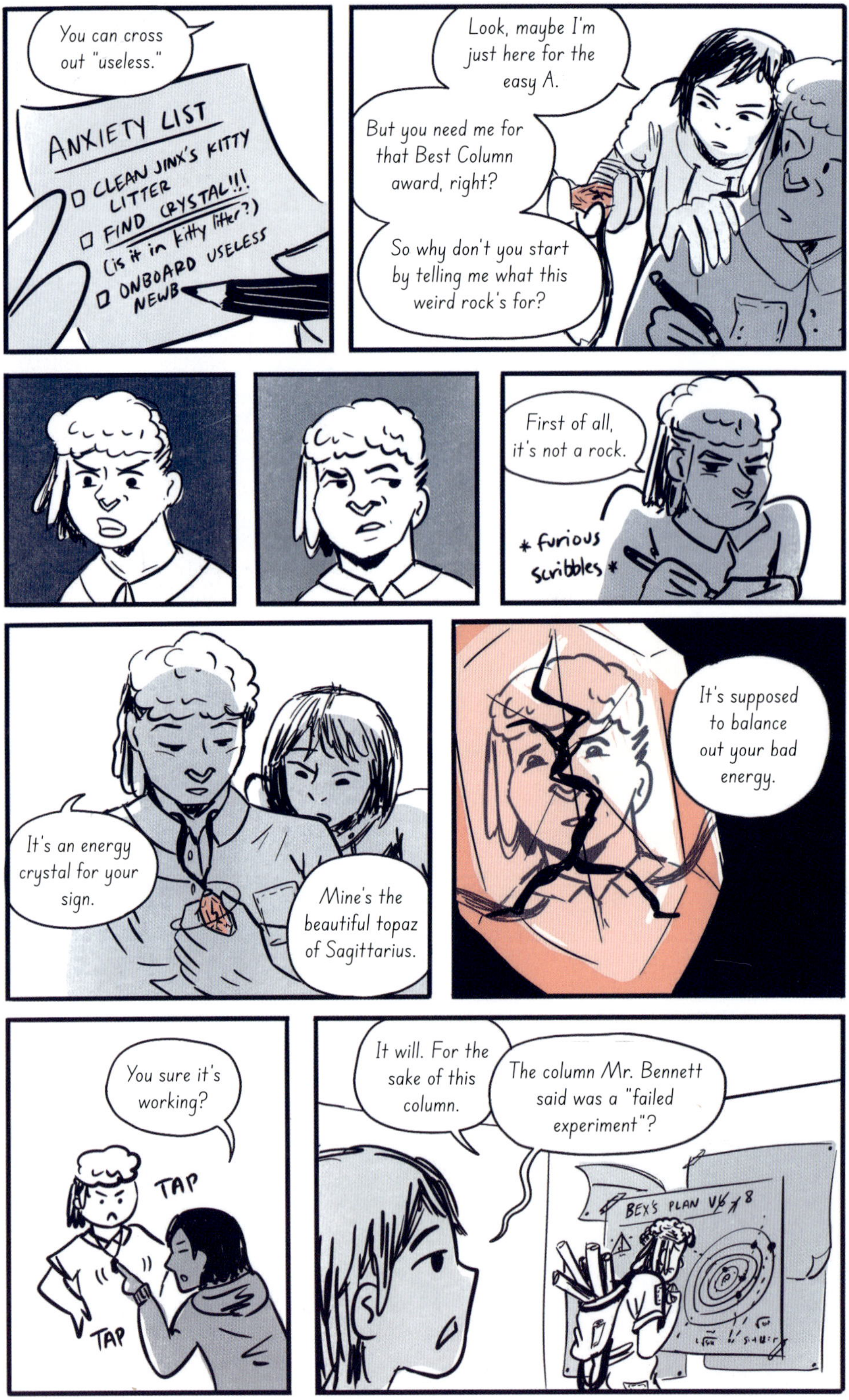

You can cross out "useless."
ANXIETY LIST
CLEAN JINX'S KITTY LITTER
FIND CRYSTAL!!! (is it in kitty litter?)
ONBOARD USELESS NEWB
Look, maybe I'm just here for the easy A.
But you need me for that Best Column award, right?
So why don't you start by telling me what this weird rock's for?
First of all, it's not a rock.
* furious scribbles *
It's an energy crystal for your sign.
Mine's the beautiful topaz of Sagittarius.
It's supposed to balance out your bad energy.
You sure it's working?
TAP
TAP
It will. For the sake of this column.
The column Mr. Bennett said was a "failed experiment"?
BEX'S PLAN V8

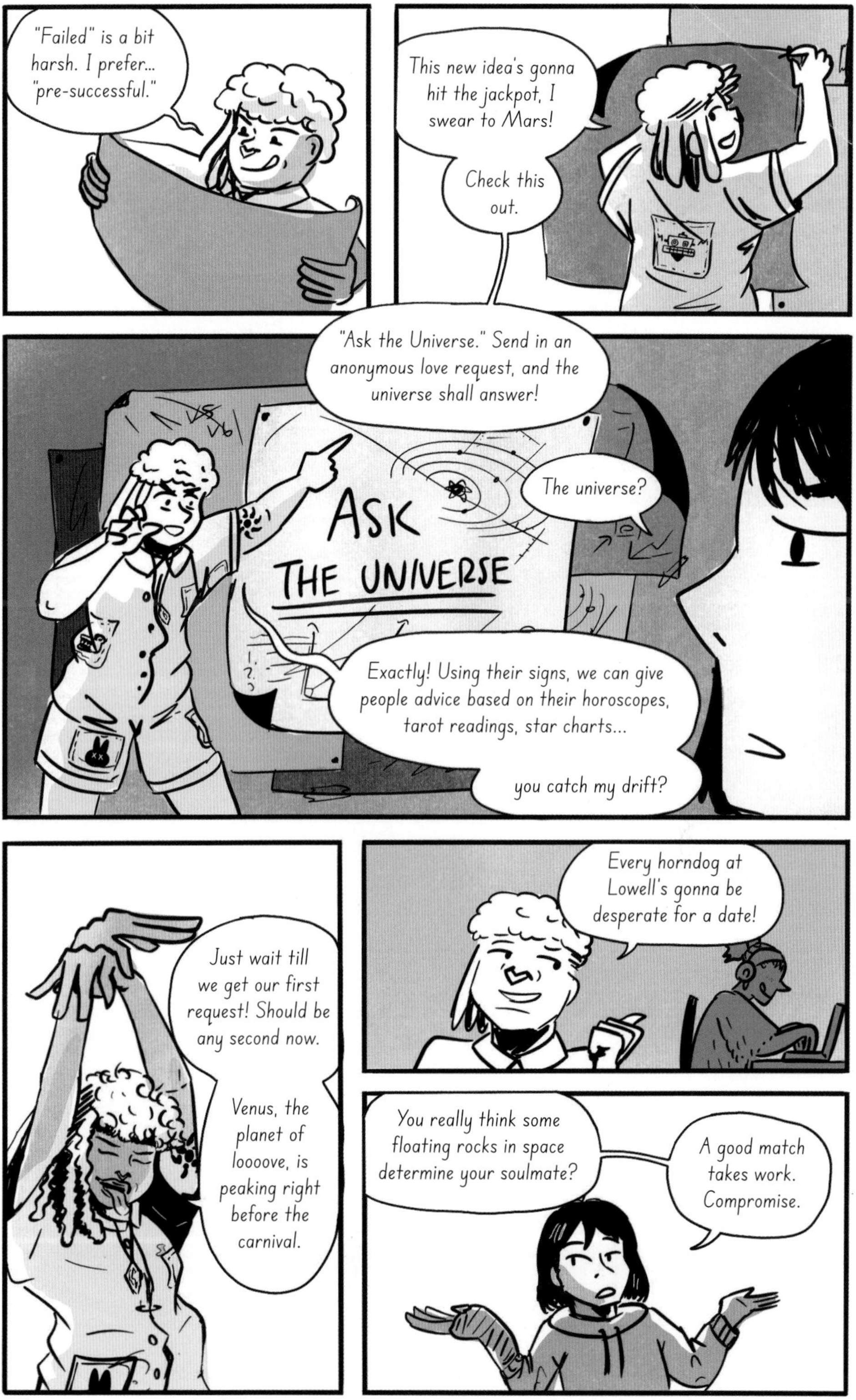
"Failed" is a bit harsh. I prefer... "pre-successful."
This new idea's gonna hit the jackpot, I swear to Mars!
Check this out.
"Ask the Universe." Send in an anonymous love request, and the universe shall answer!
ASK THE UNIVERSE
The universe?
Exactly! Using their signs, we can give people advice based on their horoscopes, tarot readings, star charts...
you catch my drift?
Just wait till we get our first request! Should be any second now.
Venus, the planet of loooove, is peaking right before the carnival.
Every horndog at Lowell's gonna be desperate for a date!
You really think some floating rocks in space determine your soulmate?
A good match takes work. Compromise.

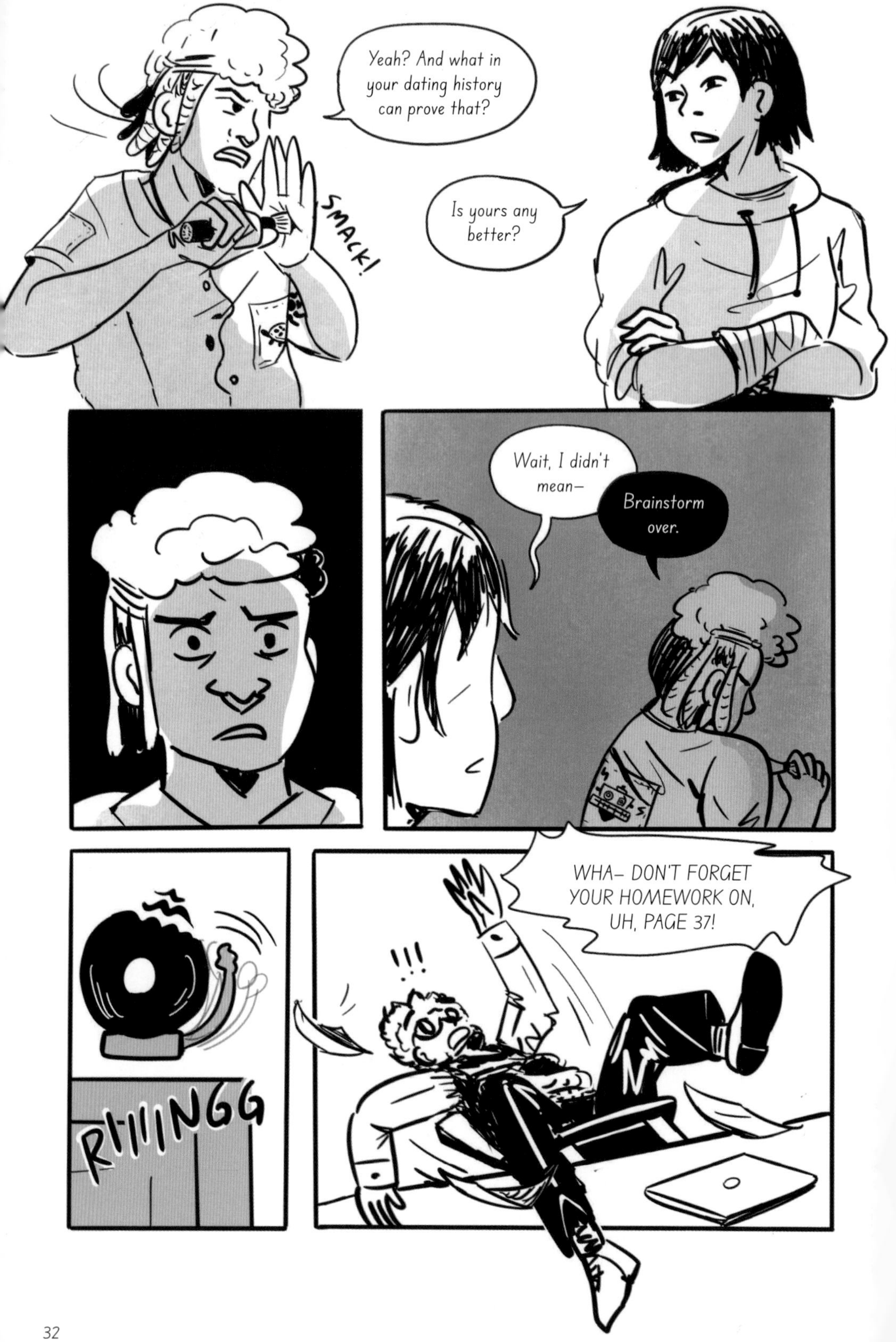
Yeah? And what in your dating history can prove that?
SMACK!
Is yours any better?
Wait, I didn't mean—
Brainstorm over.
RIIIINGG
!!!
WHA– DON'T FORGET YOUR HOMEWORK ON, UH, PAGE 37!

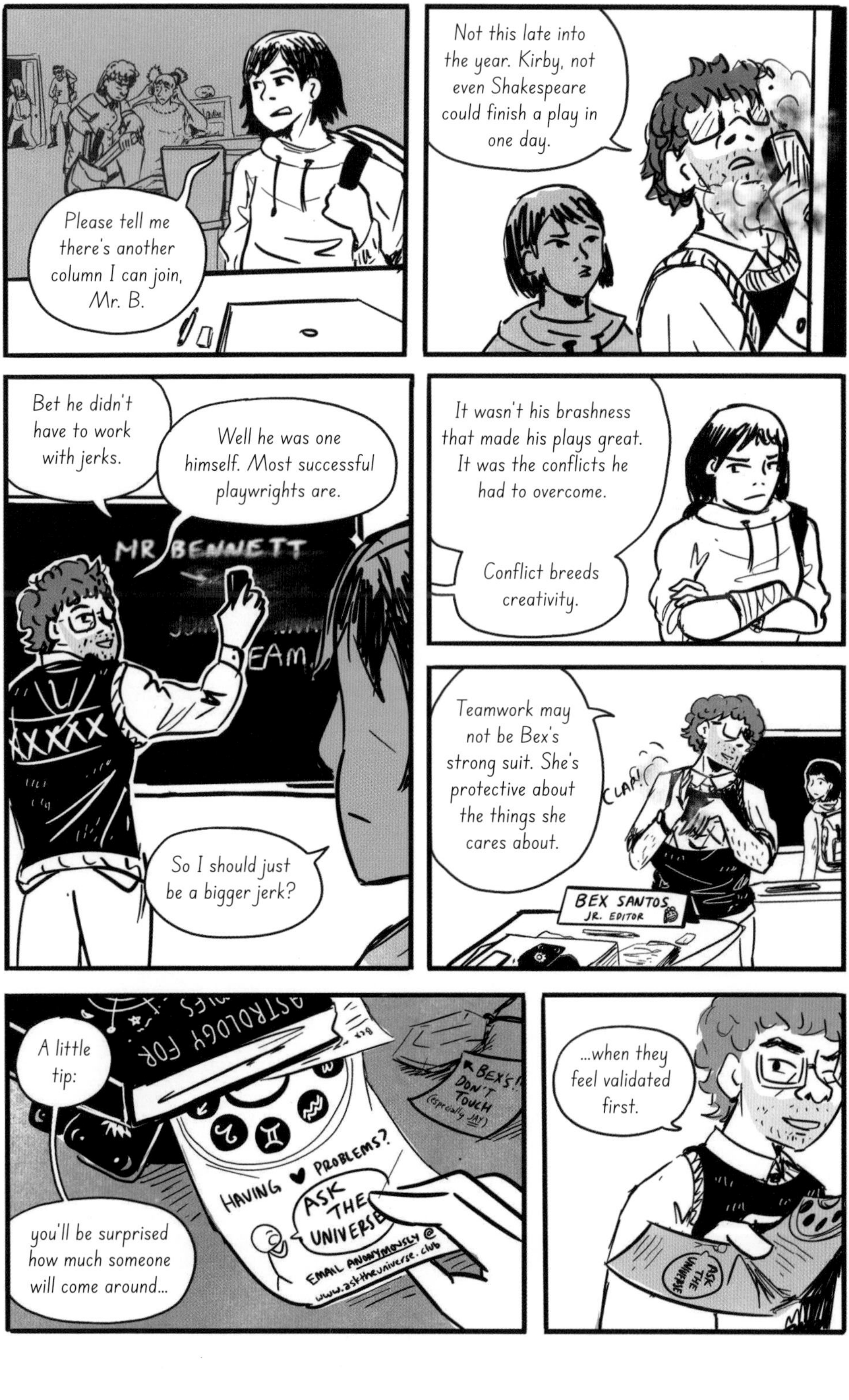
Please tell me there's another column I can join, Mr. B.
Not this late into the year. Kirby, not even Shakespeare could finish a play in one day.
Bet he didn't have to work with jerks.
Well he was one himself. Most successful playwrights are.
MR BENNETT
So I should just be a bigger jerk?
It wasn't his brashness that made his plays great. It was the conflicts he had to overcome.
Conflict breeds creativity.
Teamwork may not be Bex's strong suit. She's protective about the things she cares about.
CLAP!
BEX SANTOS
JR. EDITOR
A little tip:
ASTROLOGY FOR
BEX'S!! DON'T TOUCH (especially JAY)
HAVING ♥ PROBLEMS?
ASK THE UNIVERSE
EMAIL ANONYMOUSLY @
www.asktheuniverse.club
you'll be surprised how much someone will come around...
...when they feel validated first.
ASK THE UNIVERSE

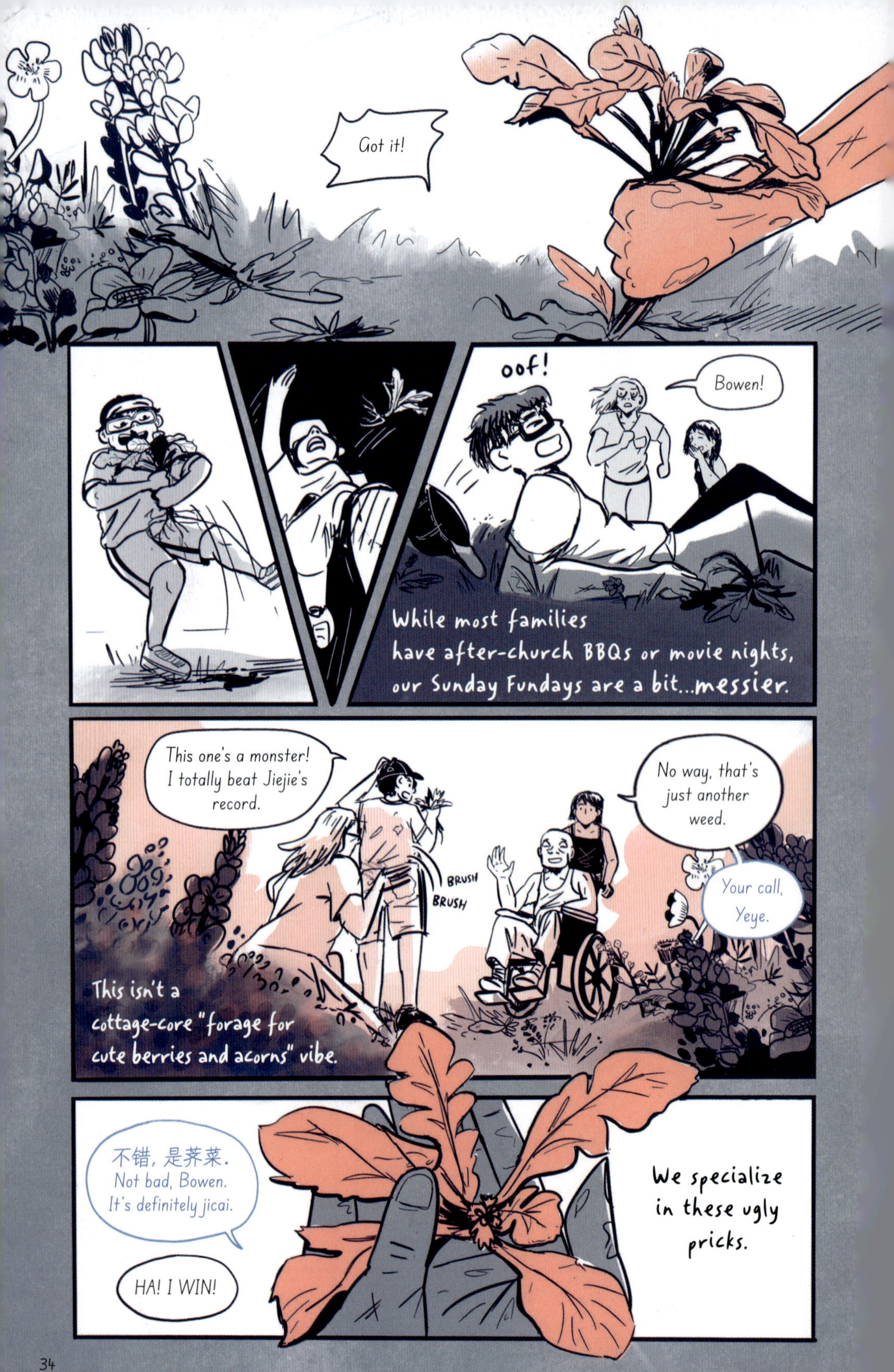
Got it!
oof!
Bowen!
While most families have after-church BBQs or movie nights, our Sunday Fundays are a bit...messier.
This one's a monster! I totally beat Jiejie's record.
BRUSH
BRUSH
No way, that's just another weed.
Your call, Yeye.
This isn't a cottage-core "forage for cute berries and acorns" vibe.
不错，是荠菜.
Not bad, Bowen. It's definitely jicai.
HA! I WIN!
We specialize in these ugly pricks.

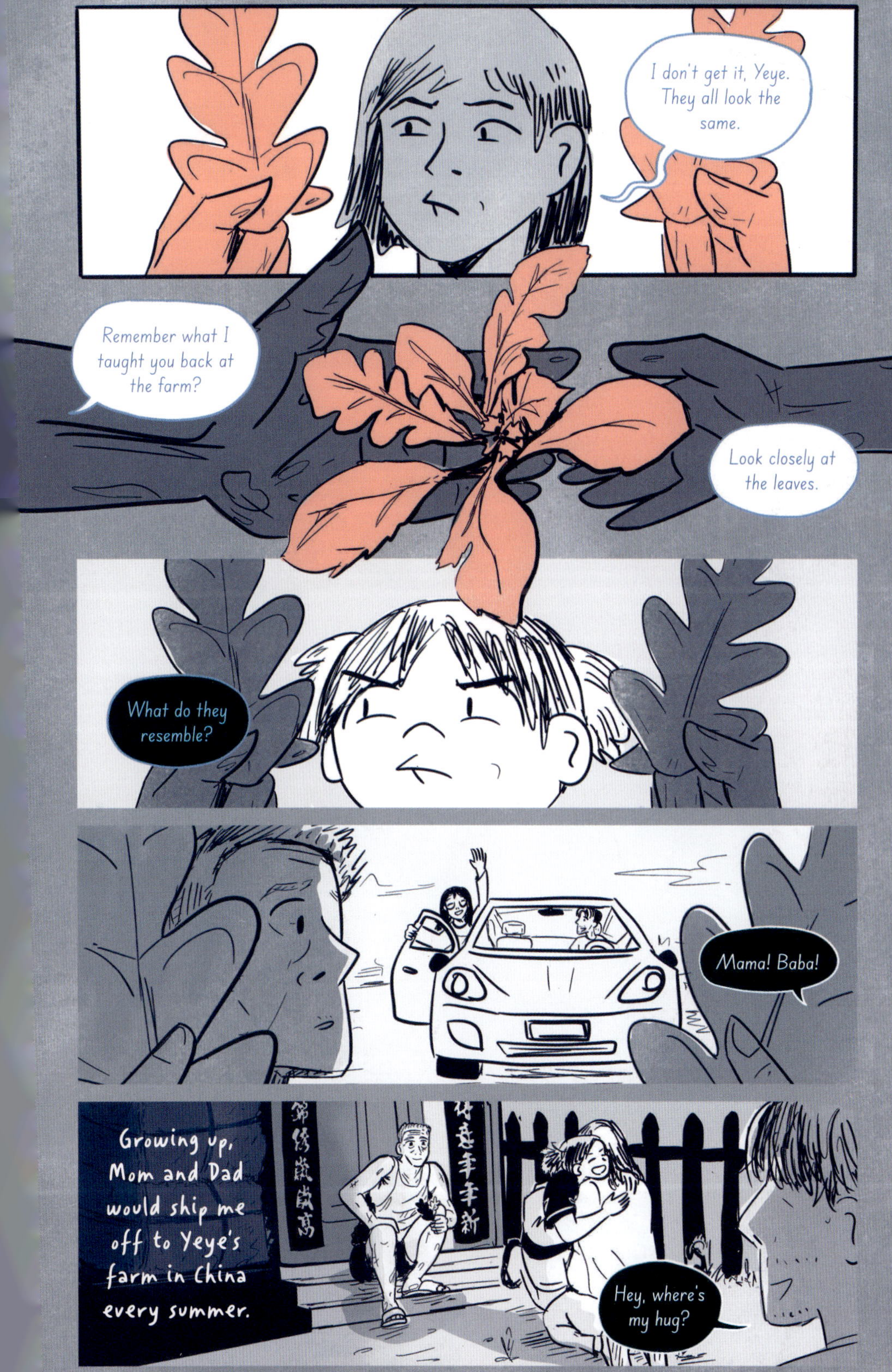

I don't get it, Yeye. They all look the same.
Remember what I taught you back at the farm?
Look closely at the leaves.
What do they resemble?
Mama! Baba!
Growing up, Mom and Dad would ship me off to Yeye's farm in China every summer.
Hey, where's my hug?

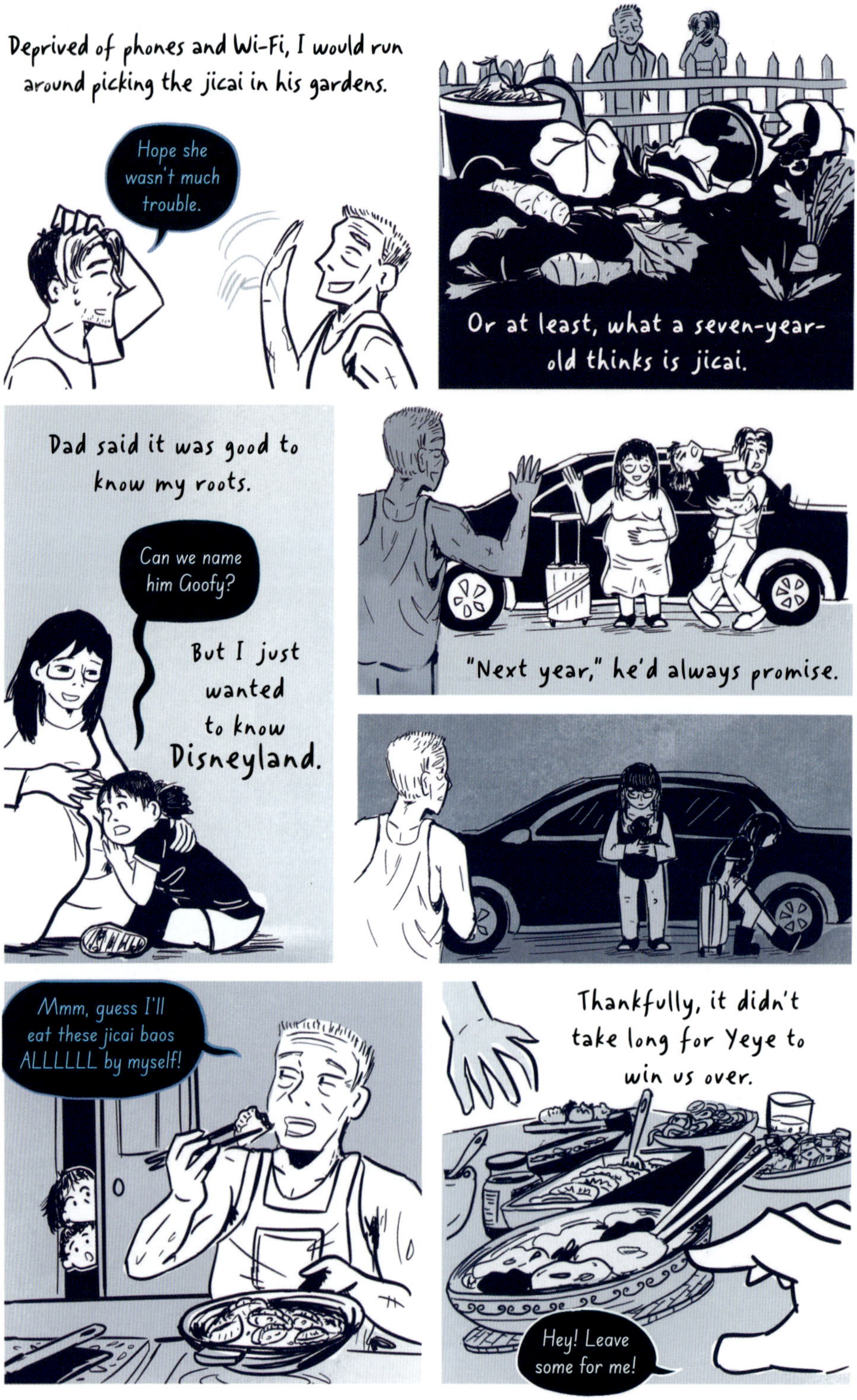
Deprived of phones and Wi-Fi, I would run around picking the jicai in his gardens.
Hope she wasn't much trouble.
Or at least, what a seven-year-old thinks is jicai.
Dad said it was good to know my roots.
Can we name him Goofy?
But I just wanted to know Disneyland.
"Next year," he'd always promise.
Mmm, guess I'll eat these jicai baos ALLLLLL by myself!
Thankfully, it didn't take long for Yeye to win us over.
Hey! Leave some for me!

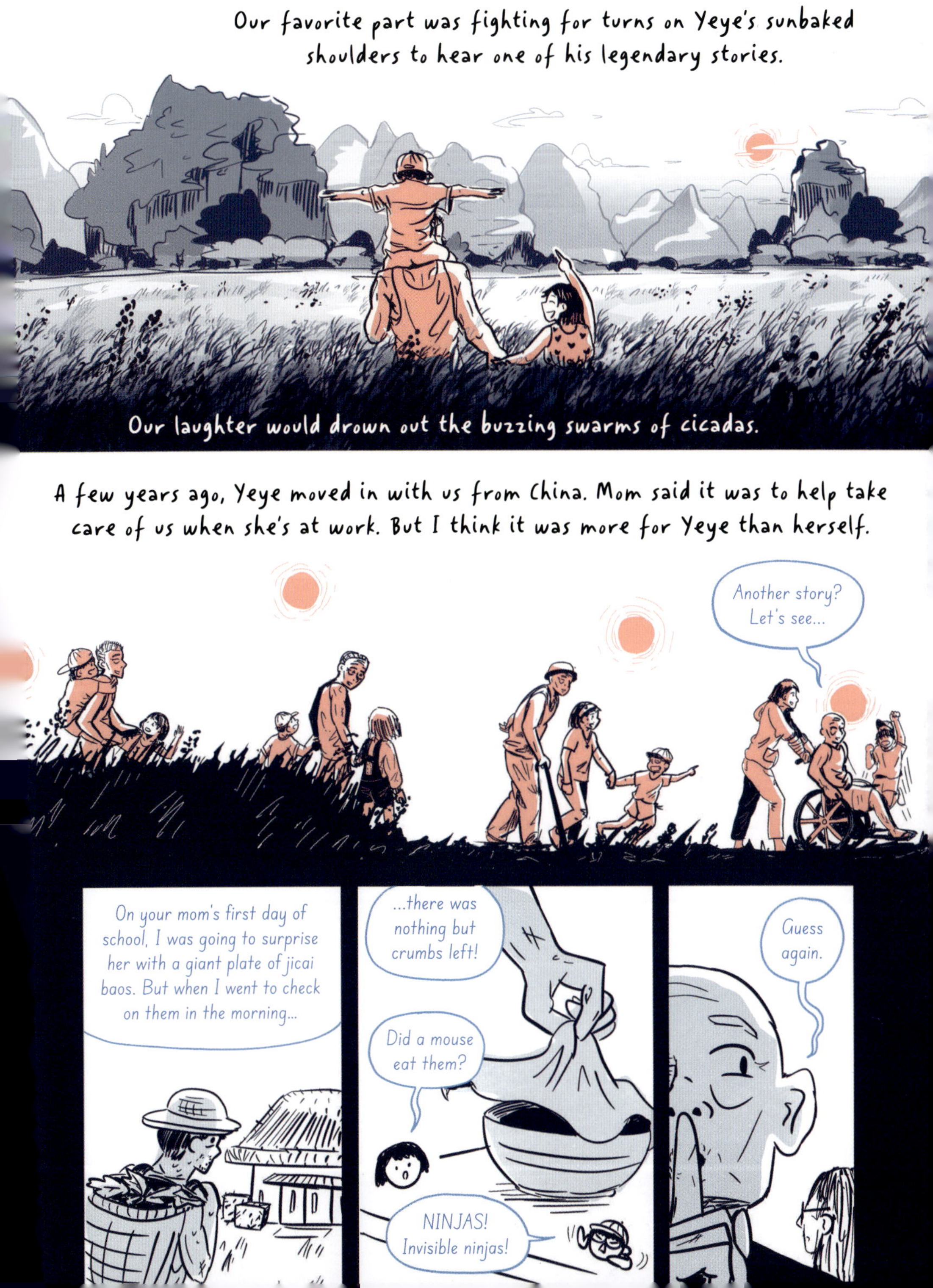
Our favorite part was fighting for turns on Yeye's sunbaked shoulders to hear one of his legendary stories.
Our laughter would drown out the buzzing swarms of cicadas.
A few years ago, Yeye moved in with us from China. Mom said it was to help take care of us when she's at work. But I think it was more for Yeye than herself.
Another story? Let's see...
On your mom's first day of school, I was going to surprise her with a giant plate of jicai baos. But when I went to check on them in the morning...
...there was nothing but crumbs left!
Did a mouse eat them?
NINJAS! Invisible ninjas!
Guess again.

"Her poop was green for a week!"

Yeye's laugh is one of my favorite sounds.

"What's so funny? I could barely hear the doctor."

"GREEN POOP!!"

Even after his memory began to fail and he repeated the same stories. They never got old.

"Ignore Bowen. He's just fighting invisible ninjas."

"Really? Well, I highly doubt that..."

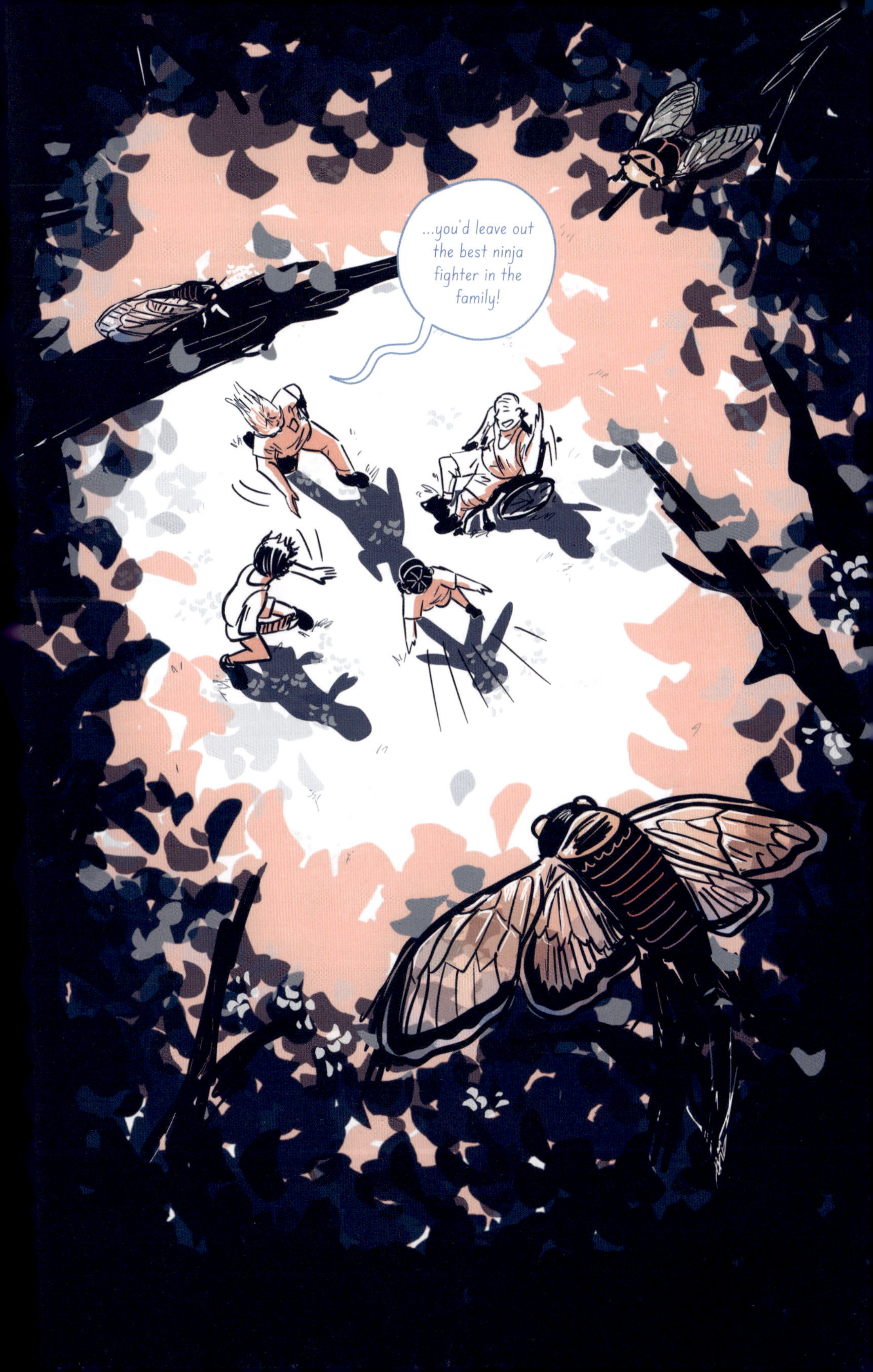
...you'd leave out the best ninja fighter in the family!

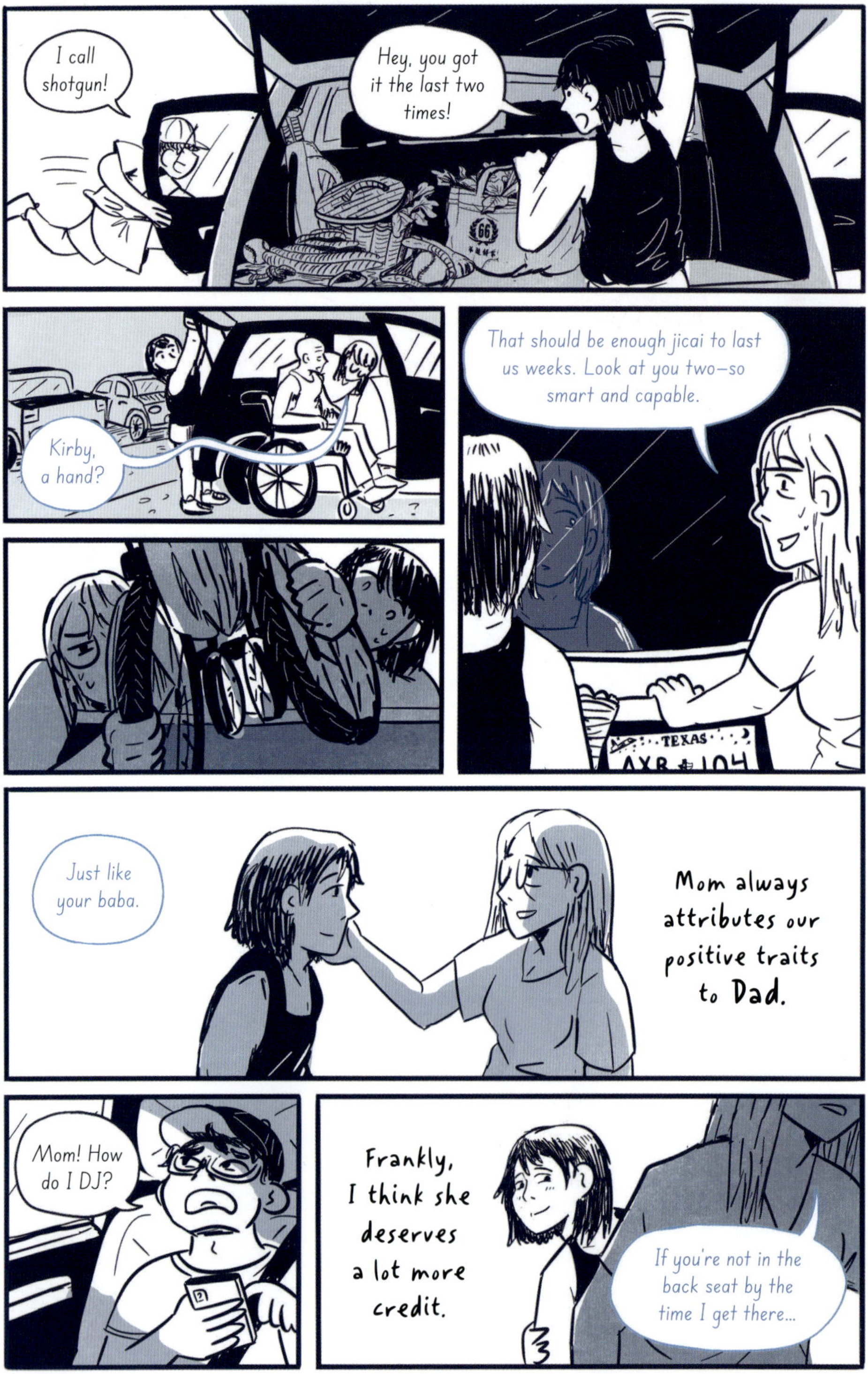
I call shotgun!
Hey, you got it the last two times!
Kirby, a hand?
That should be enough jicai to last us weeks. Look at you two—so smart and capable.
TEXAS
Just like your baba.
Mom always attributes our positive traits to Dad.
Mom! How do I DJ?
Frankly, I think she deserves a lot more credit.
If you're not in the back seat by the time I get there...

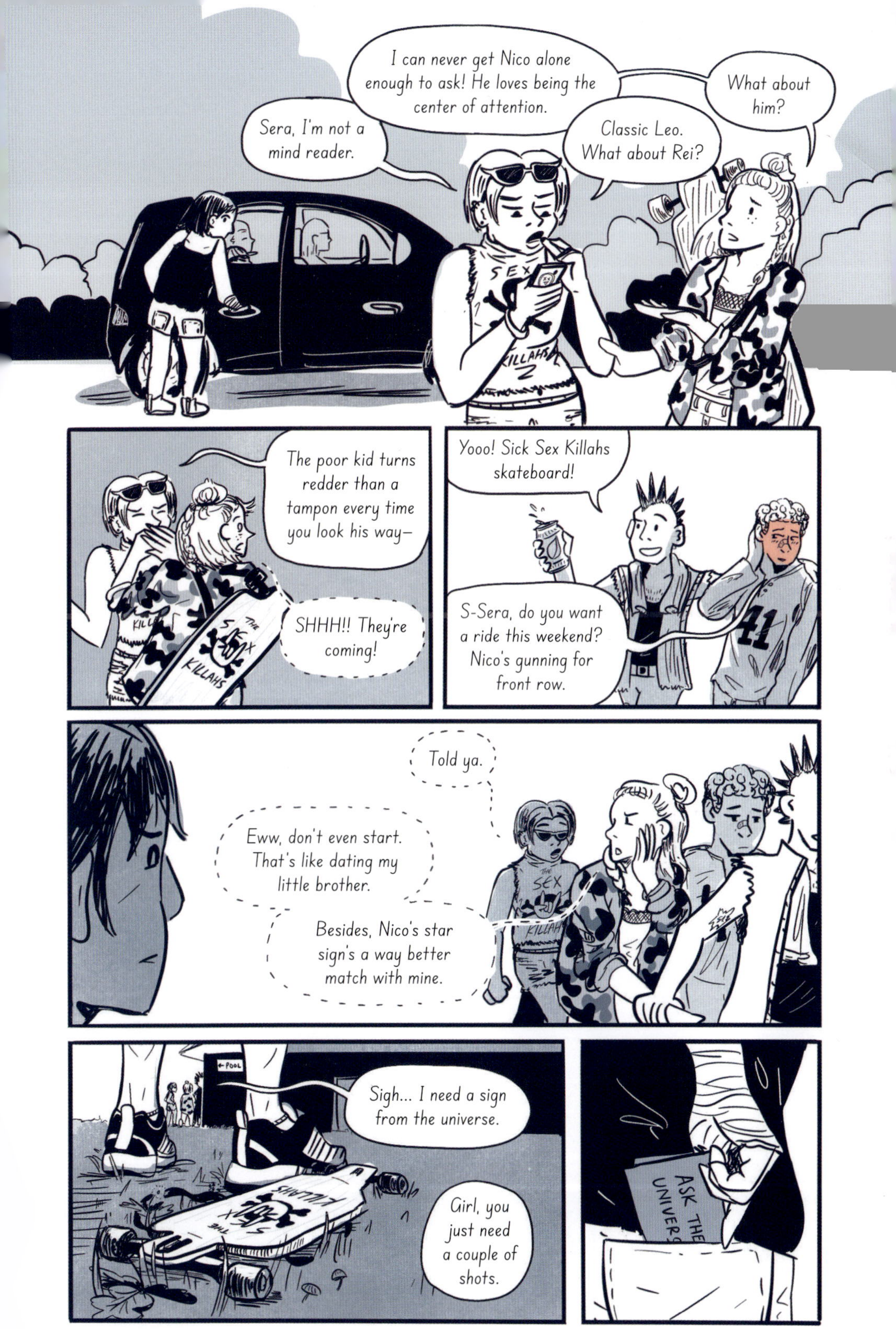
Sera, I'm not a mind reader.
I can never get Nico alone enough to ask! He loves being the center of attention.
Classic Leo. What about Rei?
What about him?
SEX KILLAHS
The poor kid turns redder than a tampon every time you look his way—
SHHH!! They're coming!
THE SEX KILLAHS
Yooo! Sick Sex Killahs skateboard!
S-Sera, do you want a ride this weekend? Nico's gunning for front row.
Told ya.
Eww, don't even start. That's like dating my little brother.
Besides, Nico's star sign's a way better match with mine.
←POOL
Sigh... I need a sign from the universe.
Girl, you just need a couple of shots.
ASK THE UNIVERS

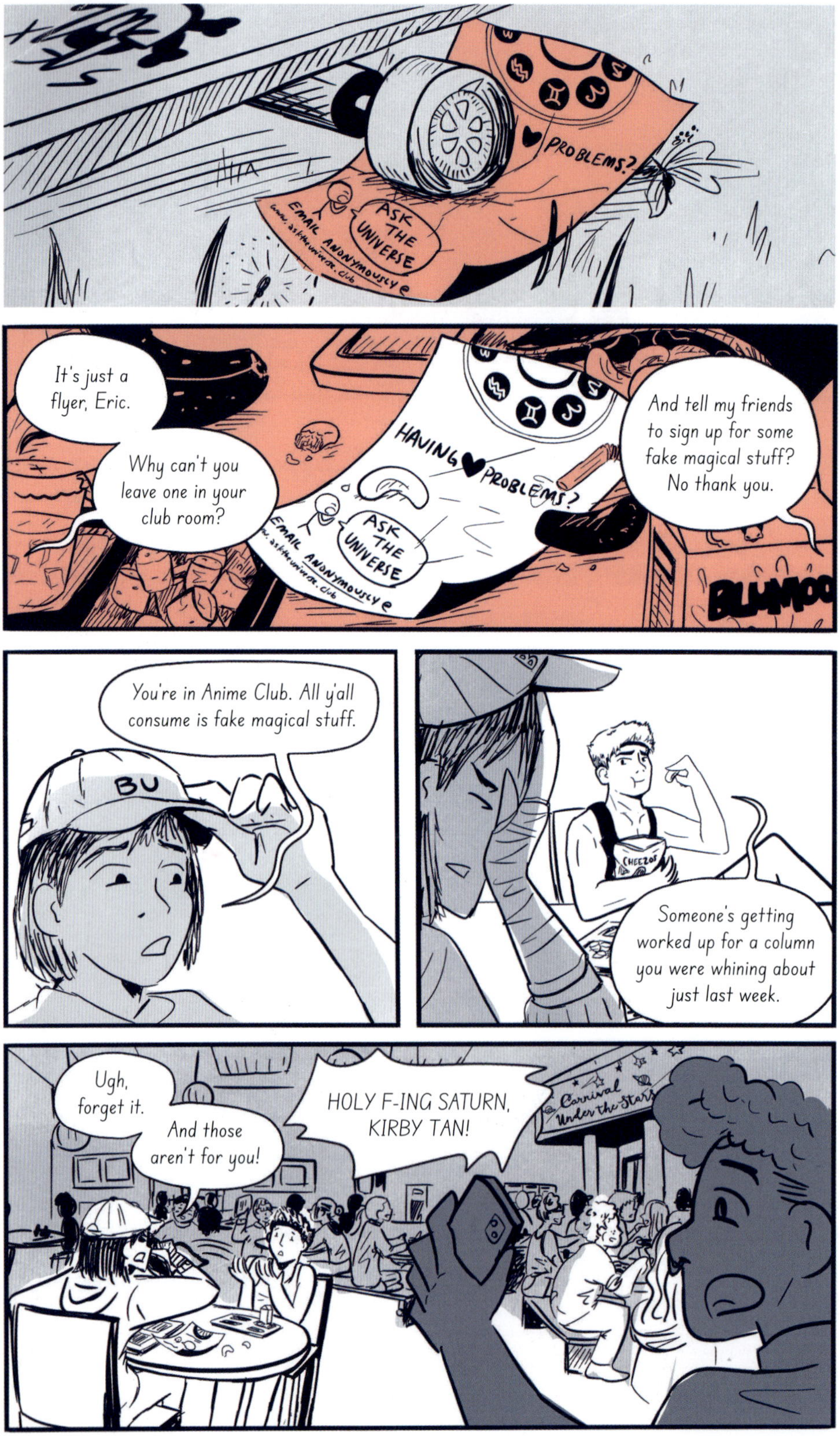
PROBLEMS?
ASK THE UNIVERSE
EMAIL ANONYMOUSLY @
www.asktheuniverse.club
It's just a flyer, Eric.
Why can't you leave one in your club room?
HAVING PROBLEMS?
ASK THE UNIVERSE
EMAIL ANONYMOUSLY @
asktheuniverse.club
And tell my friends to sign up for some fake magical stuff? No thank you.
BLMMO
You're in Anime Club. All y'all consume is fake magical stuff.
BU
CHEEZOS
Someone's getting worked up for a column you were whining about just last week.
Ugh, forget it.
And those aren't for you!
HOLY F-ING SATURN, KIRBY TAN!
Carnival Under the Stars

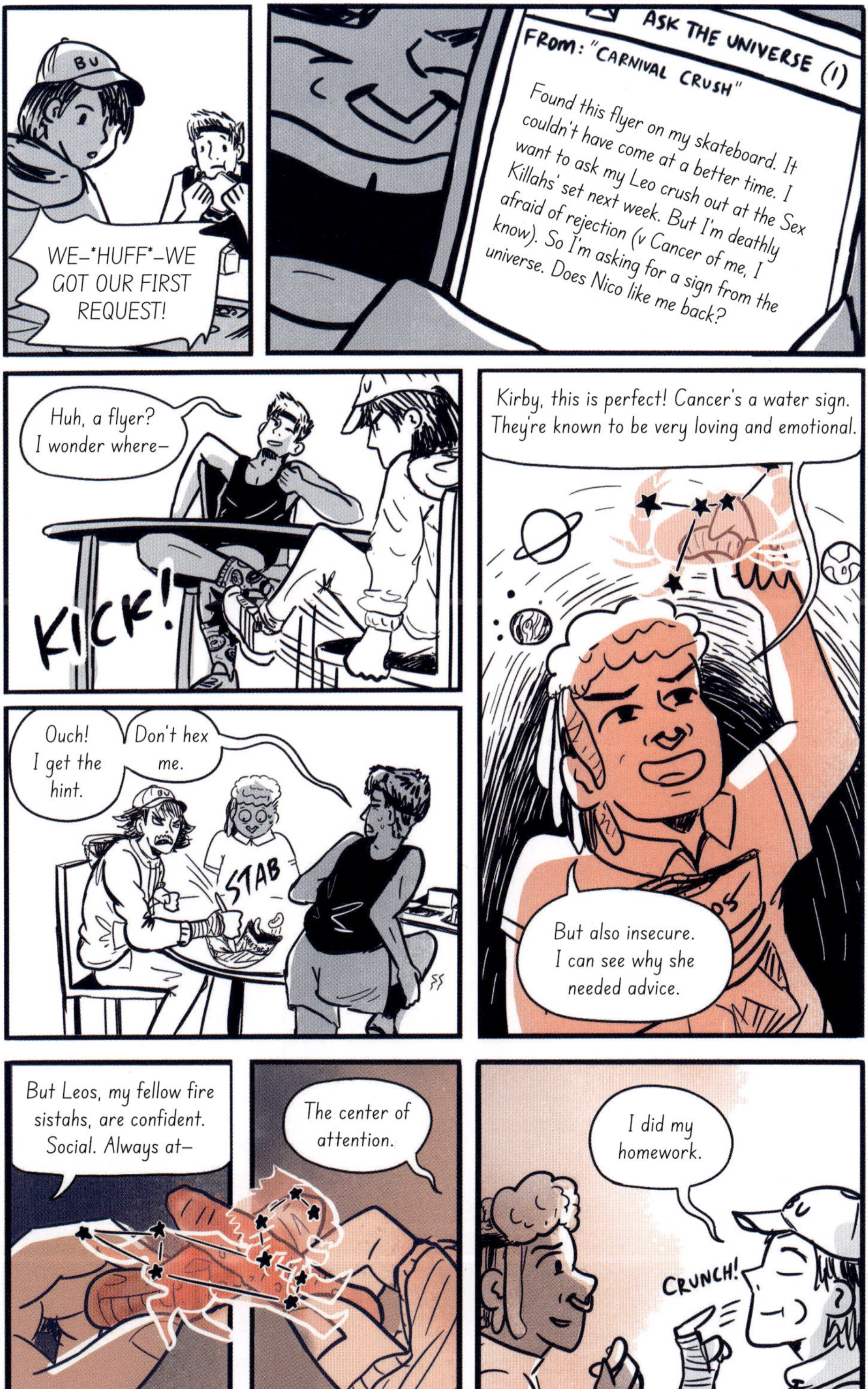
WE–*HUFF*–WE GOT OUR FIRST REQUEST!
ASK THE UNIVERSE (1)
FROM: "CARNIVAL CRUSH"
Found this flyer on my skateboard. It couldn't have come at a better time. I want to ask my Leo crush out at the Sex Killahs' set next week. But I'm deathly afraid of rejection (v Cancer of me, I know). So I'm asking for a sign from the universe. Does Nico like me back?
Huh, a flyer? I wonder where–
KICK!
Kirby, this is perfect! Cancer's a water sign. They're known to be very loving and emotional.
Ouch! I get the hint.
Don't hex me.
STAB
But also insecure. I can see why she needed advice.
But Leos, my fellow fire sistahs, are confident. Social. Always at–
The center of attention.
I did my homework.
CRUNCH!

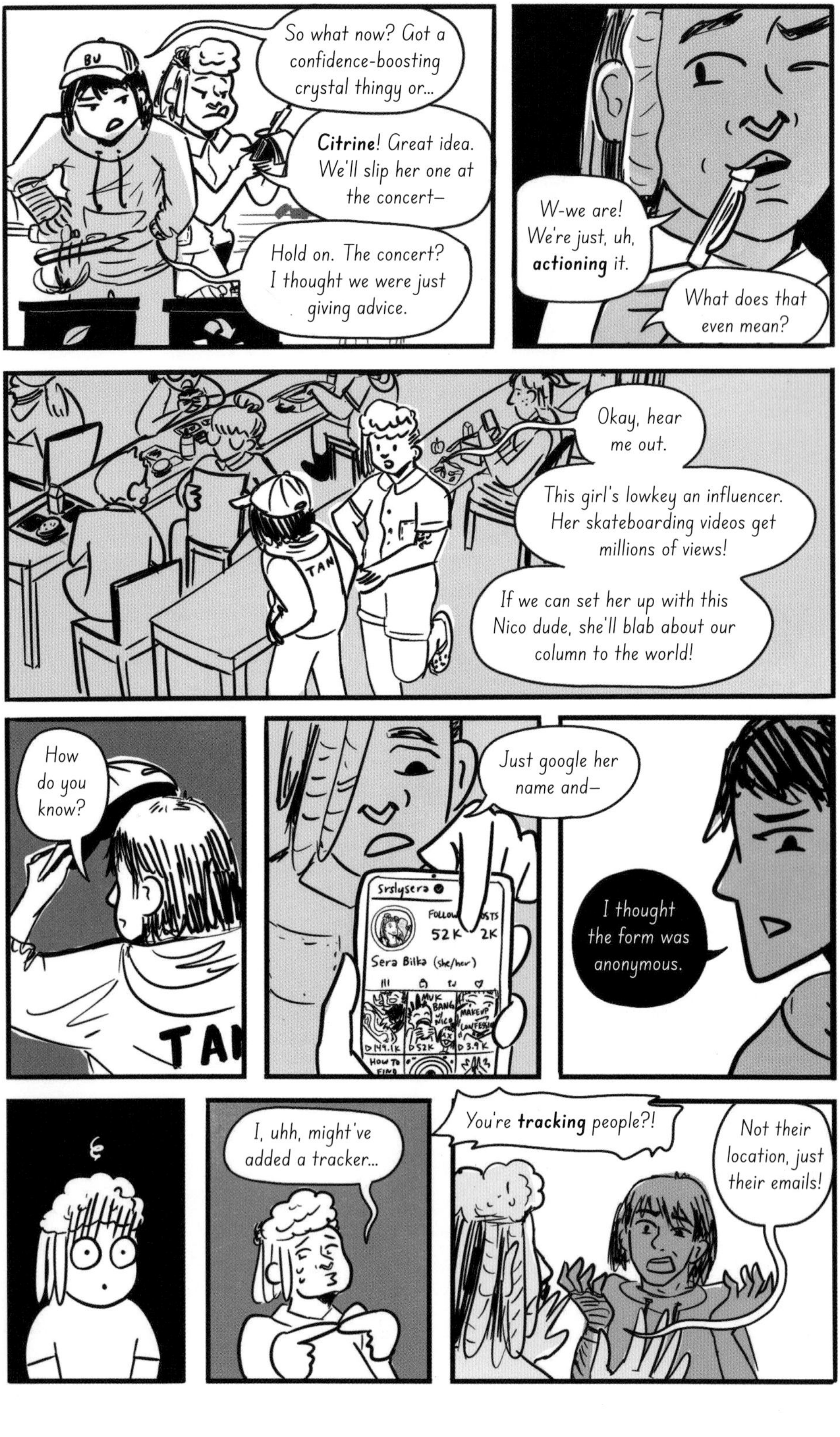
So what now? Got a confidence-boosting crystal thingy or...
Citrine! Great idea. We'll slip her one at the concert—
Hold on. The concert? I thought we were just giving advice.
W-we are! We're just, uh, **actioning** it.
What does that even mean?
Okay, hear me out.
This girl's lowkey an influencer. Her skateboarding videos get millions of views!
If we can set her up with this Nico dude, she'll blab about our column to the world!
How do you know?
Just google her name and—
Srslysera
52K
2K
Sera Bilka (she/her)
I thought the form was anonymous.
I, uhh, might've added a tracker...
You're **tracking** people?!
Not their location, just their emails!

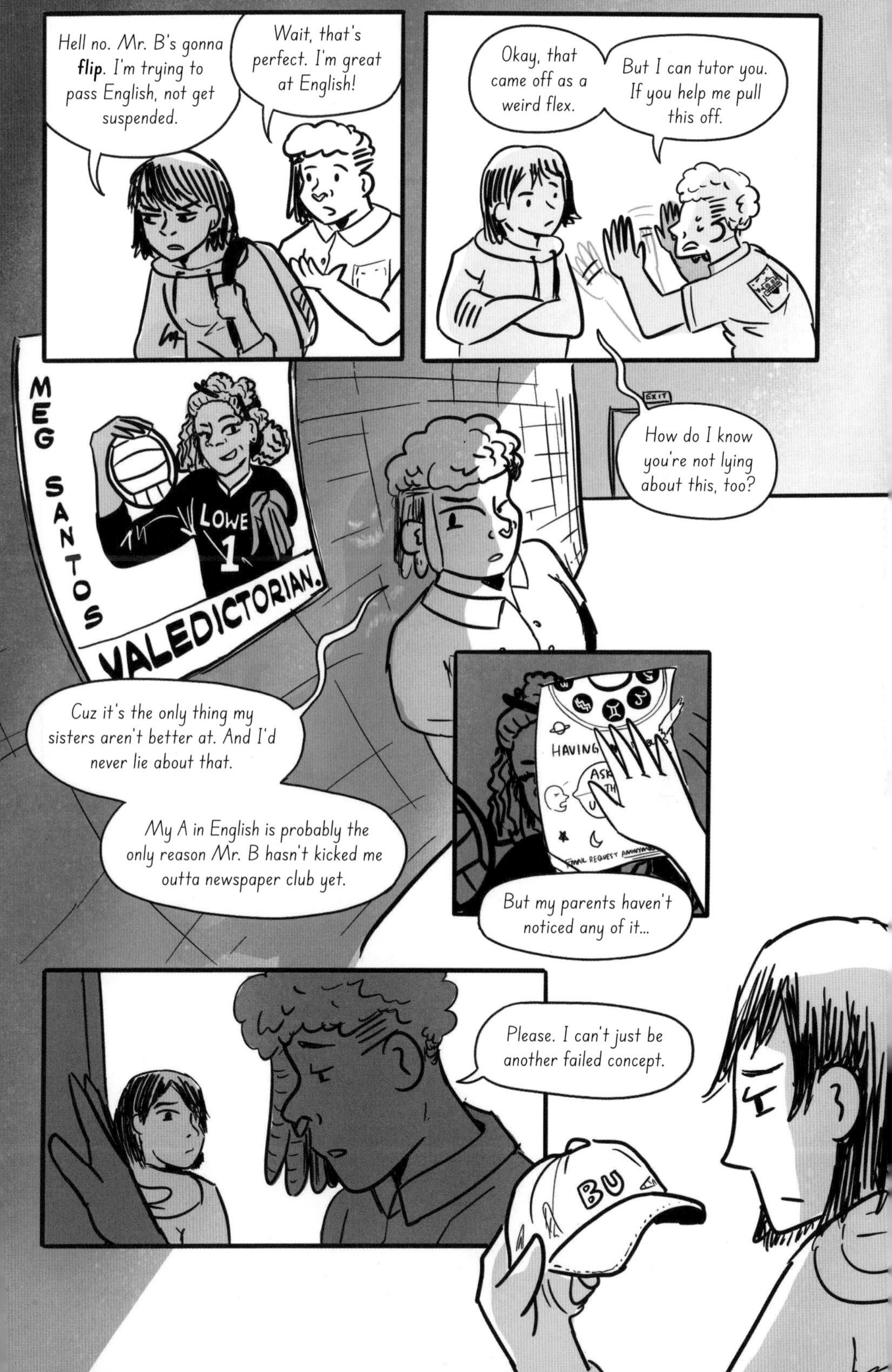

Hell no. Mr. B's gonna **flip**. I'm trying to pass English, not get suspended.
Wait, that's perfect. I'm great at English!
Okay, that came off as a weird flex.
But I can tutor you. If you help me pull this off.
MEG SANTOS
LOWE
1
VALEDICTORIAN.
EXIT
How do I know you're not lying about this, too?
Cuz it's the only thing my sisters aren't better at. And I'd never lie about that.
My A in English is probably the only reason Mr. B hasn't kicked me outta newspaper club yet.
HAVING
But my parents haven't noticed any of it...
Please. I can't just be another failed concept.
BU

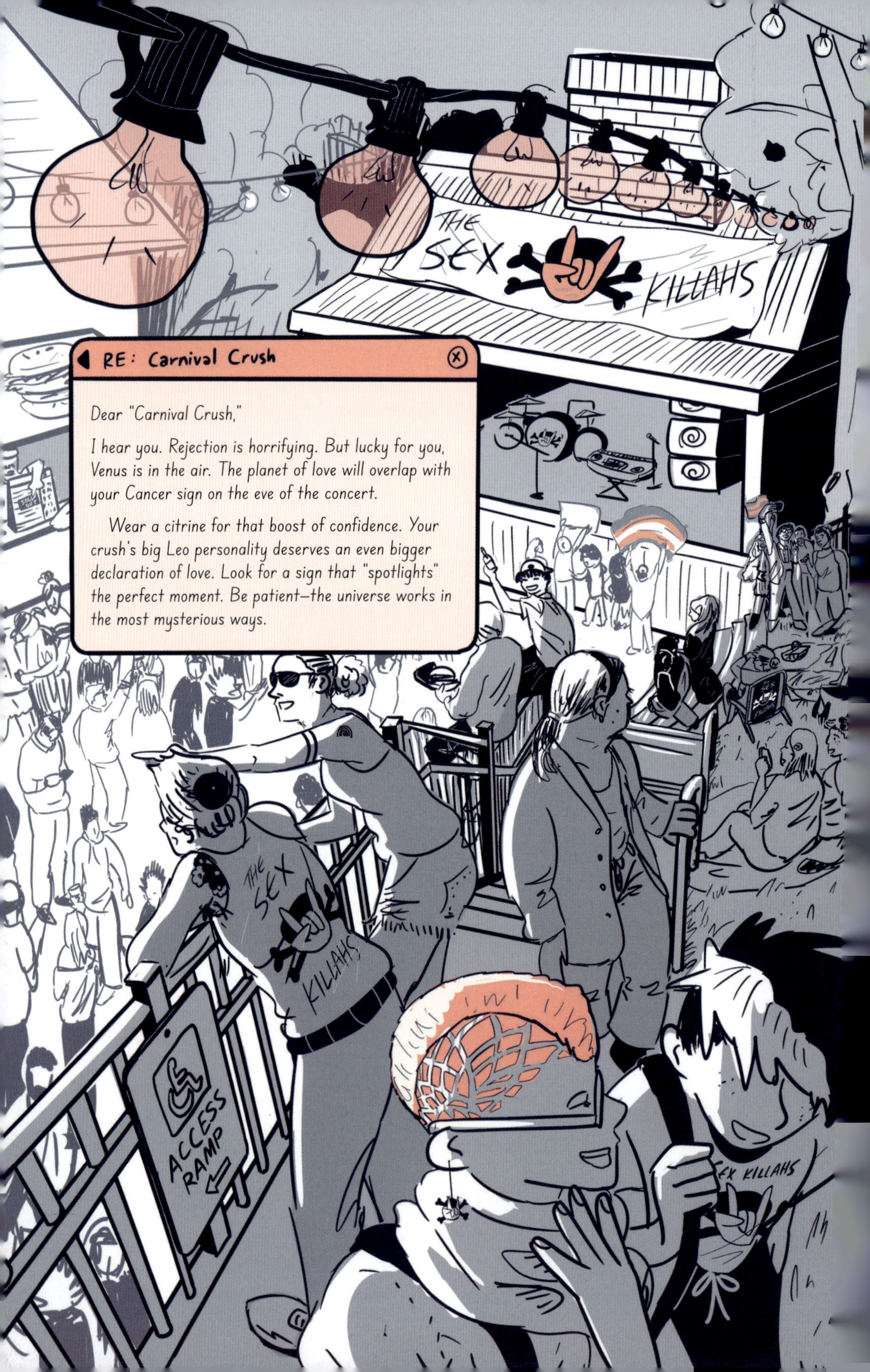
THE SEX KILLAHS
RE: Carnival Crush
Dear "Carnival Crush,"
I hear you. Rejection is horrifying. But lucky for you, Venus is in the air. The planet of love will overlap with your Cancer sign on the eve of the concert.
Wear a citrine for that boost of confidence. Your crush's big Leo personality deserves an even bigger declaration of love. Look for a sign that "spotlights" the perfect moment. Be patient—the universe works in the most mysterious ways.
THE SEX KILLAHS
ACCESS RAMP
SEX KILLAHS

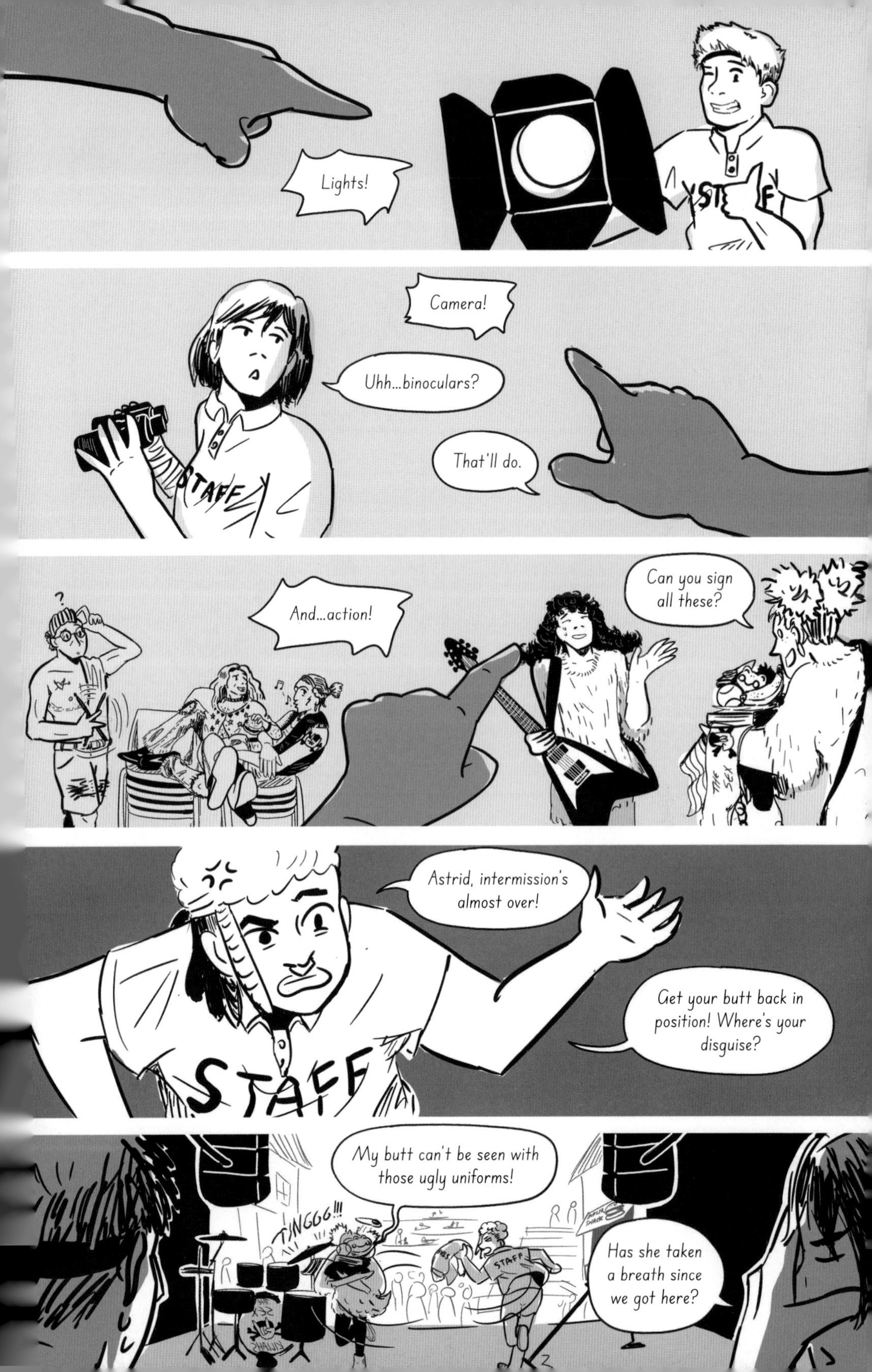
Lights!
Camera!
Uhh...binoculars?
That'll do.
And...action!
Can you sign all these?
Astrid, intermission's almost over!
Get your butt back in position! Where's your disguise?
STAFF
My butt can't be seen with those ugly uniforms!
Has she taken a breath since we got here?

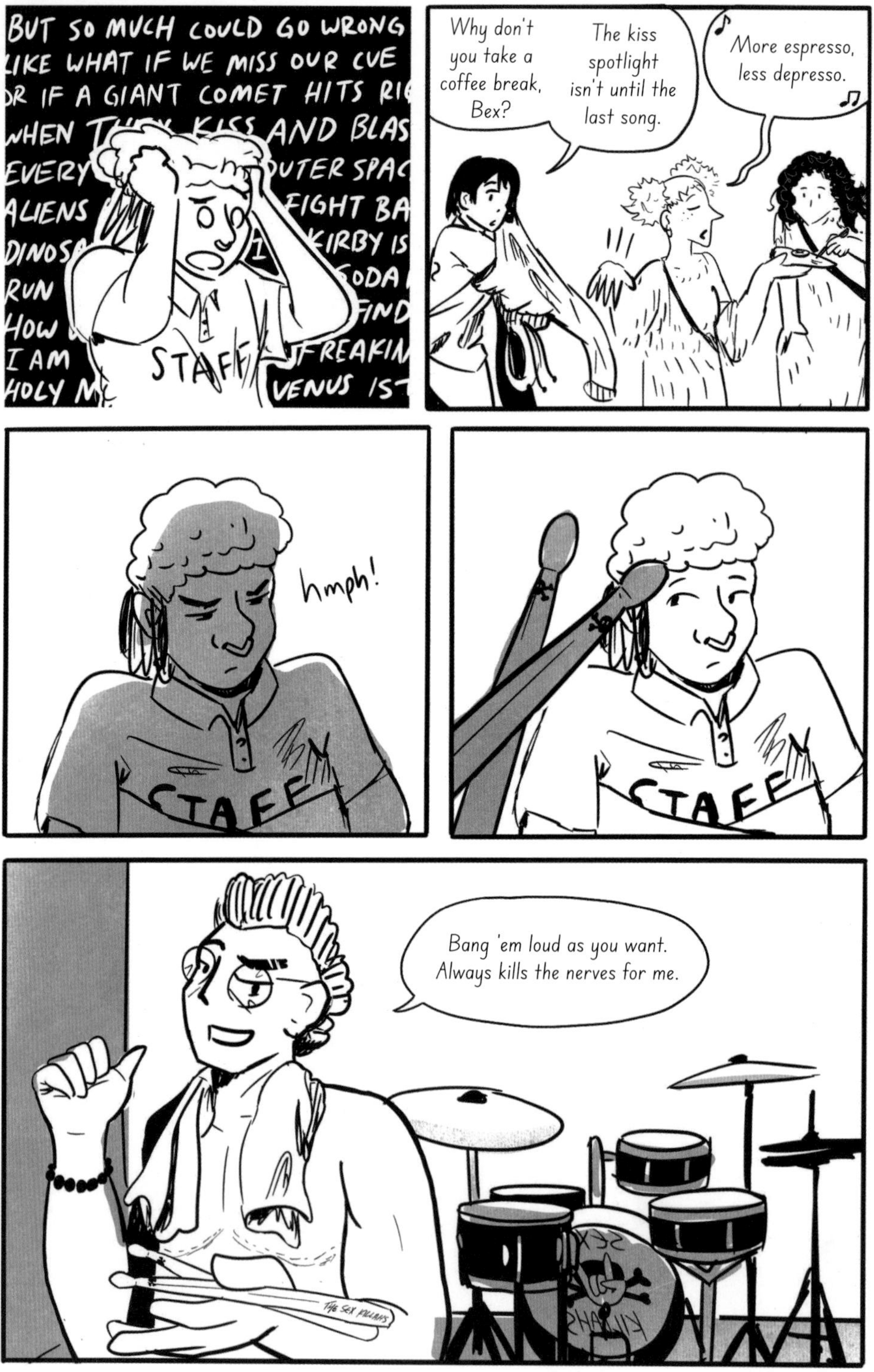
BUT SO MUCH COULD GO WRONG
STAFF
Why don't you take a coffee break, Bex?
The kiss spotlight isn't until the last song.
More espresso, less depresso.
hmph!
STAFF
STAFF
Bang 'em loud as you want. Always kills the nerves for me.

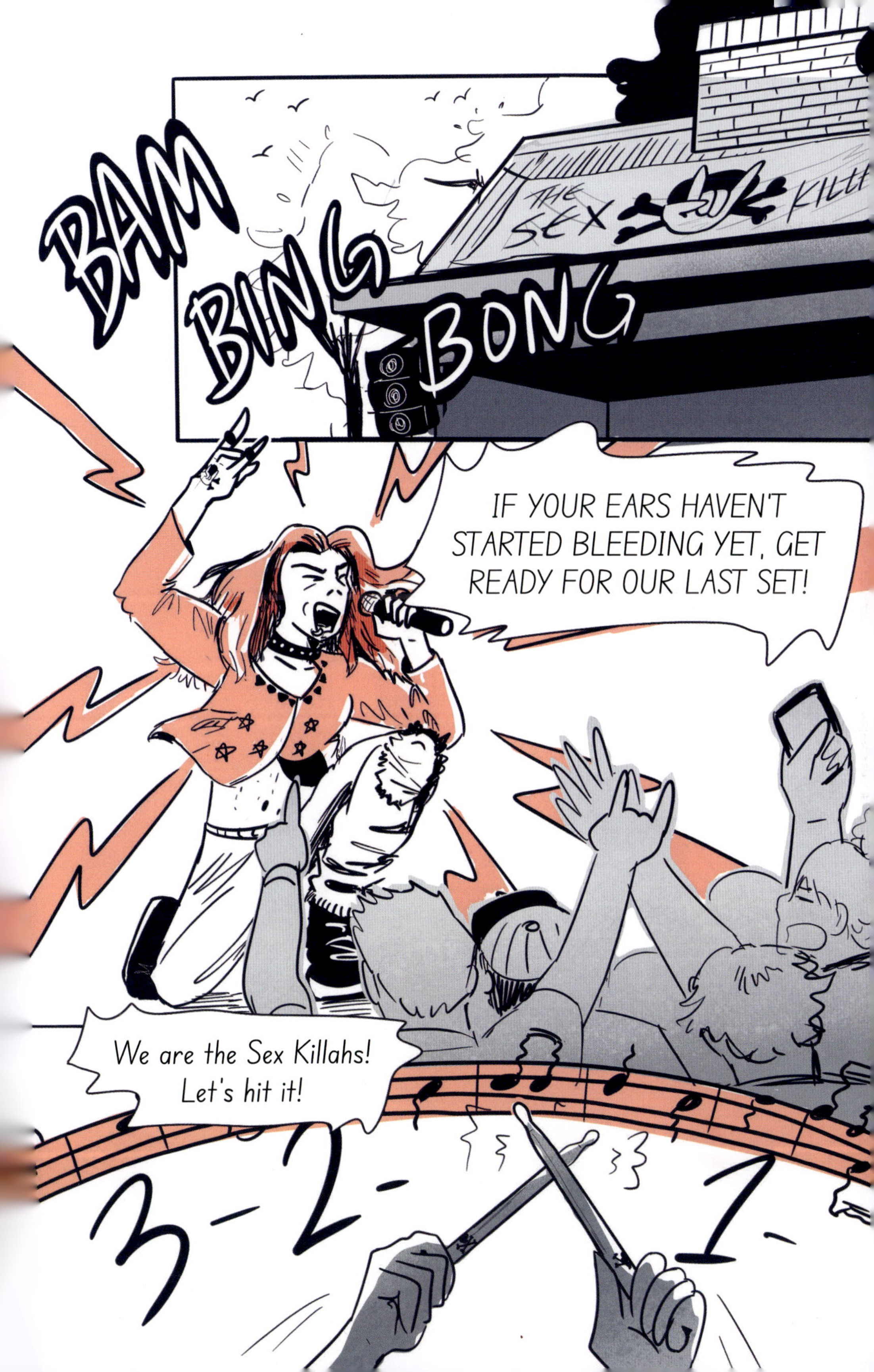
BAM
BING
BONG
IF YOUR EARS HAVEN'T STARTED BLEEDING YET, GET READY FOR OUR LAST SET!
We are the Sex Killahs! Let's hit it!
3-2-1

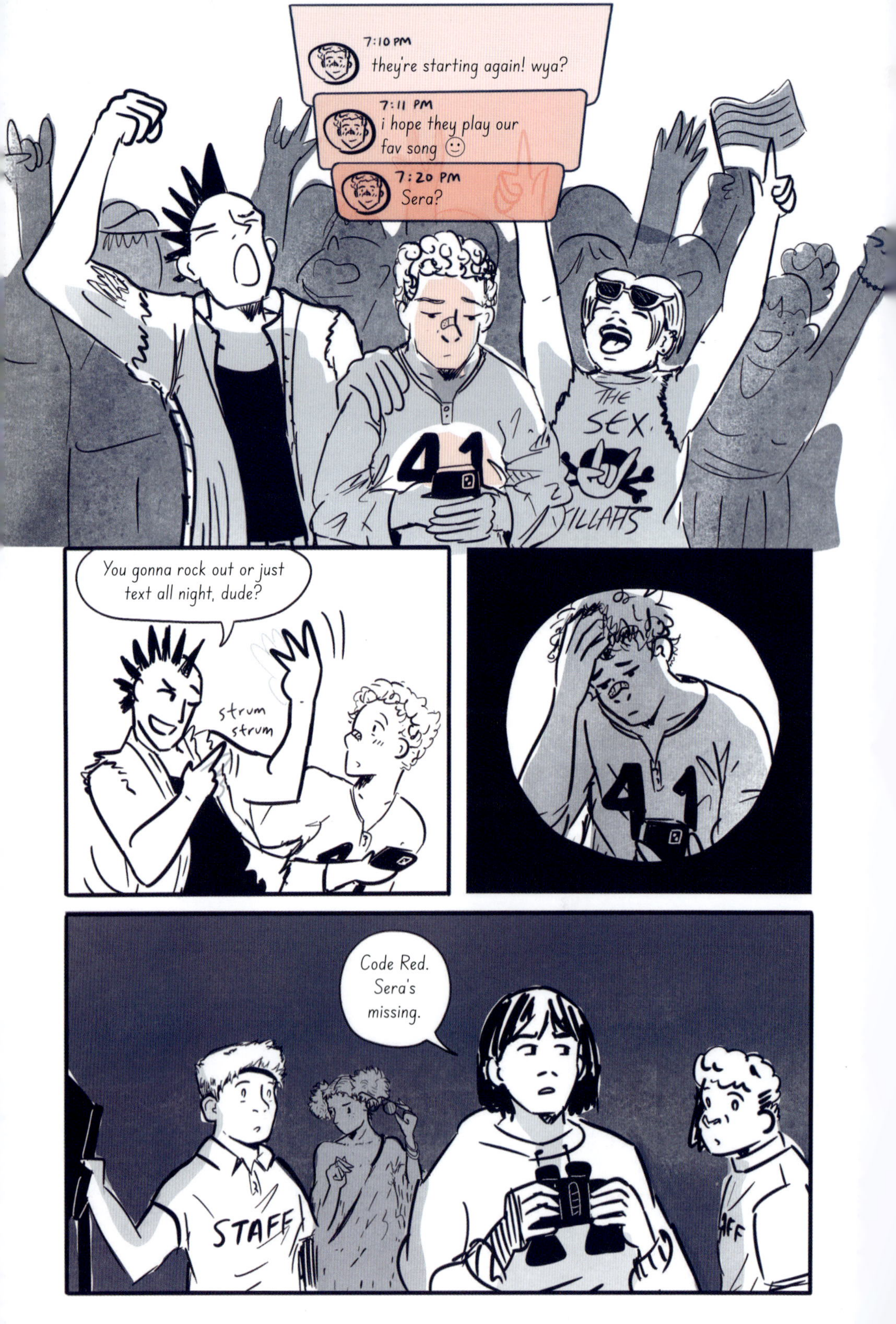
7:10 PM
they're starting again! wya?
7:11 PM
i hope they play our fav song ☺
7:20 PM
Sera?
THE SEX VILLAINS
You gonna rock out or just text all night, dude?
strum strum
Code Red. Sera's missing.
STAFF

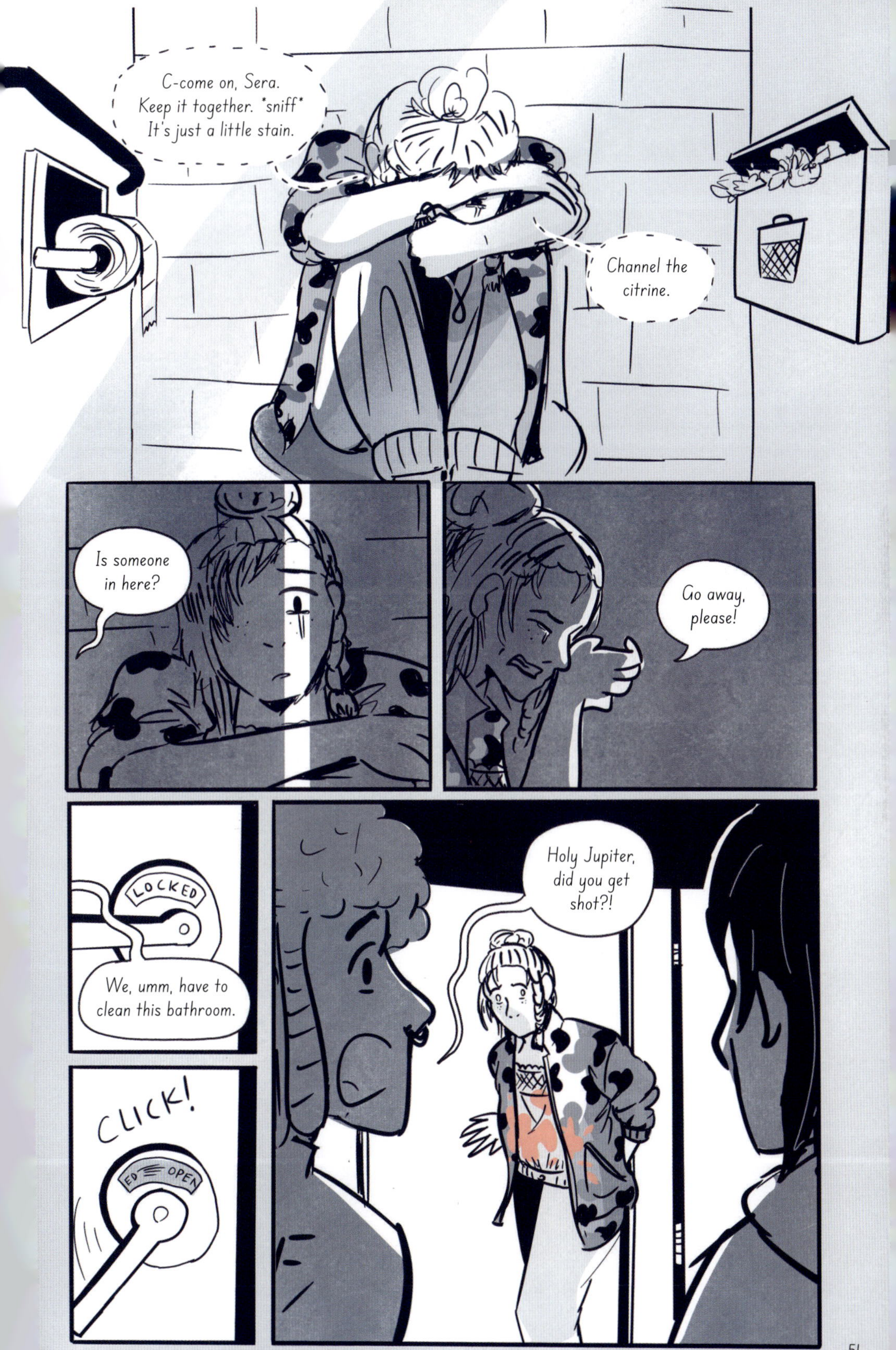
C-come on, Sera.
Keep it together. *sniff*
It's just a little stain.
Channel the citrine.
Is someone in here?
Go away, please!
LOCKED
We, umm, have to clean this bathroom.
CLICK!
OPEN
Holy Jupiter, did you get shot?!

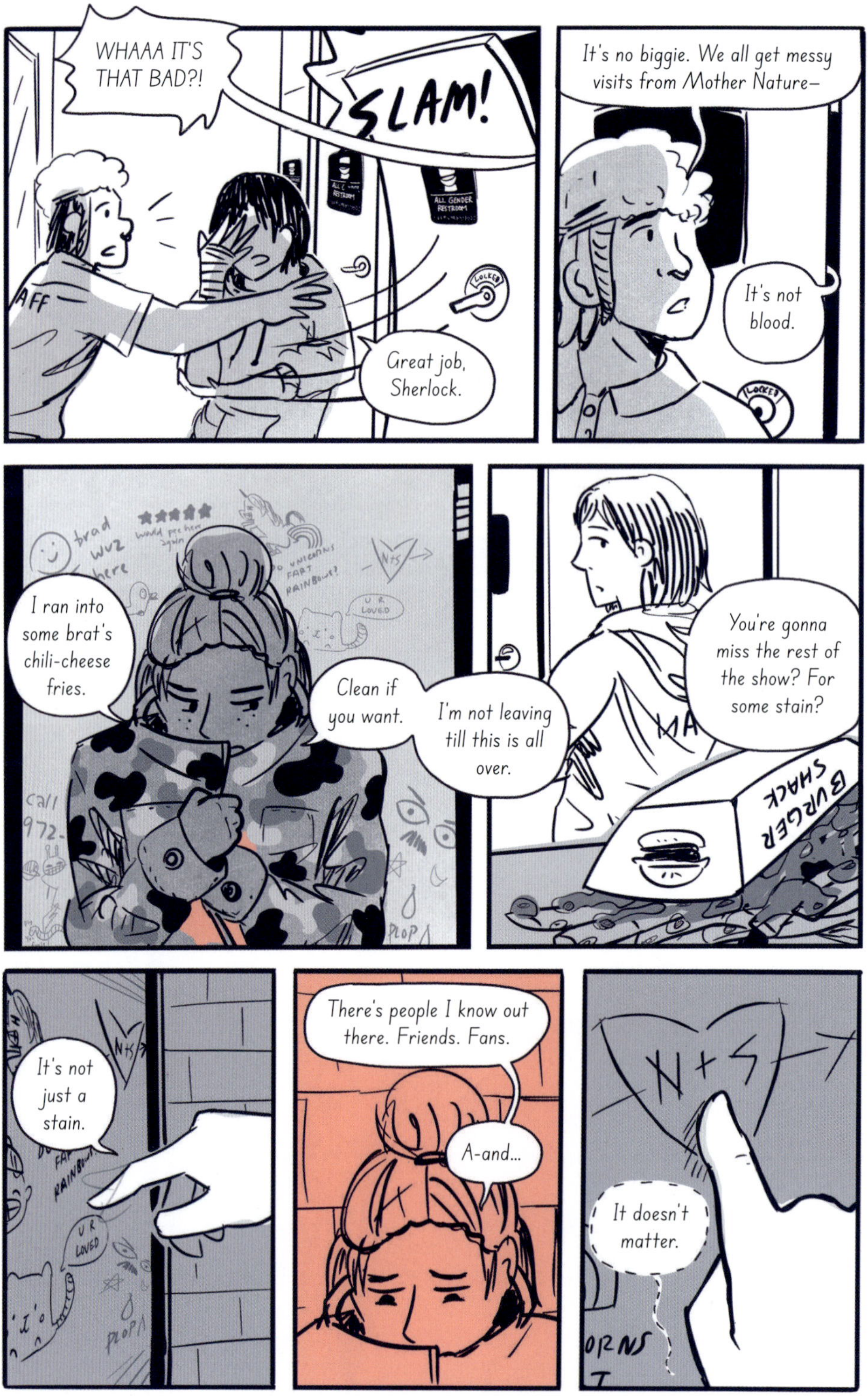
WHAAA IT'S THAT BAD?!
SLAM!
Great job, Sherlock.
It's no biggie. We all get messy visits from Mother Nature–
It's not blood.
I ran into some brat's chili-cheese fries.
Clean if you want.
I'm not leaving till this is all over.
You're gonna miss the rest of the show? For some stain?
BURGER SHACK
It's not just a stain.
There's people I know out there. Friends. Fans.
A-and...
It doesn't matter.

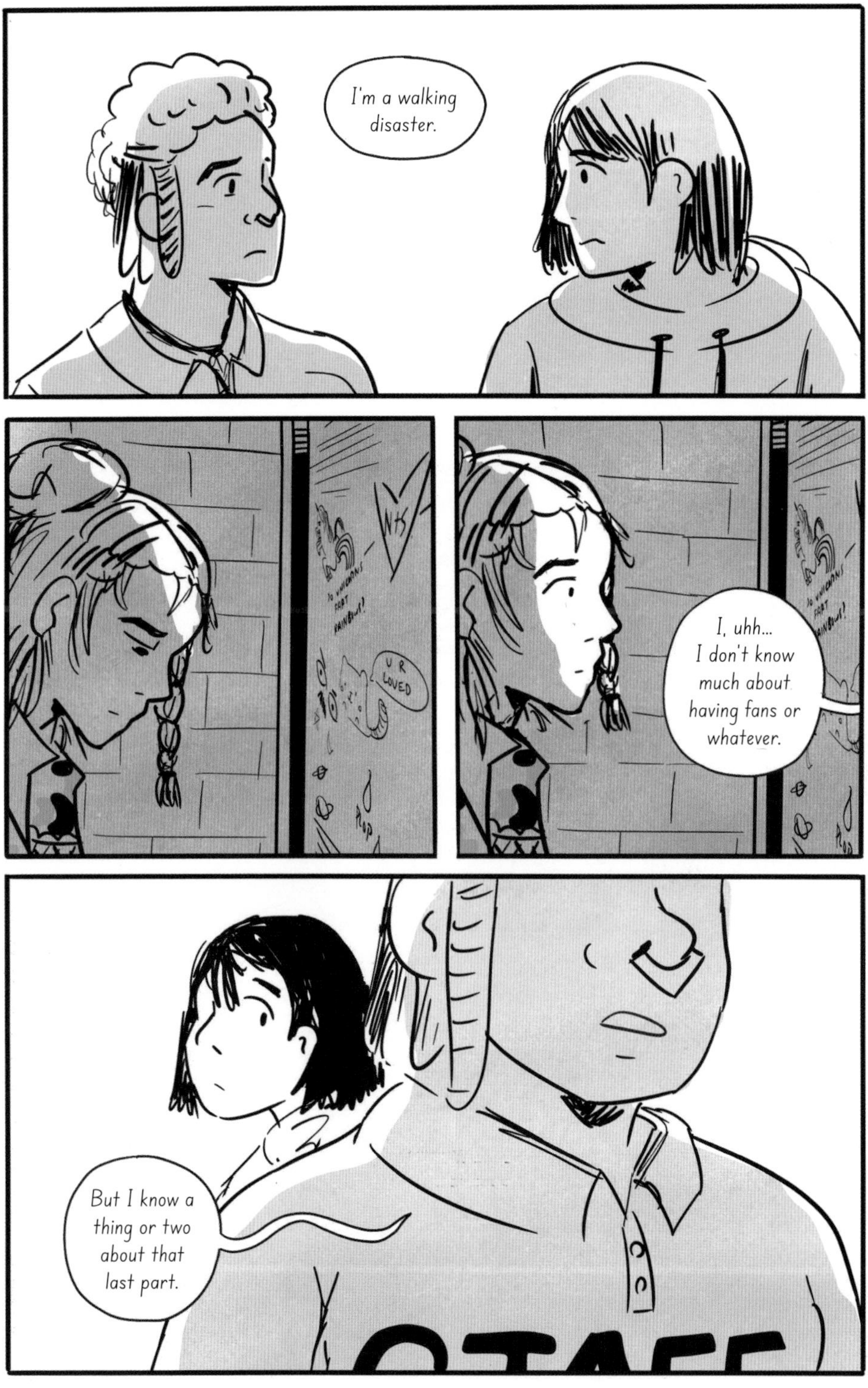
I'm a walking disaster.
U R LOVED
I, uhh... I don't know much about having fans or whatever.
But I know a thing or two about that last part.

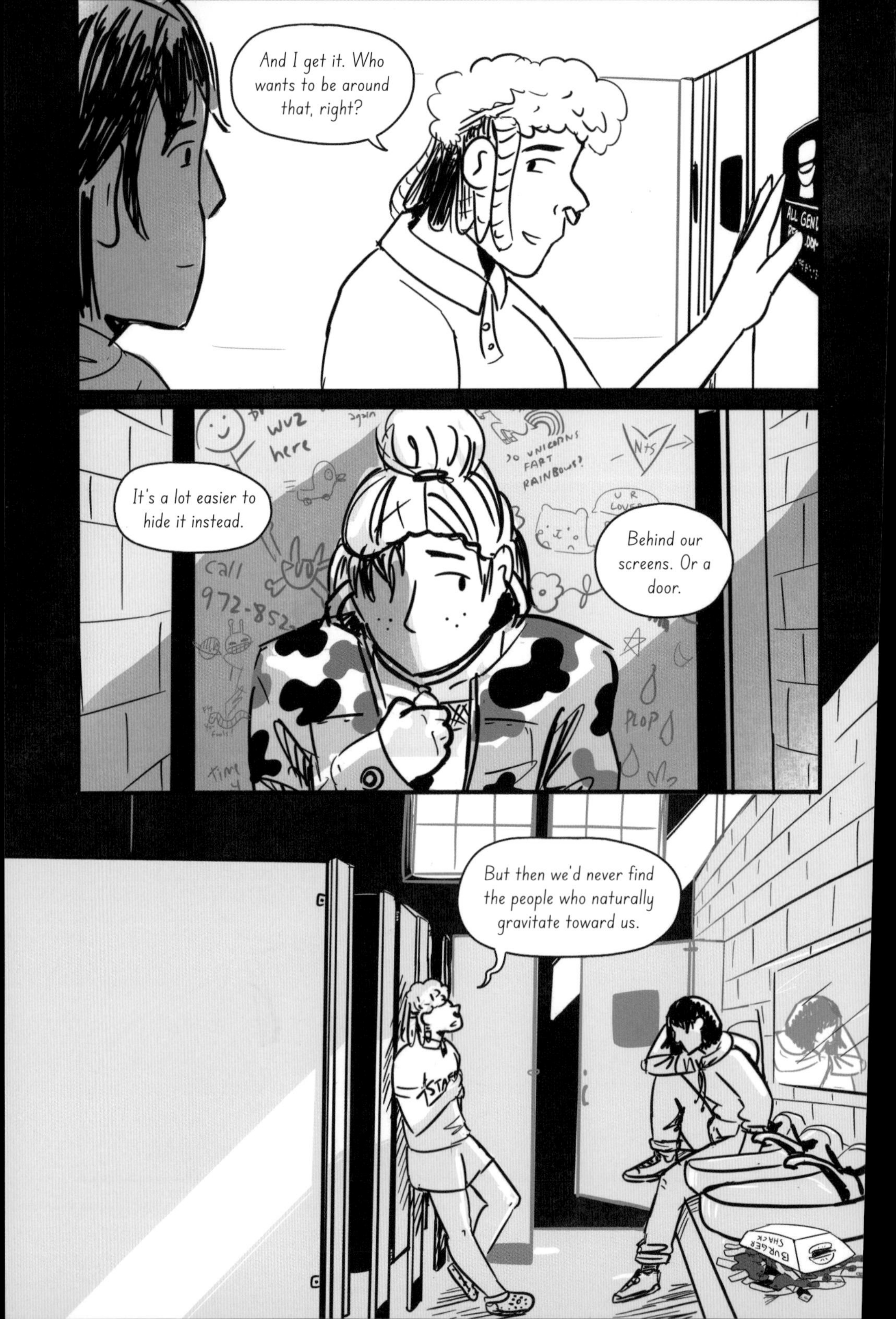
And I get it. Who wants to be around that, right?
ALL GEND
It's a lot easier to hide it instead.
Behind our screens. Or a door.
wuz here
DO UNICORNS FART RAINBOWS?
call 972-852
PLOP
But then we'd never find the people who naturally gravitate toward us.
STAFF
BURGER SHACK

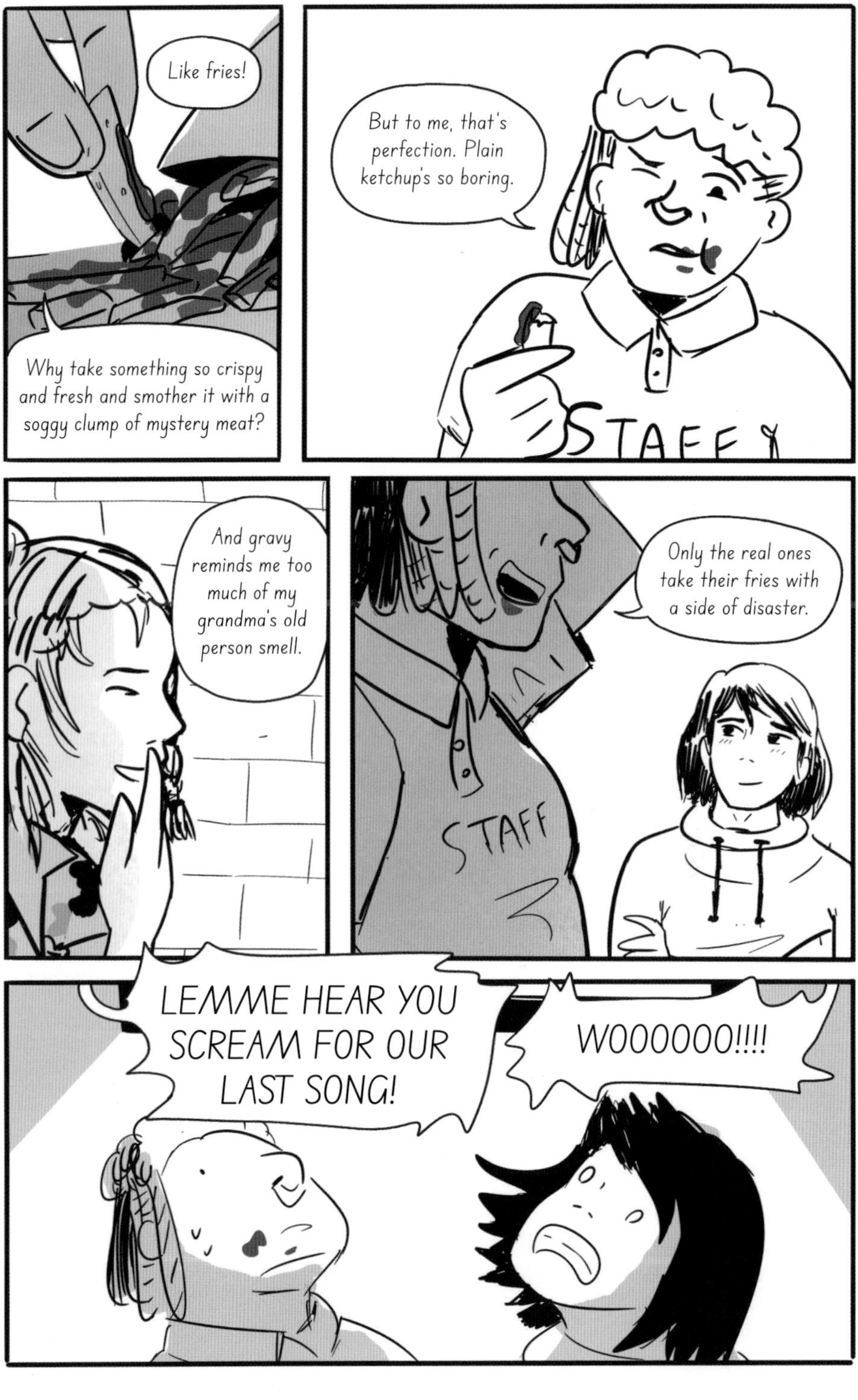
Like fries!
Why take something so crispy and fresh and smother it with a soggy clump of mystery meat?
But to me, that's perfection. Plain ketchup's so boring.
STAFF
And gravy reminds me too much of my grandma's old person smell.
Only the real ones take their fries with a side of disaster.
STAFF
LEMME HEAR YOU SCREAM FOR OUR LAST SONG!
WOOOOOO!!!!

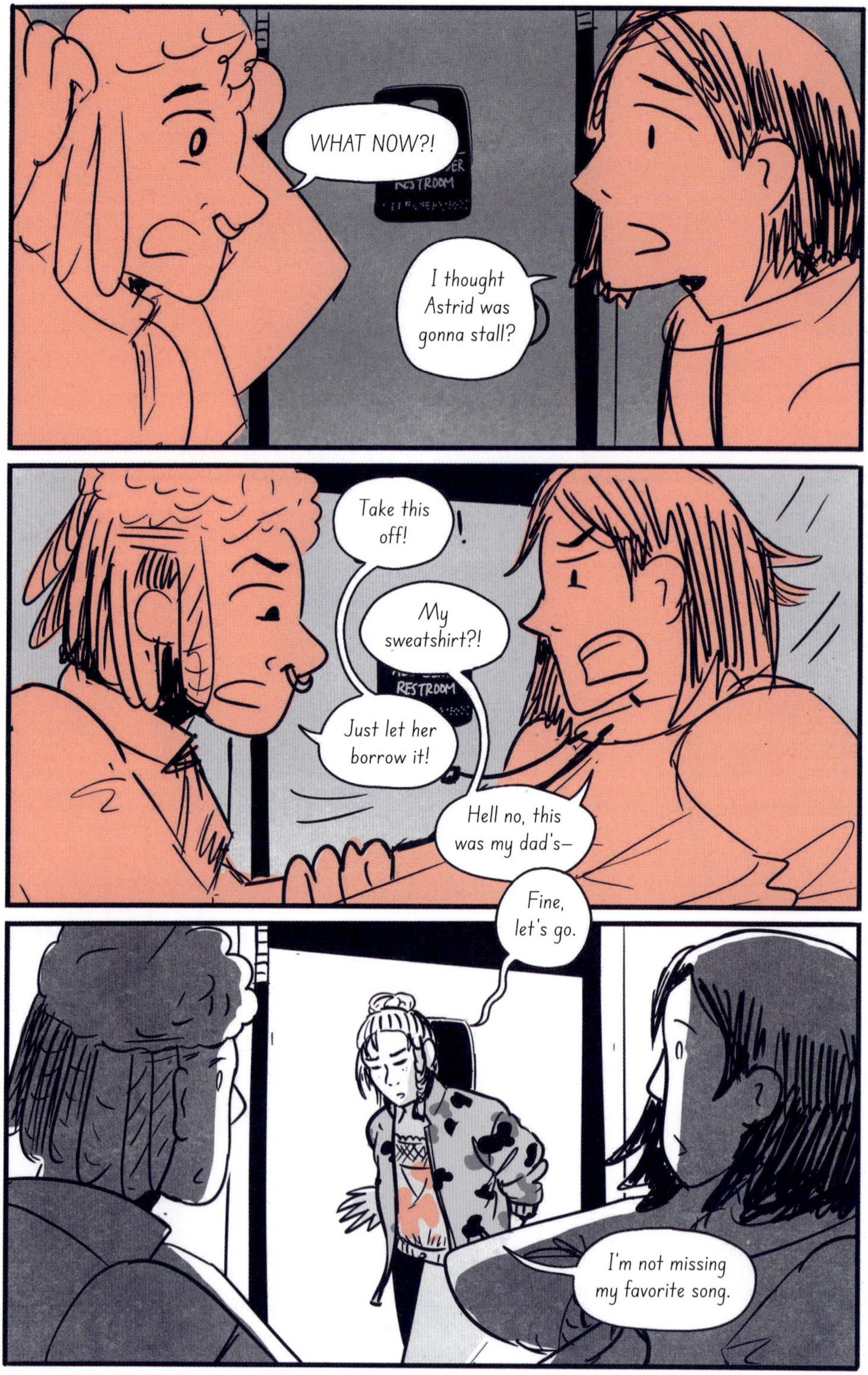
WHAT NOW?!
I thought Astrid was gonna stall?
Take this off!
My sweatshirt?!
Just let her borrow it!
Hell no, this was my dad's—
Fine, let's go.
I'm not missing my favorite song.

STAGE

Crap, it's locked! Where's the ticket person—

CLICK!

I got you.

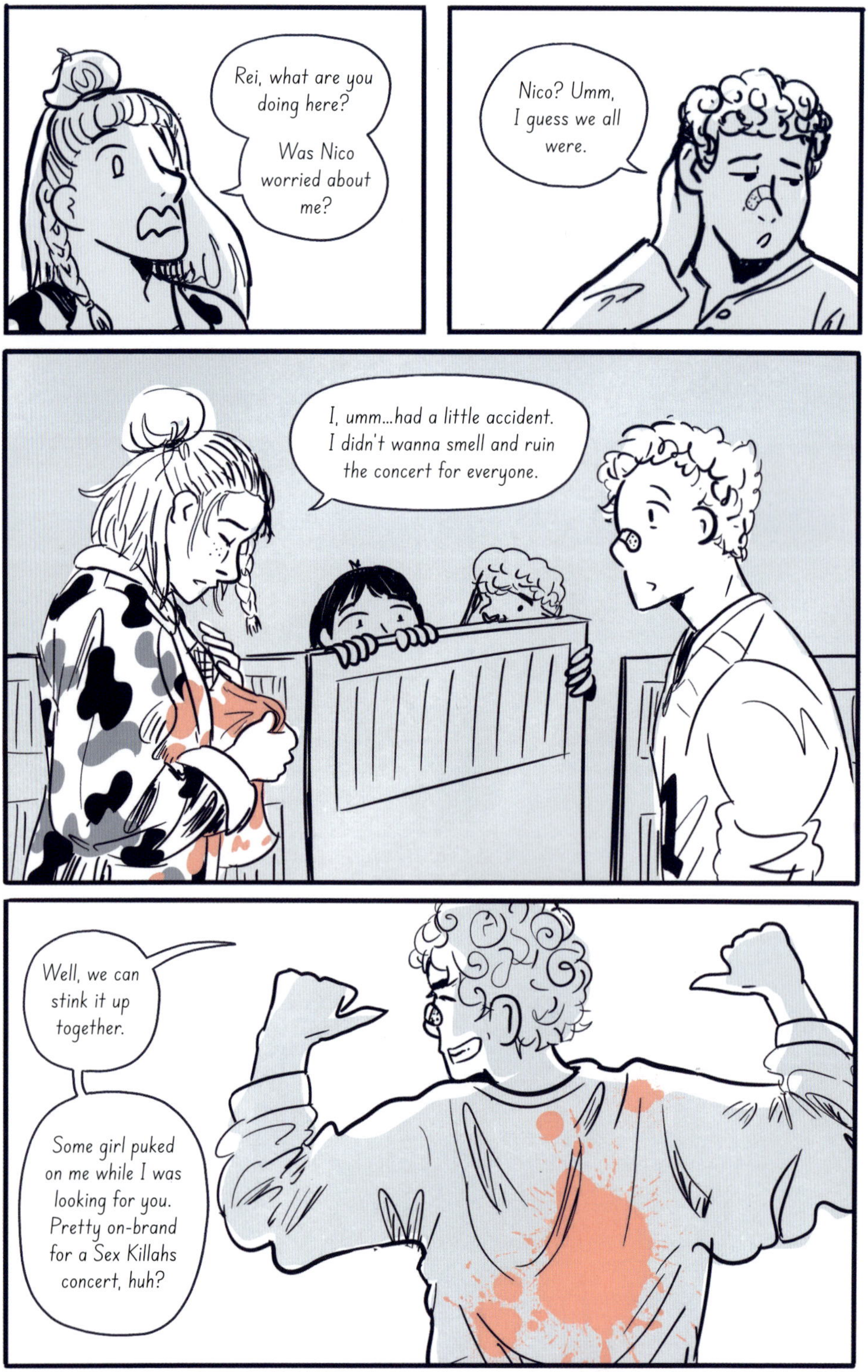
Rei, what are you doing here?
Was Nico worried about me?
Nico? Umm, I guess we all were.
I, umm...had a little accident. I didn't wanna smell and ruin the concert for everyone.
Well, we can stink it up together.
Some girl puked on me while I was looking for you. Pretty on-brand for a Sex Killahs concert, huh?

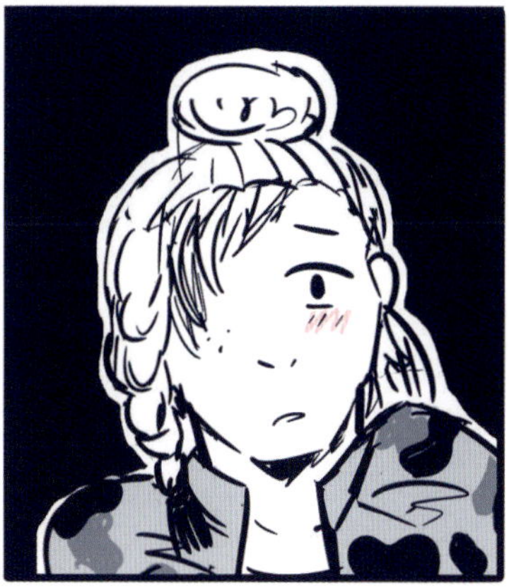

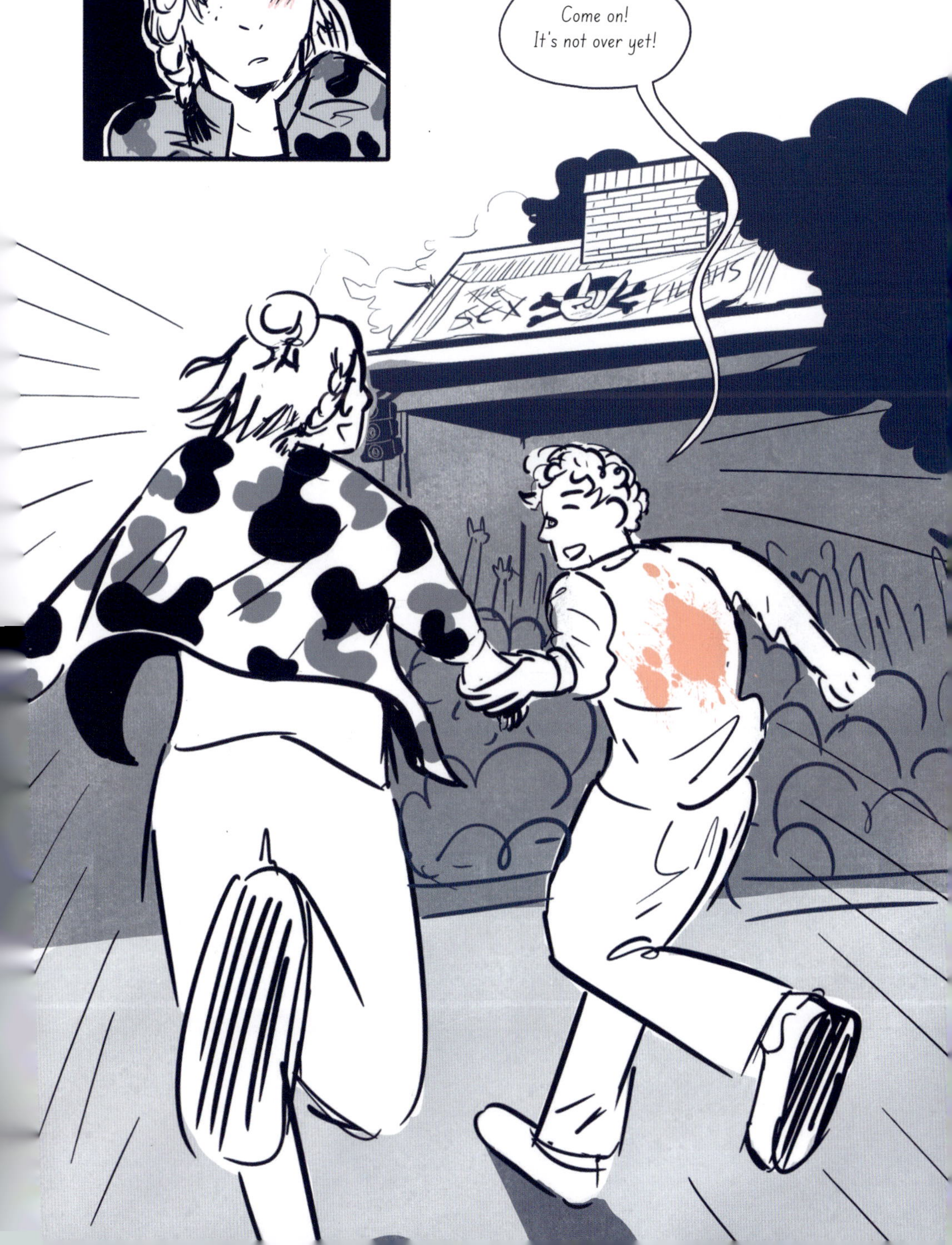
Come on!
It's not over yet!

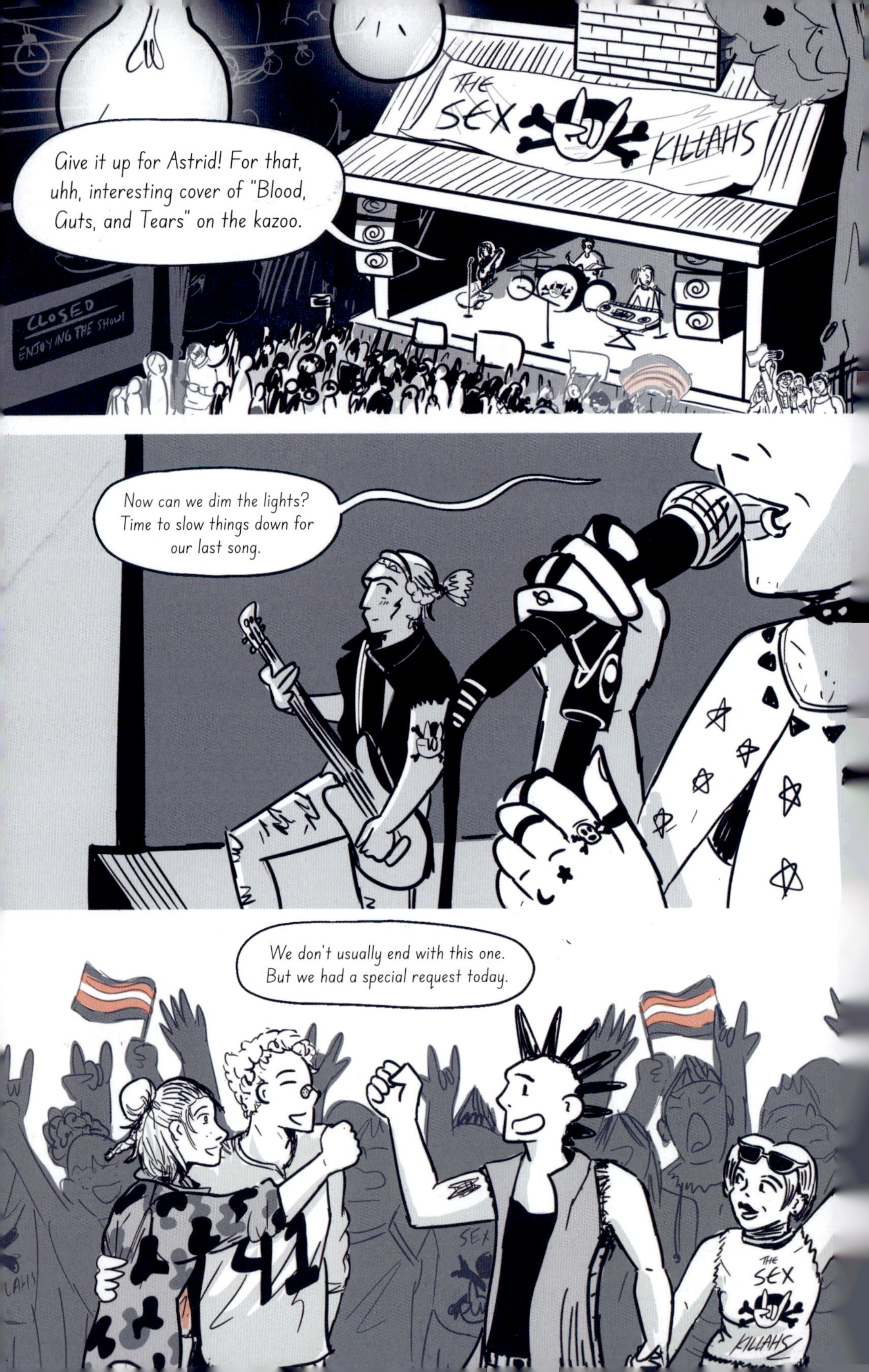
THE SEX KILLAHS
CLOSED
ENJOYING THE SHOW!
Give it up for Astrid! For that, uhh, interesting cover of "Blood, Guts, and Tears" on the kazoo.
Now can we dim the lights? Time to slow things down for our last song.
We don't usually end with this one. But we had a special request today.
THE SEX KILLAHS

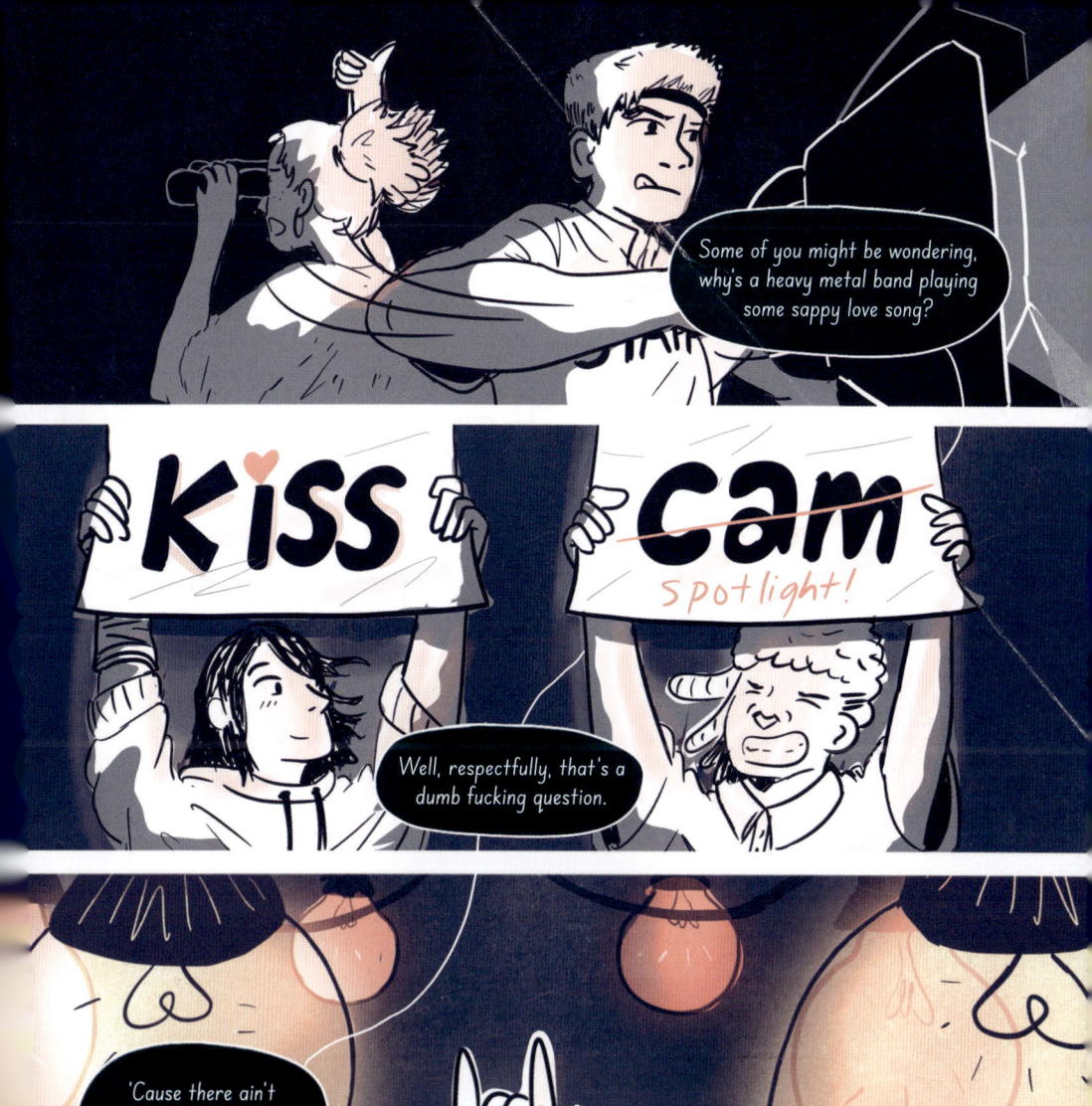

Some of you might be wondering, why's a heavy metal band playing some sappy love song?

KISS cam ~~cam~~ spotlight!

Well, respectfully, that's a dumb fucking question.

'Cause there ain't nothing more metal...

...than loving who you want.

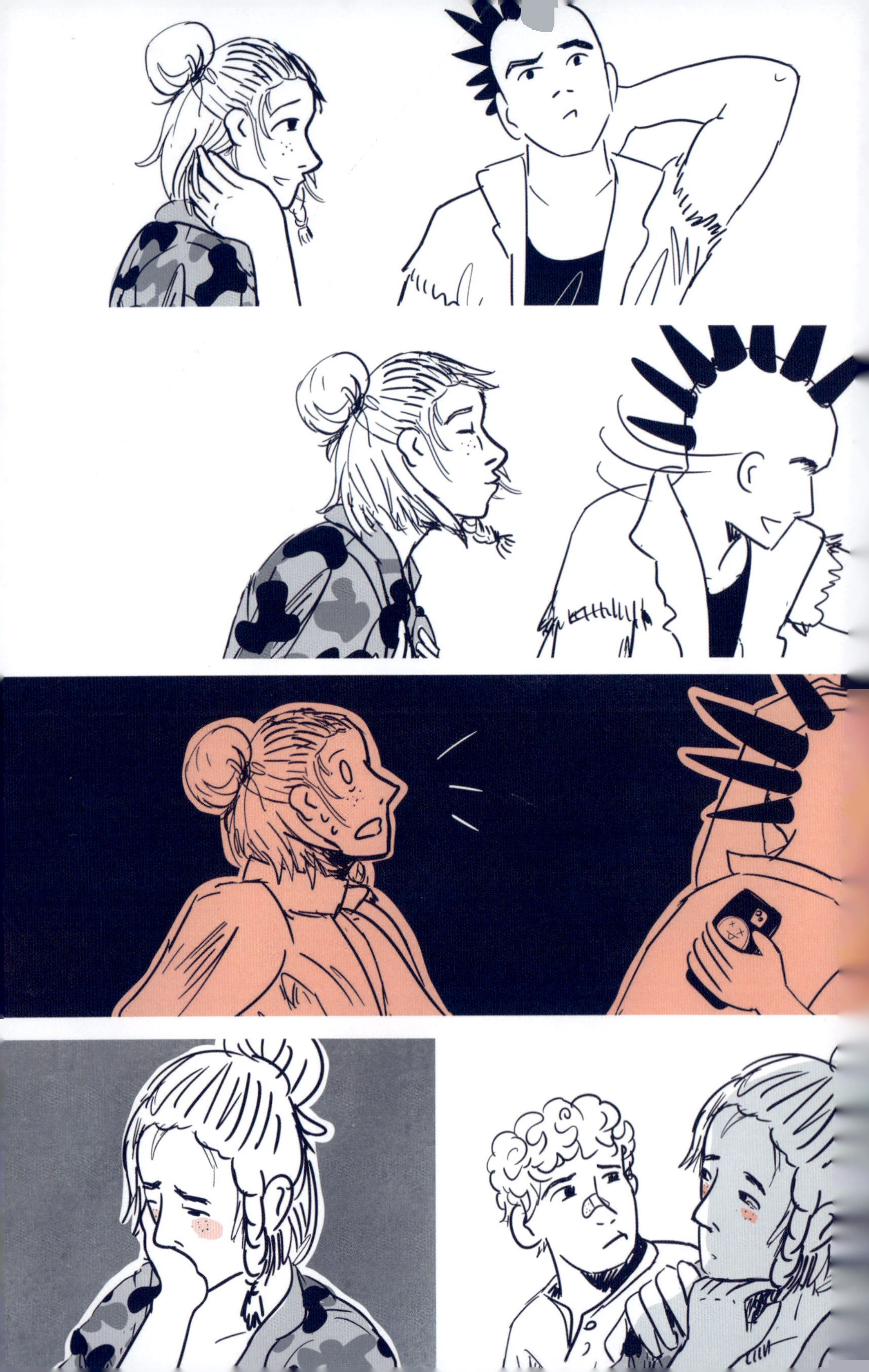

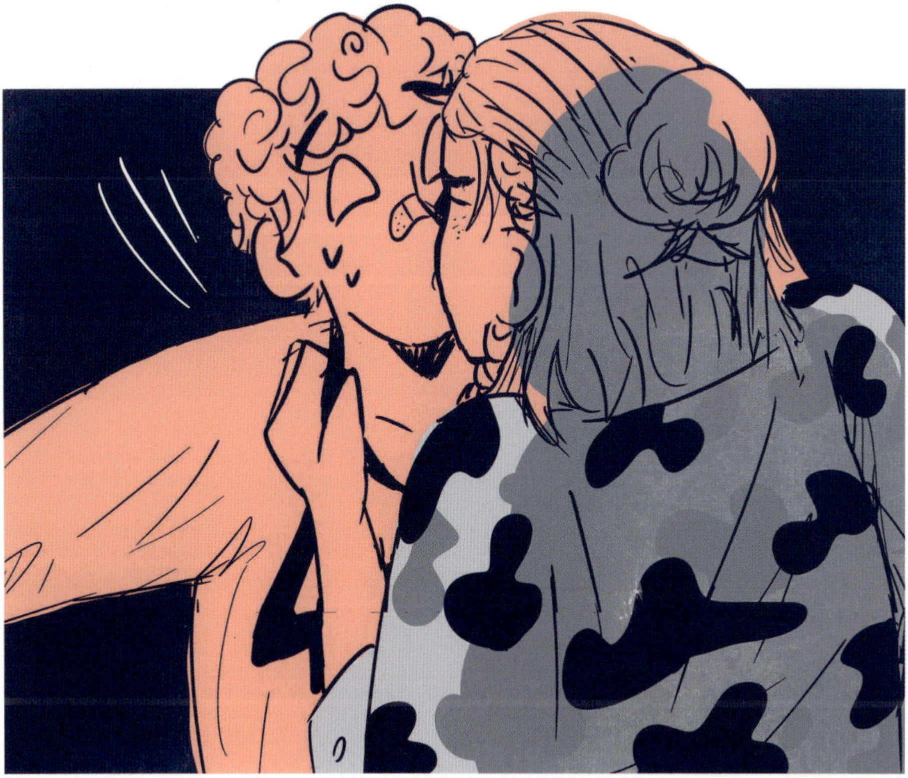

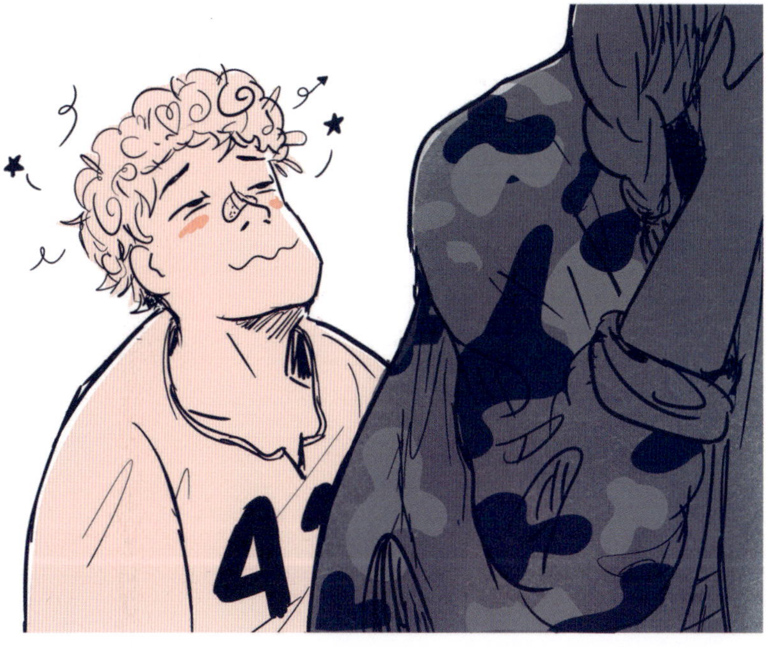

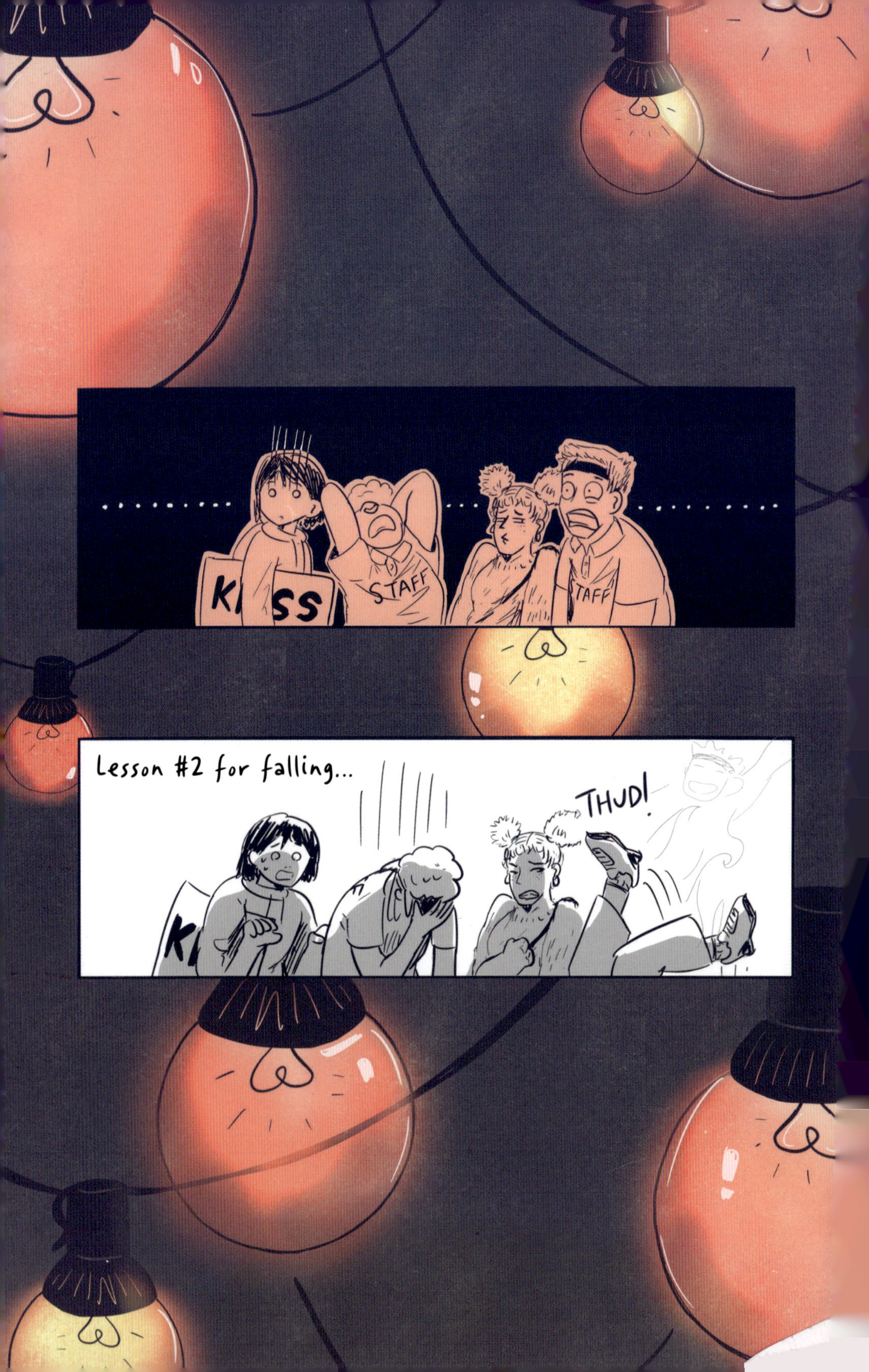
KISS
STAFF
STAFF
Lesson #2 for falling...
THUD!

PART 2

The Star
FAITH
INSECURITY

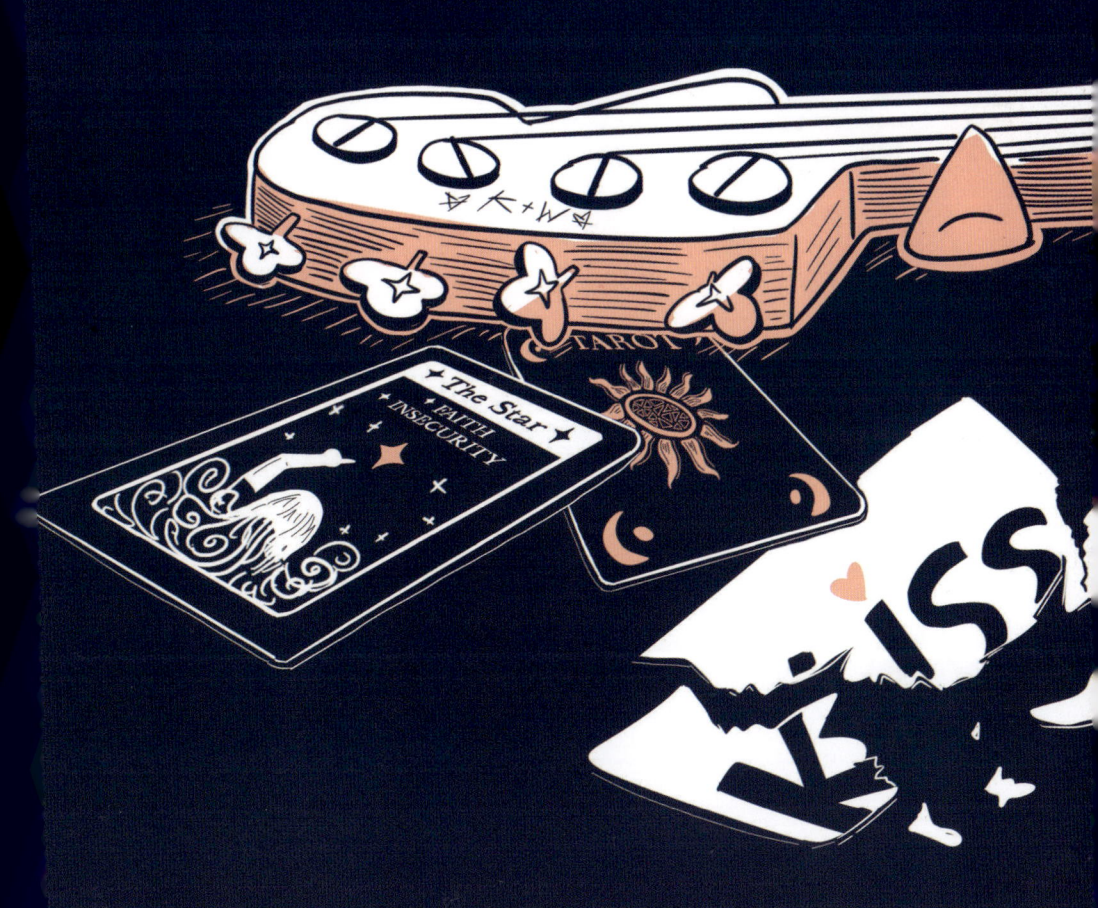

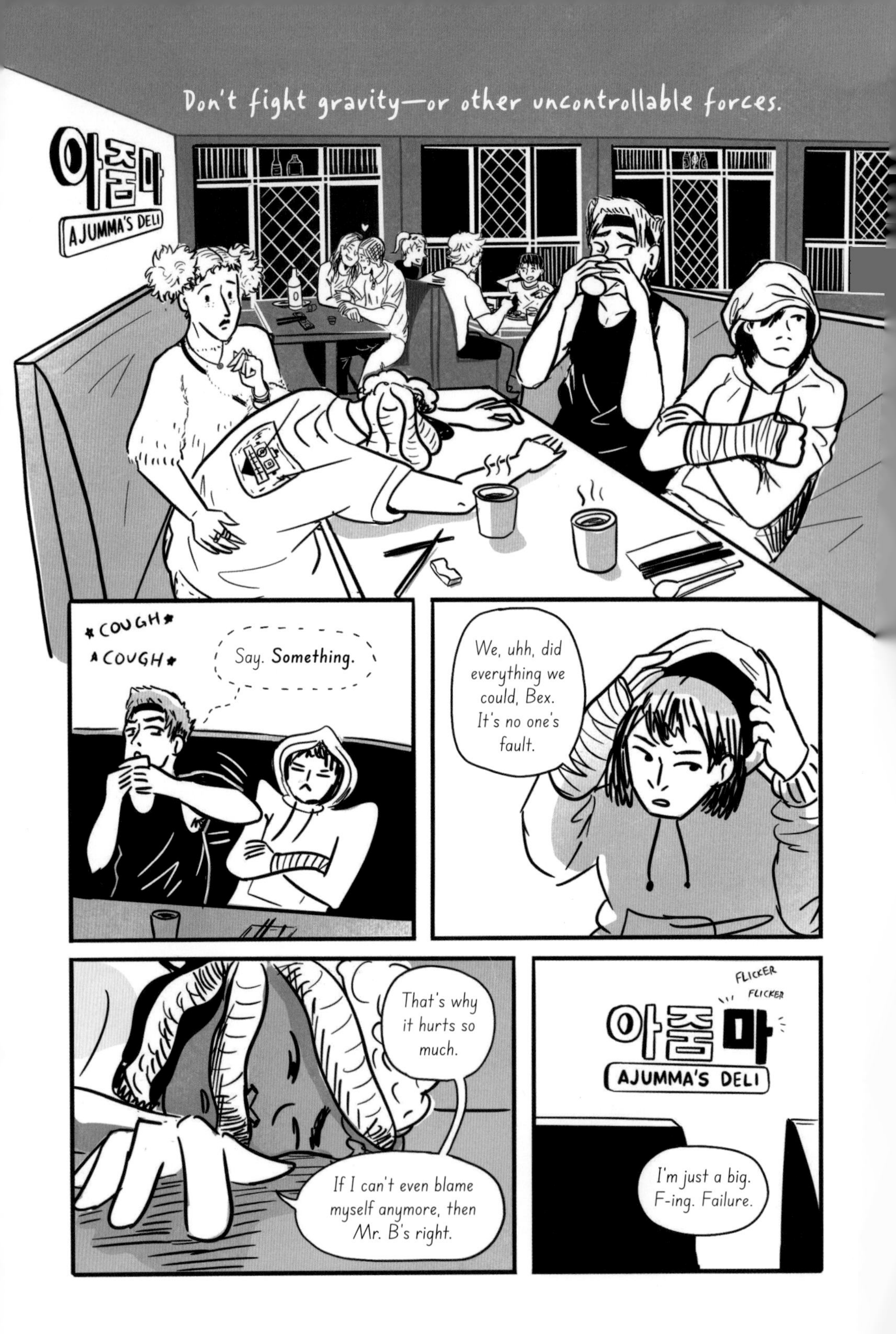
Don't fight gravity—or other uncontrollable forces.
아줌마
AJUMMA'S DELI
COUGH
COUGH
Say. Something.
We, uhh, did everything we could, Bex. It's no one's fault.
That's why it hurts so much.
If I can't even blame myself anymore, then Mr. B's right.
FLICKER
FLICKER
아줌마
AJUMMA'S DELI
I'm just a big. F-ing. Failure.

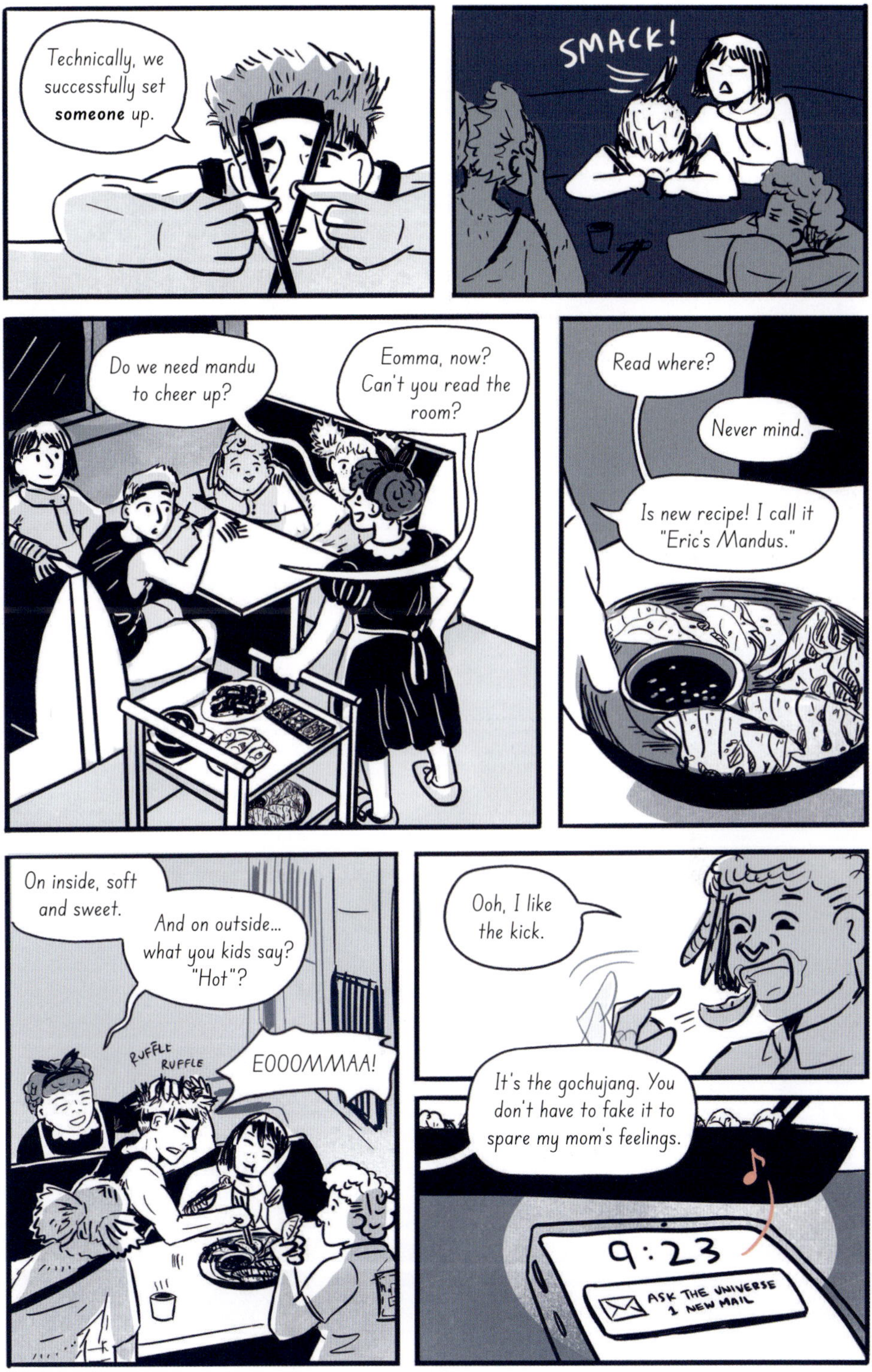
Technically, we successfully set **someone** up.
SMACK!
Do we need mandu to cheer up?
Eomma, now? Can't you read the room?
Read where?
Never mind.
Is new recipe! I call it "Eric's Mandus."
On inside, soft and sweet.
And on outside... what you kids say? "Hot"?
RUFFLE RUFFLE
EOOOMMAA!
Ooh, I like the kick.
It's the gochujang. You don't have to fake it to spare my mom's feelings.
9:23
ASK THE UNIVERSE 1 NEW MAIL

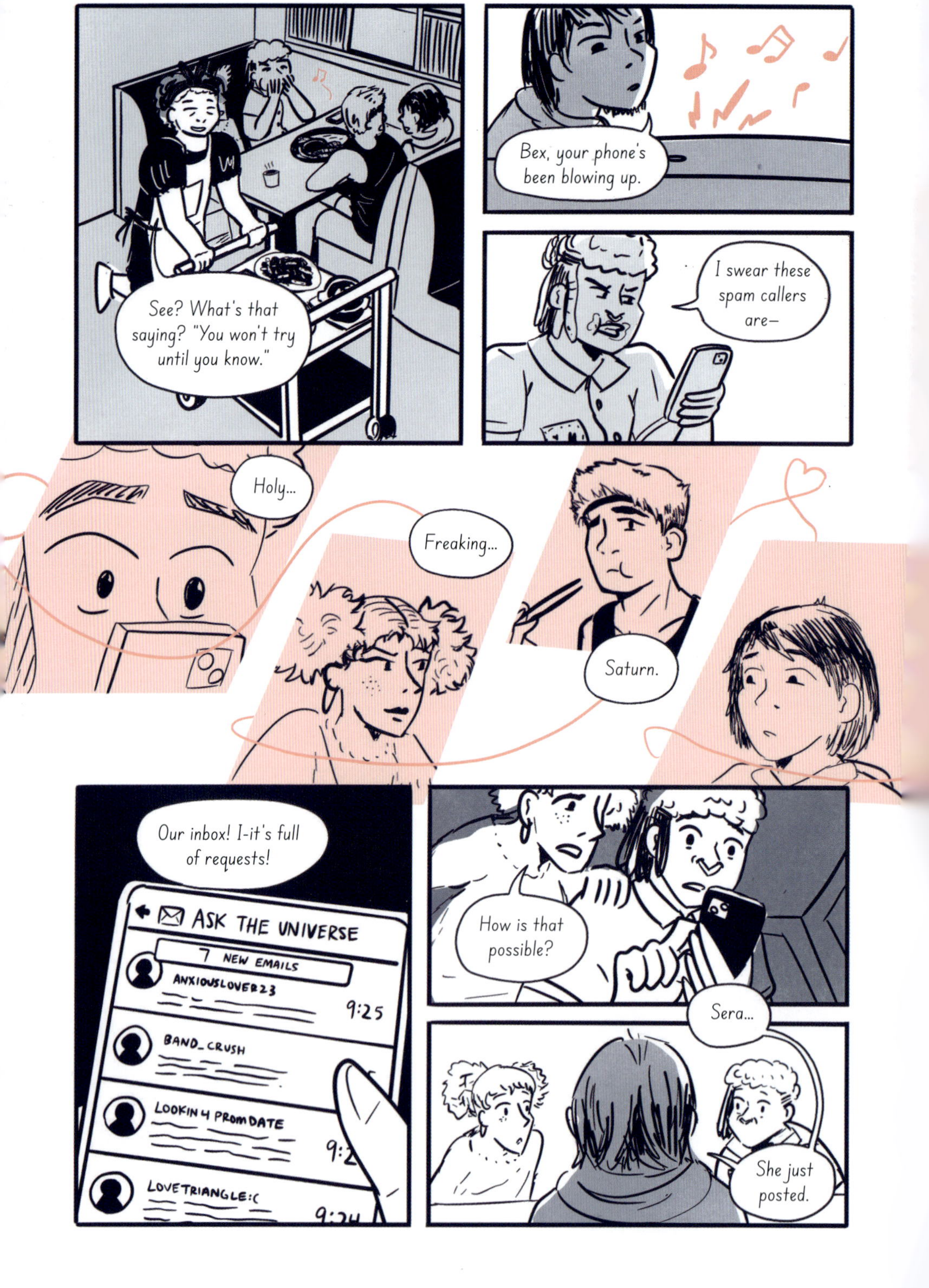
See? What's that saying? "You won't try until you know."
Bex, your phone's been blowing up.
I swear these spam callers are—
Holy...
Freaking...
Saturn.
Our inbox! I-it's full of requests!
ASK THE UNIVERSE
7 NEW EMAILS
ANXIOUSLOVER23
9:25
BAND_CRUSH
LOOKIN 4 PROMDATE
LOVETRIANGLE:(
How is that possible?
Sera...
She just posted.

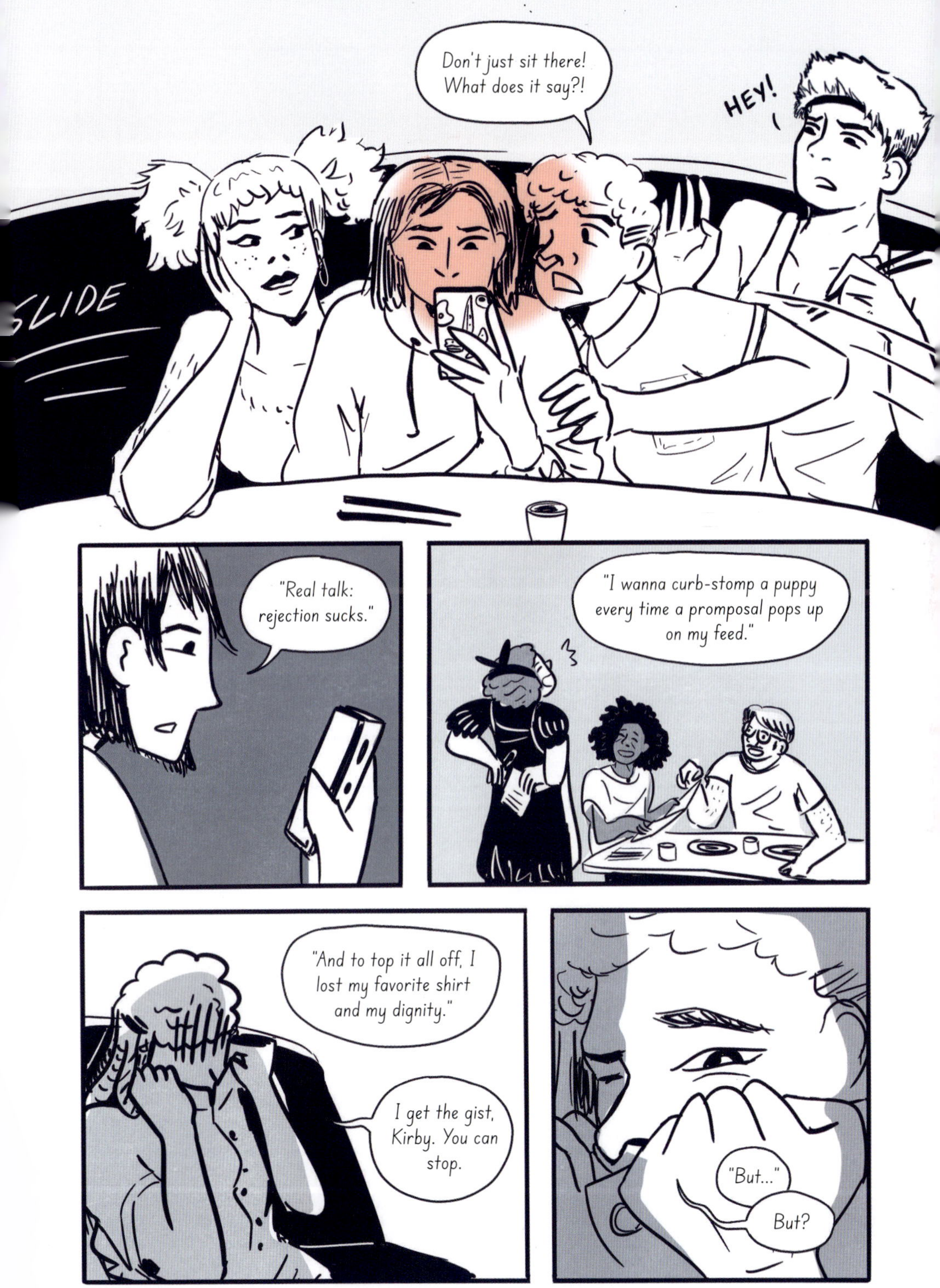
Don't just sit there! What does it say?!
HEY!
SLIDE
"Real talk: rejection sucks."
"I wanna curb-stomp a puppy every time a promposal pops up on my feed."
"And to top it all off, I lost my favorite shirt and my dignity."
I get the gist, Kirby. You can stop.
"But..."
But?

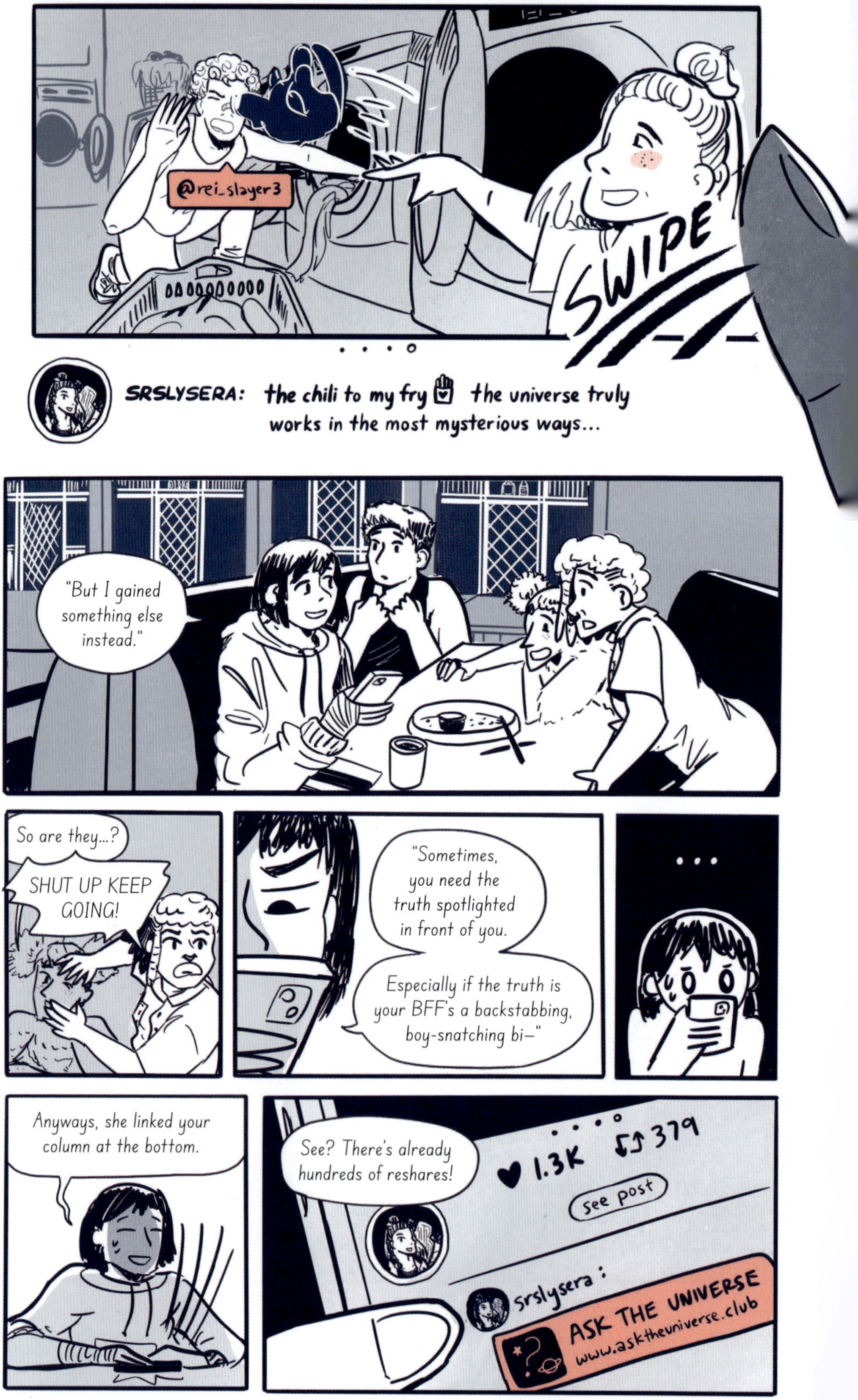

@rei_slayer3
SWIPE
SRSLYSERA: the chili to my fry the universe truly works in the most mysterious ways...
"But I gained something else instead."
So are they...?
SHUT UP KEEP GOING!
"Sometimes, you need the truth spotlighted in front of you.
Especially if the truth is your BFF's a backstabbing, boy-snatching bi–"
Anyways, she linked your column at the bottom.
See? There's already hundreds of reshares!
1.3K
379
see post
srslysera:
ASK THE UNIVERSE
www.asktheuniverse.club

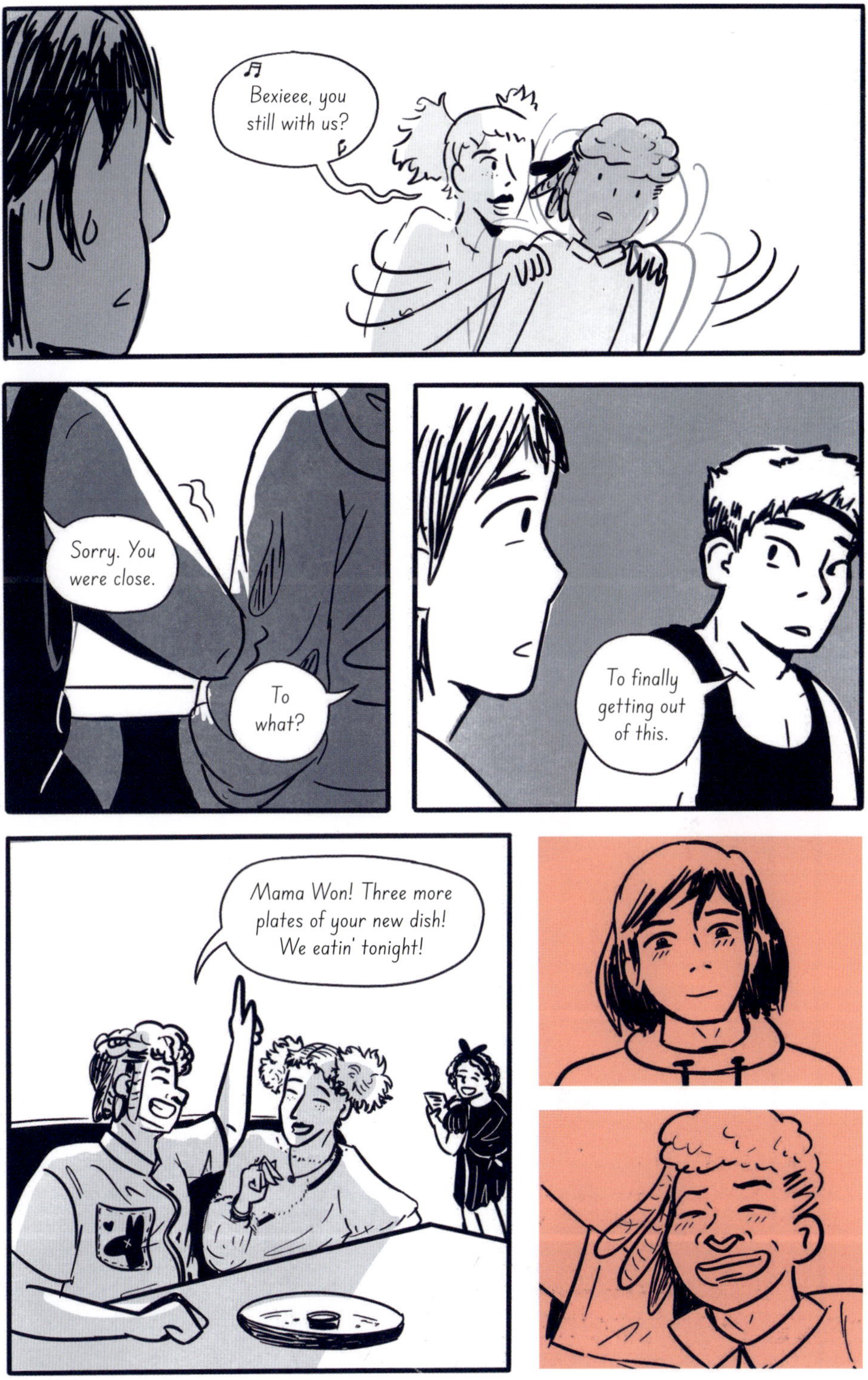
Bexieee, you still with us?
Sorry. You were close.
To what?
To finally getting out of this.
Mama Won! Three more plates of your new dish! We eatin' tonight!

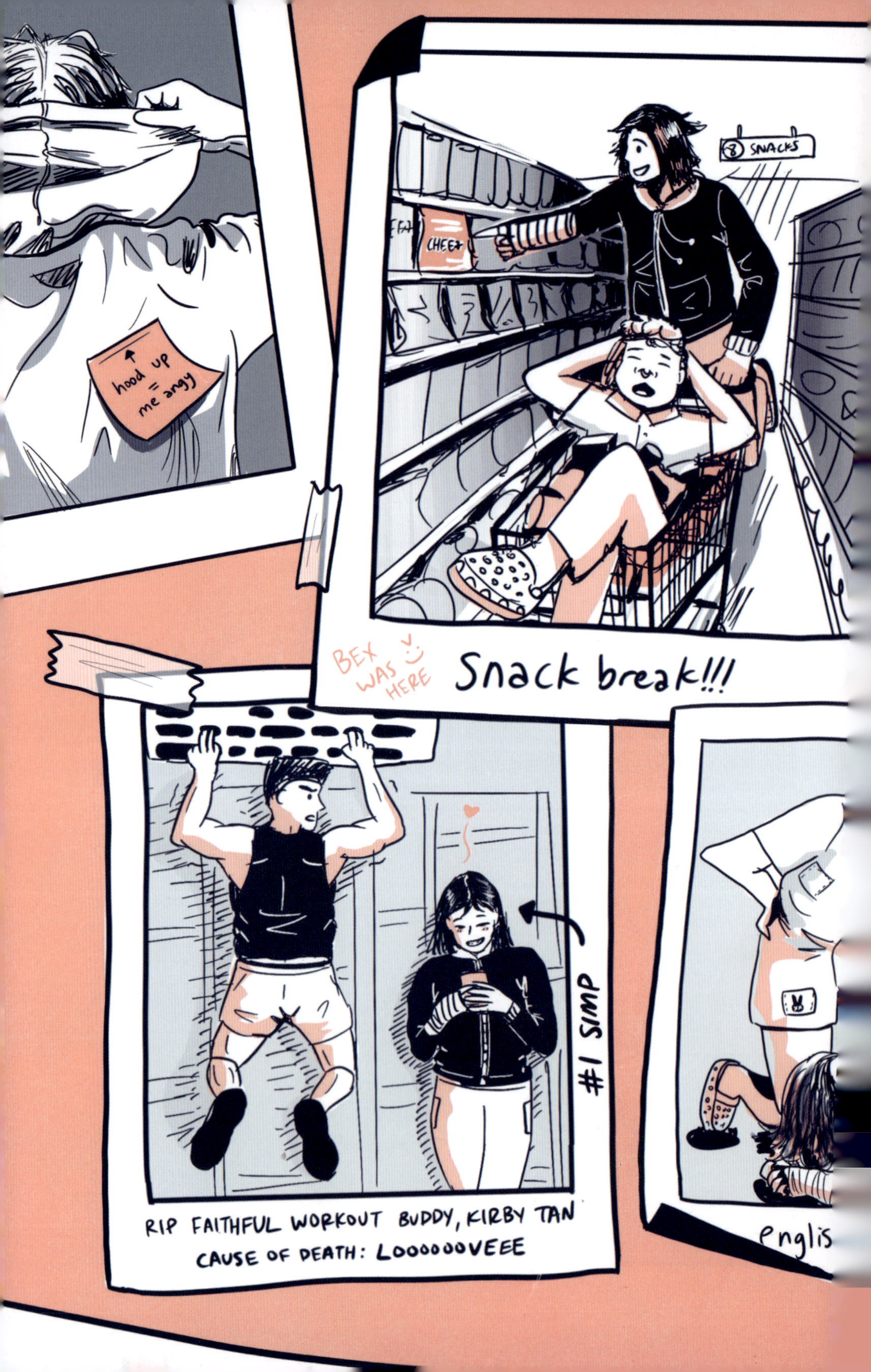
hood up = me angy
CHEEZ
8 SNACKS
BEX WAS HERE
Snack break!!!
#1 SIMP
RIP FAITHFUL WORKOUT BUDDY, KIRBY TAN
CAUSE OF DEATH: LOOOOOOVEEE
englis

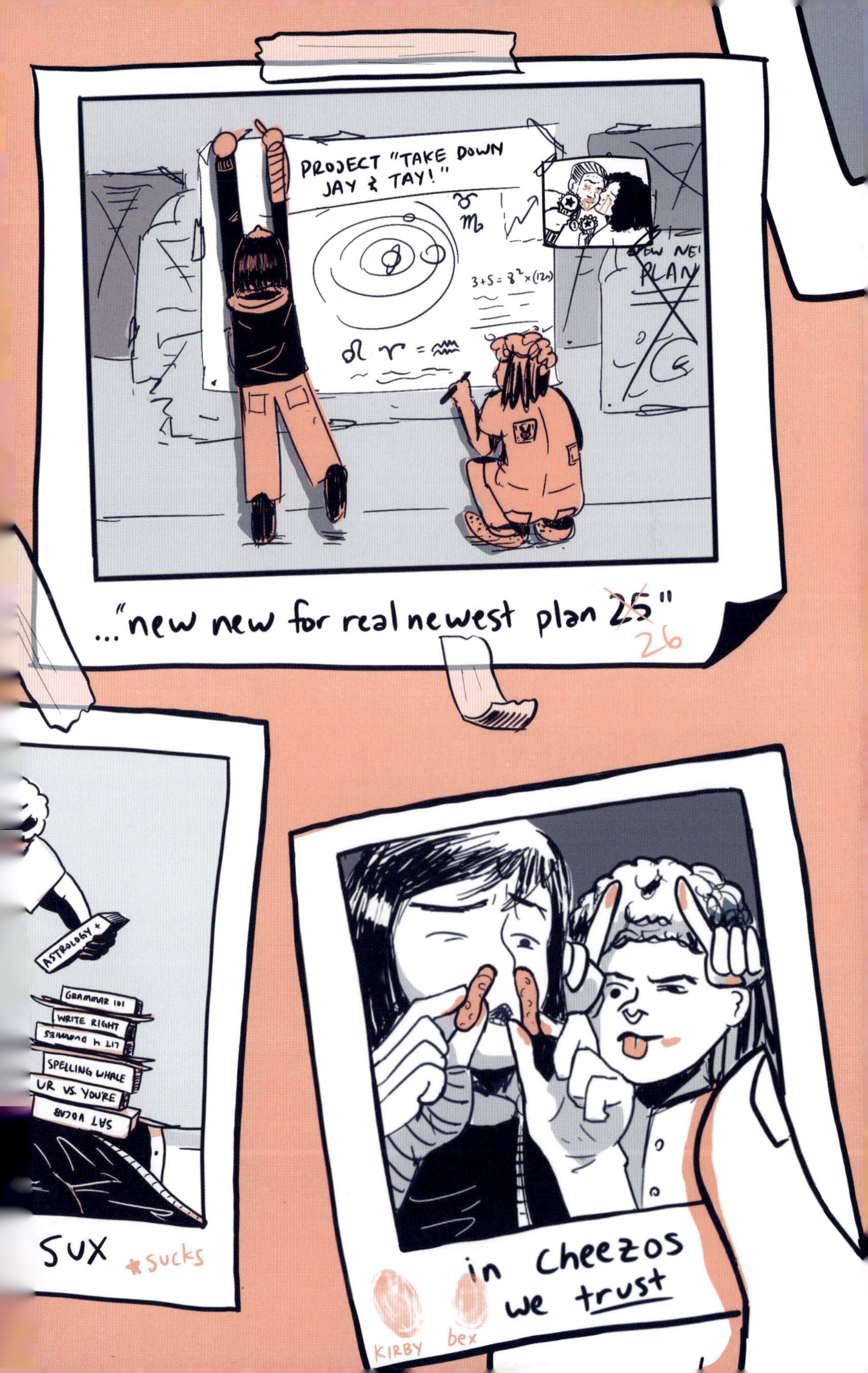
PROJECT "TAKE DOWN JAY & TAY!"
..."new new for real newest plan ~~25~~ 26"
ASTROLOGY +
GRAMMAR 101
WRITE RIGHT
LIT 4 DUMMIES
SPELLING WHALE
UR VS. YOU'RE
SAT VOCAB
SUX *sucks
in cheezos we trust
KIRBY
bex

Over the next couple months, the four of us hung out almost every day to orchestrate dates.

RE: boy next door

Dear Boy Next Door:
The marching band's charity show is the perfect date to march into his life. Pisces are romantics at heart. You can't go wrong with your heart on your sleeve.

Some panned out.

Most didn't.

But the feedback was the same:

"It's nice to know the universe is rooting for you."

"Makes it a bit less terrifying to try."

74

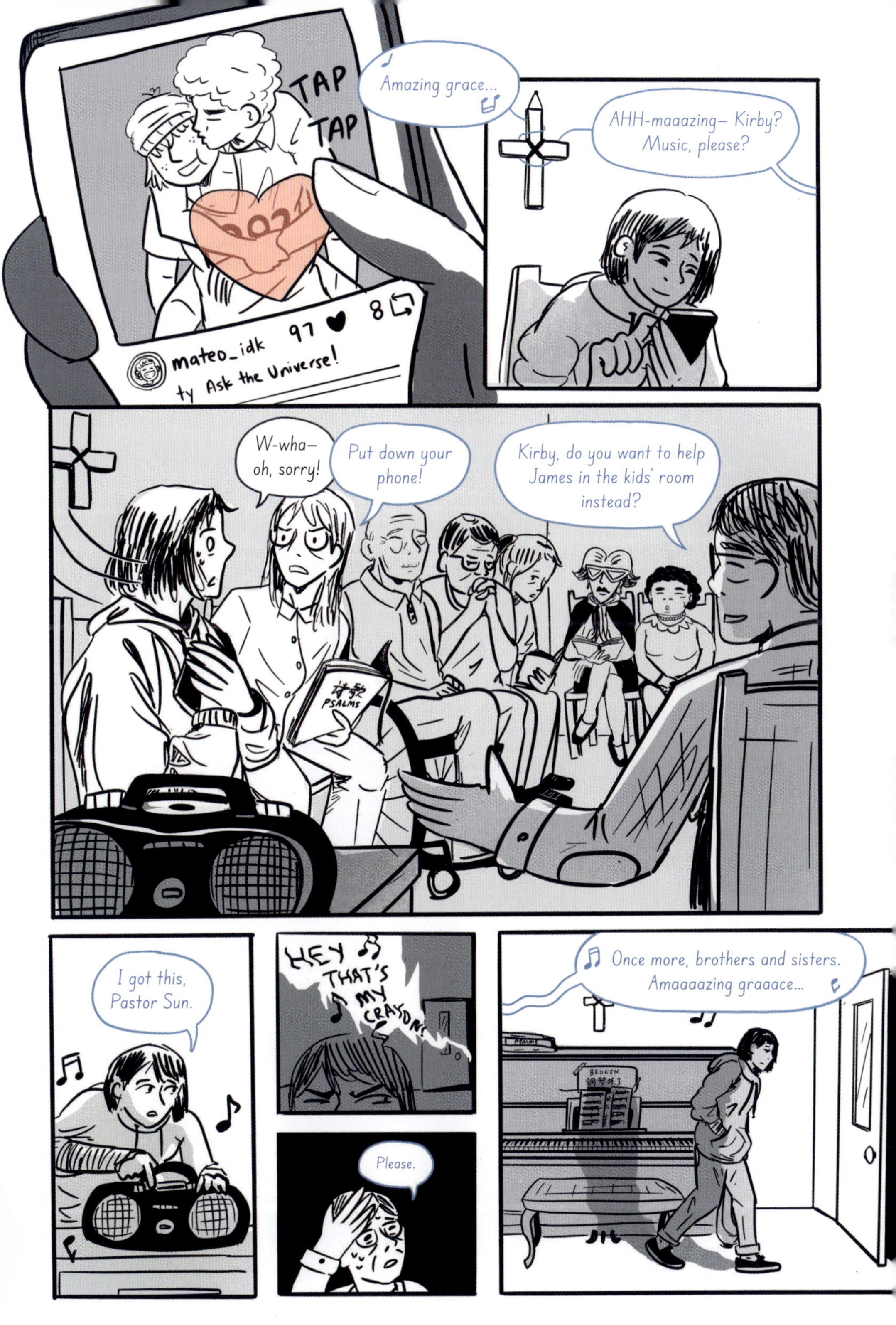
TAP
TAP
2021
@mateo_idk 97 8
ty Ask the Universe!
Amazing grace...
AHH-maaazing— Kirby? Music, please?
W-wha— oh, sorry!
Put down your phone!
Kirby, do you want to help James in the kids' room instead?
PSALMS
I got this, Pastor Sun.
HEY THAT'S MY CRAYON!
Please.
Once more, brothers and sisters. Amaaaazing graaace...
BROKEN

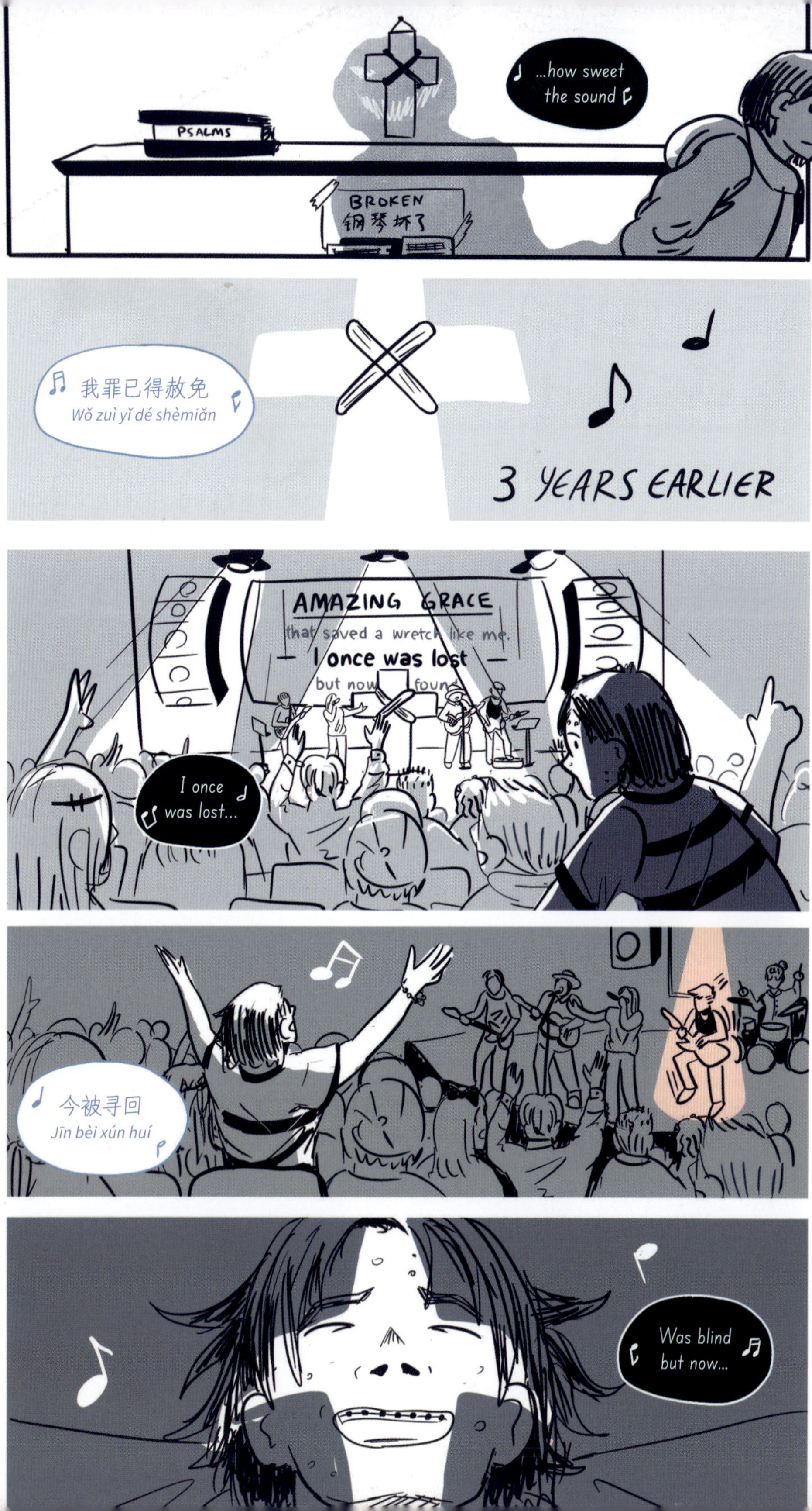
PSALMS
BROKEN
钢琴坏了
...how sweet the sound
我罪已得赦免
Wǒ zuì yǐ dé shèmiǎn
3 YEARS EARLIER
AMAZING GRACE
that saved a wretch like me.
I once was lost
but now found
I once was lost...
今被寻回
Jīn bèi xún huí
Was blind but now...

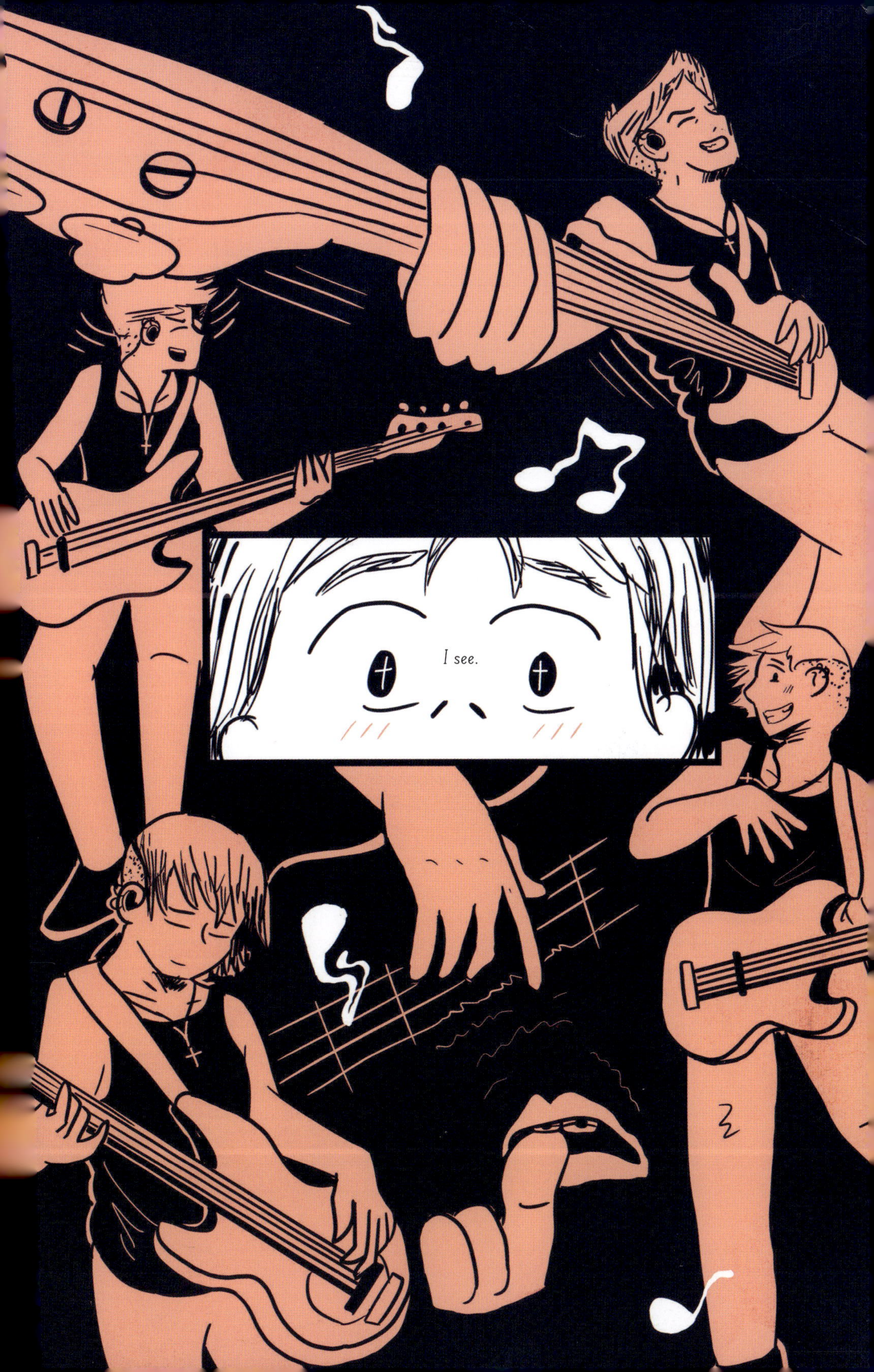
I see.

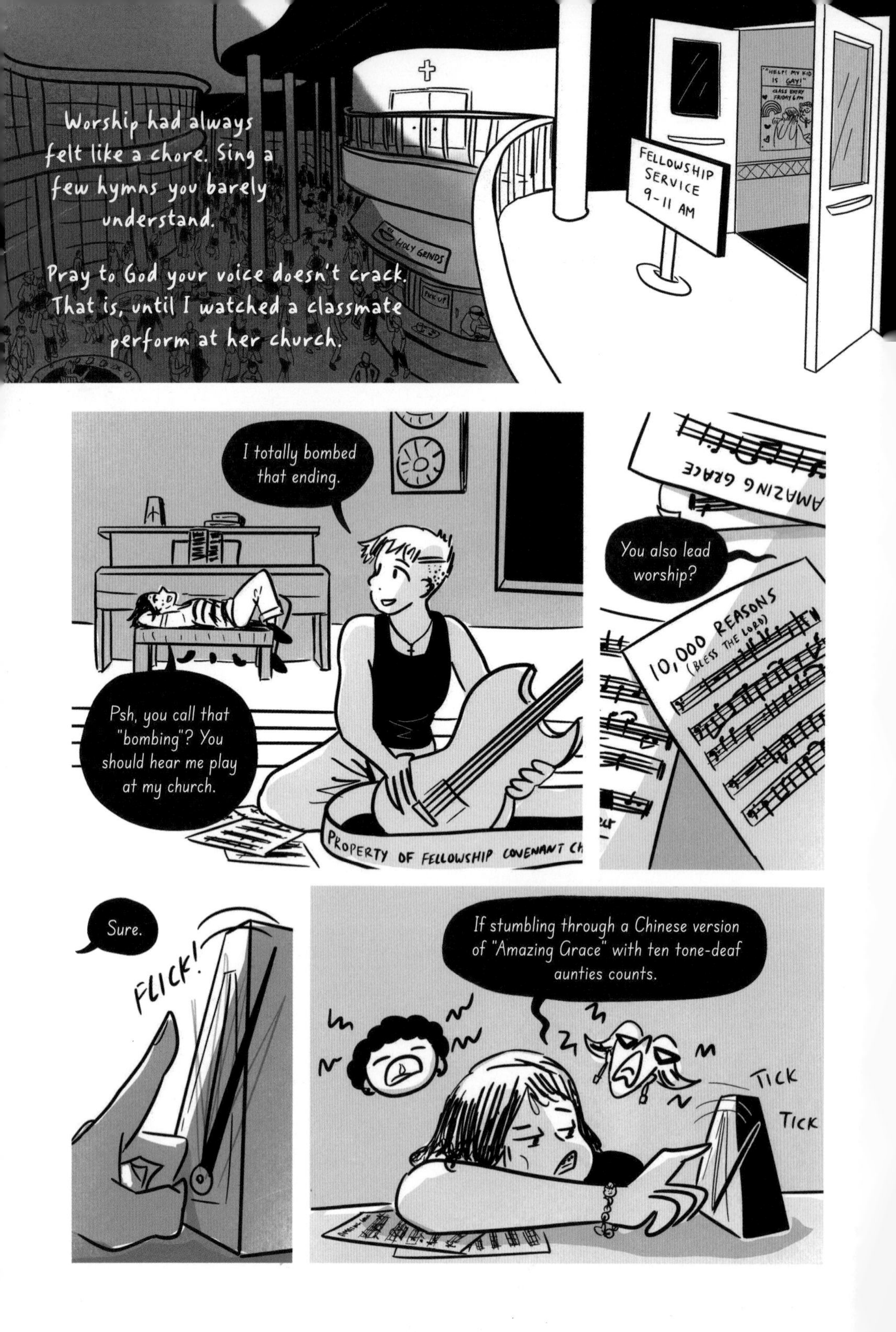
Worship had always felt like a chore. Sing a few hymns you barely understand.
Pray to God your voice doesn't crack. That is, until I watched a classmate perform at her church.
HOLY GRINDS
PICK UP
FELLOWSHIP SERVICE 9–11 AM
"HELP! MY KID IS GAY!"
CLASS EVERY FRIDAY 6 PM
I totally bombed that ending.
Psh, you call that "bombing"? You should hear me play at my church.
PROPERTY OF FELLOWSHIP COVENANT CH
AMAZING GRACE
You also lead worship?
10,000 REASONS (BLESS THE LORD)
Sure.
FLICK!
If stumbling through a Chinese version of "Amazing Grace" with ten tone-deaf aunties counts.
TICK
TICK

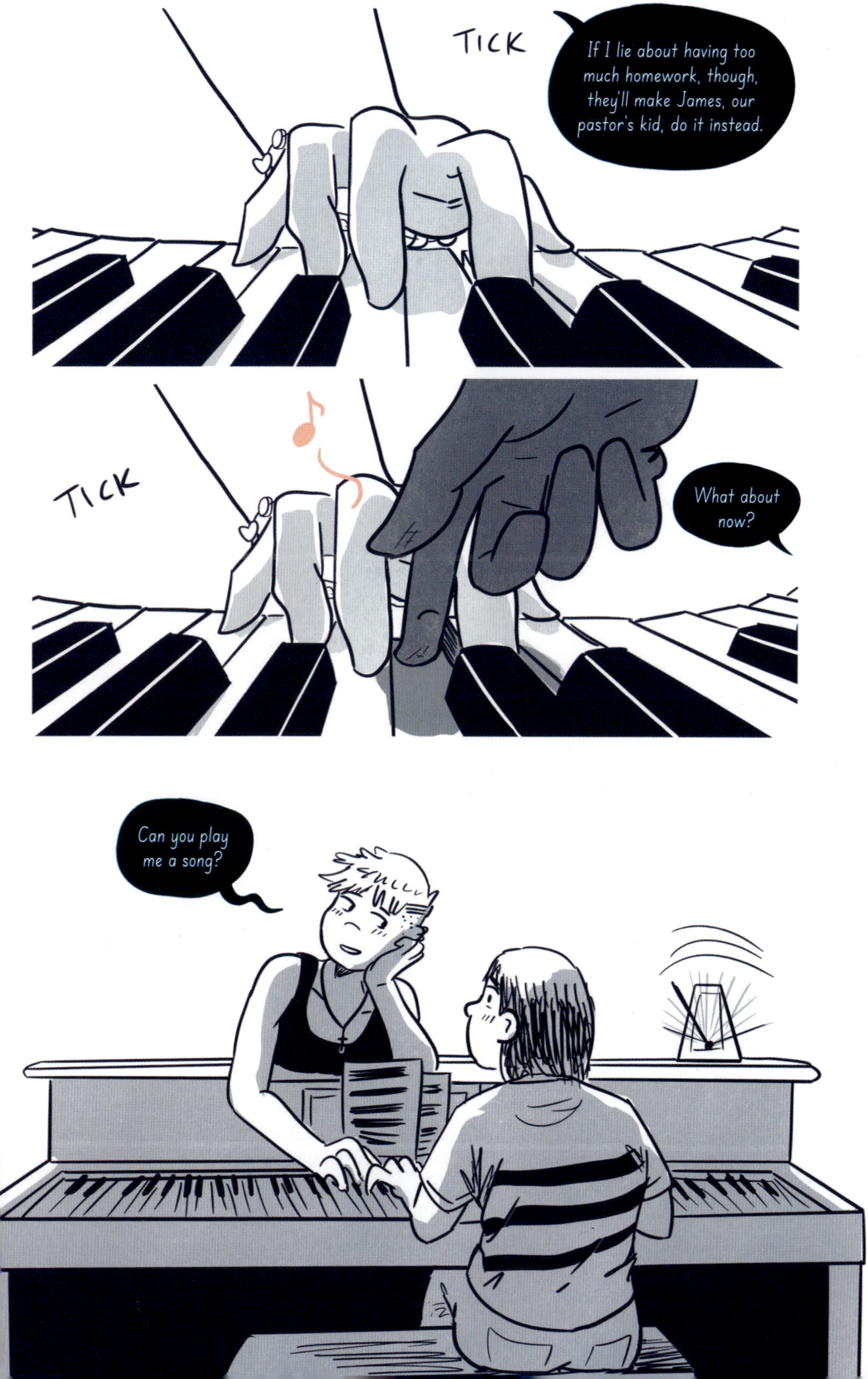
TICK
If I lie about having too much homework, though, they'll make James, our pastor's kid, do it instead.
TICK
What about now?
Can you play me a song?

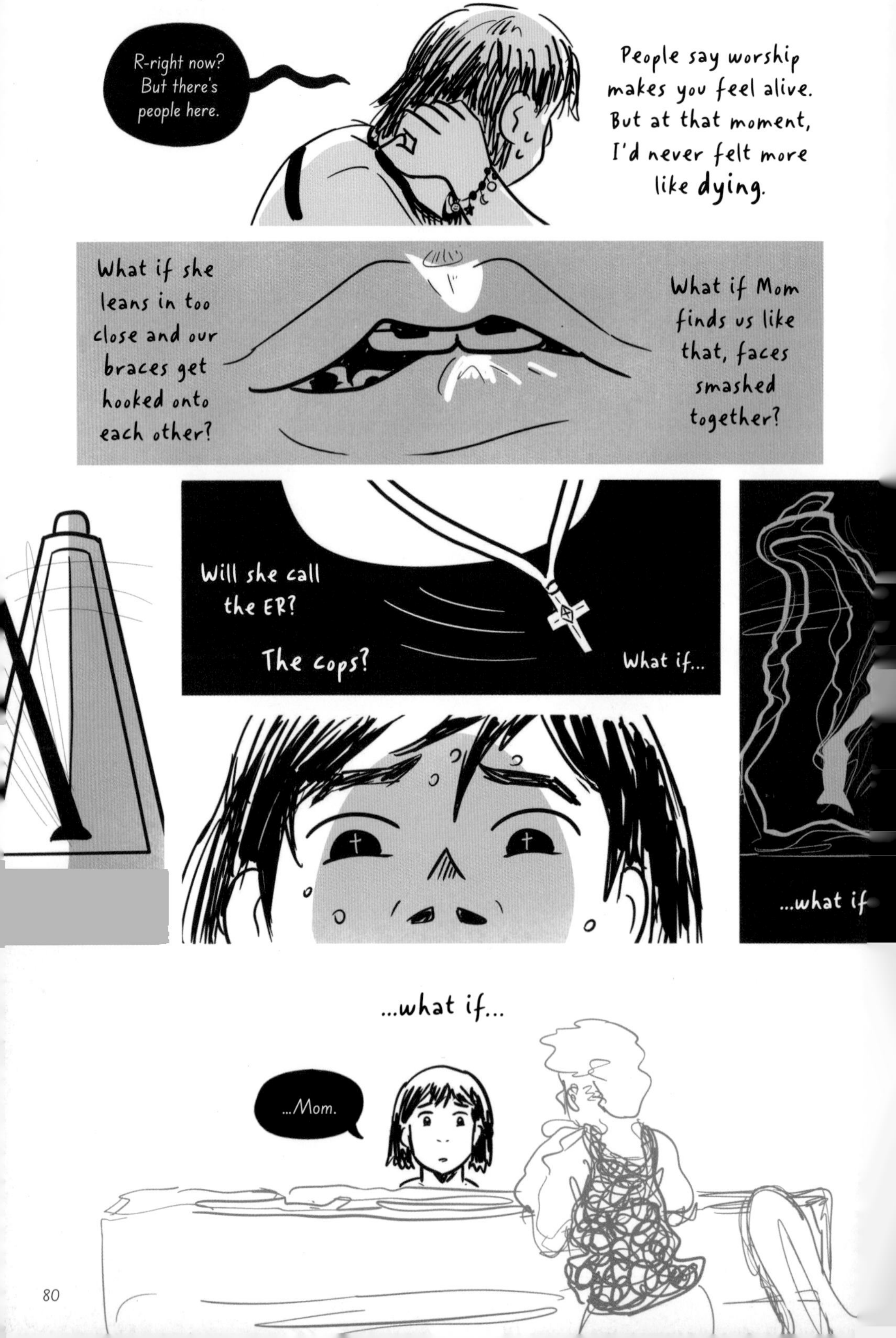
R-right now? But there's people here.
People say worship makes you feel alive. But at that moment, I'd never felt more like dying.
What if she leans in too close and our braces get hooked onto each other?
What if Mom finds us like that, faces smashed together?
Will she call the ER?
The cops?
What if...
...what if
...what if...
...Mom.

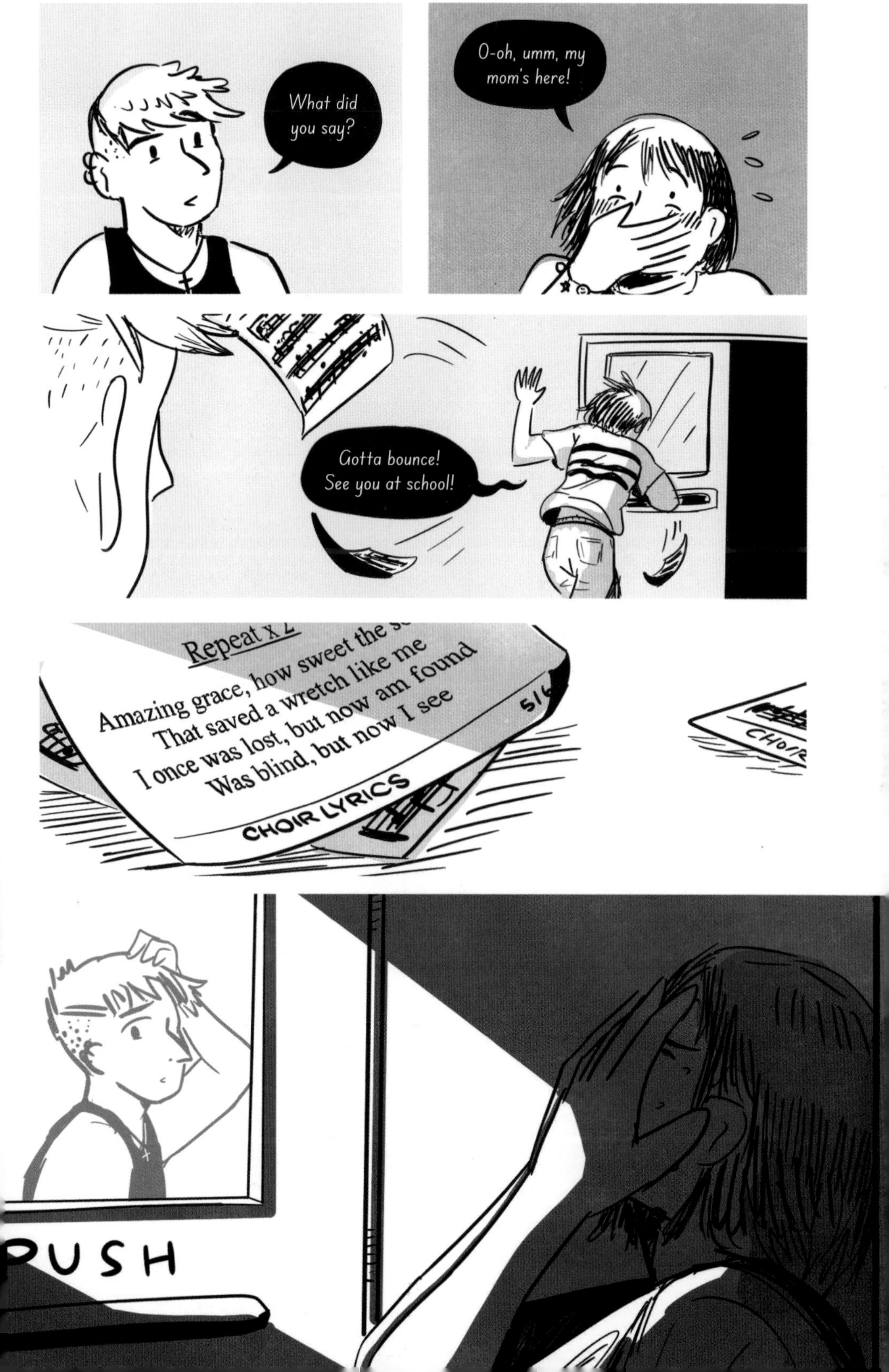
What did you say?
O-oh, umm, my mom's here!
Gotta bounce! See you at school!
Repeat x 2
Amazing grace, how sweet the so
That saved a wretch like me
I once was lost, but now am found
Was blind, but now I see
5/6
CHOIR LYRICS
CHOIR
USH

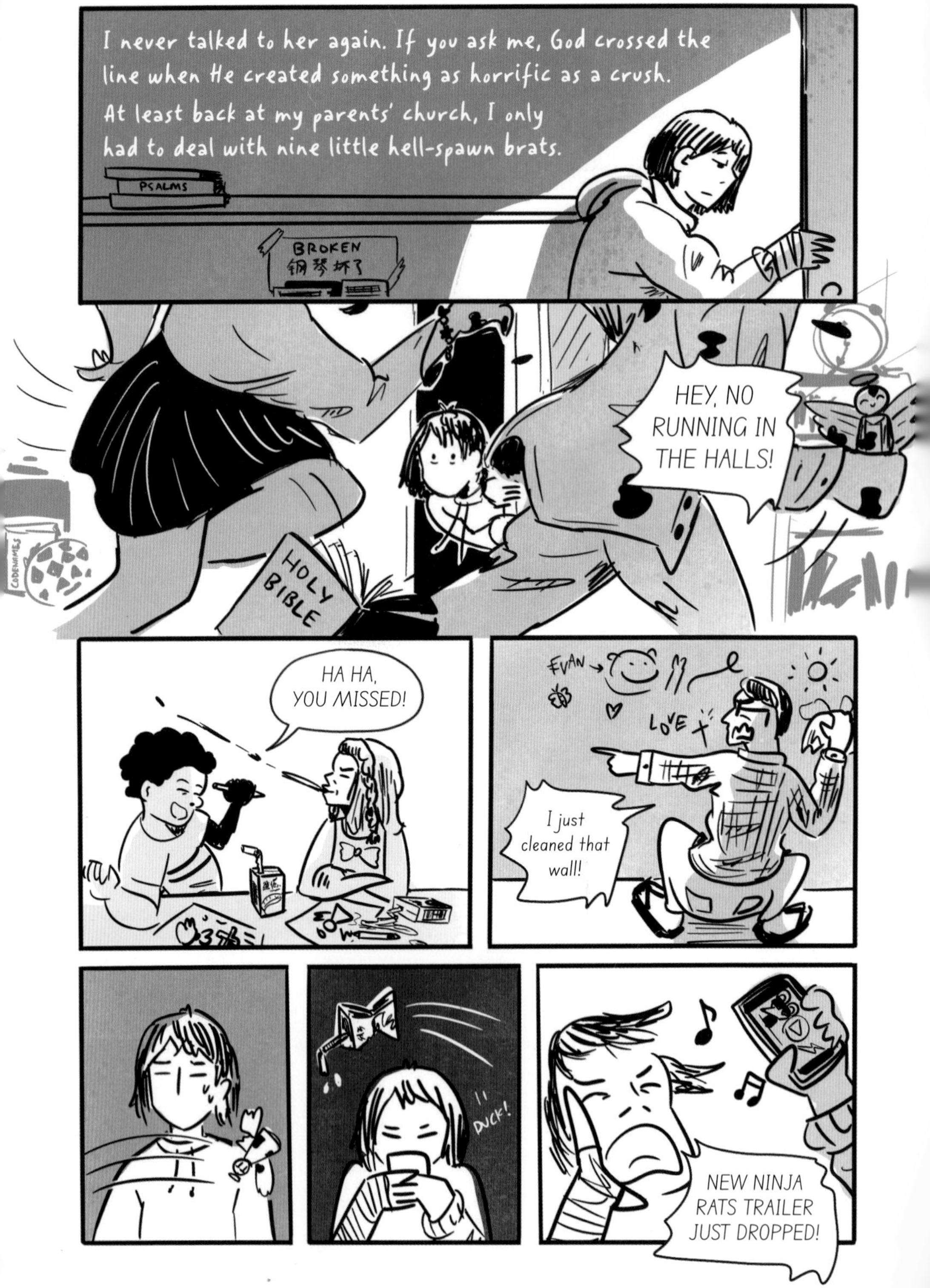
I never talked to her again. If you ask me, God crossed the line when He created something as horrific as a crush.
At least back at my parents' church, I only had to deal with nine little hell-spawn brats.
PSALMS
BROKEN
钢琴坏了
HEY, NO RUNNING IN THE HALLS!
HOLY BIBLE
CODENAMES
HA HA, YOU MISSED!
EVAN
LOVE
I just cleaned that wall!
DUCK!
NEW NINJA RATS TRAILER JUST DROPPED!

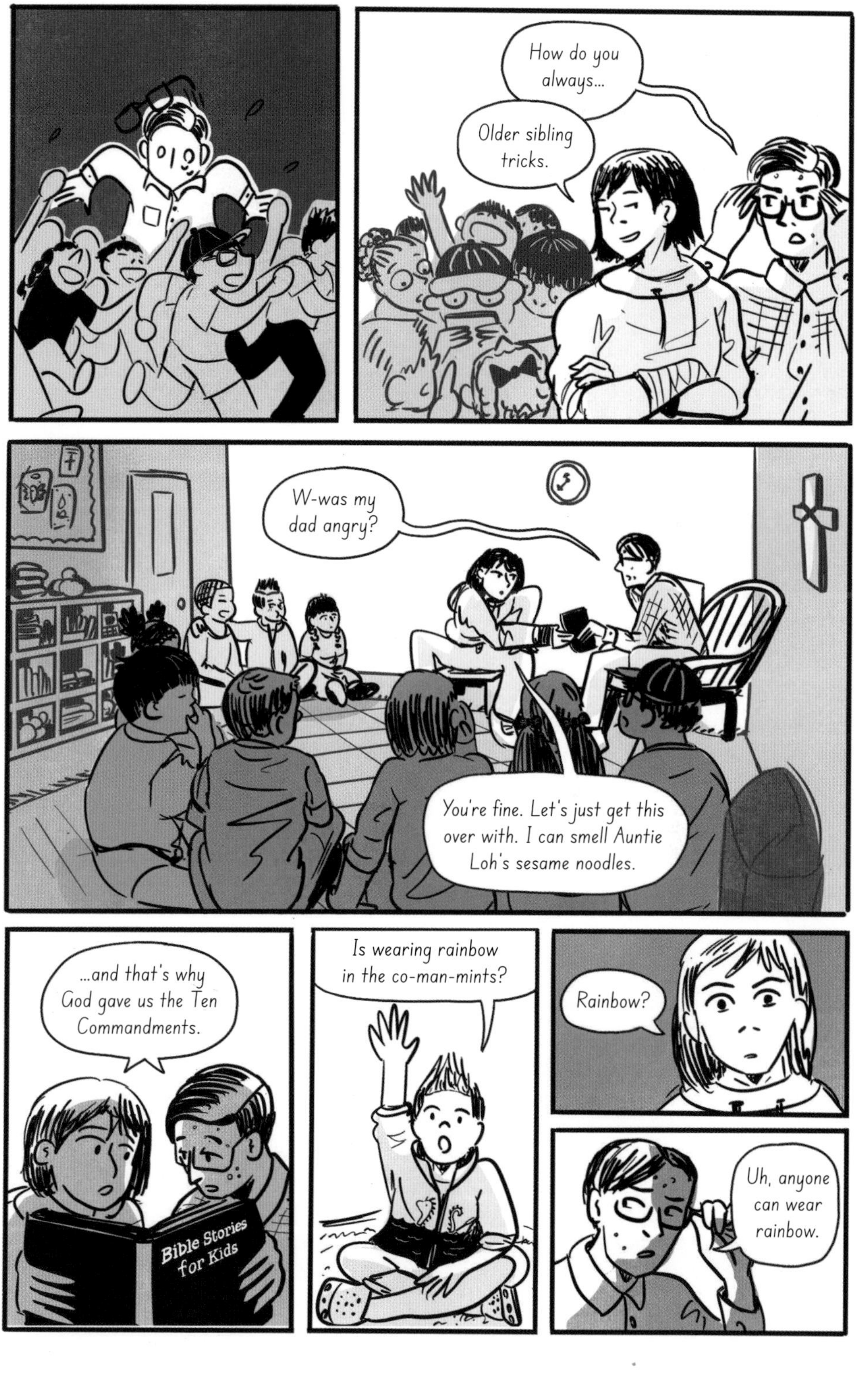
How do you always...
Older sibling tricks.
W-was my dad angry?
You're fine. Let's just get this over with. I can smell Auntie Loh's sesame noodles.
...and that's why God gave us the Ten Commandments.
Bible Stories for Kids
Is wearing rainbow in the co-man-mints?
Rainbow?
Uh, anyone can wear rainbow.

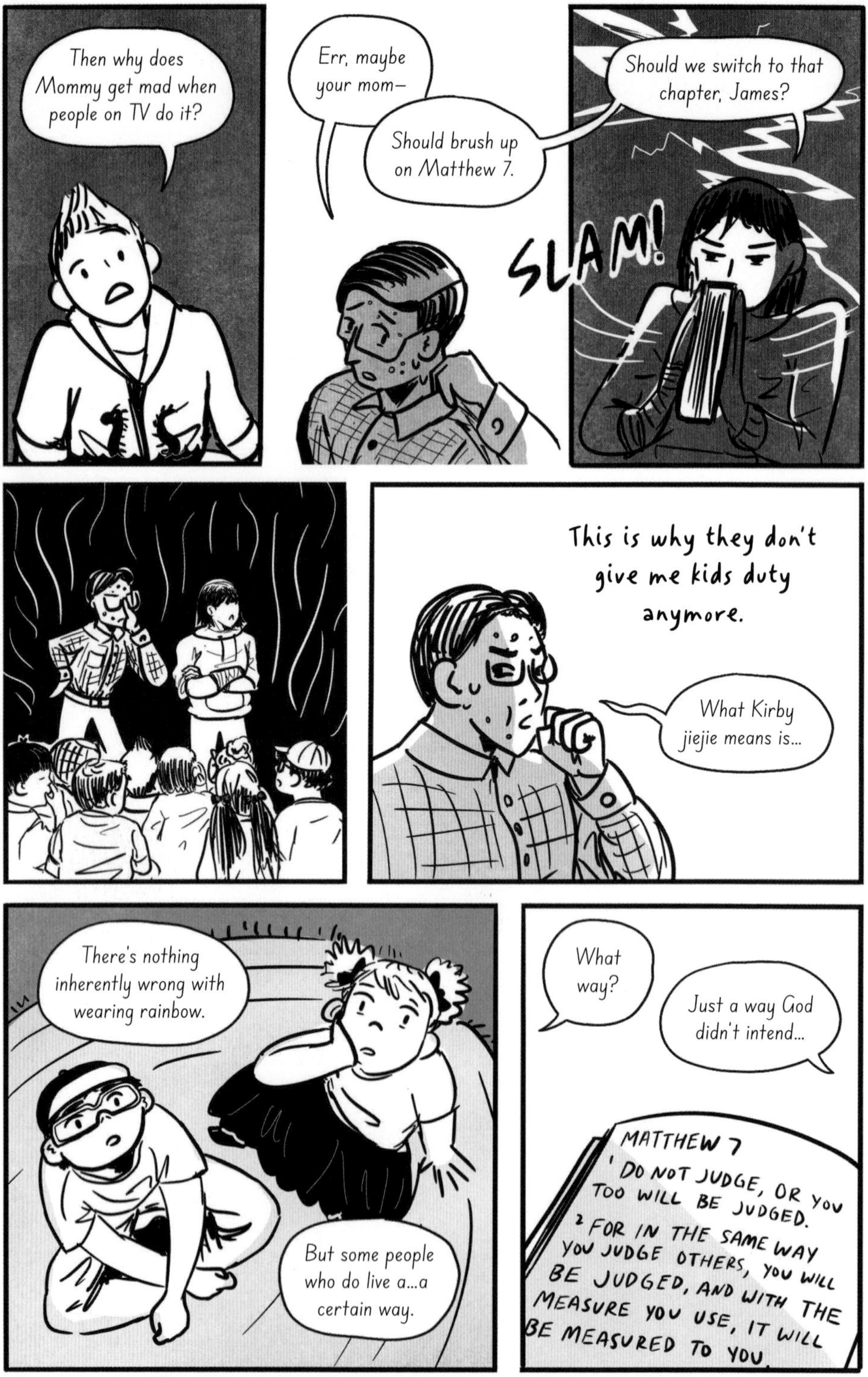

Then why does Mommy get mad when people on TV do it?
Err, maybe your mom—
Should brush up on Matthew 7.
Should we switch to that chapter, James?
SLAM!
This is why they don't give me kids duty anymore.
What Kirby jiejie means is...
There's nothing inherently wrong with wearing rainbow.
But some people who do live a...a certain way.
What way?
Just a way God didn't intend...
MATTHEW 7
1 DO NOT JUDGE, OR YOU TOO WILL BE JUDGED.
2 FOR IN THE SAME WAY YOU JUDGE OTHERS, YOU WILL BE JUDGED, AND WITH THE MEASURE YOU USE, IT WILL BE MEASURED TO YOU.

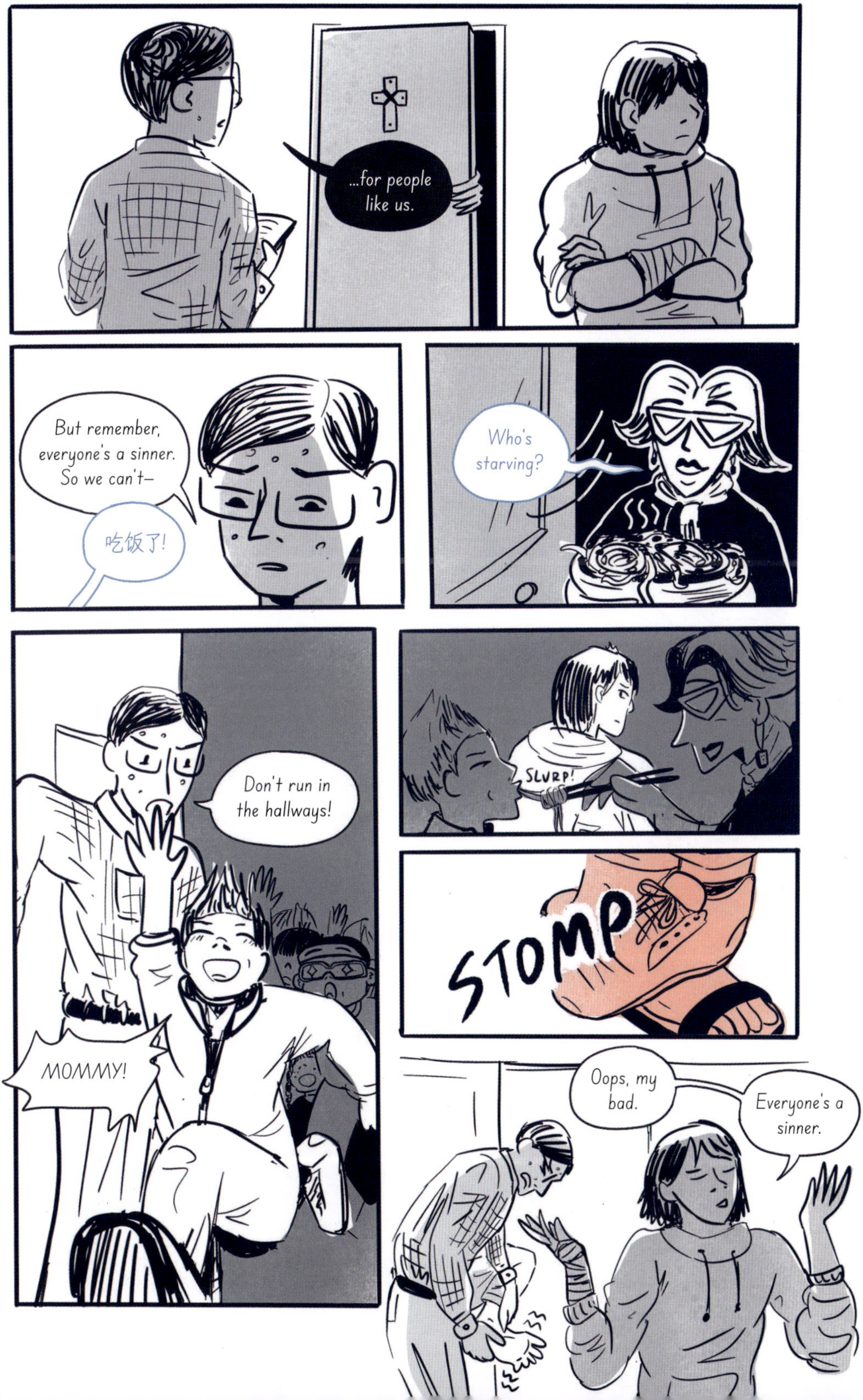
...for people like us.
But remember, everyone's a sinner. So we can't—
吃饭了!
Who's starving?
Don't run in the hallways!
MOMMY!
SLURP!
STOMP
Oops, my bad.
Everyone's a sinner.

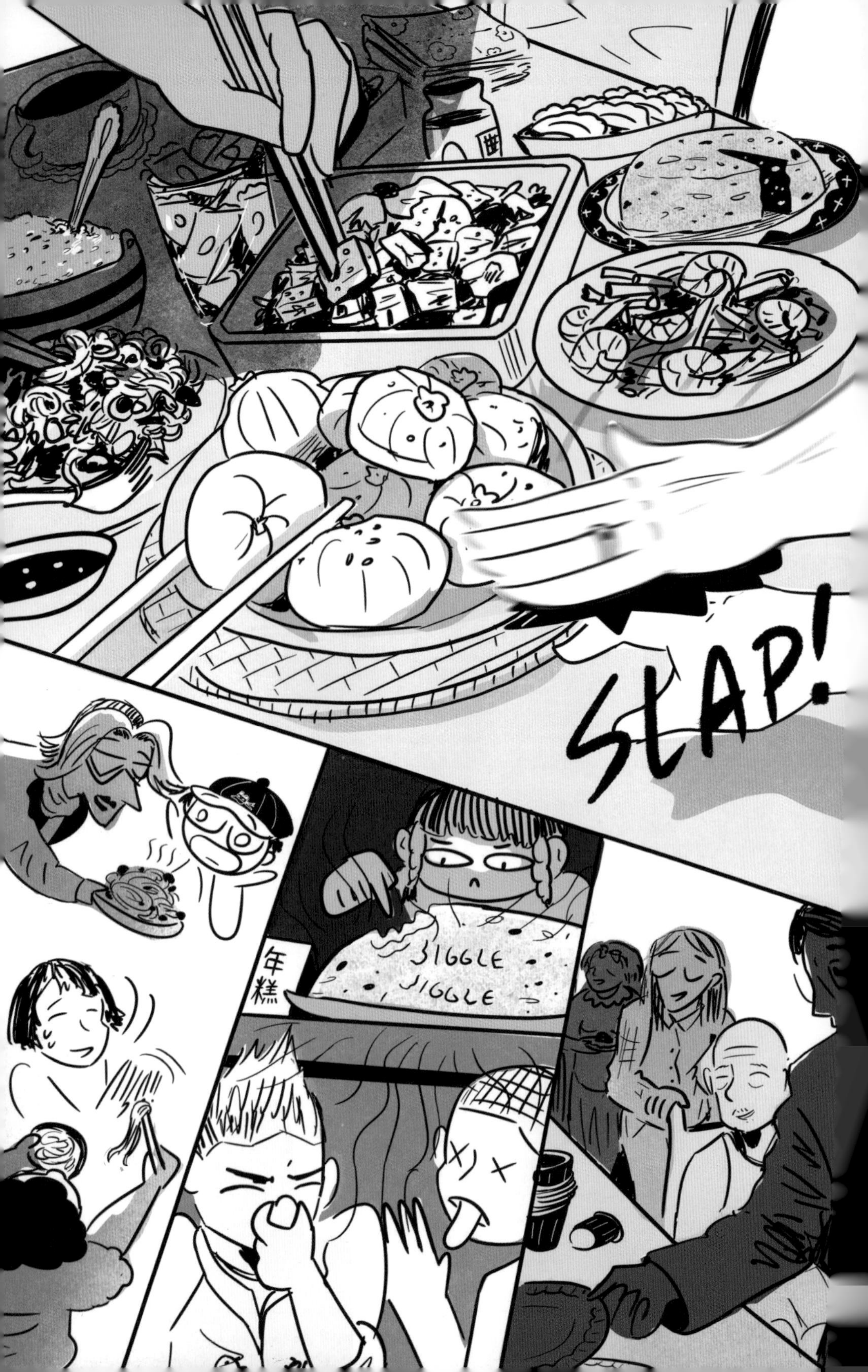
SLAP!
年糕
JIGGLE
JIGGLE

"James, want to lead us today? Give us a taste of what you've been learning in college."

"Oh, uhh, sure. L-let's bow our heads, then."

I've said grace at this table since even before I learned my ABCs.

Instead of closing my eyes, I always look at Mom.

It's the only time I can catch her like this.

Breath soft, jaw relaxed. Like somehow...

...everything will be okay.

"In Your name we pray:"

"Amen."

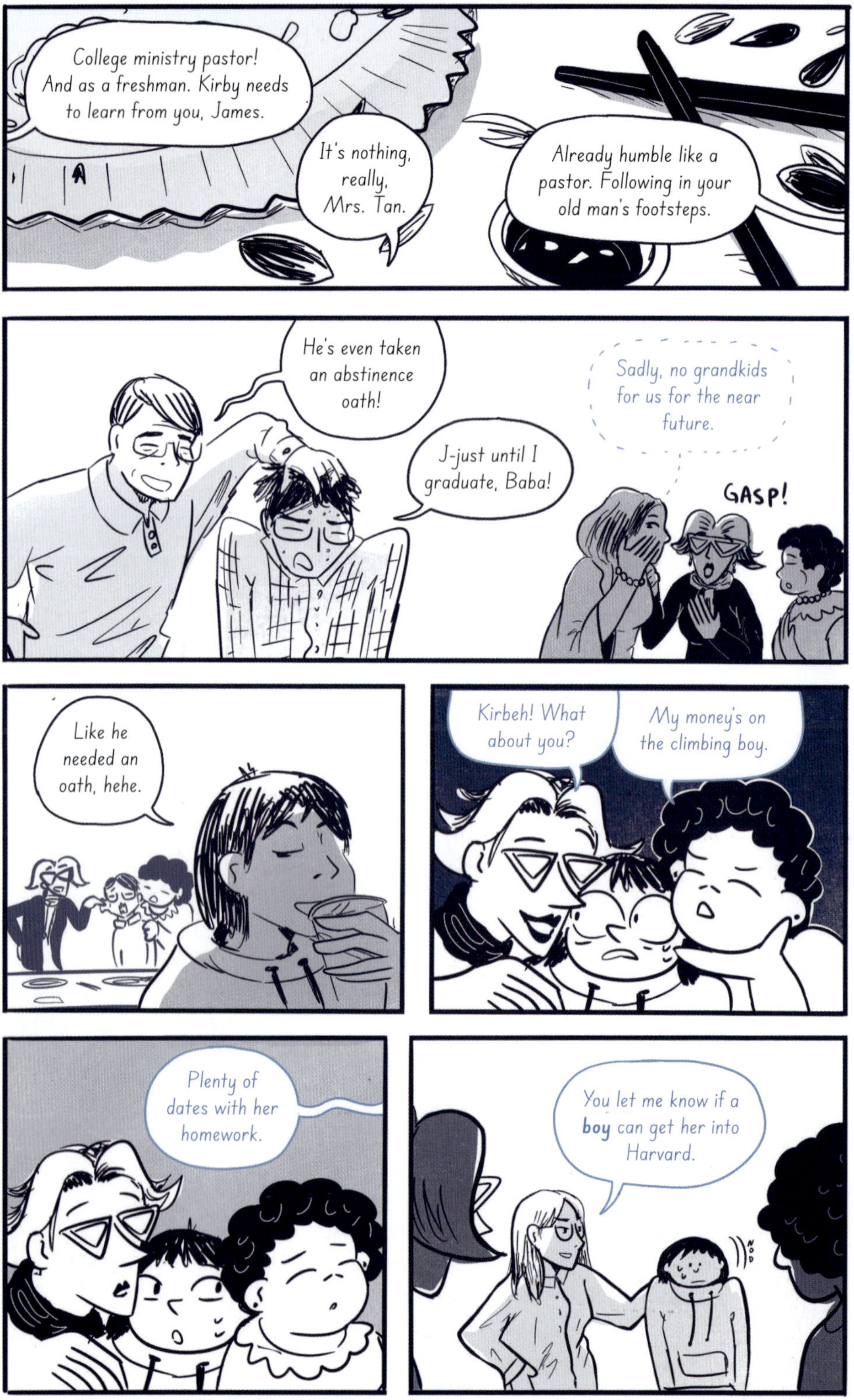
College ministry pastor! And as a freshman. Kirby needs to learn from you, James.
It's nothing, really, Mrs. Tan.
Already humble like a pastor. Following in your old man's footsteps.
He's even taken an abstinence oath!
J-just until I graduate, Baba!
Sadly, no grandkids for us for the near future.
GASP!
Like he needed an oath, hehe.
Kirbeh! What about you?
My money's on the climbing boy.
Plenty of dates with her homework.
You let me know if a **boy** can get her into Harvard.
NOD

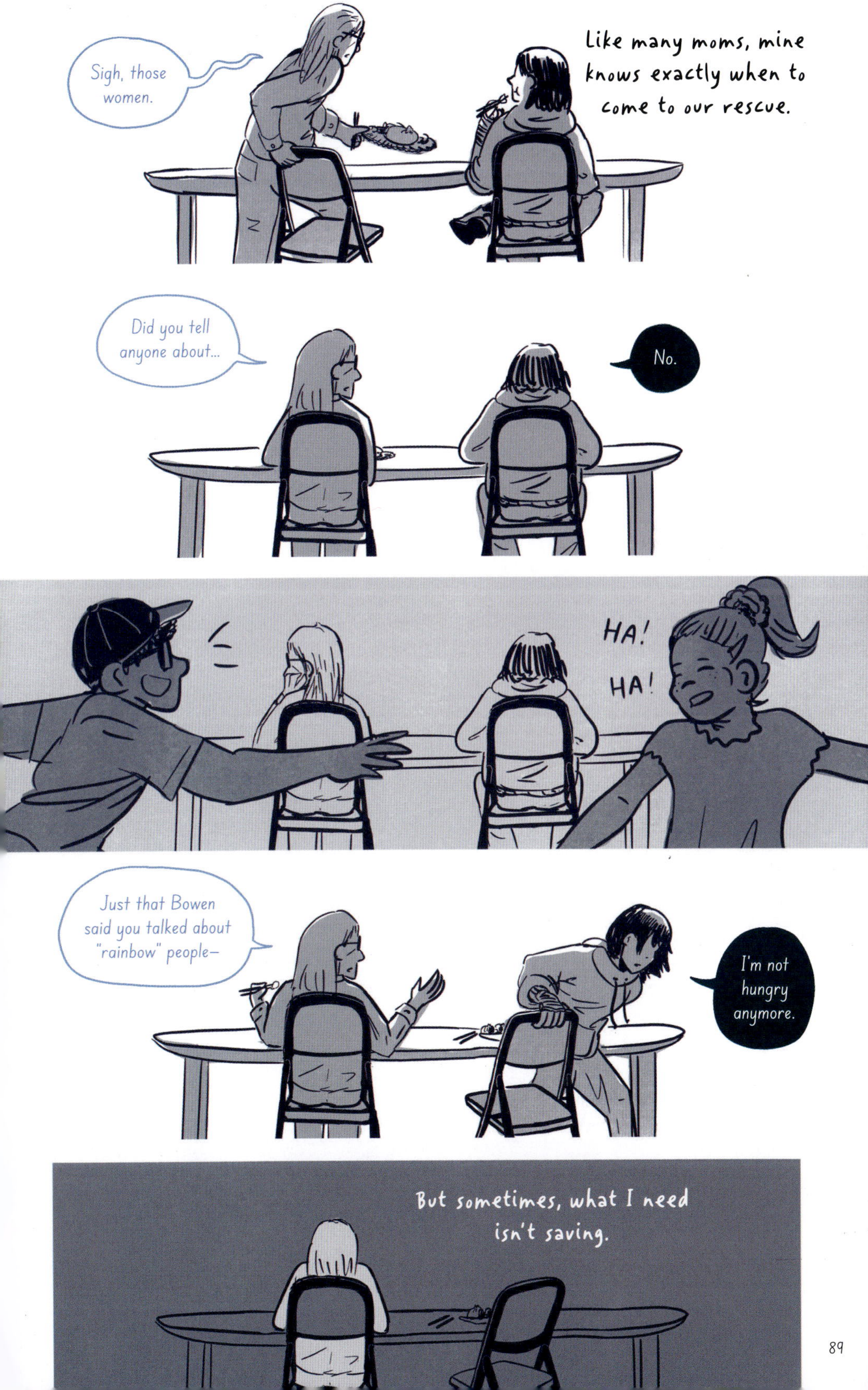
Sigh, those women.
Like many moms, mine knows exactly when to come to our rescue.
Did you tell anyone about...
No.
HA!
HA!
Just that Bowen said you talked about "rainbow" people—
I'm not hungry anymore.
But sometimes, what I need isn't saving.

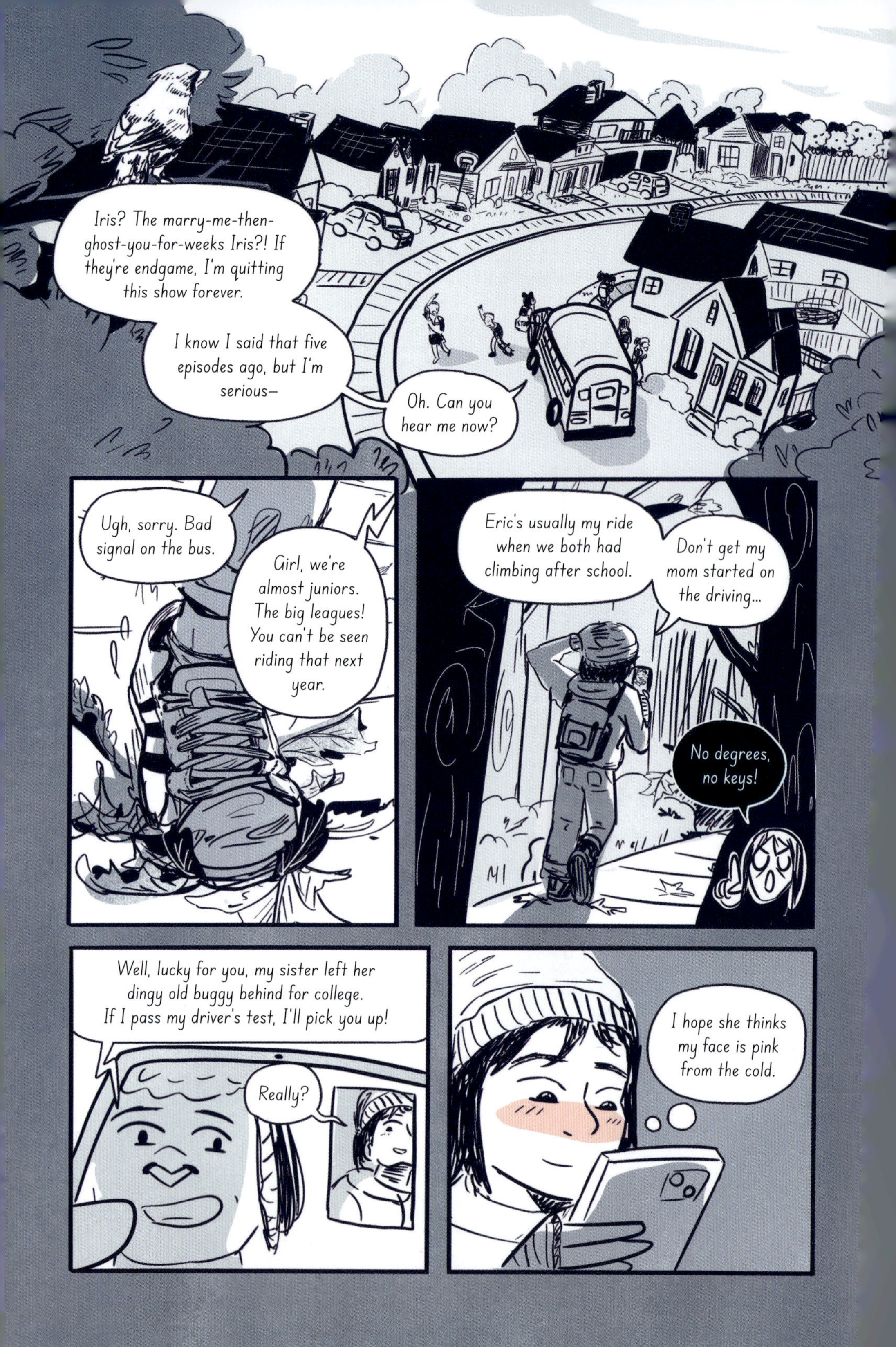

Iris? The marry-me-then-ghost-you-for-weeks Iris?! If they're endgame, I'm quitting this show forever.
I know I said that five episodes ago, but I'm serious—
Oh. Can you hear me now?
Ugh, sorry. Bad signal on the bus.
Girl, we're almost juniors. The big leagues! You can't be seen riding that next year.
Eric's usually my ride when we both had climbing after school.
Don't get my mom started on the driving...
No degrees, no keys!
Well, lucky for you, my sister left her dingy old buggy behind for college. If I pass my driver's test, I'll pick you up!
Really?
I hope she thinks my face is pink from the cold.

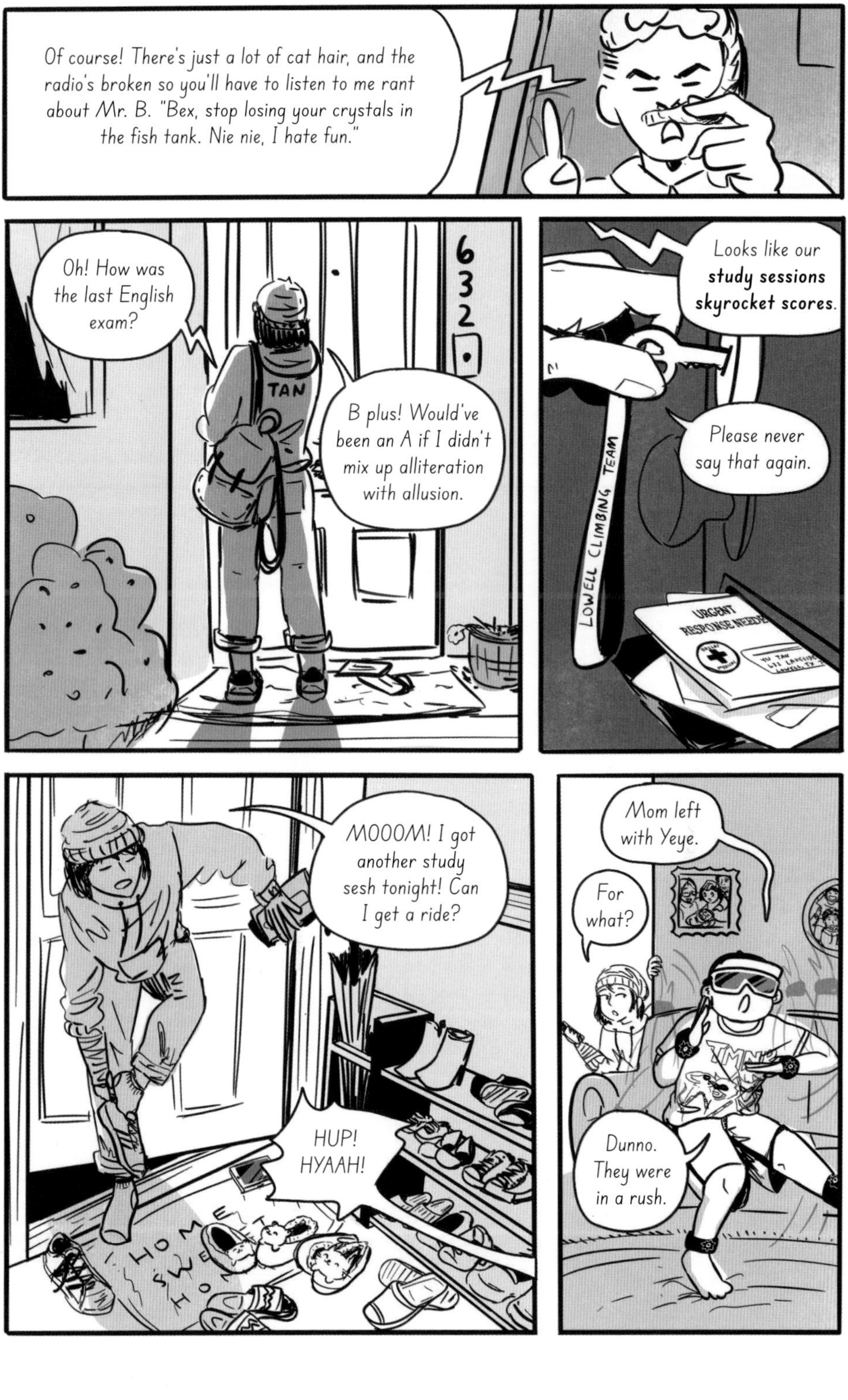
Of course! There's just a lot of cat hair, and the radio's broken so you'll have to listen to me rant about Mr. B. "Bex, stop losing your crystals in the fish tank. Nie nie, I hate fun."
Oh! How was the last English exam?
632
TAN
B plus! Would've been an A if I didn't mix up alliteration with allusion.
Looks like our **study sessions skyrocket scores**.
Please never say that again.
LOWELL CLIMBING TEAM
URGENT RESPONSE NEEDED
MOOOM! I got another study sesh tonight! Can I get a ride?
HUP! HYAAH!
HOME SWEET HOME
Mom left with Yeye.
For what?
Dunno. They were in a rush.

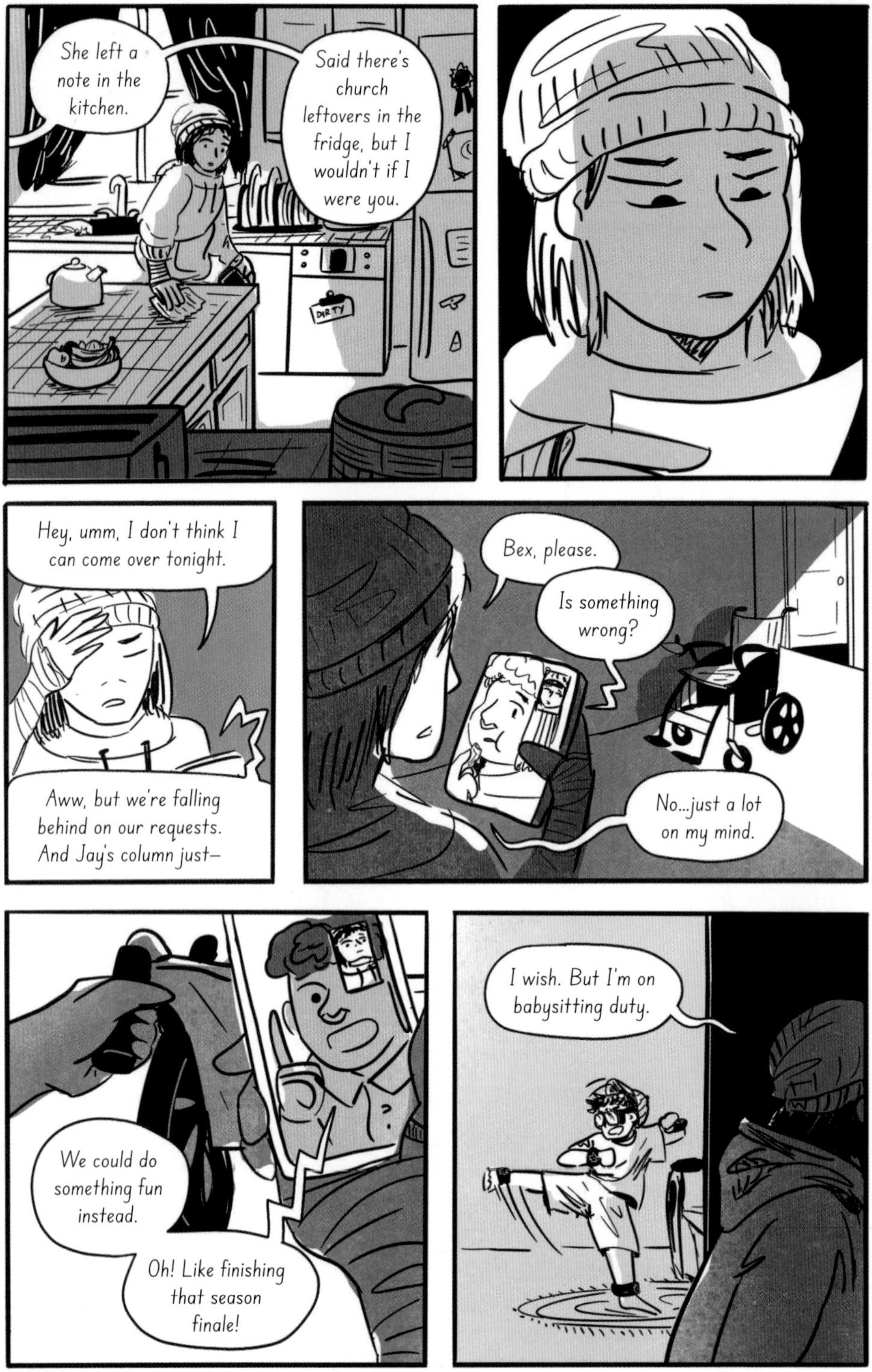
She left a note in the kitchen.
Said there's church leftovers in the fridge, but I wouldn't if I were you.
DIRTY
Hey, umm, I don't think I can come over tonight.
Aww, but we're falling behind on our requests. And Jay's column just–
Bex, please.
Is something wrong?
No...just a lot on my mind.
We could do something fun instead.
Oh! Like finishing that season finale!
I wish. But I'm on babysitting duty.

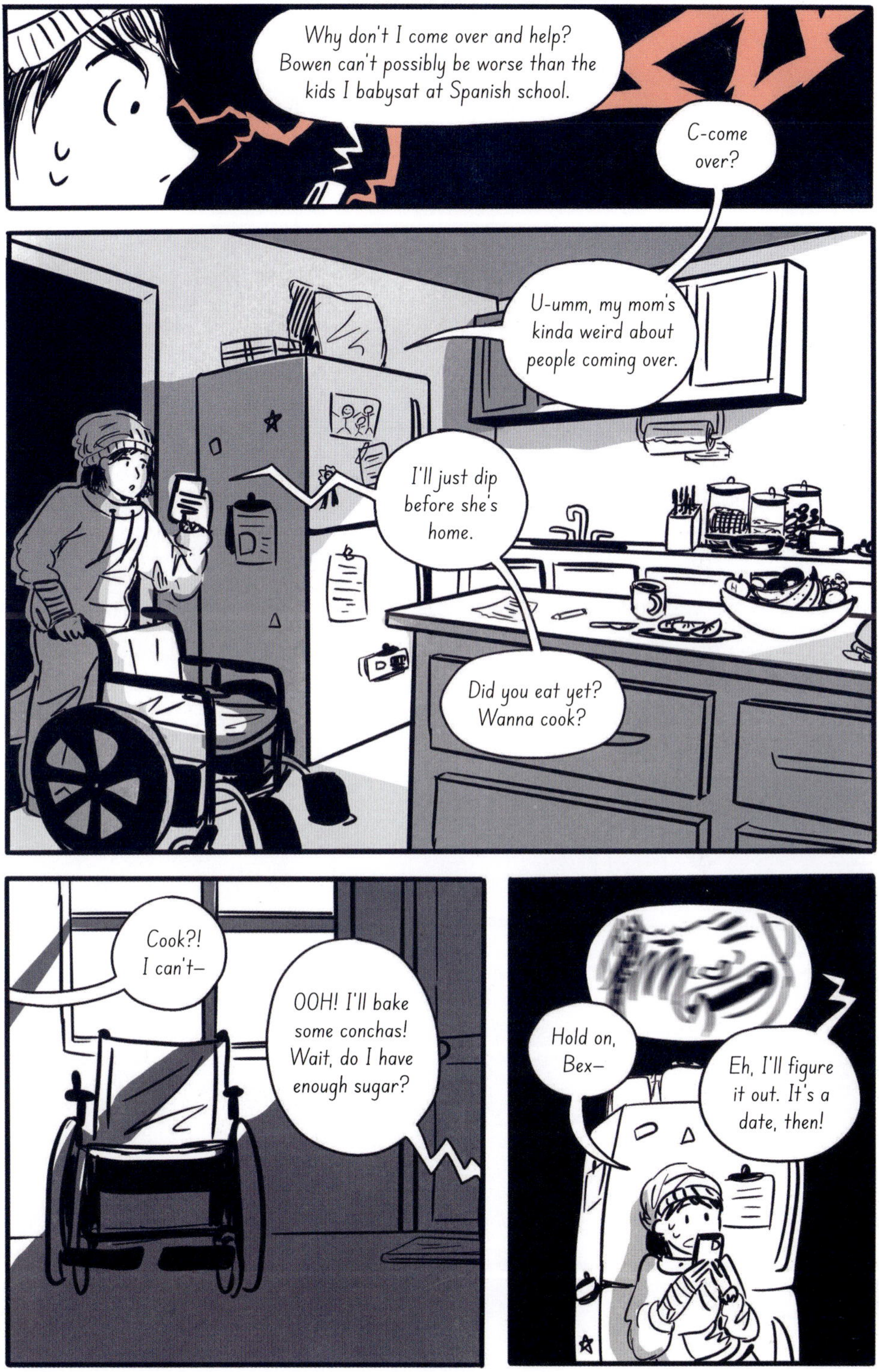
Why don't I come over and help? Bowen can't possibly be worse than the kids I babysat at Spanish school.
C-come over?
U-umm, my mom's kinda weird about people coming over.
I'll just dip before she's home.
Did you eat yet? Wanna cook?
Cook?! I can't–
OOH! I'll bake some conchas! Wait, do I have enough sugar?
Hold on, Bex–
Eh, I'll figure it out. It's a date, then!

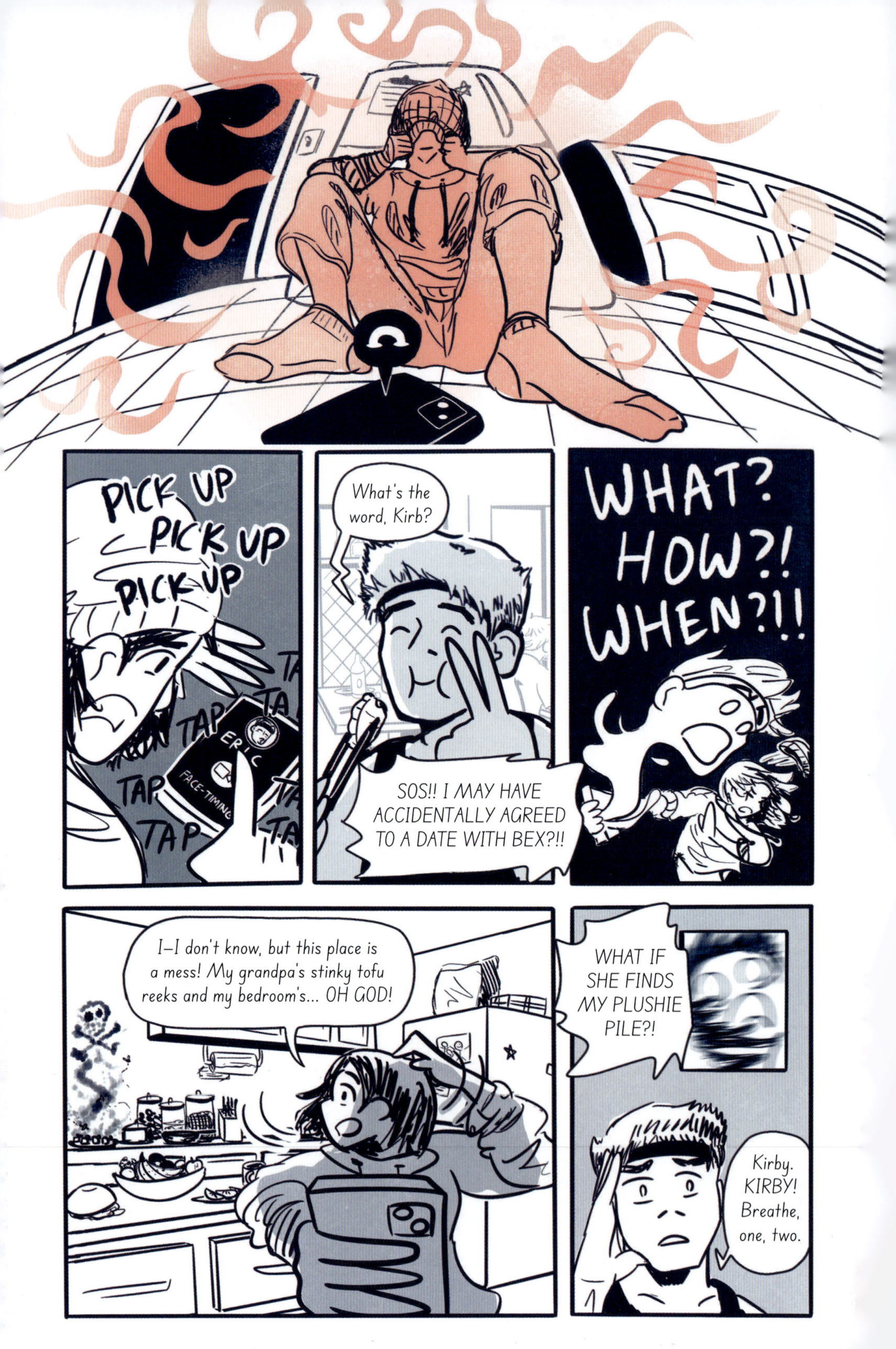

PICK UP
PICK UP
PICK UP
TAP TAP TAP TAP TAP
ERIC
FACE-TIMING
What's the word, Kirb?
SOS!! I MAY HAVE ACCIDENTALLY AGREED TO A DATE WITH BEX?!!
WHAT? HOW?! WHEN?!!
I–I don't know, but this place is a mess! My grandpa's stinky tofu reeks and my bedroom's... OH GOD!
WHAT IF SHE FINDS MY PLUSHIE PILE?!
Kirby. KIRBY! Breathe, one, two.

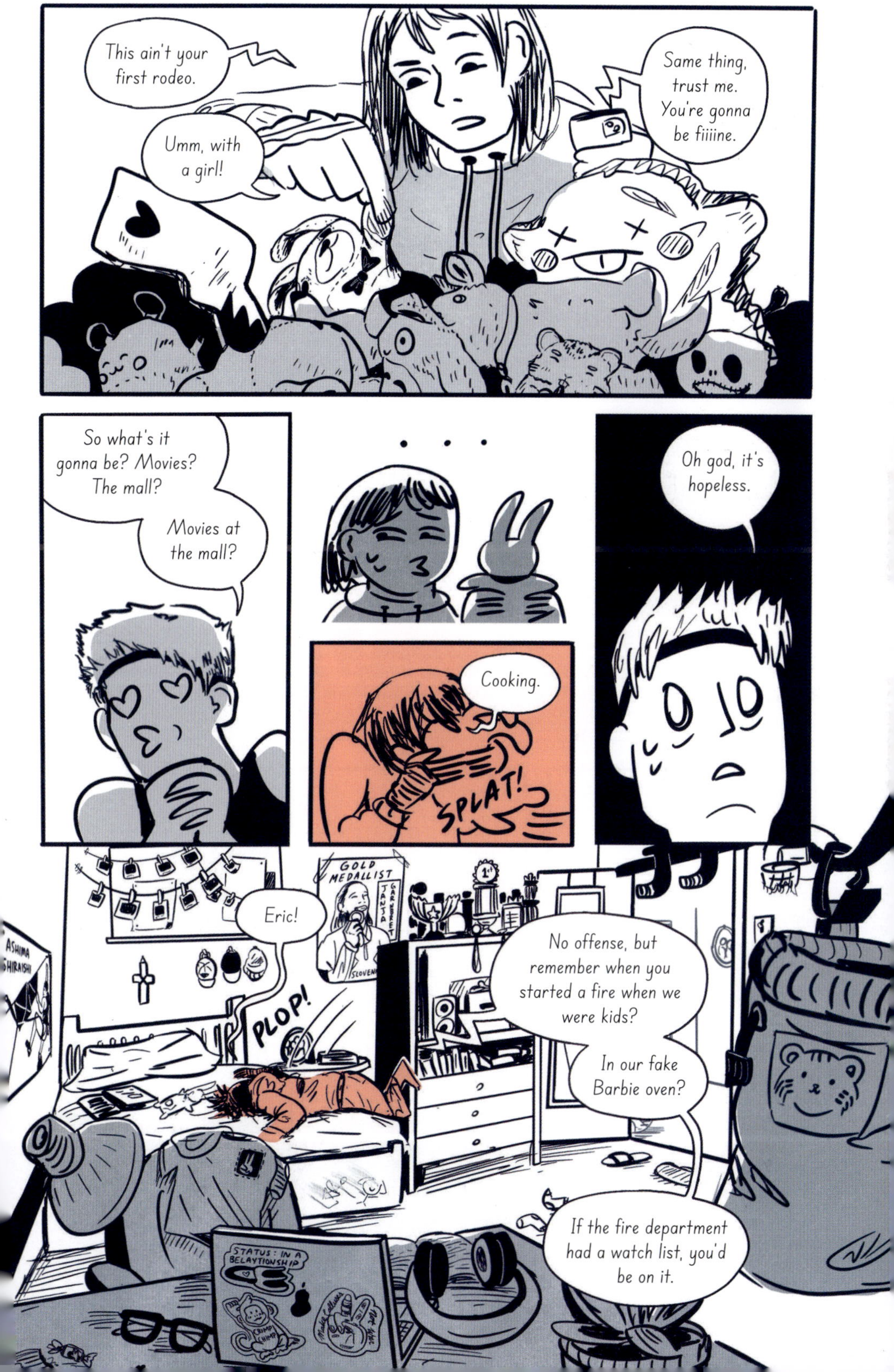
This ain't your first rodeo.
Umm, with a girl!
Same thing, trust me. You're gonna be fiiiine.
So what's it gonna be? Movies? The mall?
Movies at the mall?
Oh god, it's hopeless.
Cooking.
SPLAT!
GOLD MEDALLIST
JANJA GARNBRET
SLOVENIA
ASHIMA SHIRAISHI
Eric!
PLOP!
No offense, but remember when you started a fire when we were kids?
In our fake Barbie oven?
If the fire department had a watch list, you'd be on it.
STATUS: IN A BELAYTIONSHIP
CRIMP CHIMP

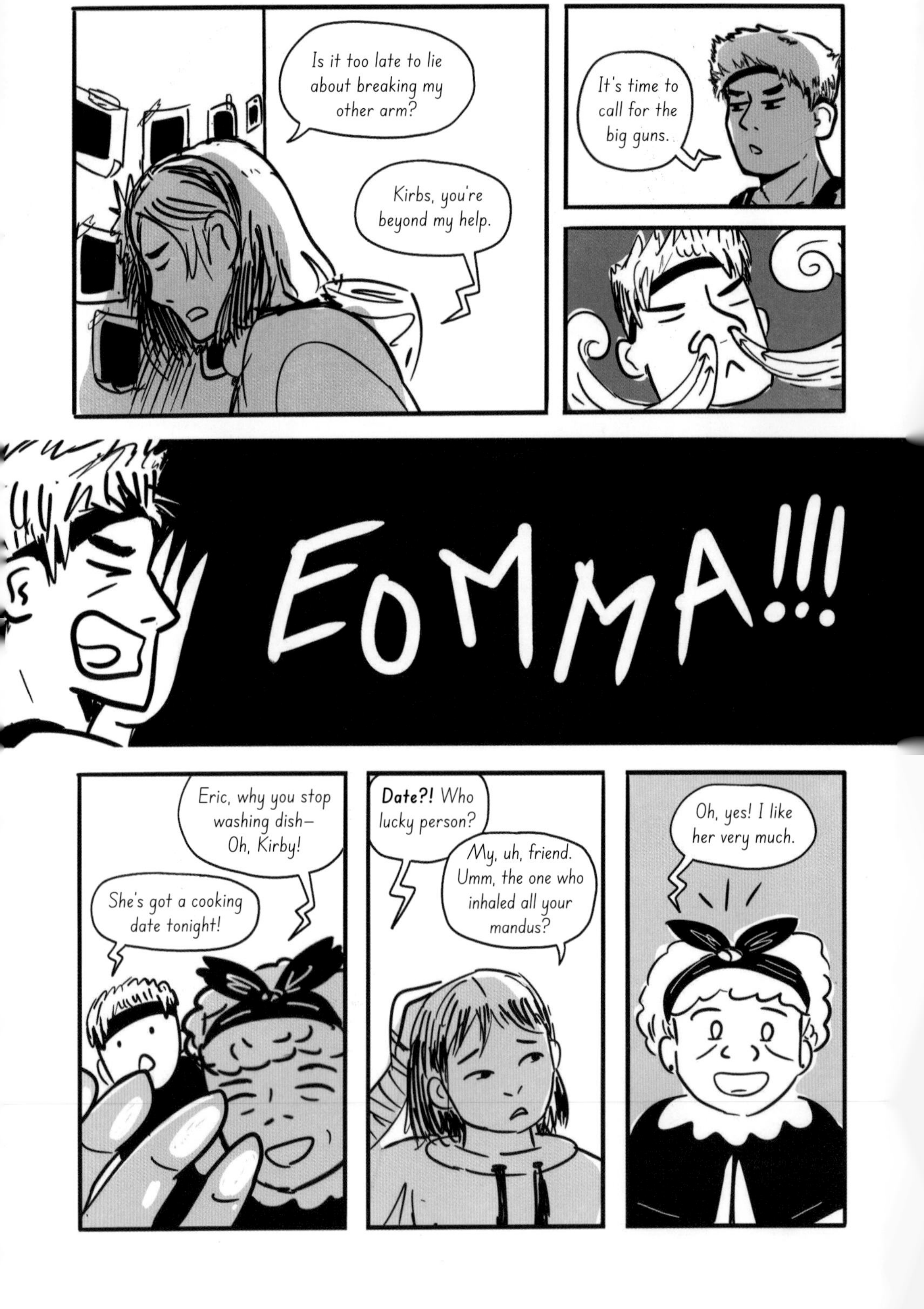
Is it too late to lie about breaking my other arm?
Kirbs, you're beyond my help.
It's time to call for the big guns.
EOMMA!!!
Eric, why you stop washing dish— Oh, Kirby!
She's got a cooking date tonight!
Date?! Who lucky person?
My, uh, friend. Umm, the one who inhaled all your mandus?
Oh, yes! I like her very much.

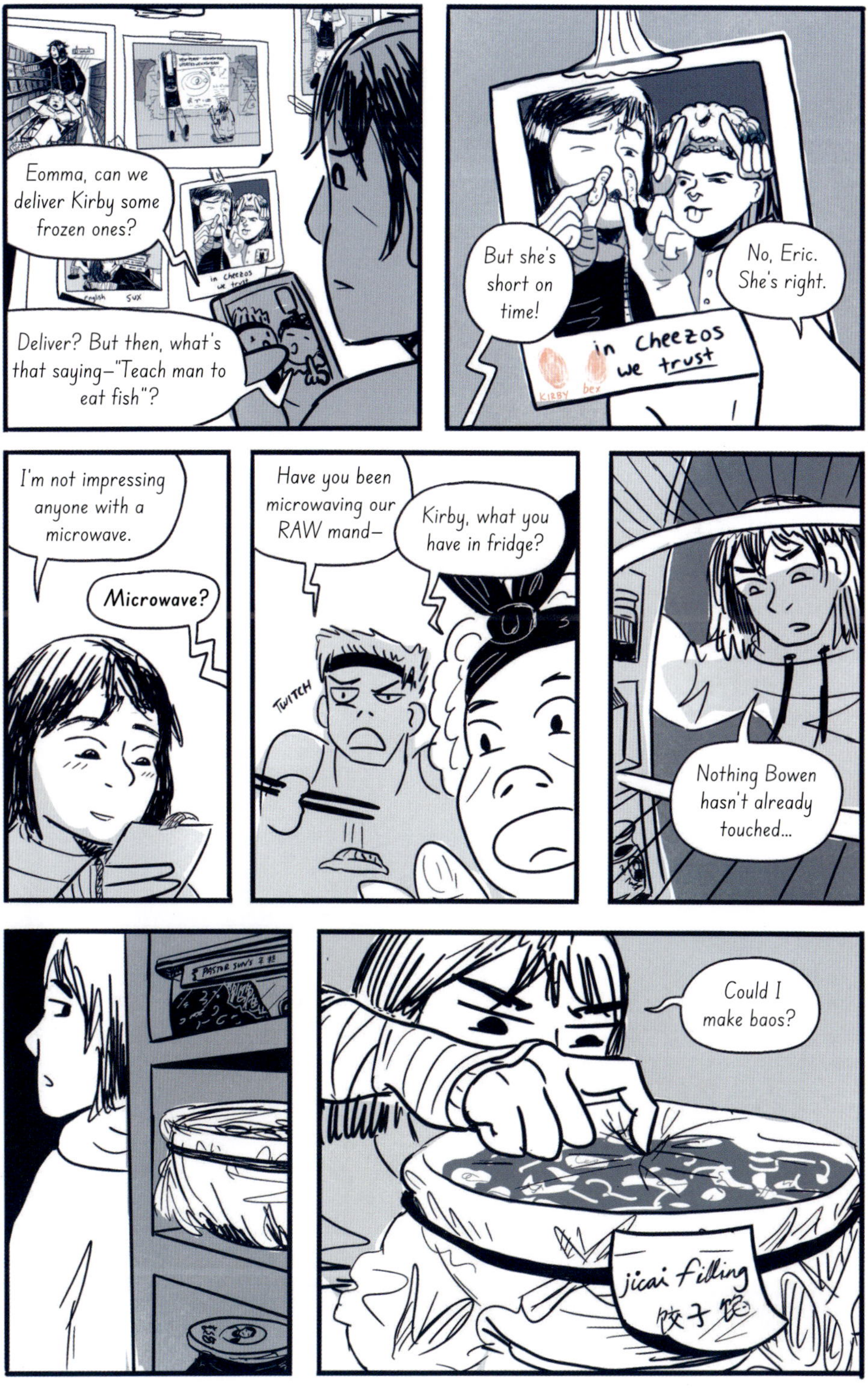
Eomma, can we deliver Kirby some frozen ones?
in cheezos we trust
english sux
Deliver? But then, what's that saying—"Teach man to eat fish"?
But she's short on time!
No, Eric. She's right.
in cheezos we trust
KIRBY
bex
I'm not impressing anyone with a microwave.
Microwave?
Have you been microwaving our RAW mand—
Kirby, what you have in fridge?
TWITCH
Nothing Bowen hasn't already touched...
Could I make baos?
jicai filling
饺子馅

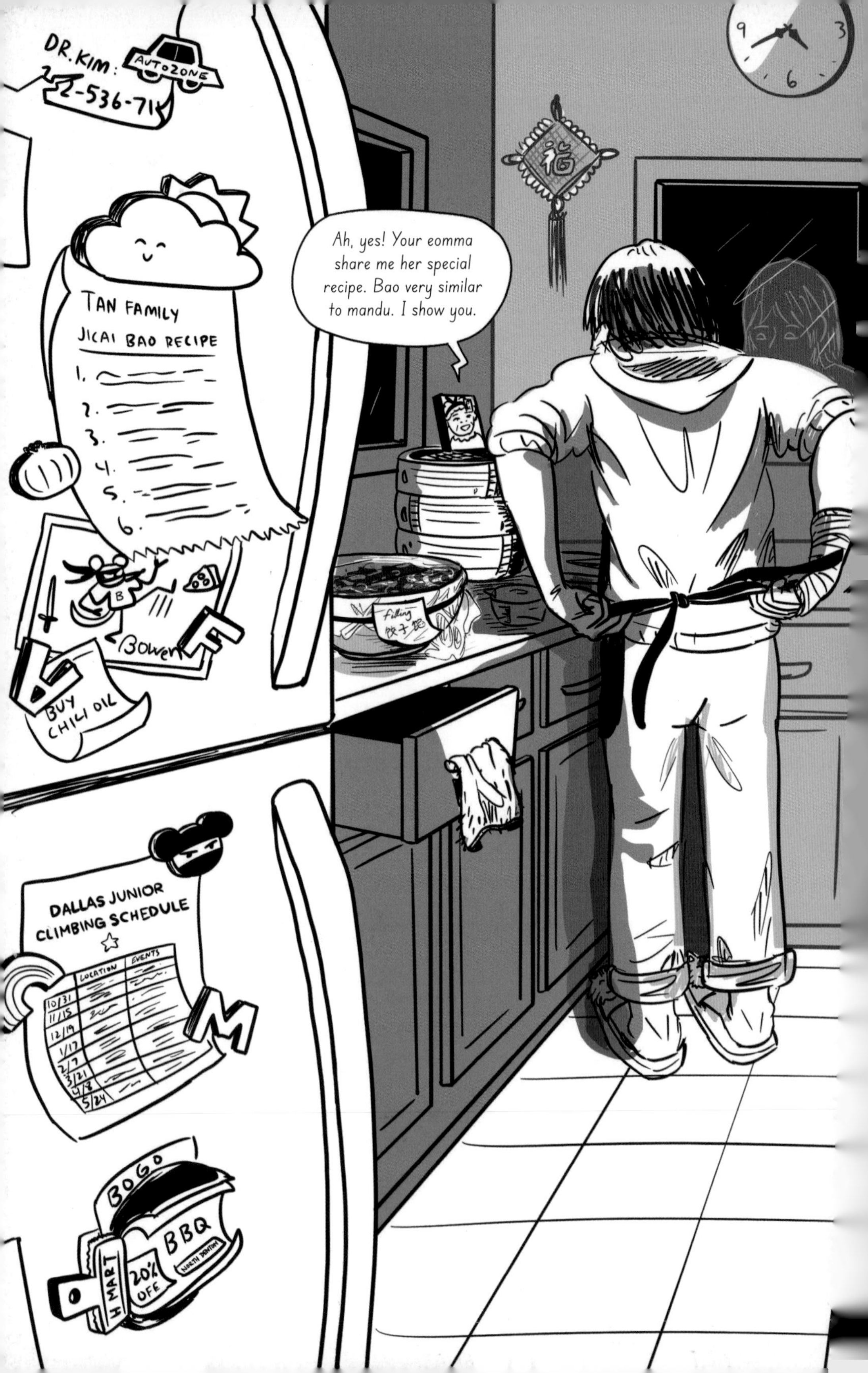
DR. KIM:
2-536-71
AUTOZONE
TAN FAMILY
JICAI BAO RECIPE
1.
2.
3.
4.
5.
6.
Ah, yes! Your eomma share me her special recipe. Bao very similar to mandu. I show you.
Filling
饺子馅
Bowen
BUY CHILI OIL
DALLAS JUNIOR CLIMBING SCHEDULE
LOCATION
EVENTS
10/31
11/15
12/19
1/17
2/7
3/21
4/8
5/24
BOGO
BBQ
NORTH DENTON
H MART
20% OFF

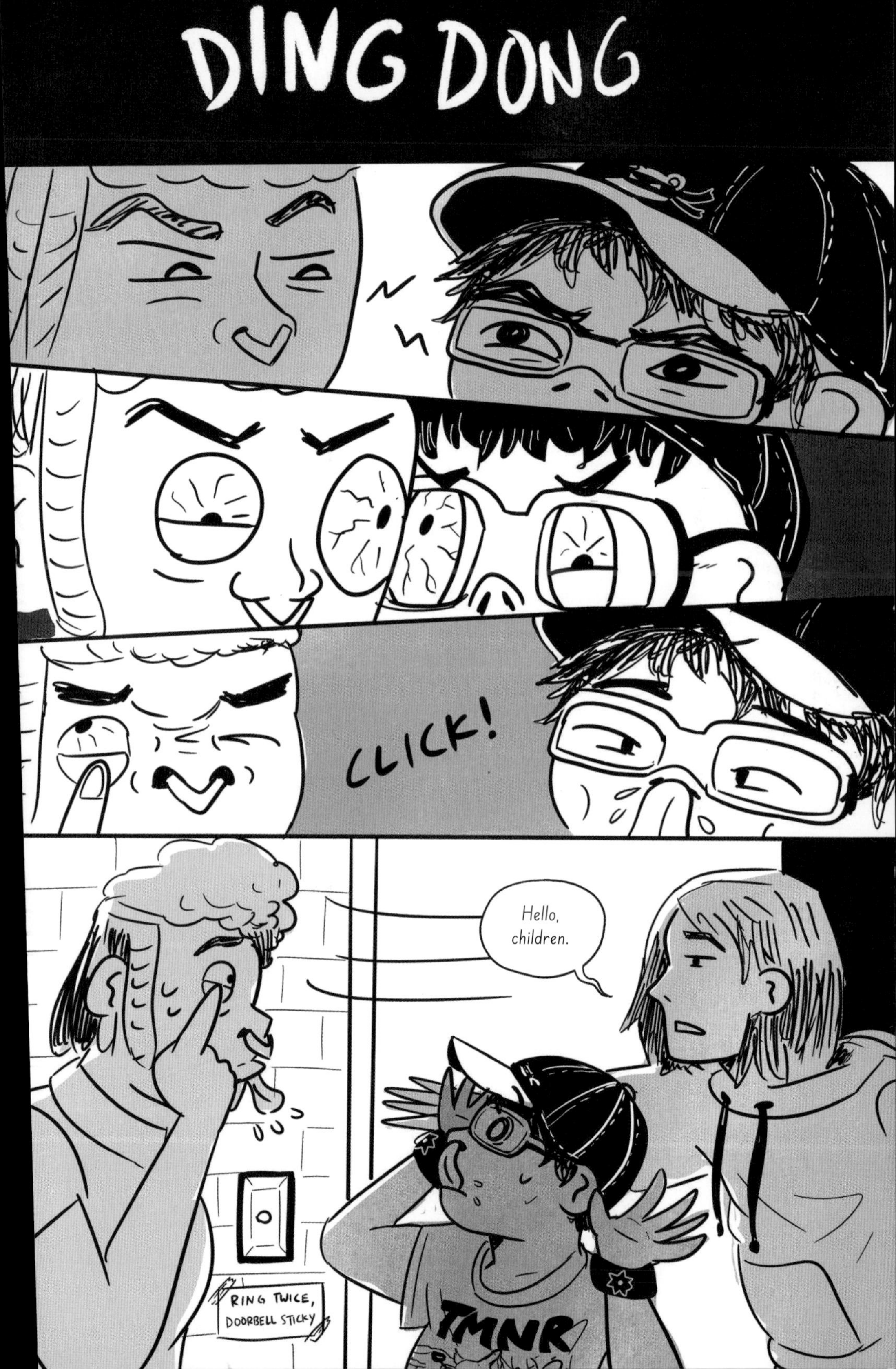
DING DONG
CLICK!
Hello, children.
RING TWICE, DOORBELL STICKY
TMNR

"Sorry I'm late! Had to wait for the conchas to cool."

"Ignore that one, I got hungry."

"What if they're poisoned? Mom says no strangers when we're home alone."

Sniff Sniff

"First of all, don't tell people we're home alone."

"And second, Bex isn't a stranger."

"If I give you a pastry will you stop whining?"

"Hmph! She hasn't even passed my test!"

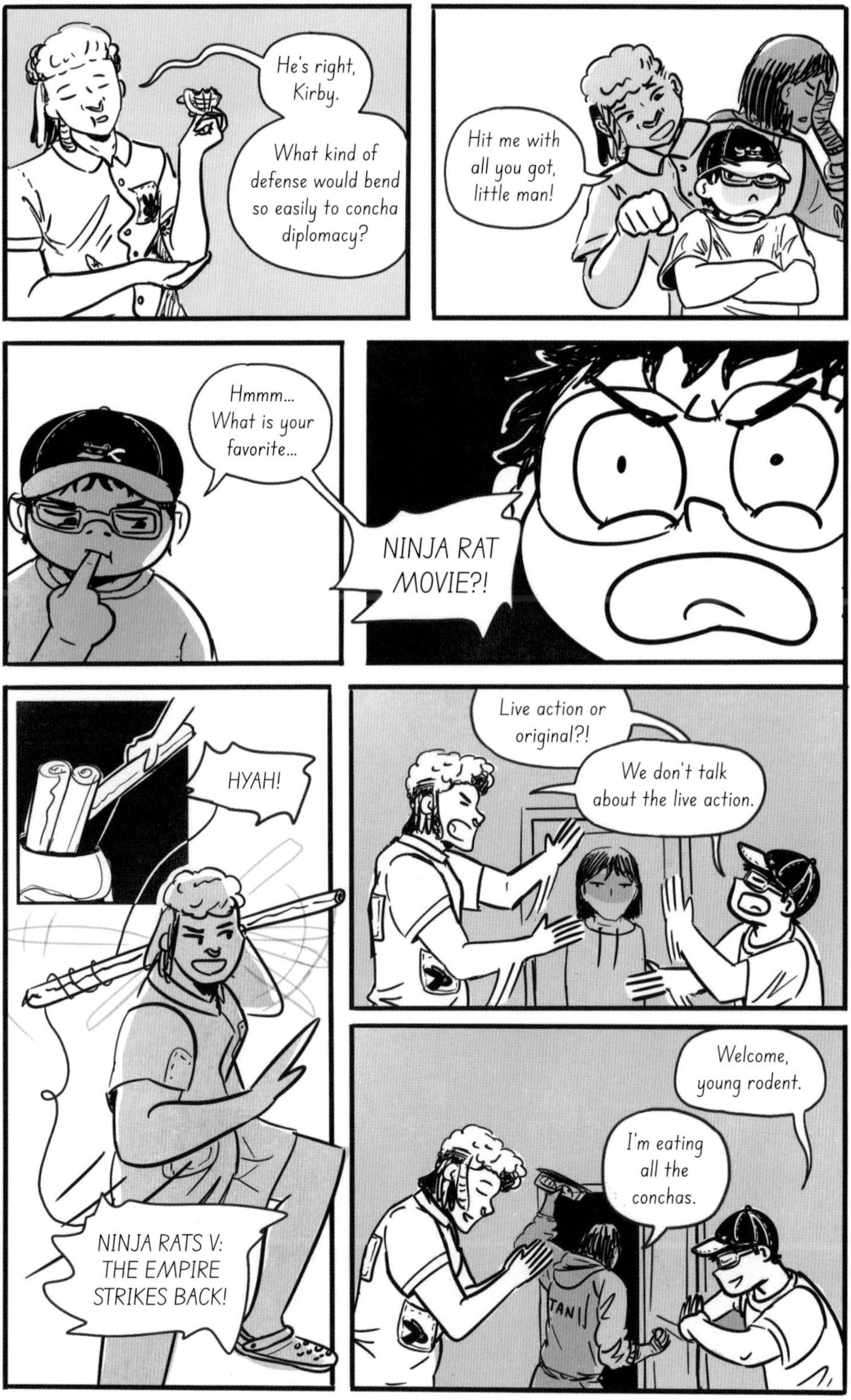
He's right, Kirby.
What kind of defense would bend so easily to concha diplomacy?
Hit me with all you got, little man!
Hmmm... What is your favorite...
NINJA RAT MOVIE?!
HYAH!
NINJA RATS V: THE EMPIRE STRIKES BACK!
Live action or original?!
We don't talk about the live action.
Welcome, young rodent.
I'm eating all the conchas.
TANI

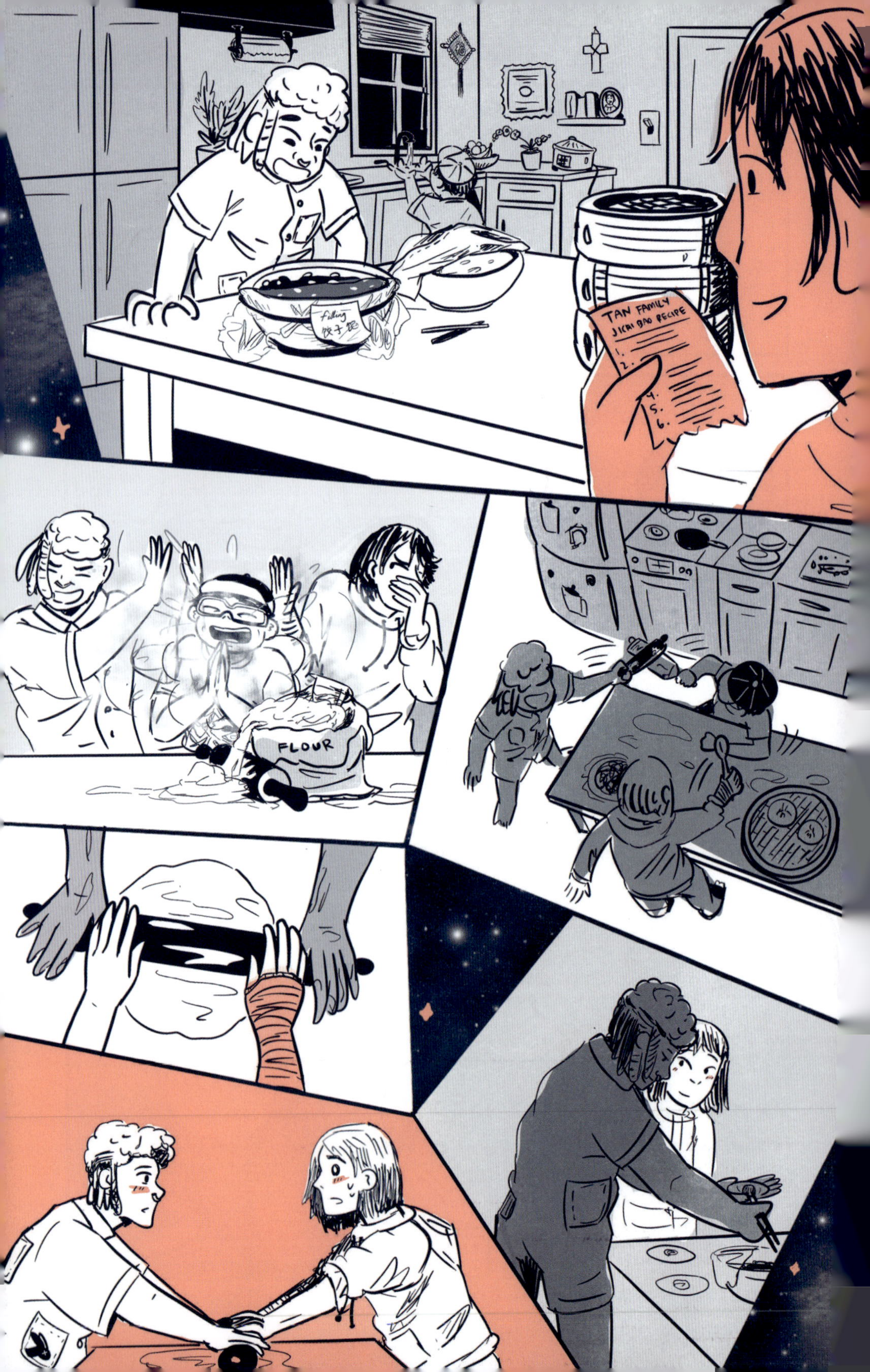
filling
饺子馅
TAN FAMILY
JICAI BAO RECIPE
1.
2.
4.
5.
6.
FLOUR

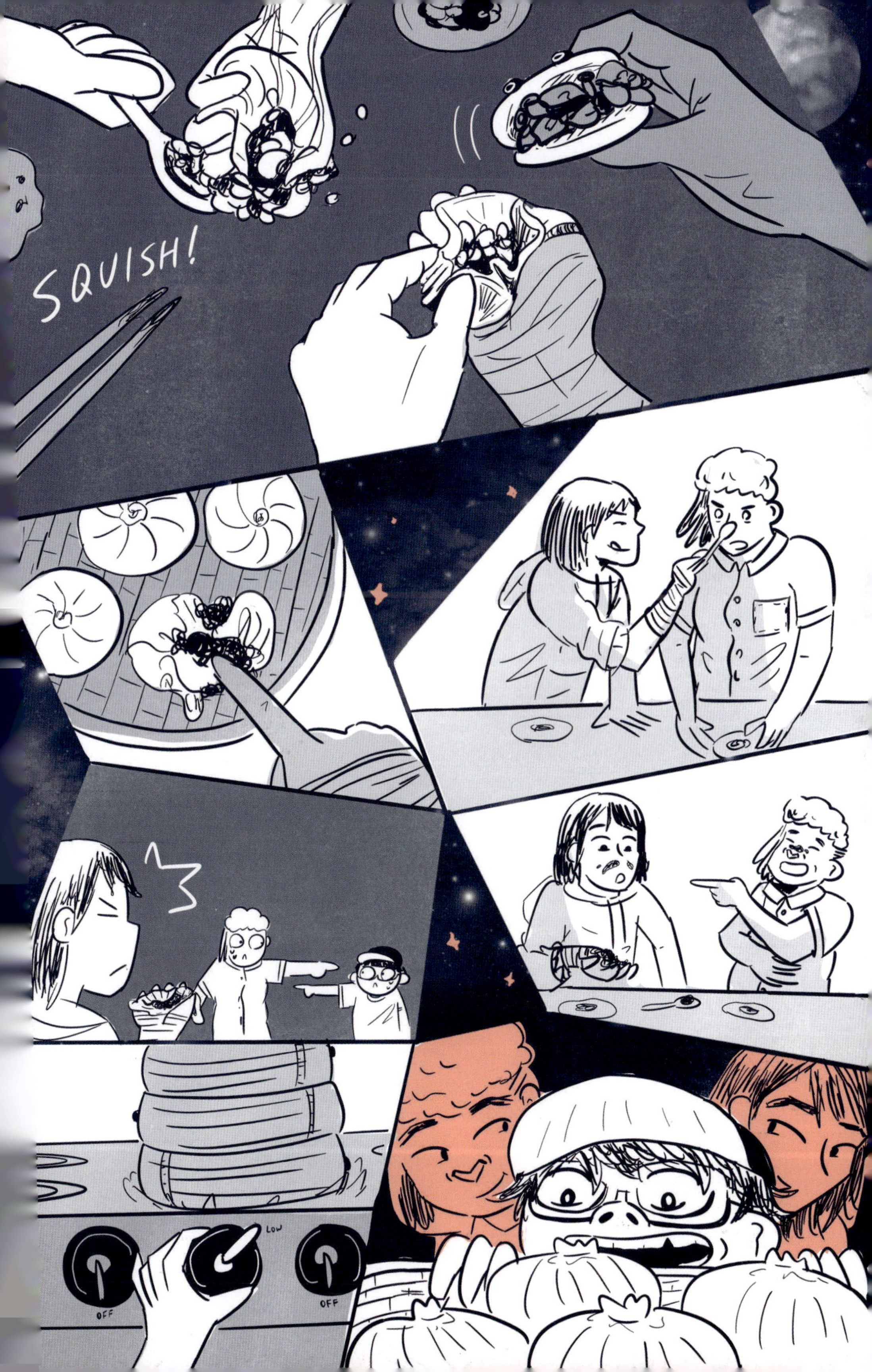
SQUISH!
LOW
OFF
OFF

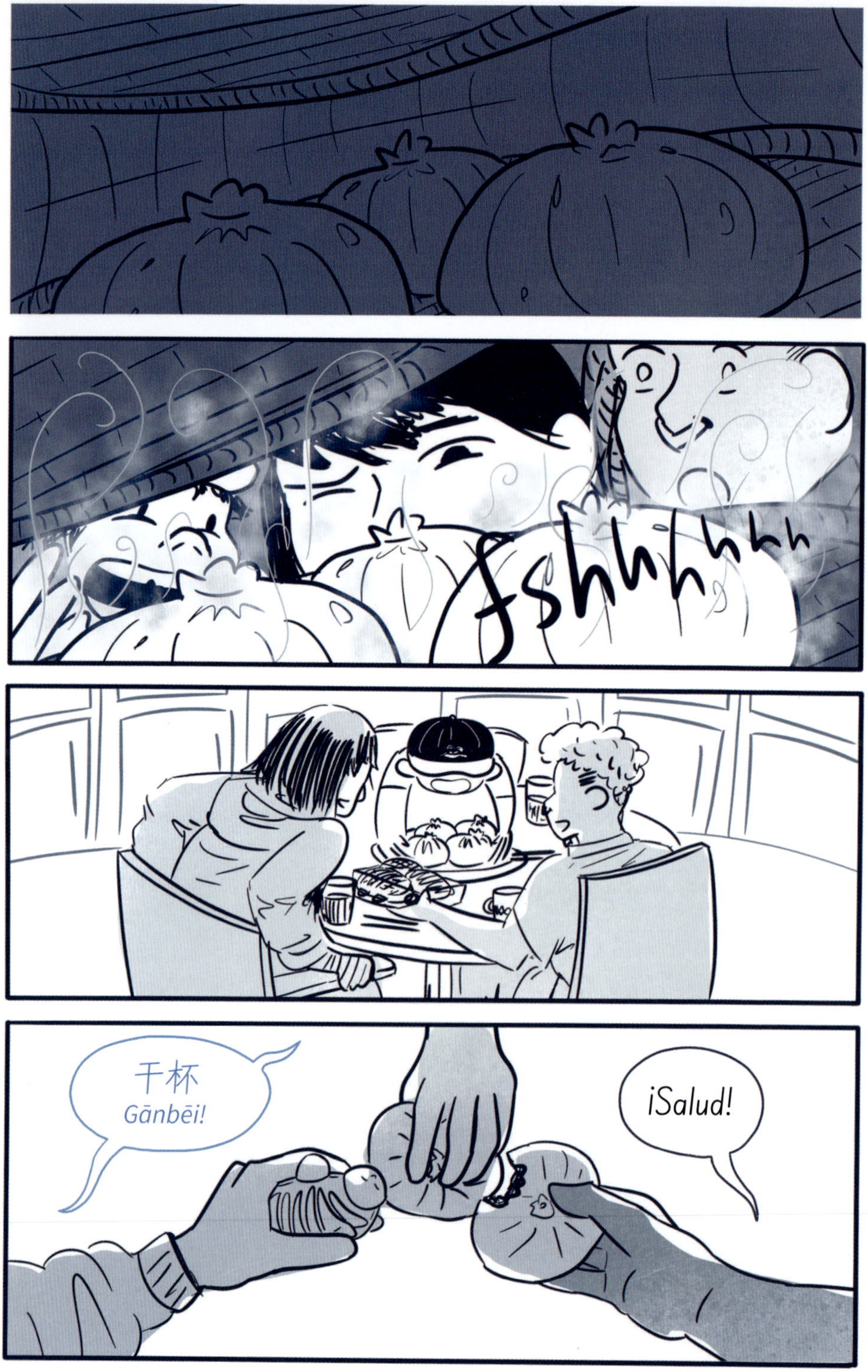
fshhhhhh
干杯
Gānbēi!
¡Salud!

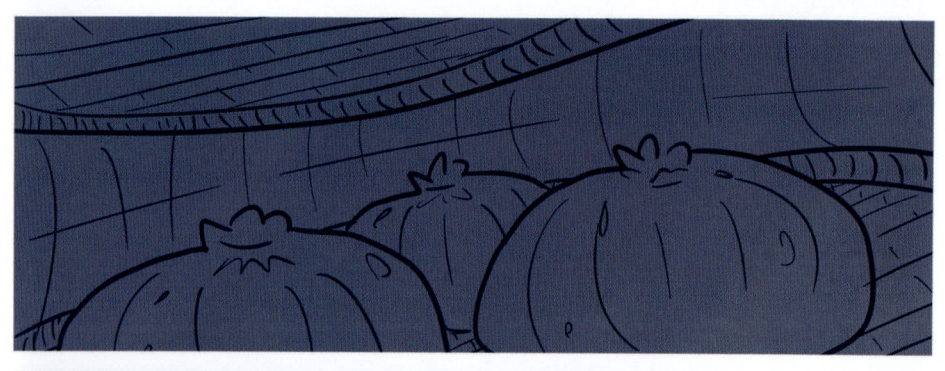

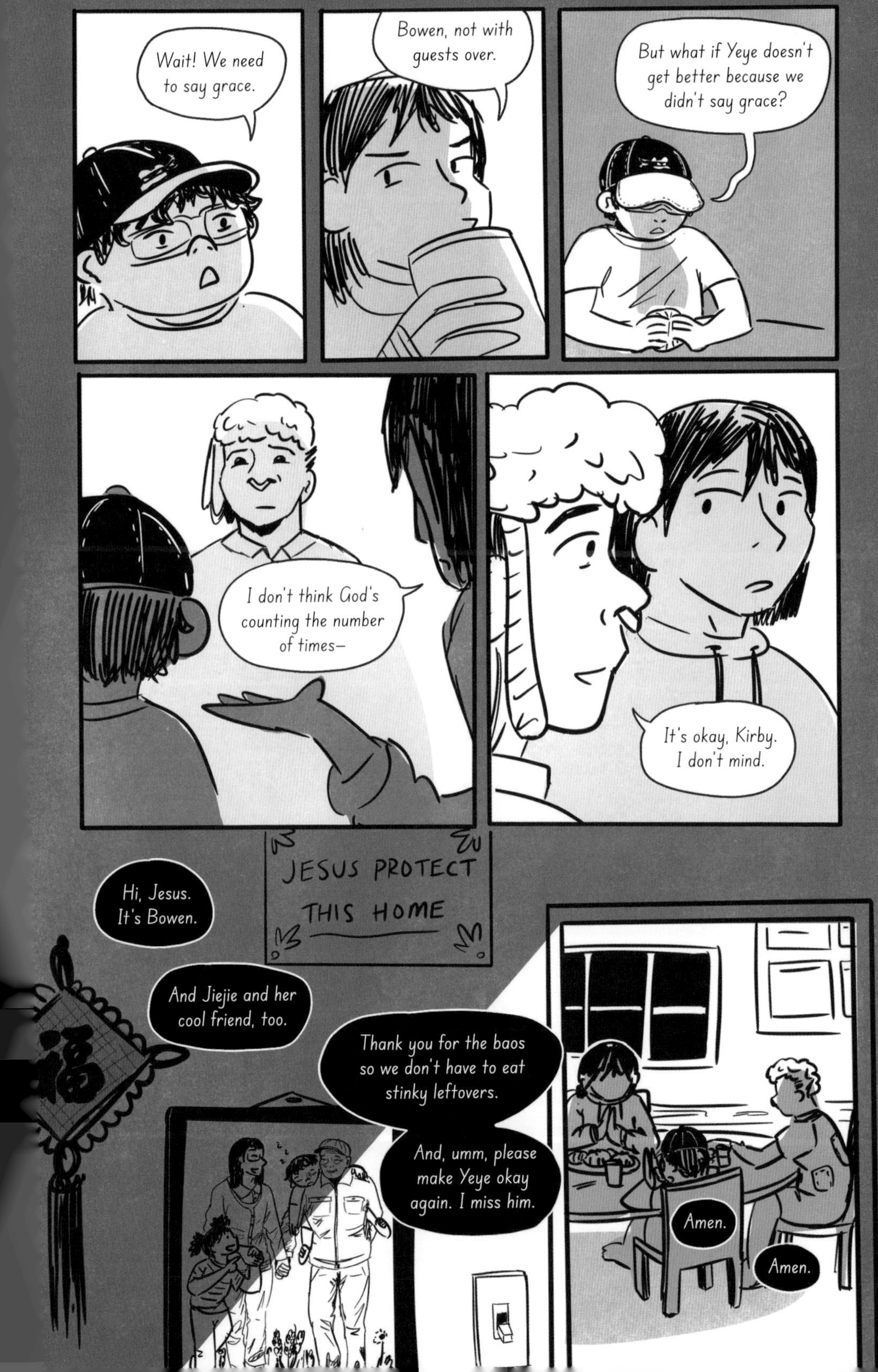

Wait! We need to say grace.
Bowen, not with guests over.
But what if Yeye doesn't get better because we didn't say grace?
I don't think God's counting the number of times—
It's okay, Kirby. I don't mind.
JESUS PROTECT THIS HOME
Hi, Jesus. It's Bowen.
And Jiejie and her cool friend, too.
Thank you for the baos so we don't have to eat stinky leftovers.
And, umm, please make Yeye okay again. I miss him.
Amen.
Amen.

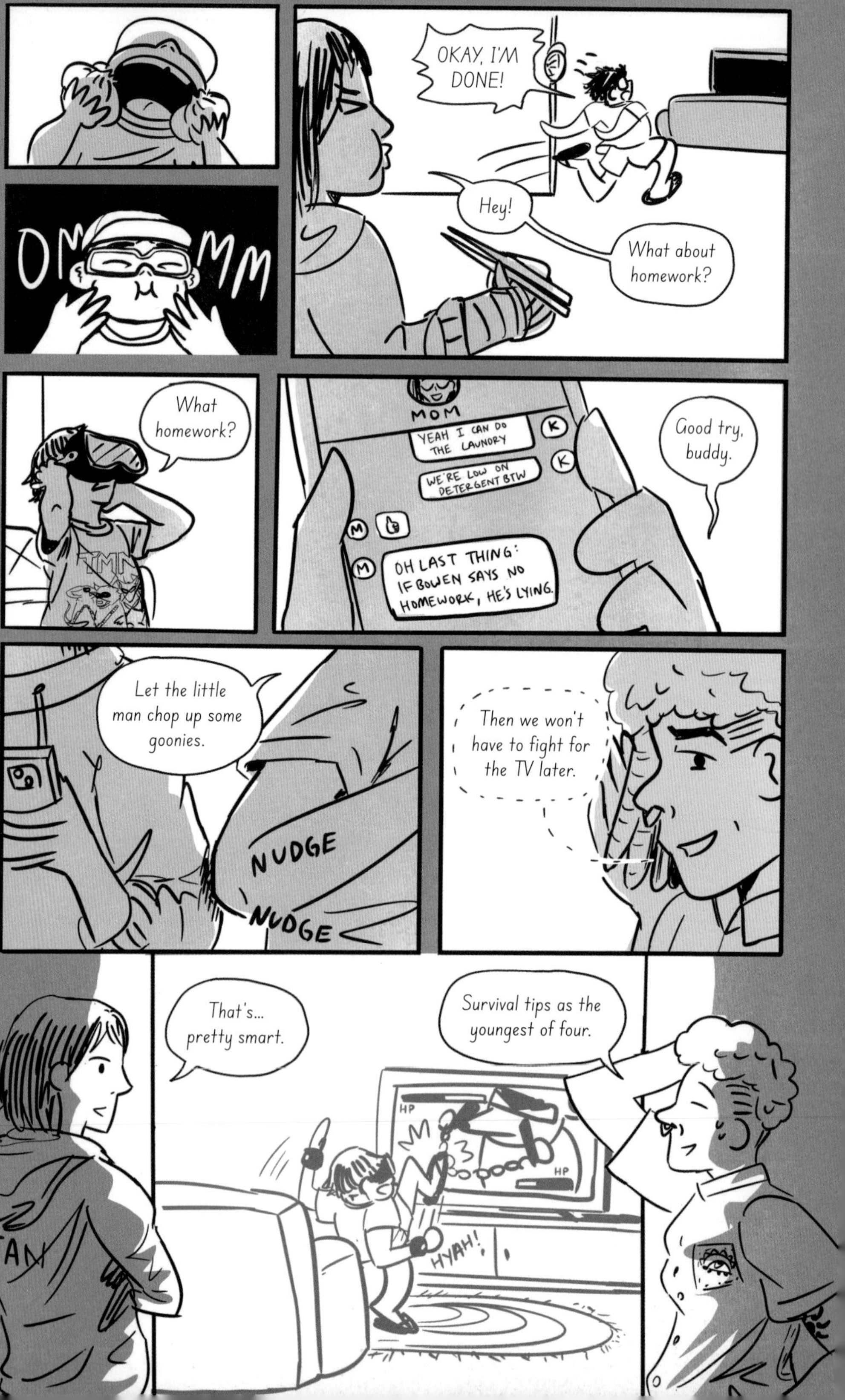
OMMMM
OKAY, I'M DONE!
Hey!
What about homework?
What homework?
MOM
YEAH I CAN DO THE LAUNDRY
K
WE'RE LOW ON DETERGENT BTW
K
M
M
OH LAST THING: IF BOWEN SAYS NO HOMEWORK, HE'S LYING.
Good try, buddy.
Let the little man chop up some goonies.
NUDGE
NUDGE
Then we won't have to fight for the TV later.
That's... pretty smart.
Survival tips as the youngest of four.
HP
HP
HYAH!
TAN

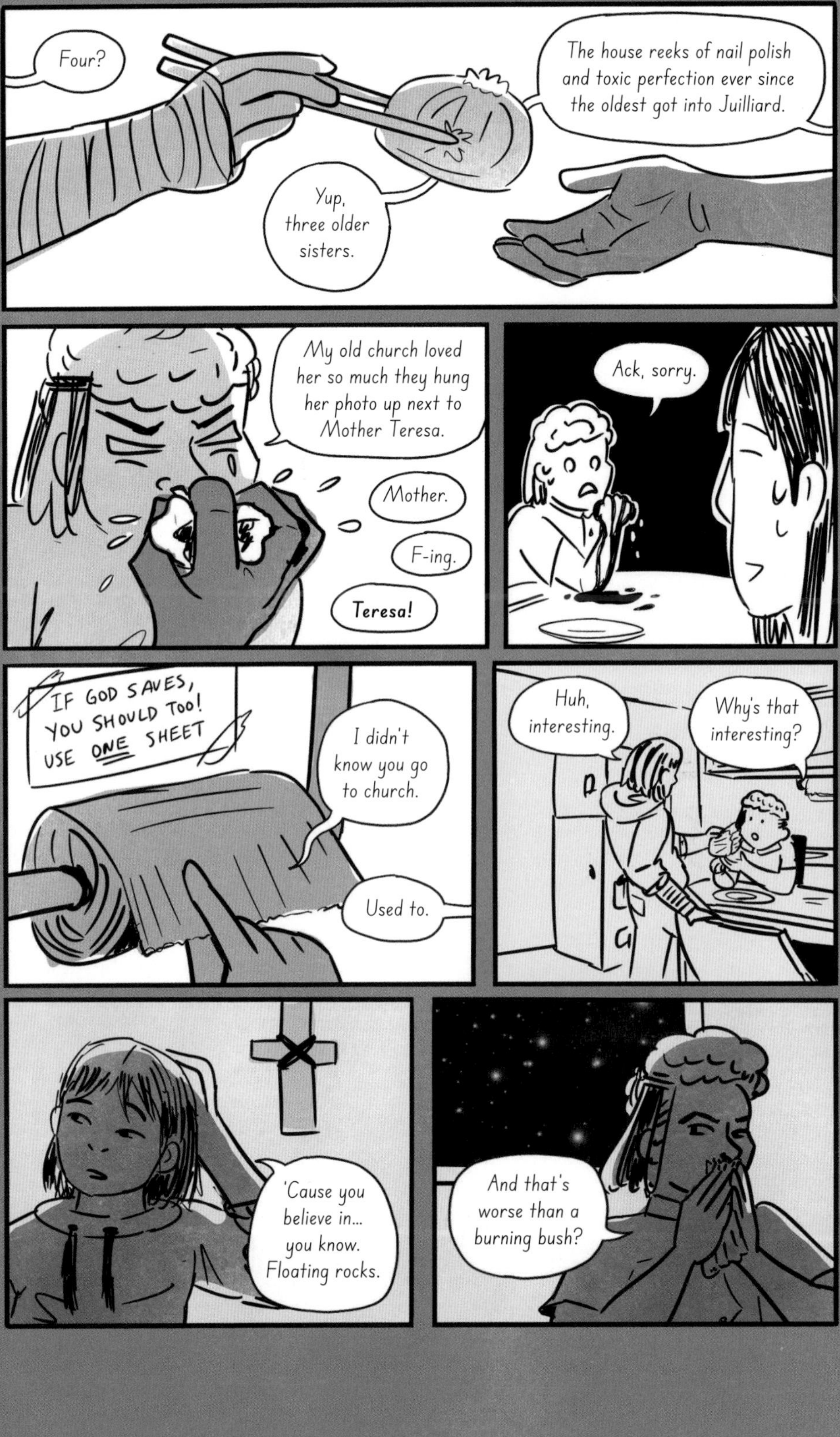

Four?
The house reeks of nail polish and toxic perfection ever since the oldest got into Juilliard.
Yup, three older sisters.
My old church loved her so much they hung her photo up next to Mother Teresa.
Mother.
F-ing.
Teresa!
Ack, sorry.
IF GOD SAVES, YOU SHOULD TOO! USE ONE SHEET
I didn't know you go to church.
Used to.
Huh, interesting.
Why's that interesting?
'Cause you believe in... you know. Floating rocks.
And that's worse than a burning bush?

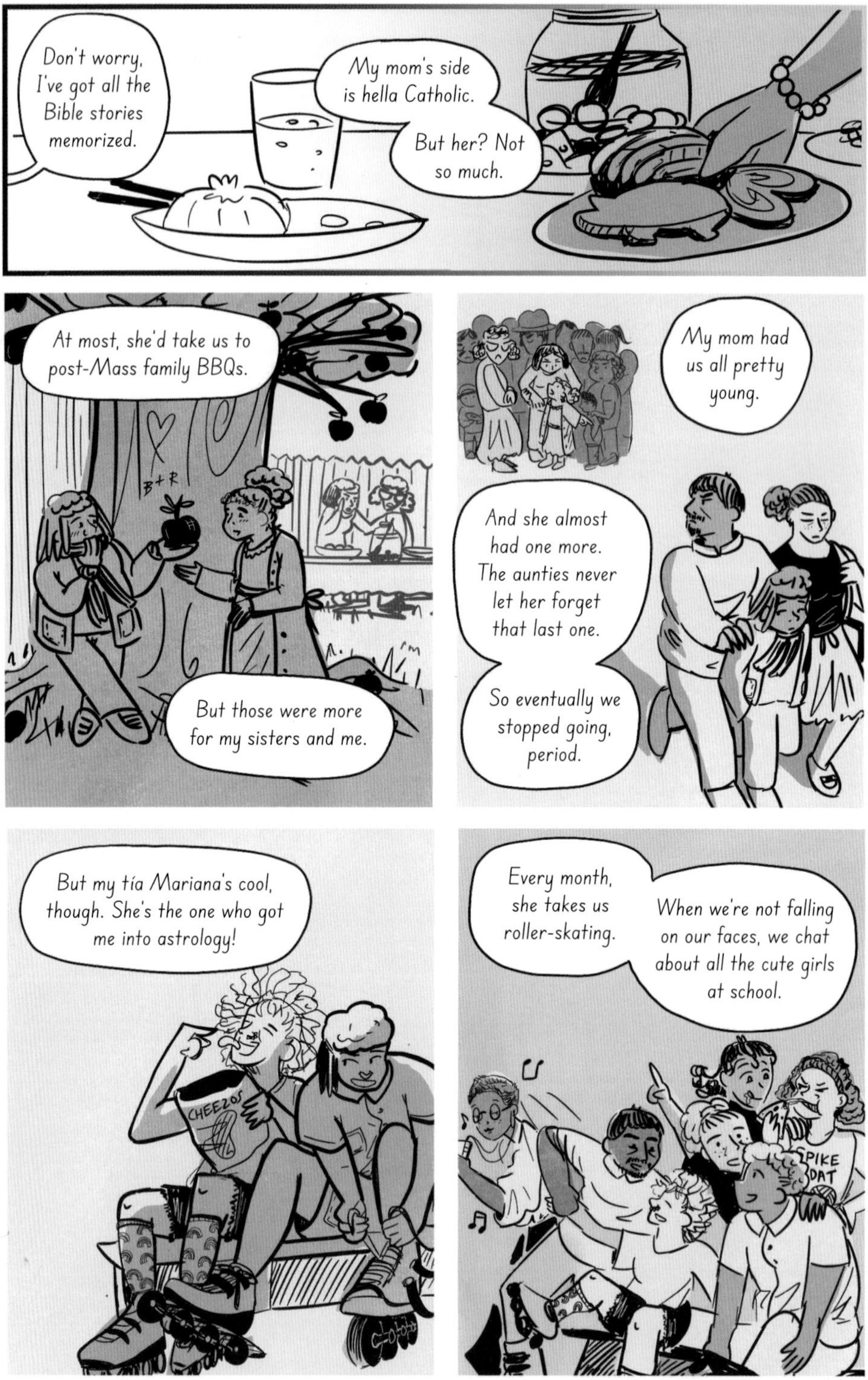
Don't worry, I've got all the Bible stories memorized.
My mom's side is hella Catholic.
But her? Not so much.
At most, she'd take us to post-Mass family BBQs.
B+R
But those were more for my sisters and me.
My mom had us all pretty young.
And she almost had one more. The aunties never let her forget that last one.
So eventually we stopped going, period.
But my tía Mariana's cool, though. She's the one who got me into astrology!
CHEEZOS
Every month, she takes us roller-skating.
When we're not falling on our faces, we chat about all the cute girls at school.
SPIKE DAT

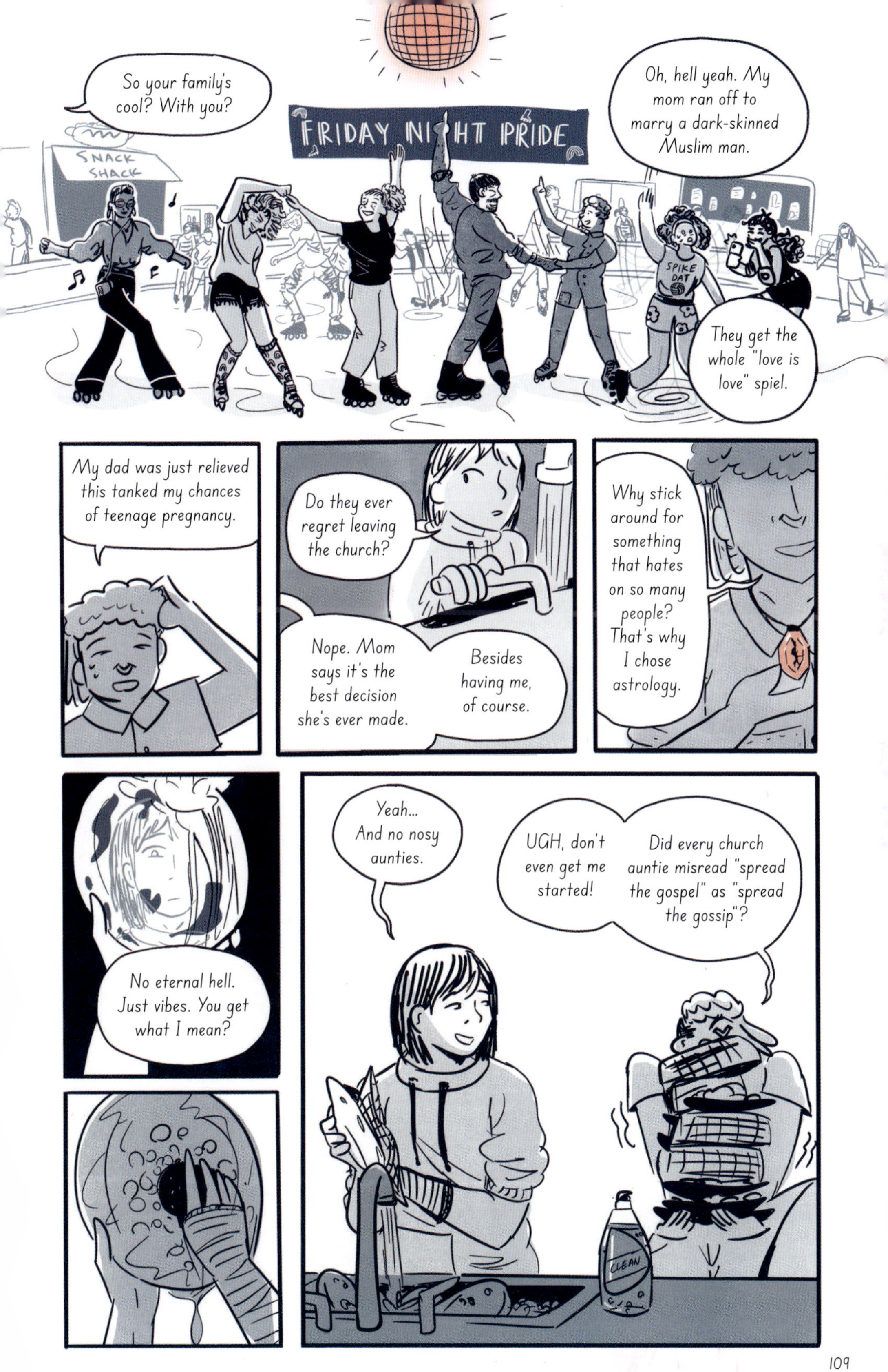

So your family's cool? With you?
FRIDAY NIGHT PRIDE
SNACK SHACK
Oh, hell yeah. My mom ran off to marry a dark-skinned Muslim man.
SPIKE DAT
They get the whole "love is love" spiel.
My dad was just relieved this tanked my chances of teenage pregnancy.
Do they ever regret leaving the church?
Nope. Mom says it's the best decision she's ever made.
Besides having me, of course.
Why stick around for something that hates on so many people? That's why I chose astrology.
No eternal hell. Just vibes. You get what I mean?
Yeah... And no nosy aunties.
UGH, don't even get me started!
Did every church auntie misread "spread the gospel" as "spread the gossip"?
CLEAN

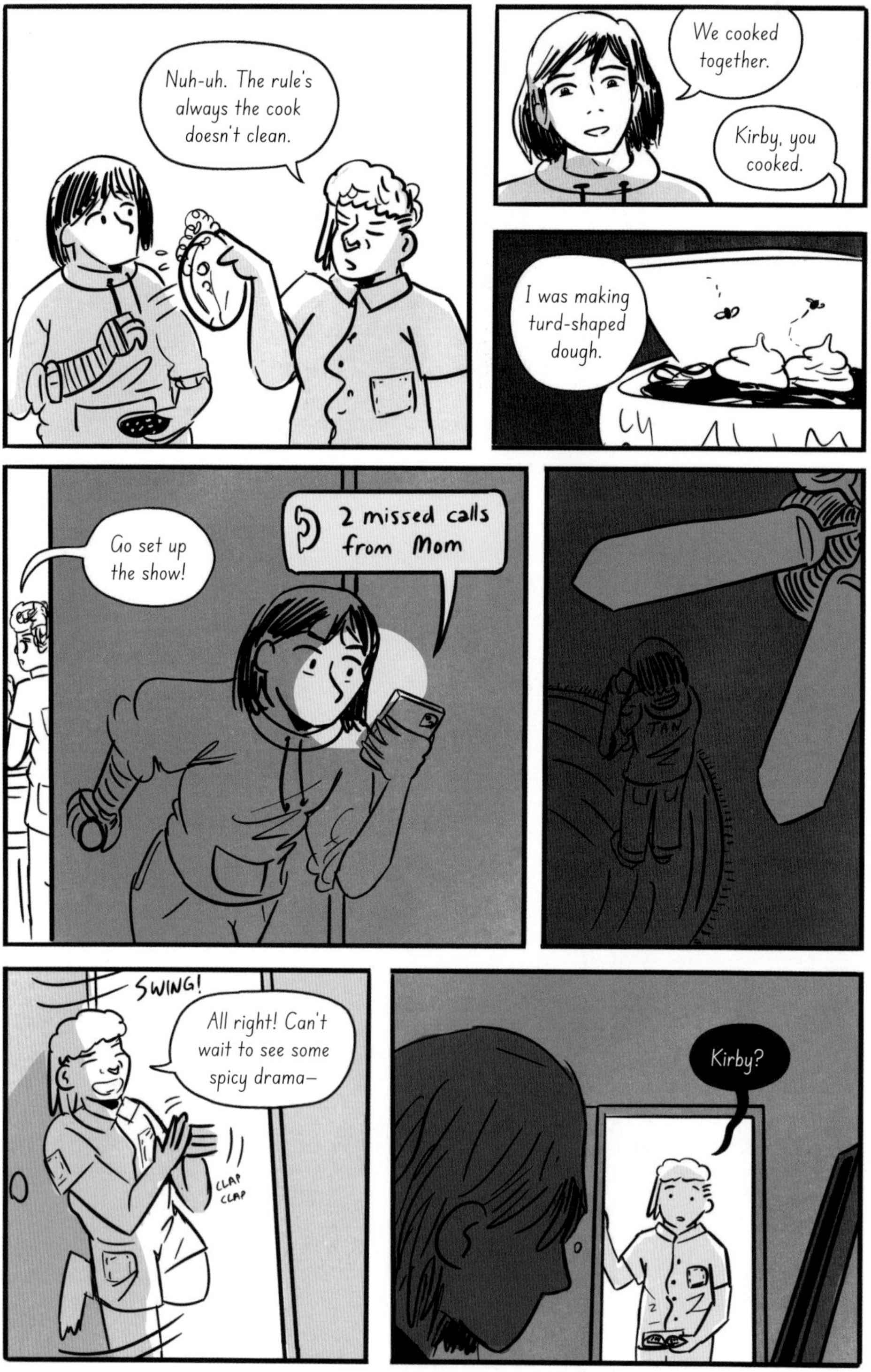

Nuh-uh. The rule's always the cook doesn't clean.
We cooked together.
Kirby, you cooked.
I was making turd-shaped dough.
2 missed calls from Mom
Go set up the show!
SWING!
All right! Can't wait to see some spicy drama—
CLAP CLAP
Kirby?

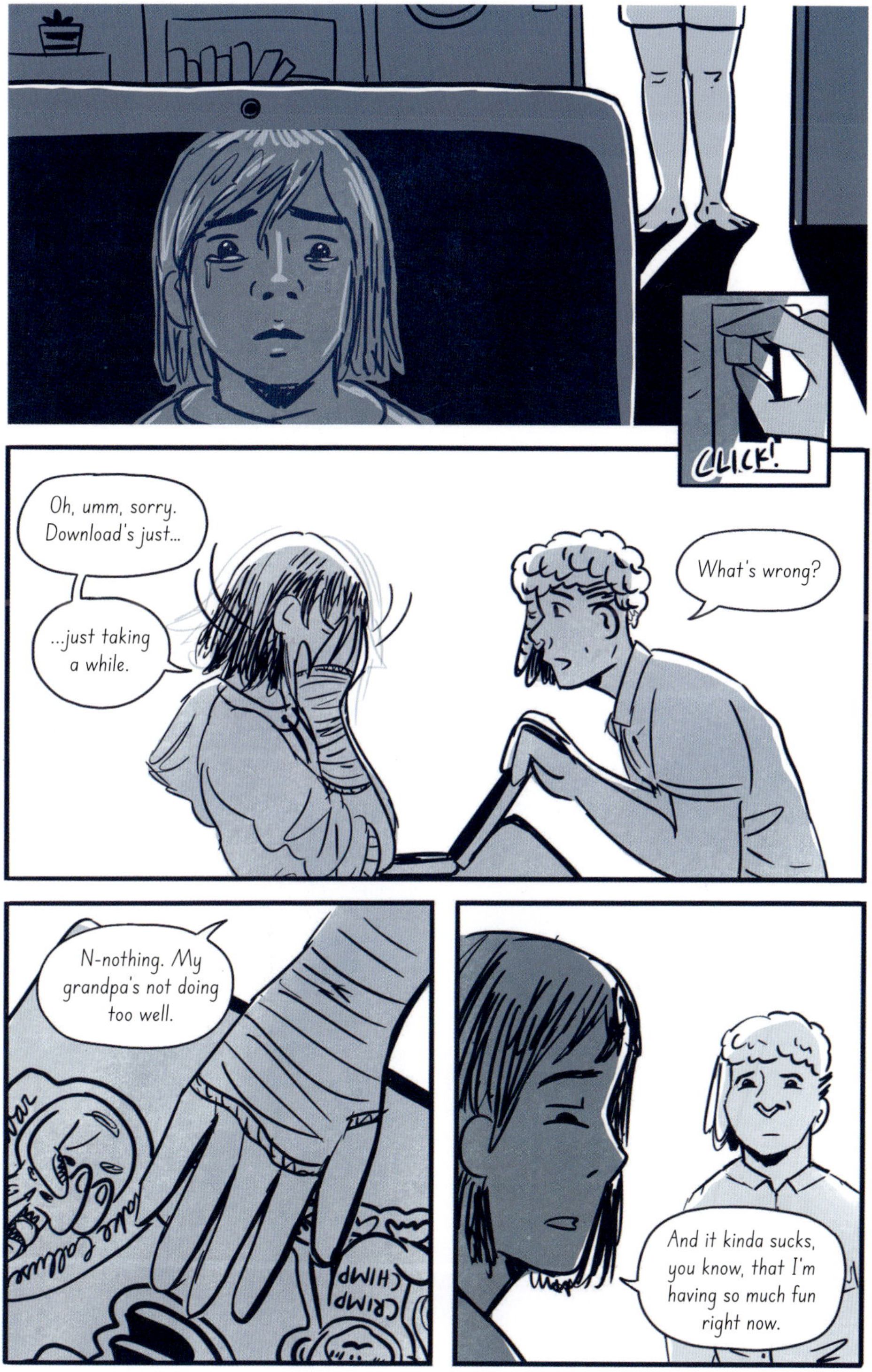
CLICK!
Oh, umm, sorry. Download's just...
...just taking a while.
What's wrong?
N-nothing. My grandpa's not doing too well.
CRIMP CHIMP
And it kinda sucks, you know, that I'm having so much fun right now.

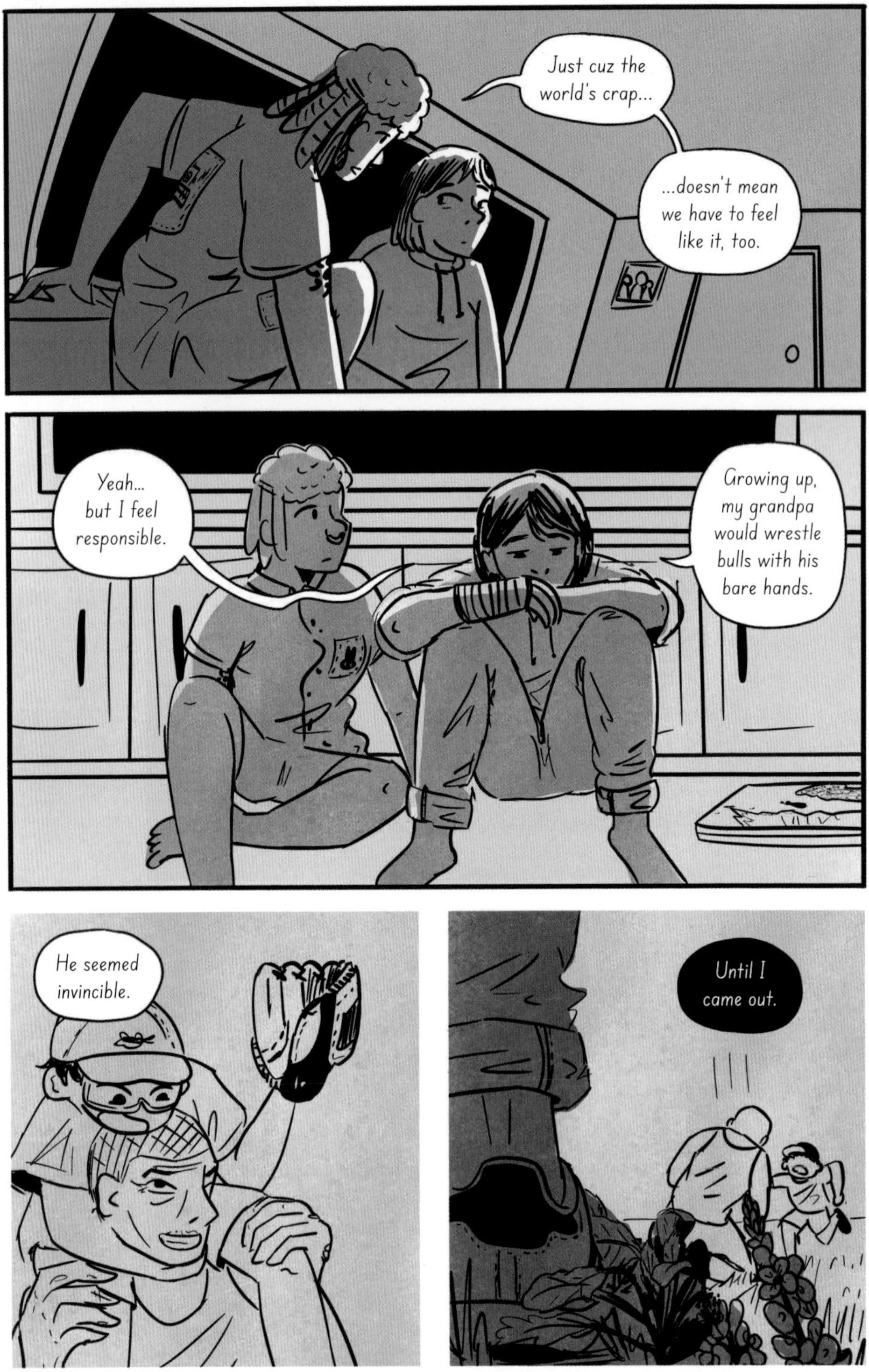
Just cuz the world's crap...
...doesn't mean we have to feel like it, too.
Yeah... but I feel responsible.
Growing up, my grandpa would wrestle bulls with his bare hands.
He seemed invincible.
Until I came out.

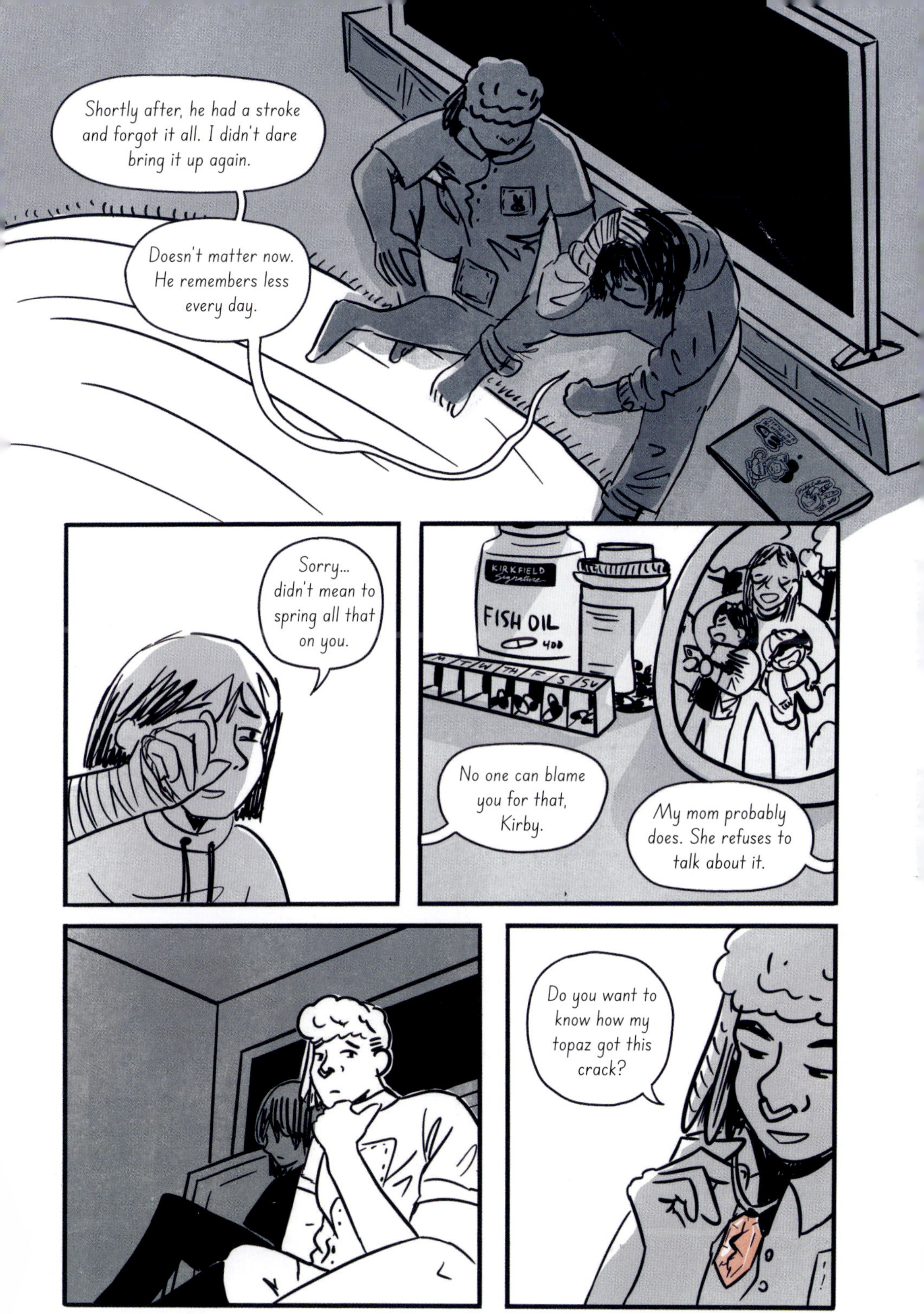
Shortly after, he had a stroke and forgot it all. I didn't dare bring it up again.
Doesn't matter now. He remembers less every day.
Sorry... didn't mean to spring all that on you.
KIRKFIELD Signature
FISH OIL
M T W TH F S SU
No one can blame you for that, Kirby.
My mom probably does. She refuses to talk about it.
Do you want to know how my topaz got this crack?

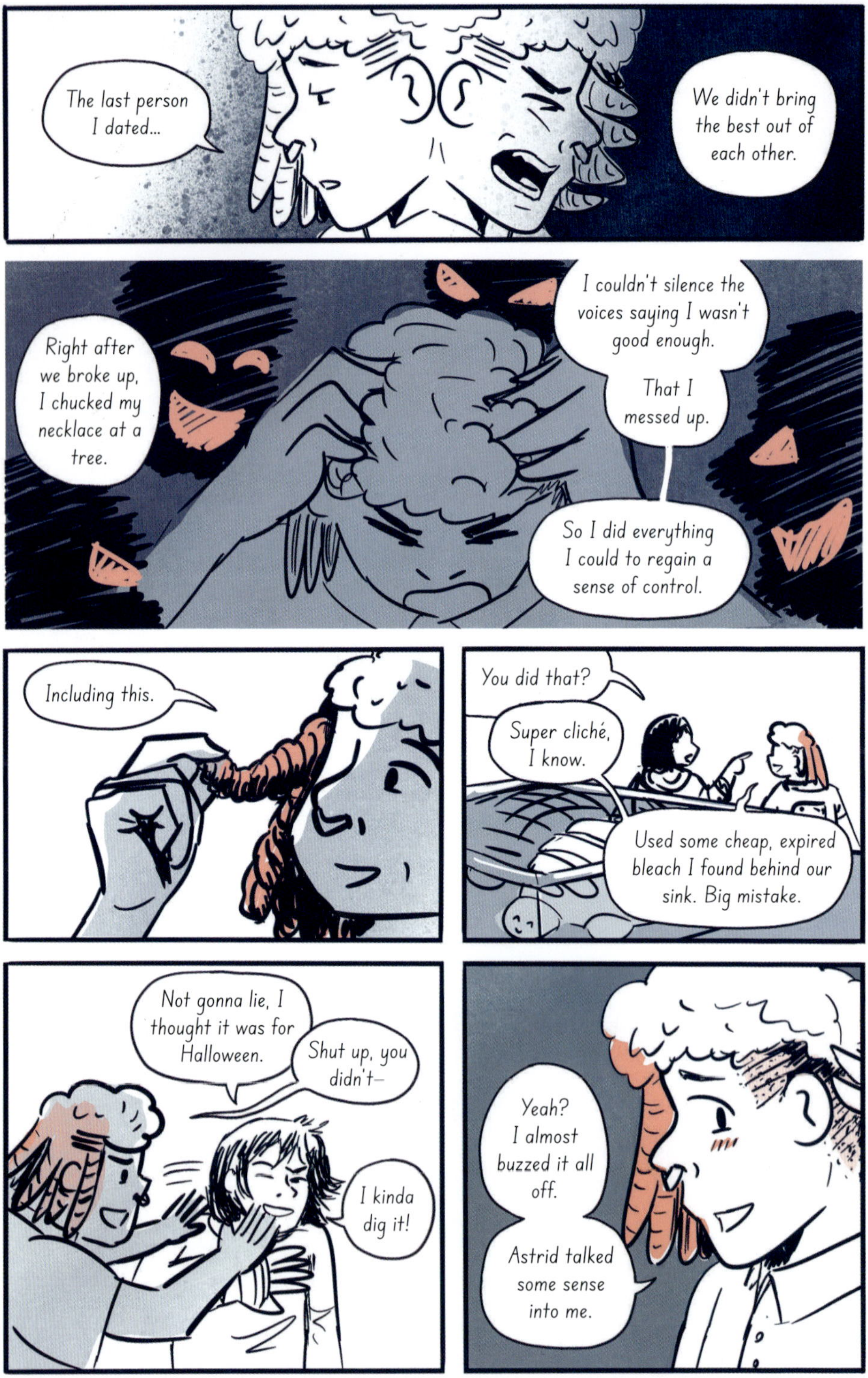
The last person I dated...
We didn't bring the best out of each other.
Right after we broke up, I chucked my necklace at a tree.
I couldn't silence the voices saying I wasn't good enough.
That I messed up.
So I did everything I could to regain a sense of control.
Including this.
You did that?
Super cliché, I know.
Used some cheap, expired bleach I found behind our sink. Big mistake.
Not gonna lie, I thought it was for Halloween.
Shut up, you didn't—
I kinda dig it!
Yeah? I almost buzzed it all off.
Astrid talked some sense into me.

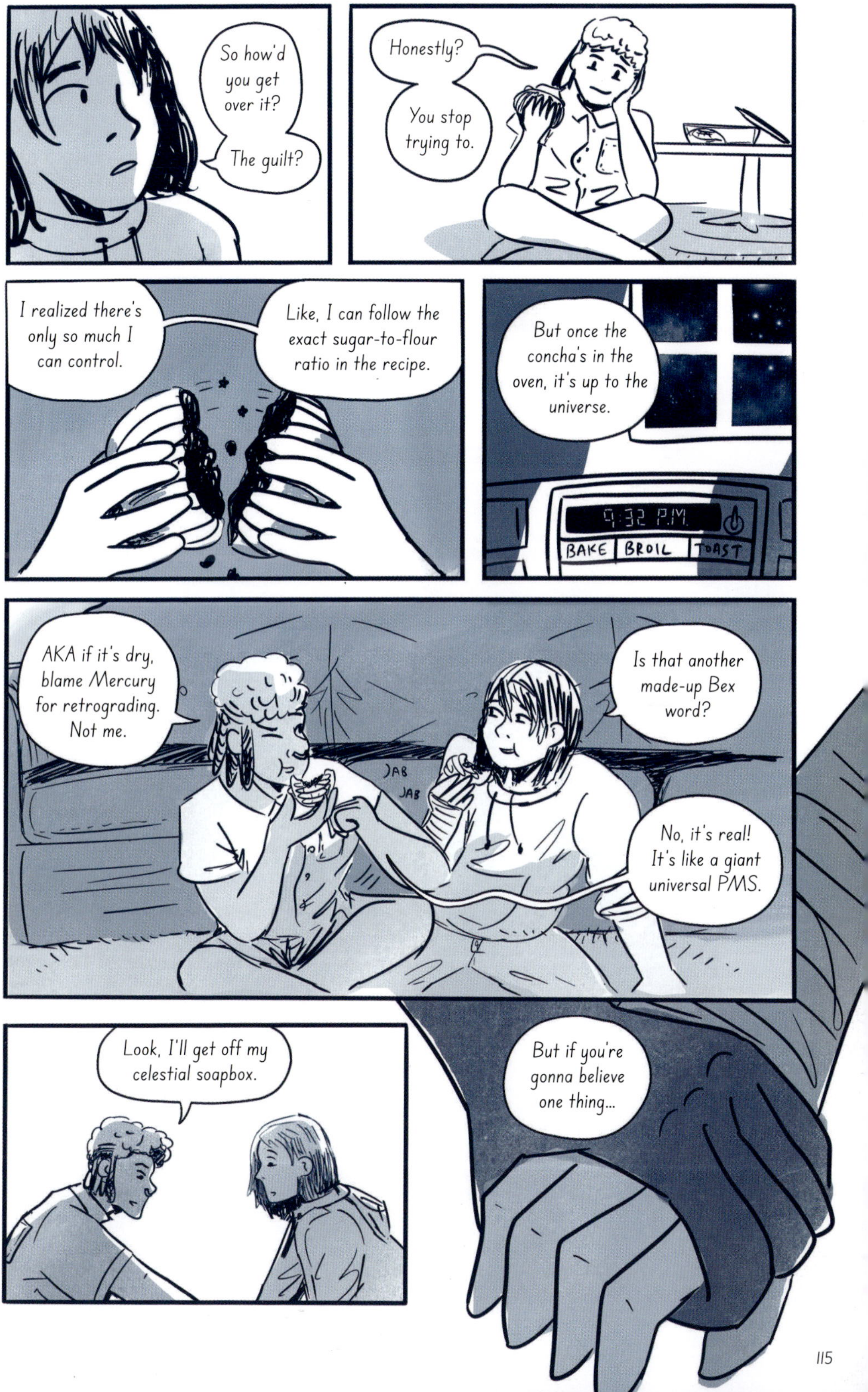

So how'd you get over it?
The guilt?
Honestly?
You stop trying to.
I realized there's only so much I can control.
Like, I can follow the exact sugar-to-flour ratio in the recipe.
But once the concha's in the oven, it's up to the universe.
9:32 P.M.
BAKE
BROIL
TOAST
AKA if it's dry, blame Mercury for retrograding. Not me.
Is that another made-up Bex word?
JAB
JAB
No, it's real! It's like a giant universal PMS.
Look, I'll get off my celestial soapbox.
But if you're gonna believe one thing...

...believe in this.

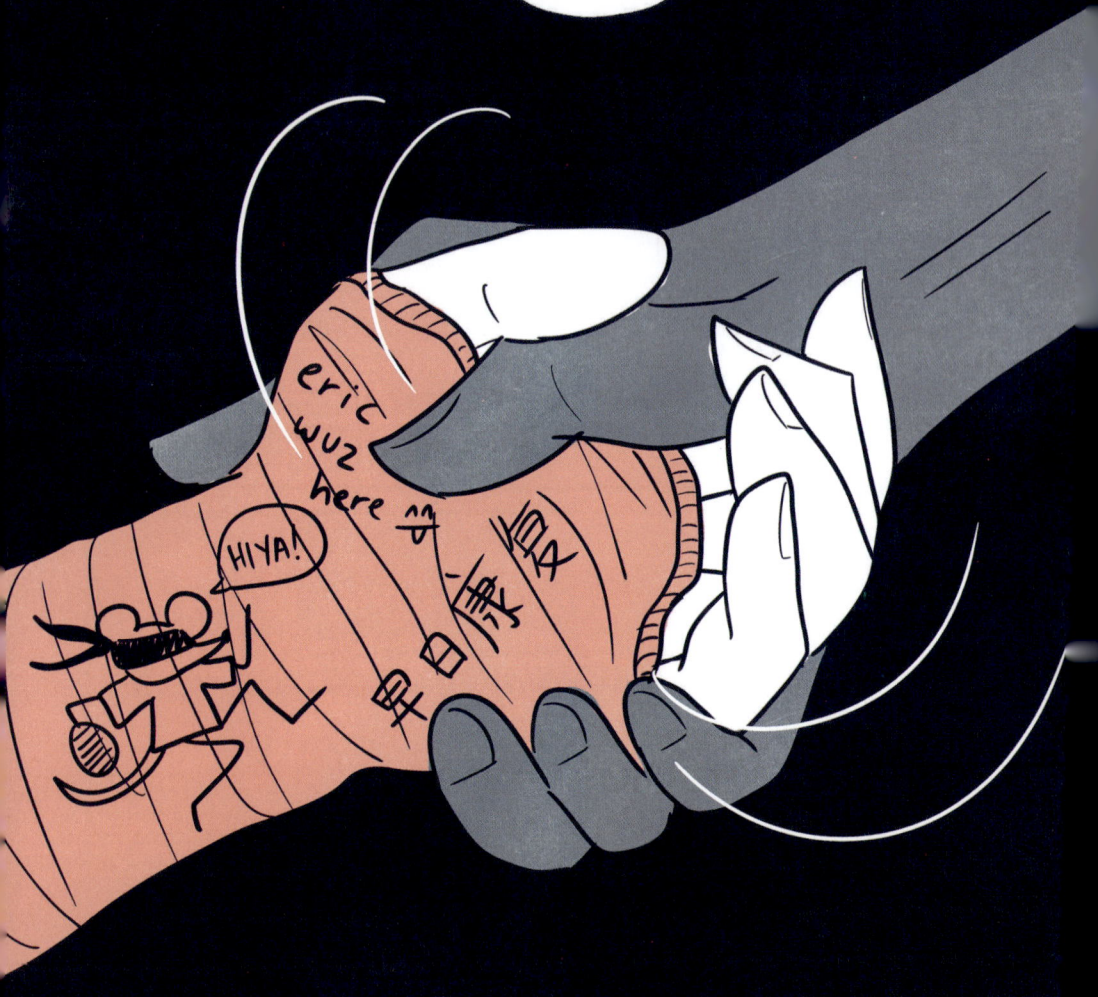

Lesson #3 for falling: Trust your partner.

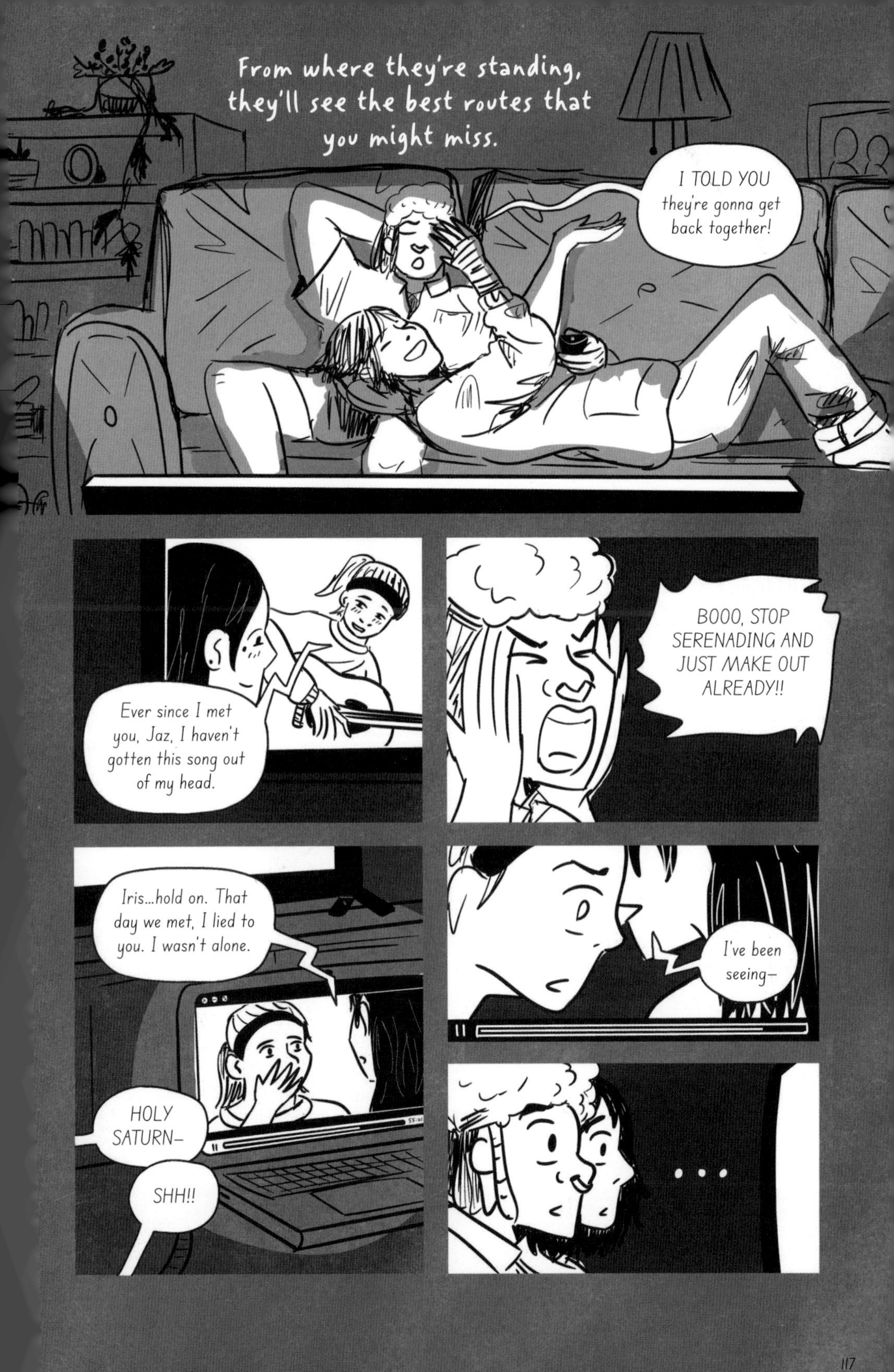
From where they're standing, they'll see the best routes that you might miss.
I TOLD YOU they're gonna get back together!
Ever since I met you, Jaz, I haven't gotten this song out of my head.
BOOO, STOP SERENADING AND JUST MAKE OUT ALREADY!!
Iris...hold on. That day we met, I lied to you. I wasn't alone.
HOLY SATURN—
SHH!!
I've been seeing—
. . .

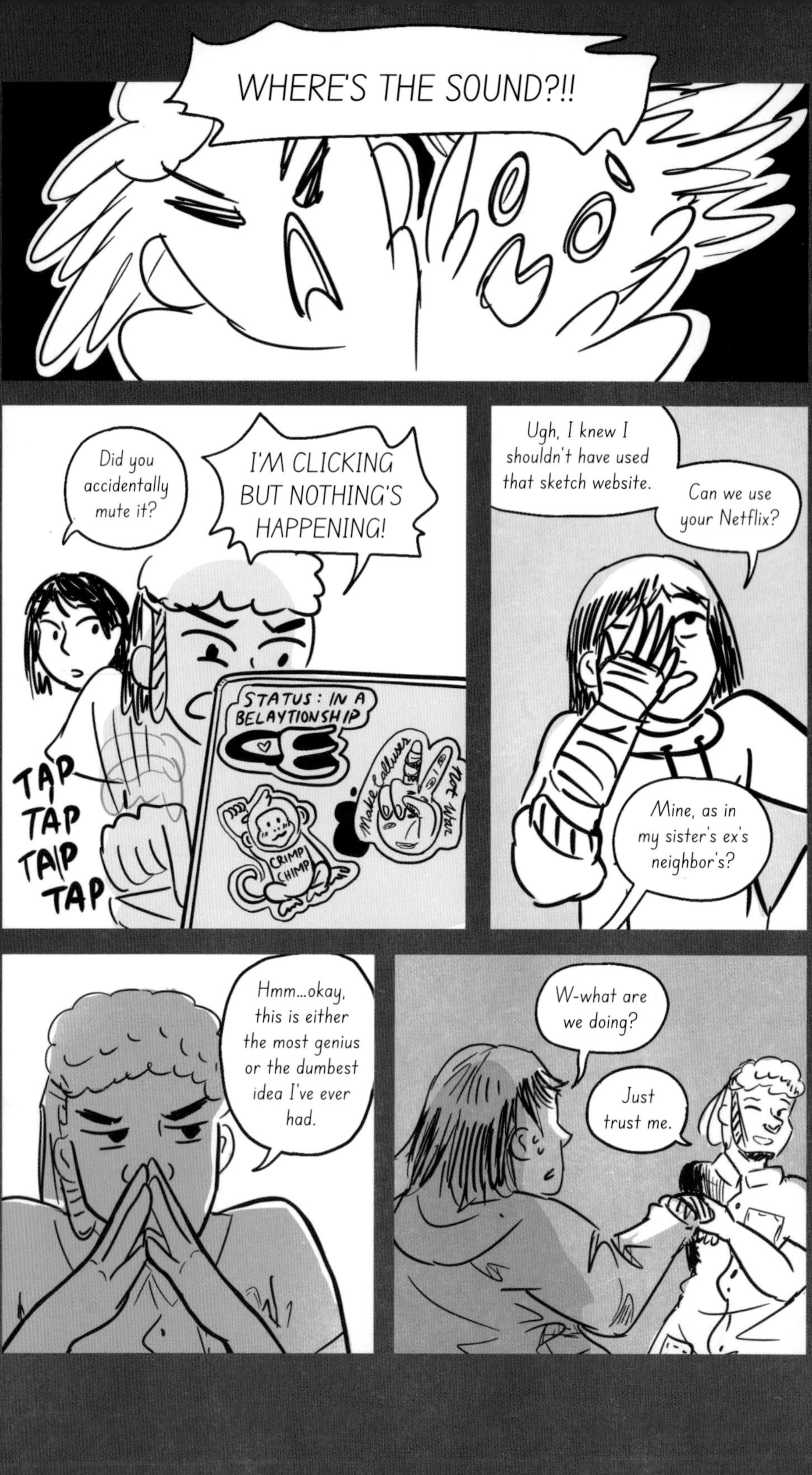
WHERE'S THE SOUND?!!
Did you accidentally mute it?
I'M CLICKING BUT NOTHING'S HAPPENING!
STATUS: IN A BELAYTIONSHIP
Make Calluses Not War
CRIMP CHIMP
TAP TAP TAP TAP
Ugh, I knew I shouldn't have used that sketch website.
Can we use your Netflix?
Mine, as in my sister's ex's neighbor's?
Hmm...okay, this is either the most genius or the dumbest idea I've ever had.
W-what are we doing?
Just trust me.

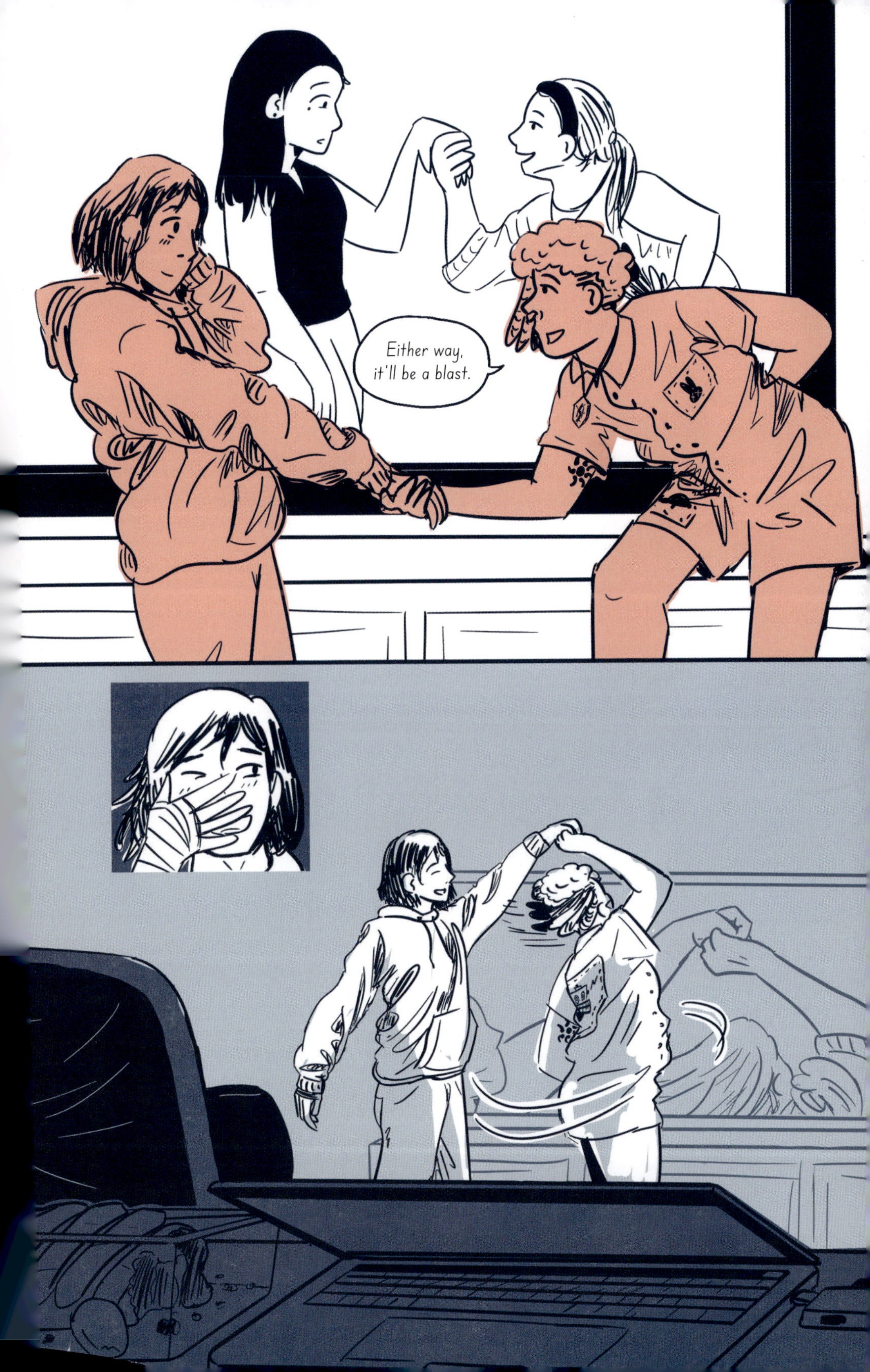
Either way, it'll be a blast.

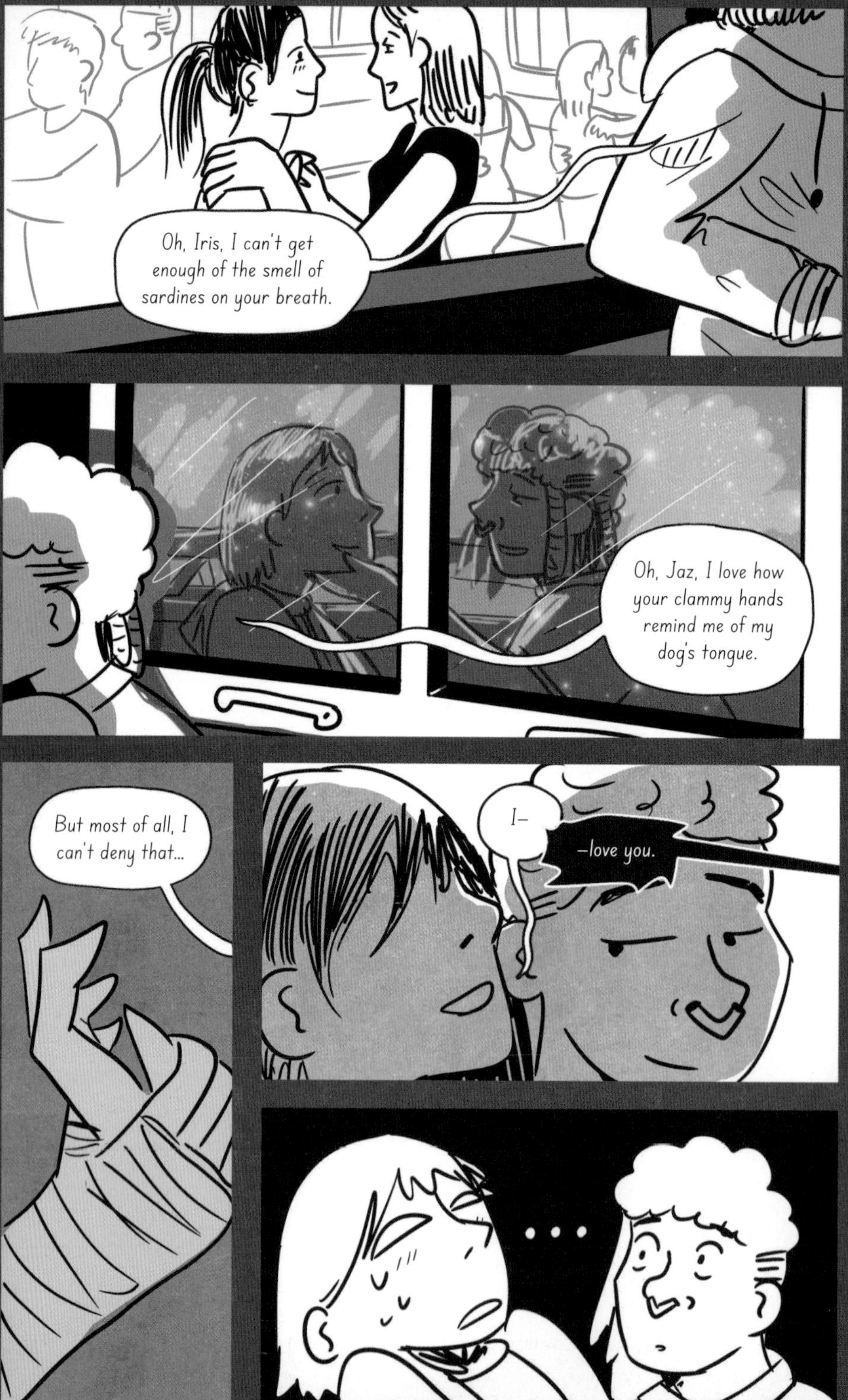
Oh, Iris, I can't get enough of the smell of sardines on your breath.
Oh, Jaz, I love how your clammy hands remind me of my dog's tongue.
But most of all, I can't deny that...
I–
–love you.
• • •

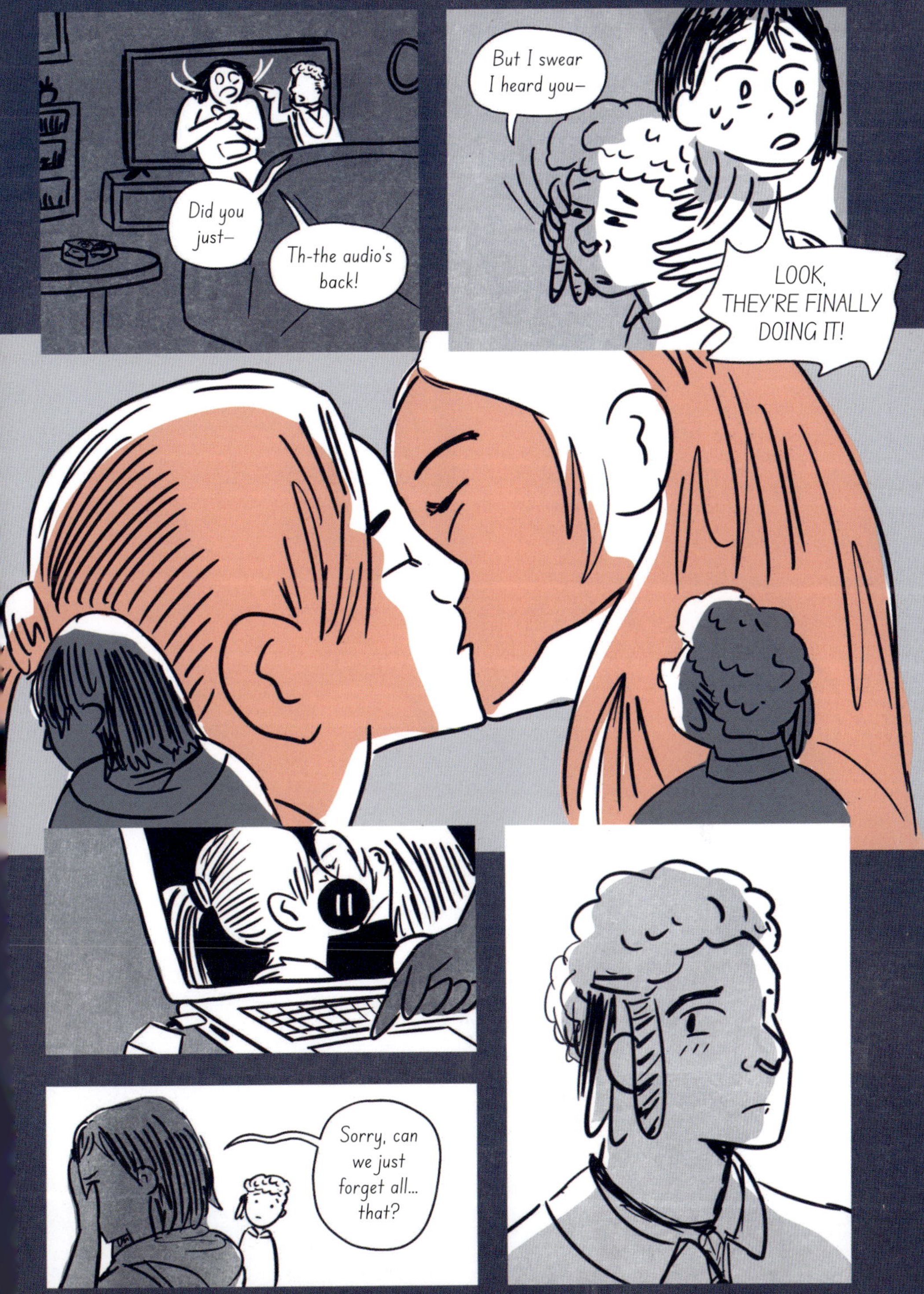
Did you just–
Th-the audio's back!
But I swear I heard you–
LOOK, THEY'RE FINALLY DOING IT!
Sorry, can we just forget all... that?

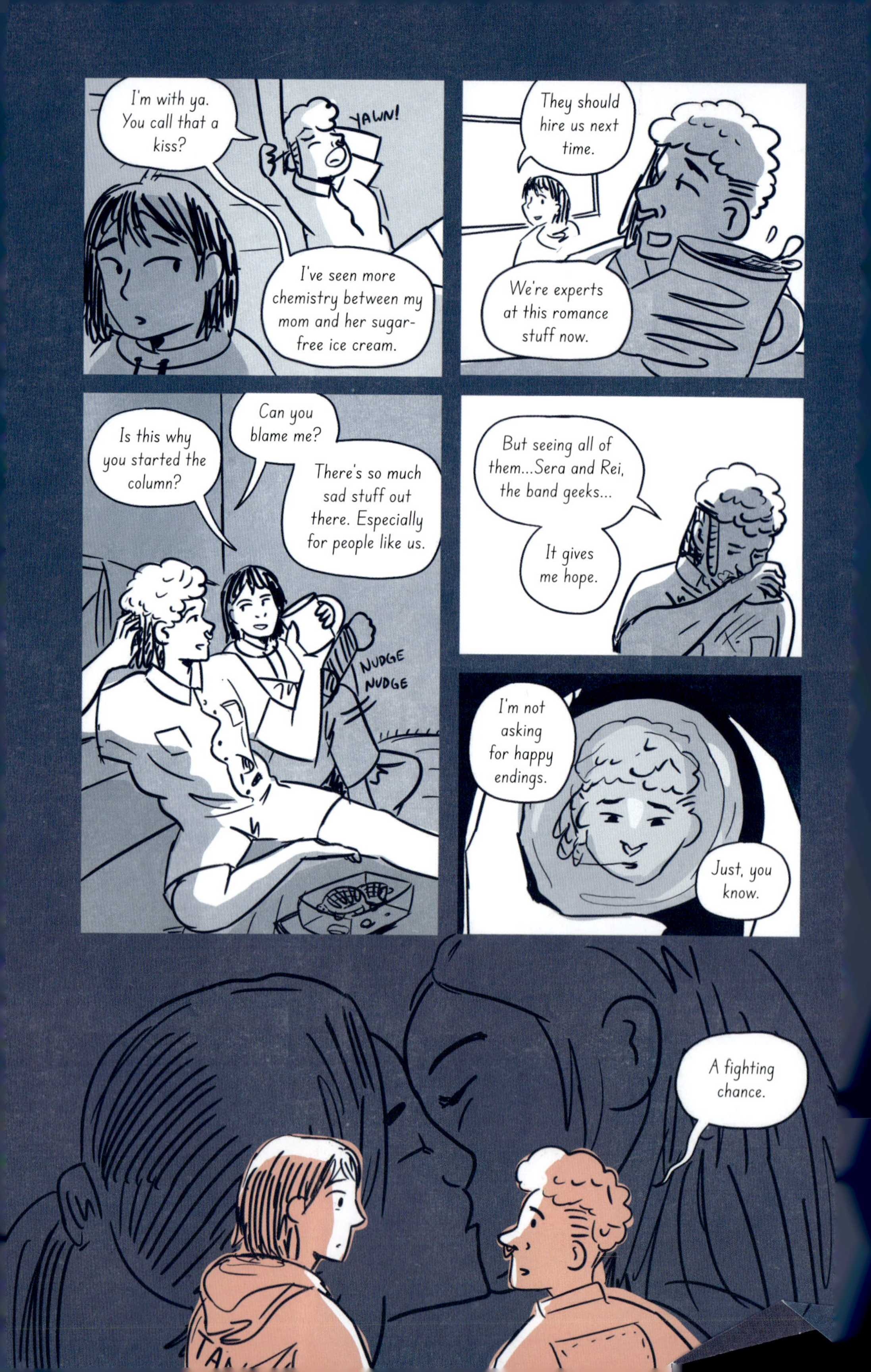
I'm with ya. You call that a kiss?
YAWN!
I've seen more chemistry between my mom and her sugar-free ice cream.
They should hire us next time.
We're experts at this romance stuff now.
Is this why you started the column?
Can you blame me?
There's so much sad stuff out there. Especially for people like us.
NUDGE NUDGE
But seeing all of them...Sera and Rei, the band geeks...
It gives me hope.
I'm not asking for happy endings.
Just, you know.
A fighting chance.

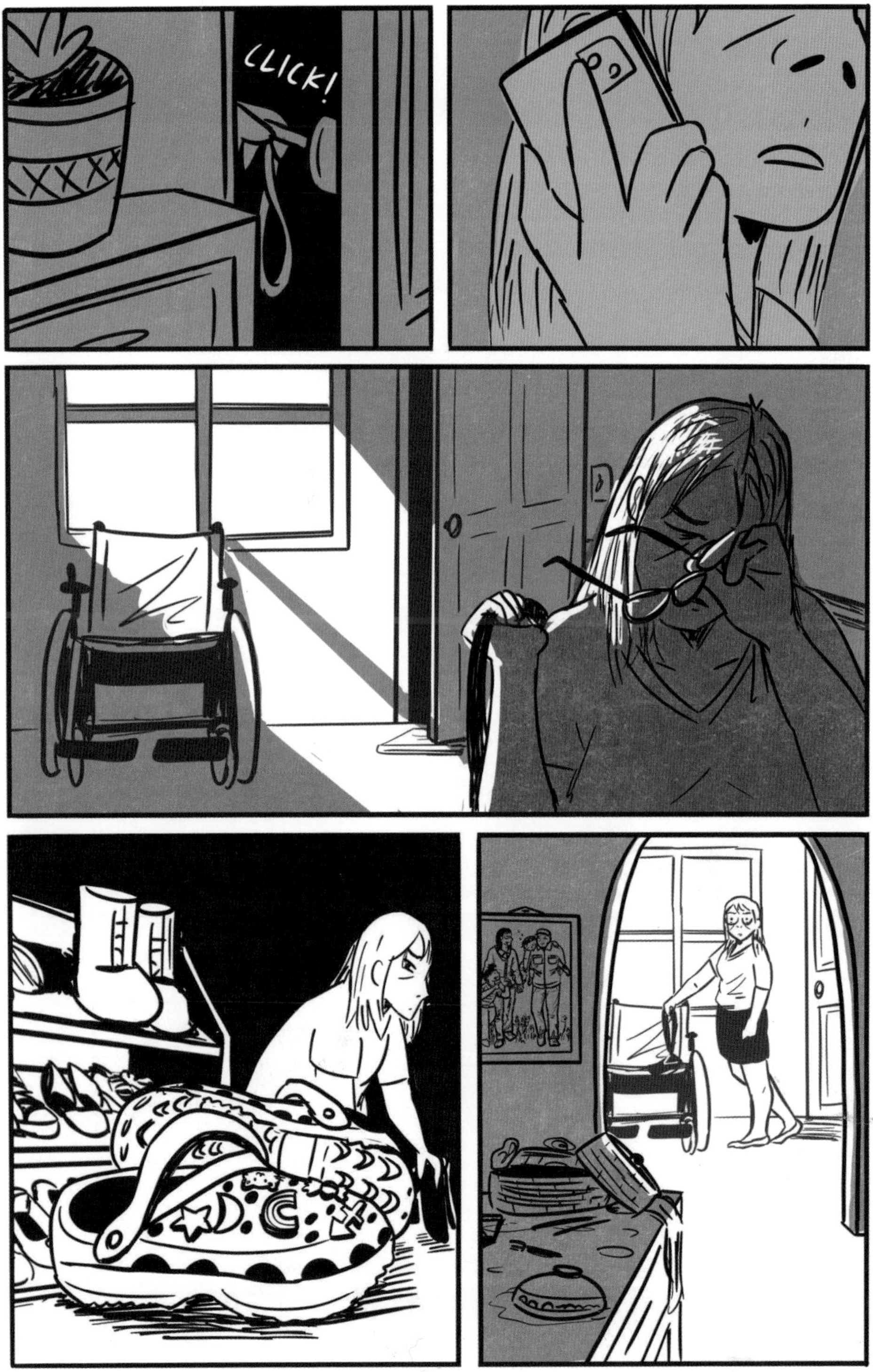
CLICK!

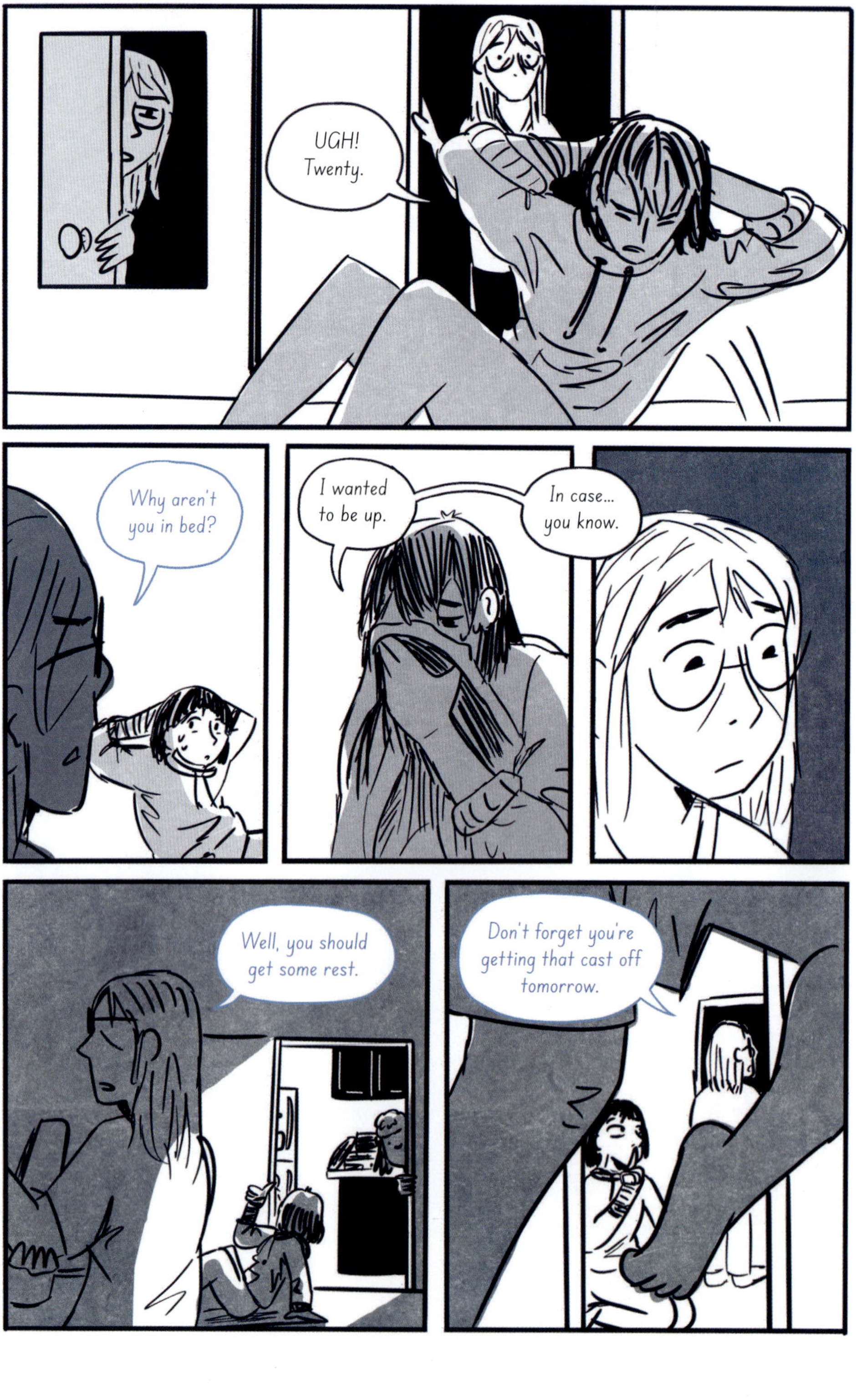
UGH! Twenty.
Why aren't you in bed?
I wanted to be up.
In case... you know.
Well, you should get some rest.
Don't forget you're getting that cast off tomorrow.

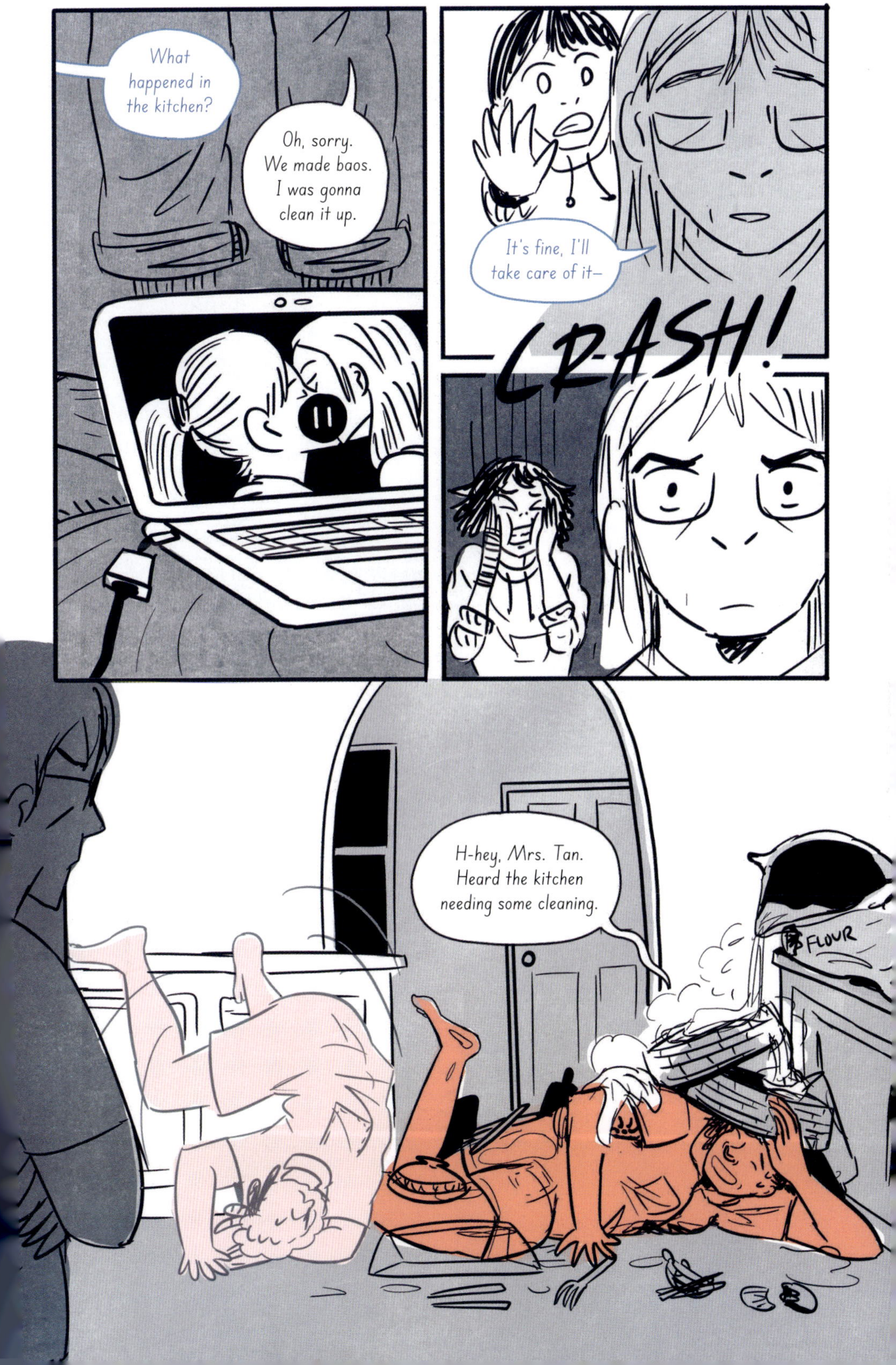
What happened in the kitchen?
Oh, sorry. We made baos. I was gonna clean it up.
It's fine, I'll take care of it—
CRASH!
H-hey, Mrs. Tan. Heard the kitchen needing some cleaning.
FLOUR

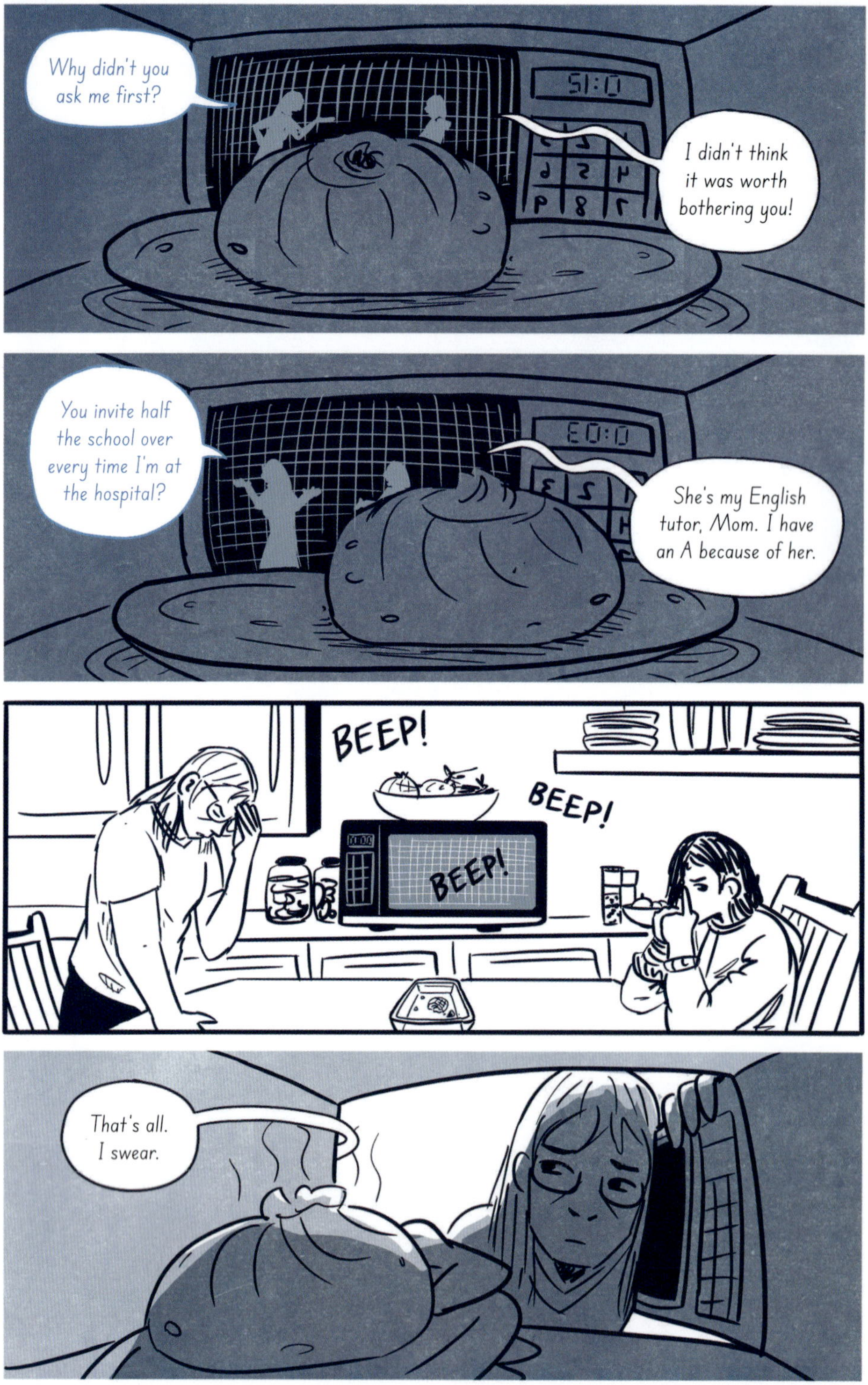
Why didn't you ask me first?
I didn't think it was worth bothering you!
You invite half the school over every time I'm at the hospital?
She's my English tutor, Mom. I have an A because of her.
BEEP!
BEEP!
BEEP!
That's all. I swear.

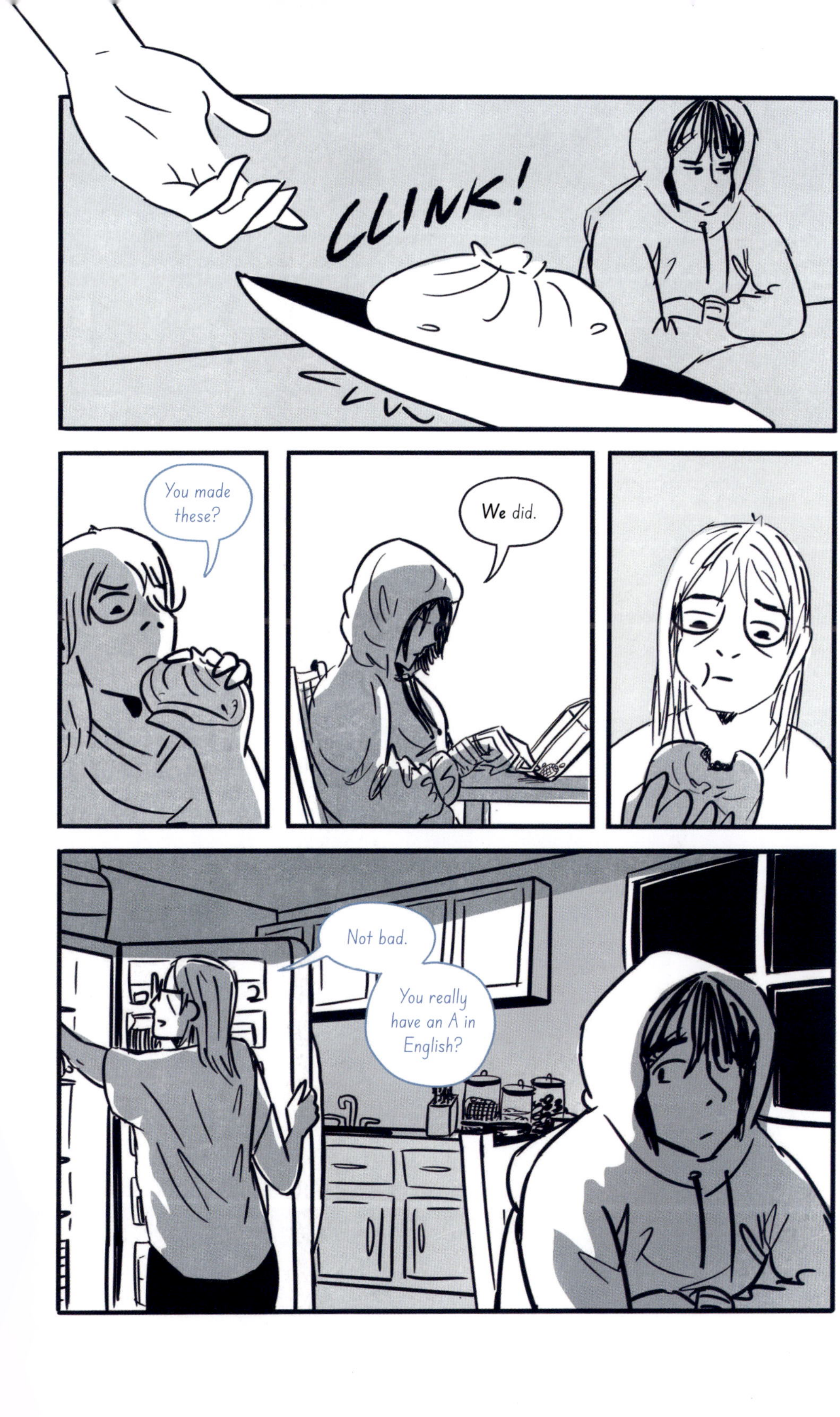
CLINK!
You made these?
We did.
Not bad.
You really have an A in English?

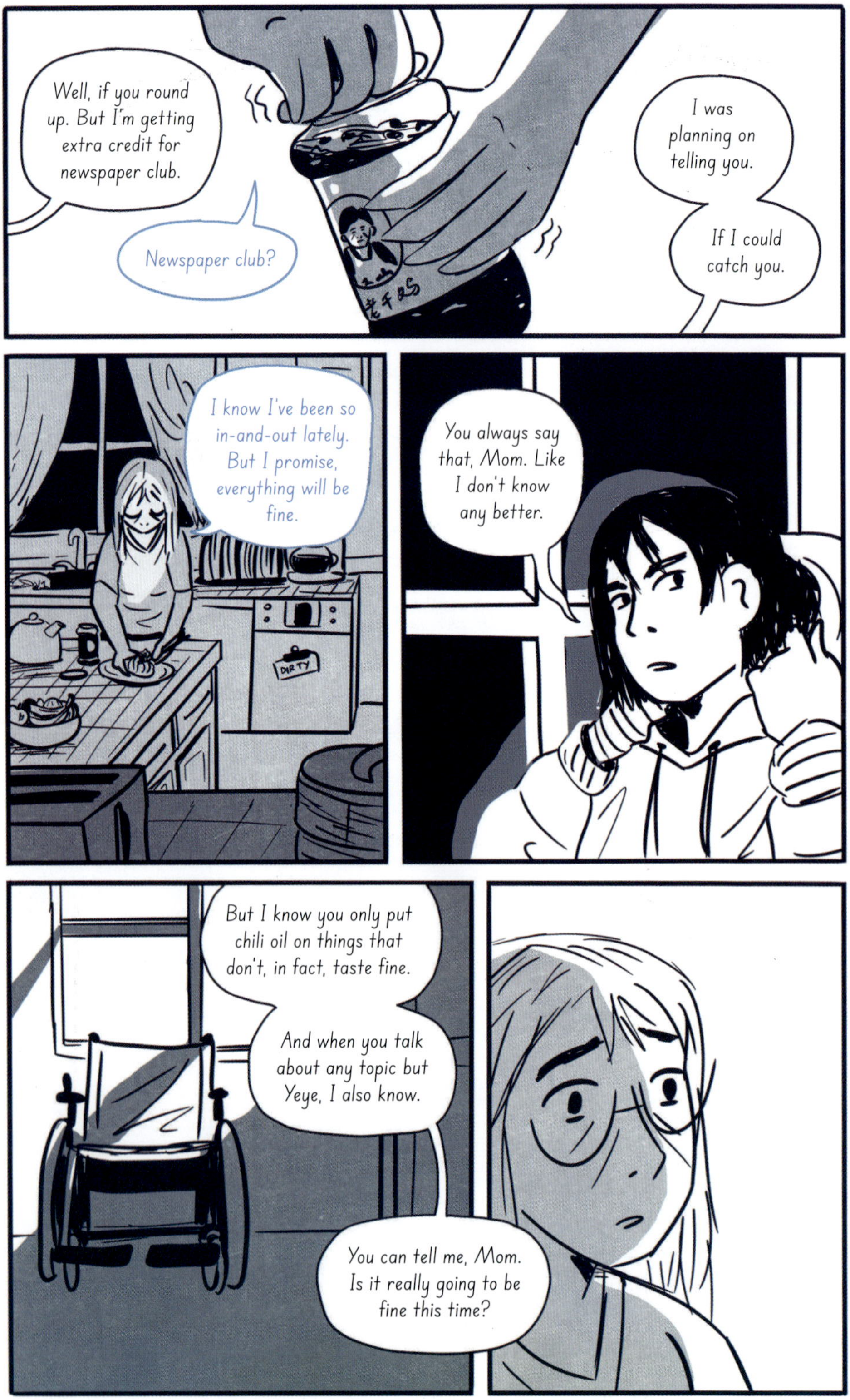
Well, if you round up. But I'm getting extra credit for newspaper club.
Newspaper club?
I was planning on telling you.
If I could catch you.
I know I've been so in-and-out lately. But I promise, everything will be fine.
You always say that, Mom. Like I don't know any better.
But I know you only put chili oil on things that don't, in fact, taste fine.
And when you talk about any topic but Yeye, I also know.
You can tell me, Mom. Is it really going to be fine this time?

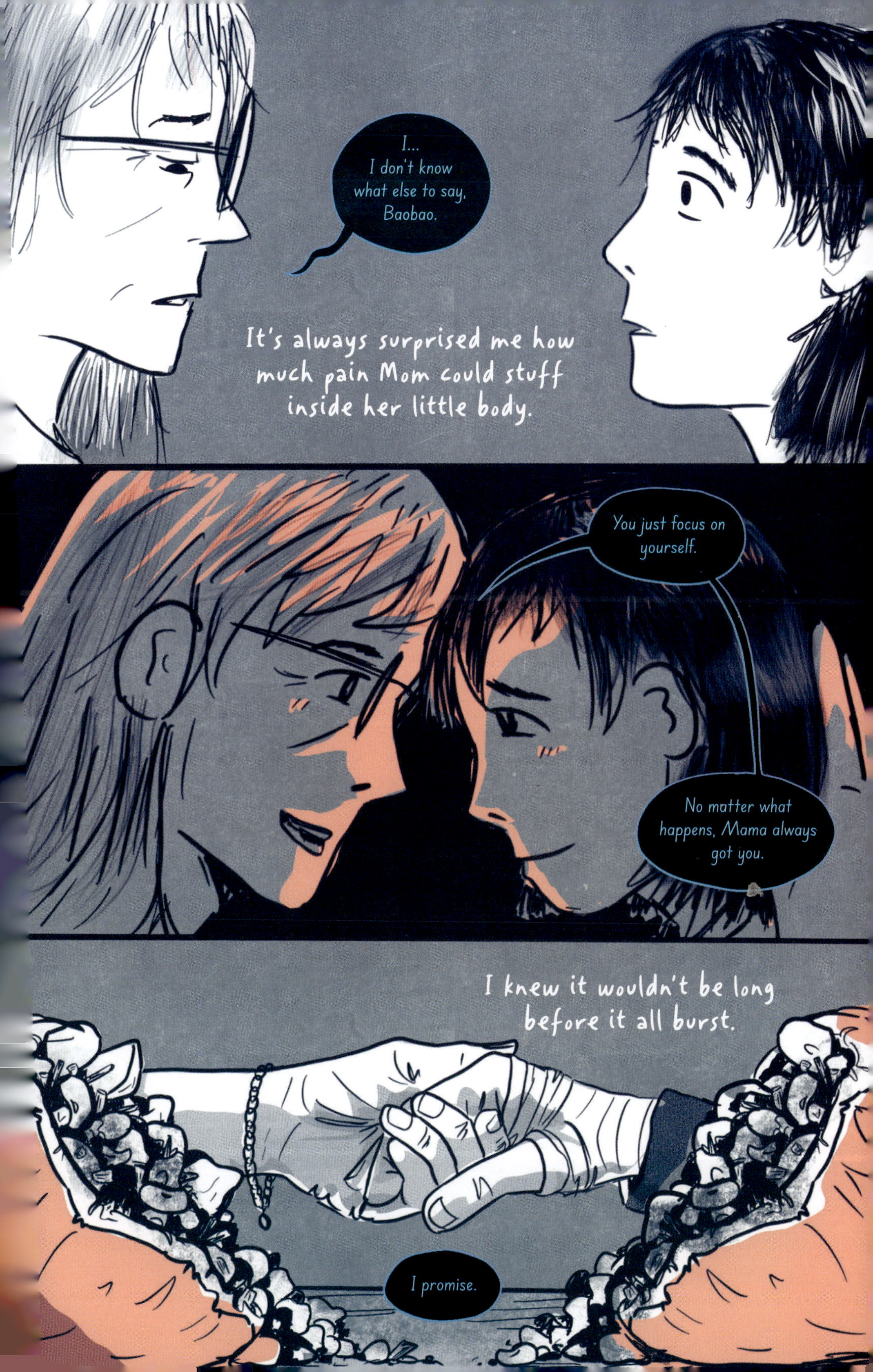
I... I don't know what else to say, Baobao.
It's always surprised me how much pain Mom could stuff inside her little body.
You just focus on yourself.
No matter what happens, Mama always got you.
I knew it wouldn't be long before it all burst.
I promise.

PART 3

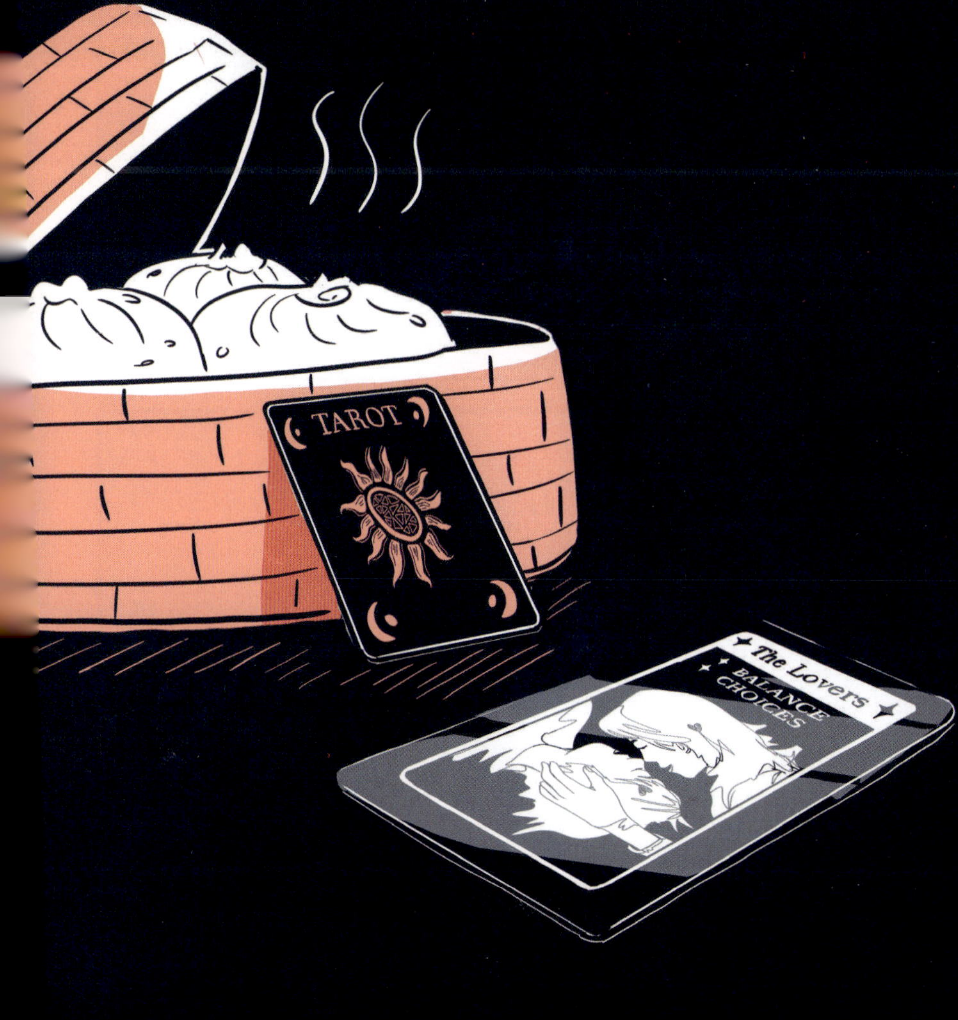
TAROT
The Lovers
BALANCE
CHOICES

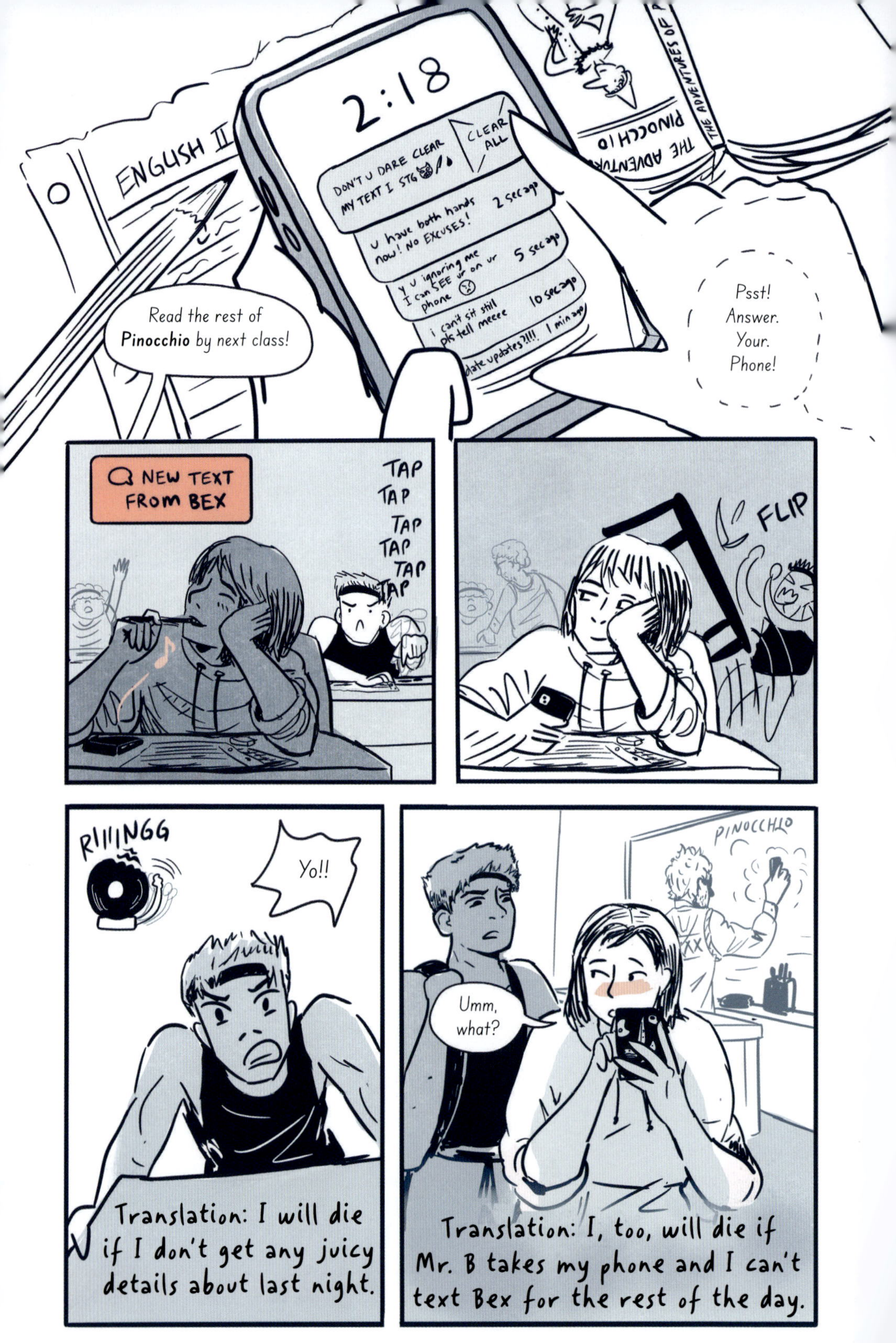

ENGLISH II
2:18
DON'T U DARE CLEAR MY TEXT I STG
CLEAR ALL
u have both hands now! NO EXCUSES! 2 sec ago
y u ignoring me I can SEE ur on ur phone 5 sec ago
i can't sit still pls tell meeee 10 sec ago
date updates?!!! 1 min ago
THE ADVENTURES OF PINOCCHIO
Read the rest of Pinocchio by next class!
Psst! Answer. Your. Phone!
NEW TEXT FROM BEX
TAP TAP TAP TAP TAP TAP
FLIP
RIIIINGG
Yo!!
Translation: I will die if I don't get any juicy details about last night.
PINOCCHIO
Umm, what?
Translation: I, too, will die if Mr. B takes my phone and I can't text Bex for the rest of the day.

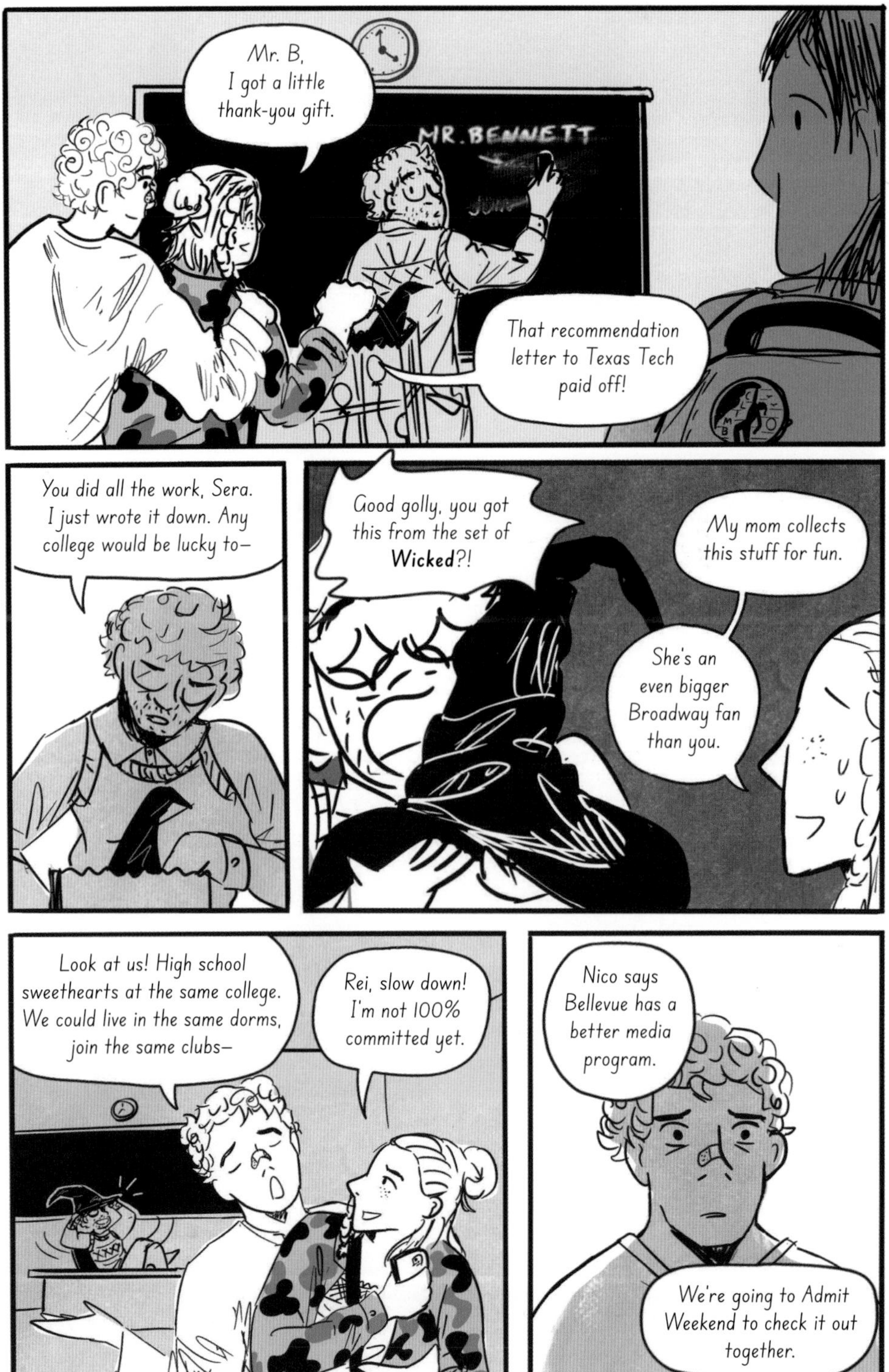

Mr. B, I got a little thank-you gift.
MR. BENNETT
That recommendation letter to Texas Tech paid off!
You did all the work, Sera. I just wrote it down. Any college would be lucky to–
Good golly, you got this from the set of **Wicked**?!
My mom collects this stuff for fun.
She's an even bigger Broadway fan than you.
Look at us! High school sweethearts at the same college. We could live in the same dorms, join the same clubs–
Rei, slow down! I'm not 100% committed yet.
Nico says Bellevue has a better media program.
We're going to Admit Weekend to check it out together.

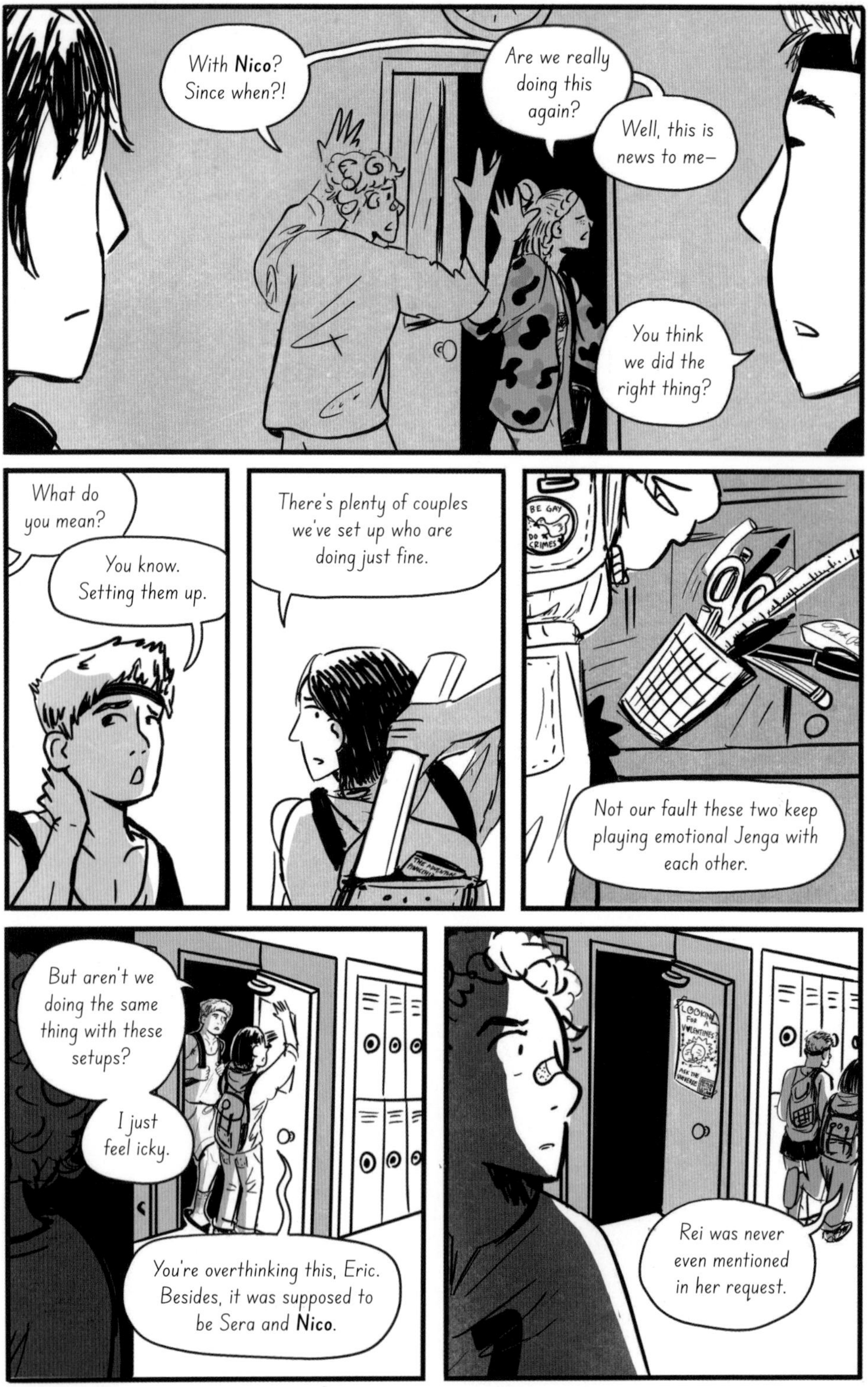
With **Nico**? Since when?!
Are we really doing this again?
Well, this is news to me—
You think we did the right thing?
What do you mean?
You know. Setting them up.
There's plenty of couples we've set up who are doing just fine.
BE GAY
DO CRIMES
Not our fault these two keep playing emotional Jenga with each other.
But aren't we doing the same thing with these setups?
I just feel icky.
You're overthinking this, Eric. Besides, it was supposed to be Sera and **Nico**.
Rei was never even mentioned in her request.

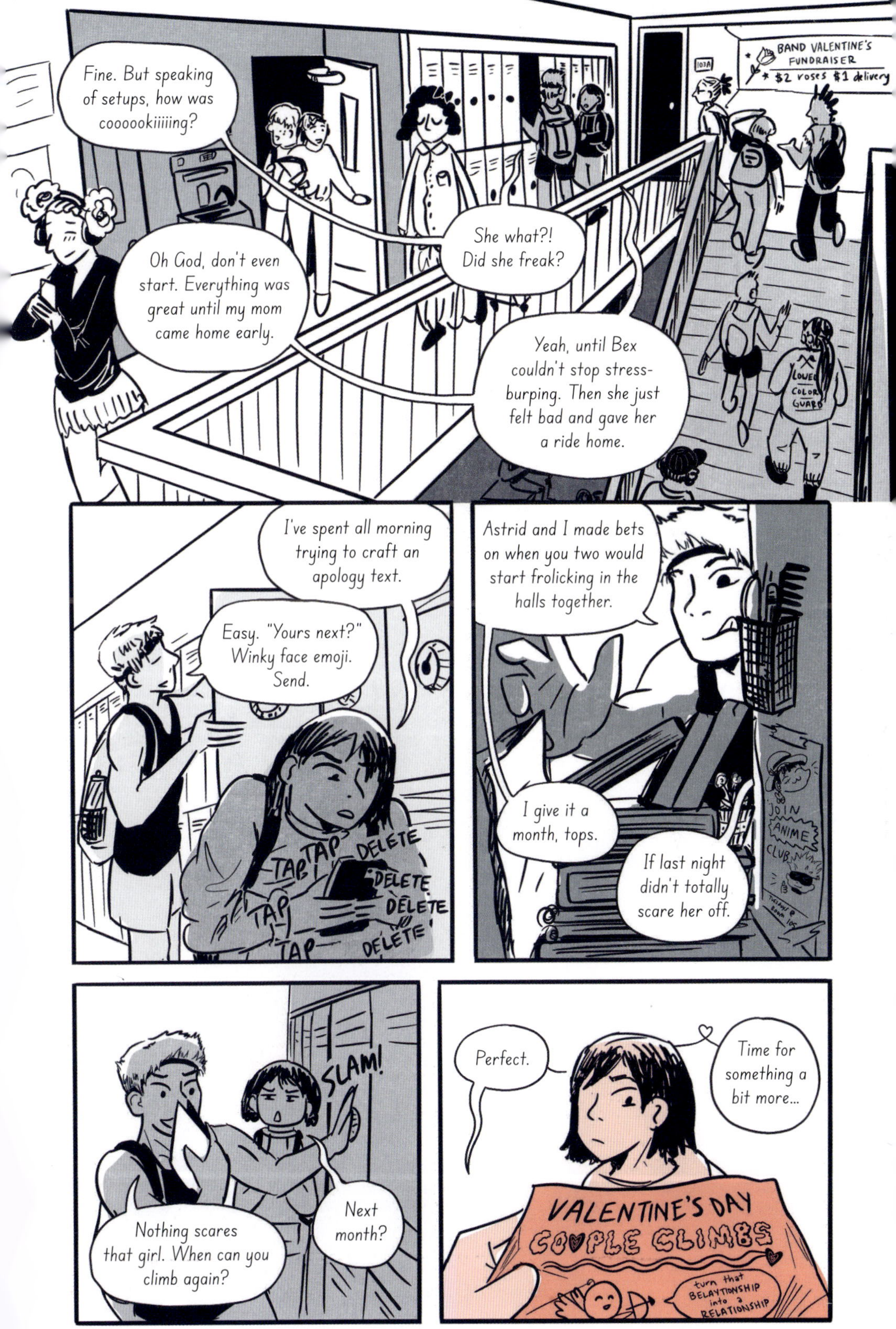
BAND VALENTINE'S FUNDRAISER
$2 roses $1 delivery
Fine. But speaking of setups, how was cooooookiiiiing?
Oh God, don't even start. Everything was great until my mom came home early.
She what?! Did she freak?
Yeah, until Bex couldn't stop stress-burping. Then she just felt bad and gave her a ride home.
LOWER COLOR GUARD
I've spent all morning trying to craft an apology text.
Easy. "Yours next?" Winky face emoji. Send.
TAP TAP TAP TAP
DELETE DELETE DELETE DELETE
Astrid and I made bets on when you two would start frolicking in the halls together.
I give it a month, tops.
If last night didn't totally scare her off.
JOIN ANIME CLUB
SLAM!
Nothing scares that girl. When can you climb again?
Next month?
Perfect.
Time for something a bit more...
VALENTINE'S DAY COUPLE CLIMBS
turn that BELAYTIONSHIP into a RELATIONSHIP

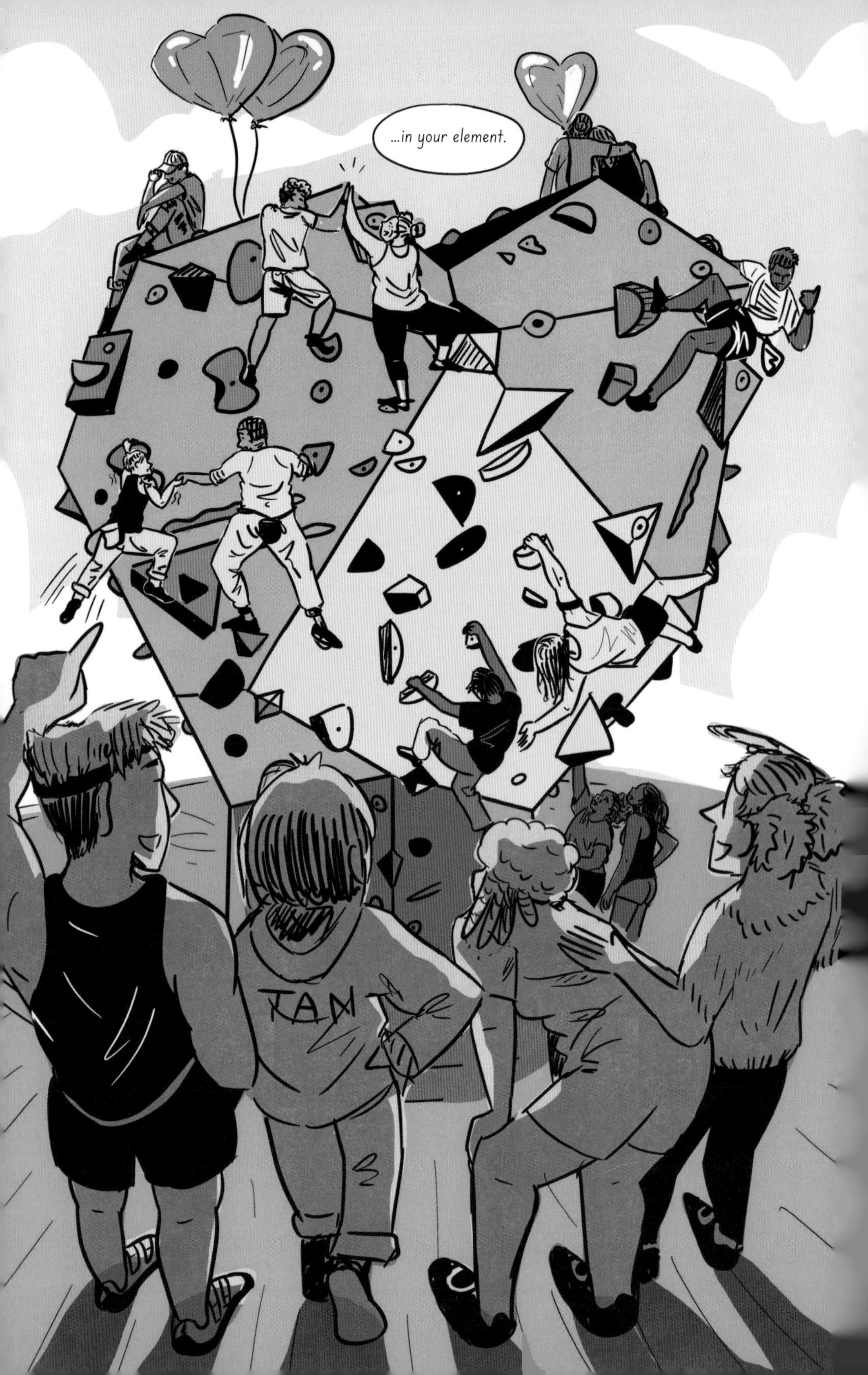
...in your element.
TAM

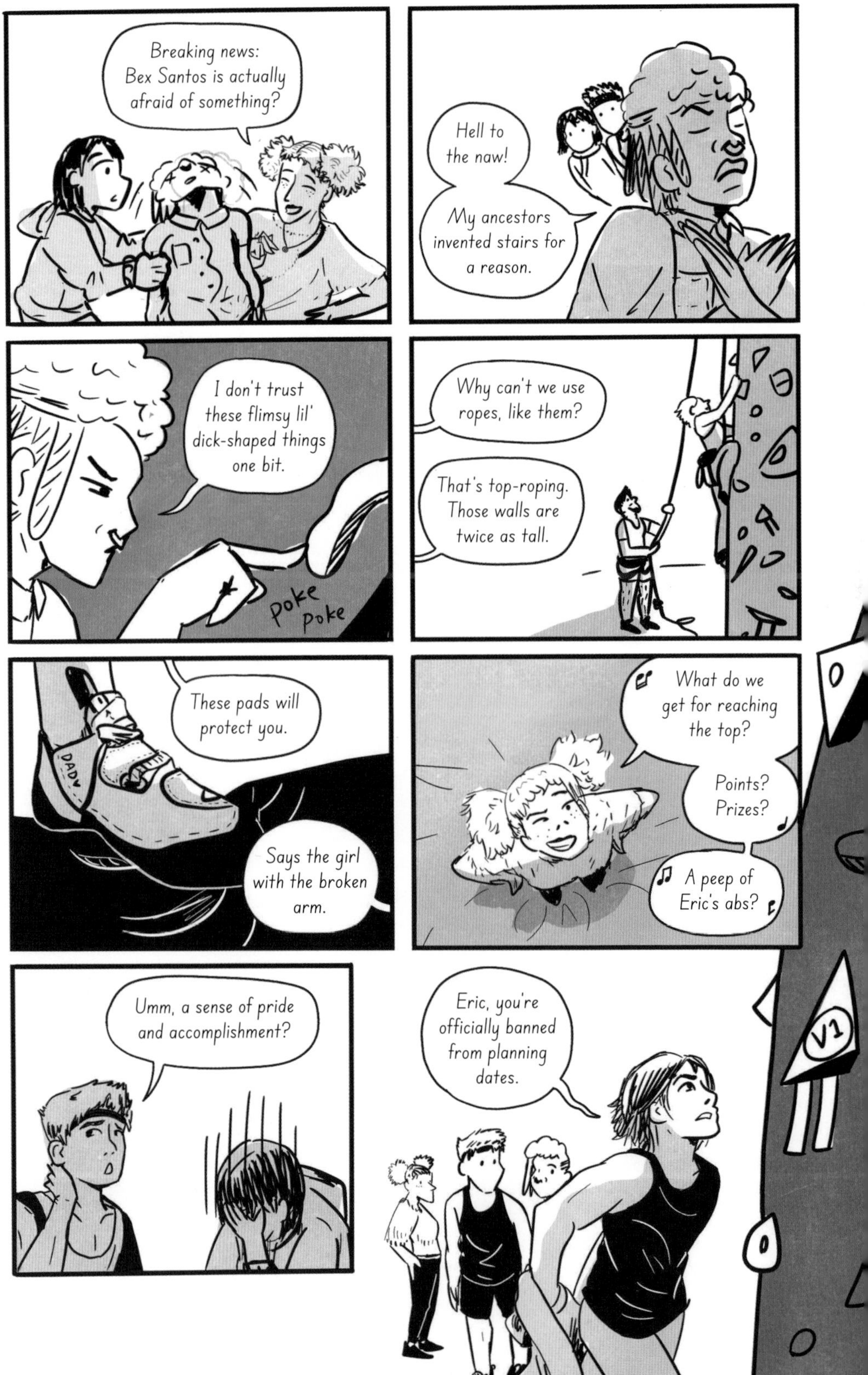
Breaking news:
Bex Santos is actually afraid of something?
Hell to the naw!
My ancestors invented stairs for a reason.
I don't trust these flimsy lil' dick-shaped things one bit.
poke poke
Why can't we use ropes, like them?
That's top-roping. Those walls are twice as tall.
These pads will protect you.
DAD
Says the girl with the broken arm.
What do we get for reaching the top?
Points? Prizes?
A peep of Eric's abs?
Umm, a sense of pride and accomplishment?
Eric, you're officially banned from planning dates.
V1

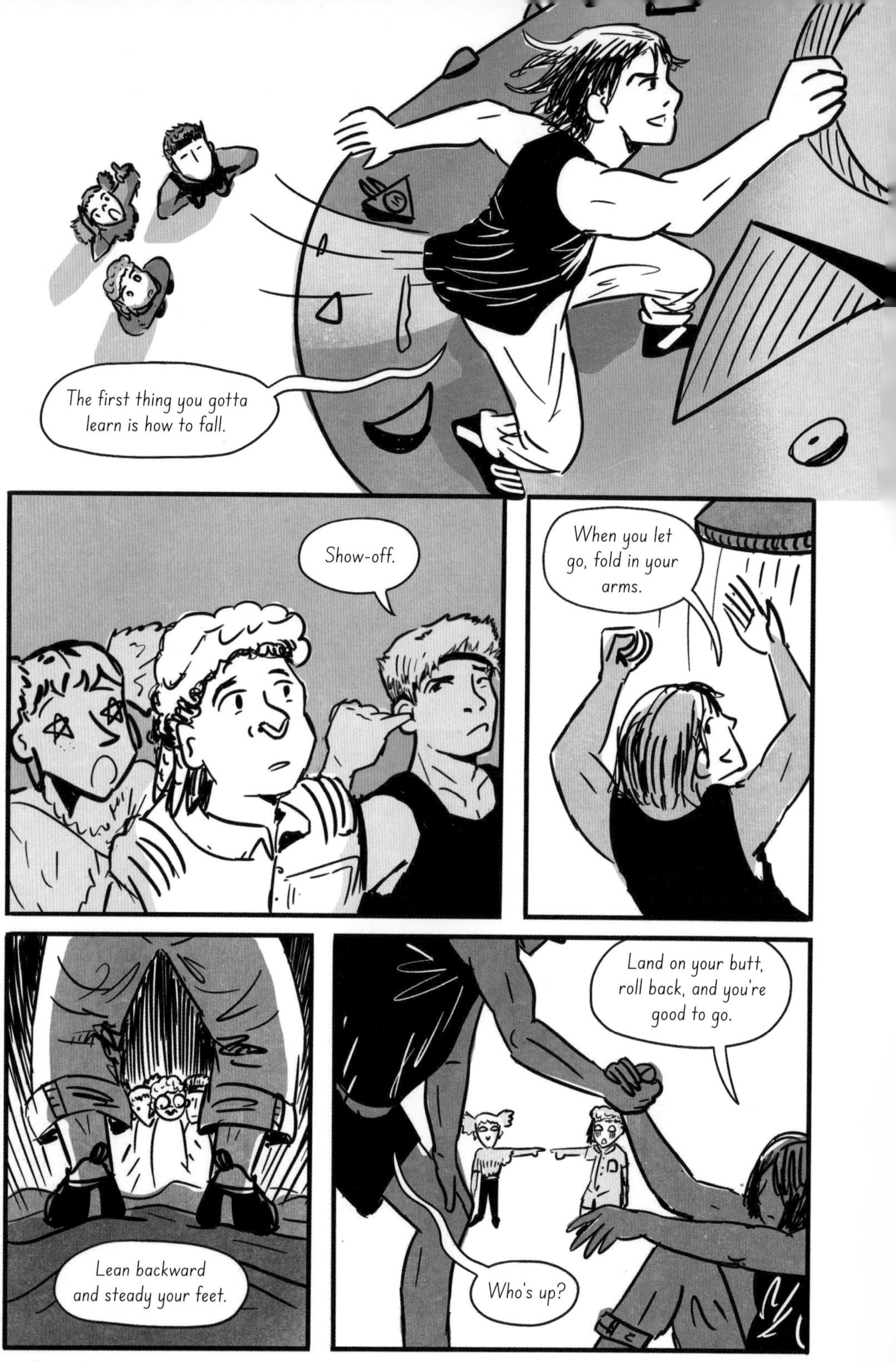
The first thing you gotta learn is how to fall.
Show-off.
When you let go, fold in your arms.
Lean backward and steady your feet.
Land on your butt, roll back, and you're good to go.
Who's up?

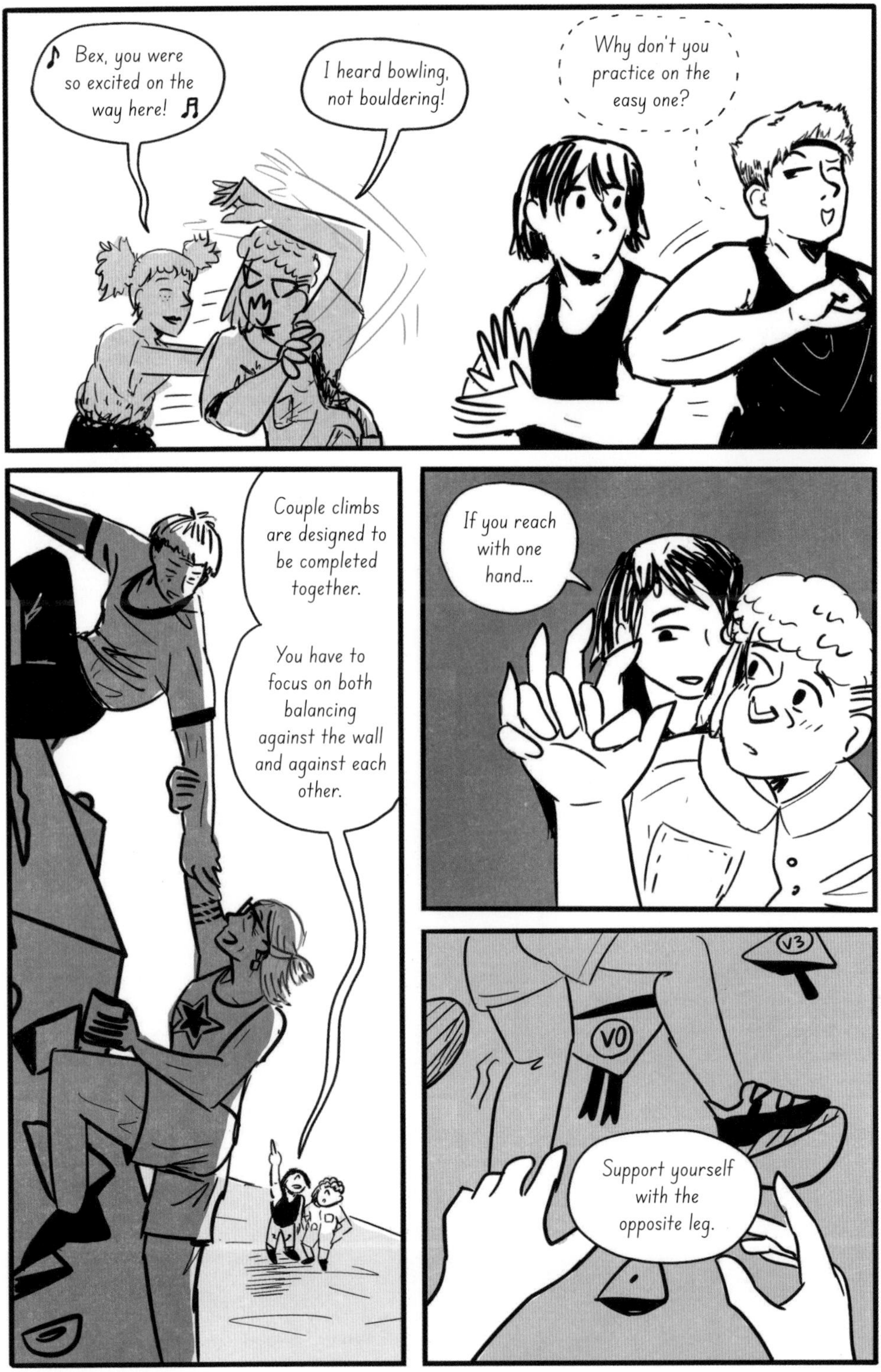
Bex, you were so excited on the way here!
I heard bowling, not bouldering!
Why don't you practice on the easy one?
Couple climbs are designed to be completed together.
You have to focus on both balancing against the wall and against each other.
If you reach with one hand...
V3
V0
Support yourself with the opposite leg.

SLIP

... ...

THUD

Get a room!

That's one way to cushion your fall!

Hehe, remember when I did that on our first date?

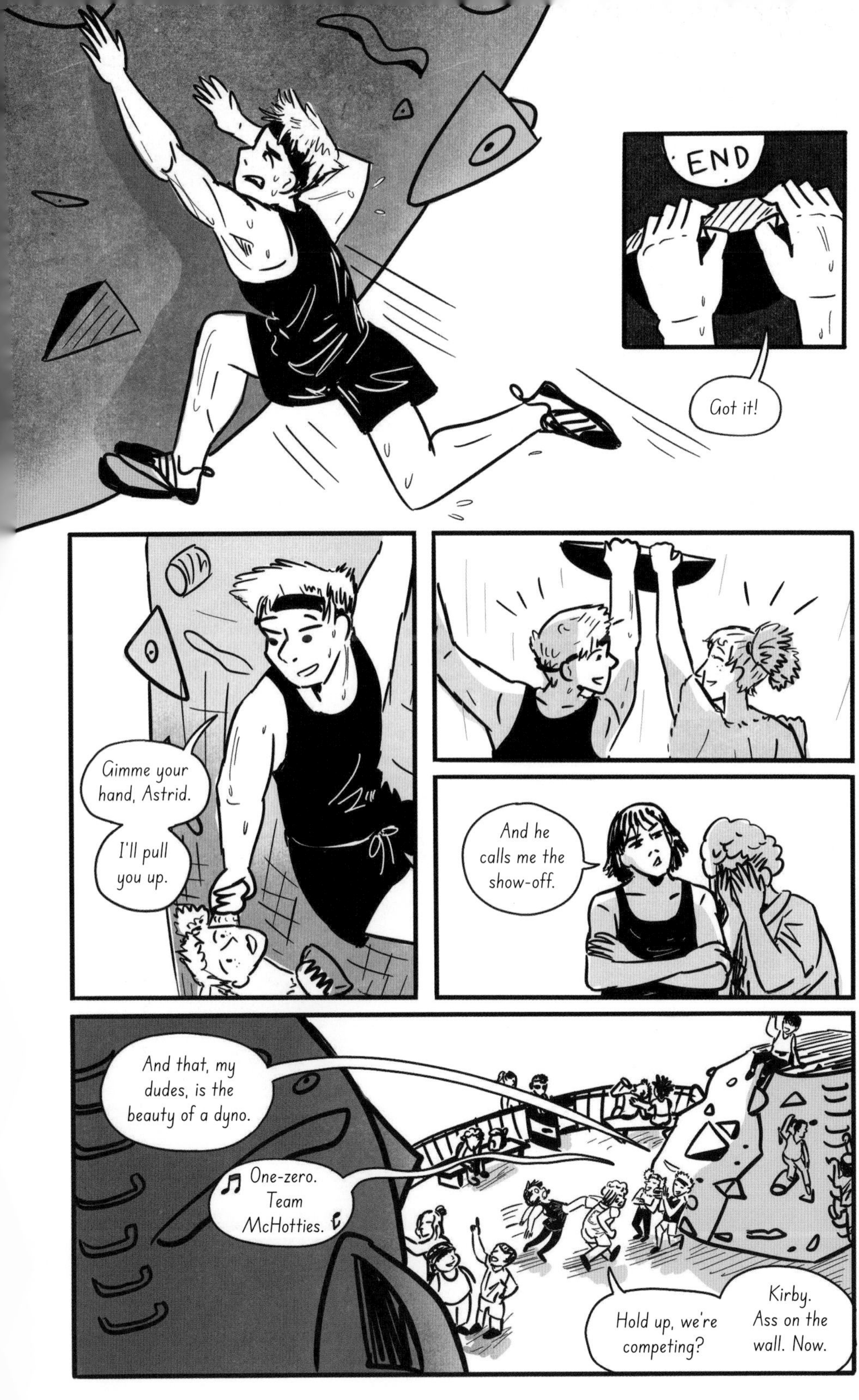
END
Got it!
Gimme your hand, Astrid.
I'll pull you up.
And he calls me the show-off.
And that, my dudes, is the beauty of a dyno.
One-zero. Team McHotties.
Hold up, we're competing?
Kirby. Ass on the wall. Now.

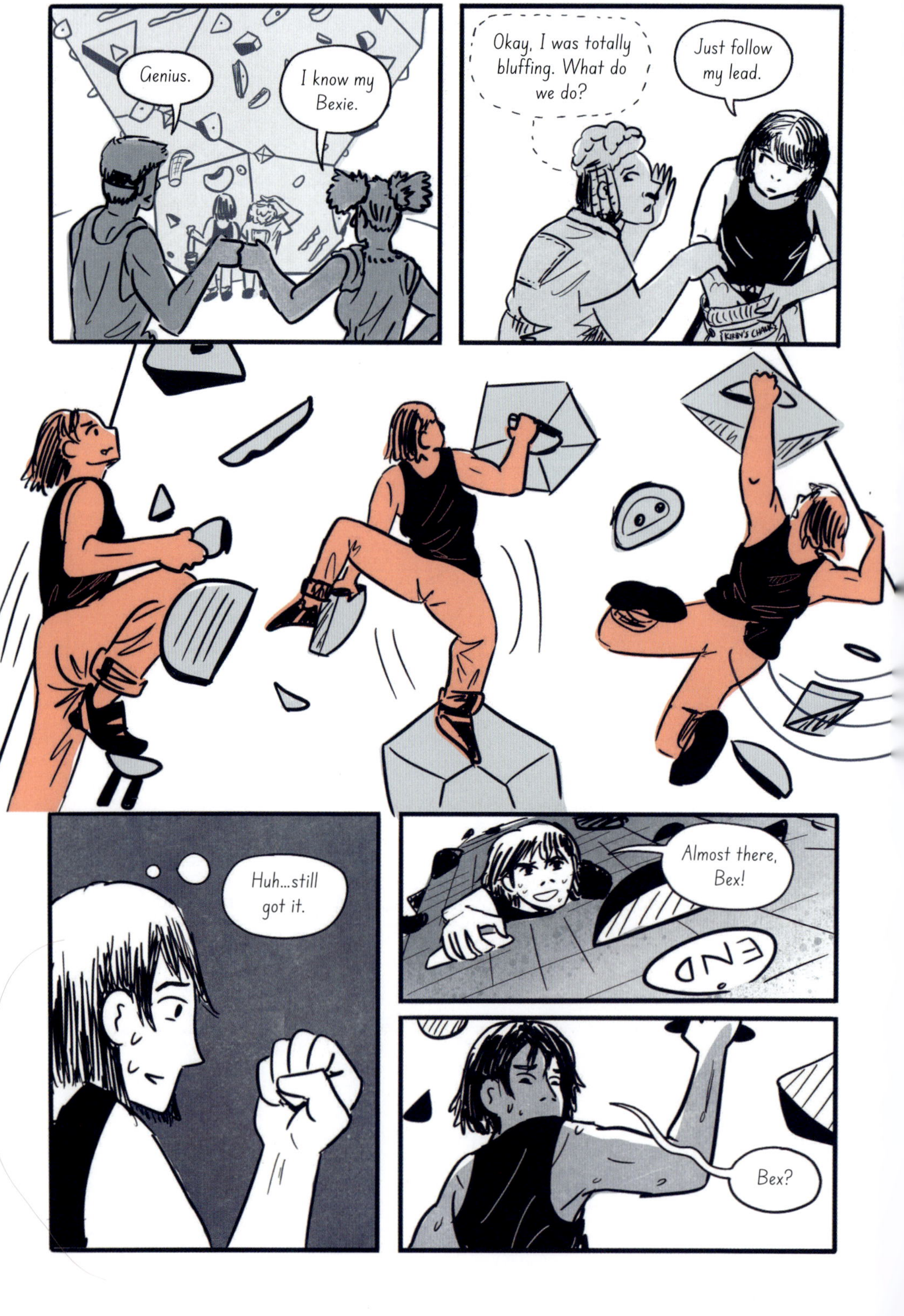
Genius.
I know my Bexie.
Okay, I was totally bluffing. What do we do?
Just follow my lead.
KIRBY'S CHALKS
Huh...still got it.
Almost there, Bex!
END
Bex?

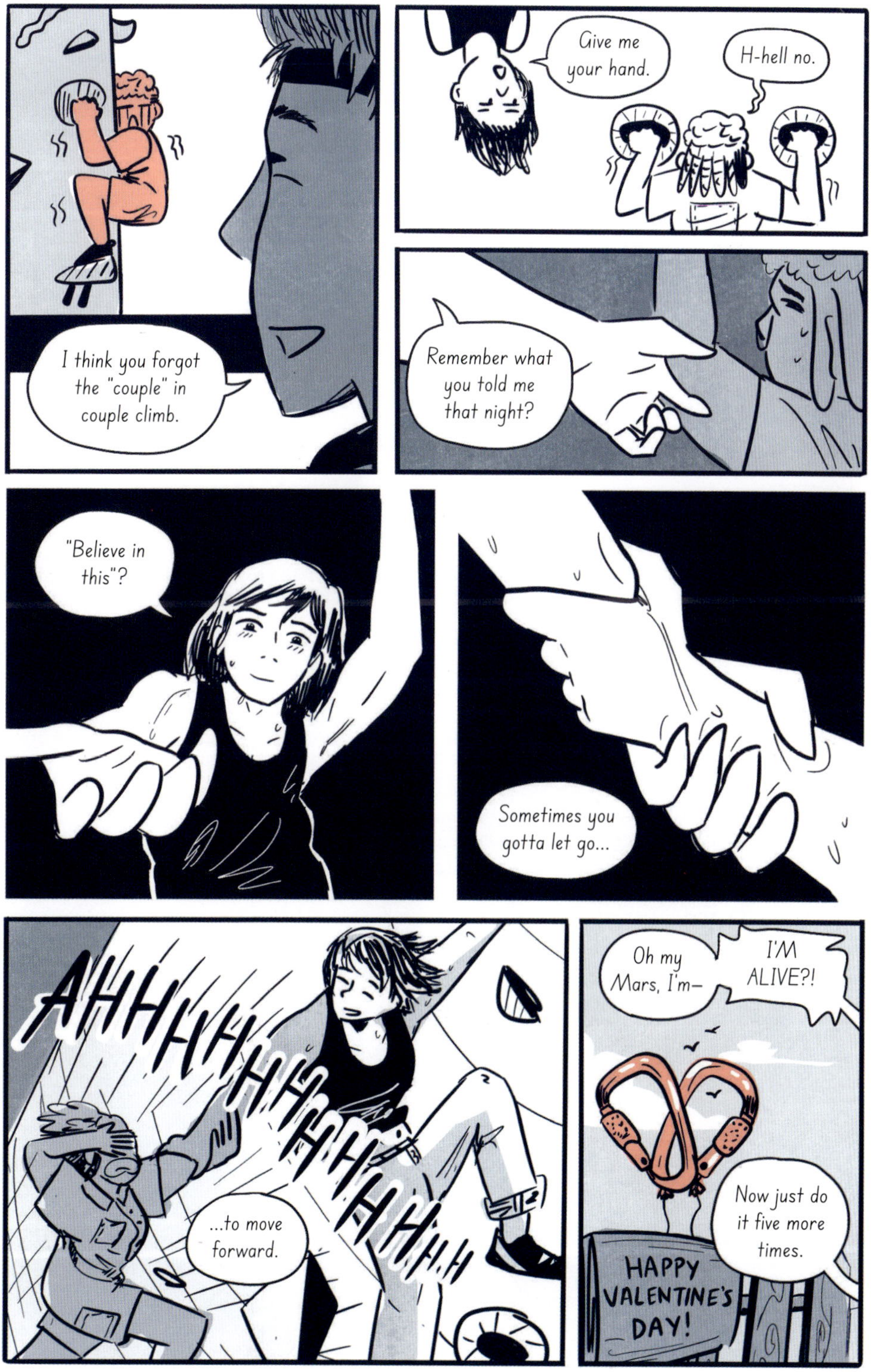
I think you forgot the "couple" in couple climb.
Give me your hand.
H-hell no.
Remember what you told me that night?
"Believe in this"?
Sometimes you gotta let go...
AHHHHHHHHHHHHHHH
...to move forward.
Oh my Mars, I'm–
I'M ALIVE?!
HAPPY VALENTINE'S DAY!
Now just do it five more times.

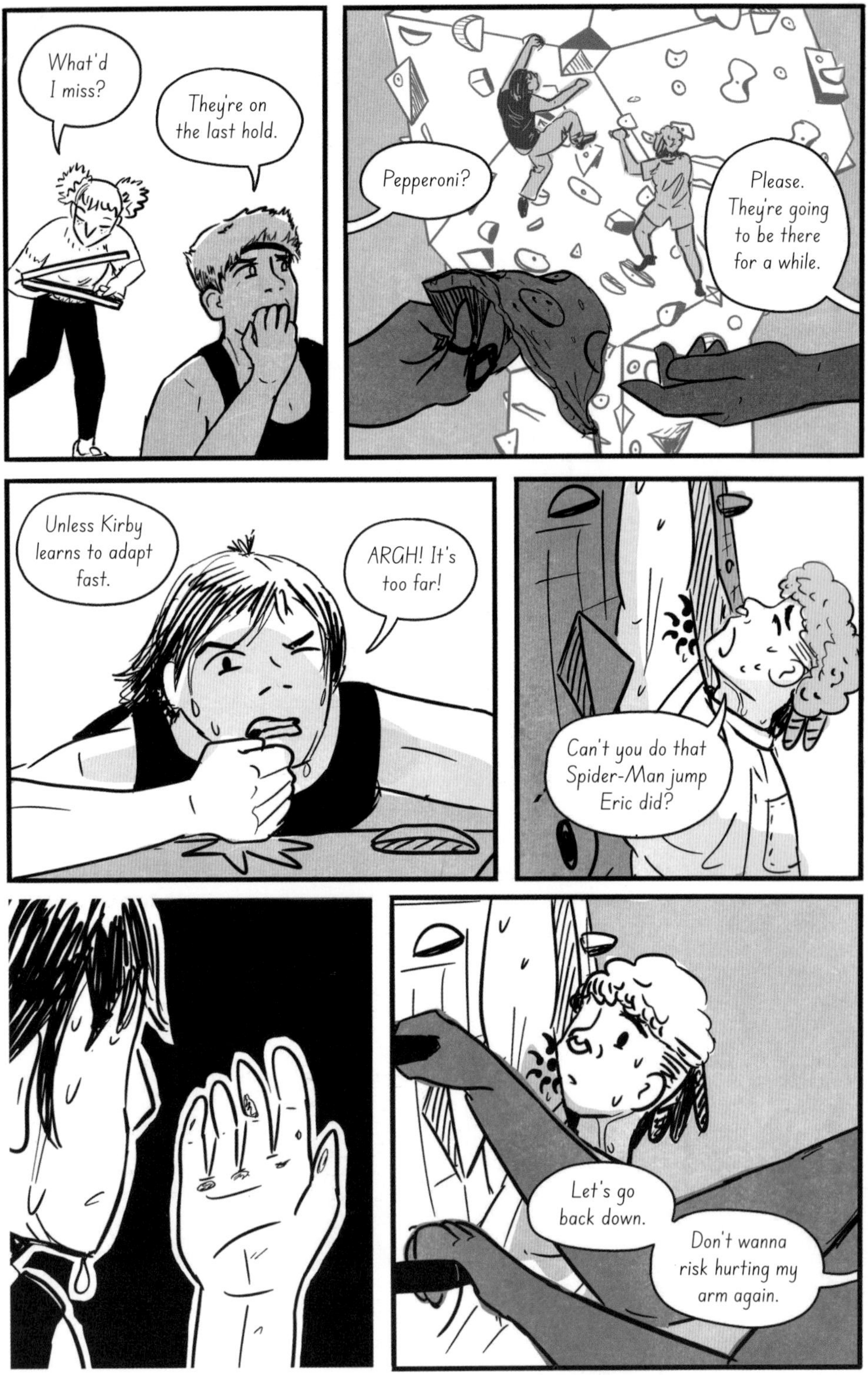
What'd I miss?
They're on the last hold.
Pepperoni?
Please. They're going to be there for a while.
Unless Kirby learns to adapt fast.
ARGH! It's too far!
Can't you do that Spider-Man jump Eric did?
Let's go back down.
Don't wanna risk hurting my arm again.

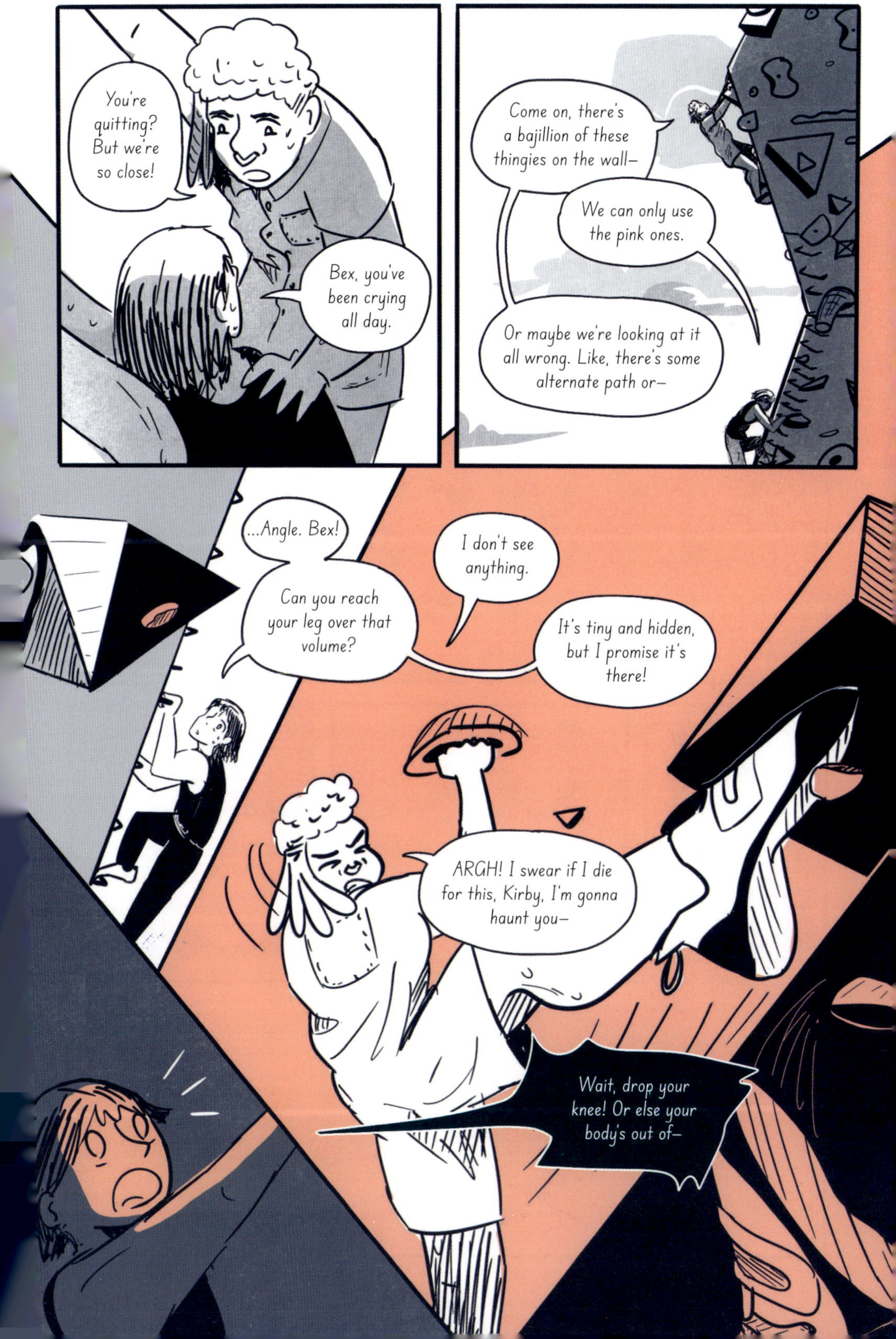
You're quitting? But we're so close!
Bex, you've been crying all day.
Come on, there's a bajillion of these thingies on the wall—
We can only use the pink ones.
Or maybe we're looking at it all wrong. Like, there's some alternate path or—
...Angle. Bex!
Can you reach your leg over that volume?
I don't see anything.
It's tiny and hidden, but I promise it's there!
ARGH! I swear if I die for this, Kirby, I'm gonna haunt you—
Wait, drop your knee! Or else your body's out of—

AHHH—
—balance.
AHHH!

ruffle ruffle
I looked more badass in my mind, haha.

You get enough B-roll for the wedding?
Get ready to fork over $20.

FINALLY. Let's go.
Hold on. I wanna show you one last thing.

END

Lesson #4 for falling: Most people are so afraid of falling...

146

...that they forget to enjoy the view.

I'm usually rushing back down for the next climb.

How'd you forget to mention this?

You made me pause and remember.

Well... thank you.

For what?

For the longest time I didn't think I could do anything right.

It's nice to remind myself that it's not true.

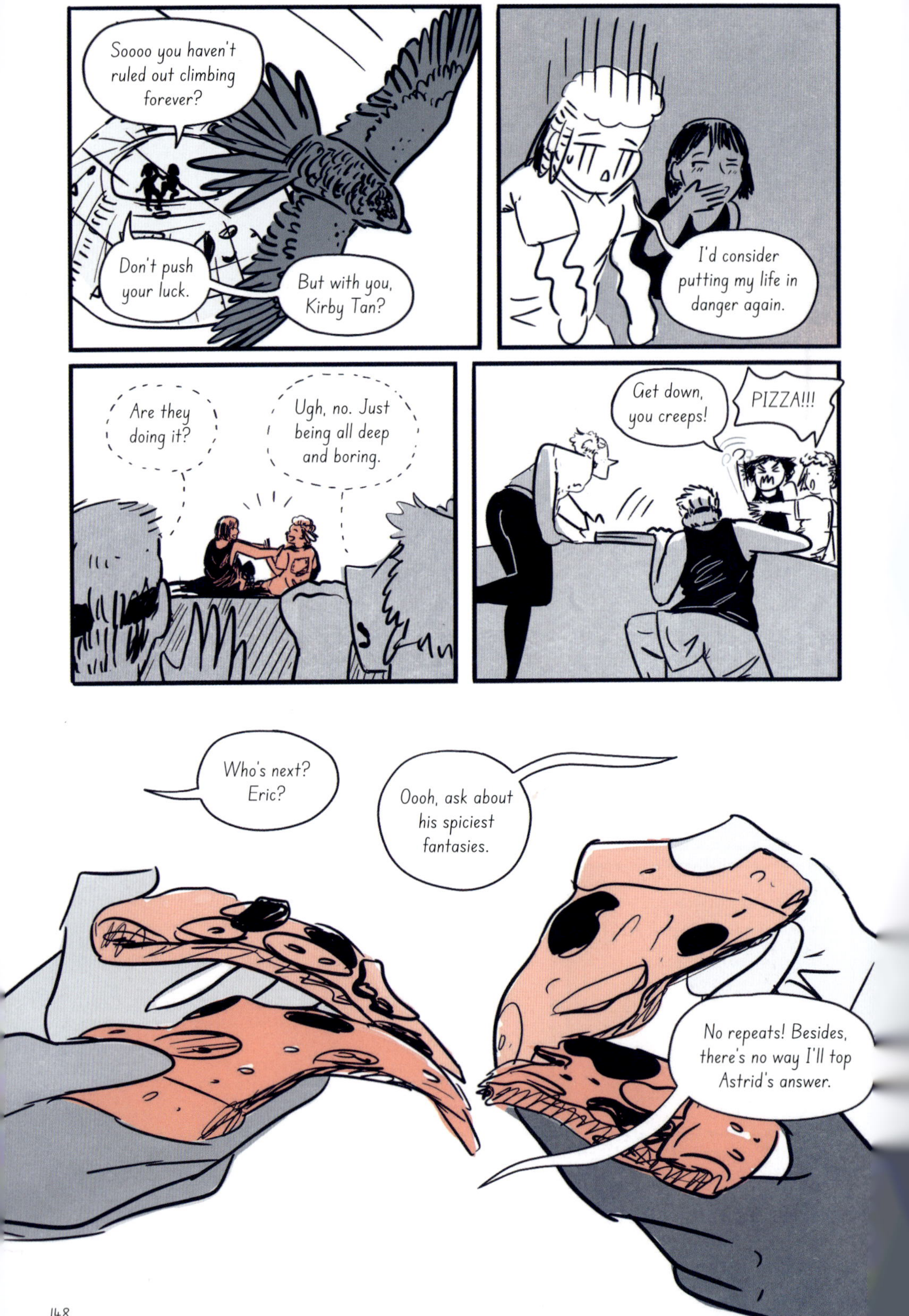

Soooo you haven't ruled out climbing forever?
Don't push your luck.
But with you, Kirby Tan?
I'd consider putting my life in danger again.
Are they doing it?
Ugh, no. Just being all deep and boring.
Get down, you creeps!
PIZZA!!!
Who's next? Eric?
Oooh, ask about his spiciest fantasies.
No repeats! Besides, there's no way I'll top Astrid's answer.

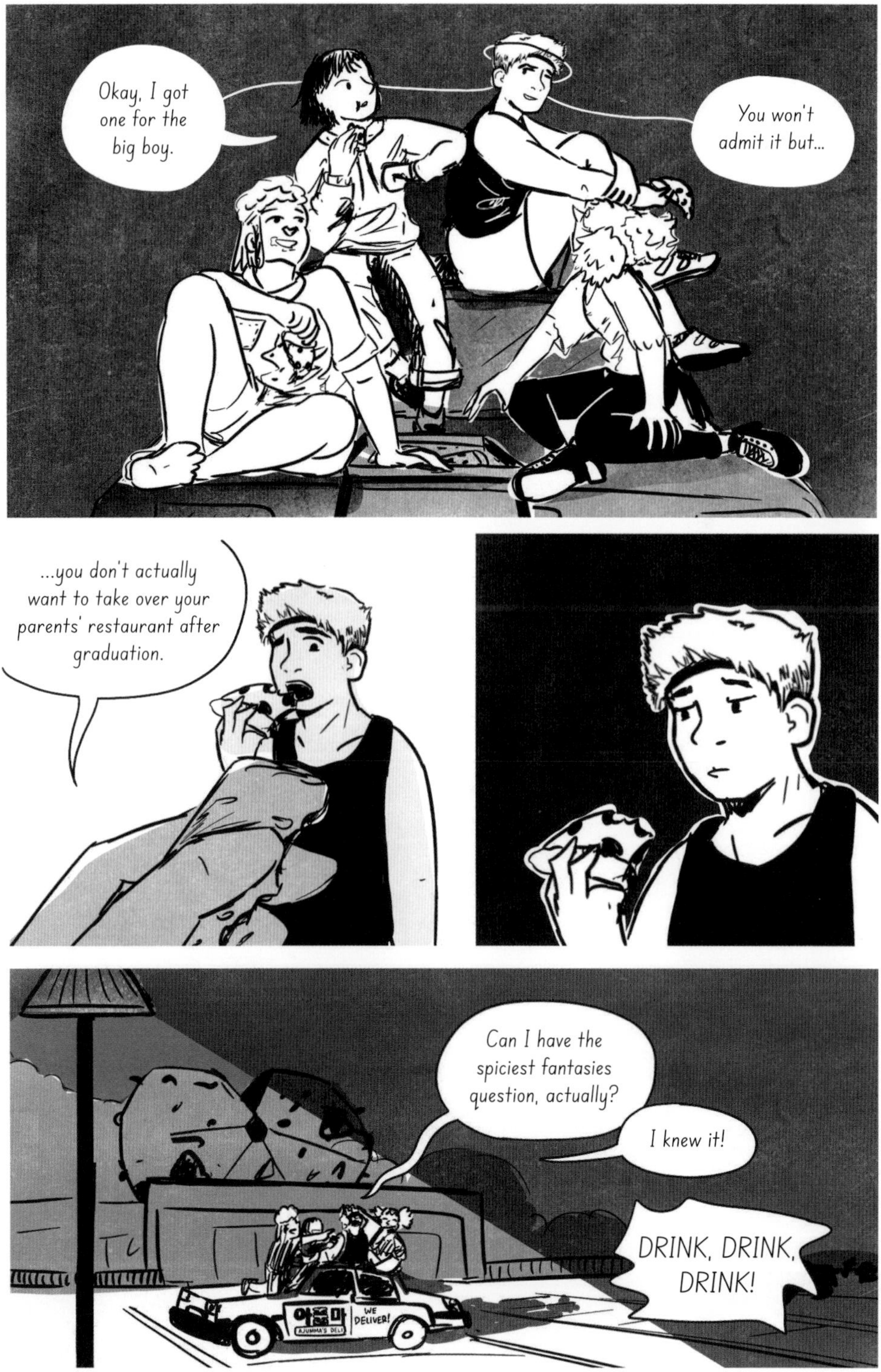

Okay, I got one for the big boy.
You won't admit it but...
...you don't actually want to take over your parents' restaurant after graduation.
Can I have the spiciest fantasies question, actually?
I knew it!
DRINK, DRINK, DRINK!
WE DELIVER!
AJUMMA'S DELI

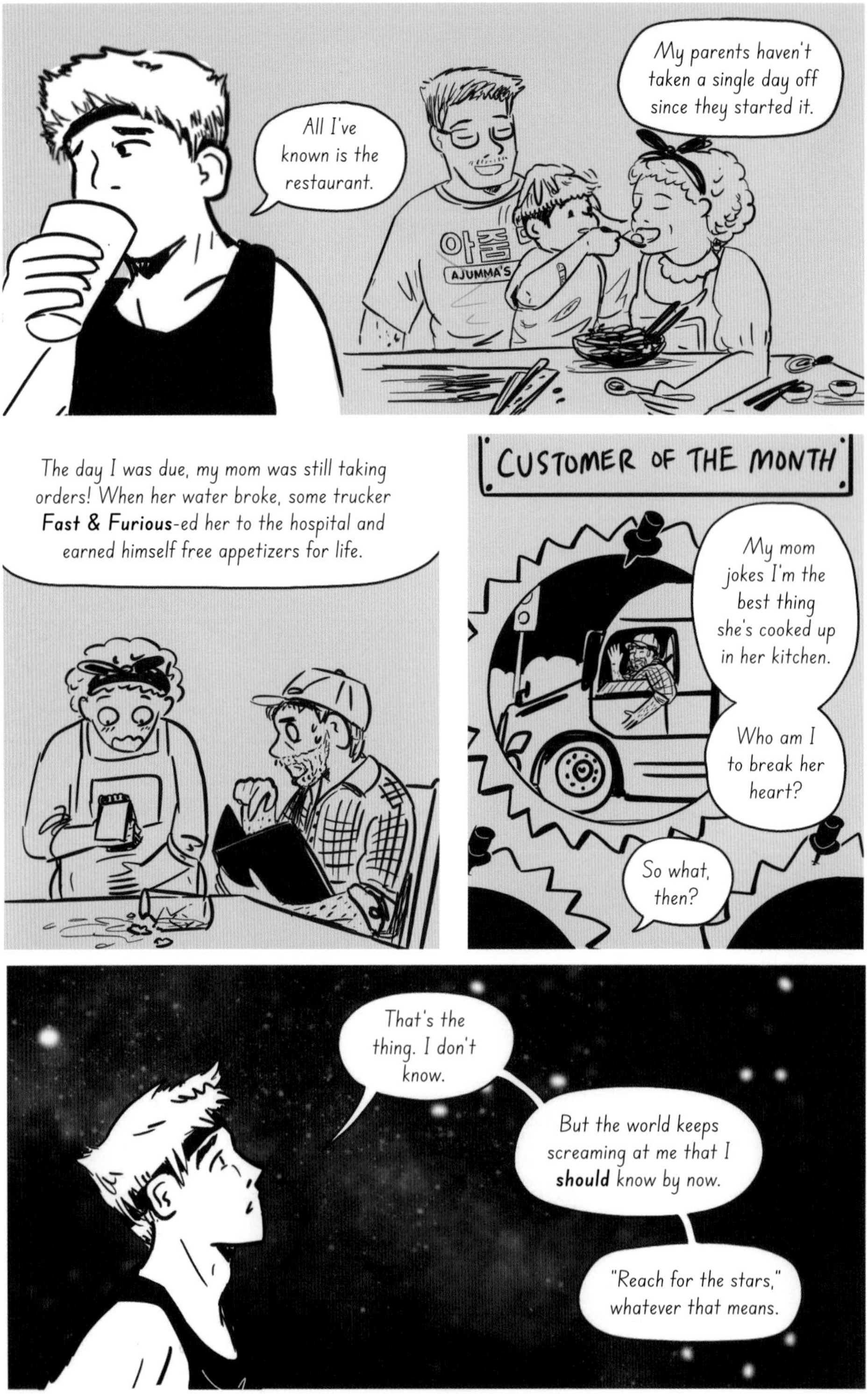
All I've known is the restaurant.
My parents haven't taken a single day off since they started it.
아줌마
AJUMMA'S
The day I was due, my mom was still taking orders! When her water broke, some trucker **Fast & Furious**-ed her to the hospital and earned himself free appetizers for life.
CUSTOMER OF THE MONTH
My mom jokes I'm the best thing she's cooked up in her kitchen.
Who am I to break her heart?
So what, then?
That's the thing. I don't know.
But the world keeps screaming at me that I **should** know by now.
"Reach for the stars," whatever that means.

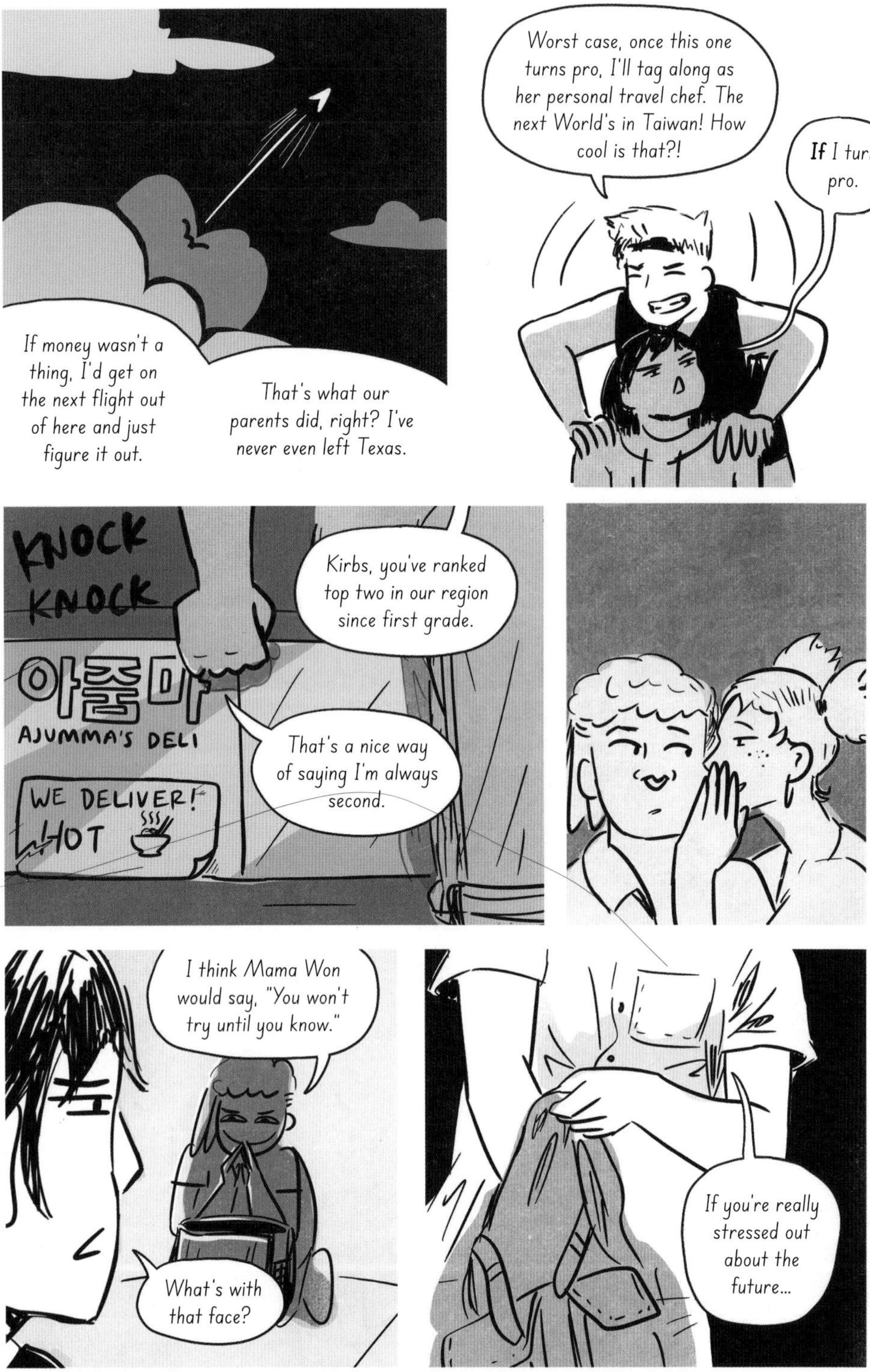
If money wasn't a thing, I'd get on the next flight out of here and just figure it out.
That's what our parents did, right? I've never even left Texas.
Worst case, once this one turns pro, I'll tag along as her personal travel chef. The next World's in Taiwan! How cool is that?!
If I turn pro.
KNOCK KNOCK
아줌마
AJUMMA'S DELI
WE DELIVER!
HOT
Kirbs, you've ranked top two in our region since first grade.
That's a nice way of saying I'm always second.
I think Mama Won would say, "You won't try until you know."
What's with that face?
If you're really stressed out about the future...

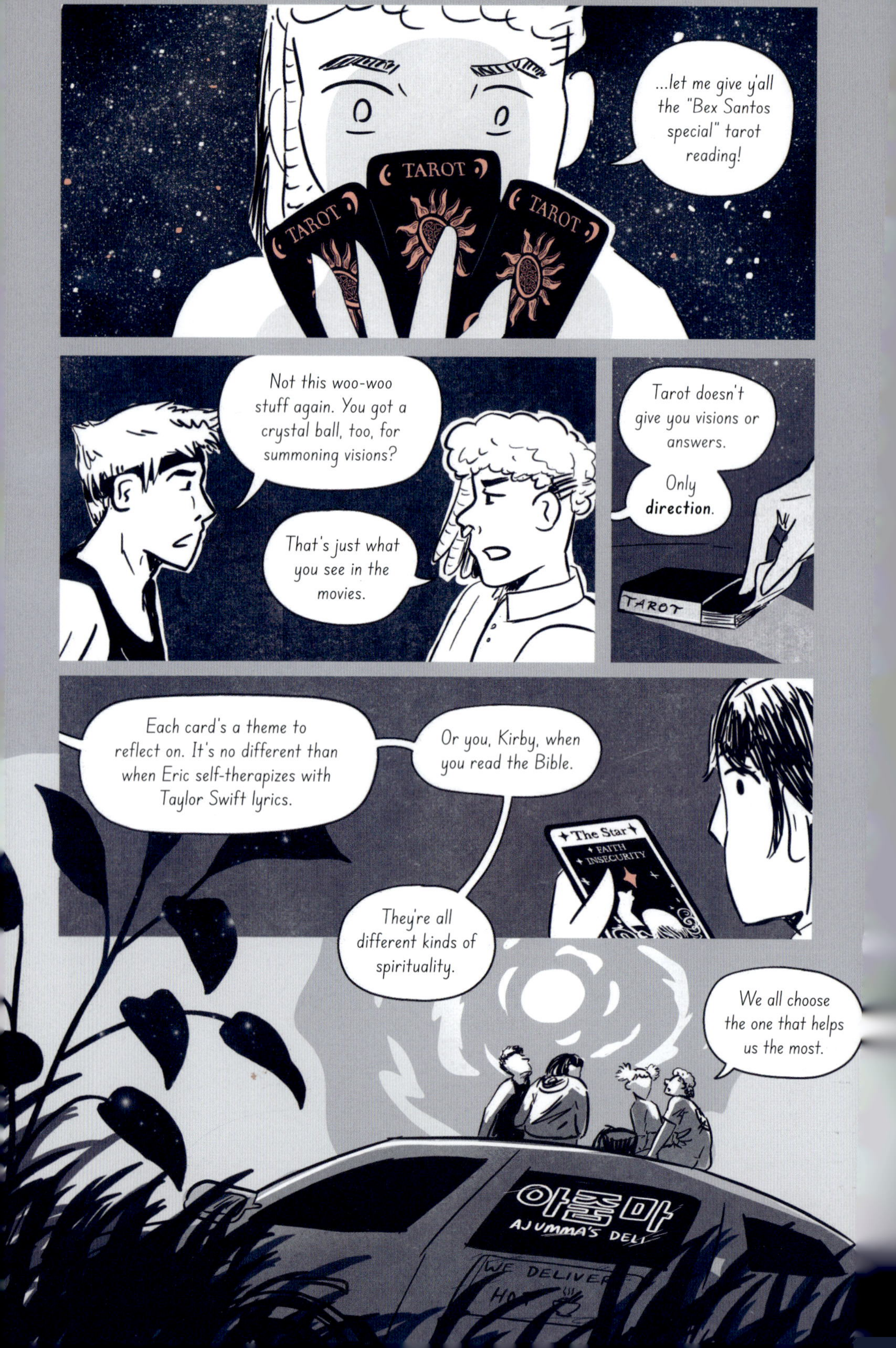
...let me give y'all the "Bex Santos special" tarot reading!
TAROT
TAROT
TAROT
Not this woo-woo stuff again. You got a crystal ball, too, for summoning visions?
That's just what you see in the movies.
Tarot doesn't give you visions or answers.
Only **direction**.
TAROT
Each card's a theme to reflect on. It's no different than when Eric self-therapizes with Taylor Swift lyrics.
Or you, Kirby, when you read the Bible.
They're all different kinds of spirituality.
The Star
FAITH
INSECURITY
We all choose the one that helps us the most.
아줌마
AJUMMA'S DELI

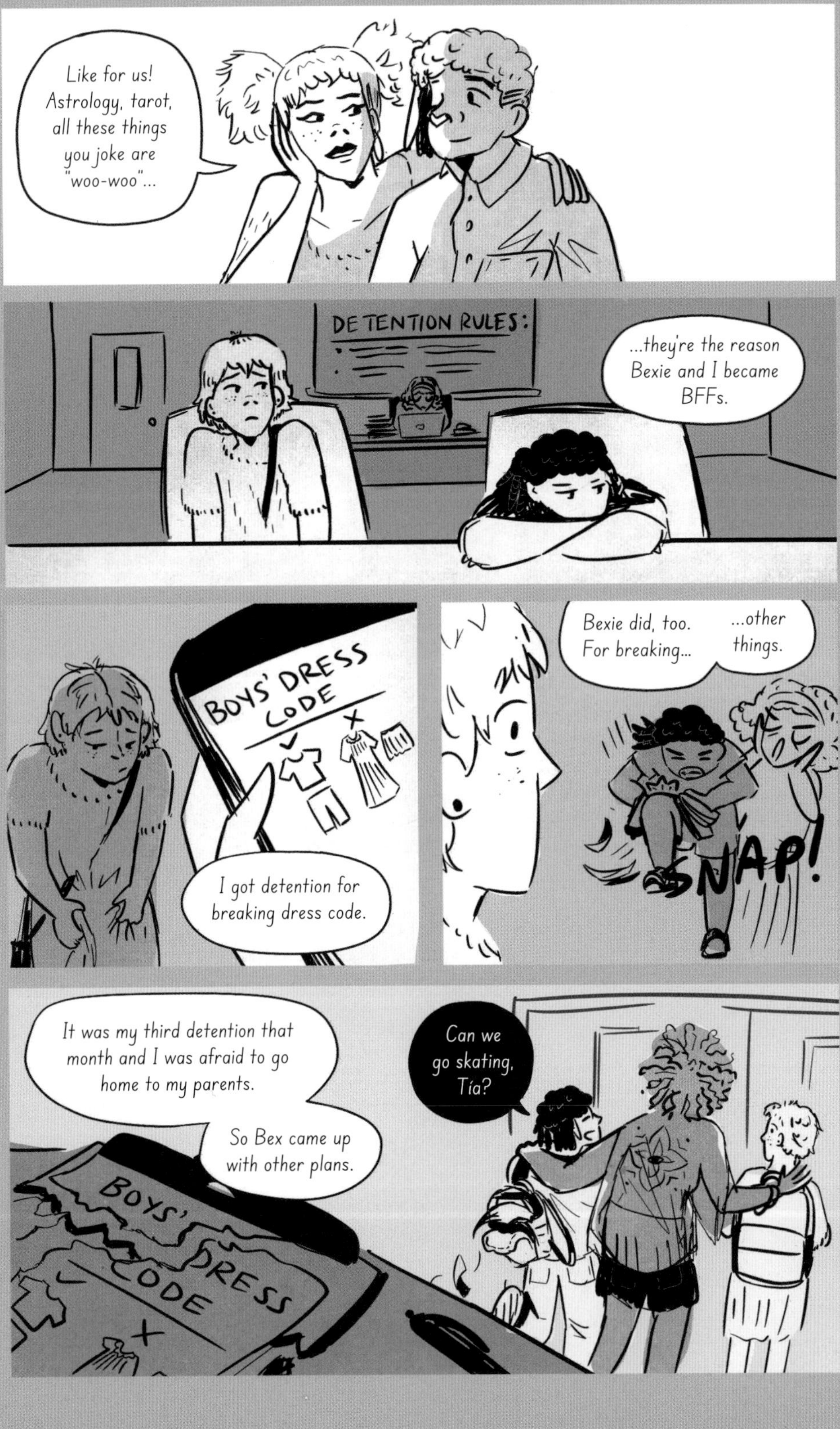

Like for us! Astrology, tarot, all these things you joke are "woo-woo"...
DETENTION RULES:
...they're the reason Bexie and I became BFFs.
BOYS' DRESS CODE
I got detention for breaking dress code.
Bexie did, too. For breaking...
...other things.
SNAP!
It was my third detention that month and I was afraid to go home to my parents.
So Bex came up with other plans.
Can we go skating, Tía?
BOYS' DRESS CODE

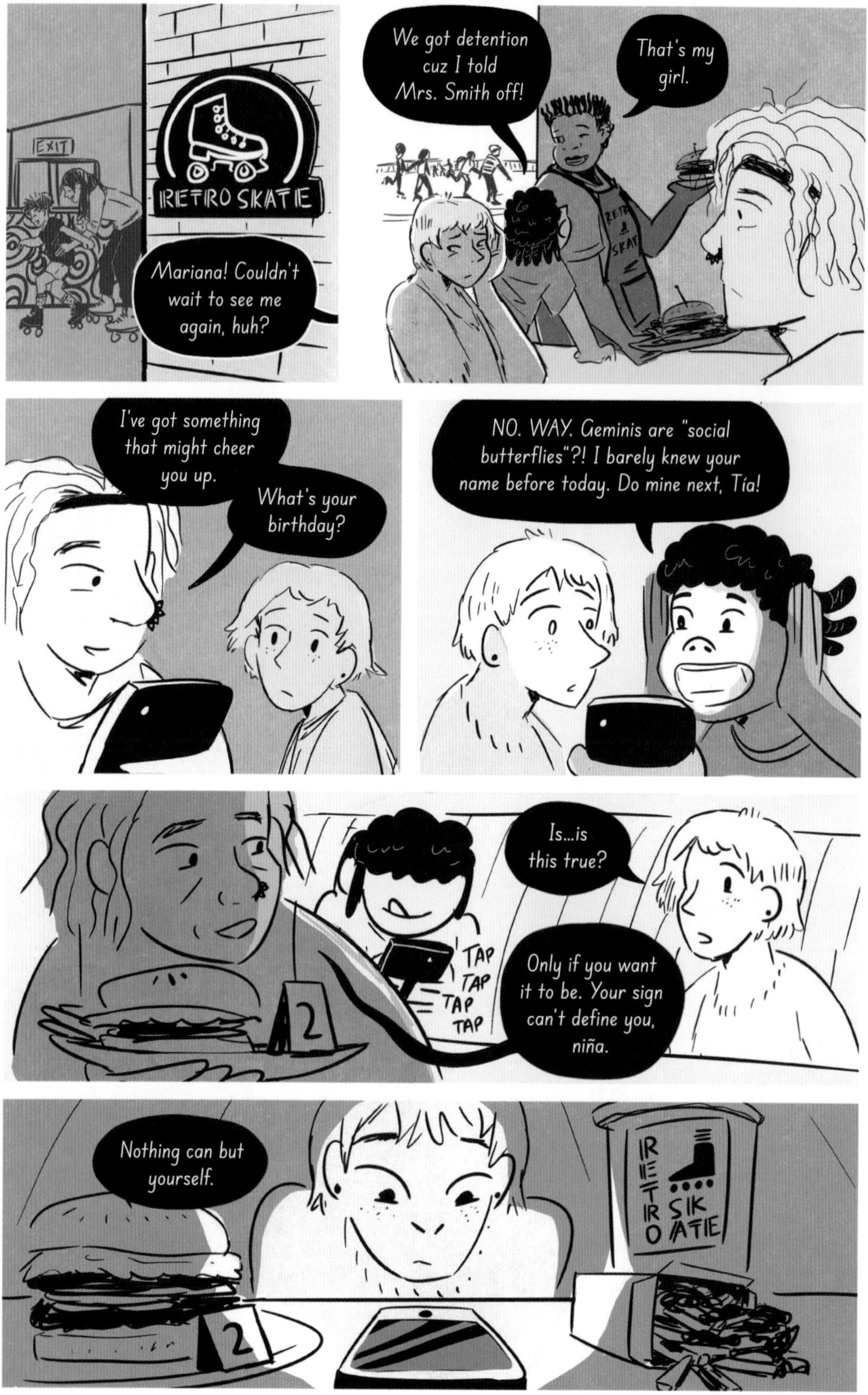
RETRO SKATE
EXIT
Mariana! Couldn't wait to see me again, huh?
We got detention cuz I told Mrs. Smith off!
That's my girl.
I've got something that might cheer you up.
What's your birthday?
NO. WAY. Geminis are "social butterflies"?! I barely knew your name before today. Do mine next, Tía!
Is...is this true?
TAP TAP TAP TAP
Only if you want it to be. Your sign can't define you, niña.
Nothing can but yourself.
RETRO SKATE

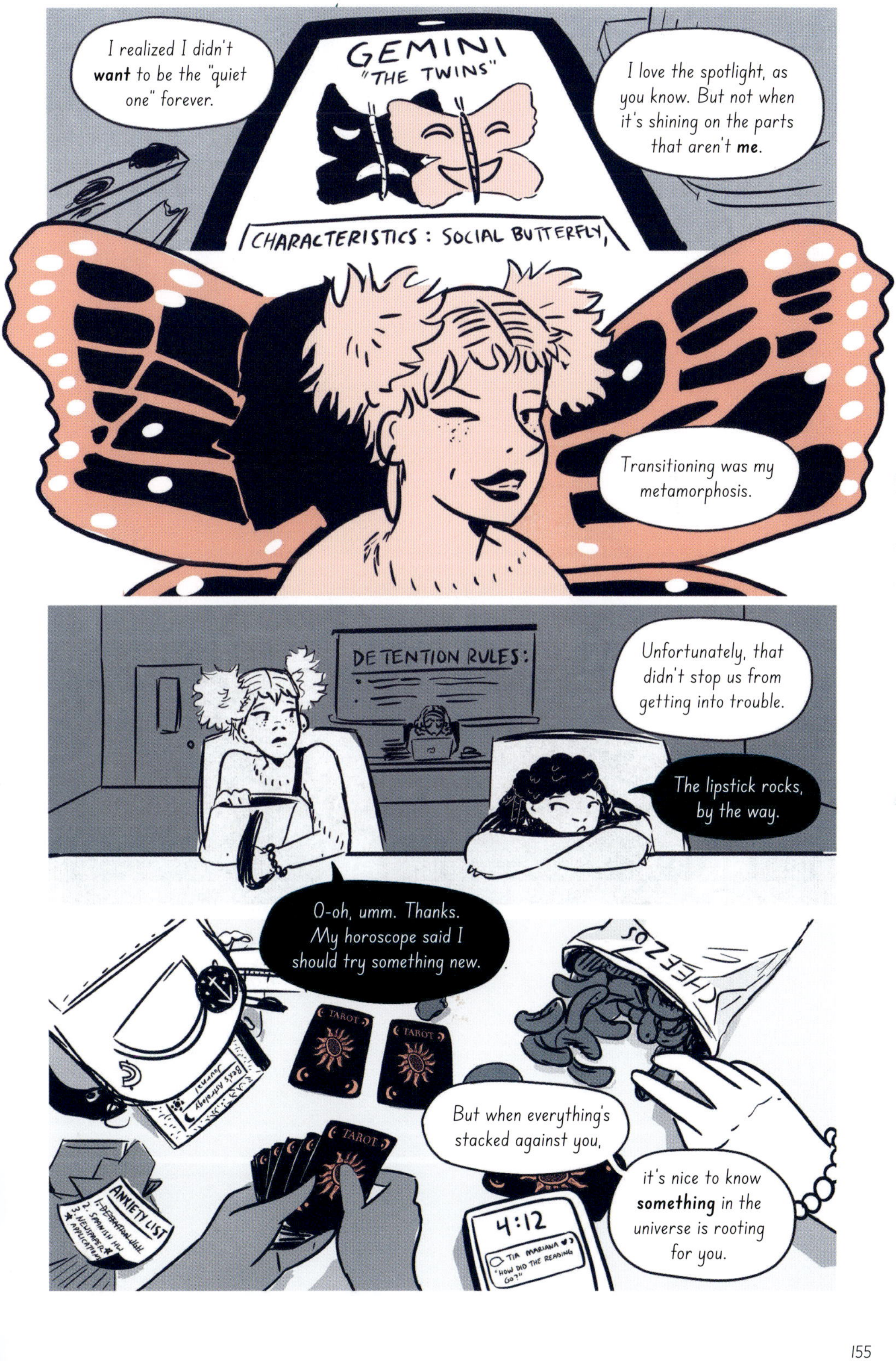
GEMINI "THE TWINS"
I realized I didn't **want** to be the "quiet one" forever.
I love the spotlight, as you know. But not when it's shining on the parts that aren't **me**.
CHARACTERISTICS : SOCIAL BUTTERFLY,
Transitioning was my metamorphosis.
DETENTION RULES:
Unfortunately, that didn't stop us from getting into trouble.
The lipstick rocks, by the way.
O-oh, umm. Thanks. My horoscope said I should try something new.
CHEEZOS
TAROT
TAROT
Bex's Astrology Journal
But when everything's stacked against you,
it's nice to know **something** in the universe is rooting for you.
TAROT
ANXIETY LIST
2. SPANISH HW
3. NEWSPAPER APPLICATION
4:12
TIA MARIANA
"HOW DID THE READING GO?"

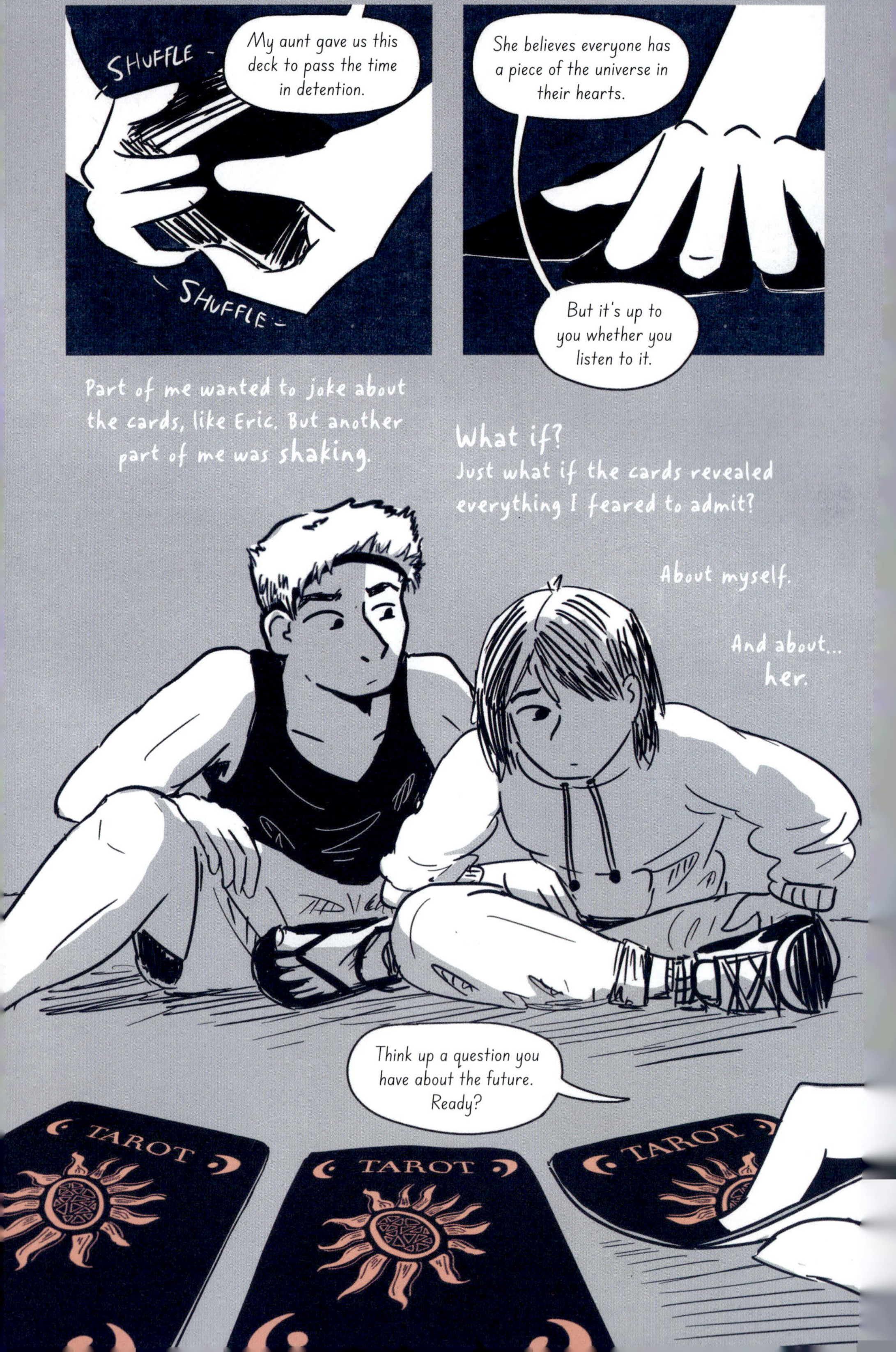
SHUFFLE
My aunt gave us this deck to pass the time in detention.
SHUFFLE
She believes everyone has a piece of the universe in their hearts.
But it's up to you whether you listen to it.
Part of me wanted to joke about the cards, like Eric. But another part of me was shaking.
What if?
Just what if the cards revealed everything I feared to admit?
About myself.
And about... her.
Think up a question you have about the future. Ready?
TAROT
TAROT
TAROT

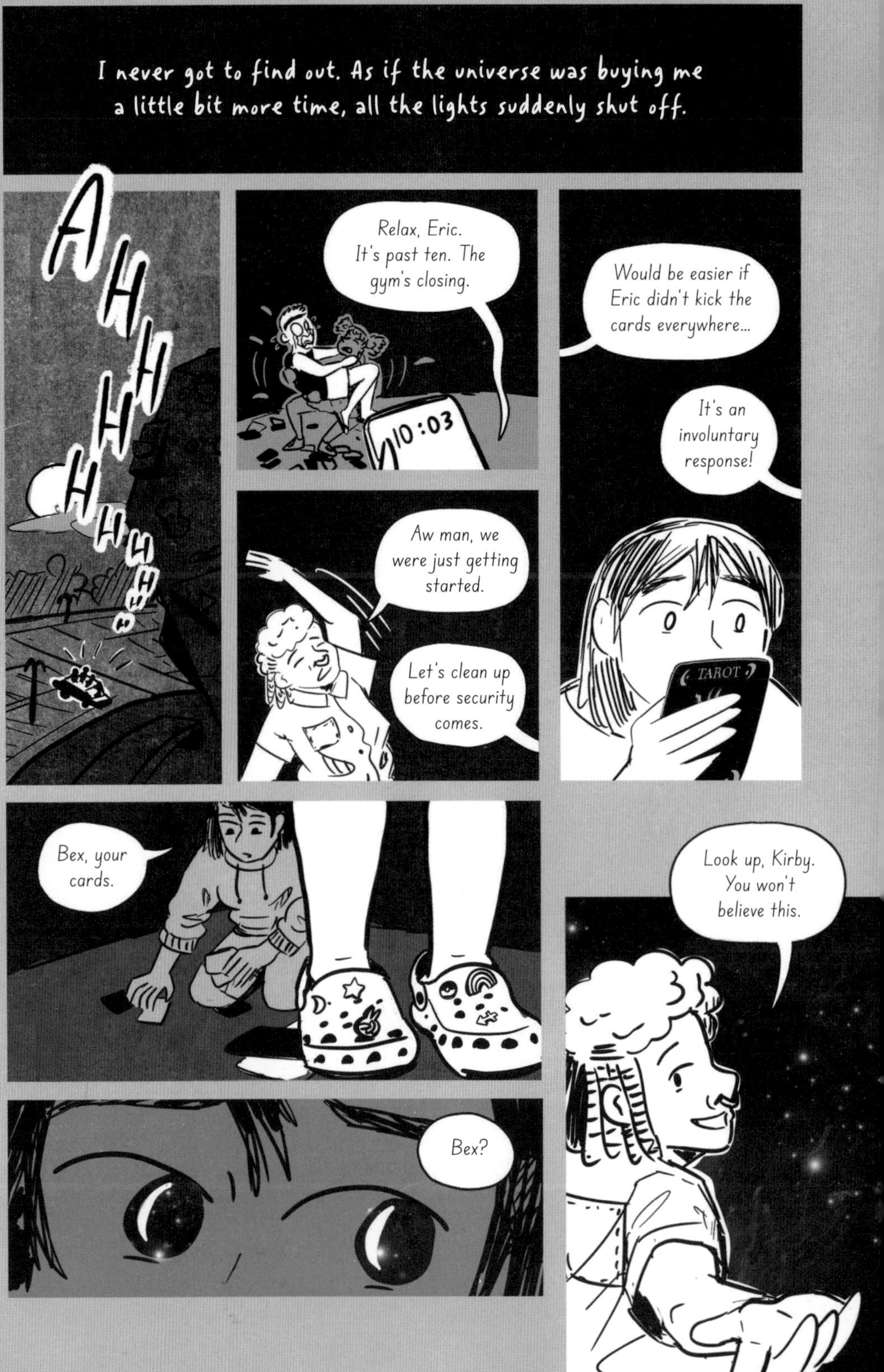
I never got to find out. As if the universe was buying me a little bit more time, all the lights suddenly shut off.
AHHHHHHHHH
Relax, Eric. It's past ten. The gym's closing.
10:03
Would be easier if Eric didn't kick the cards everywhere...
It's an involuntary response!
Aw man, we were just getting started.
Let's clean up before security comes.
TAROT
Bex, your cards.
Bex?
Look up, Kirby. You won't believe this.

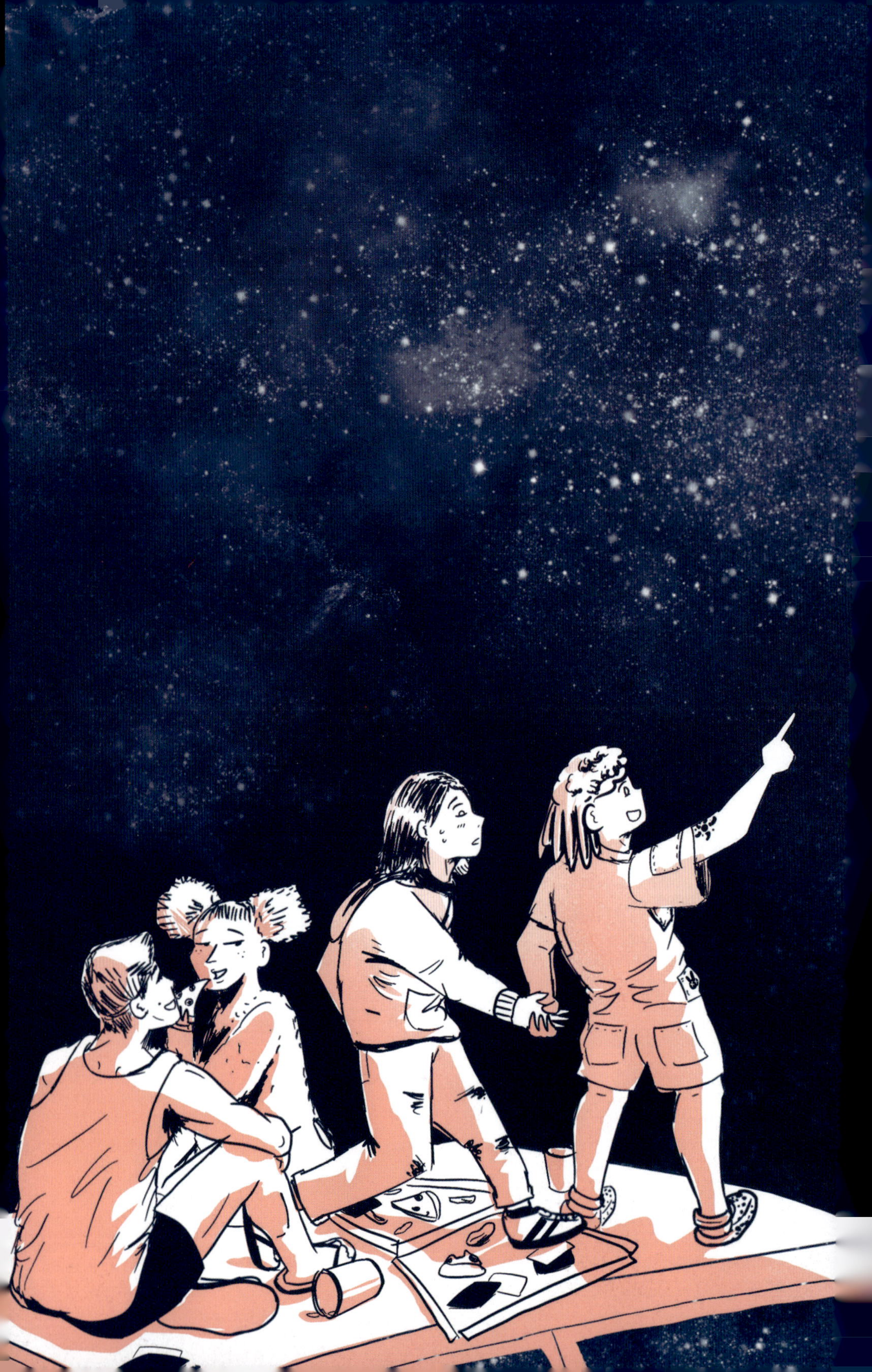

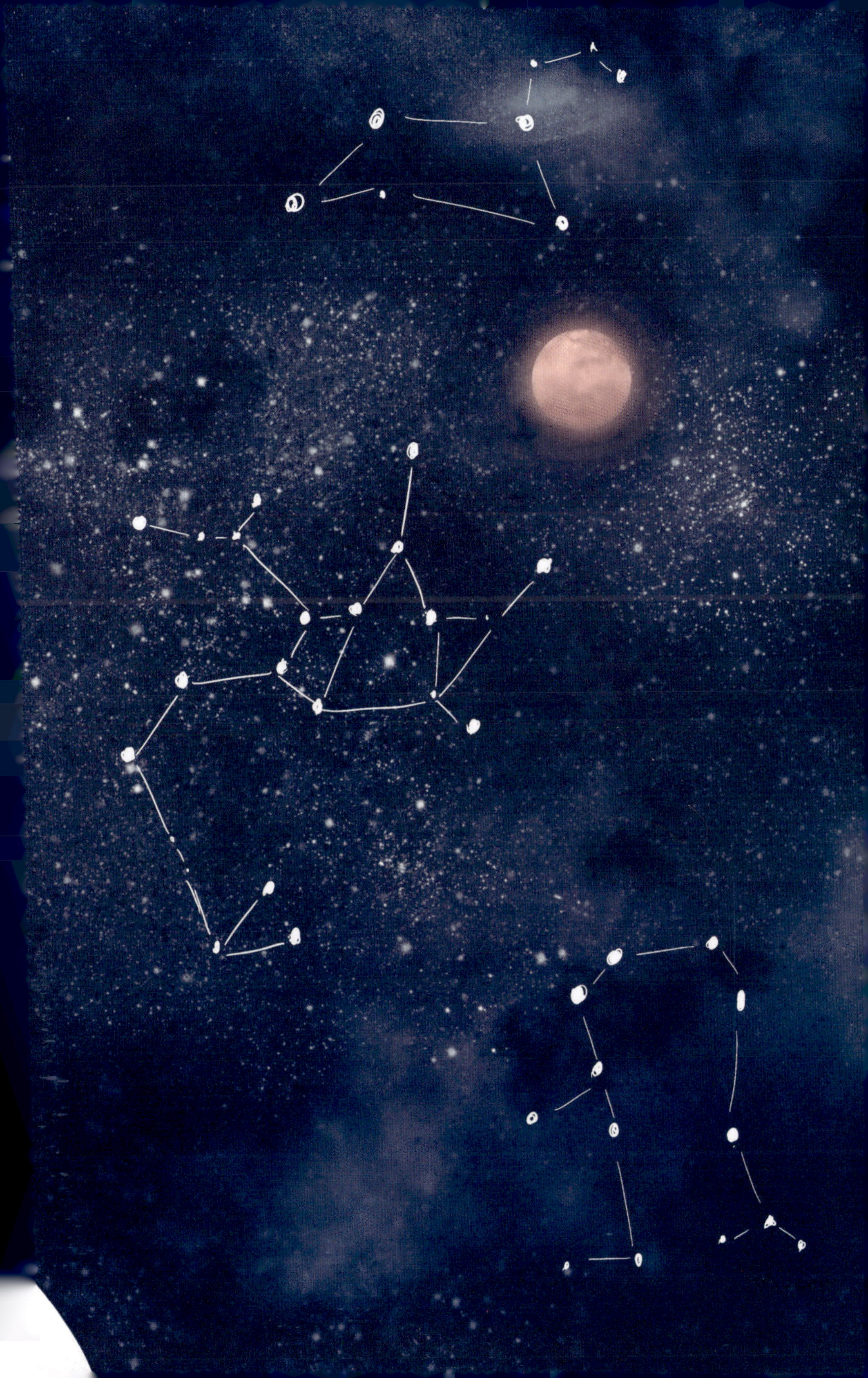

"See that triangle of stars?"

"That's you, **Libra**. The scale the universe balances on."

"What's that shimmering to its right?"

"That's me, Sagittarius, the centaur archer."

"So you get to be a badass warrior, and I'm just an inanimate object?!"

"Hey, I don't make the rules."

"I used to hate my sign's traits."

"Reminded me of what my parents would always say about me."

"Loud. Inconsistent. Emotional."

"But you have a point, Kirby."

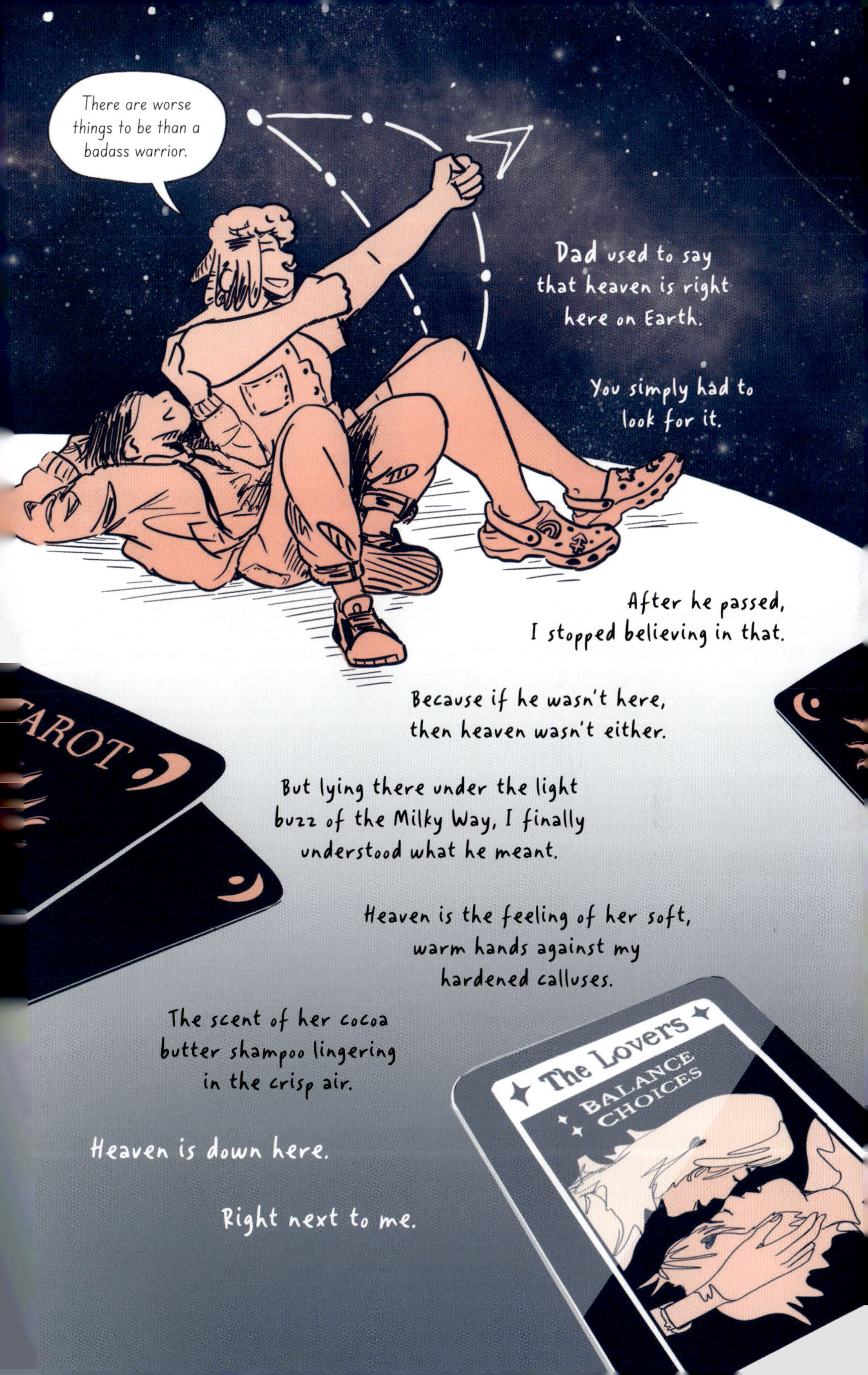

There are worse things to be than a badass warrior.
Dad used to say that heaven is right here on Earth.
You simply had to look for it.
After he passed, I stopped believing in that.
Because if he wasn't here, then heaven wasn't either.
But lying there under the light buzz of the Milky Way, I finally understood what he meant.
Heaven is the feeling of her soft, warm hands against my hardened calluses.
The scent of her cocoa butter shampoo lingering in the crisp air.
Heaven is down here.
Right next to me.
TAROT
The Lovers
BALANCE
CHOICES

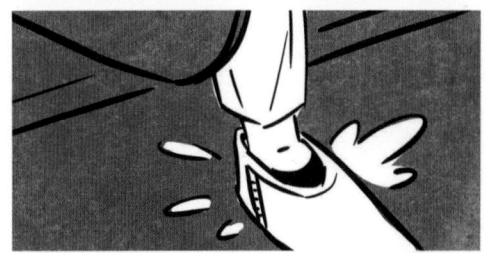

SCREECH

Hey, kids, we're closing down.

Kirby? That you?

H-hey, Coach. Just getting some practice in.

Why didn't you tell me you're back?

I—I must've forgotten.

You're just in time for the Spring Classic!

Bellevue's sending scouts again. We better get you back to peak condition, ASAP.

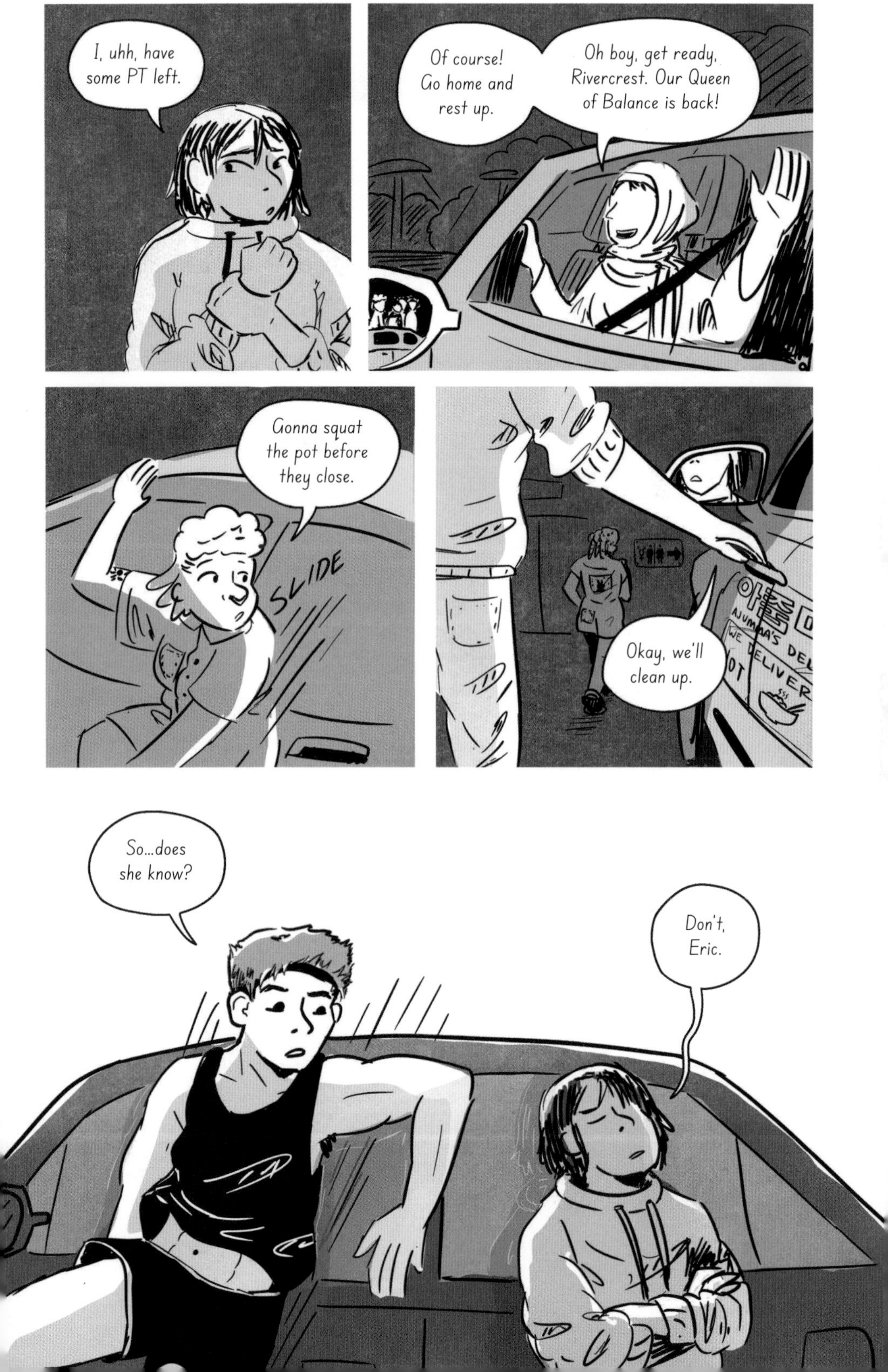
I, uhh, have some PT left.
Of course! Go home and rest up.
Oh boy, get ready, Rivercrest. Our Queen of Balance is back!
Gonna squat the pot before they close.
SLIDE
Okay, we'll clean up.
So...does she know?
Don't, Eric.

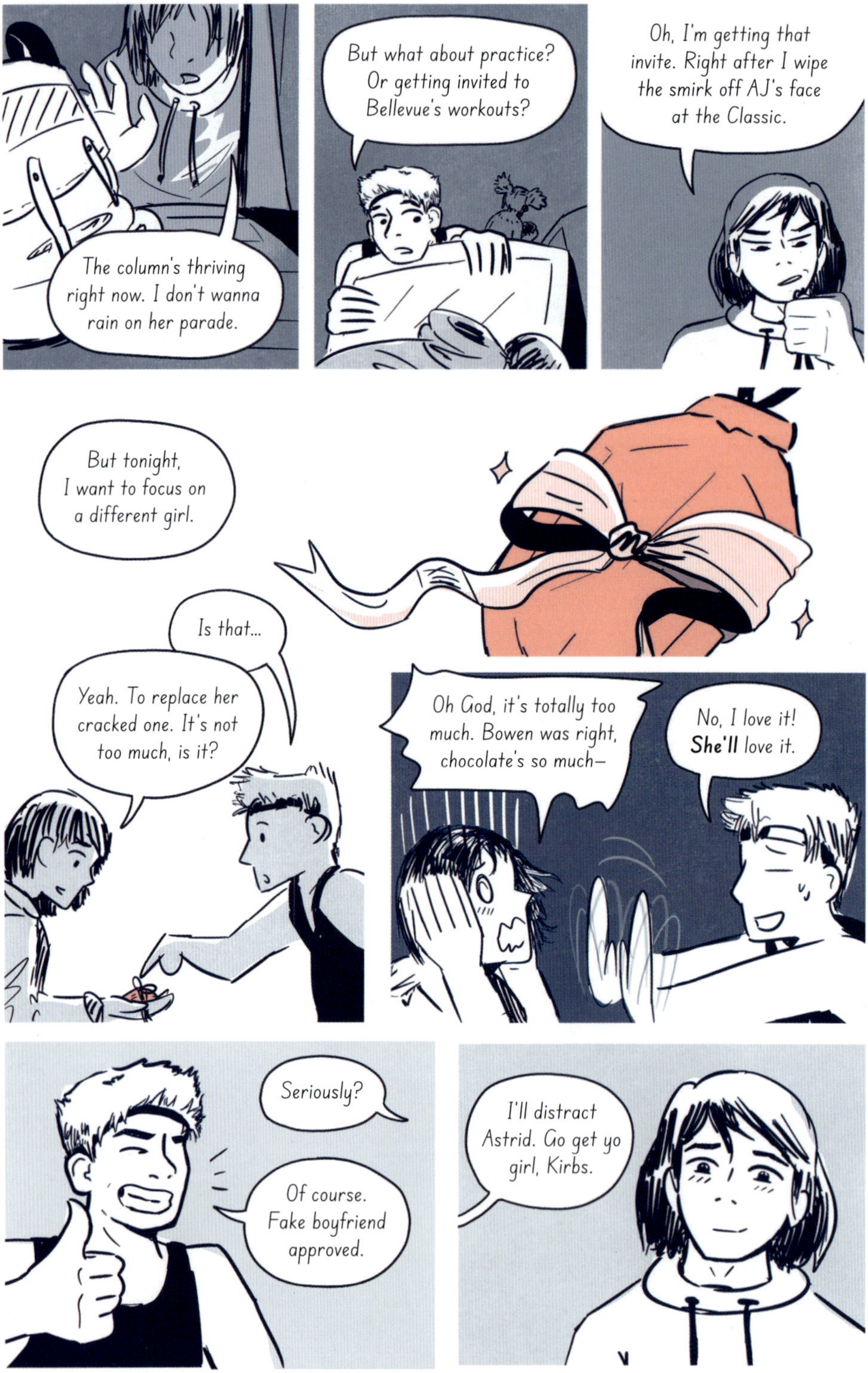
The column's thriving right now. I don't wanna rain on her parade.
But what about practice? Or getting invited to Bellevue's workouts?
Oh, I'm getting that invite. Right after I wipe the smirk off AJ's face at the Classic.
But tonight, I want to focus on a different girl.
Is that...
Yeah. To replace her cracked one. It's not too much, is it?
Oh God, it's totally too much. Bowen was right, chocolate's so much—
No, I love it! **She'll** love it.
Seriously?
Of course. Fake boyfriend approved.
I'll distract Astrid. Go get yo girl, Kirbs.

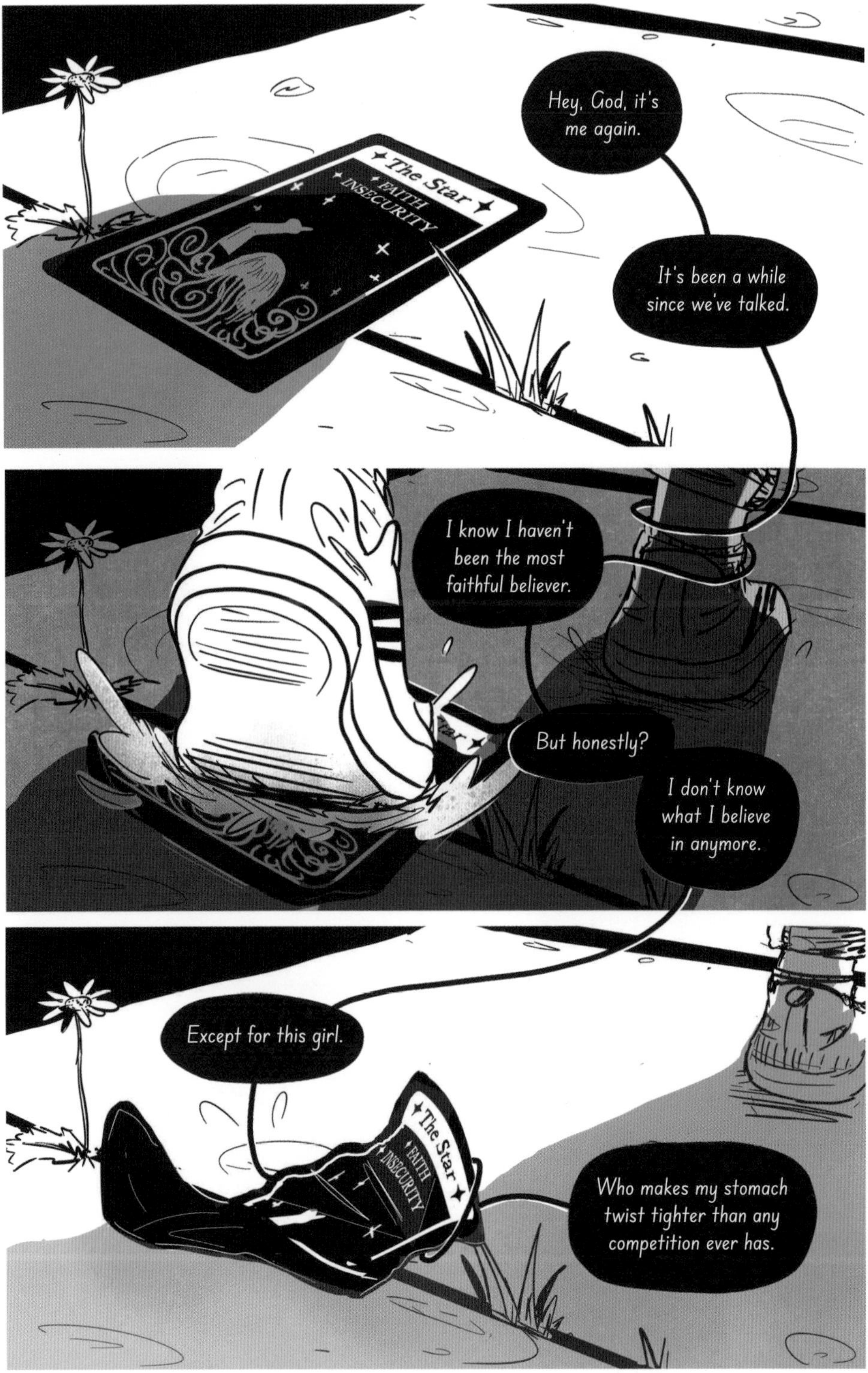
The Star
FAITH
INSECURITY
Hey, God, it's me again.
It's been a while since we've talked.
I know I haven't been the most faithful believer.
But honestly?
I don't know what I believe in anymore.
Except for this girl.
The Star
FAITH
INSECURITY
Who makes my stomach twist tighter than any competition ever has.

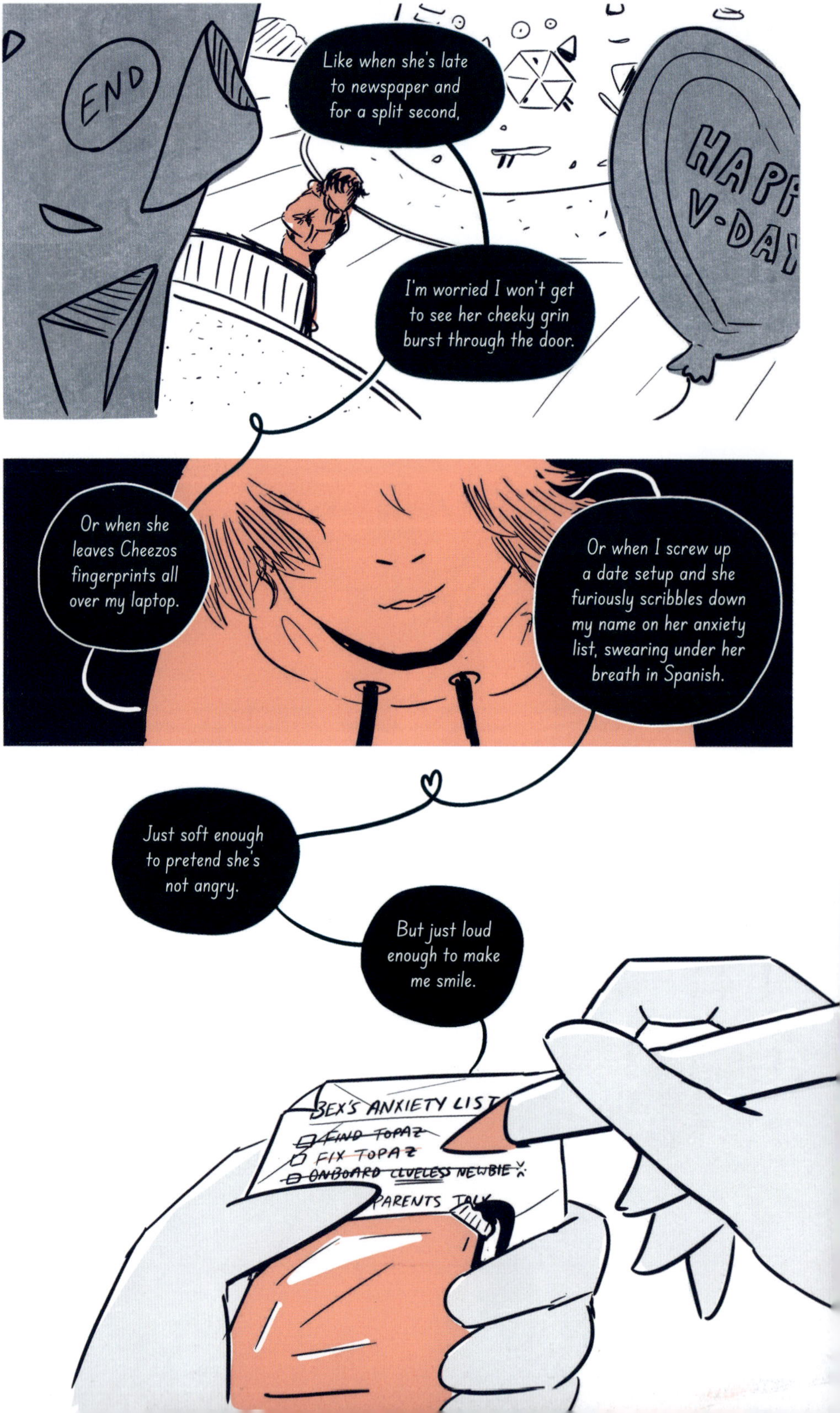
END
Like when she's late to newspaper and for a split second,
HAPP
V-DAY
I'm worried I won't get to see her cheeky grin burst through the door.
Or when she leaves Cheezos fingerprints all over my laptop.
Or when I screw up a date setup and she furiously scribbles down my name on her anxiety list, swearing under her breath in Spanish.
Just soft enough to pretend she's not angry.
But just loud enough to make me smile.
BEX'S ANXIETY LIST
FIND TOPAZ
FIX TOPAZ
ONBOARD CLUELESS NEWBIE
PARENTS

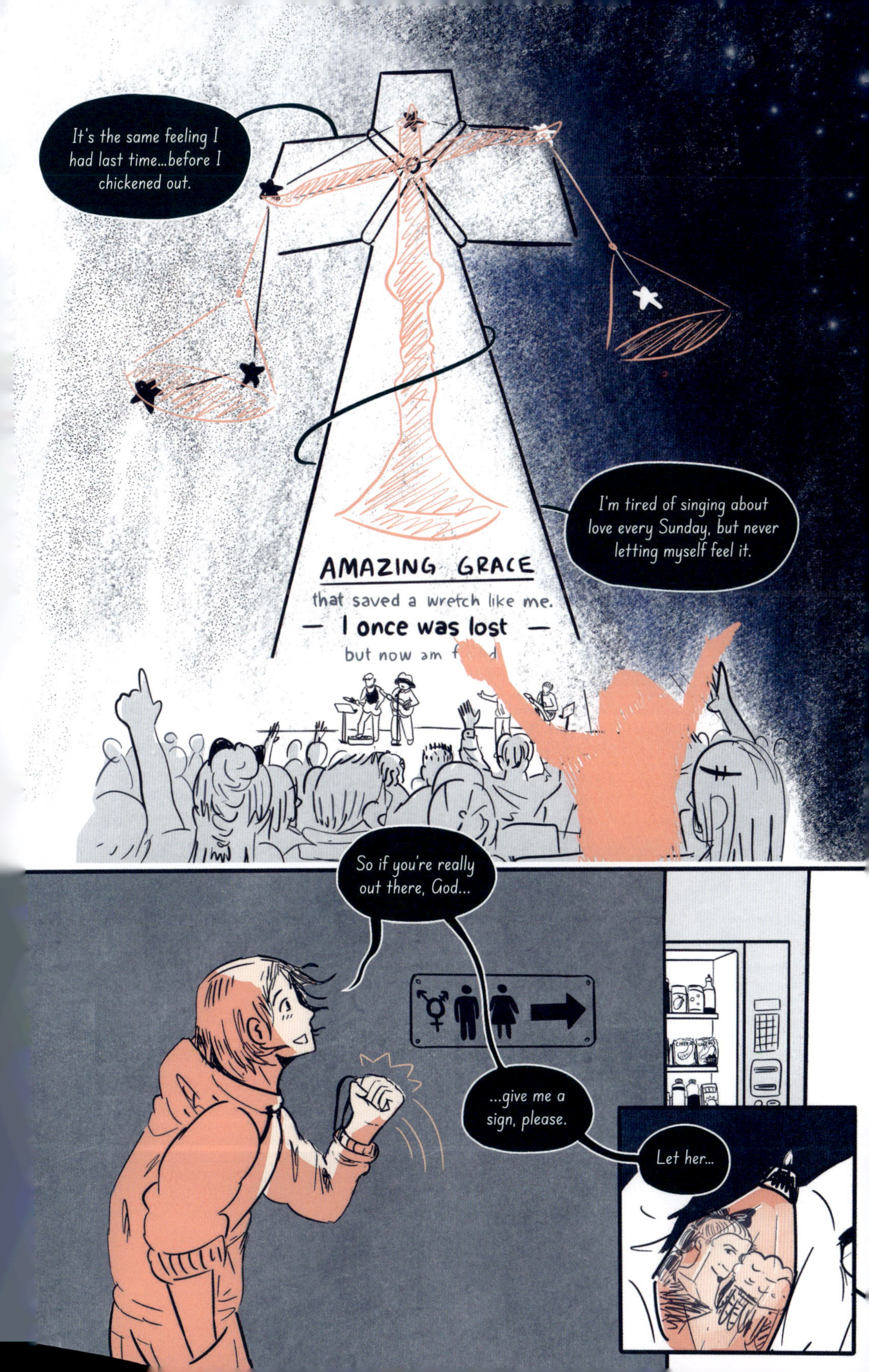
It's the same feeling I had last time...before I chickened out.
AMAZING GRACE
that saved a wretch like me.
— I once was lost —
but now am
I'm tired of singing about love every Sunday, but never letting myself feel it.
So if you're really out there, God...
...give me a sign, please.
Let her...

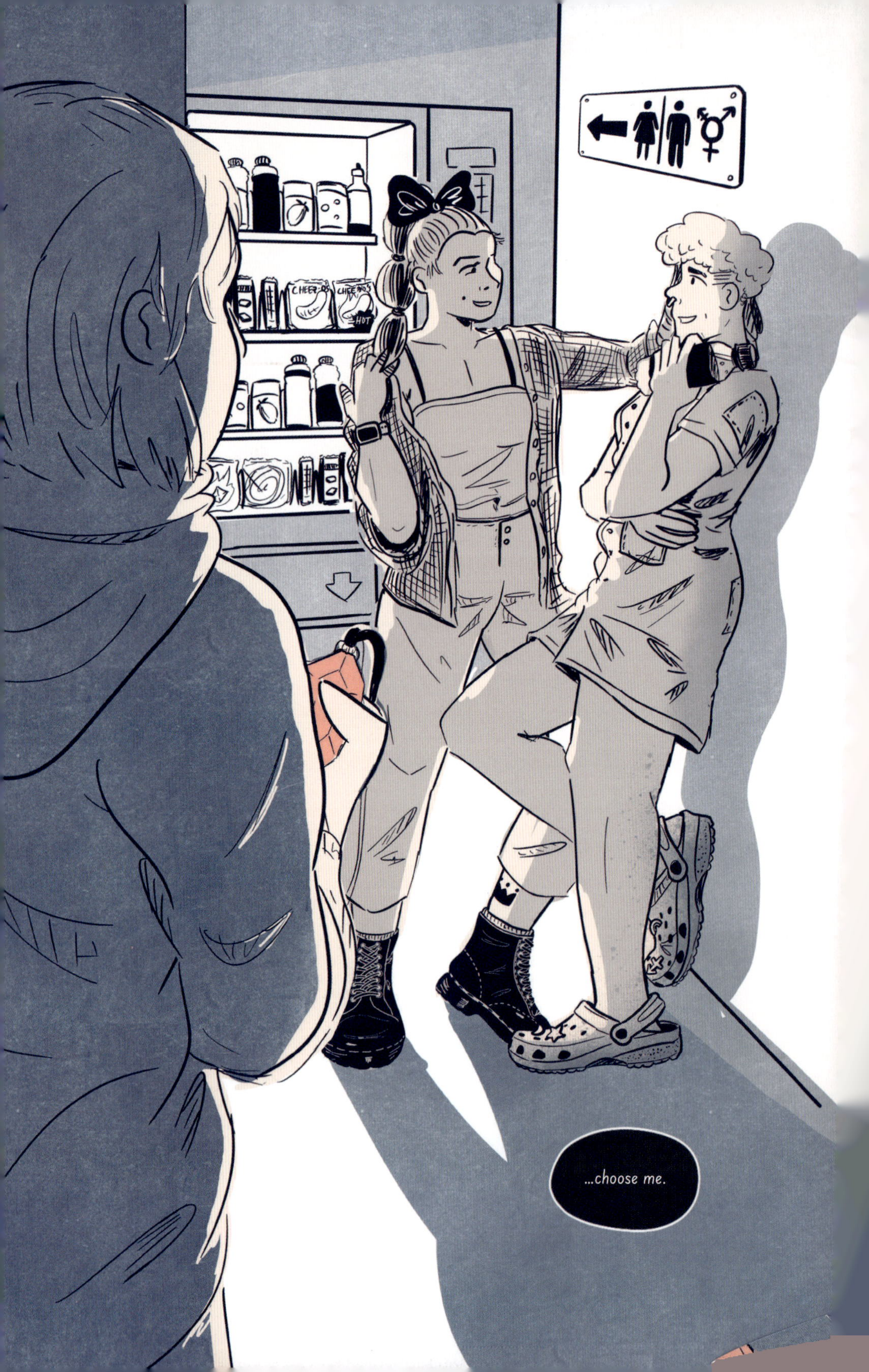
...choose me.

PART 4

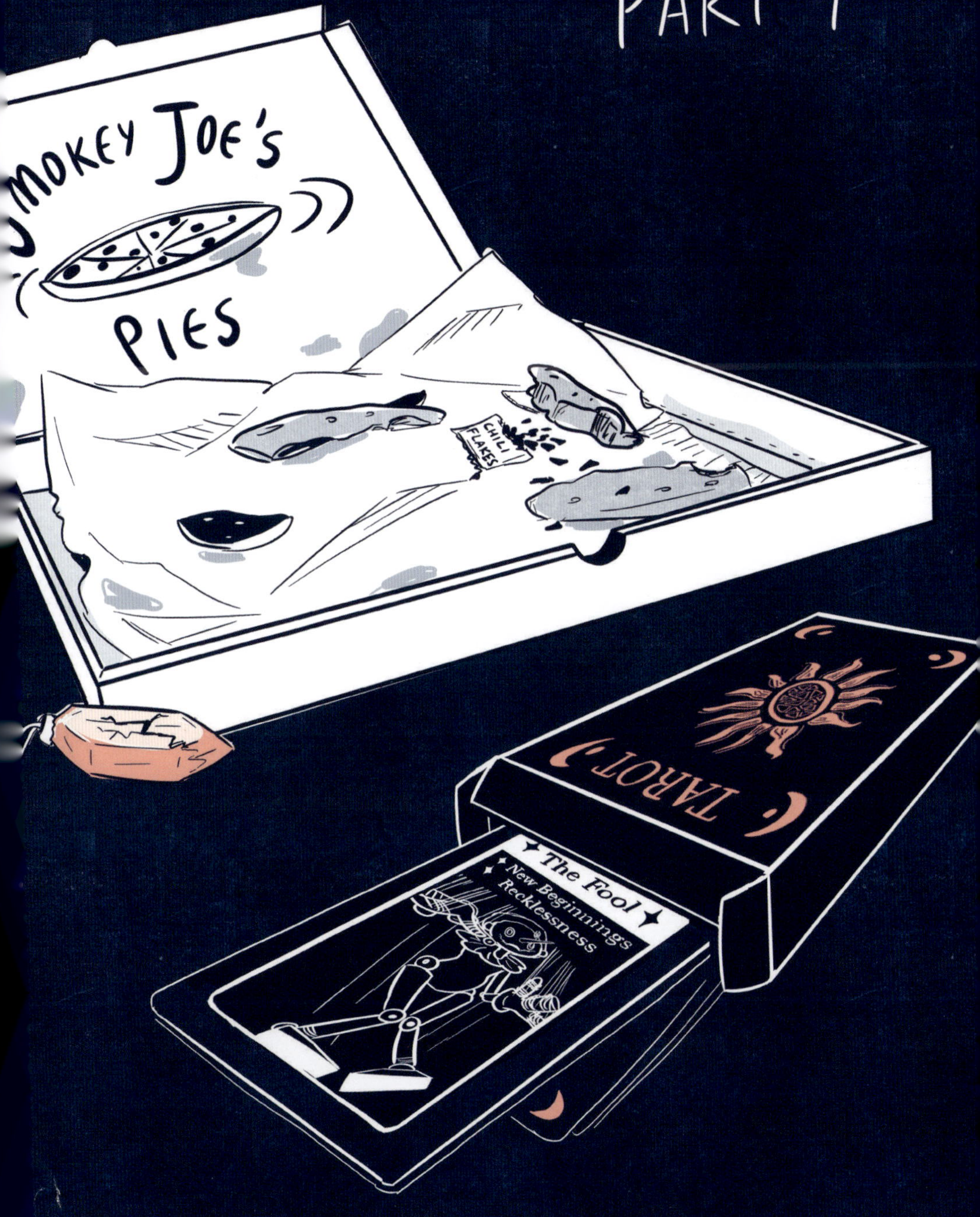
MOKEY JOE'S
PIES
CHILI FLAKES
TAROT
The Fool
New Beginnings
Recklessness

YOUTH CLIMBING SPRING CLASSIC
HOSTED BY RIVERCREST ACADEMY

ROYALS

AJ DAVIS

What a battle today, folks!

Kirby Tan is seconds away from victory!

END

Can she steal the crown away from the reigning champion?

YES!

Look who finally made it.

170

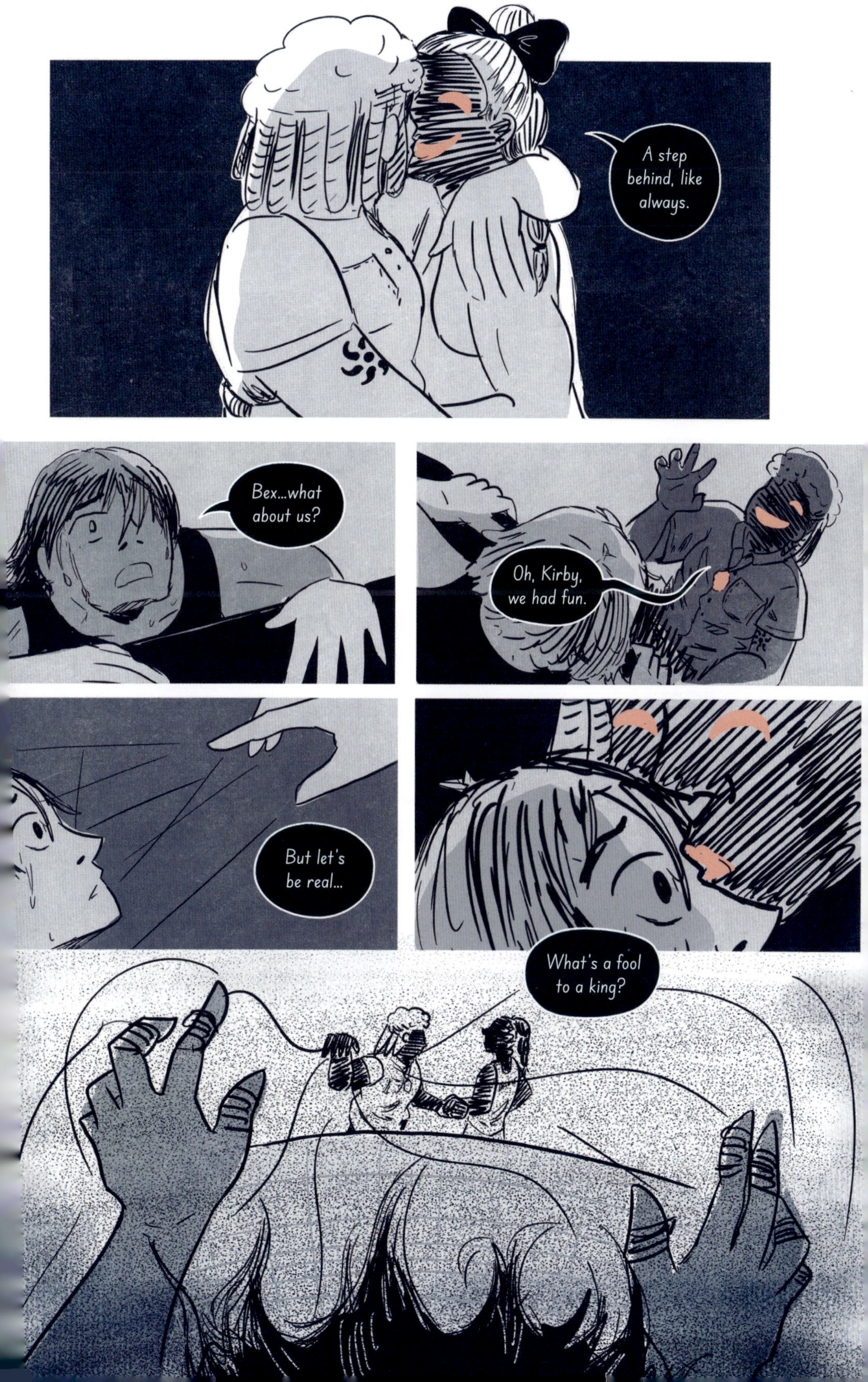
A step behind, like always.
Bex...what about us?
Oh, Kirby, we had fun.
But let's be real...
What's a fool to a king?

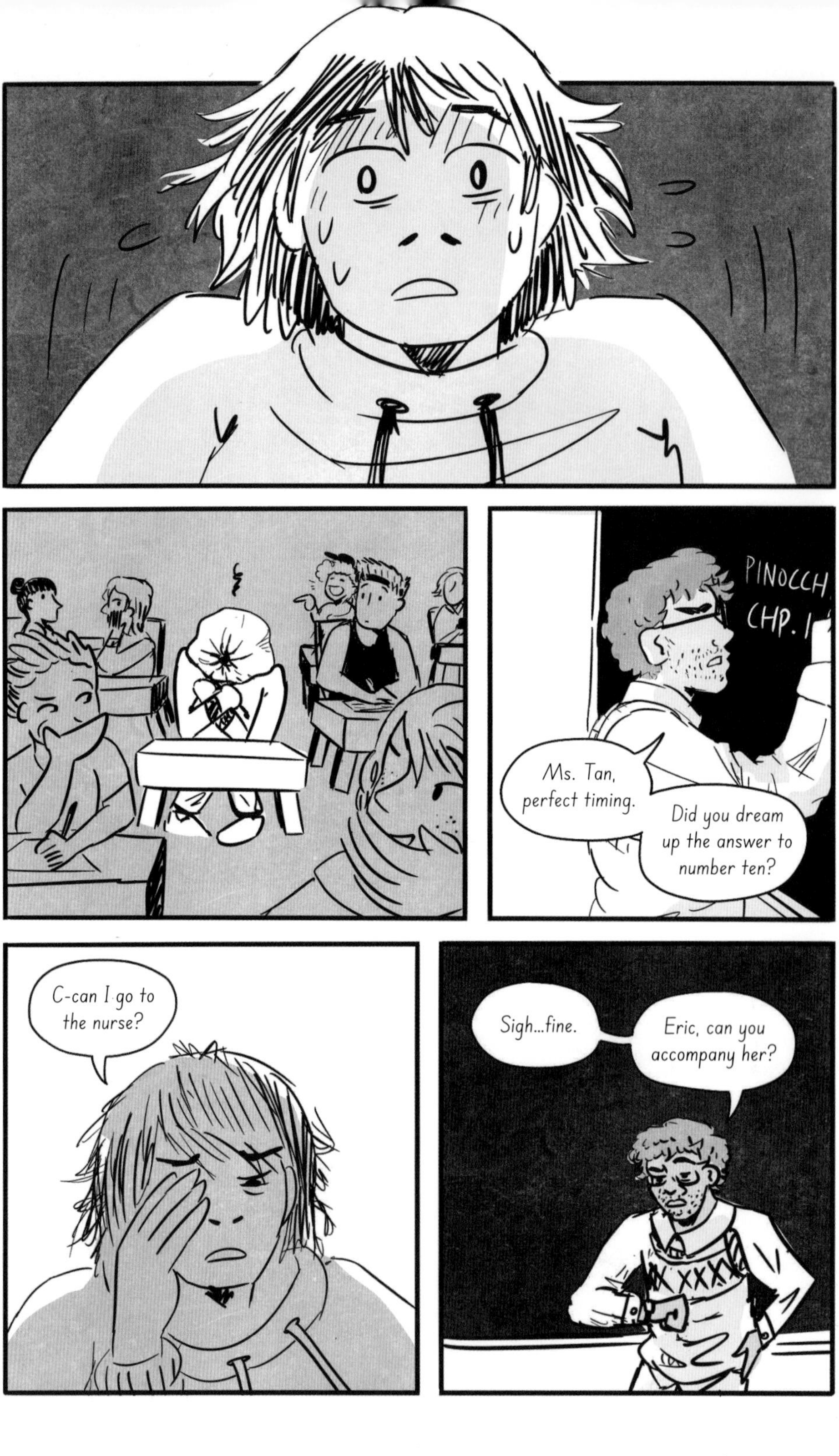
PINOCCH
CHP. 1
Ms. Tan, perfect timing.
Did you dream up the answer to number ten?
C-can I go to the nurse?
Sigh...fine.
Eric, can you accompany her?

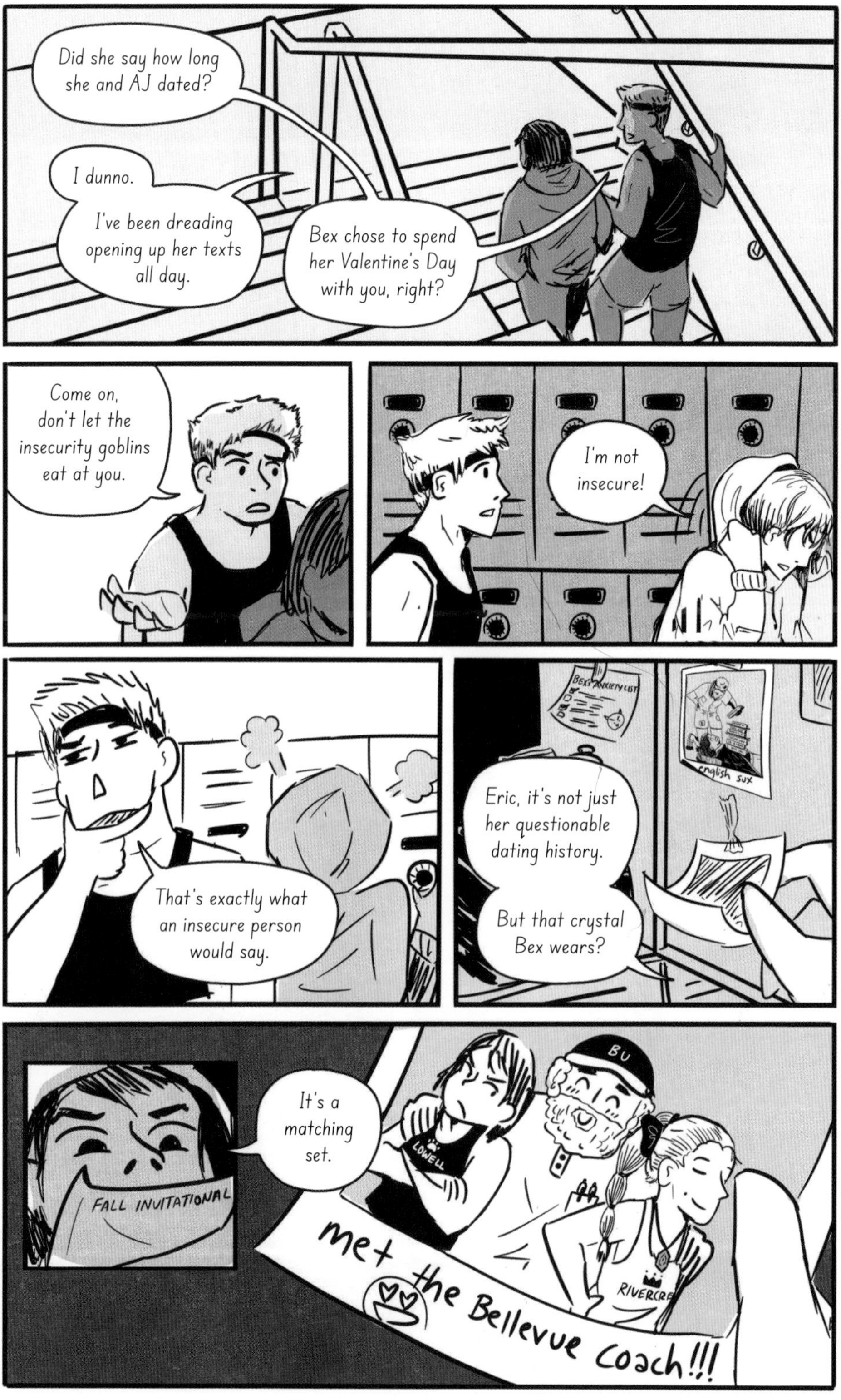

Did she say how long she and AJ dated?
I dunno.
I've been dreading opening up her texts all day.
Bex chose to spend her Valentine's Day with you, right?
Come on, don't let the insecurity goblins eat at you.
I'm not insecure!
That's exactly what an insecure person would say.
english sux
Eric, it's not just her questionable dating history.
But that crystal Bex wears?
It's a matching set.
FALL INVITATIONAL
BU
LOWELL
met the Bellevue coach!!!

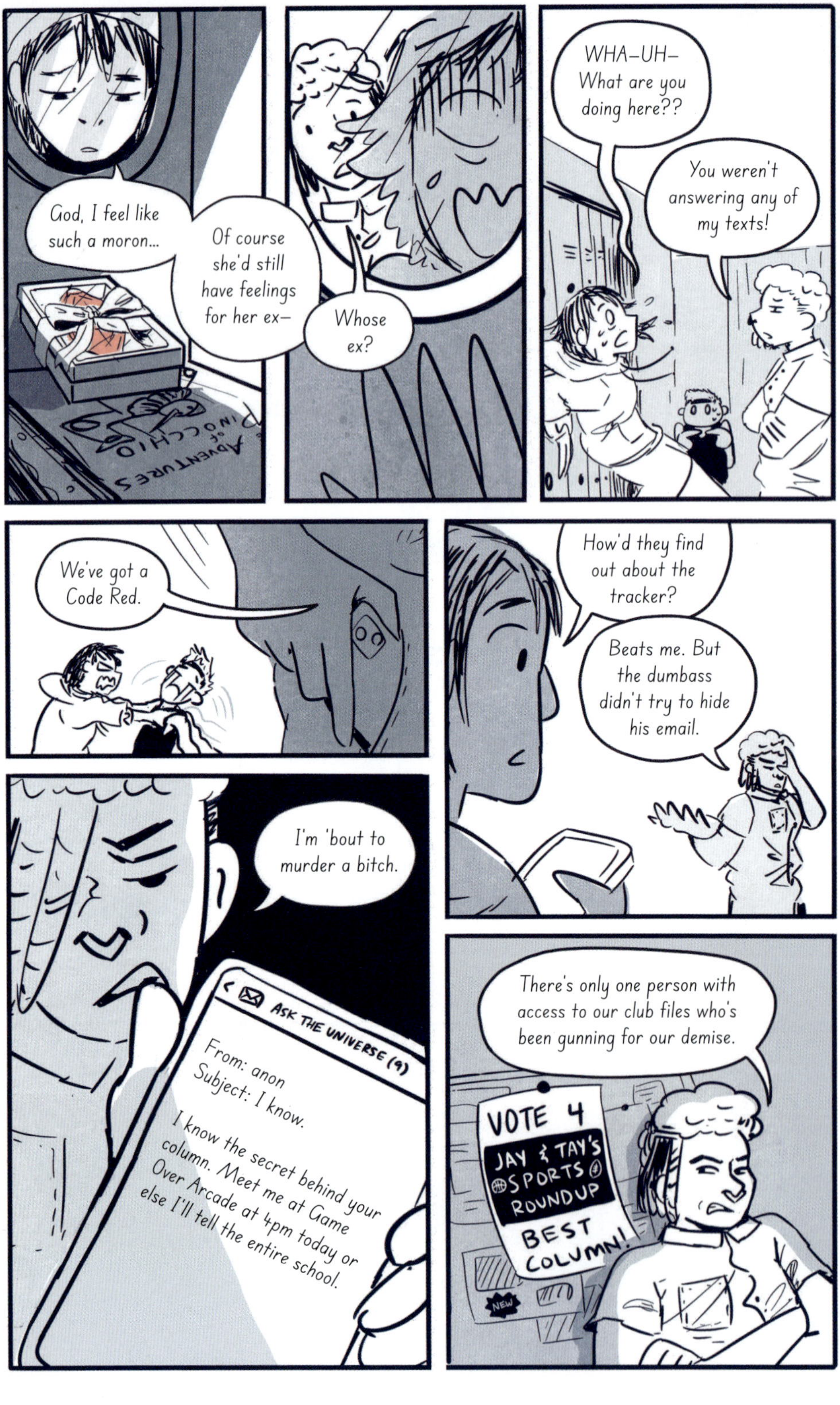
God, I feel like such a moron...
Of course she'd still have feelings for her ex—
Whose ex?
WHA—UH— What are you doing here??
You weren't answering any of my texts!
We've got a Code Red.
How'd they find out about the tracker?
Beats me. But the dumbass didn't try to hide his email.
I'm 'bout to murder a bitch.
ASK THE UNIVERSE (9)
From: anon
Subject: I know.
I know the secret behind your column. Meet me at Game Over Arcade at 4pm today or else I'll tell the entire school.
There's only one person with access to our club files who's been gunning for our demise.
VOTE 4
JAY & TAY'S SPORTS ROUNDUP
BEST COLUMN!
NEW

JAY BUTLER, YA BETTER SHOW YOUR UGLY FACE WHILE YOU STILL HAVE ONE!

RE: I know

Are you trying to get kicked out?! Go into Mecha War VR Machine. Player 2. Don't try anything or you'll be sorry.

4:42
NEW EMAIL

"You'll be sorry," pfft. Is he trying to sound like some cartoon villain?

175

I **told you** the trackers were a bad idea.

And I told you I'd handle it.

Right. Whatever you say.

SIR STABBY

CLAWABUNGA

All right, Jay. No more games.

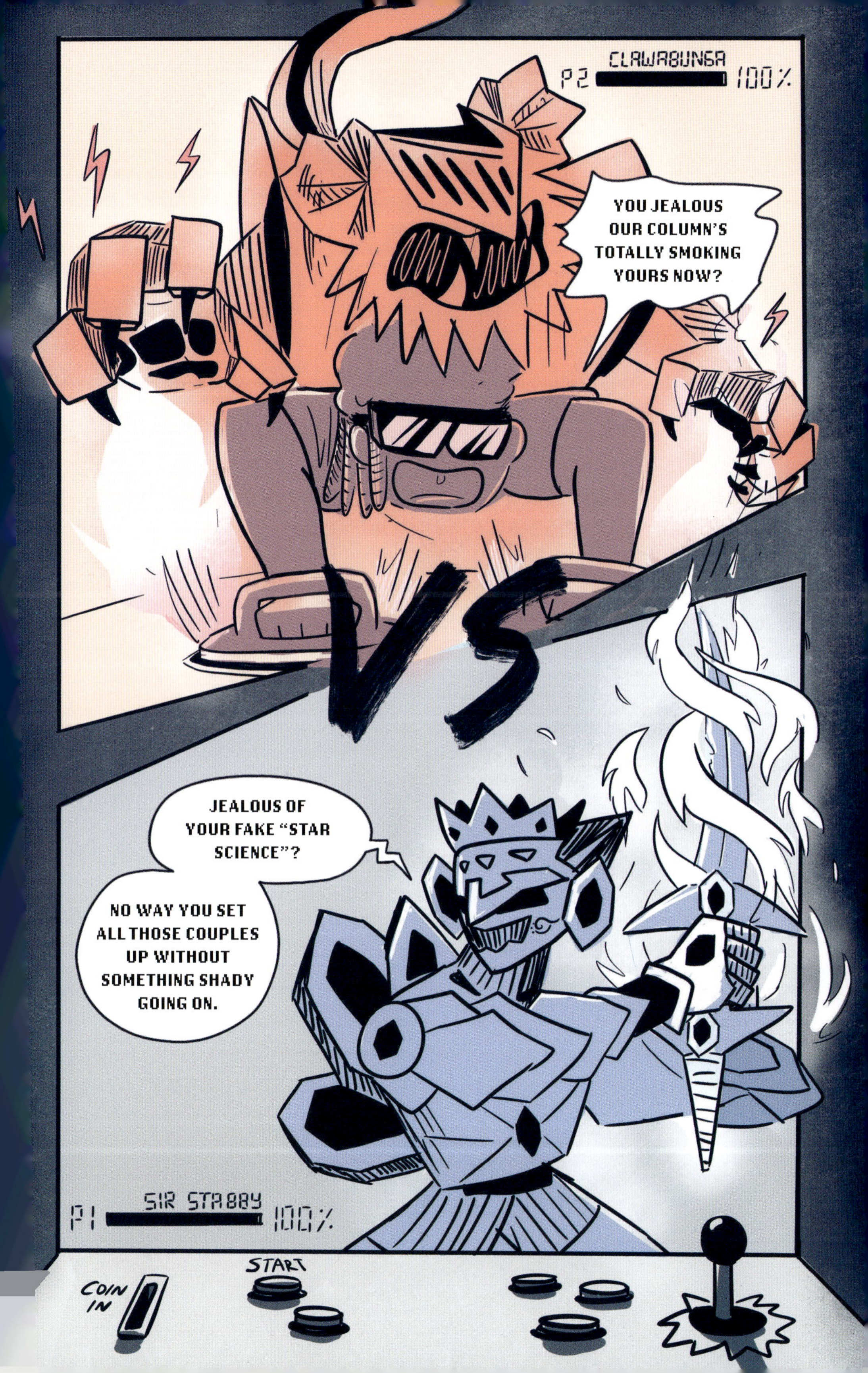
P2 CLAWABUNGA 100%
YOU JEALOUS OUR COLUMN'S TOTALLY SMOKING YOURS NOW?
VS
JEALOUS OF YOUR FAKE "STAR SCIENCE"?
NO WAY YOU SET ALL THOSE COUPLES UP WITHOUT SOMETHING SHADY GOING ON.
P1 SIR STABBY 100%
COIN IN
START

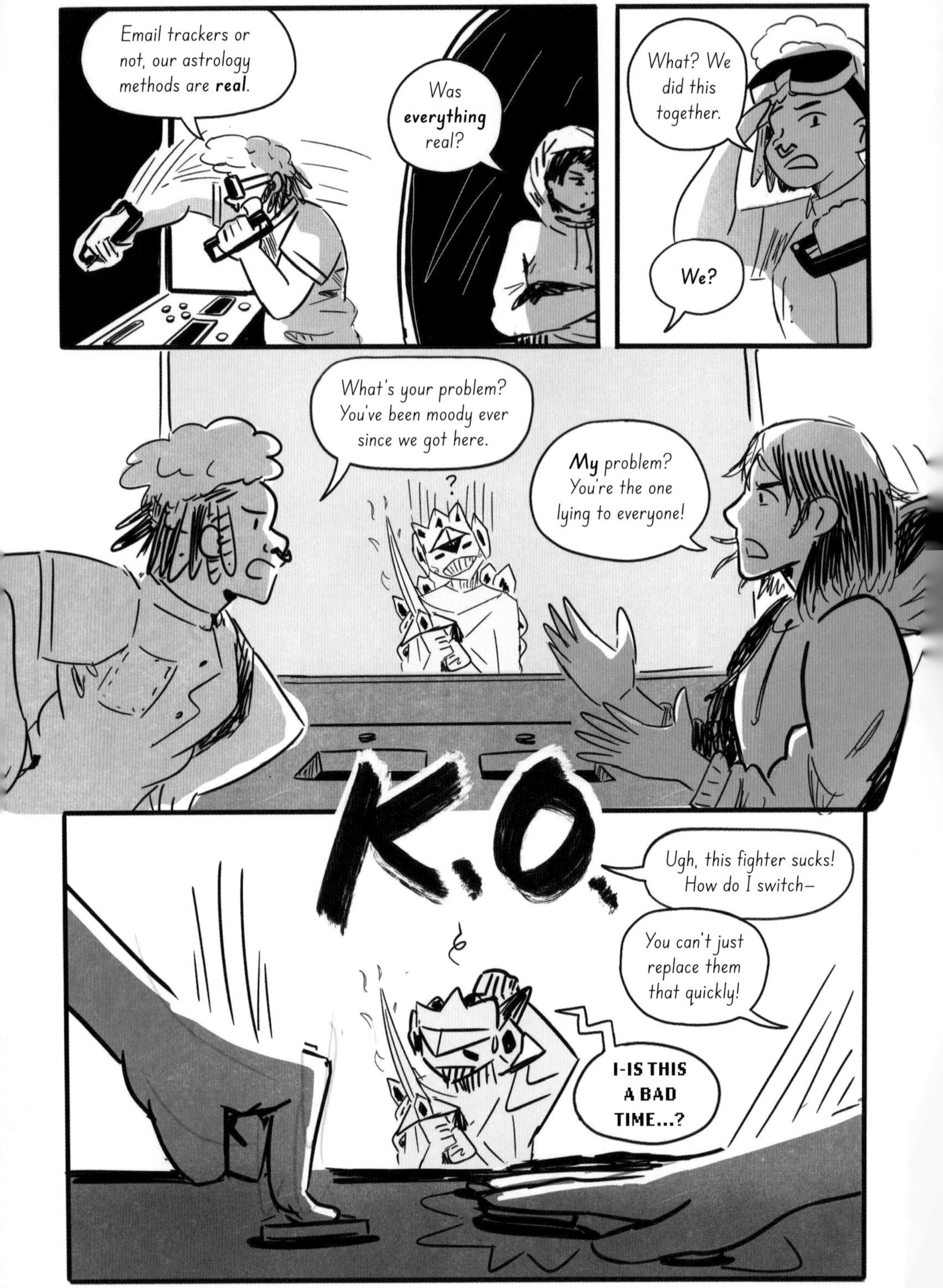
Email trackers or not, our astrology methods are **real**.
Was **everything** real?
What? We did this together.
We?
What's your problem? You've been moody ever since we got here.
?
My problem? You're the one lying to everyone!
K.O.
Ugh, this fighter sucks! How do I switch—
You can't just replace them that quickly!
I-IS THIS A BAD TIME...?

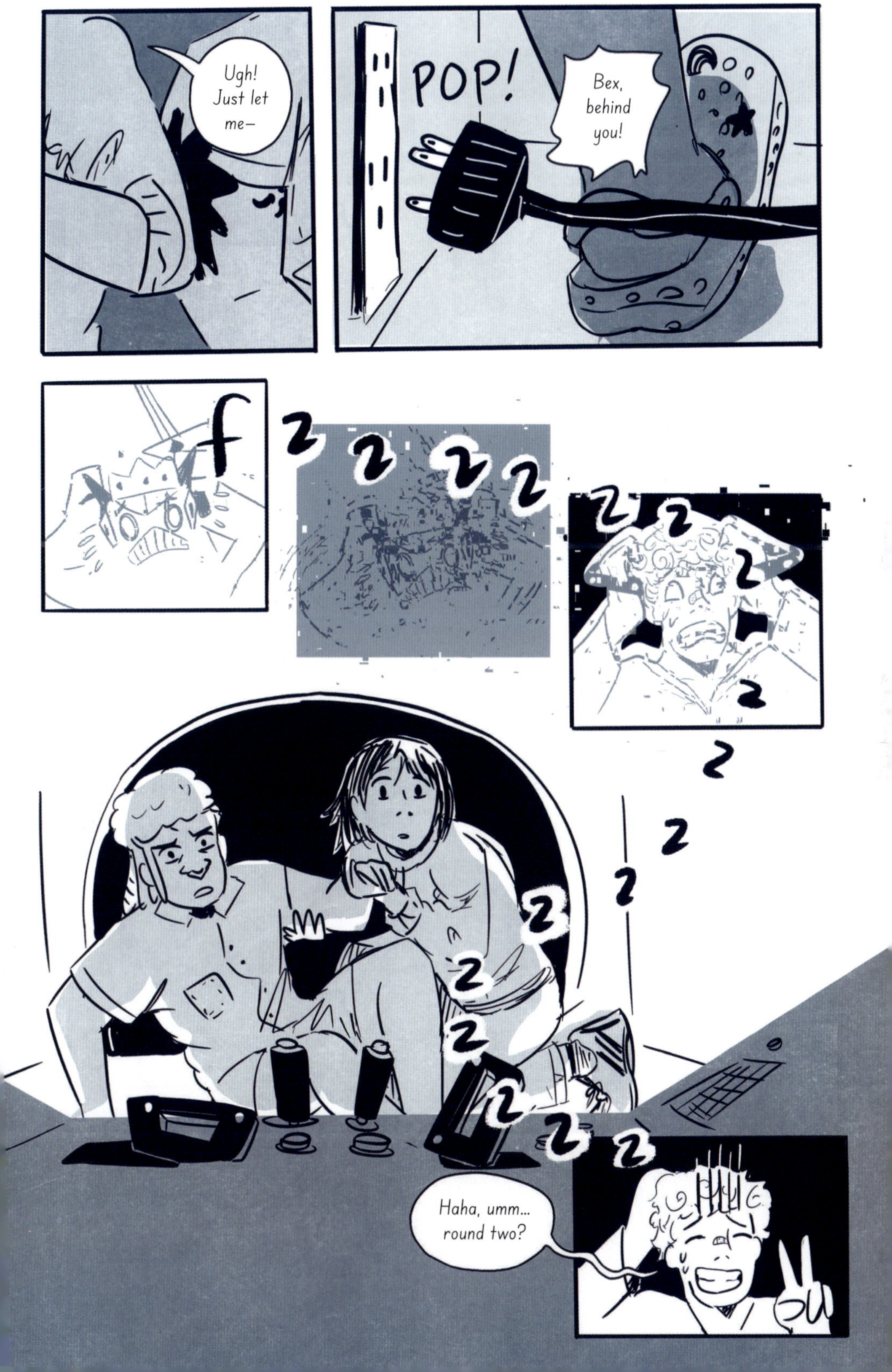
Ugh! Just let me—
POP!
Bex, behind you!
fzzzzzzzzzzzzzzz
Haha, umm… round two?

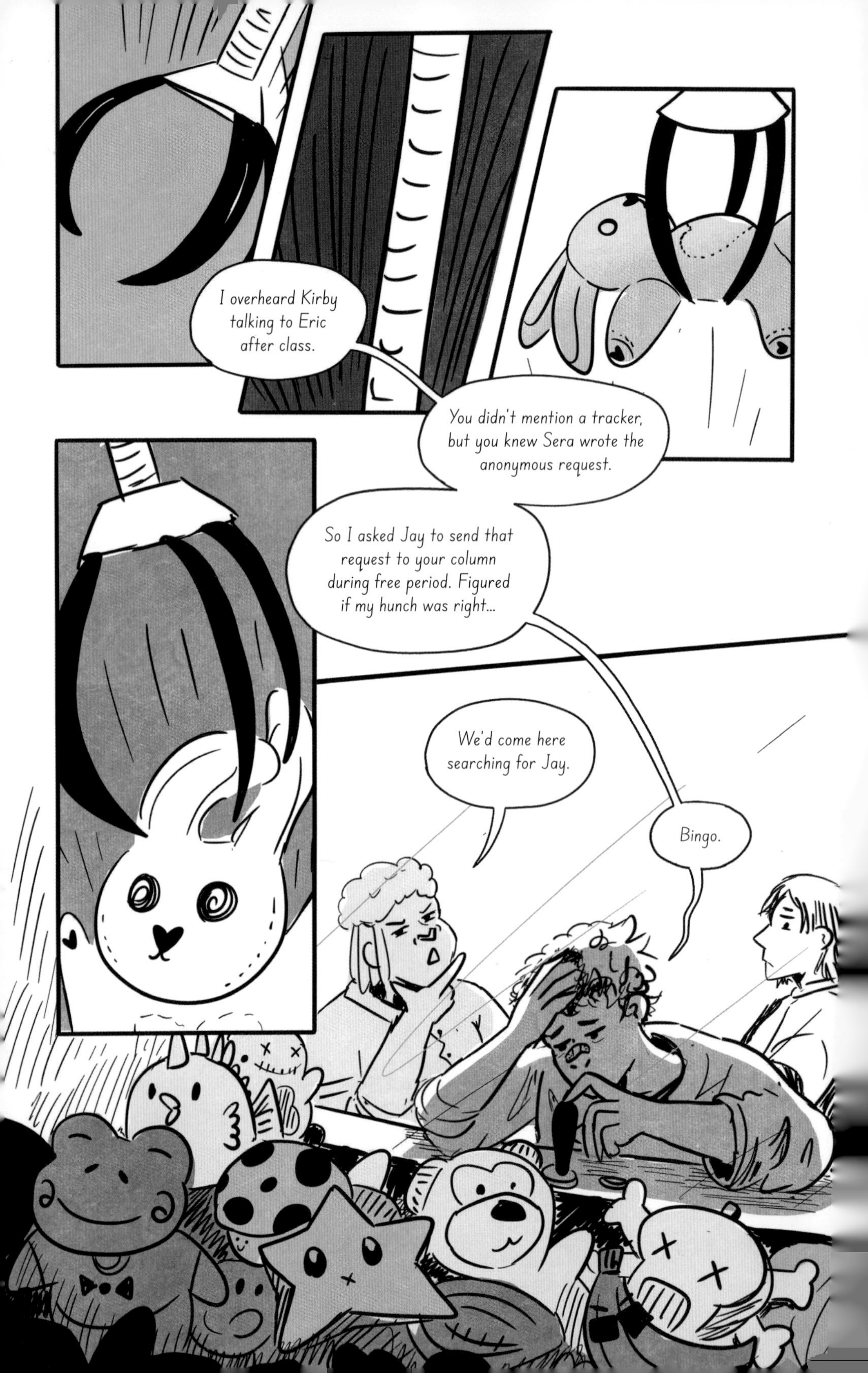
I overheard Kirby talking to Eric after class.
You didn't mention a tracker, but you knew Sera wrote the anonymous request.
So I asked Jay to send that request to your column during free period. Figured if my hunch was right...
We'd come here searching for Jay.
Bingo.

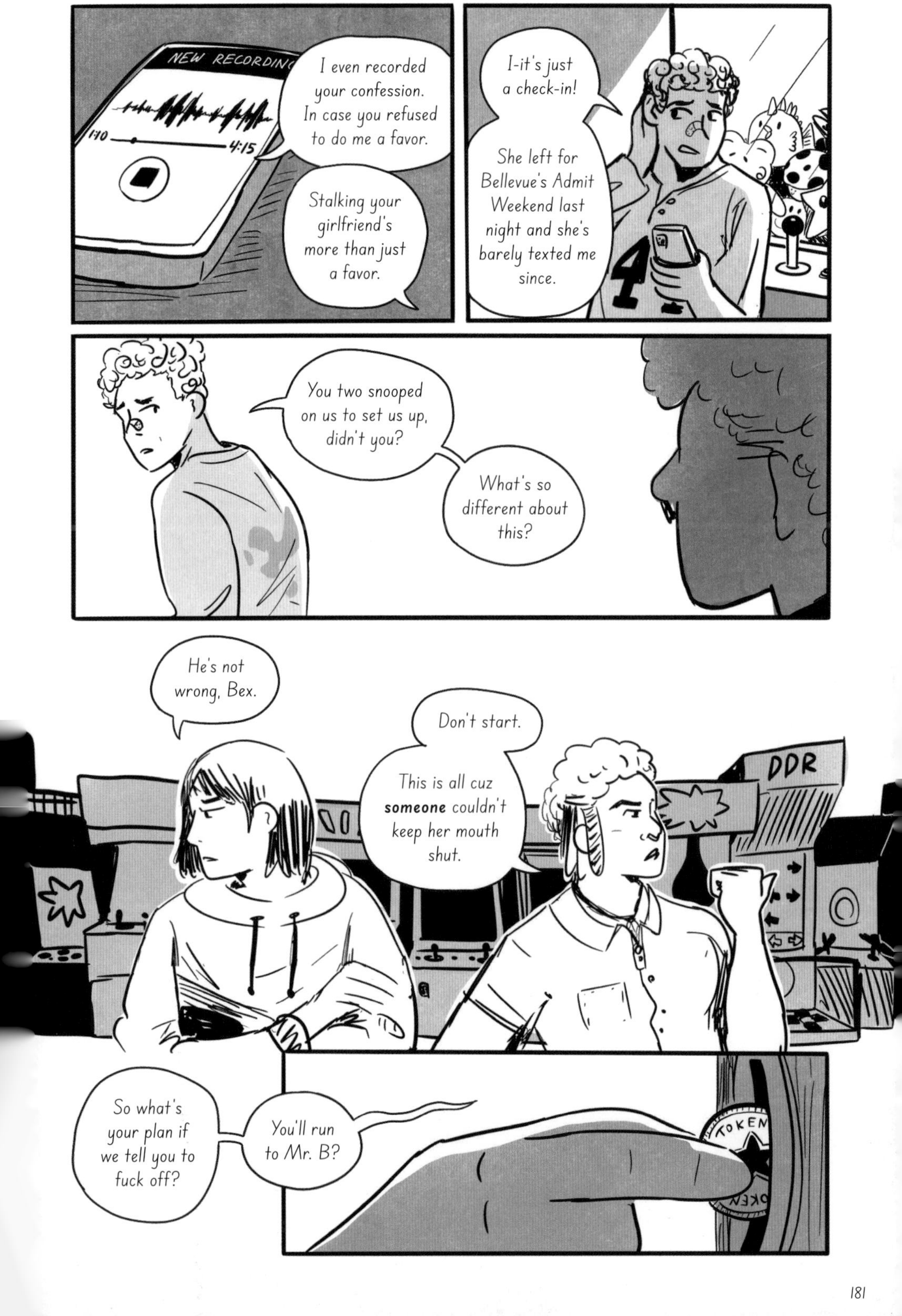
NEW RECORDING
1:10
4:15
I even recorded your confession. In case you refused to do me a favor.
Stalking your girlfriend's more than just a favor.
I-it's just a check-in!
She left for Bellevue's Admit Weekend last night and she's barely texted me since.
You two snooped on us to set us up, didn't you?
What's so different about this?
He's not wrong, Bex.
Don't start.
This is all cuz **someone** couldn't keep her mouth shut.
DDR
So what's your plan if we tell you to fuck off?
You'll run to Mr. B?
TOKEN

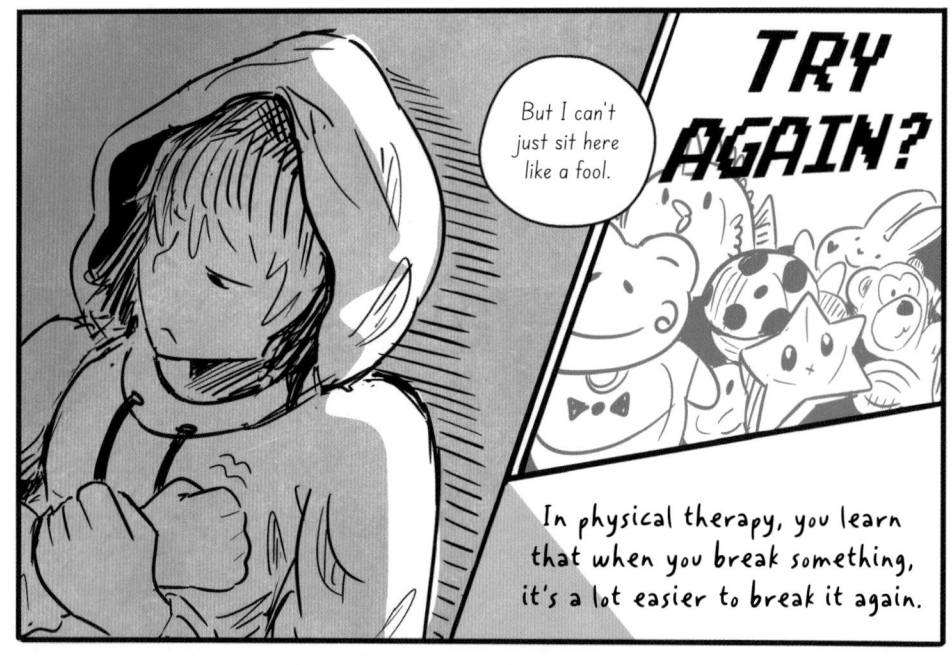

"I don't— No... I don't even have the guts to talk to my own girlfriend."

"Ever since I overheard you talk about Nico, I can't shake off this awful feeling."

TRY AGAIN?

"I'm so...scared. That I'm her second choice. That I've been playing a game I was always bound to lose."

"I don't know what's worse. Knowing or not knowing."

"But I can't just sit here like a fool."

TRY AGAIN?

In physical therapy, you learn that when you break something, it's a lot easier to break it again.

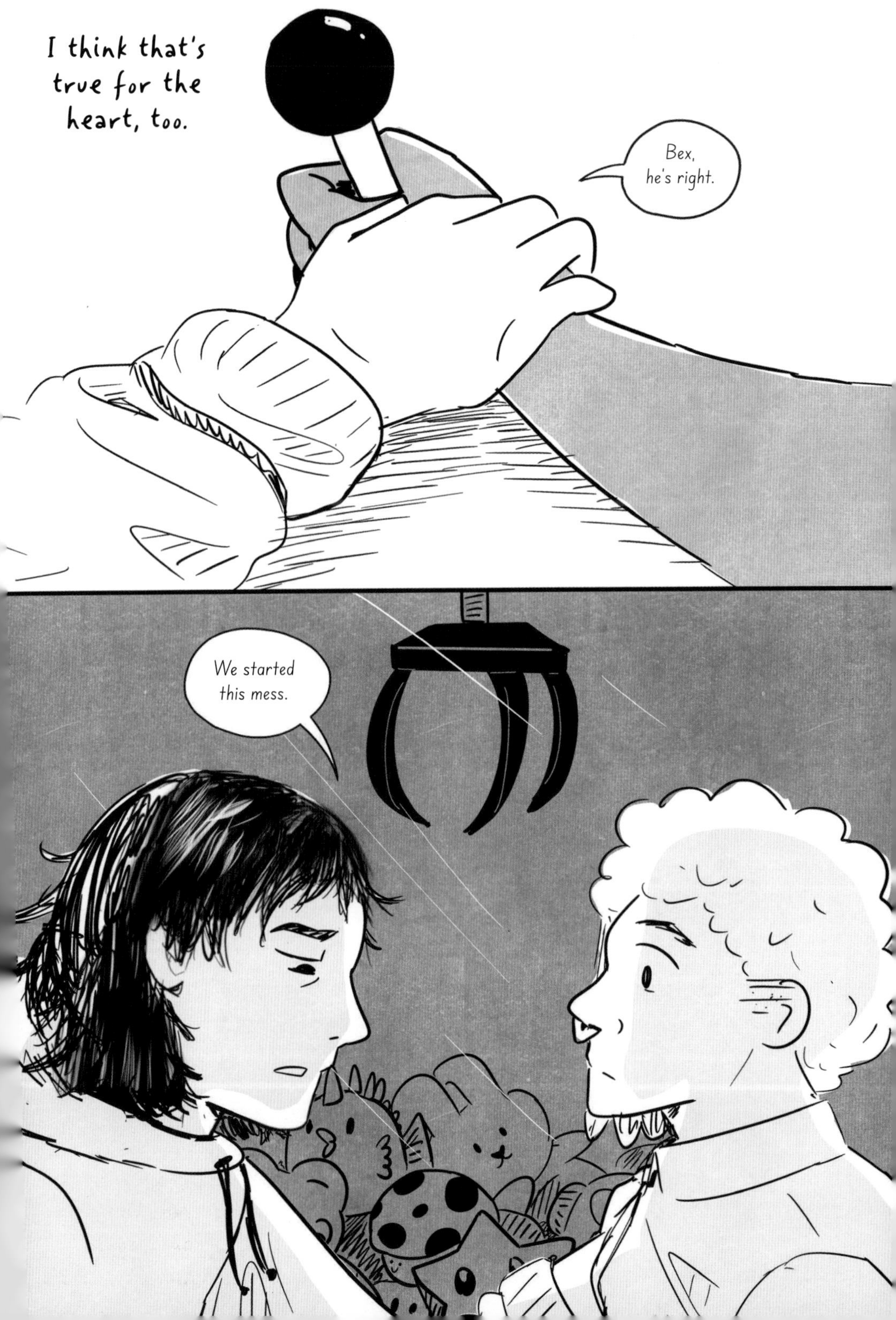
I think that's true for the heart, too.
Bex, he's right.
We started this mess.

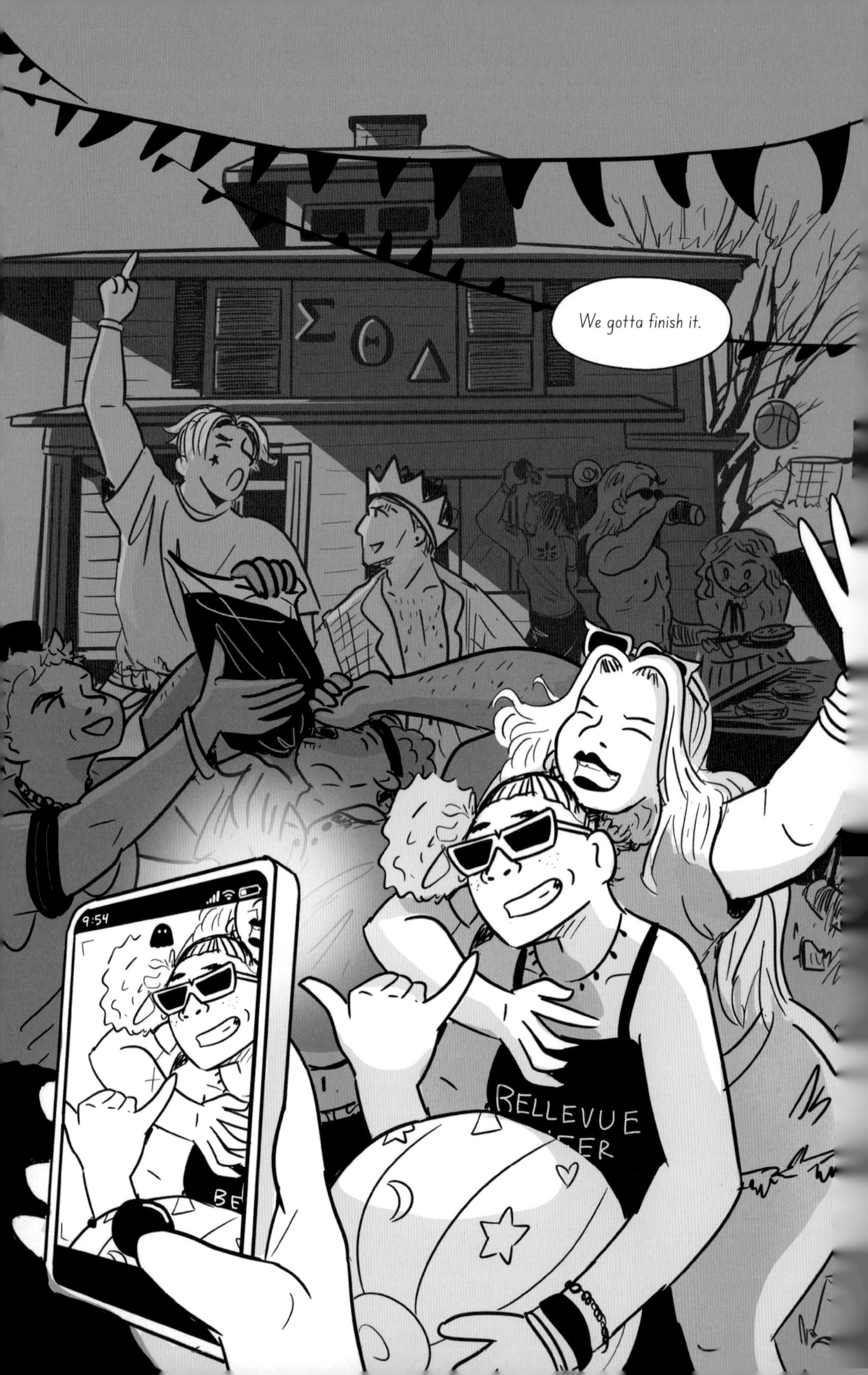
ΣΘΔ
We gotta finish it.
9:54
RELLEVUE

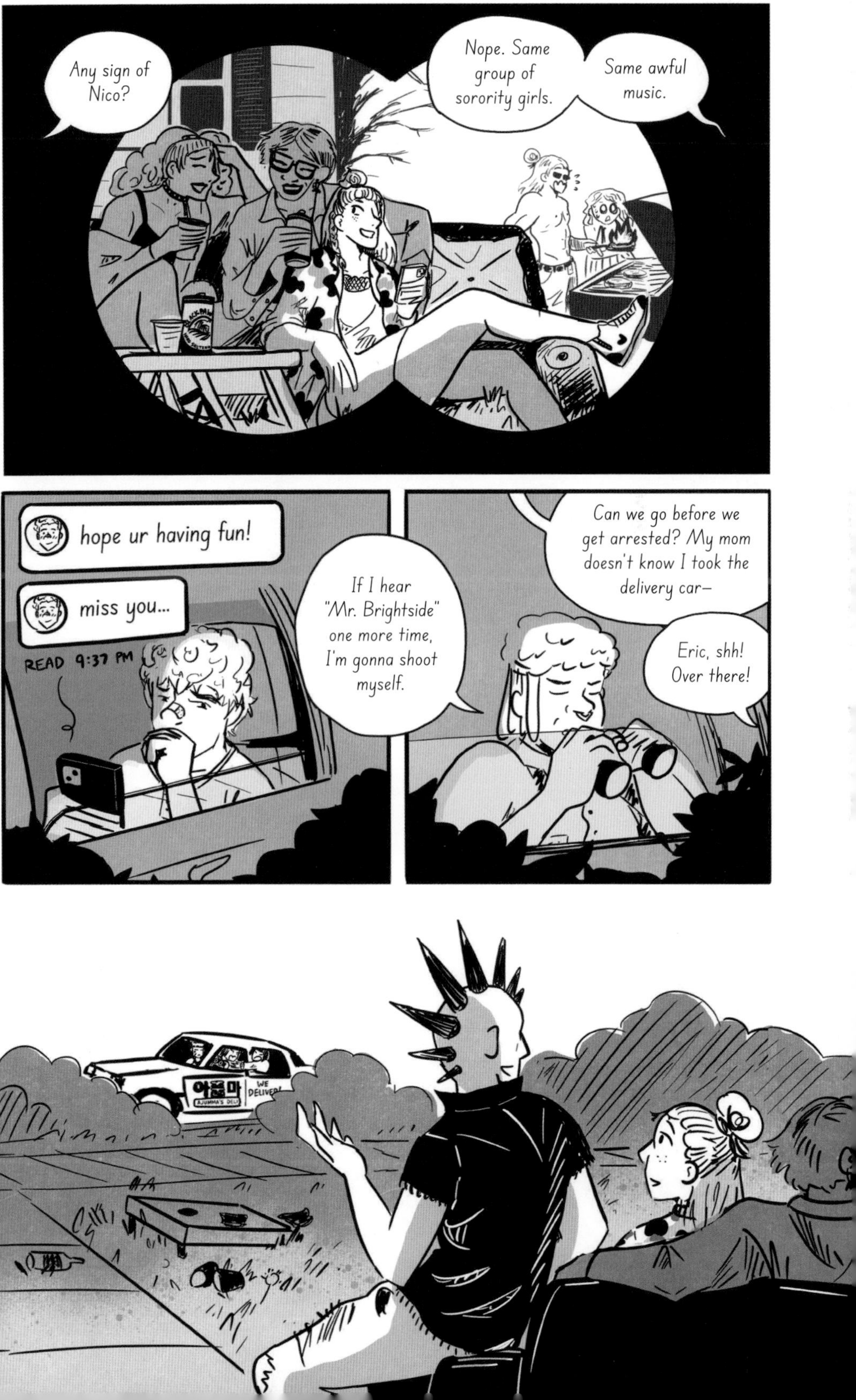

Any sign of Nico?
Nope. Same group of sorority girls.
Same awful music.
hope ur having fun!
miss you...
READ 9:37 PM
If I hear "Mr. Brightside" one more time, I'm gonna shoot myself.
Can we go before we get arrested? My mom doesn't know I took the delivery car—
Eric, shh! Over there!
아줌마
AJUMMA'S DELI
WE

NOD

I knew it! I need to—

SLAM

Get back in here! I bet she'd just love to find out her boyfriend's spying on her!

I can't just sit here!

They're going inside the frat house!

GULP W-what if we call up Kirby's church aunties instead? Right, K-Kirby?

Go, Eric! These are your people!

M-m-my people?!

KIRBY?!

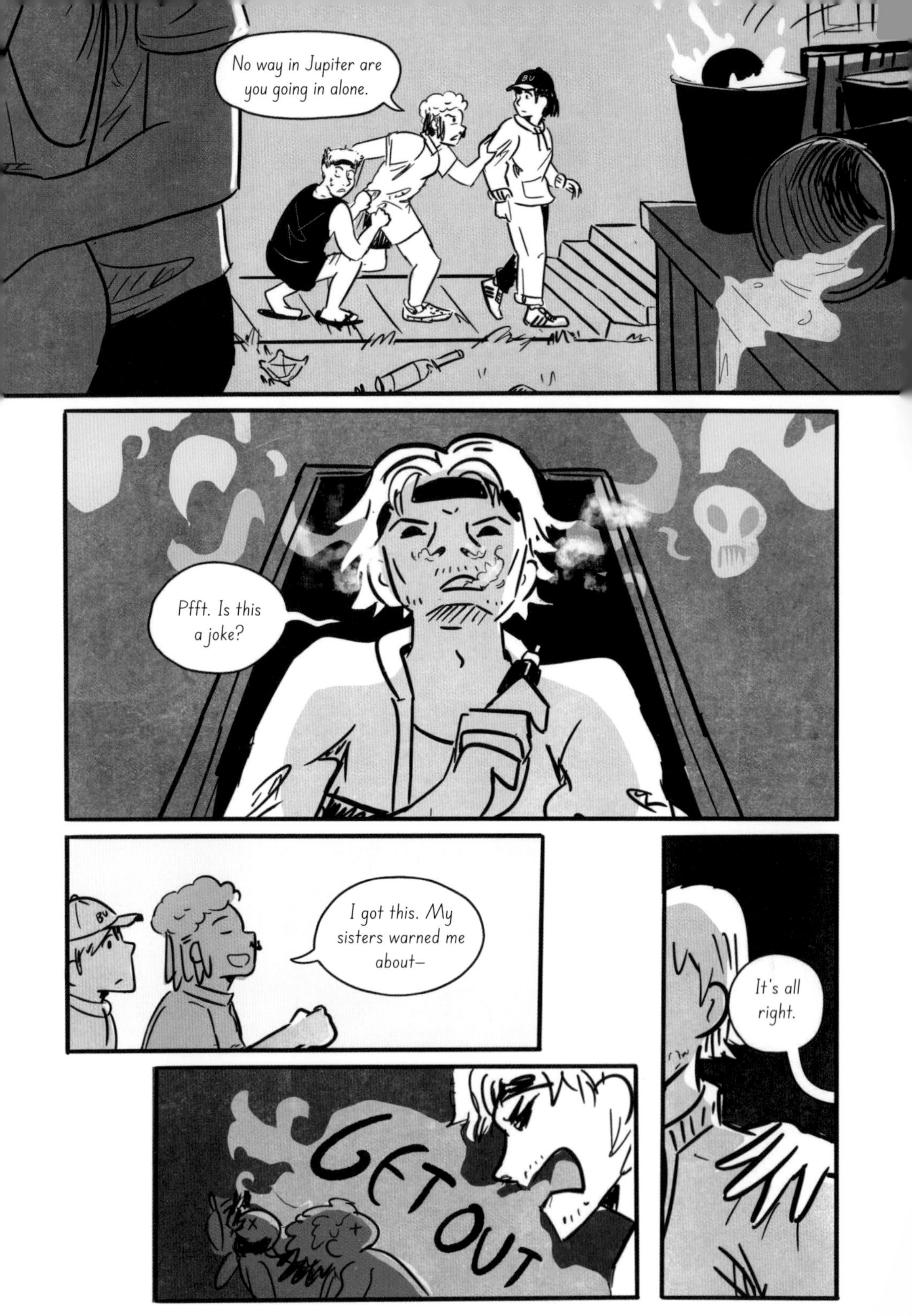
No way in Jupiter are you going in alone.
Pfft. Is this a joke?
I got this. My sisters warned me about–
It's all right.
GET OUT

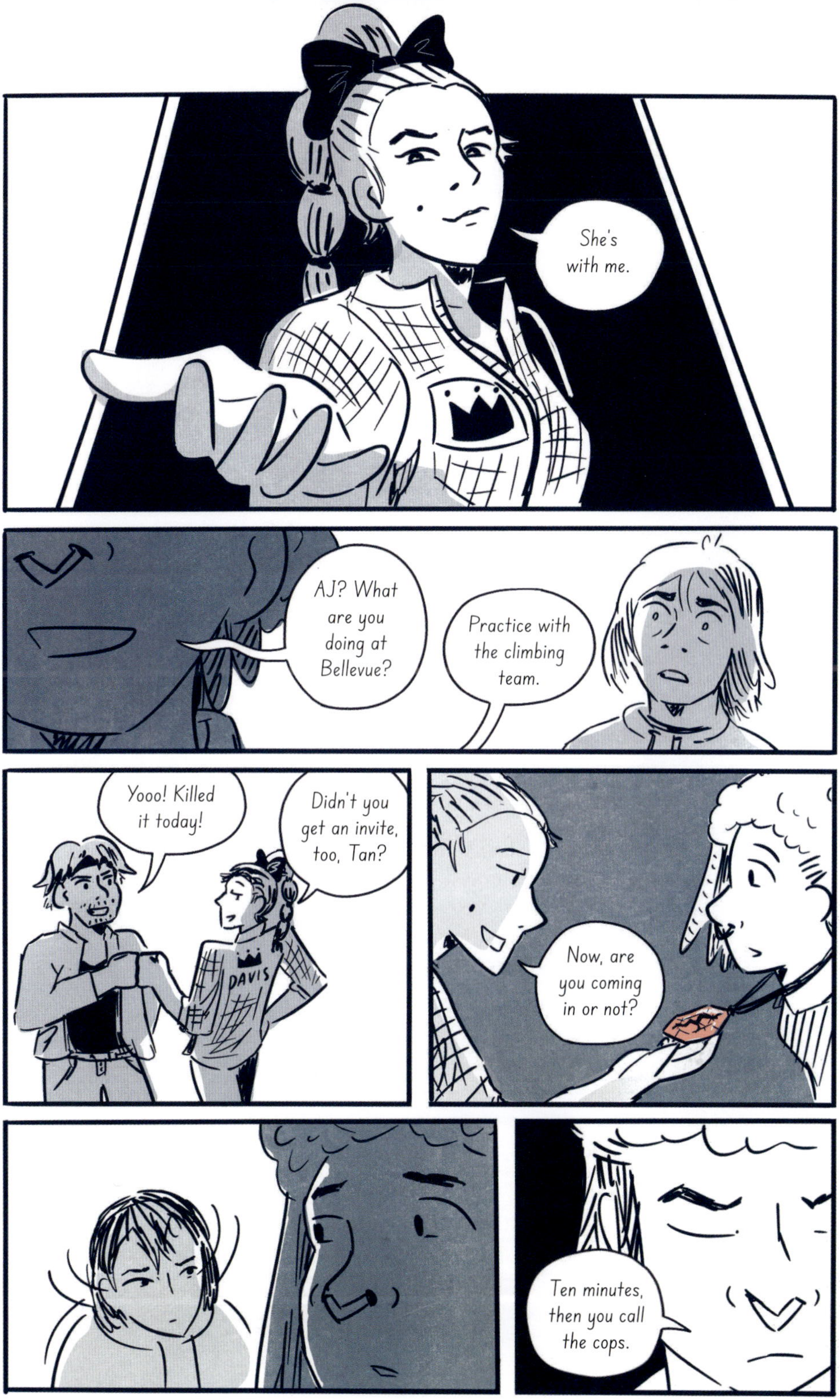
She's with me.
AJ? What are you doing at Bellevue?
Practice with the climbing team.
Yooo! Killed it today!
Didn't you get an invite, too, Tan?
DAVIS
Now, are you coming in or not?
Ten minutes, then you call the cops.

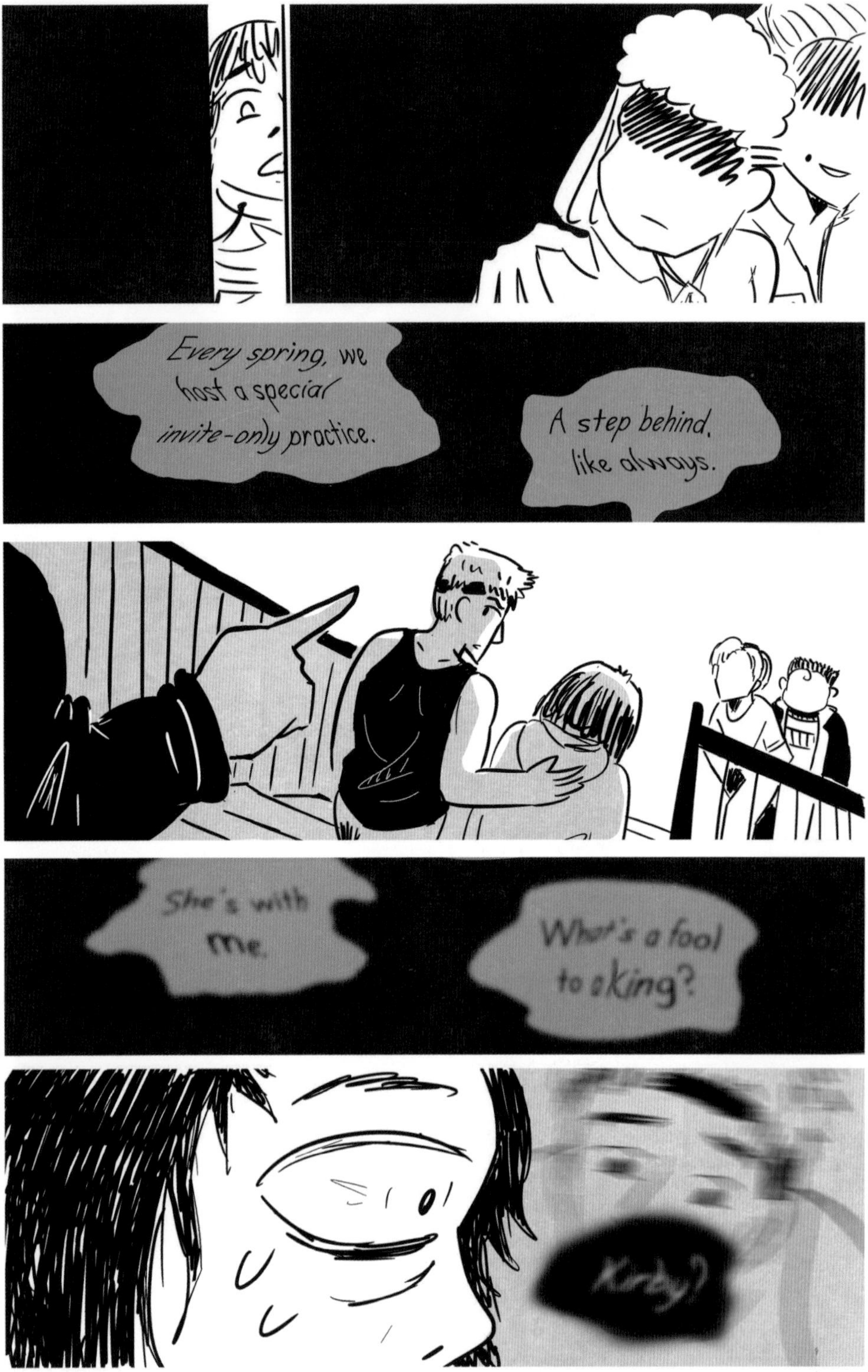
Every spring, we host a special invite-only practice.
A step behind, like always.
She's with me.
What's a fool to a King?

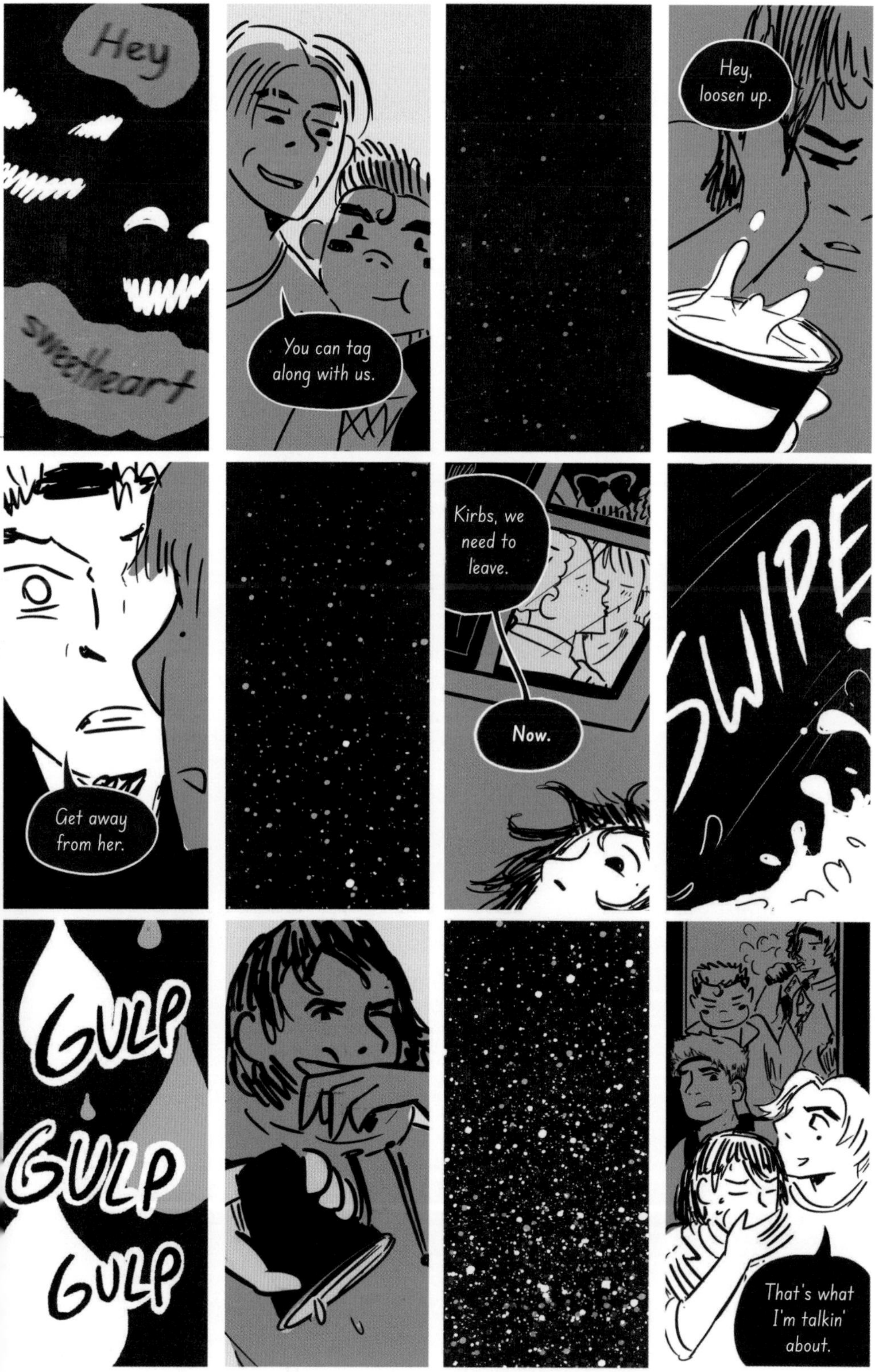
Hey
sweetheart
You can tag along with us.
Hey, loosen up.
Get away from her.
Kirbs, we need to leave.
Now.
SWIPE
GULP
GULP
GULP
That's what I'm talkin' about.

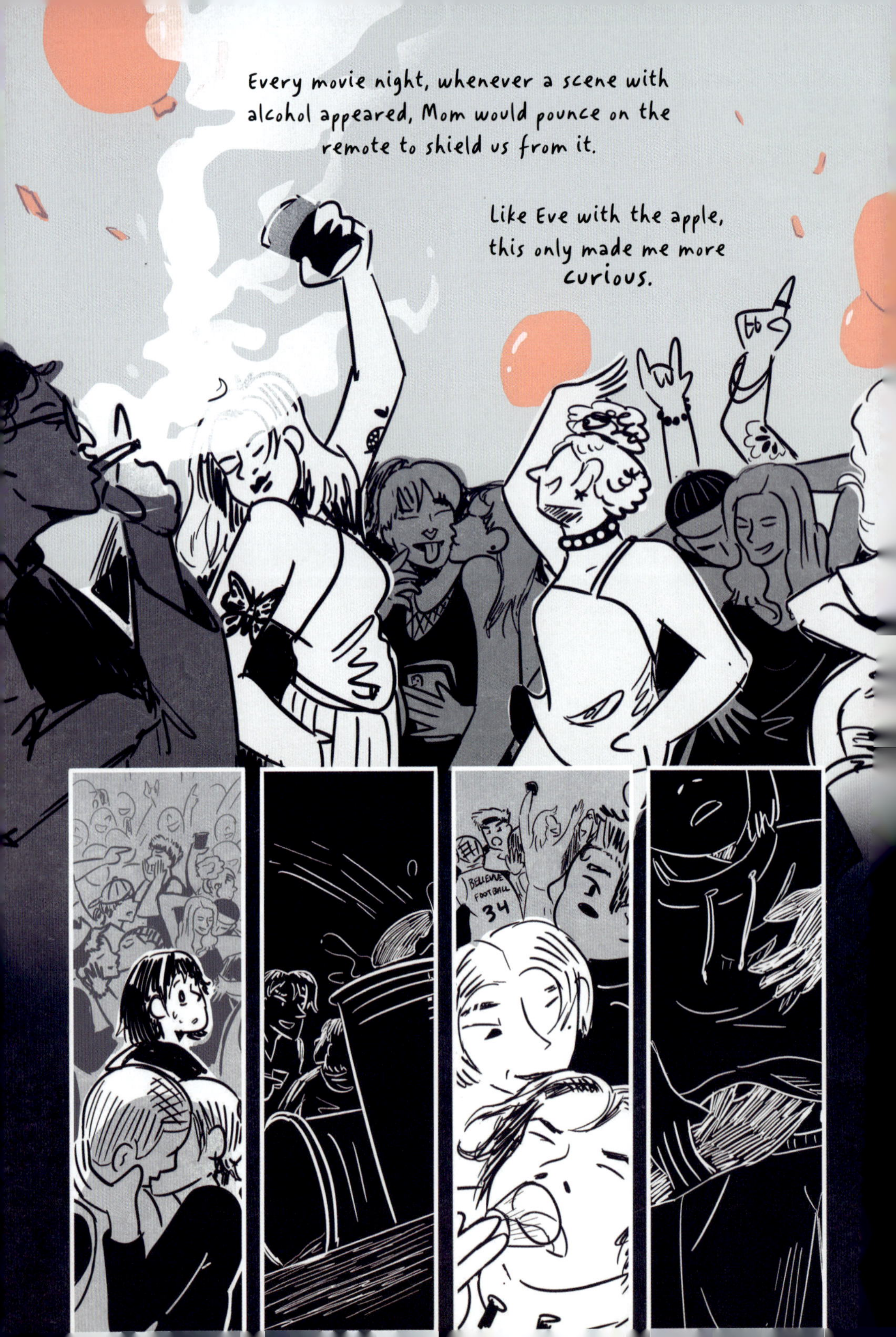
Every movie night, whenever a scene with alcohol appeared, Mom would pounce on the remote to shield us from it.
Like Eve with the apple, this only made me more curious.
BELLEVUE FOOTBALL 34

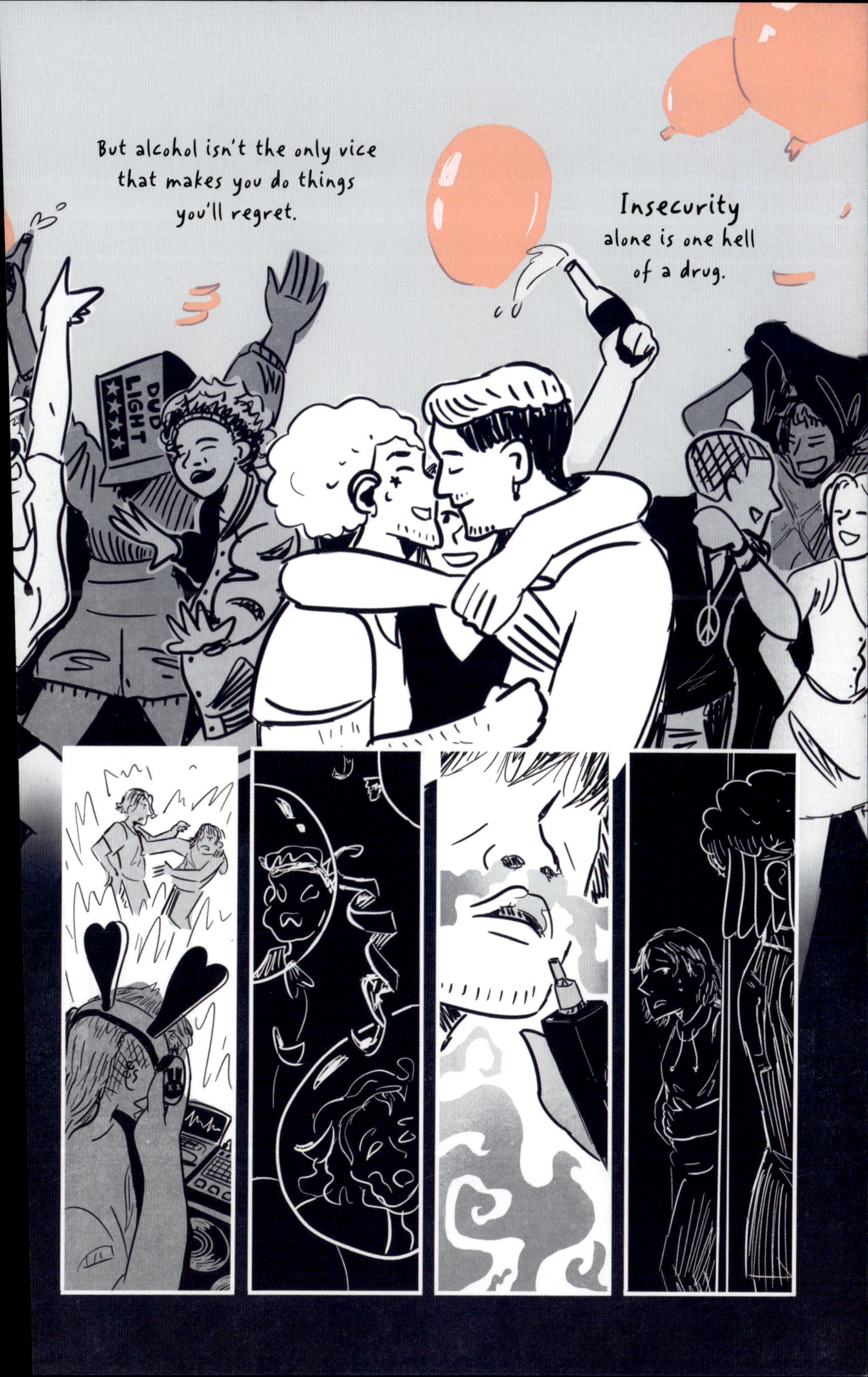
But alcohol isn't the only vice that makes you do things you'll regret.
Insecurity alone is one hell of a drug.
DUD LIGHT

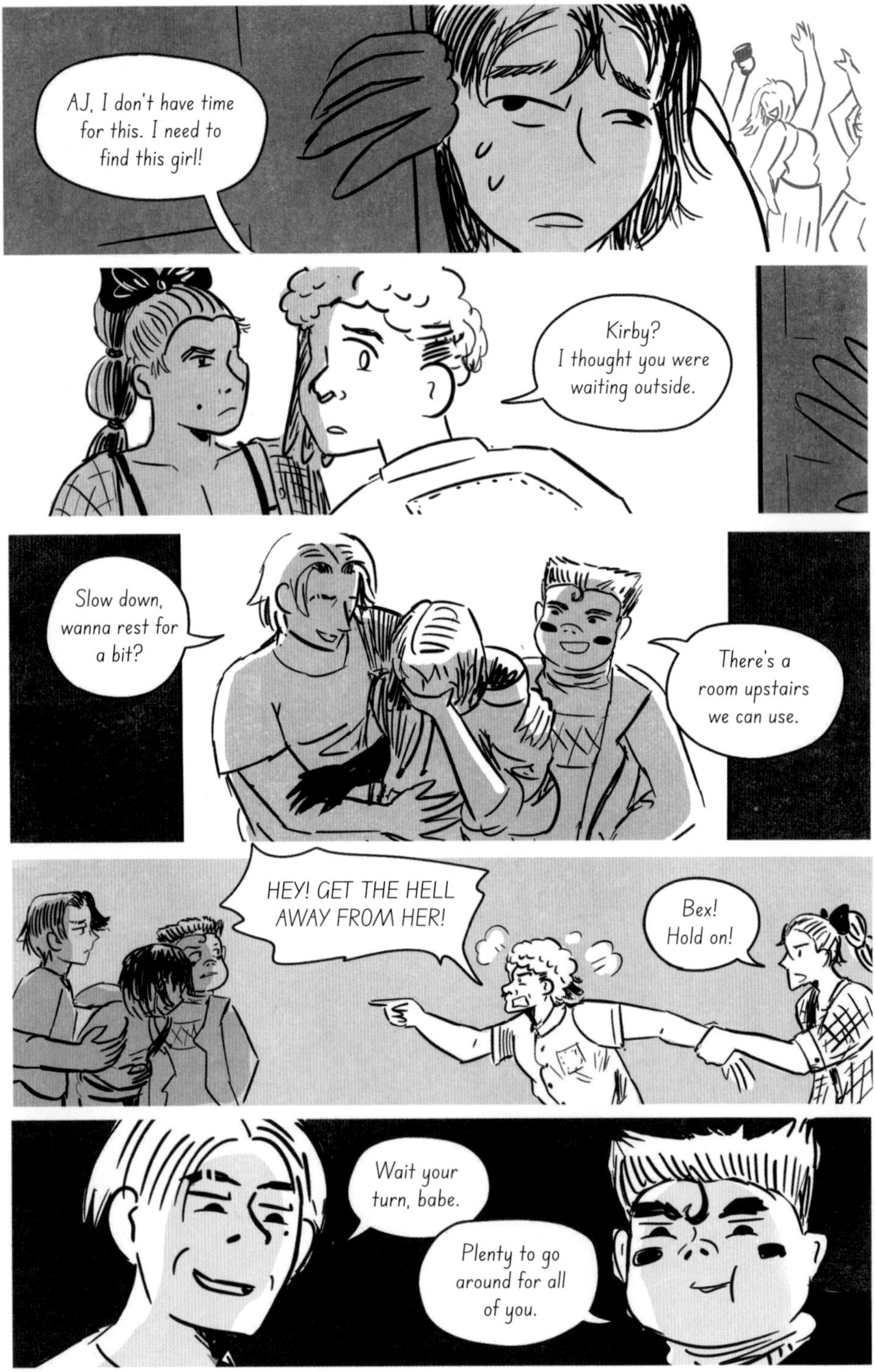

AJ, I don't have time for this. I need to find this girl!
Kirby? I thought you were waiting outside.
Slow down, wanna rest for a bit?
There's a room upstairs we can use.
HEY! GET THE HELL AWAY FROM HER!
Bex! Hold on!
Wait your turn, babe.
Plenty to go around for all of you.

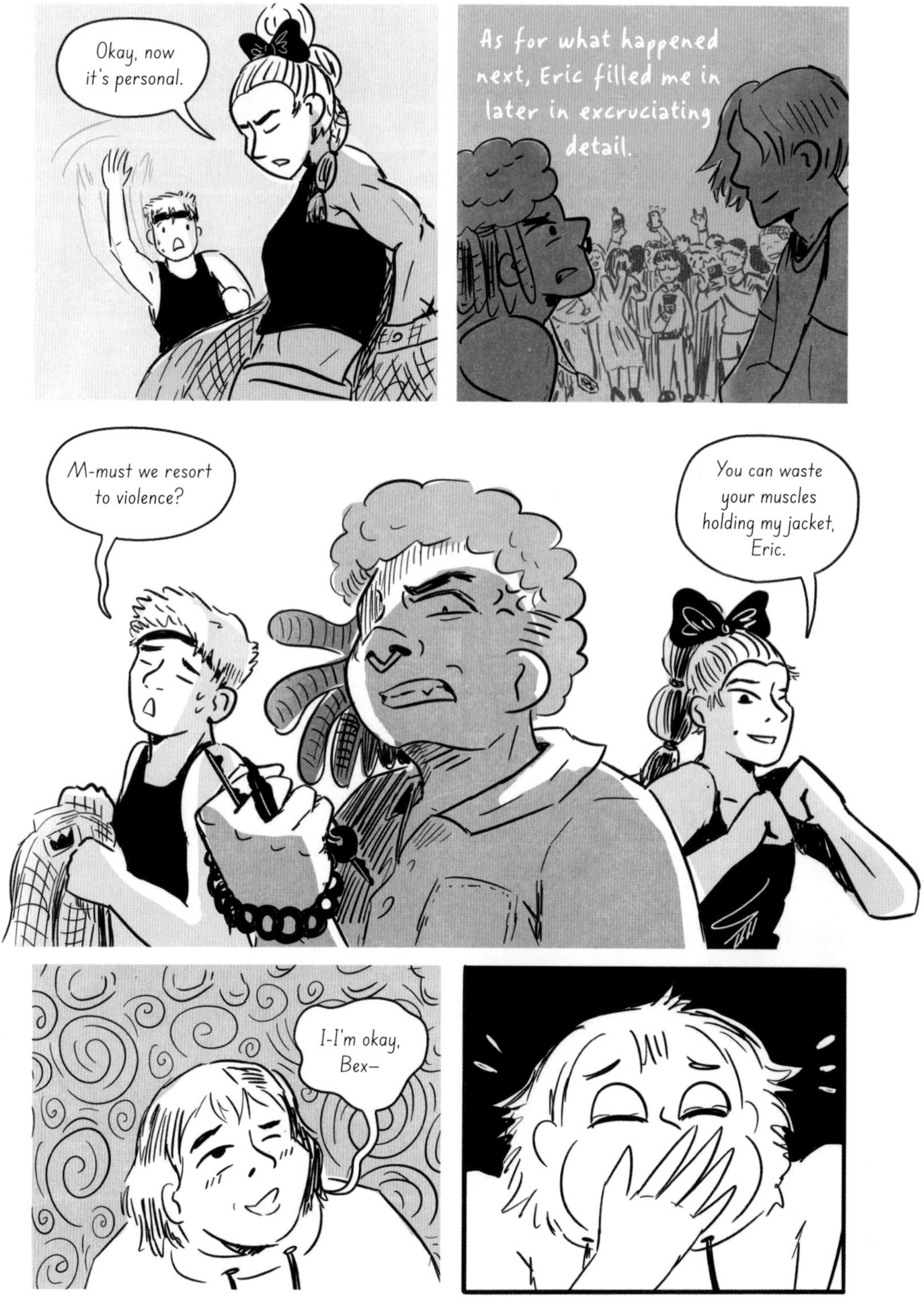
Okay, now it's personal.
As for what happened next, Eric filled me in later in excruciating detail.
M-must we resort to violence?
You can waste your muscles holding my jacket, Eric.
I-I'm okay, Bex–

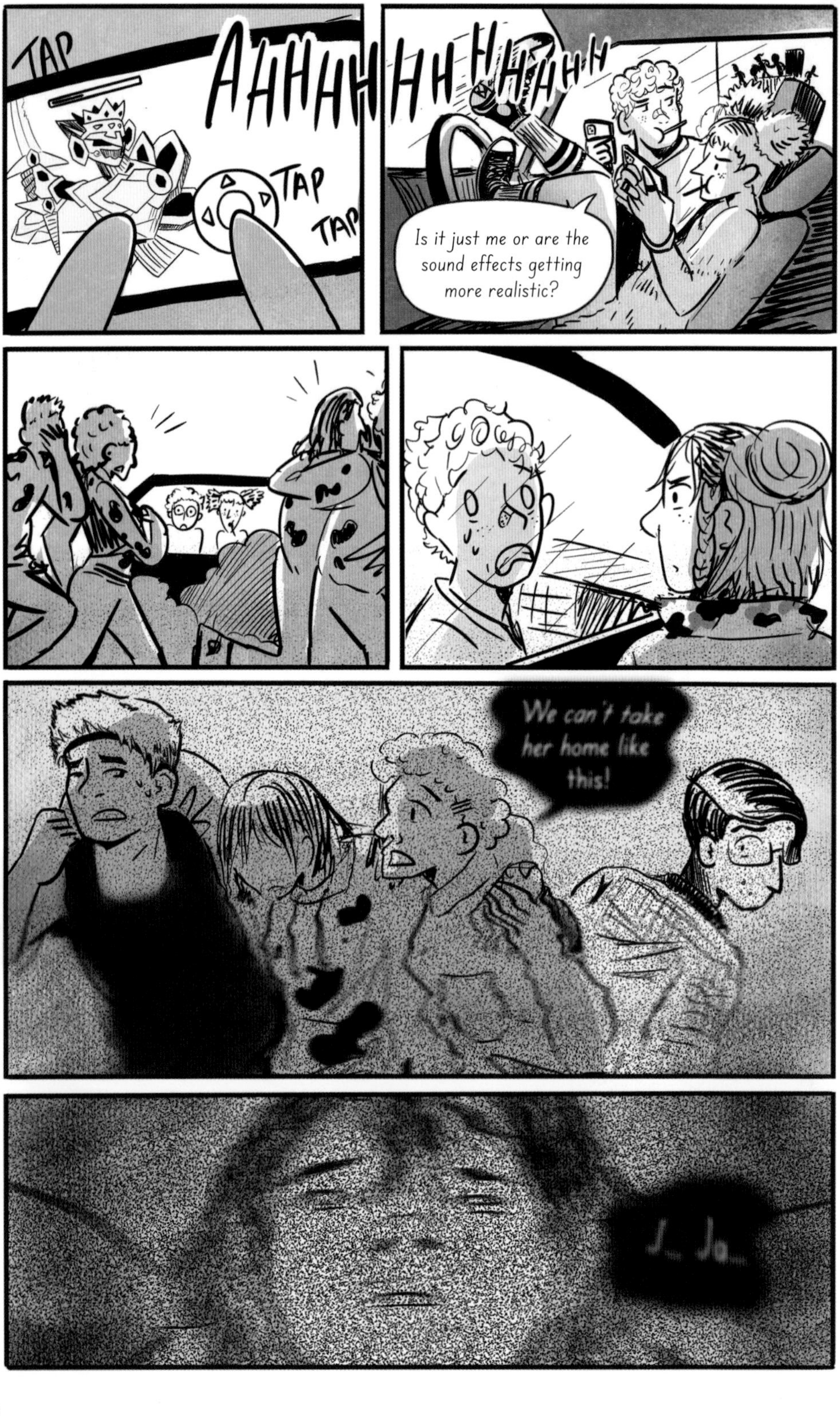
TAP
AHHHHHHHHHHHH
TAP
TAP
Is it just me or are the sound effects getting more realistic?
We can't take her home like this!
J... Jo...

James, stop crying!

W-we shouldn't be back here!

Eww...what do you think Jesus's blood tastes like?

This is the Blood of Christ, which was shed for you.

What if my dad finds us?

Can you stop being a PK for once?

I'm literally the pastor's kid! What does that even mean?

See? You're so innocent you don't even know!

Fine, go be chicken.

Aren't you even a little curious?

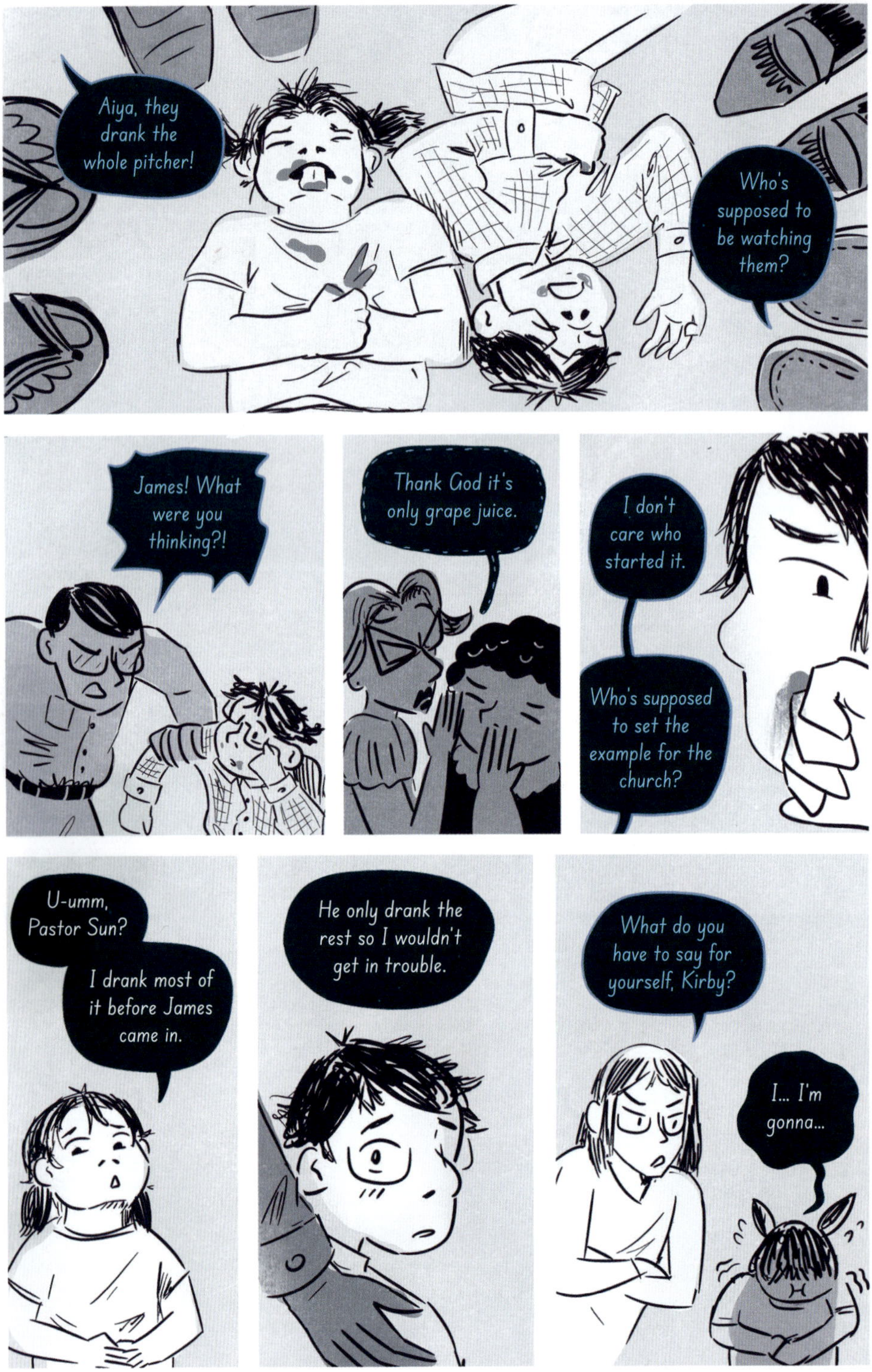
Aiya, they drank the whole pitcher!
Who's supposed to be watching them?
James! What were you thinking?!
Thank God it's only grape juice.
I don't care who started it.
Who's supposed to set the example for the church?
U-umm, Pastor Sun?
I drank most of it before James came in.
He only drank the rest so I wouldn't get in trouble.
What do you have to say for yourself, Kirby?
I... I'm gonna...

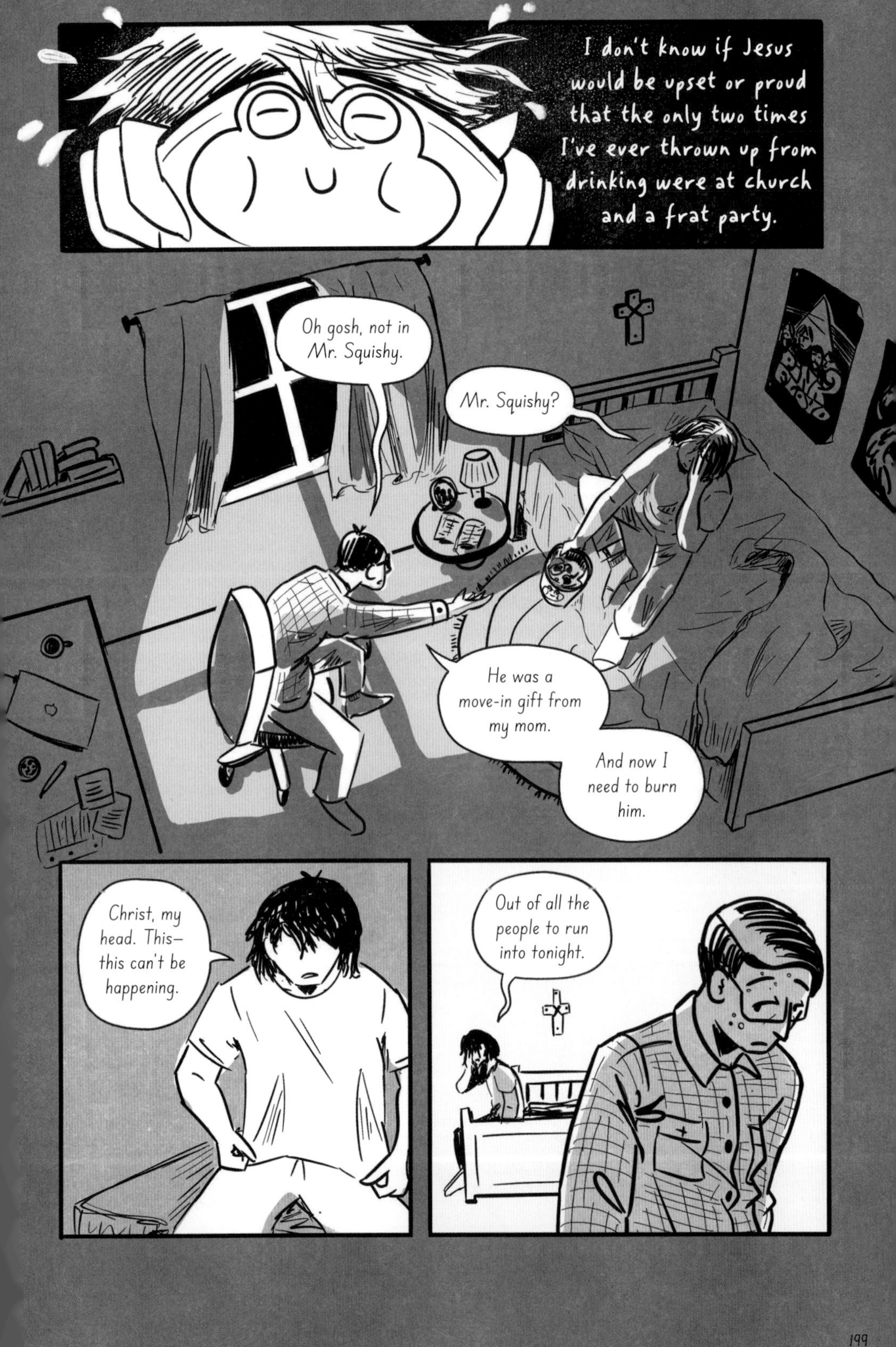

I don't know if Jesus would be upset or proud that the only two times I've ever thrown up from drinking were at church and a frat party.
Oh gosh, not in Mr. Squishy.
Mr. Squishy?
He was a move-in gift from my mom.
And now I need to burn him.
Christ, my head. This— this can't be happening.
Out of all the people to run into tonight.

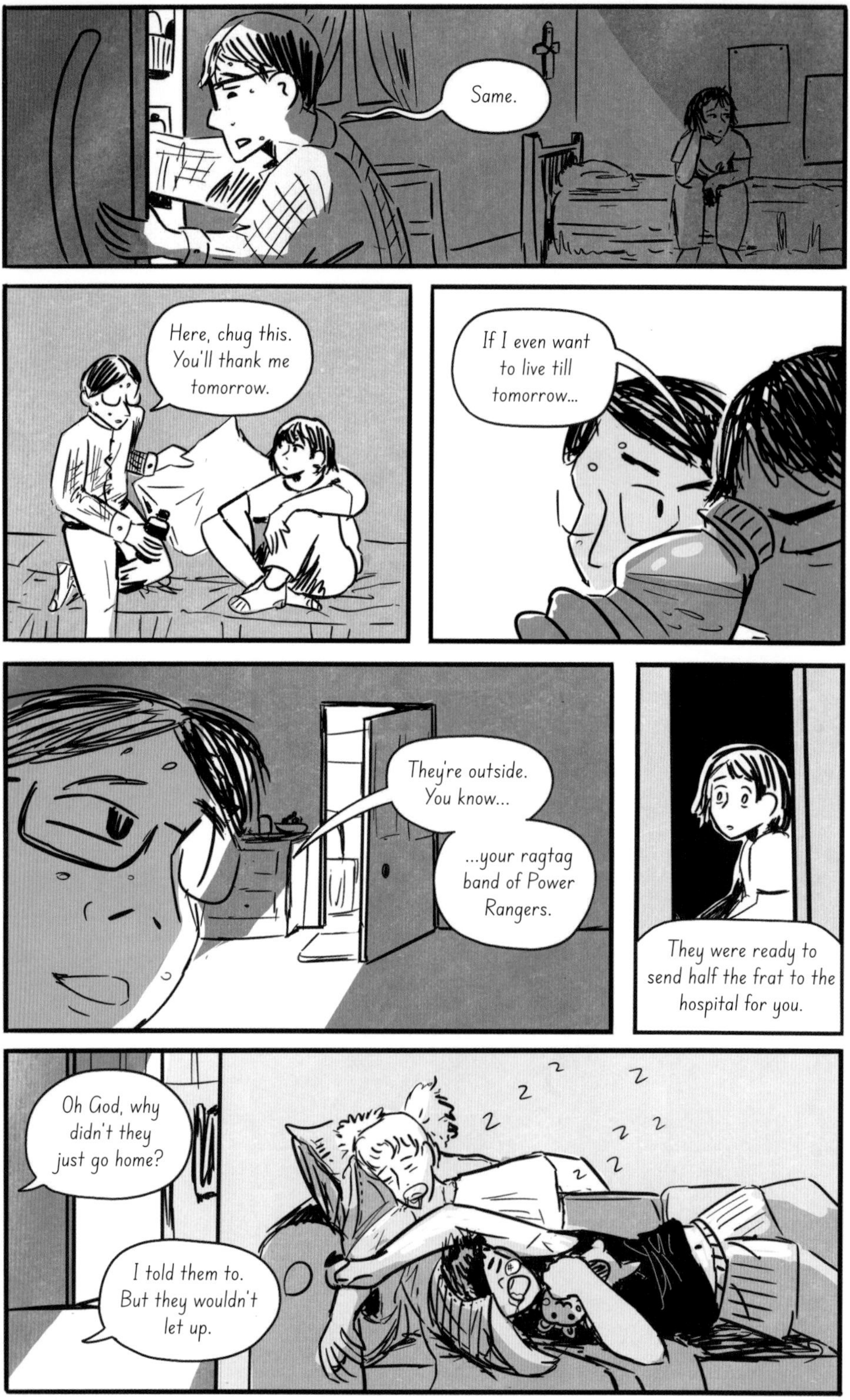

Same.
Here, chug this. You'll thank me tomorrow.
If I even want to live till tomorrow...
They're outside. You know...
...your ragtag band of Power Rangers.
They were ready to send half the frat to the hospital for you.
Oh God, why didn't they just go home?
I told them to. But they wouldn't let up.

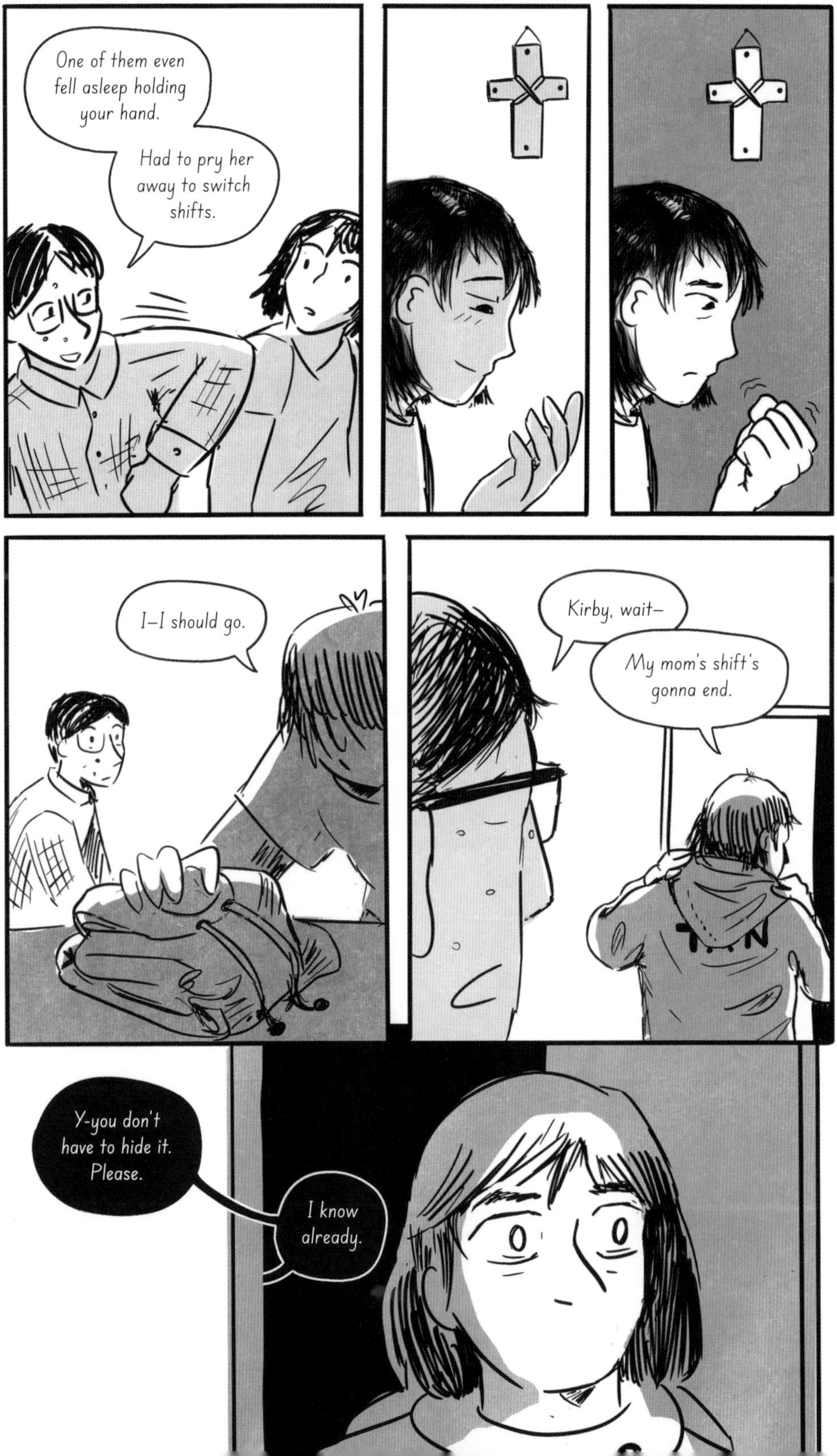
One of them even fell asleep holding your hand.
Had to pry her away to switch shifts.
I–I should go.
Kirby, wait–
My mom's shift's gonna end.
Y-you don't have to hide it. Please.
I know already.

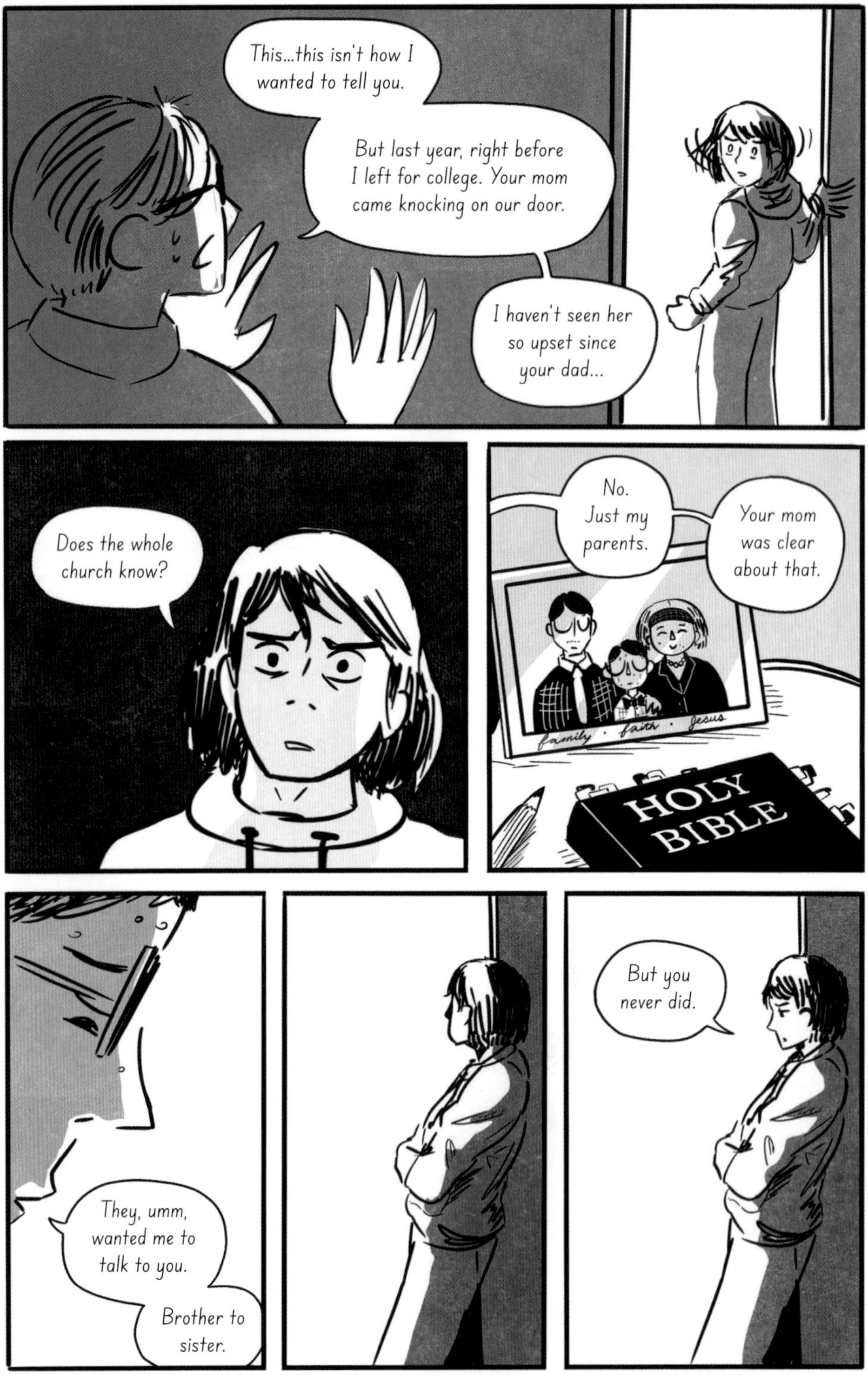
This...this isn't how I wanted to tell you.
But last year, right before I left for college. Your mom came knocking on our door.
I haven't seen her so upset since your dad...
Does the whole church know?
No. Just my parents.
Your mom was clear about that.
family · faith · Jesus
HOLY BIBLE
They, umm, wanted me to talk to you.
Brother to sister.
But you never did.

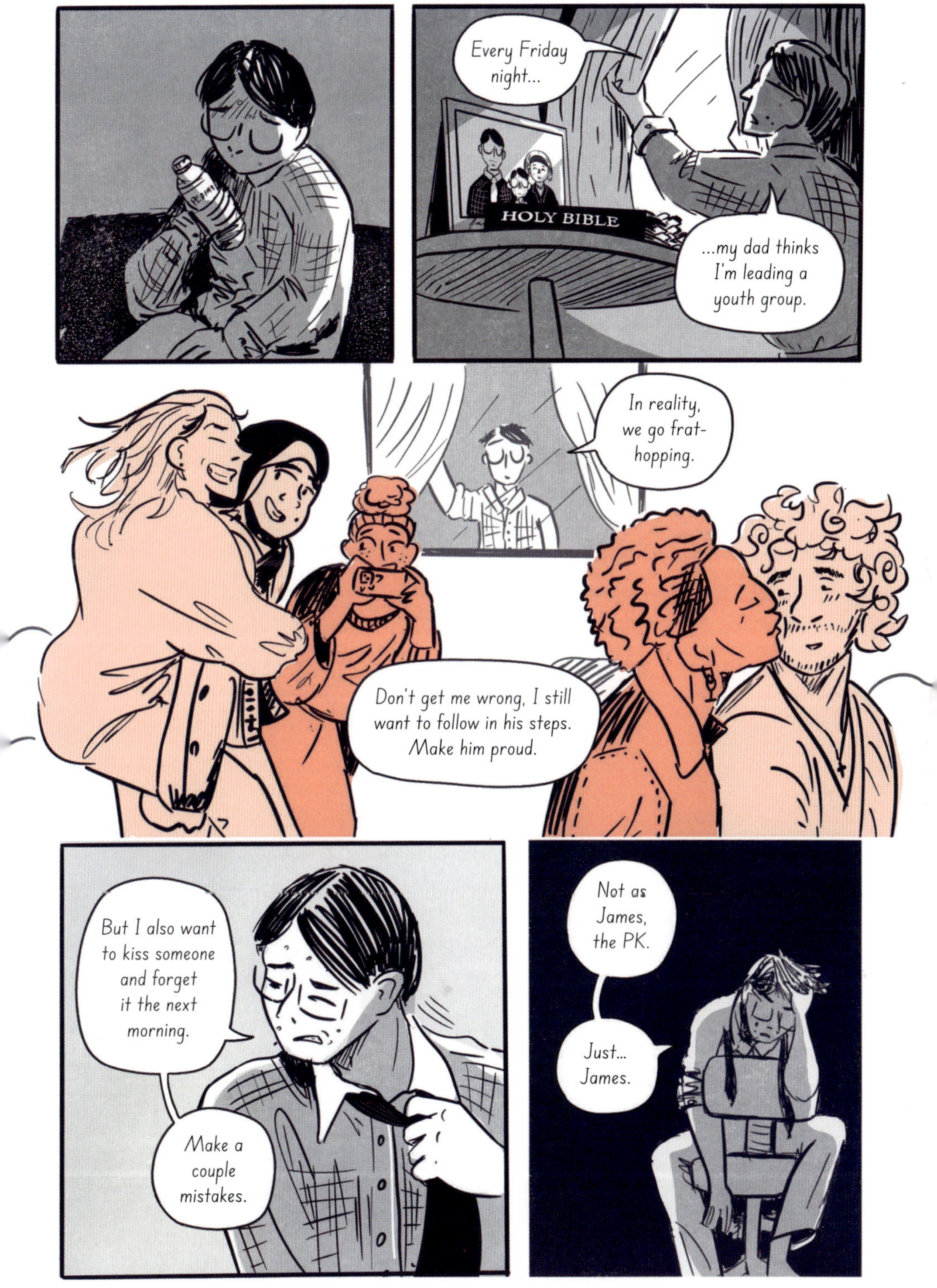
Every Friday night...
HOLY BIBLE
...my dad thinks I'm leading a youth group.
In reality, we go frat-hopping.
Don't get me wrong, I still want to follow in his steps. Make him proud.
But I also want to kiss someone and forget it the next morning.
Make a couple mistakes.
Not as James, the PK.
Just... James.

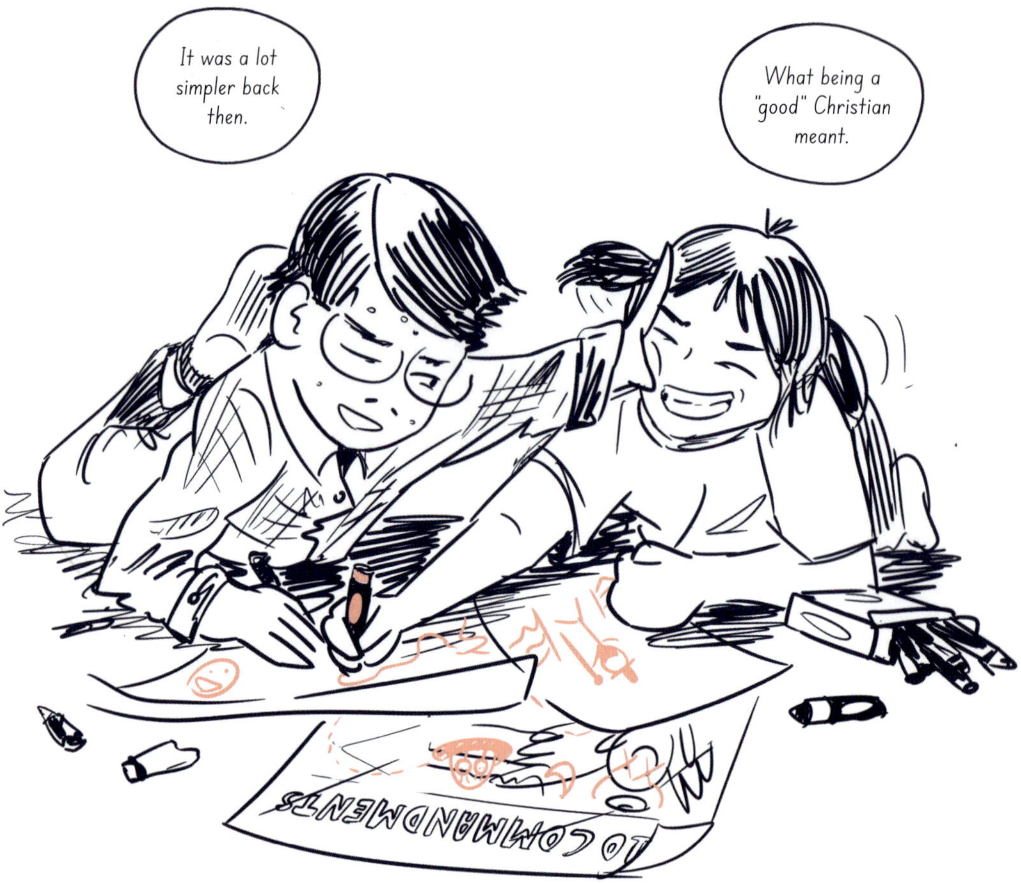
It was a lot simpler back then.
What being a "good" Christian meant.
10 COMMANDMENTS

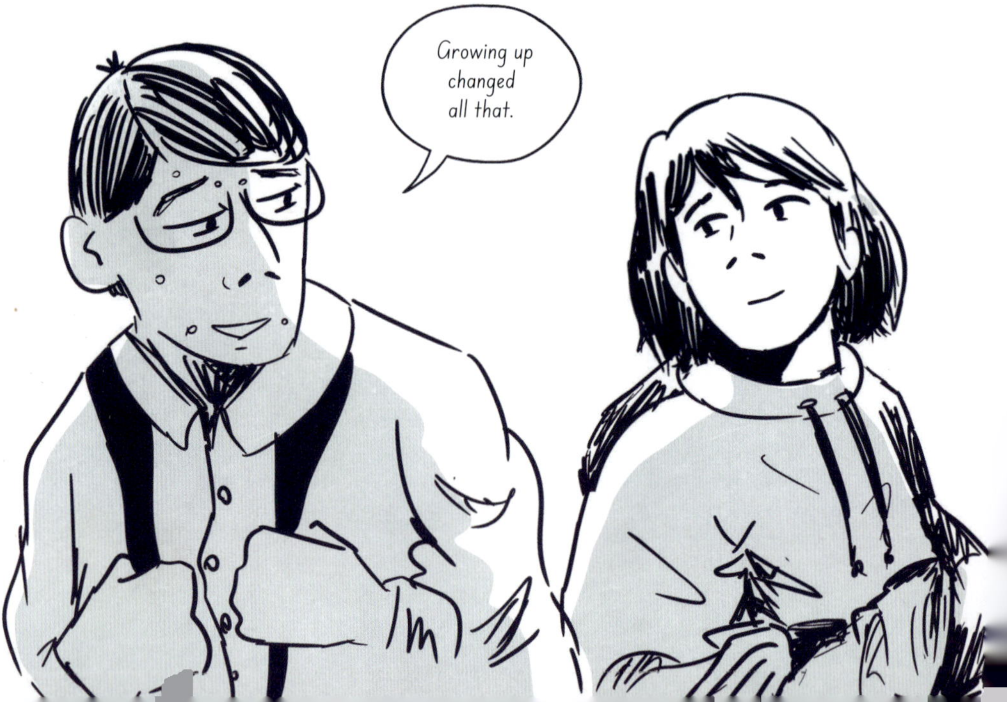
Growing up changed all that.

First step to growing up: learning how to dress well.	Keep the first two undone.

Screams less Bible-verse-correcting, gelled-up PK.

Same gel. Hopefully less, well...

...everything else.

I used to envy that, you know.

Not the gel.

But how you knew exactly how to get the parents to love you.

Yeah, I know...

Guai.

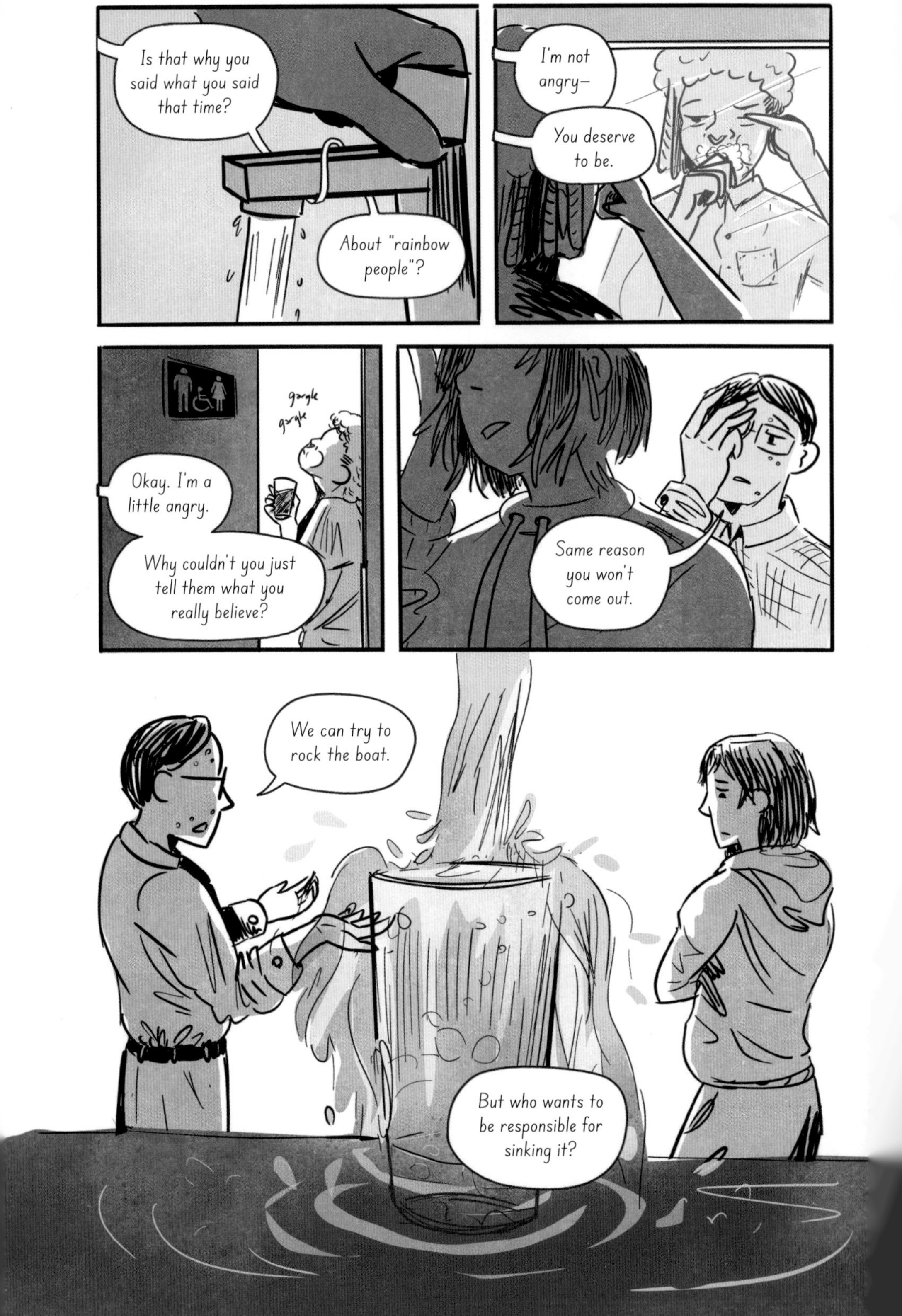
Is that why you said what you said that time?
About "rainbow people"?
I'm not angry—
You deserve to be.
gargle
gargle
Okay. I'm a little angry.
Why couldn't you just tell them what you really believe?
Same reason you won't come out.
We can try to rock the boat.
But who wants to be responsible for sinking it?

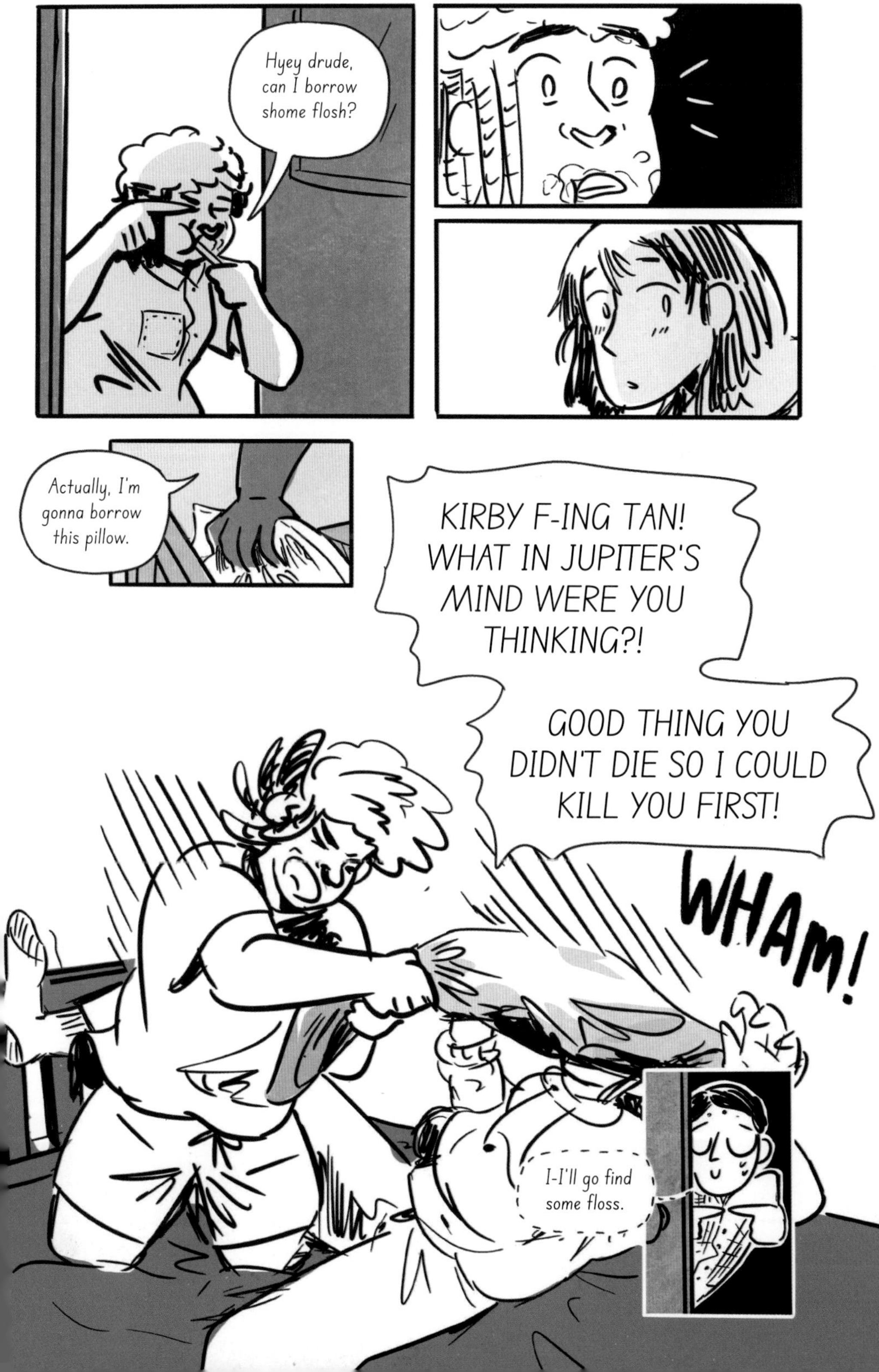
Hyey drude, can I borrow shome flosh?
Actually, I'm gonna borrow this pillow.
KIRBY F-ING TAN! WHAT IN JUPITER'S MIND WERE YOU THINKING?!
GOOD THING YOU DIDN'T DIE SO I COULD KILL YOU FIRST!
WHAM!
I-I'll go find some floss.

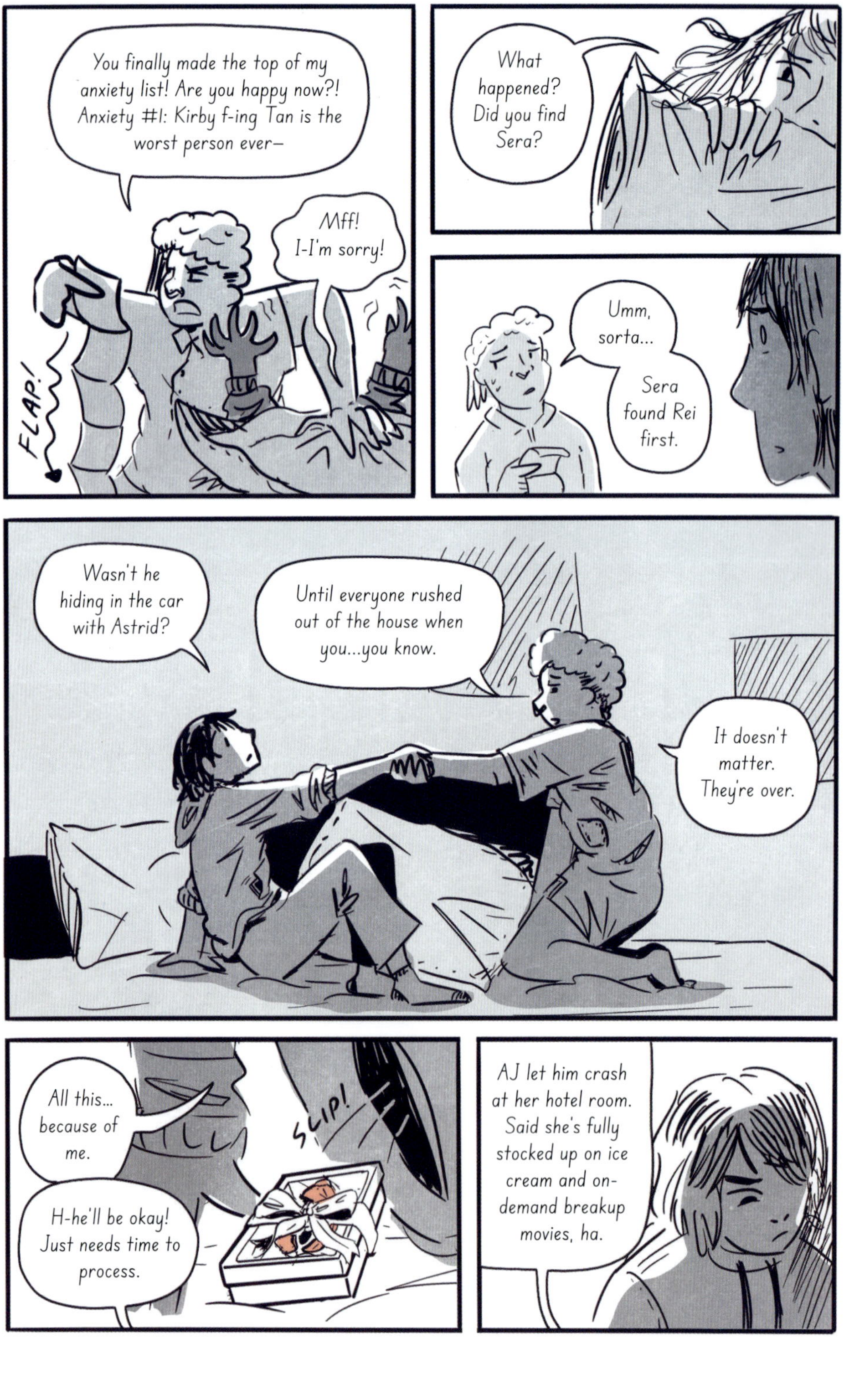
You finally made the top of my anxiety list! Are you happy now?! Anxiety #1: Kirby f-ing Tan is the worst person ever—
Mff! I-I'm sorry!
FLAP!
What happened? Did you find Sera?
Umm, sorta...
Sera found Rei first.
Wasn't he hiding in the car with Astrid?
Until everyone rushed out of the house when you...you know.
It doesn't matter. They're over.
All this... because of me.
SLIP!
H-he'll be okay! Just needs time to process.
AJ let him crash at her hotel room. Said she's fully stocked up on ice cream and on-demand breakup movies, ha.

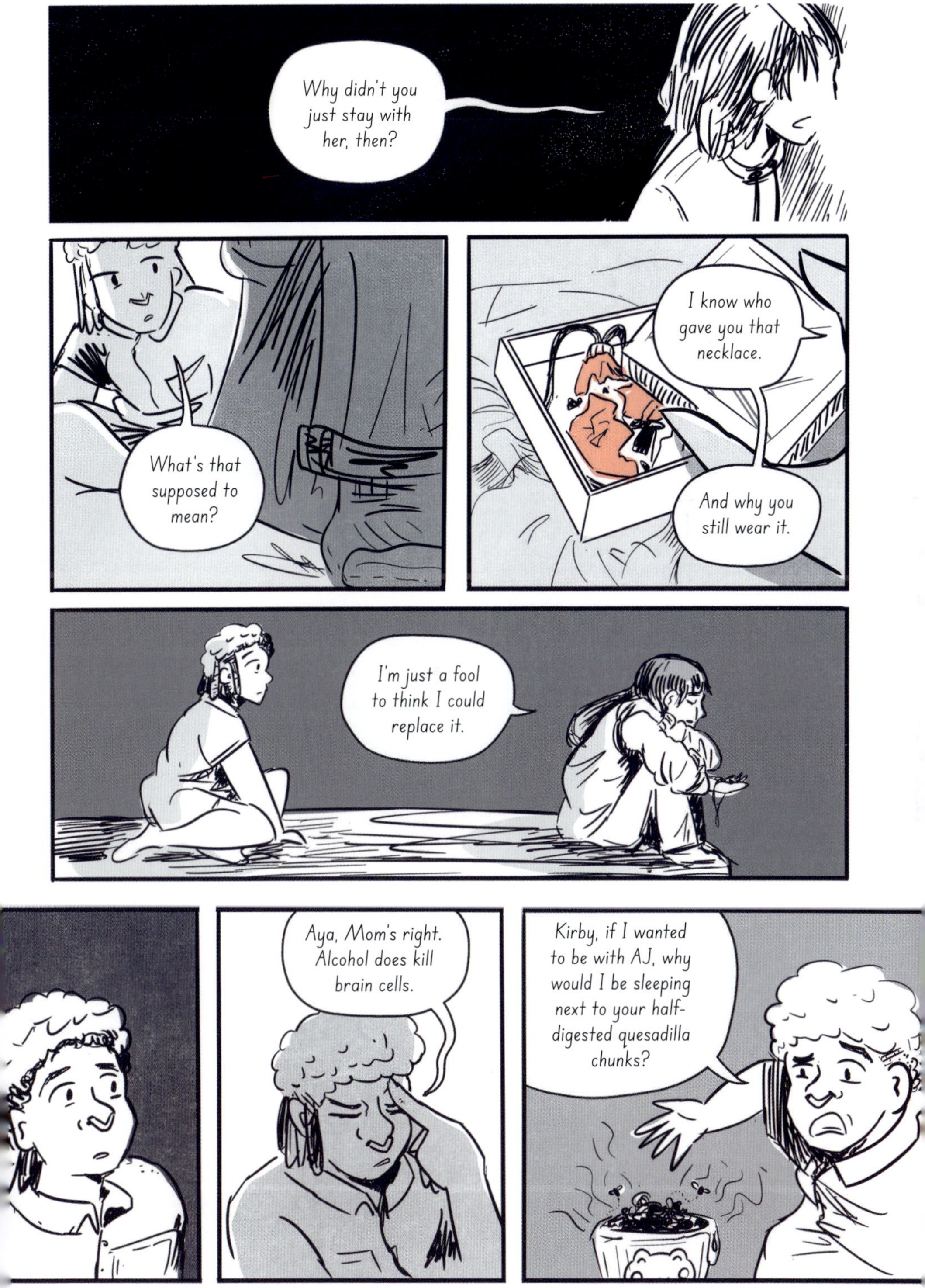
Why didn't you just stay with her, then?
What's that supposed to mean?
I know who gave you that necklace.
And why you still wear it.
I'm just a fool to think I could replace it.
Aya, Mom's right. Alcohol does kill brain cells.
Kirby, if I wanted to be with AJ, why would I be sleeping next to your half-digested quesadilla chunks?

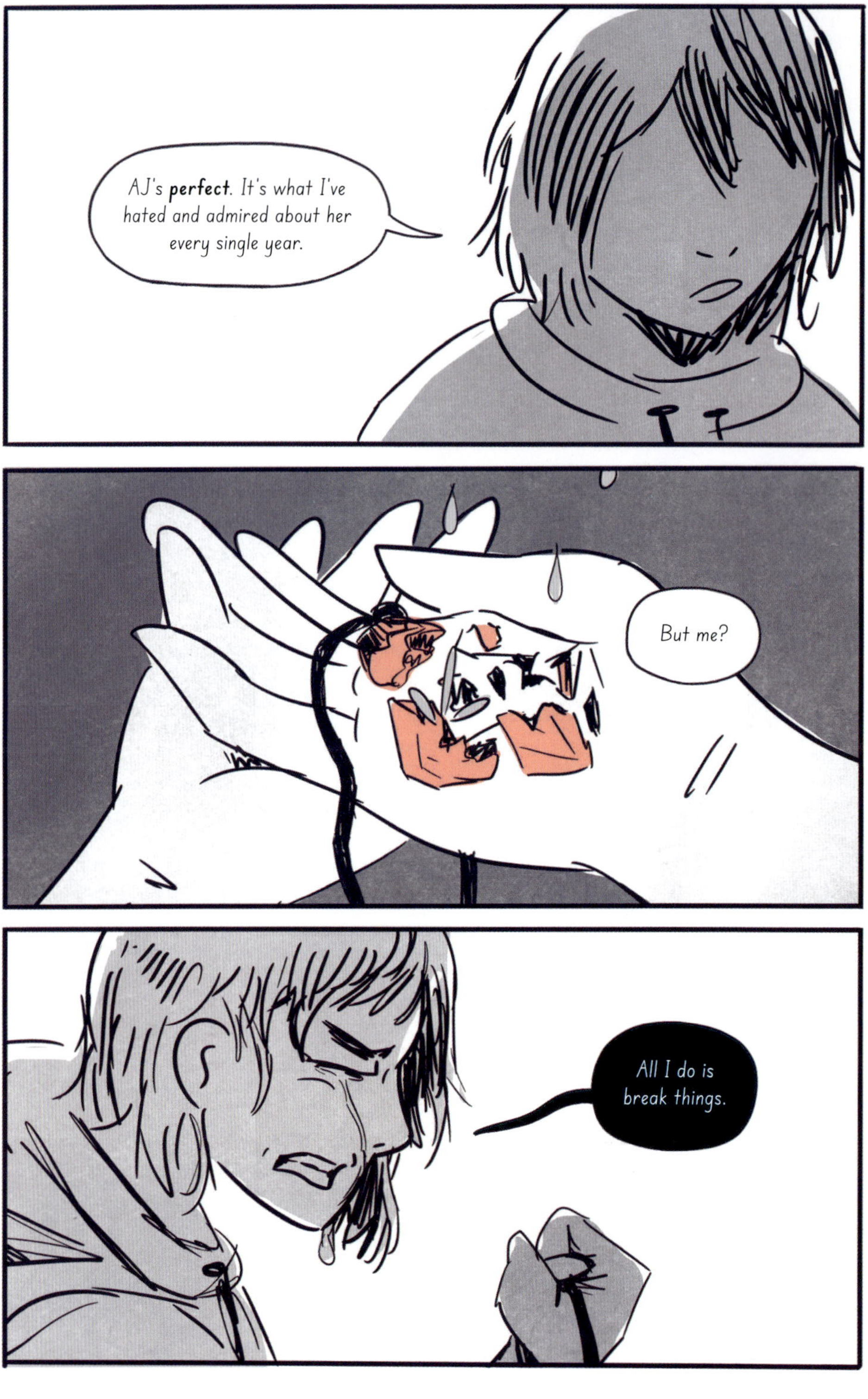
AJ's **perfect**. It's what I've hated and admired about her every single year.
But me?
All I do is break things.

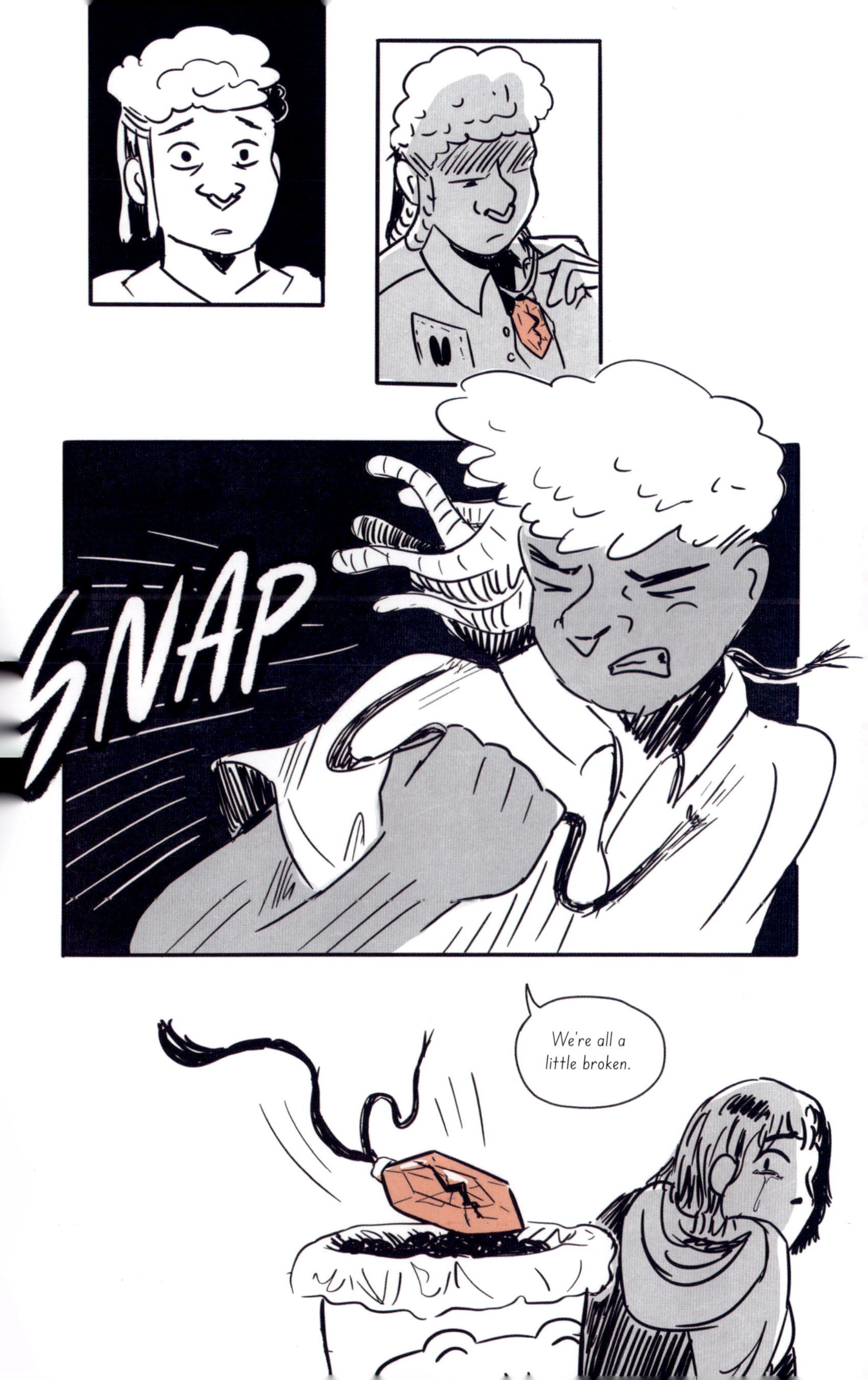
SNAP
We're all a
little broken.

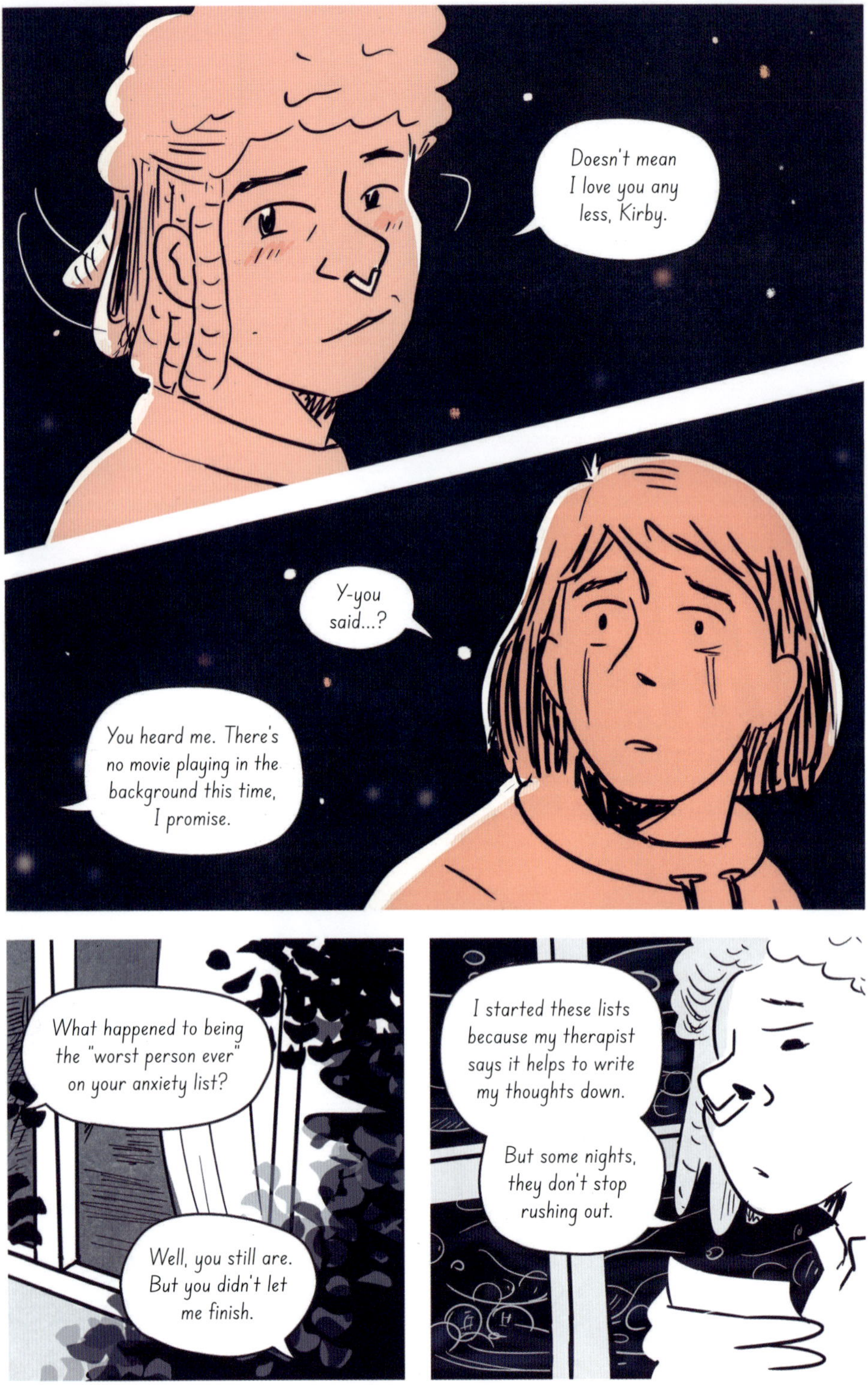
Doesn't mean I love you any less, Kirby.
Y-you said...?
You heard me. There's no movie playing in the background this time, I promise.
What happened to being the "worst person ever" on your anxiety list?
Well, you still are. But you didn't let me finish.
I started these lists because my therapist says it helps to write my thoughts down.
But some nights, they don't stop rushing out.

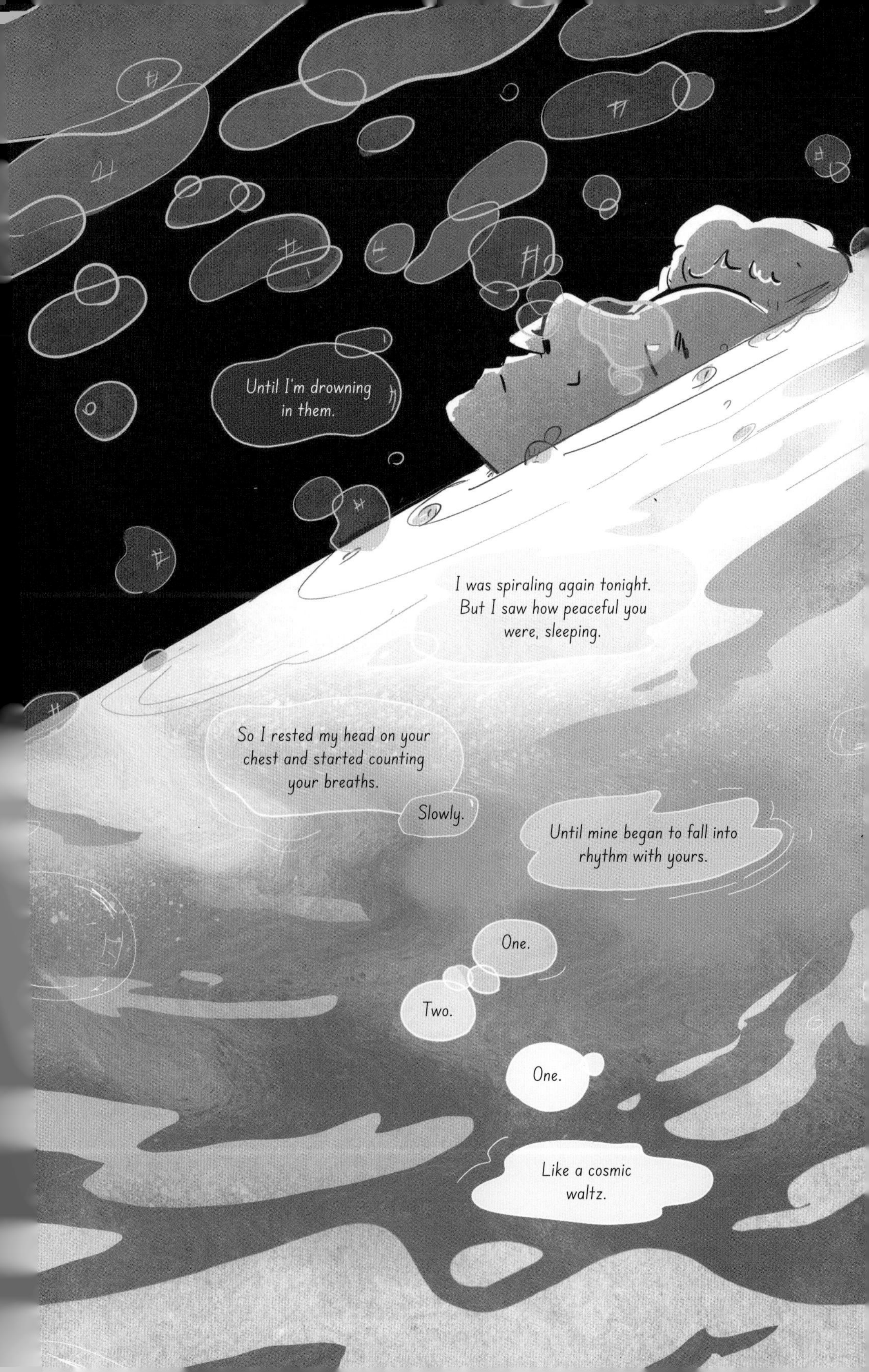
Until I'm drowning in them.
I was spiraling again tonight. But I saw how peaceful you were, sleeping.
So I rested my head on your chest and started counting your breaths.
Slowly.
Until mine began to fall into rhythm with yours.
One.
Two.
One.
Like a cosmic waltz.

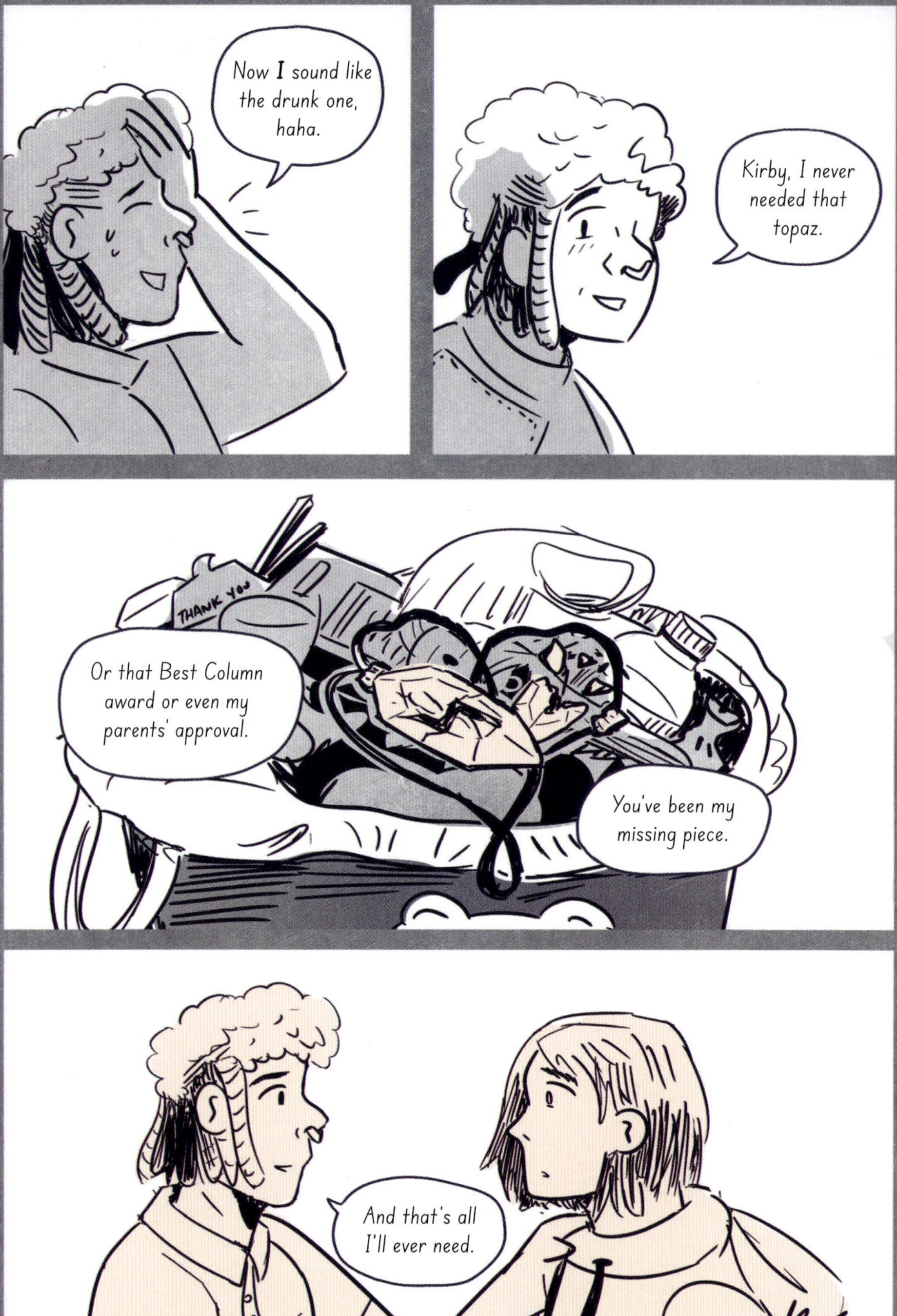
Now I sound like the drunk one, haha.
Kirby, I never needed that topaz.
THANK YOU
Or that Best Column award or even my parents' approval.
You've been my missing piece.
And that's all I'll ever need.

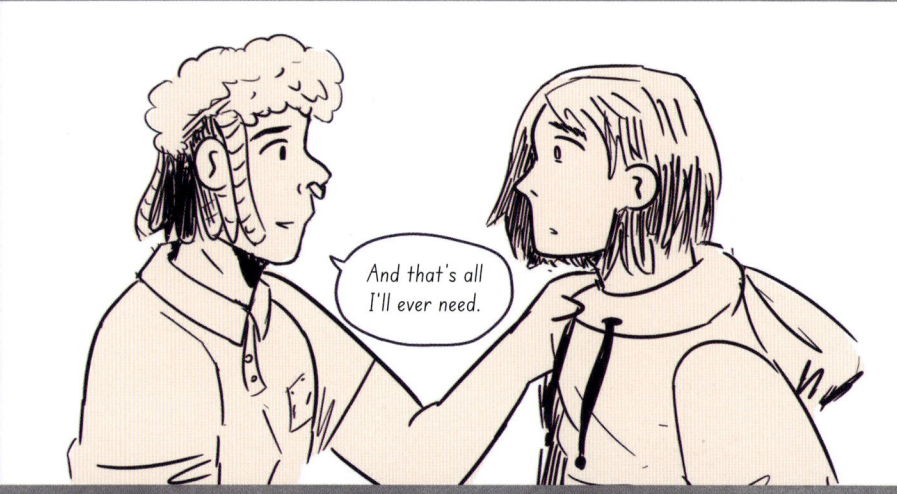

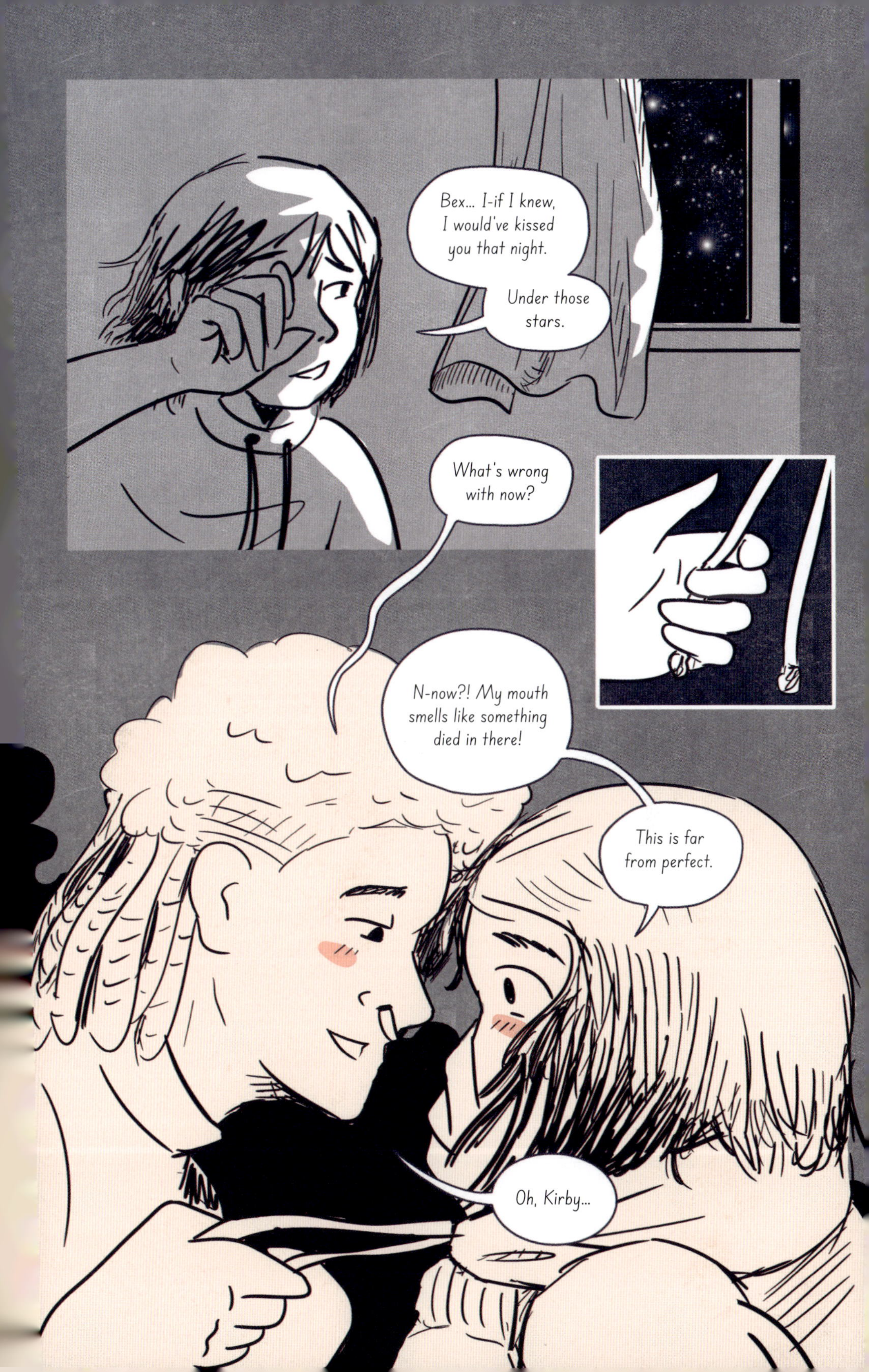

Bex... I-if I knew, I would've kissed you that night.
Under those stars.
What's wrong with now?
N-now?! My mouth smells like something died in there!
This is far from perfect.
Oh, Kirby...

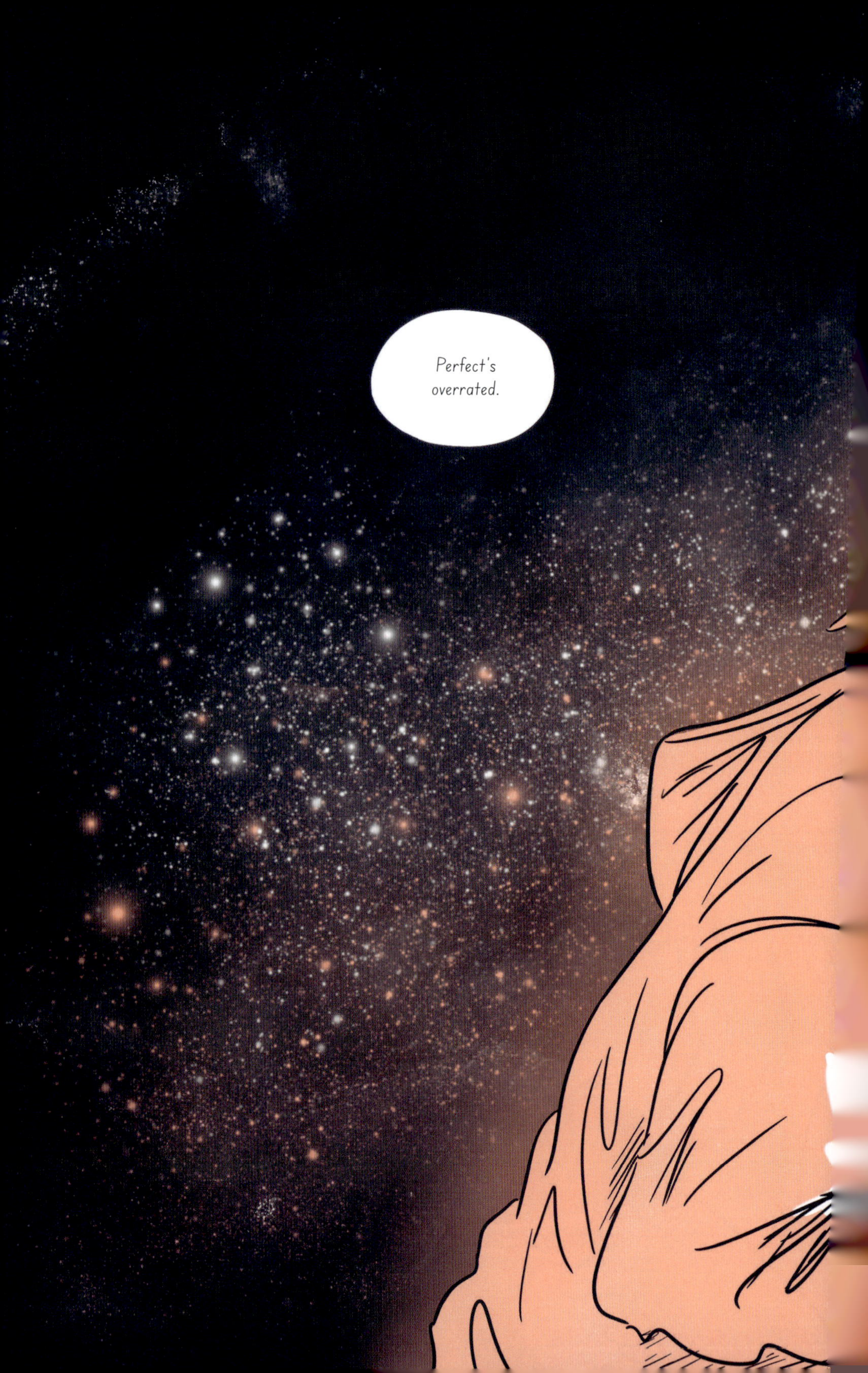
Perfect's overrated.

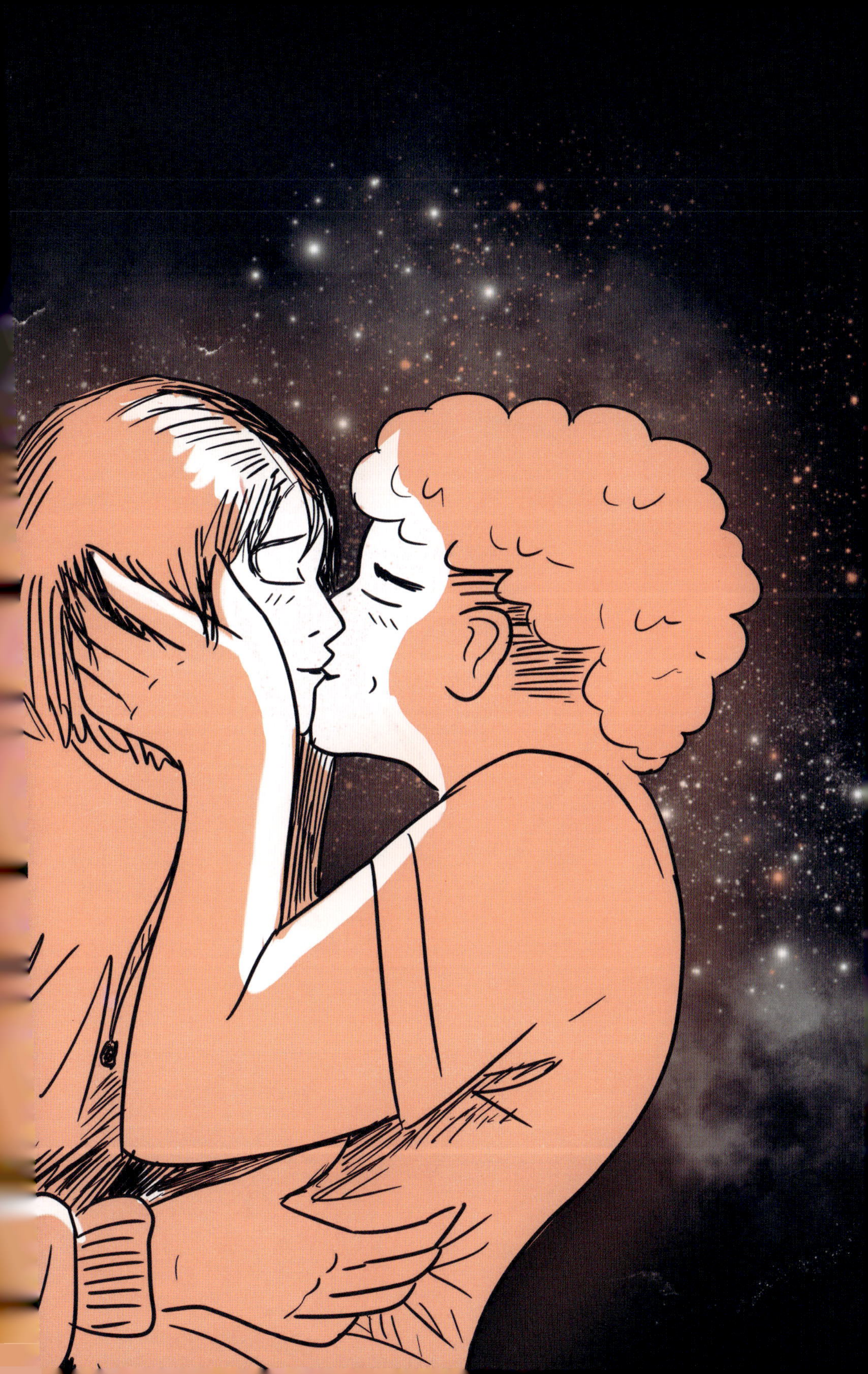

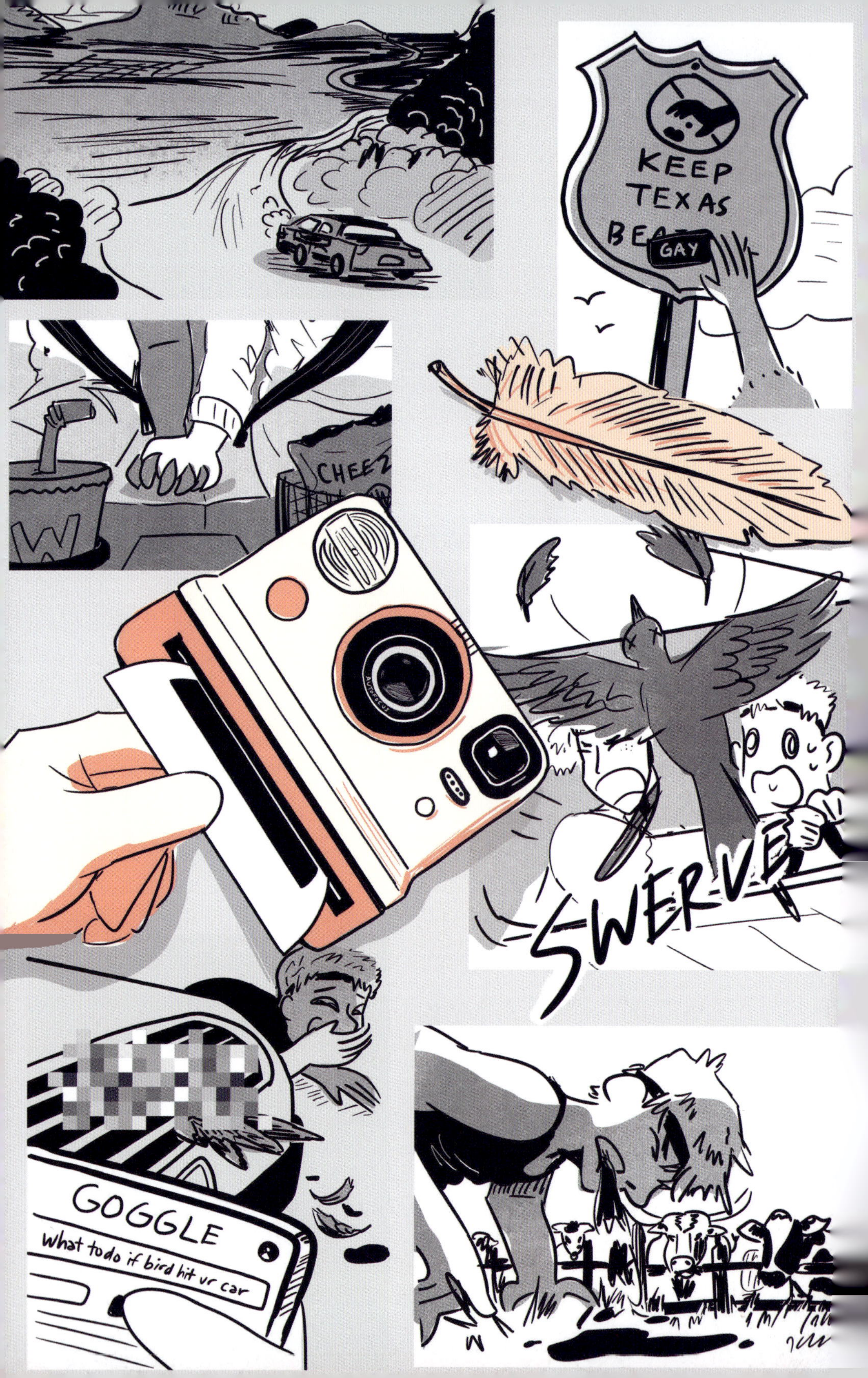
KEEP
TEXAS
BEA
GAY
CHEEZ
SWERVE
GOGGLE
what todo if bird hit ur car

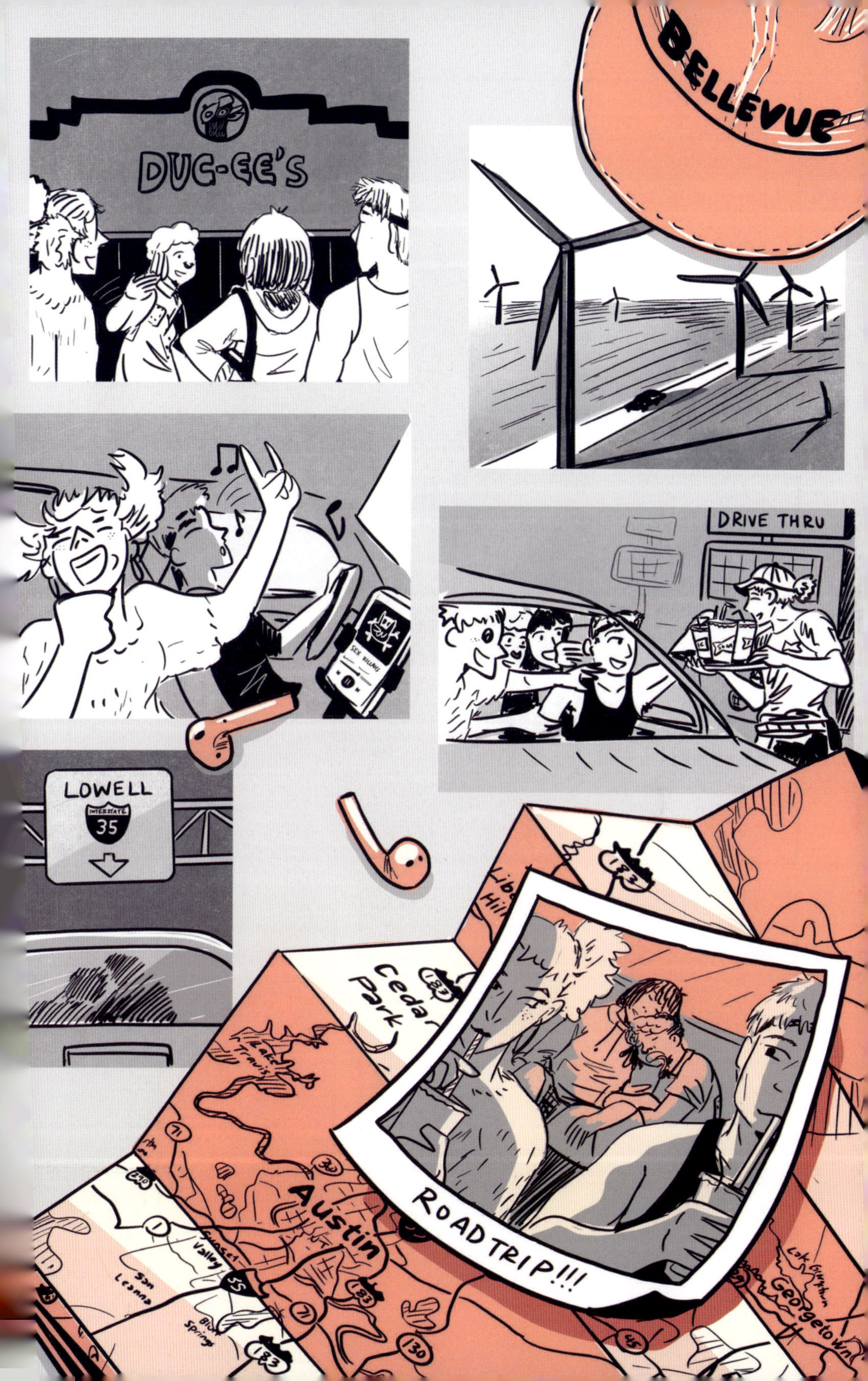

DUC-EE'S
BELLEVUE
DRIVE THRU
LOWELL
INTERSTATE
35
Cedar Park
Lake Travis
Austin
Sunset Valley
San Leanna
Georgetown
ROADTRIP!!!

RE: new column idea?

wb this?
KITTY-VOYANT: Horoscopes based on what container Jinx decides to squeeze into today.

After the whole Bellevue fiasco, Bex and I decided to take a break from date setups.

Weirdly enough, Mr. B didn't react as harshly as we feared.

He's probably surprised we even lasted this long.

wdya think this means 🙂

umm that truly nothing is safe from that demon cat 💀

I think having a daughter's softening him up.

CLICK!

I'm coming in, Yeye.

Are you, umm, done?

Kirby! It's good to see you.

Why are we here again?

Sooner or later, I'll have to tell Bex I'm quitting newspaper.

And tell Mom that I have a new...you know.

But there never seems to be a good time.

I'd never trust Evan at a non-Christian college. I hear they pass out drugs like candy!

Sisters, I appreciate the concern. But for James, we put our trust in our Lord and Savior.

The Bellevue Parents WeChat group.

I swear my mom spends more time reading that chat than the Bible.

They have EVERYTHING!

School news, gossip, crime, which internships their kids got—

LOOK! THERE'S EVEN A PICTURE OF SOME PARTY THAT HAPPENED FRIDAY!

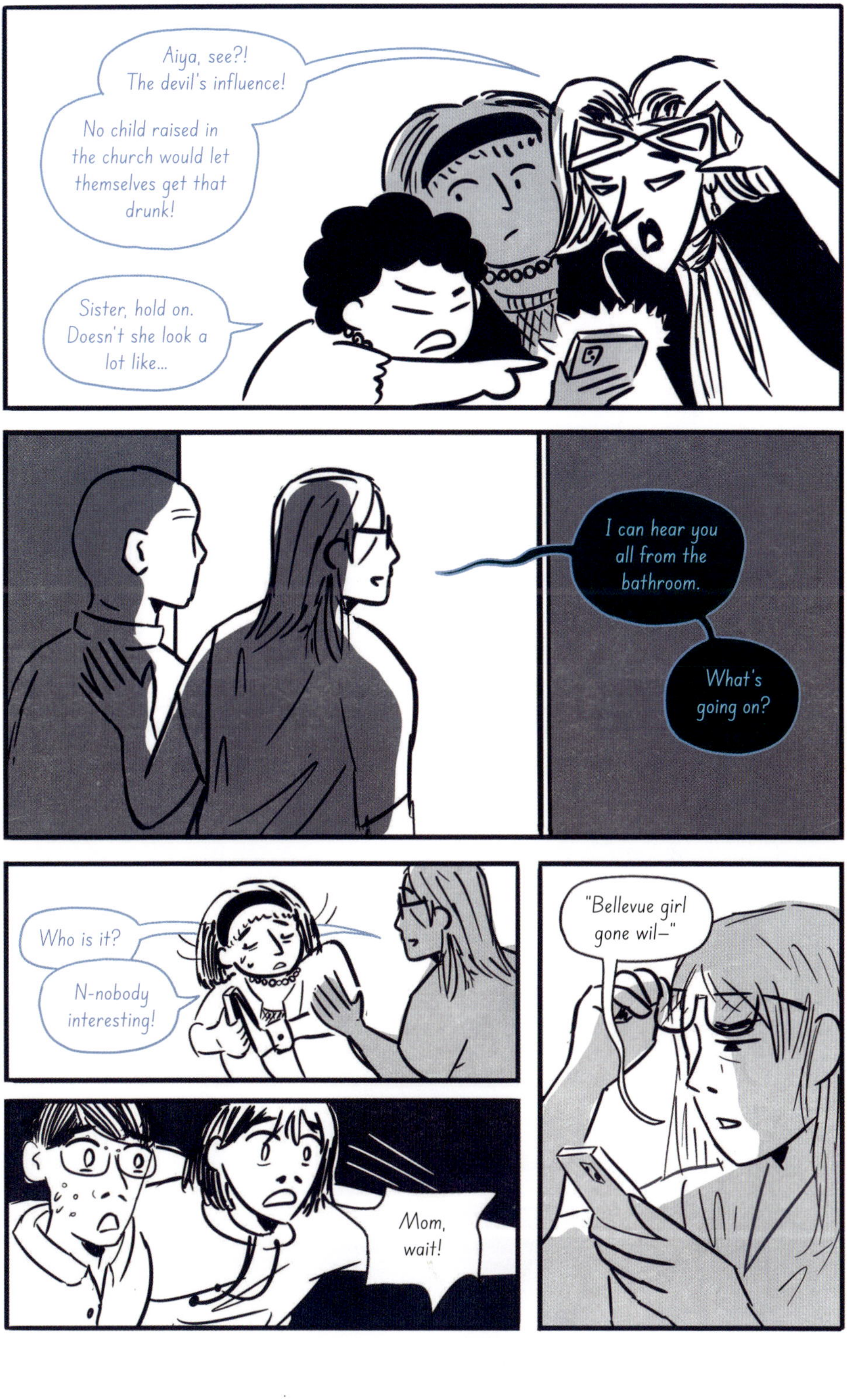
Aiya, see?! The devil's influence!
No child raised in the church would let themselves get that drunk!
Sister, hold on. Doesn't she look a lot like...
I can hear you all from the bathroom.
What's going on?
Who is it?
N-nobody interesting!
"Bellevue girl gone wil—"
Mom, wait!

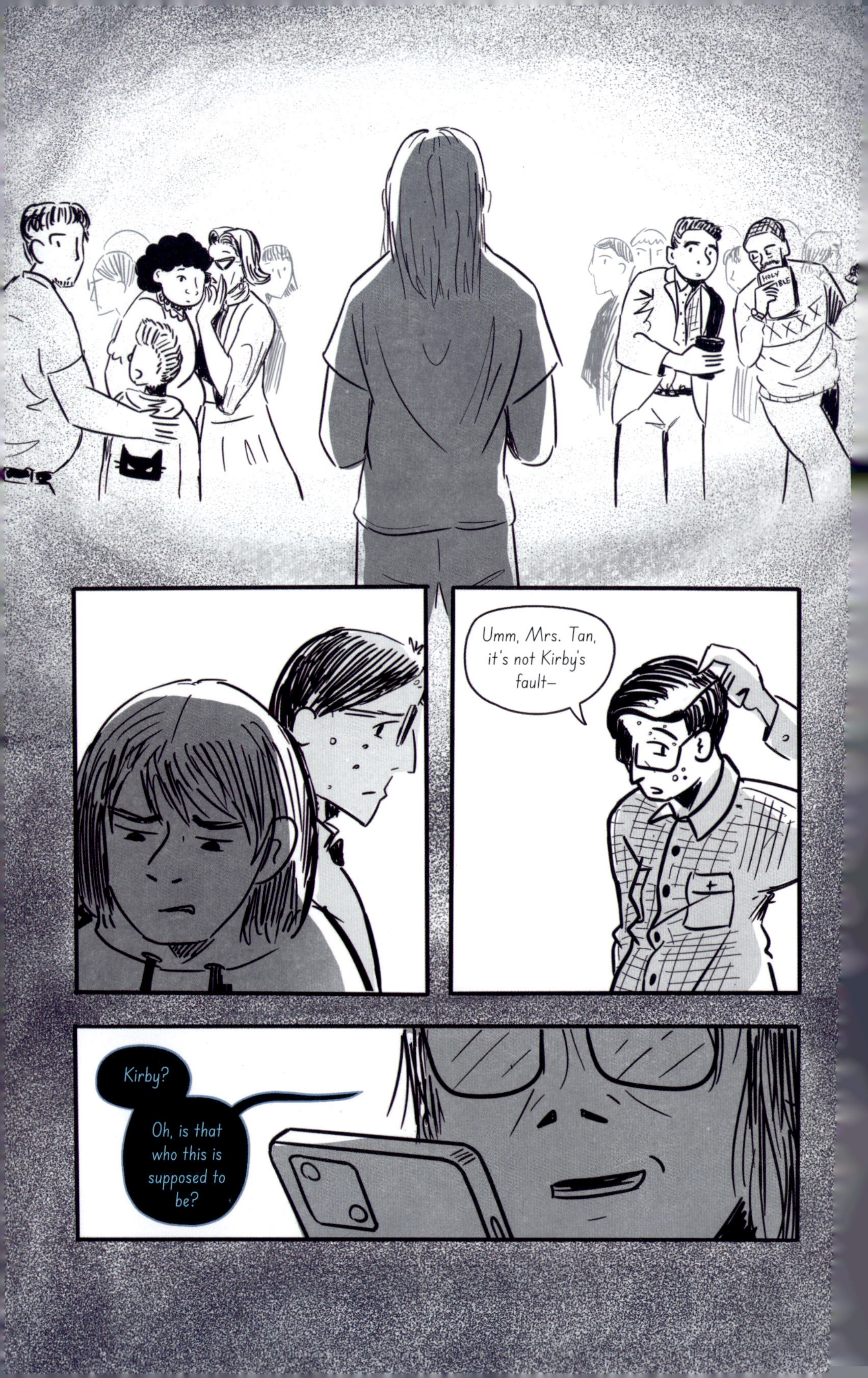
Umm, Mrs. Tan, it's not Kirby's fault—
Kirby?
Oh, is that who this is supposed to be?

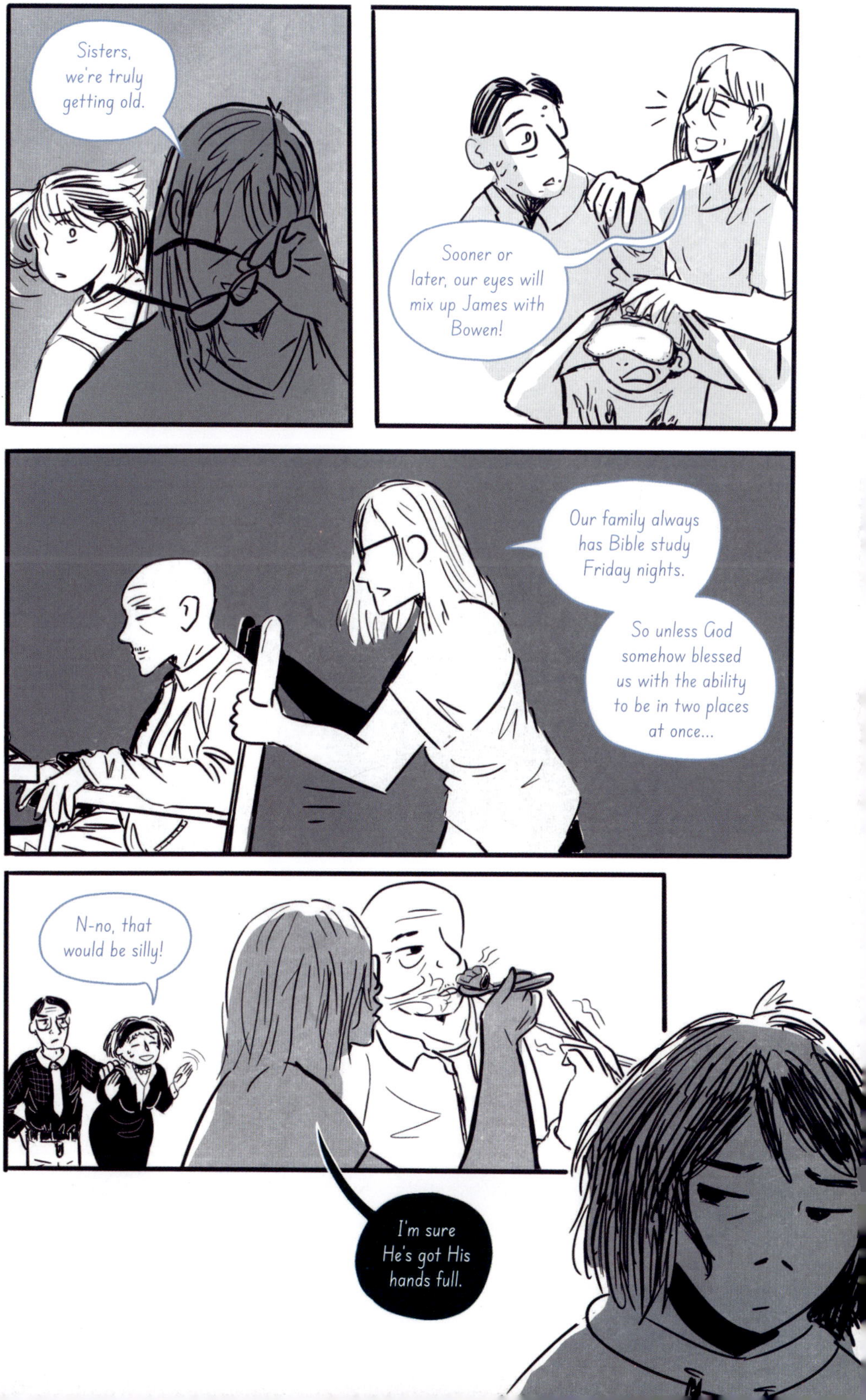
Sisters, we're truly getting old.
Sooner or later, our eyes will mix up James with Bowen!
Our family always has Bible study Friday nights.
So unless God somehow blessed us with the ability to be in two places at once...
N-no, that would be silly!
I'm sure He's got His hands full.

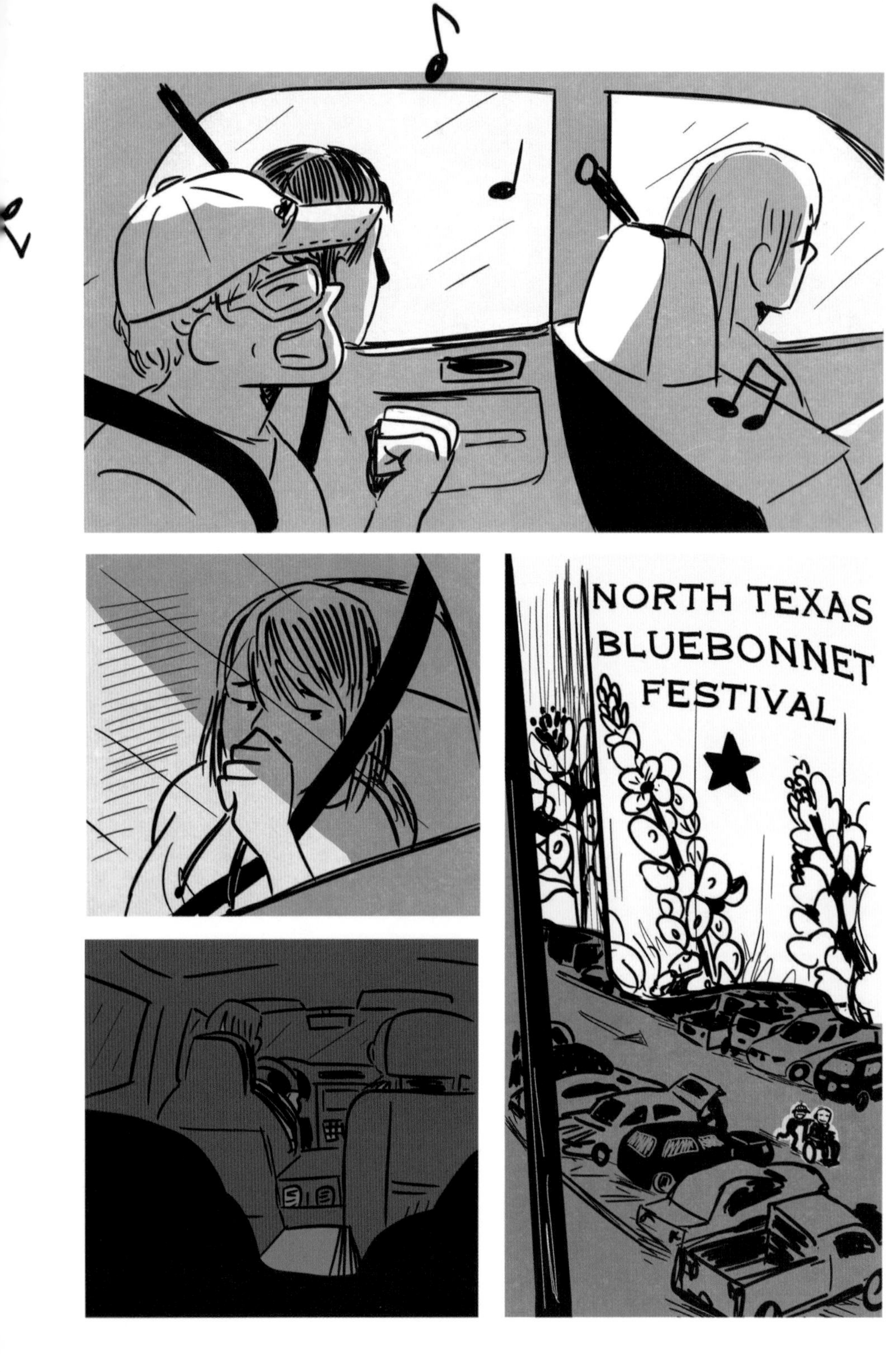
NORTH TEXAS
BLUEBONNET
FESTIVAL

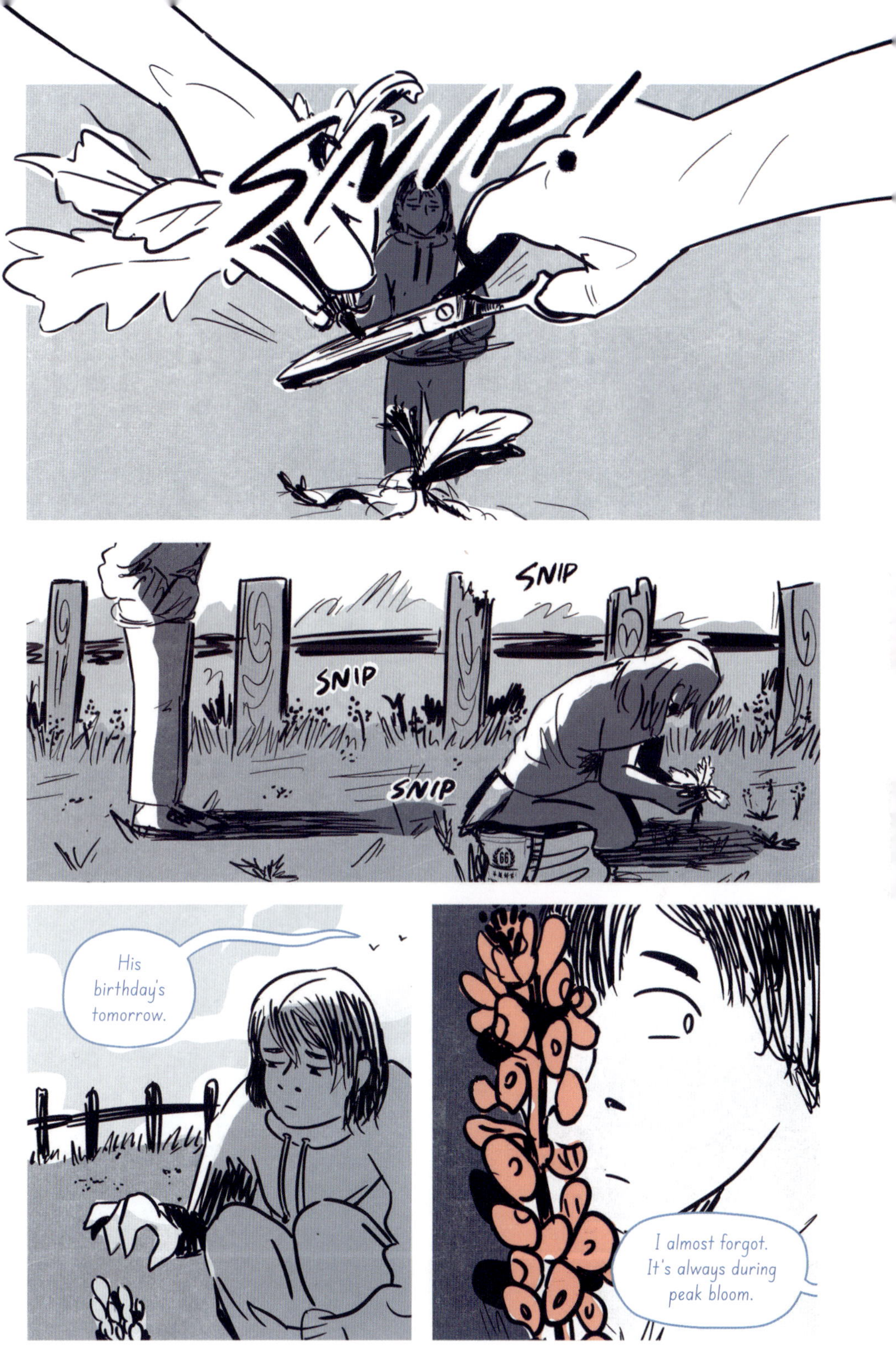
SNIP!
SNIP
SNIP
SNIP
His birthday's tomorrow.
I almost forgot. It's always during peak bloom.

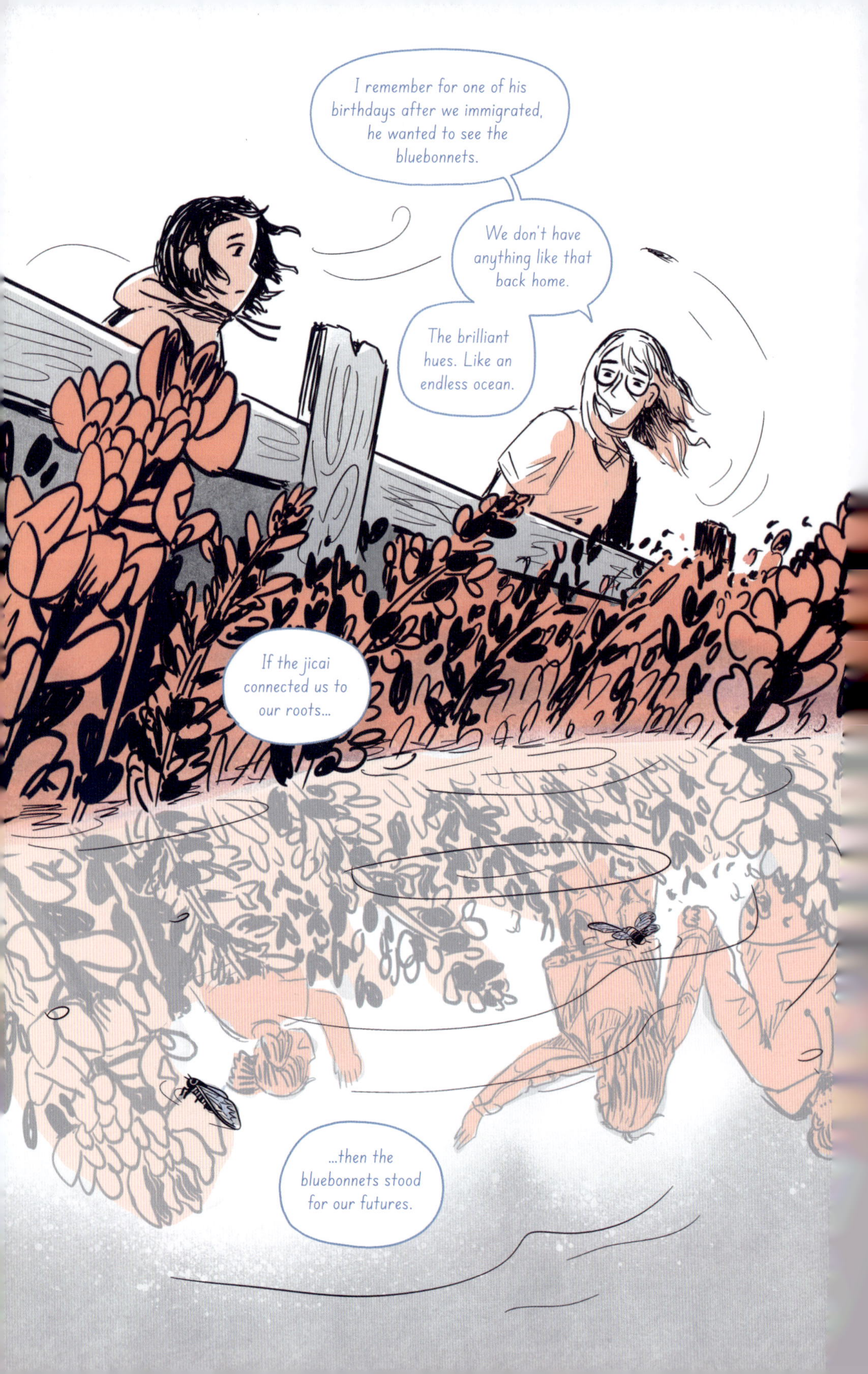
I remember for one of his birthdays after we immigrated, he wanted to see the bluebonnets.
We don't have anything like that back home.
The brilliant hues. Like an endless ocean.
If the jicai connected us to our roots...
...then the bluebonnets stood for our futures.

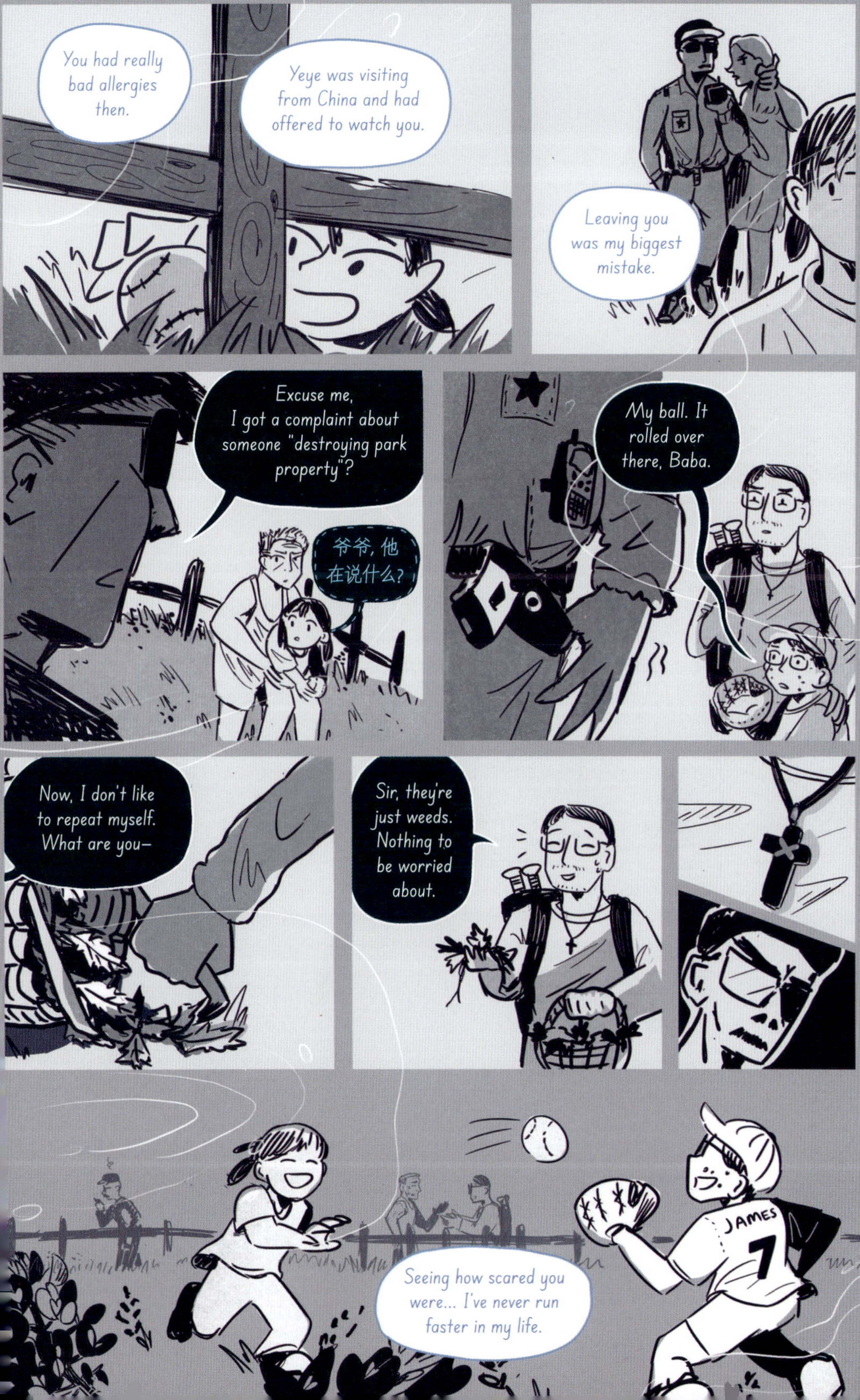
You had really bad allergies then.
Yeye was visiting from China and had offered to watch you.
Leaving you was my biggest mistake.
Excuse me, I got a complaint about someone "destroying park property"?
爷爷, 他在说什么?
My ball. It rolled over there, Baba.
Now, I don't like to repeat myself. What are you—
Sir, they're just weeds. Nothing to be worried about.
JAMES 7
Seeing how scared you were... I've never run faster in my life.

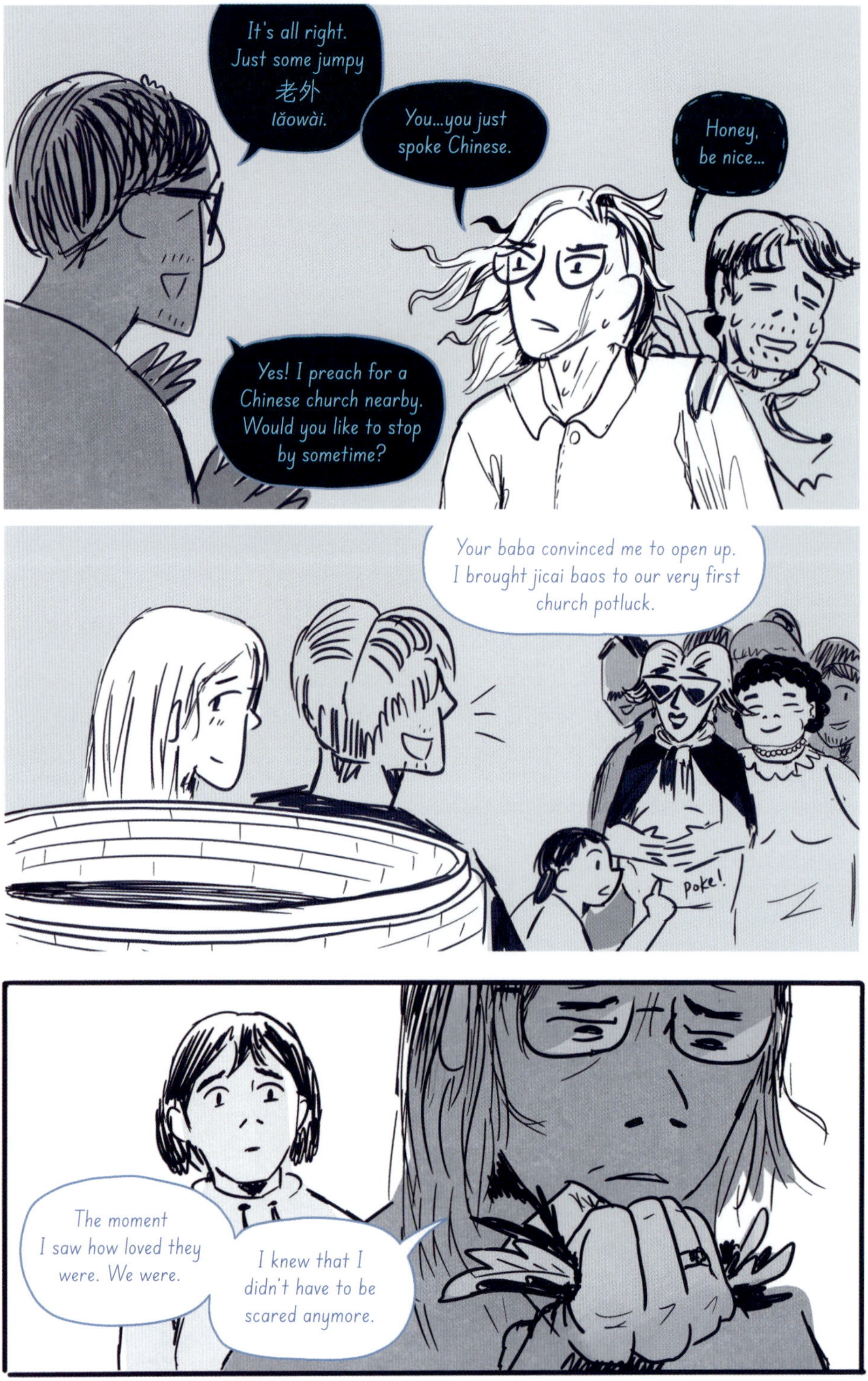
It's all right. Just some jumpy 老外 lǎowài.
You...you just spoke Chinese.
Honey, be nice...
Yes! I preach for a Chinese church nearby. Would you like to stop by sometime?
Your baba convinced me to open up. I brought jicai baos to our very first church potluck.
Poke!
The moment I saw how loved they were. We were.
I knew that I didn't have to be scared anymore.

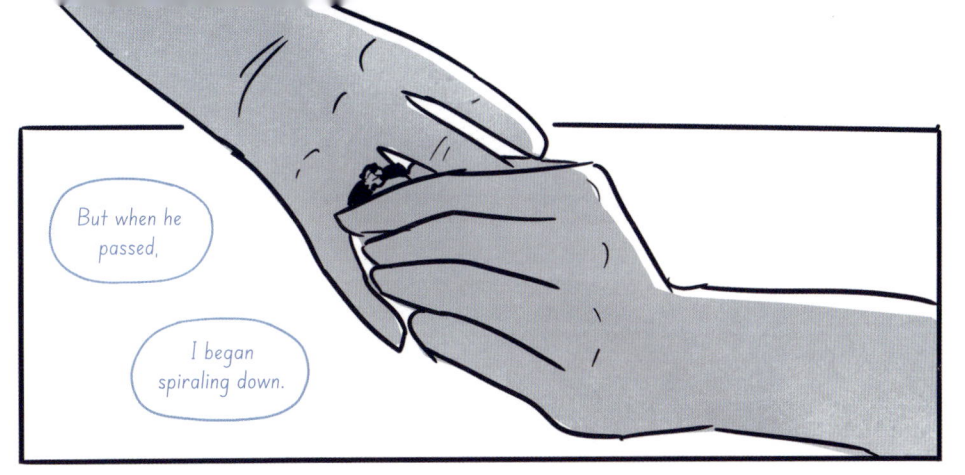

But when he passed,

I began spiraling down.

You and the church were the only things keeping me afloat.

Mom, why...

Why aren't you mad at me?

Because I'm afraid I'm one step away from losing everything.

Nothing's been the same. Ever since that night you told me. I was so lost!

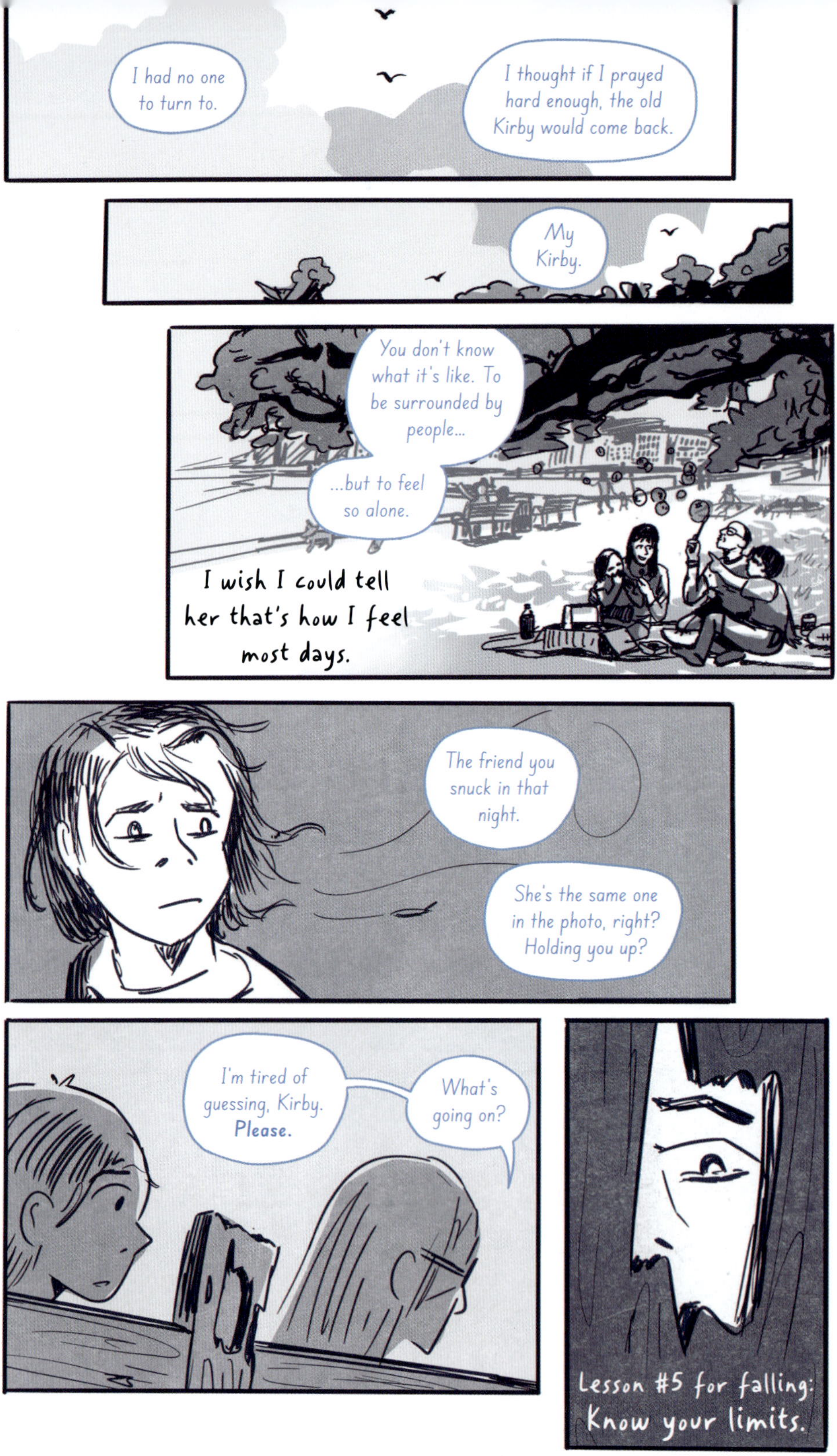
I had no one to turn to.
I thought if I prayed hard enough, the old Kirby would come back.
My Kirby.
You don't know what it's like. To be surrounded by people...
...but to feel so alone.
I wish I could tell her that's how I feel most days.
The friend you snuck in that night.
She's the same one in the photo, right? Holding you up?
I'm tired of guessing, Kirby. **Please.**
What's going on?
Lesson #5 for falling: Know your limits.

"I...I got invited to Bellevue. To practice with the team."

Unfortunately, I was never great at this one.

"They wanted to go out afterward. I—I got carried away."

"Bex came to pick me up once she realized I was in trouble."

"Why didn't you tell me?"

"You never cared about Bellevue—"

"But I care about your safety!"

"Do you? 'Cause you didn't even notice I was gone during your night shift!"

"Don't you dare bring work into this—"

RING! RING!

"Get in the car."

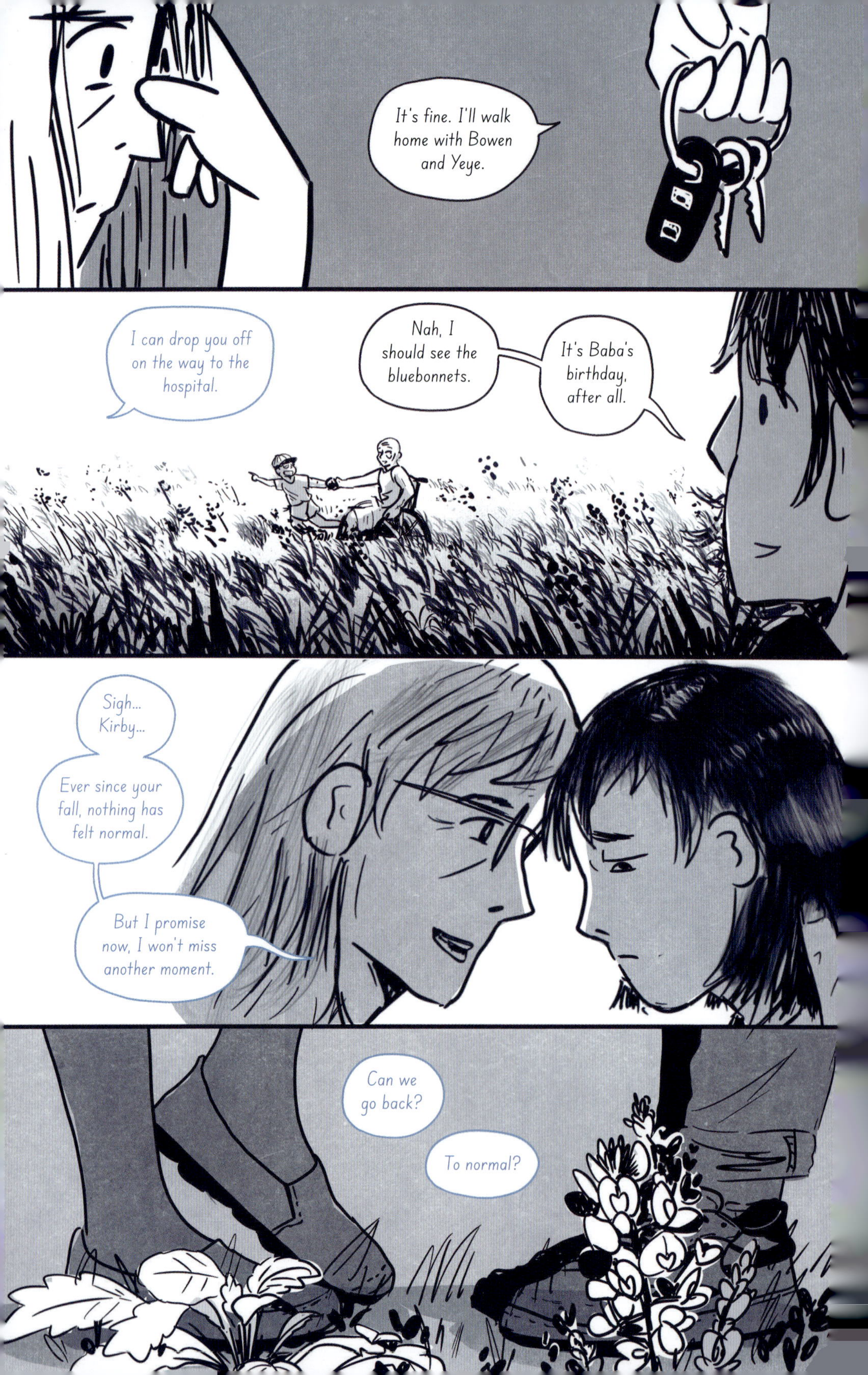
It's fine. I'll walk home with Bowen and Yeye.
I can drop you off on the way to the hospital.
Nah, I should see the bluebonnets.
It's Baba's birthday, after all.
Sigh... Kirby...
Ever since your fall, nothing has felt normal.
But I promise now, I won't miss another moment.
Can we go back?
To normal?

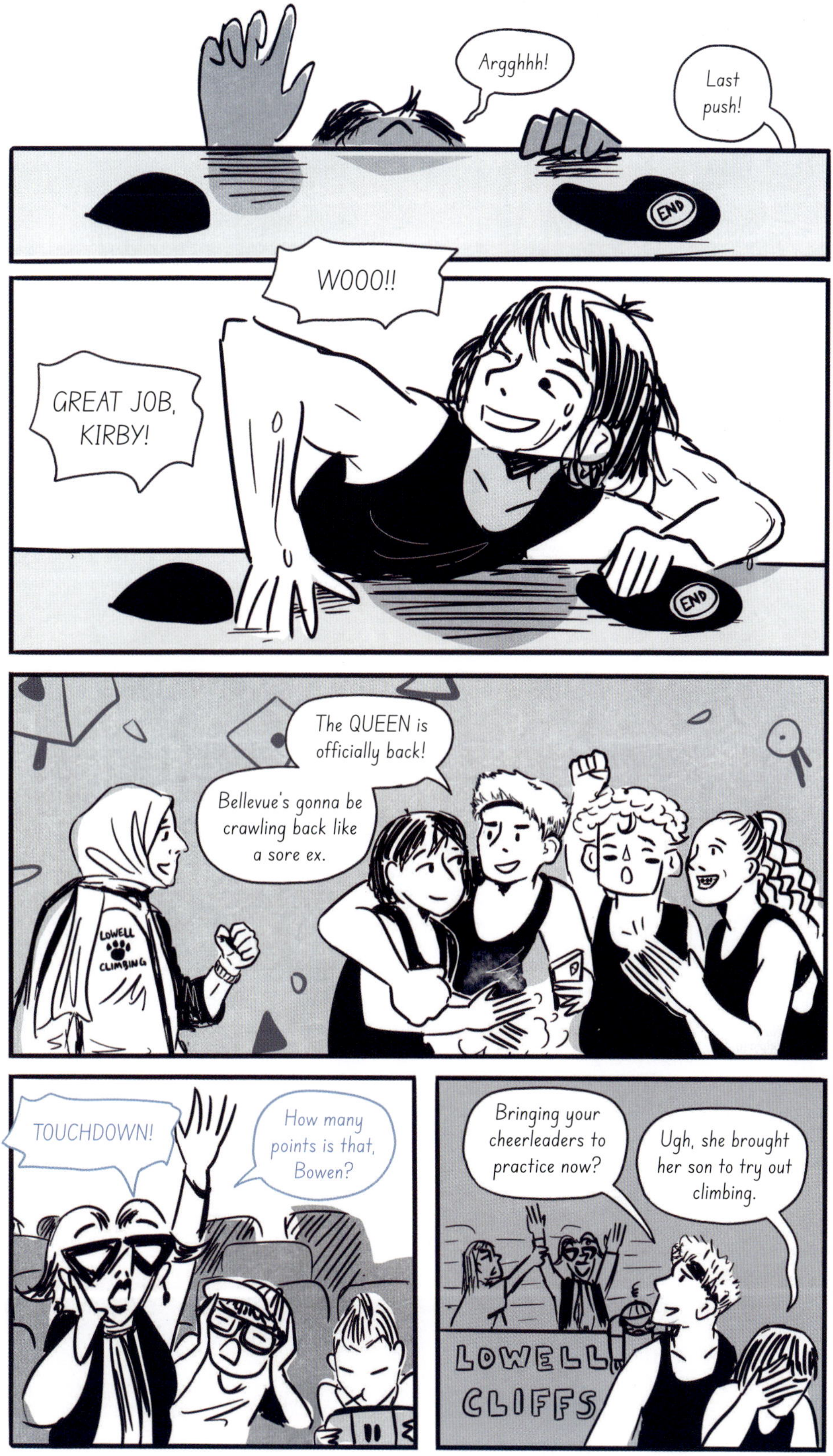
Argghhh!
Last push!
END
WOOO!!
GREAT JOB, KIRBY!
END
The QUEEN is officially back!
Bellevue's gonna be crawling back like a sore ex.
LOWELL CLIMBING
TOUCHDOWN!
How many points is that, Bowen?
Bringing your cheerleaders to practice now?
Ugh, she brought her son to try out climbing.
LOWELL CLIFFS

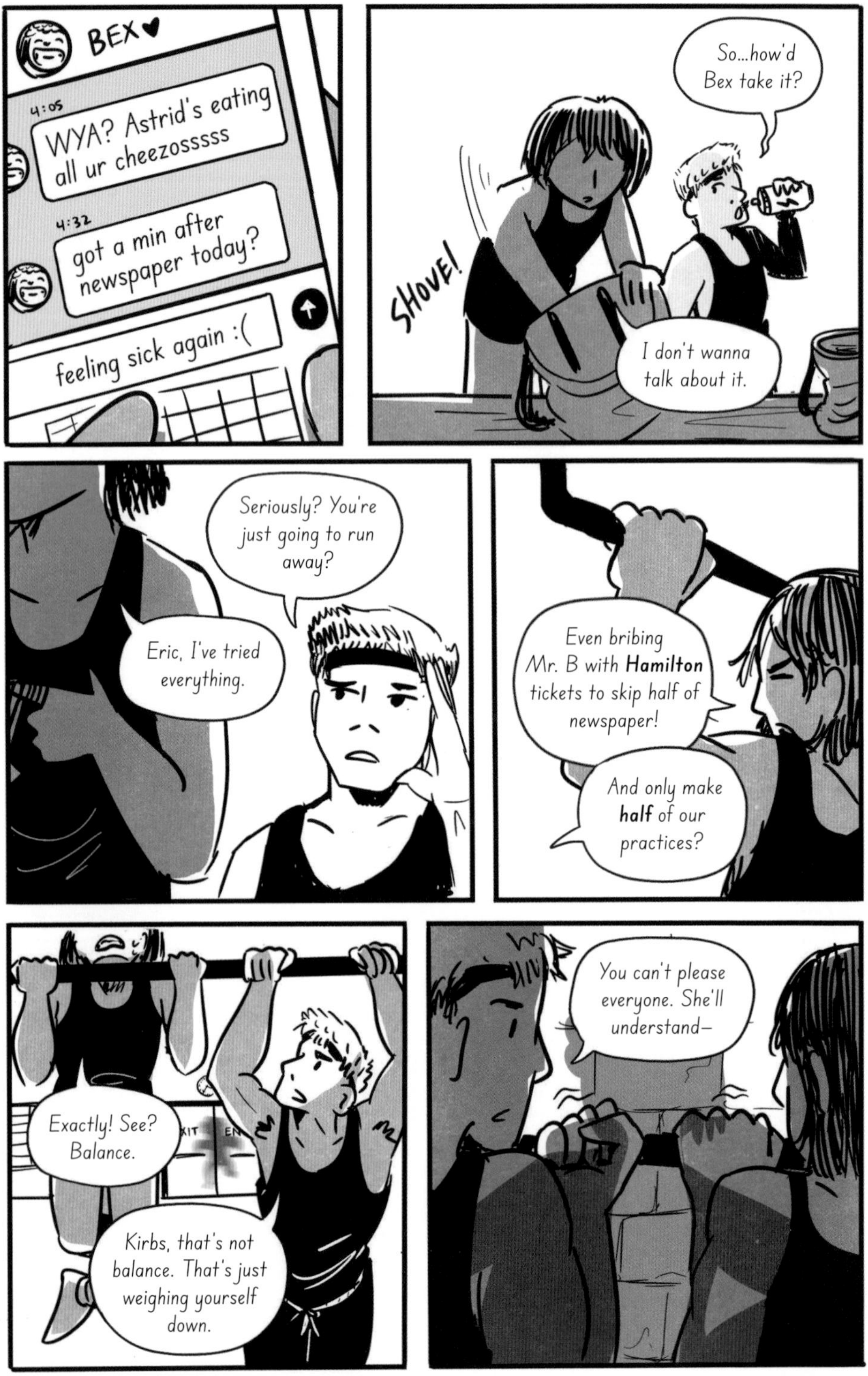
BEX
4:05
WYA? Astrid's eating all ur cheezosssss
4:32
got a min after newspaper today?
feeling sick again :(
So...how'd Bex take it?
SHOVE!
I don't wanna talk about it.
Seriously? You're just going to run away?
Eric, I've tried everything.
Even bribing Mr. B with **Hamilton** tickets to skip half of newspaper!
And only make **half** of our practices?
Exactly! See? Balance.
Kirbs, that's not balance. That's just weighing yourself down.
You can't please everyone. She'll understand—

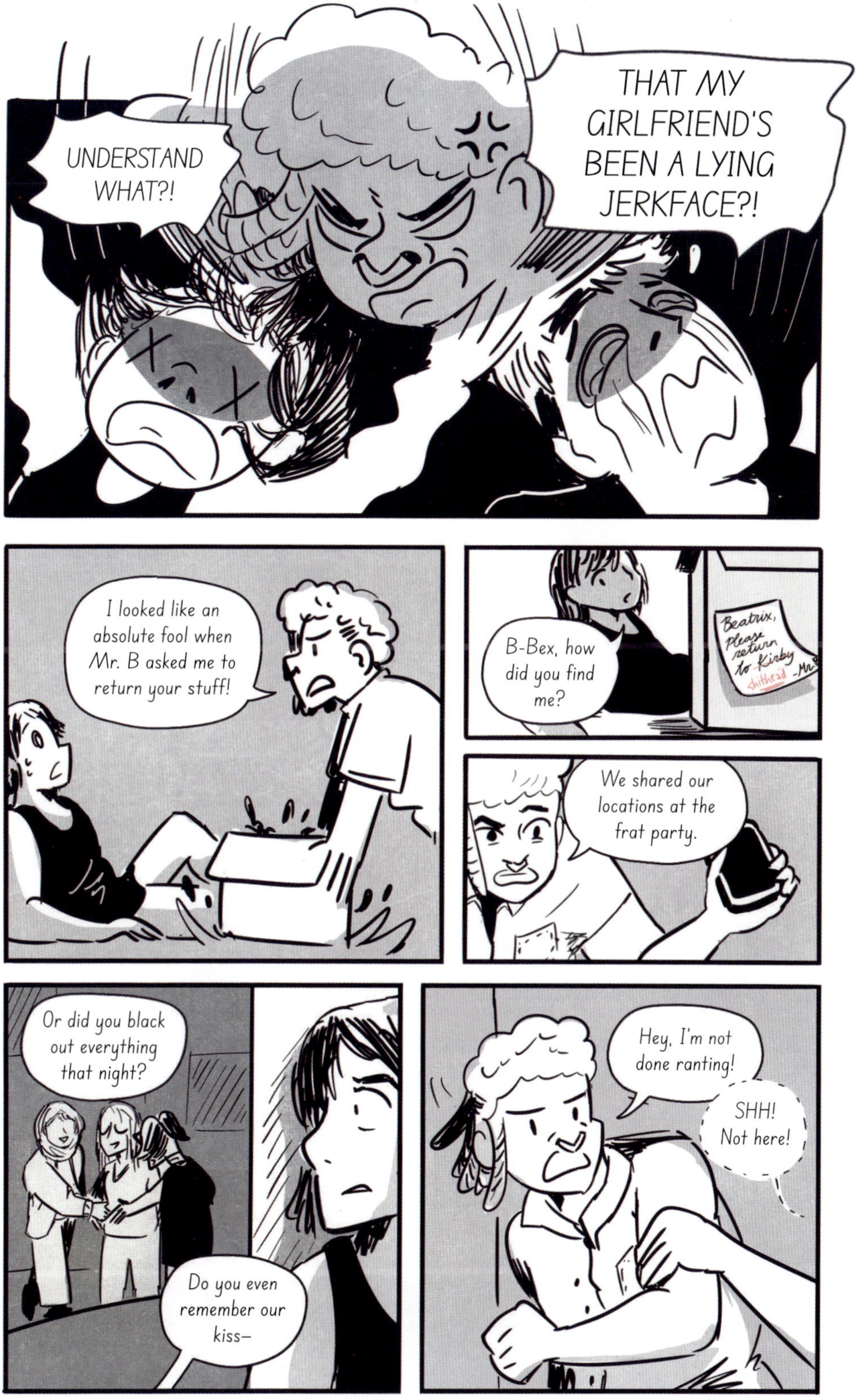
UNDERSTAND WHAT?!
THAT MY GIRLFRIEND'S BEEN A LYING JERKFACE?!
I looked like an absolute fool when Mr. B asked me to return your stuff!
B-Bex, how did you find me?
Beatrix, Please return to Kirby
shithead
-Mr
We shared our locations at the frat party.
Or did you black out everything that night?
Do you even remember our kiss–
Hey, I'm not done ranting!
SHH! Not here!

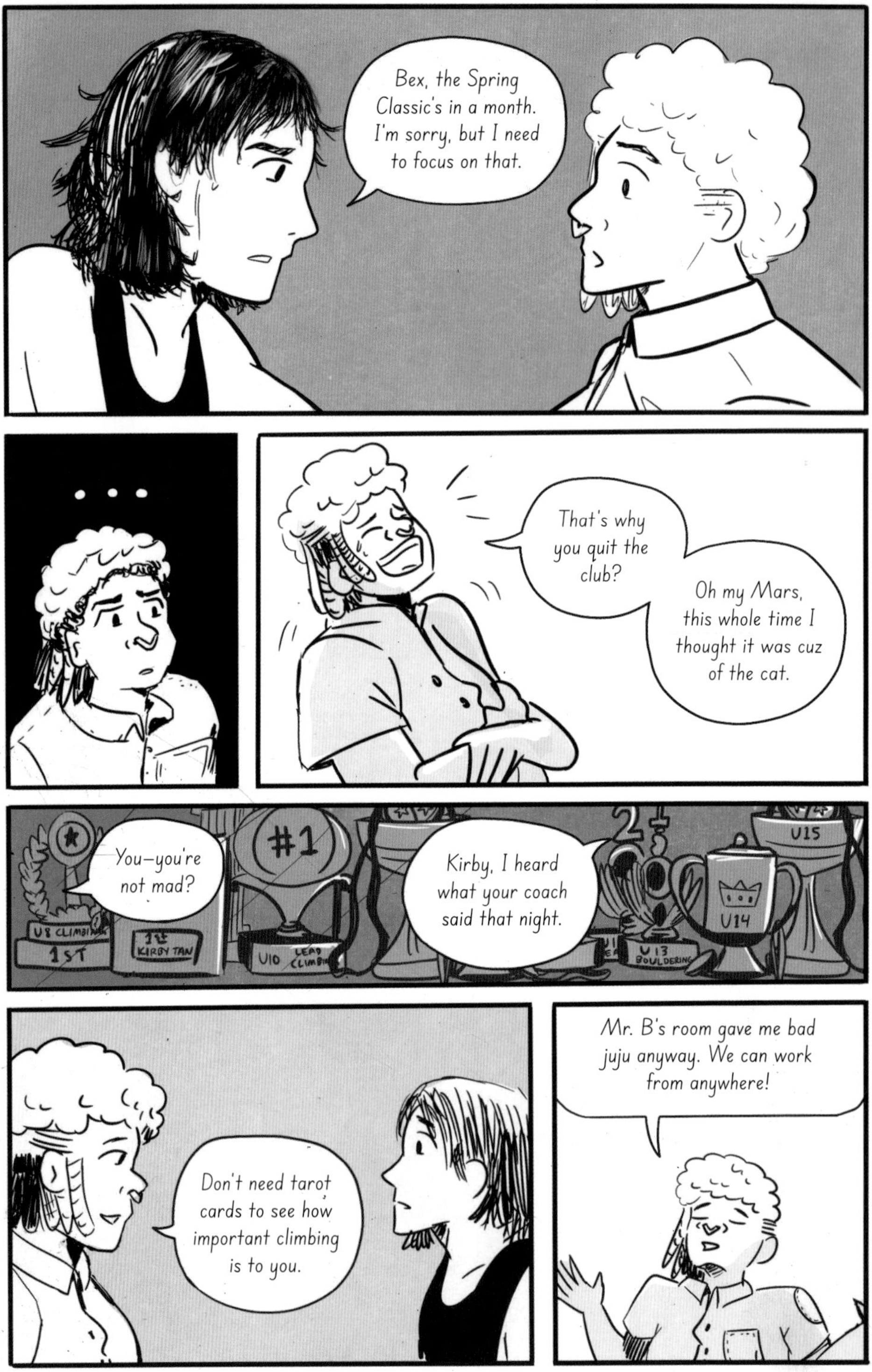
Bex, the Spring Classic's in a month. I'm sorry, but I need to focus on that.
...
That's why you quit the club?
Oh my Mars, this whole time I thought it was cuz of the cat.
You—you're not mad?
#1
U8 CLIMBING
1ST
1ST KIRBY TAN
U10 LEAD CLIMBING
Kirby, I heard what your coach said that night.
U13 BOULDERING
U14
U15
Don't need tarot cards to see how important climbing is to you.
Mr. B's room gave me bad juju anyway. We can work from anywhere!

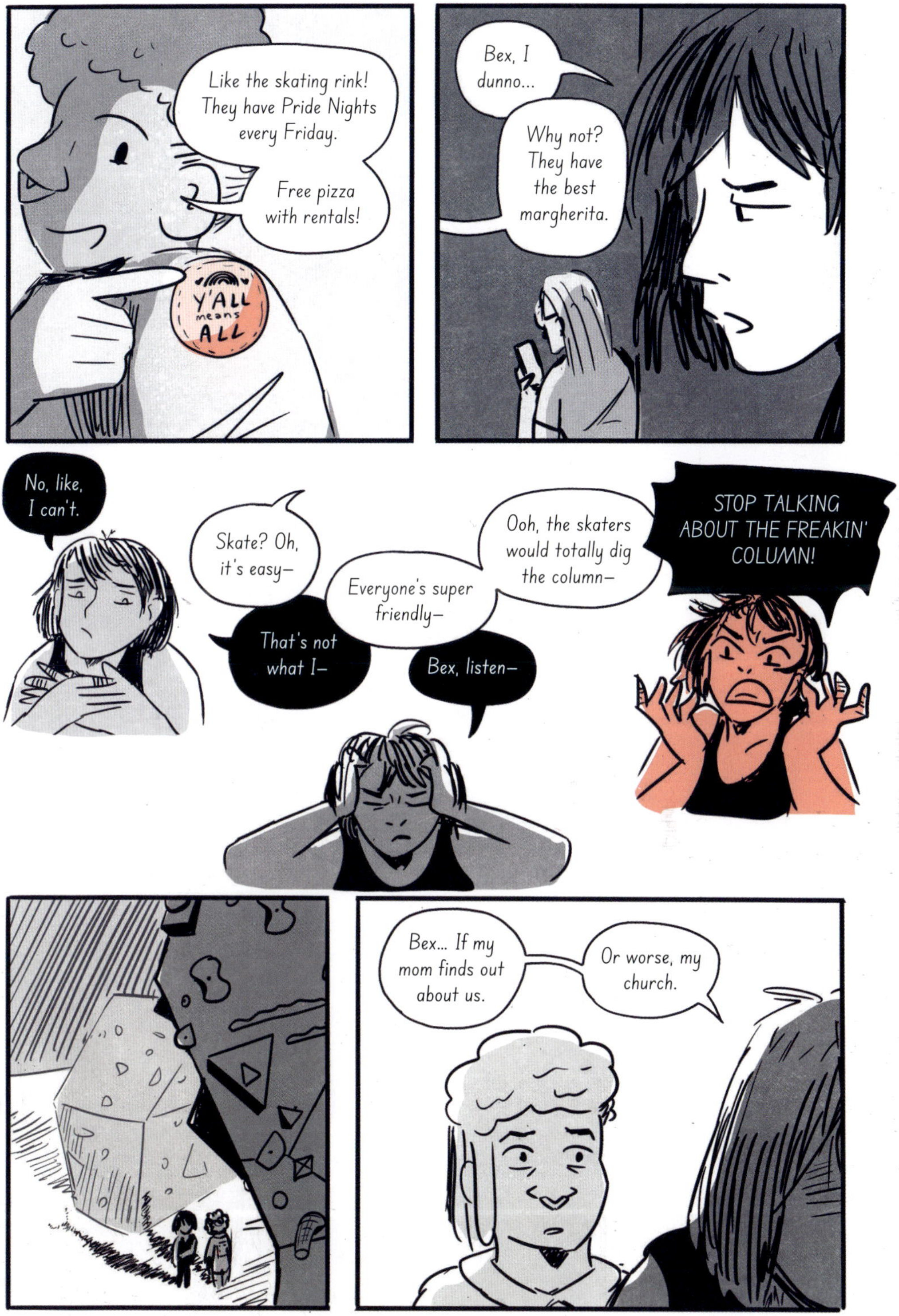

Like the skating rink! They have Pride Nights every Friday.
Free pizza with rentals!
Y'ALL means ALL
Bex, I dunno...
Why not? They have the best margherita.
No, like, I can't.
Skate? Oh, it's easy–
That's not what I–
Everyone's super friendly–
Bex, listen–
Ooh, the skaters would totally dig the column–
STOP TALKING ABOUT THE FREAKIN' COLUMN!
Bex... If my mom finds out about us.
Or worse, my church.

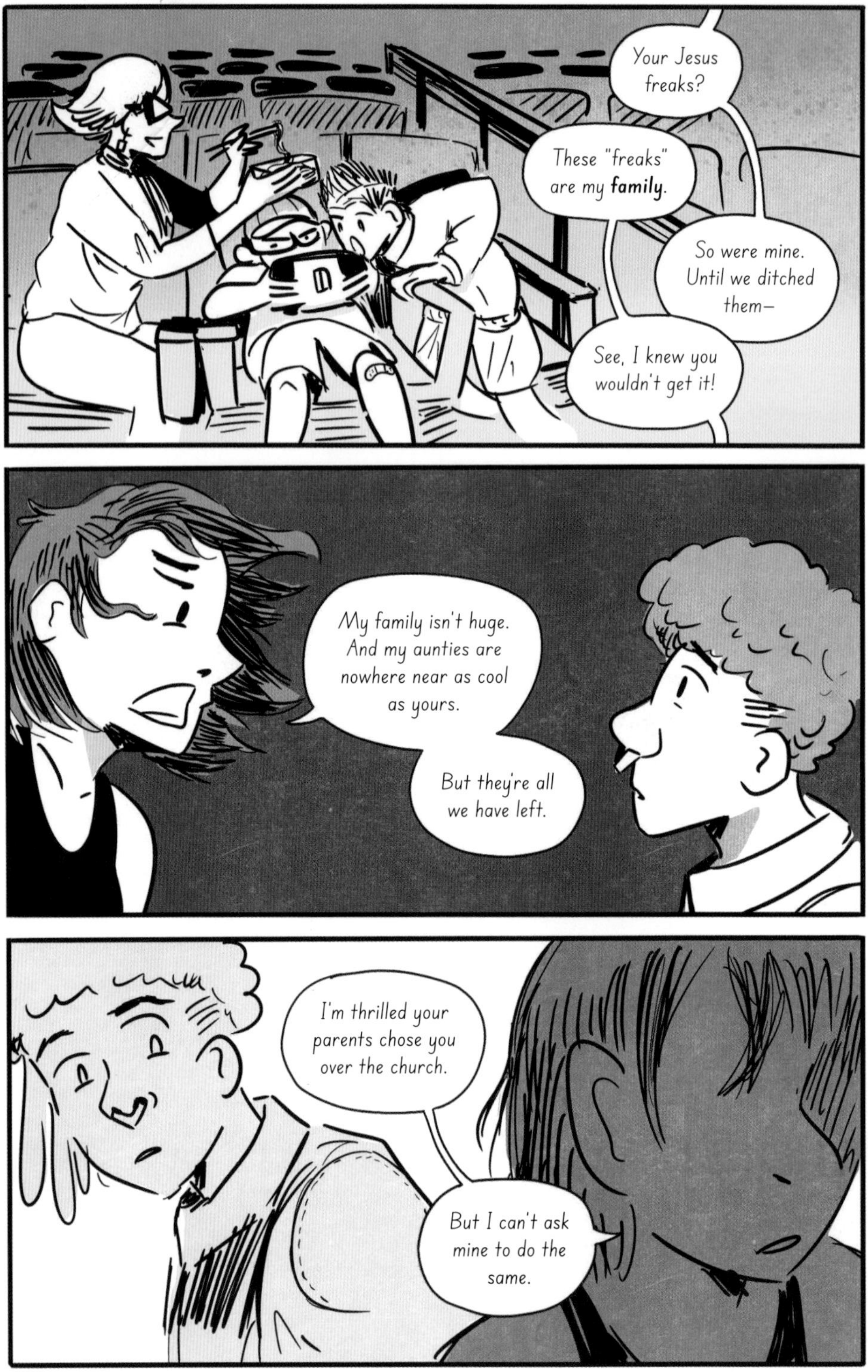
Your Jesus freaks?
These "freaks" are my **family**.
So were mine. Until we ditched them—
See, I knew you wouldn't get it!
My family isn't huge. And my aunties are nowhere near as cool as yours.
But they're all we have left.
I'm thrilled your parents chose you over the church.
But I can't ask mine to do the same.

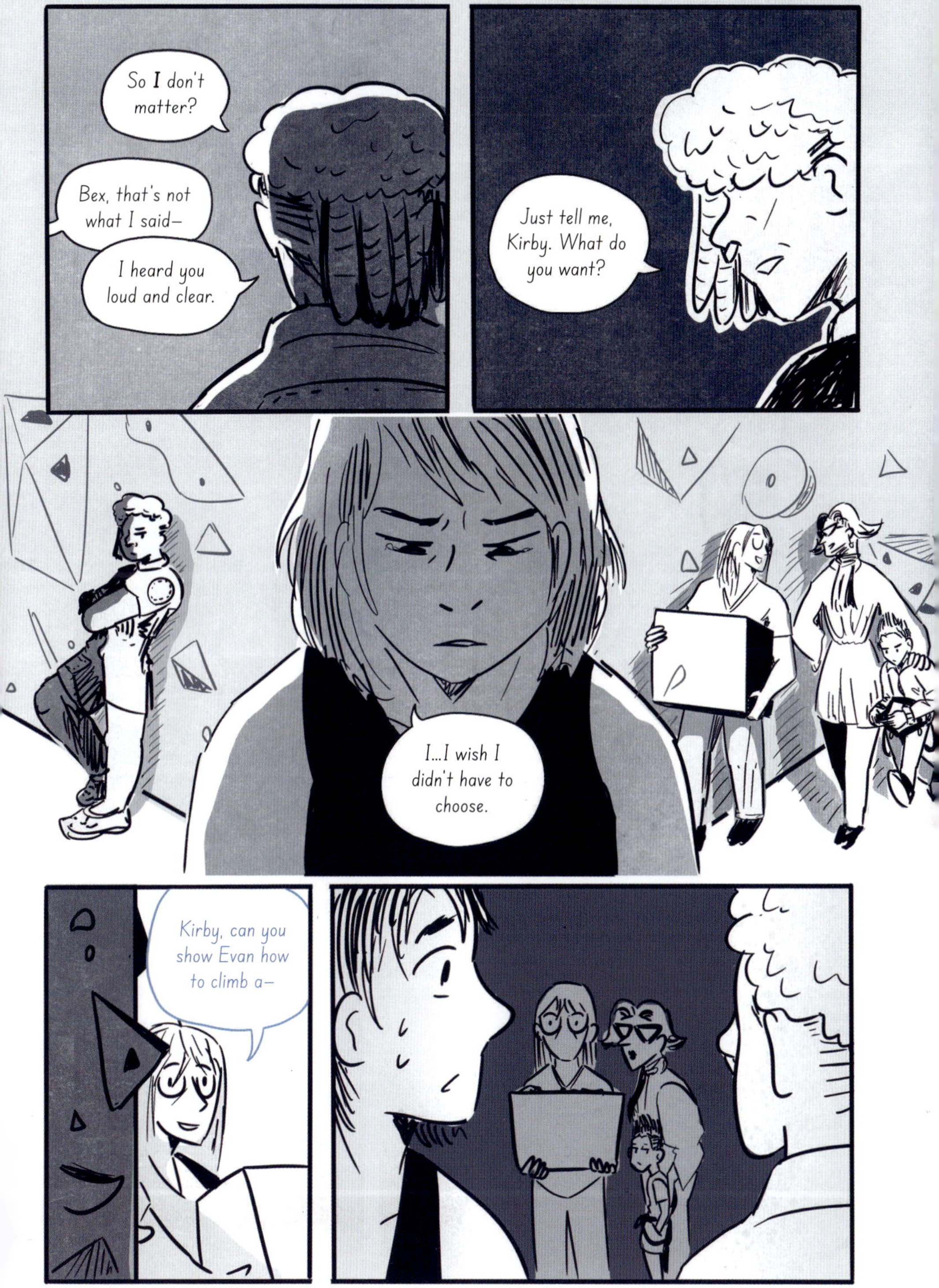
So **I** don't matter?
Bex, that's not what I said—
I heard you loud and clear.
Just tell me, Kirby. What do you want?
I...I wish I didn't have to choose.
Kirby, can you show Evan how to climb a—

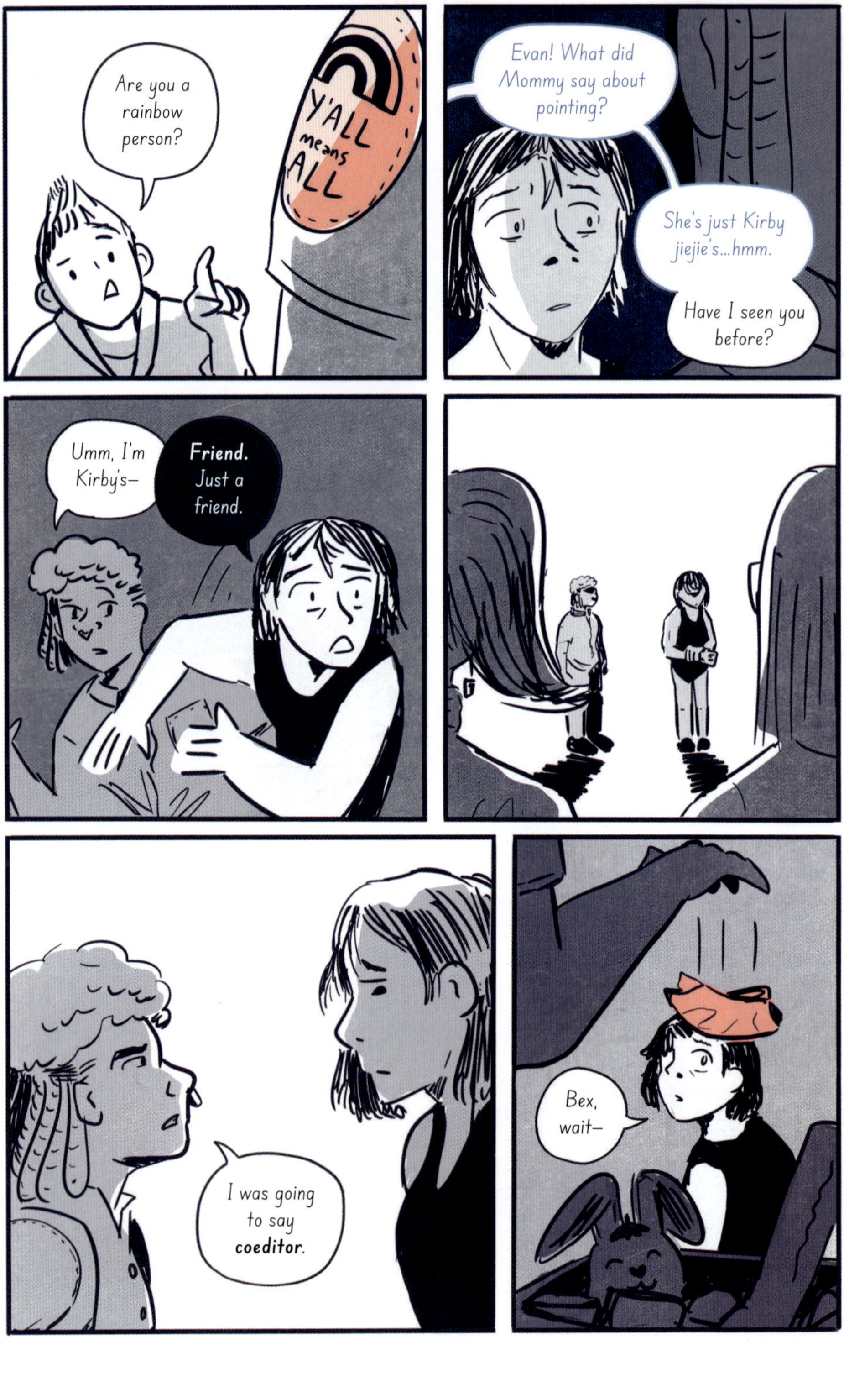
Are you a rainbow person?
Y'ALL means ALL
Evan! What did Mommy say about pointing?
She's just Kirby jiejie's...hmm.
Have I seen you before?
Umm, I'm Kirby's—
Friend. Just a friend.
I was going to say **coeditor**.
Bex, wait—

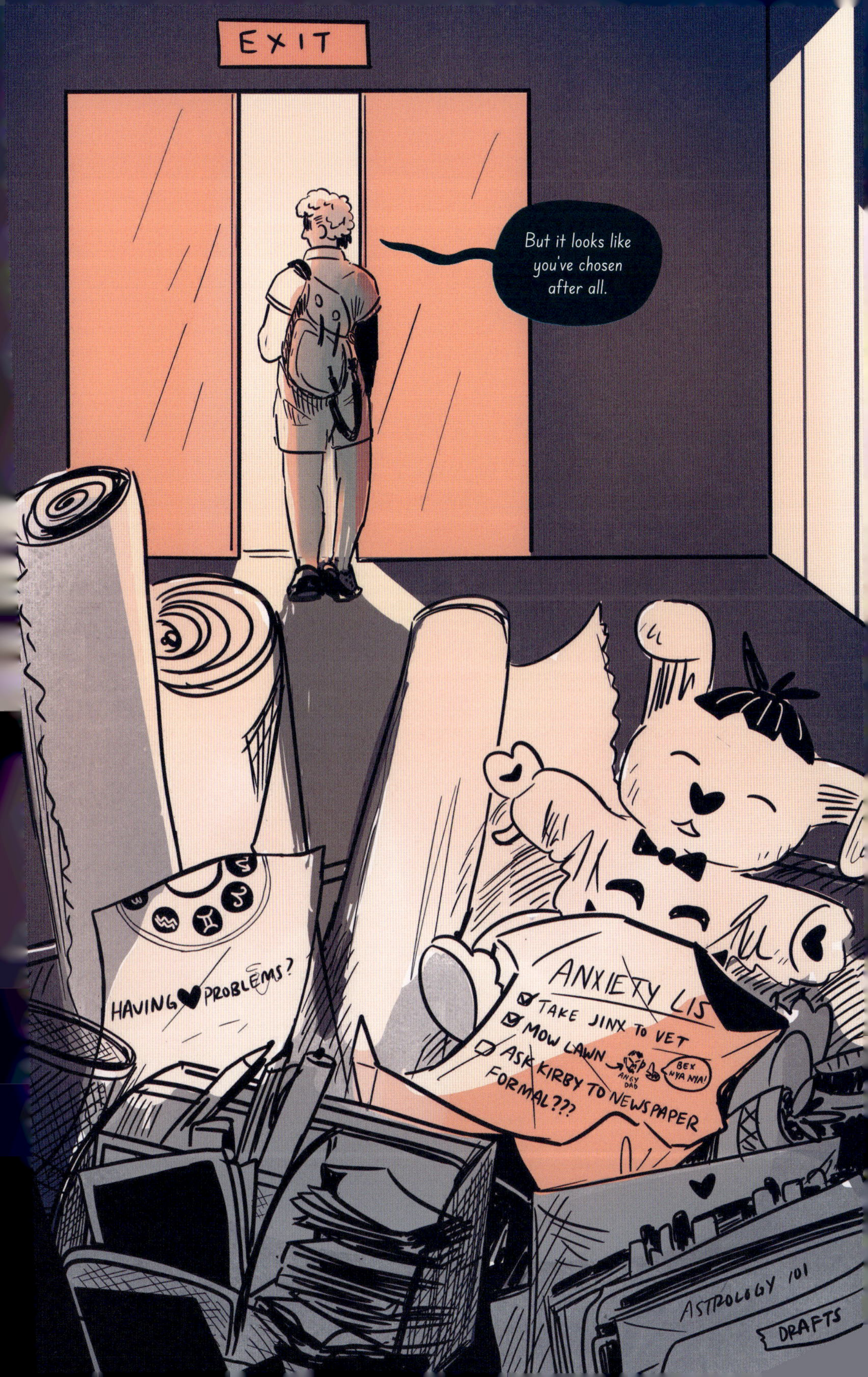
EXIT
But it looks like you've chosen after all.
HAVING ♥ PROBLEMS?
ANXIETY LIS
TAKE JINX TO VET
MOW LAWN
ASK KIRBY TO NEWSPAPER FORMAL???
BEX NYA NYA!
ASTROLOGY 101
DRAFTS

PART 5

TAROT

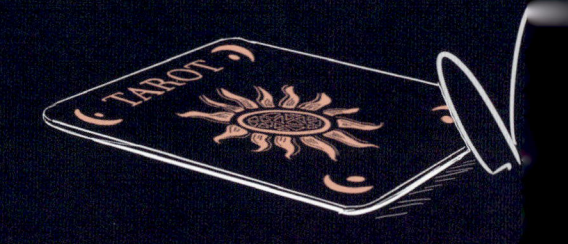

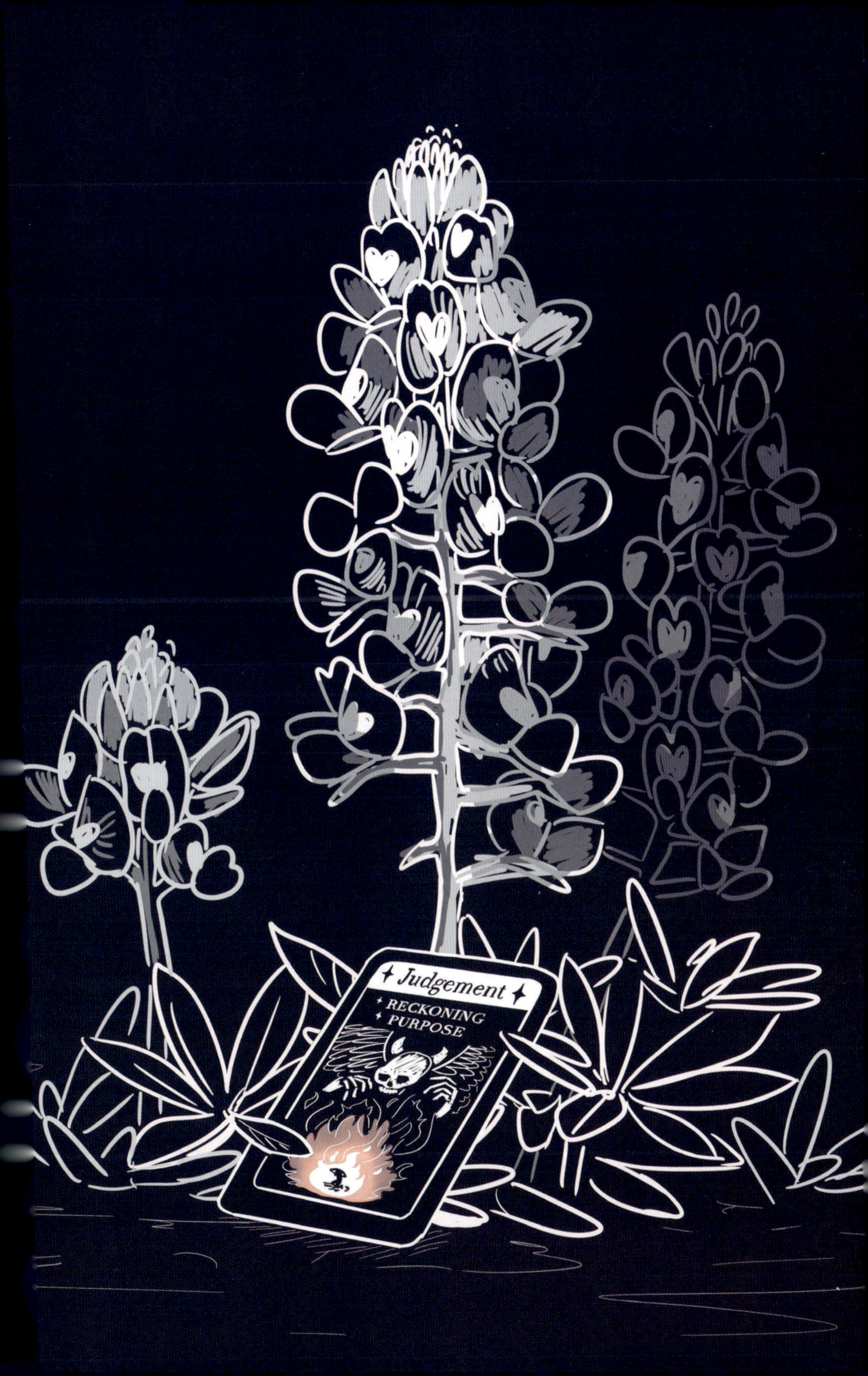
Judgement
RECKONING
PURPOSE

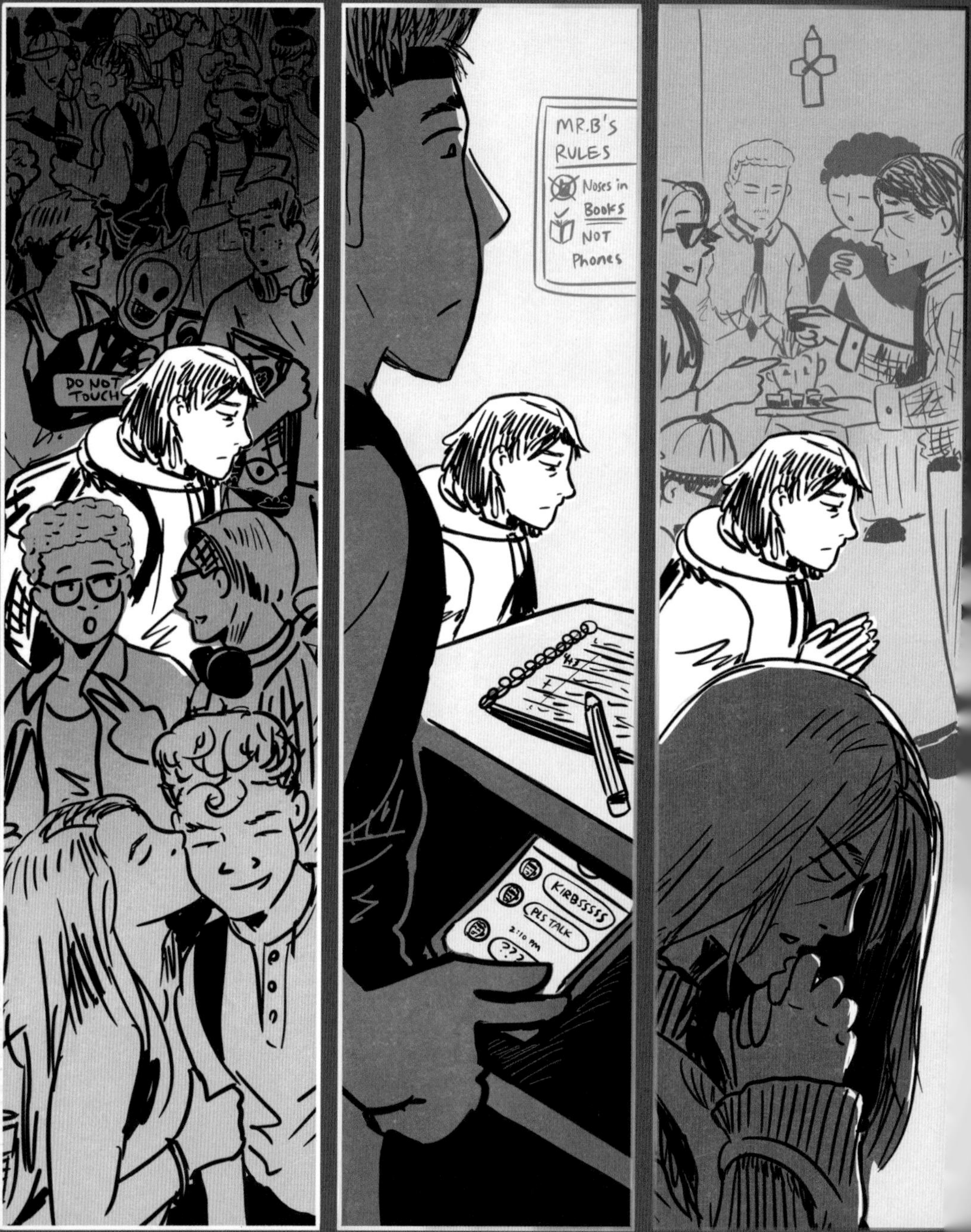

DO NOT TOUCH
MR.B'S RULES
Noses in Books
NOT Phones
KIRBSSSSS
PLS TALK
2:10 PM
???

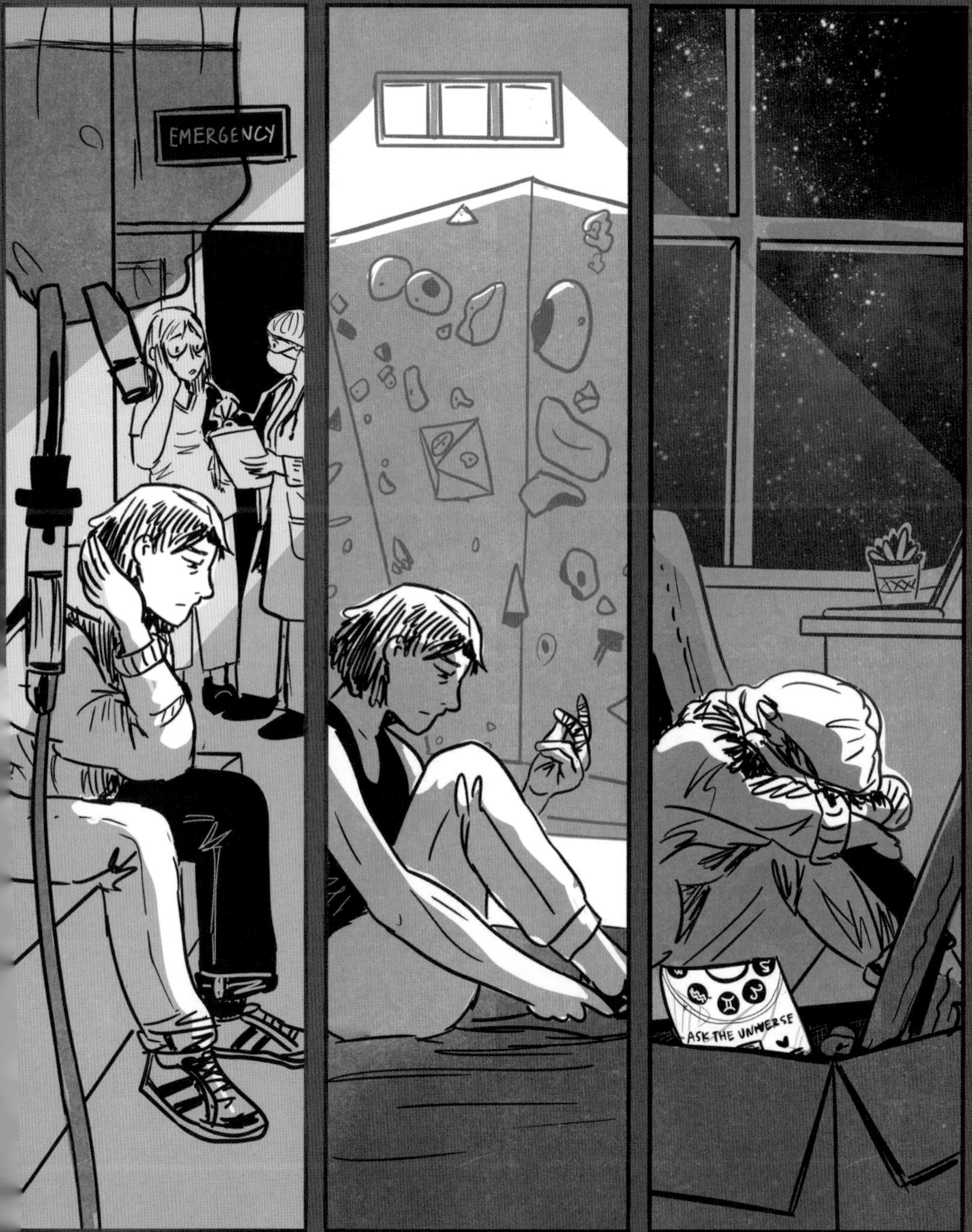
EMERGENCY
ASK THE UNIVERSE

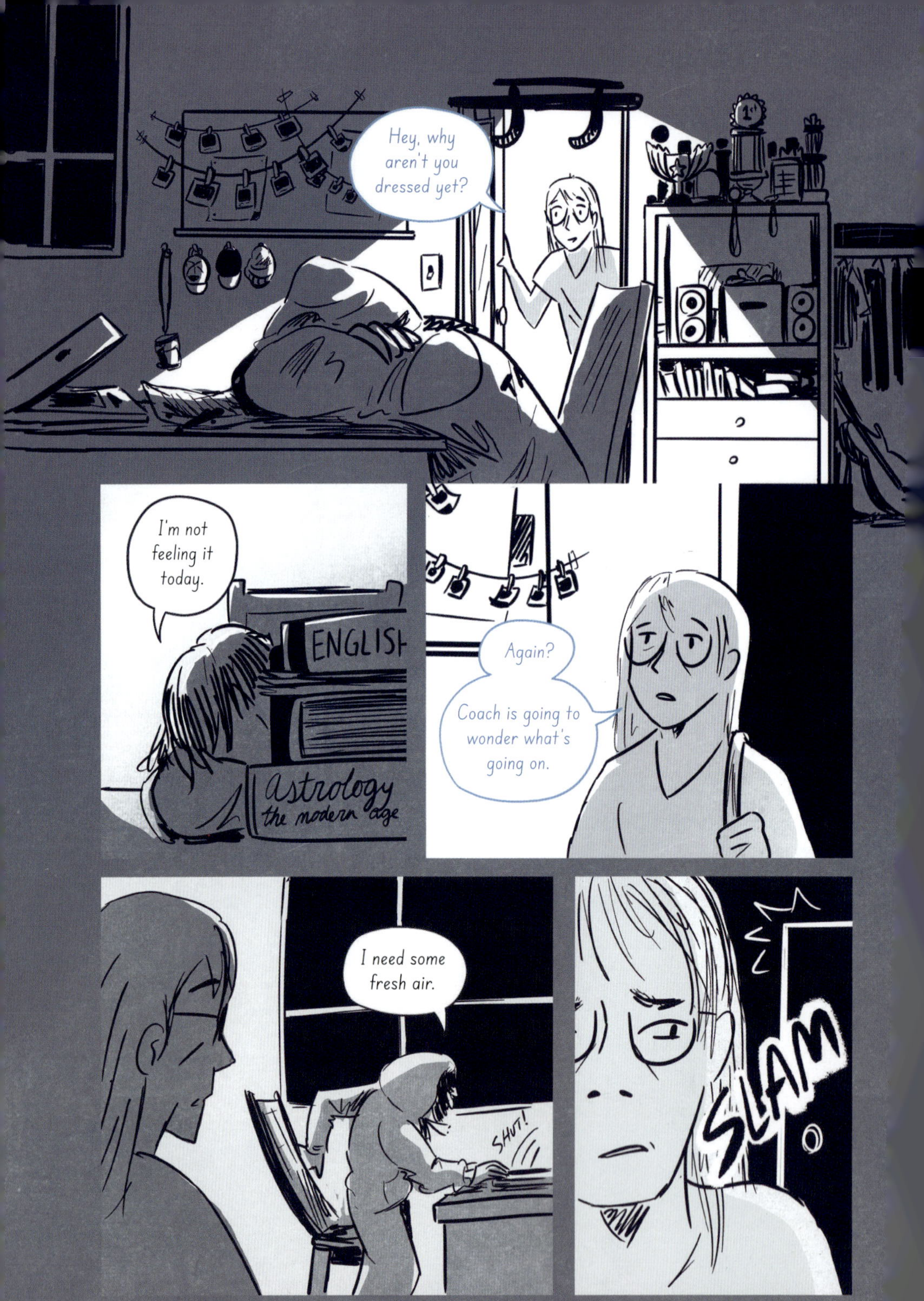
Hey, why aren't you dressed yet?
I'm not feeling it today.
ENGLISH
astrology the modern age
Again?
Coach is going to wonder what's going on.
I need some fresh air.
SHUT!
SLAM

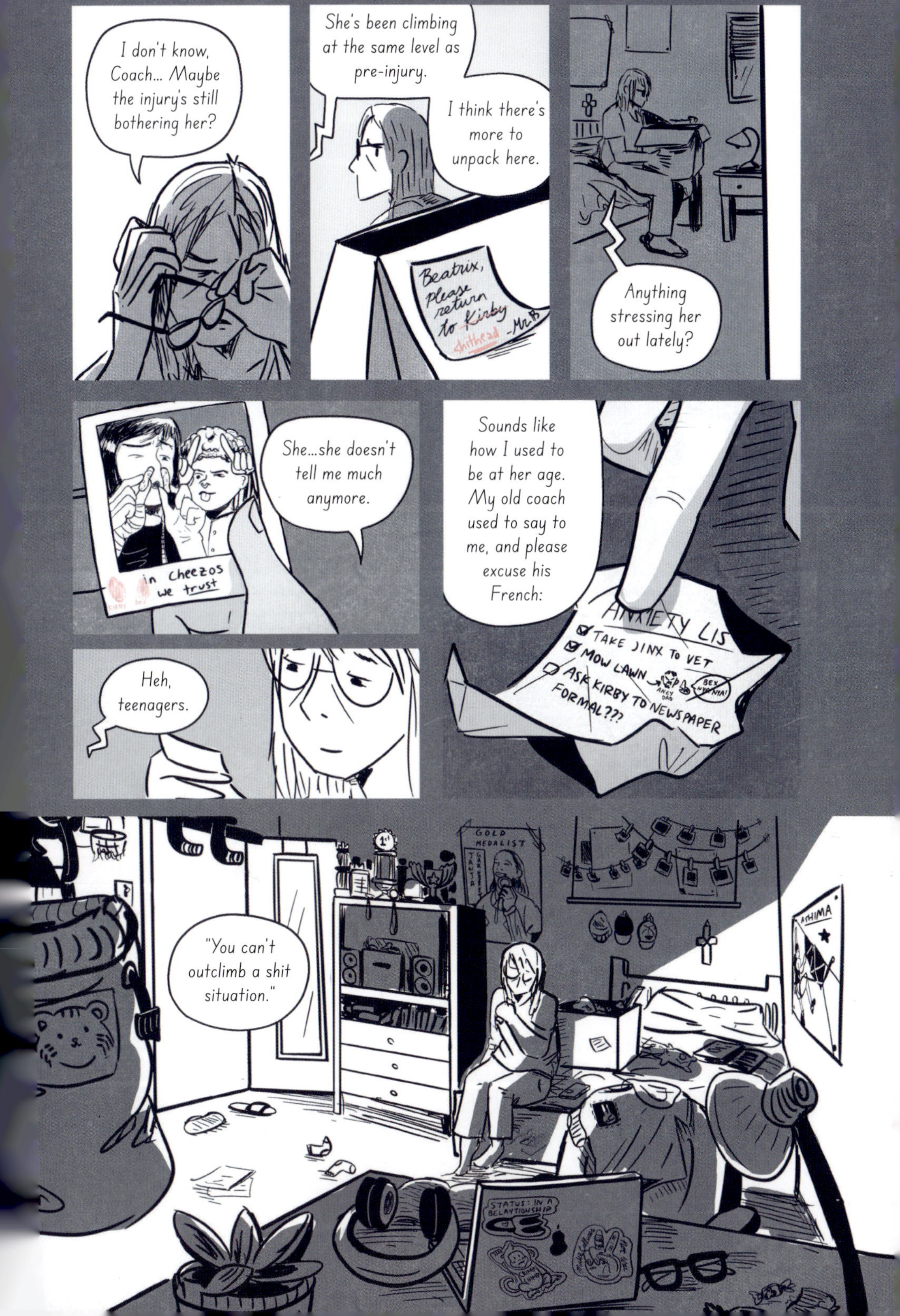

I don't know, Coach... Maybe the injury's still bothering her?
She's been climbing at the same level as pre-injury.
I think there's more to unpack here.
Beatrix, please return to Kirby shithead -Mr.B
Anything stressing her out lately?
in Cheezos we trust
She...she doesn't tell me much anymore.
Sounds like how I used to be at her age. My old coach used to say to me, and please excuse his French:
ANXIETY LIS
TAKE JINX TO VET
MOW LAWN
ASK KIRBY TO NEWSPAPER FORMAL???
Heh, teenagers.
GOLD MEDALIST
ASHIMA
"You can't outclimb a shit situation."
STATUS: IN A BELAYTIONSHIP

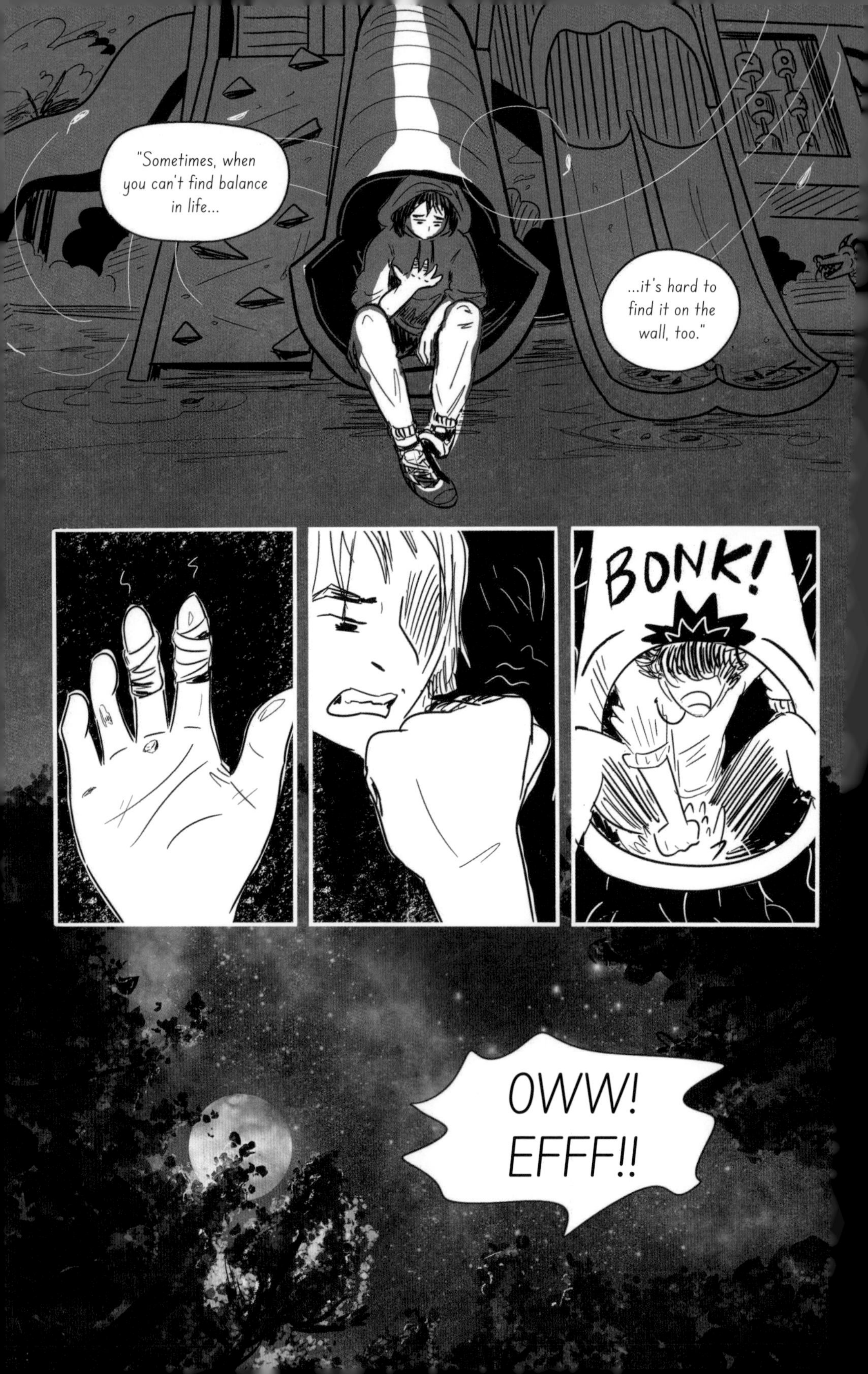
"Sometimes, when you can't find balance in life...
...it's hard to find it on the wall, too."
BONK!
OWW! EFFF!!

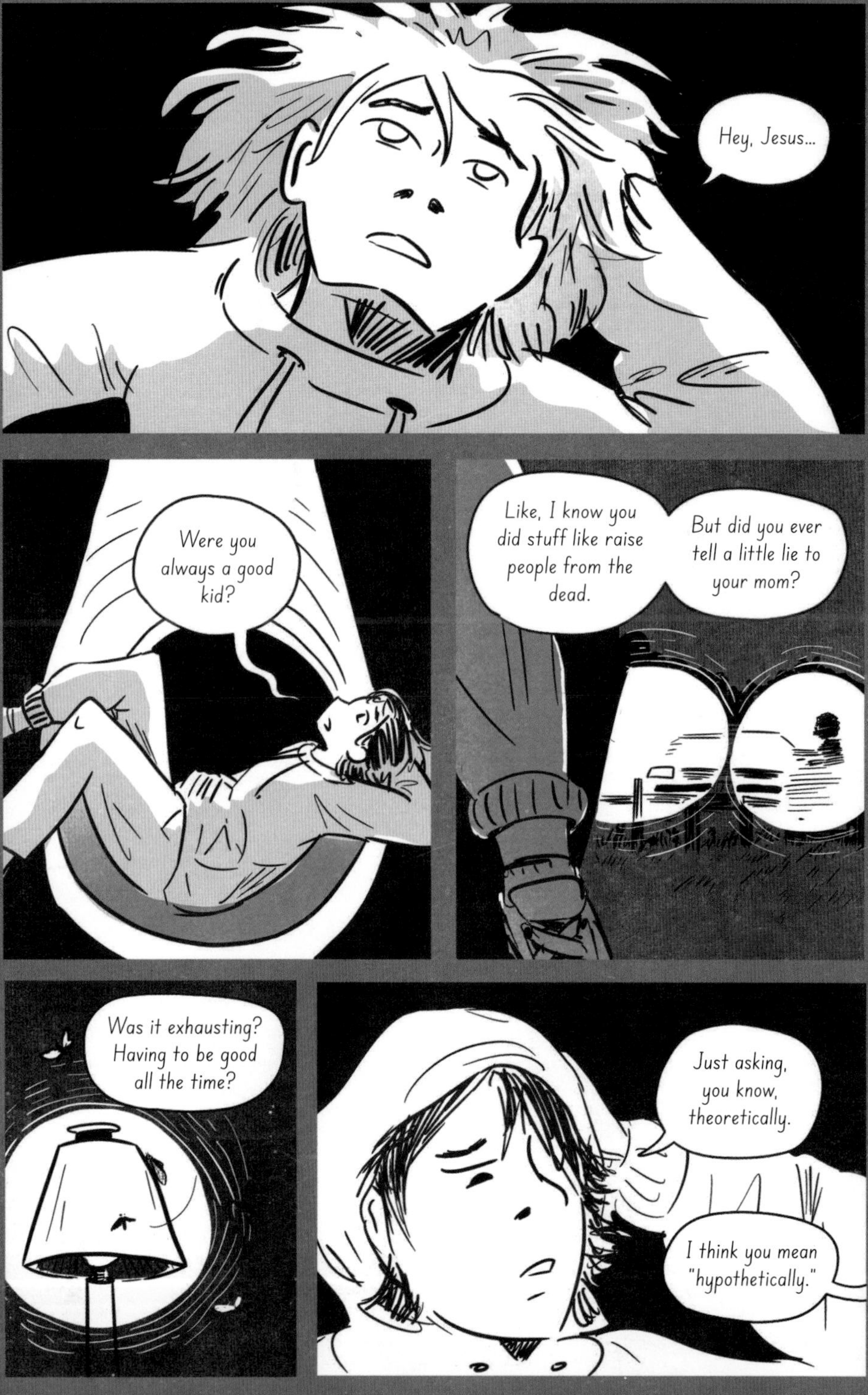
Hey, Jesus...
Were you always a good kid?
Like, I know you did stuff like raise people from the dead.
But did you ever tell a little lie to your mom?
Was it exhausting? Having to be good all the time?
Just asking, you know, theoretically.
I think you mean "hypothetically."

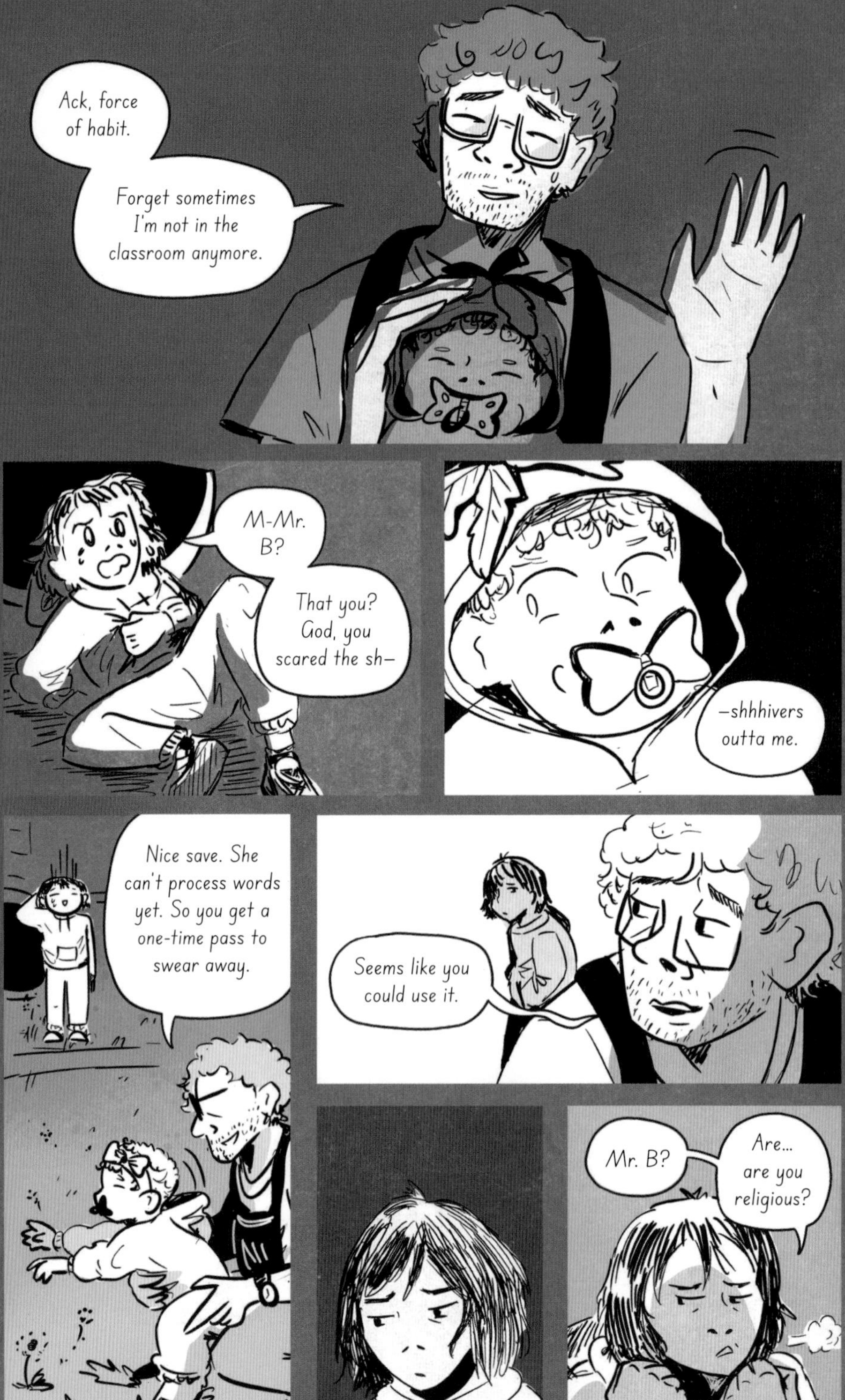
Ack, force of habit.
Forget sometimes I'm not in the classroom anymore.
M-Mr. B?
That you? God, you scared the sh—
—shhhivers outta me.
Nice save. She can't process words yet. So you get a one-time pass to swear away.
Seems like you could use it.
Mr. B?
Are... are you religious?

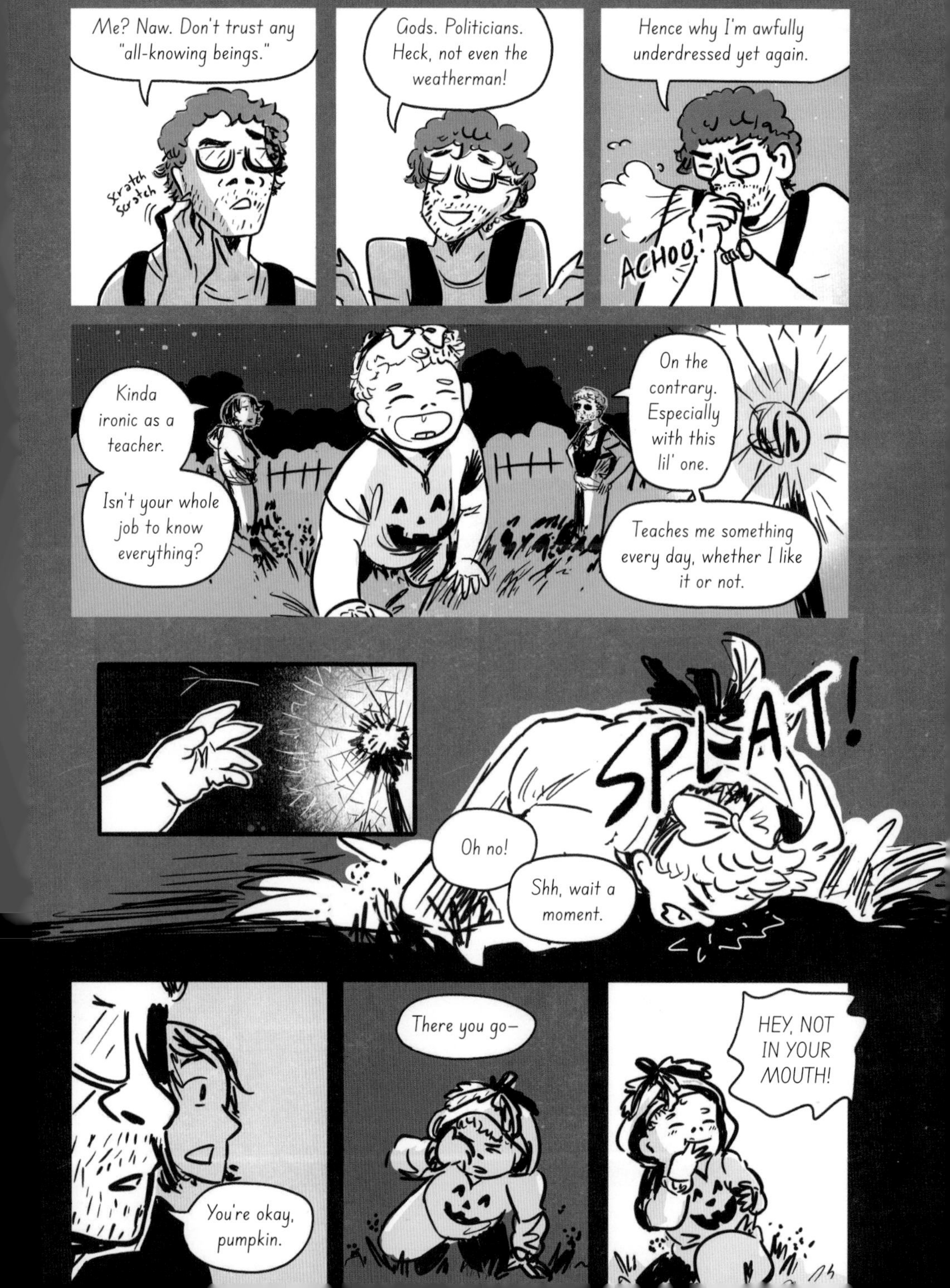

Me? Naw. Don't trust any "all-knowing beings."
Scratch scratch
Gods. Politicians. Heck, not even the weatherman!
Hence why I'm awfully underdressed yet again.
ACHOO!
Kinda ironic as a teacher.
Isn't your whole job to know everything?
On the contrary. Especially with this lil' one.
Teaches me something every day, whether I like it or not.
SPLAT!
Oh no!
Shh, wait a moment.
You're okay, pumpkin.
There you go—
HEY, NOT IN YOUR MOUTH!

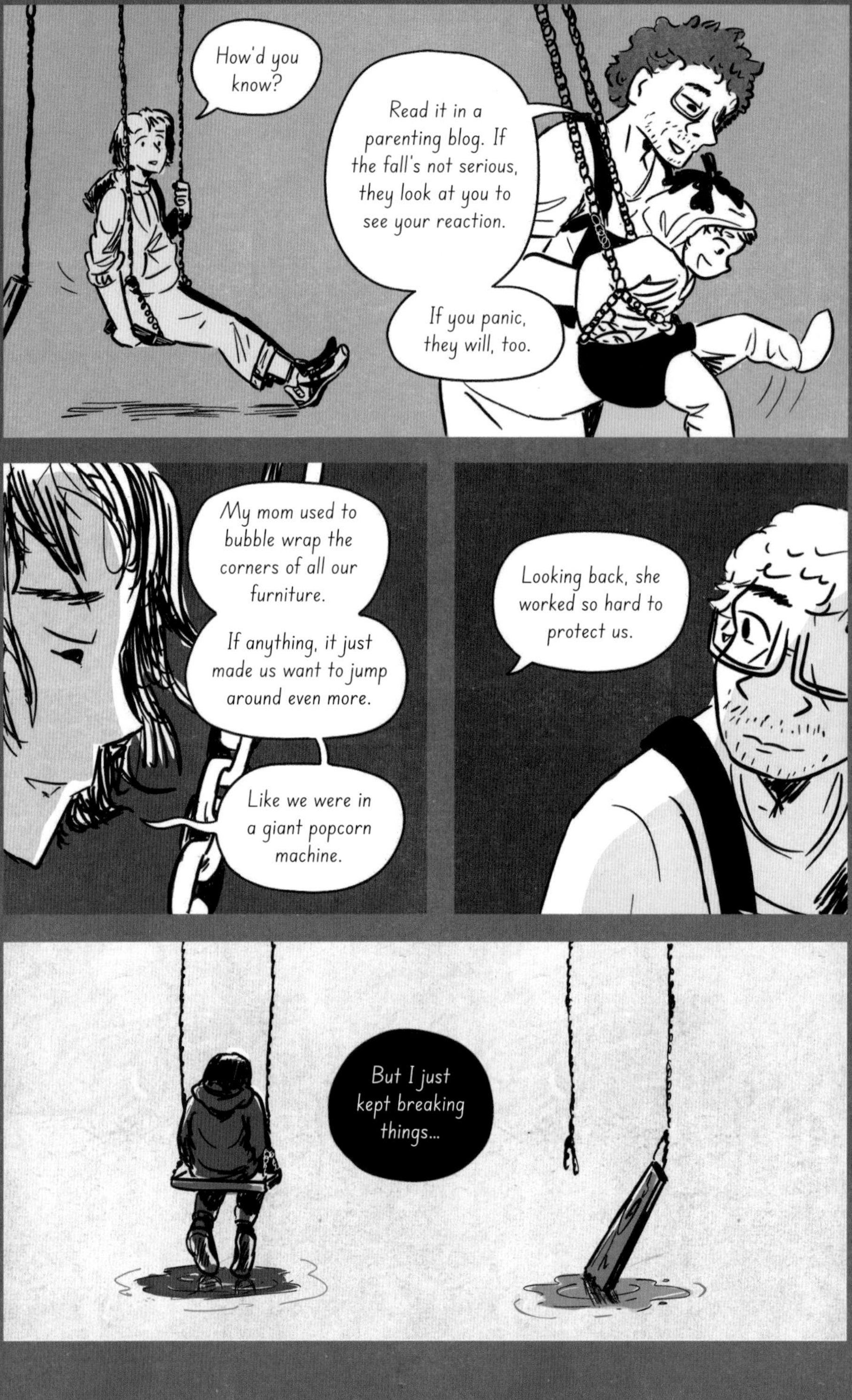
How'd you know?
Read it in a parenting blog. If the fall's not serious, they look at you to see your reaction.
If you panic, they will, too.
My mom used to bubble wrap the corners of all our furniture.
If anything, it just made us want to jump around even more.
Like we were in a giant popcorn machine.
Looking back, she worked so hard to protect us.
But I just kept breaking things...

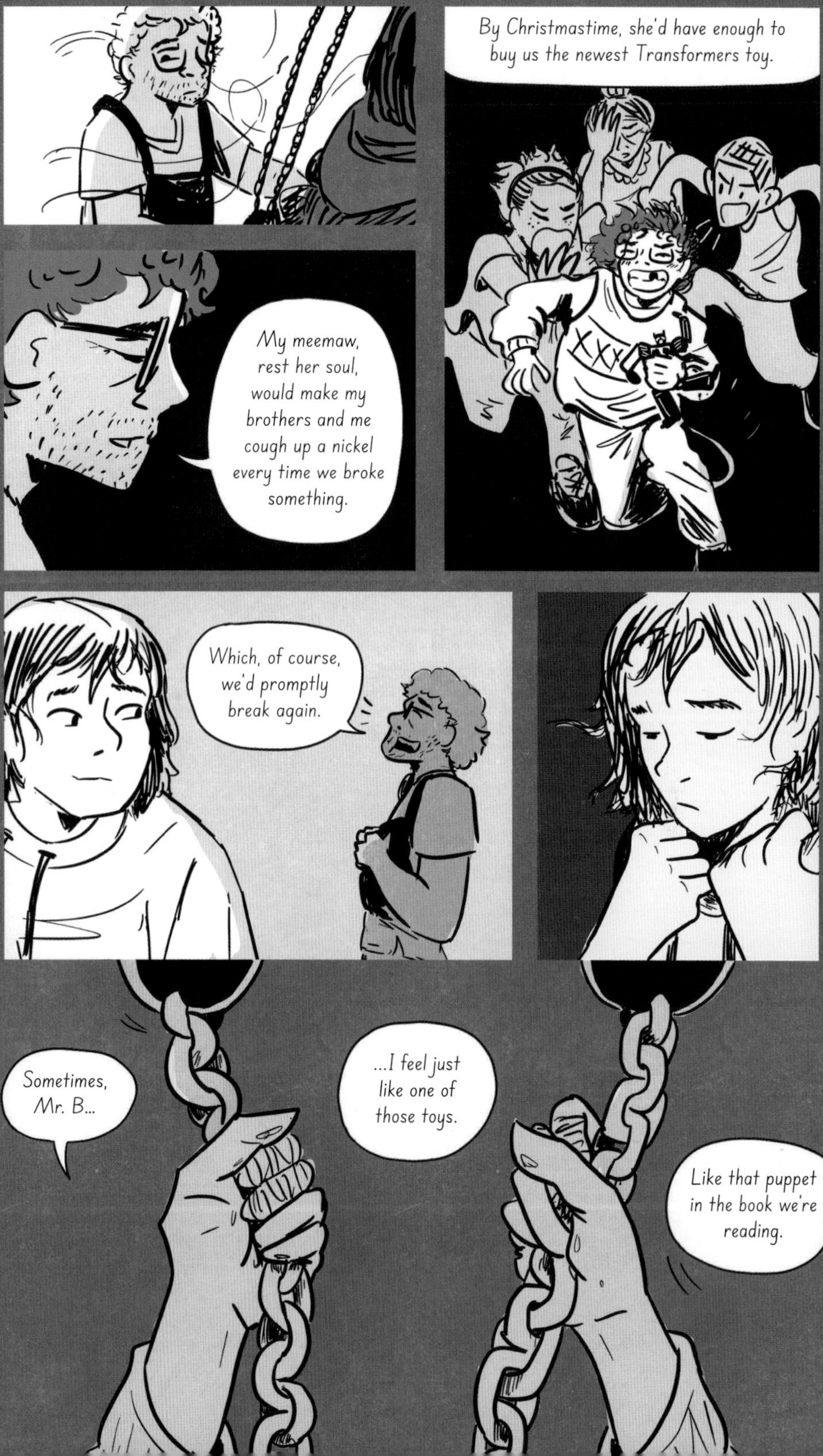

By Christmastime, she'd have enough to buy us the newest Transformers toy.
My meemaw, rest her soul, would make my brothers and me cough up a nickel every time we broke something.
Which, of course, we'd promptly break again.
Sometimes, Mr. B...
...I feel just like one of those toys.
Like that puppet in the book we're reading.

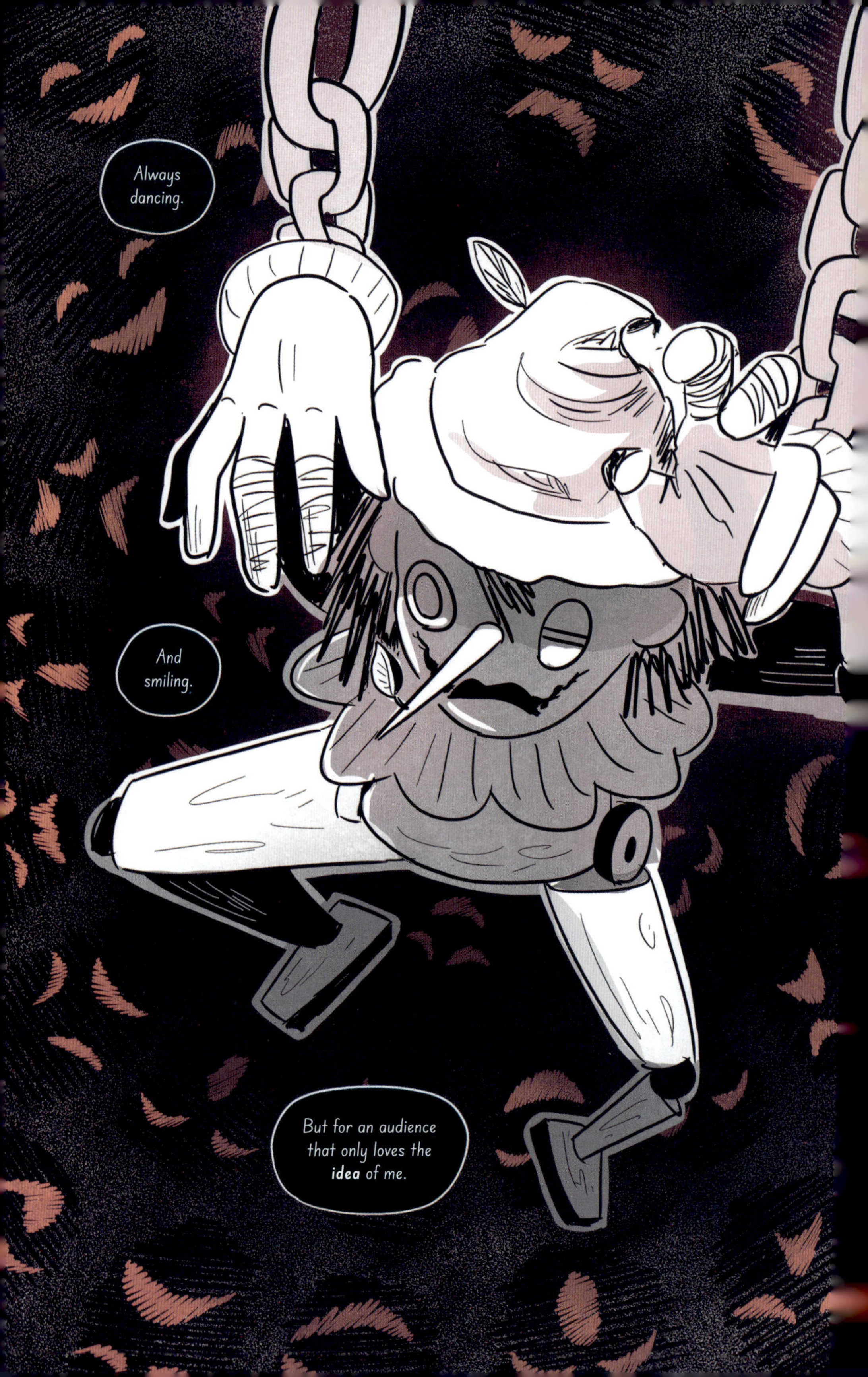
Always dancing.
And smiling.
But for an audience that only loves the **idea** of me.

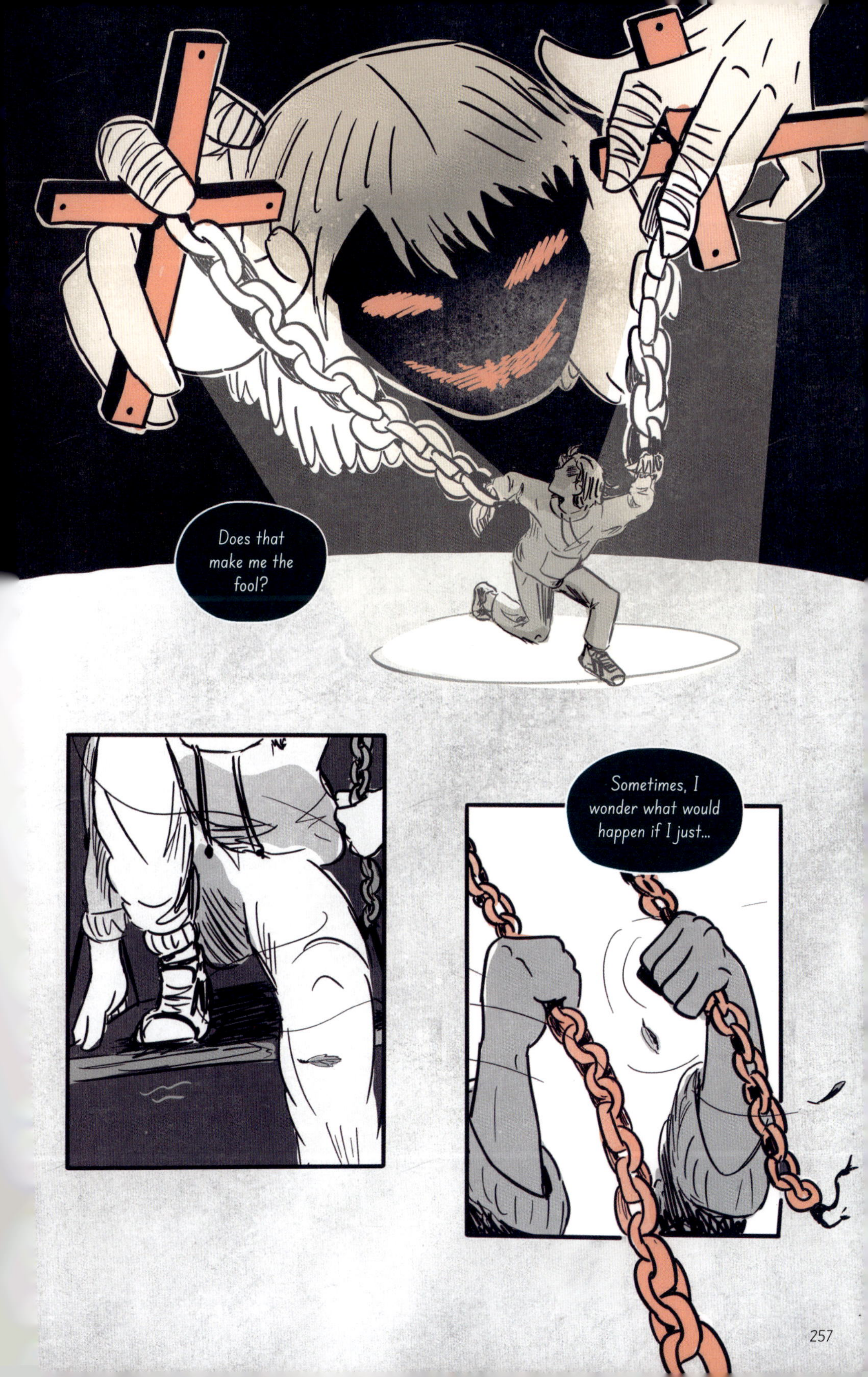
Does that make me the fool?
Sometimes, I wonder what would happen if I just...

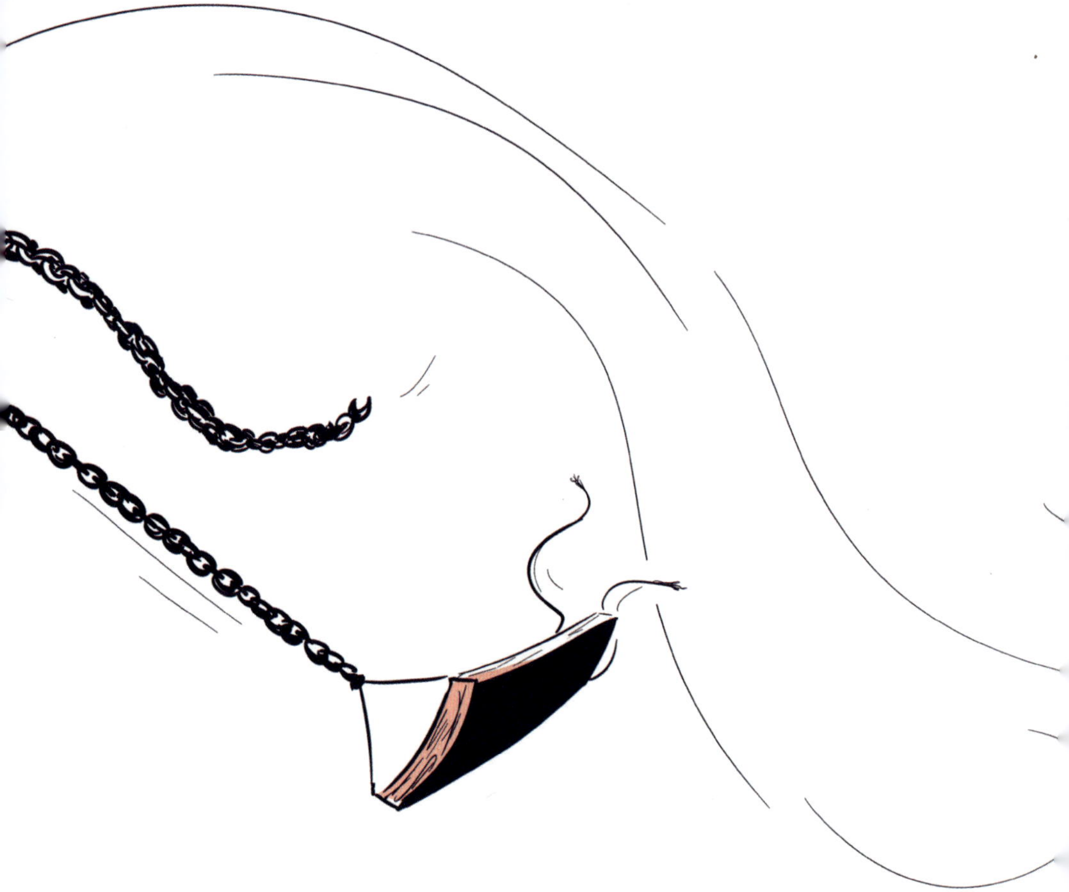

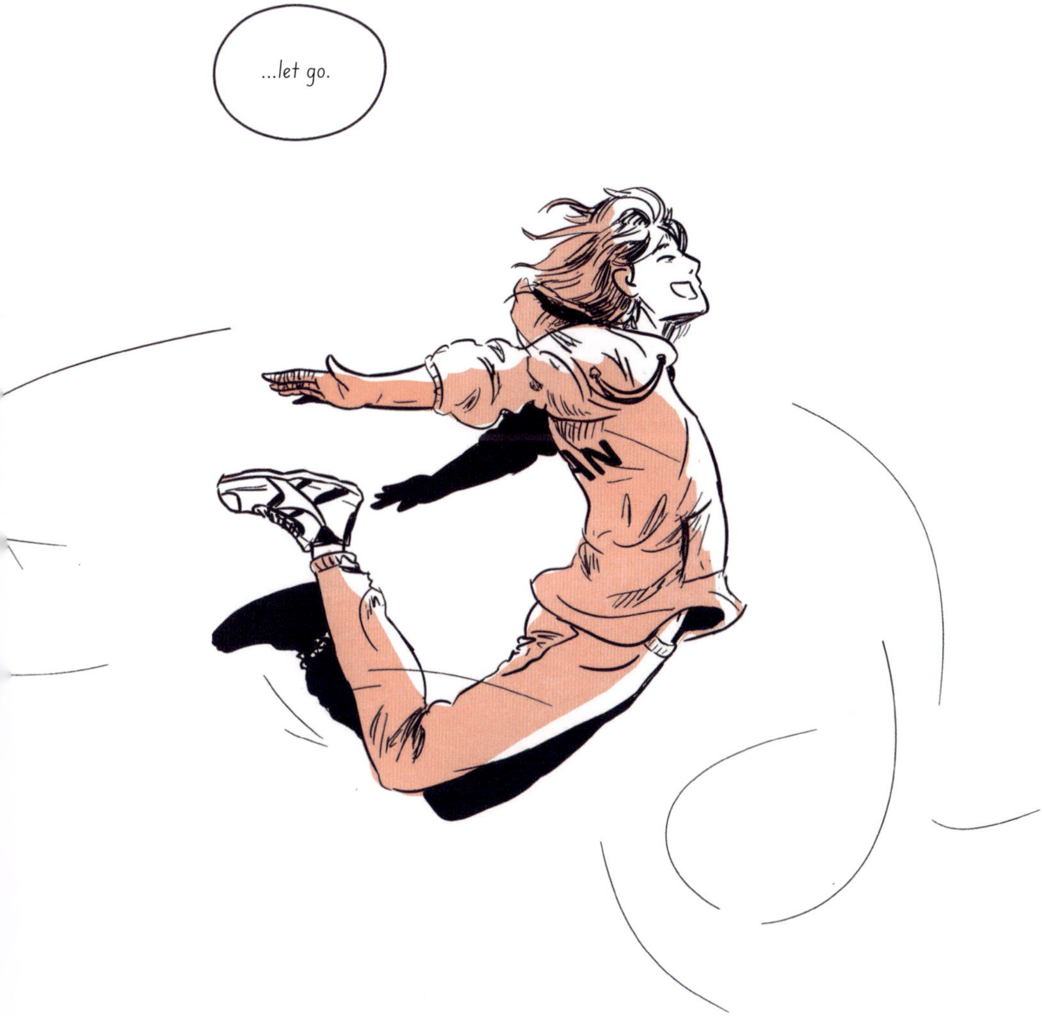
...let go.
AN

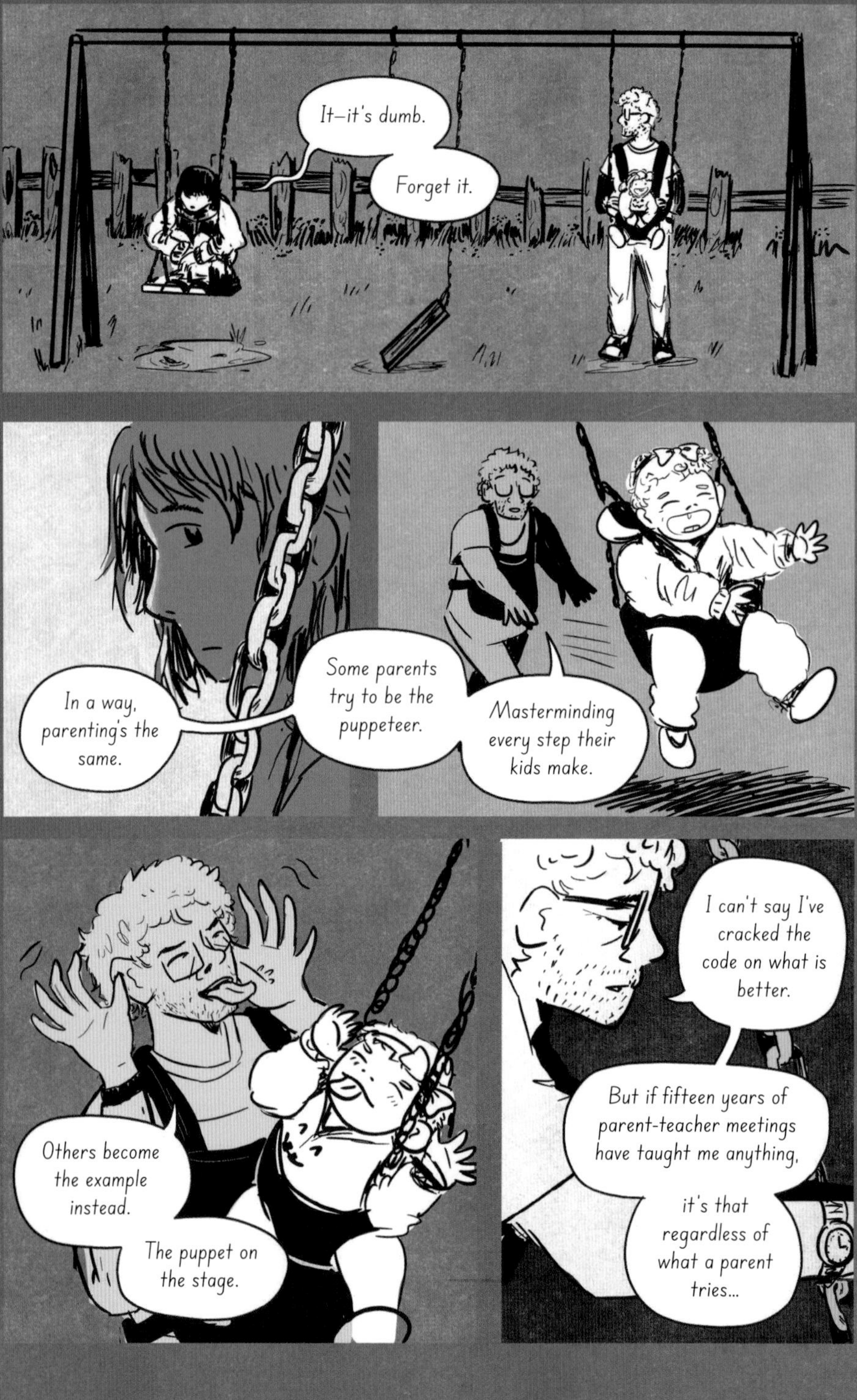
It–it's dumb.
Forget it.
In a way, parenting's the same.
Some parents try to be the puppeteer.
Masterminding every step their kids make.
Others become the example instead.
The puppet on the stage.
I can't say I've cracked the code on what is better.
But if fifteen years of parent-teacher meetings have taught me anything,
it's that regardless of what a parent tries...

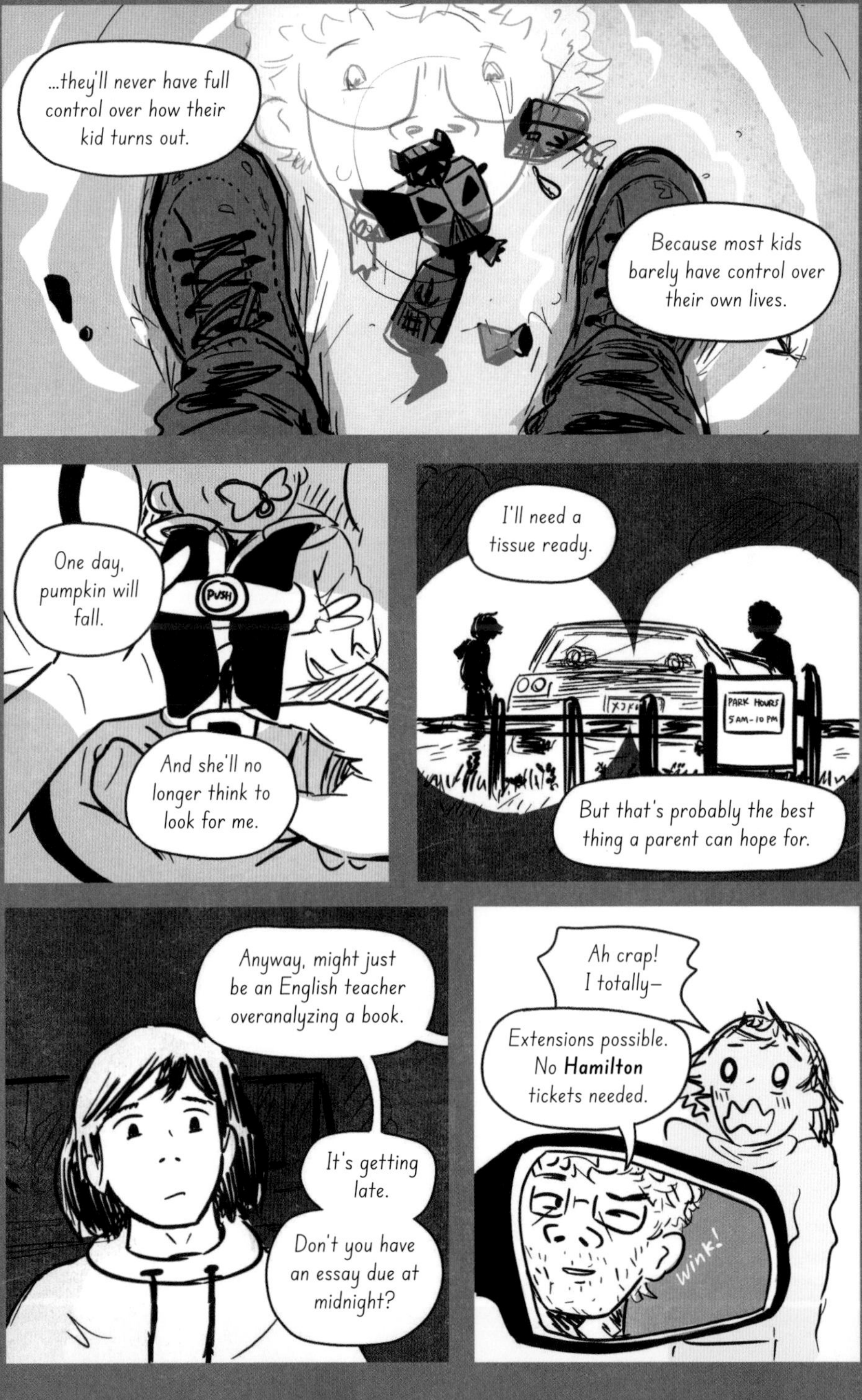
...they'll never have full control over how their kid turns out.
Because most kids barely have control over their own lives.
One day, pumpkin will fall.
PUSH
And she'll no longer think to look for me.
I'll need a tissue ready.
PARK HOURS 5AM-10PM
But that's probably the best thing a parent can hope for.
Anyway, might just be an English teacher overanalyzing a book.
It's getting late.
Don't you have an essay due at midnight?
Ah crap! I totally–
Extensions possible. No **Hamilton** tickets needed.
wink!

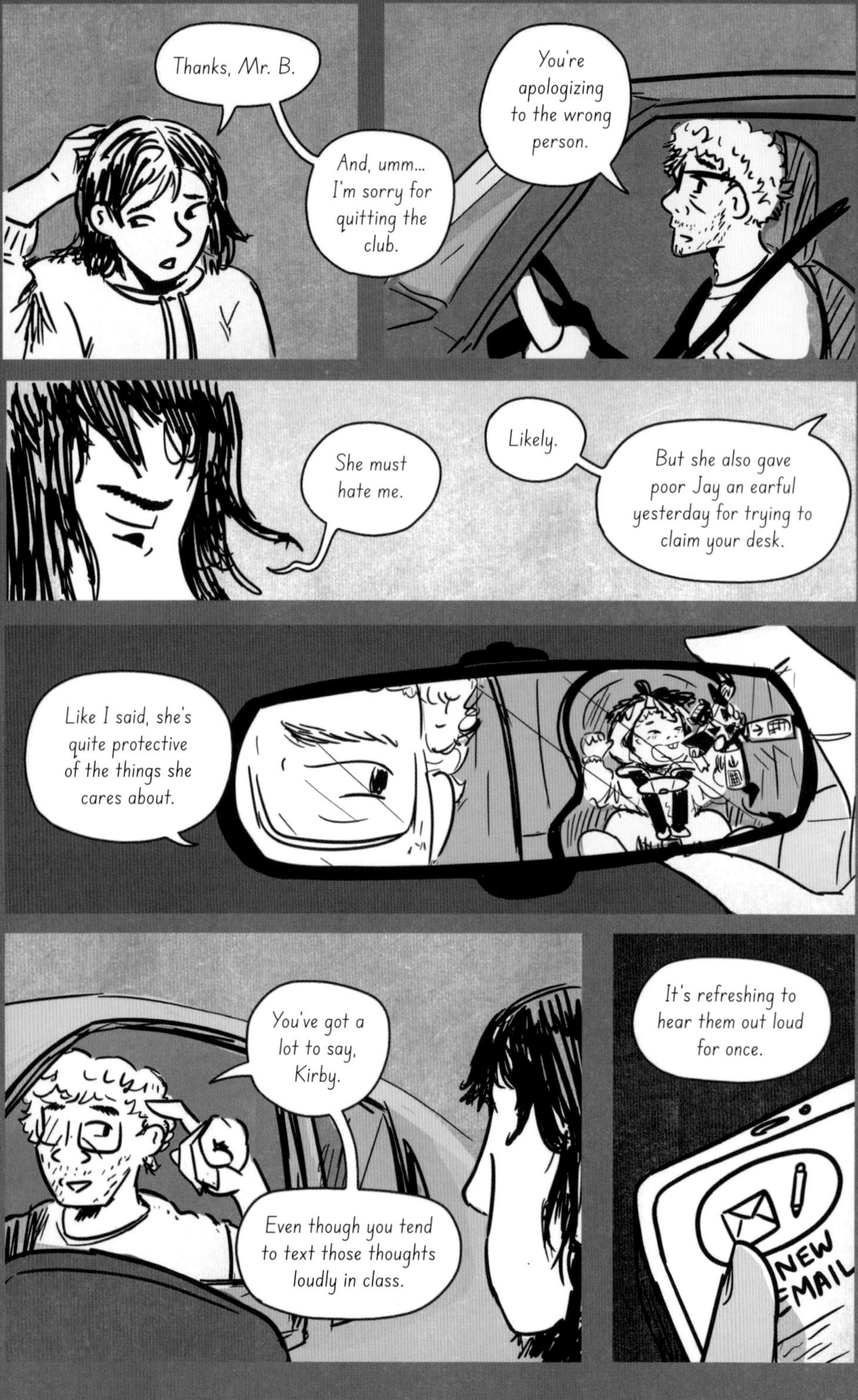
Thanks, Mr. B.
And, umm... I'm sorry for quitting the club.
You're apologizing to the wrong person.
She must hate me.
Likely.
But she also gave poor Jay an earful yesterday for trying to claim your desk.
Like I said, she's quite protective of the things she cares about.
You've got a lot to say, Kirby.
Even though you tend to text those thoughts loudly in class.
It's refreshing to hear them out loud for once.
NEW EMAIL

"Here lies "Ask the Universe," the greatest column to have ever lived."

This is so dramatic. Even for you.

Beatrix Santos, put out that candle!!

You need to talk to Kirby—

Nuh-uh. The rules, Astrid.

Last one's kinda harsh, no?

Astrid... it's her.

'Sigh... "We don't talk **about** exes. We don't talk **to** exes. We hope they **die** stepping on a Lego—"

263

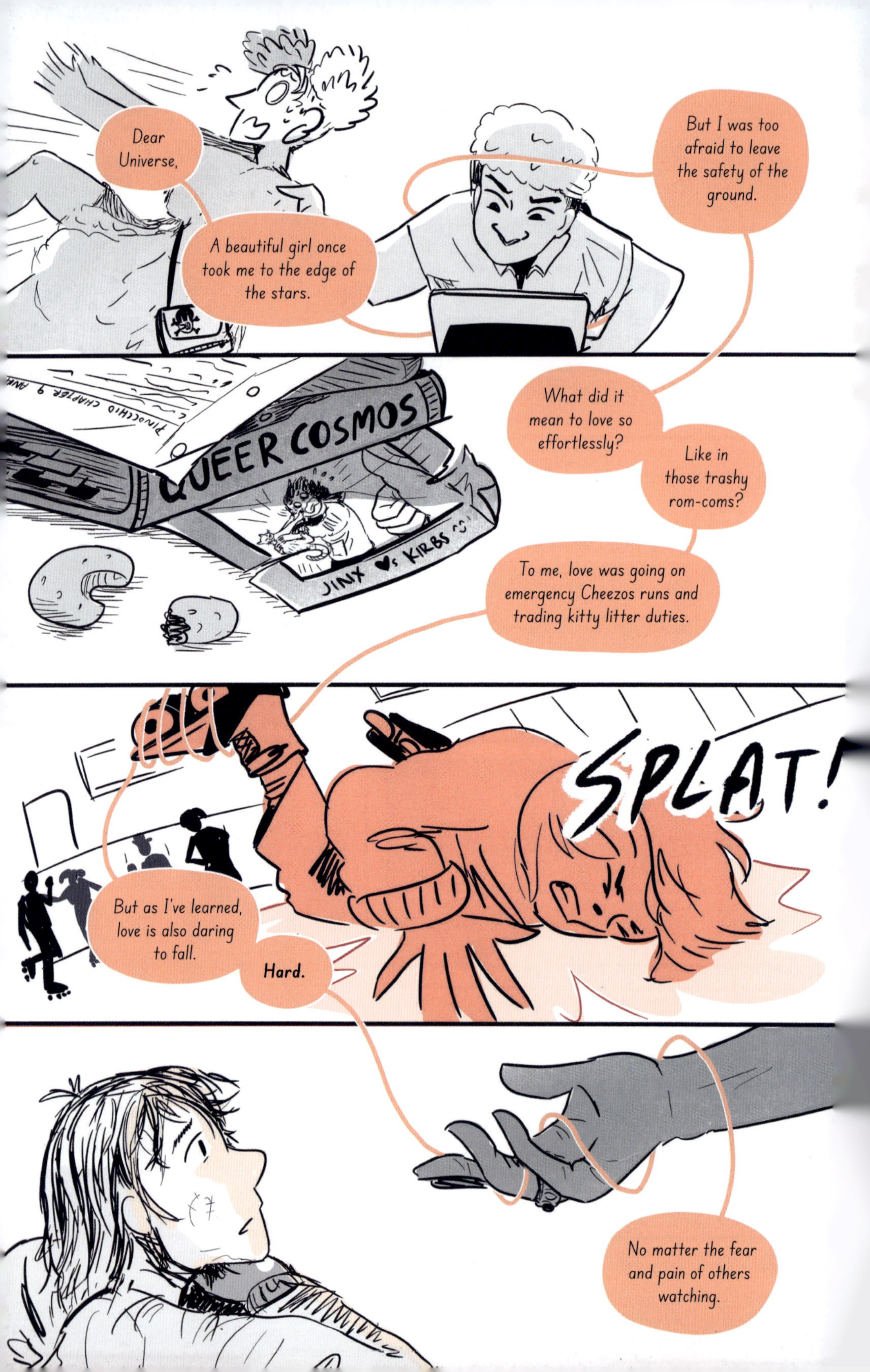

Dear Universe,
A beautiful girl once took me to the edge of the stars.
But I was too afraid to leave the safety of the ground.
PINOCCHIO CHAPTER 9 ANA
QUEER COSMOS
JINX ♥s KIRBS
What did it mean to love so effortlessly?
Like in those trashy rom-coms?
To me, love was going on emergency Cheezos runs and trading kitty litter duties.
SPLAT!
But as I've learned, love is also daring to fall.
Hard.
No matter the fear and pain of others watching.

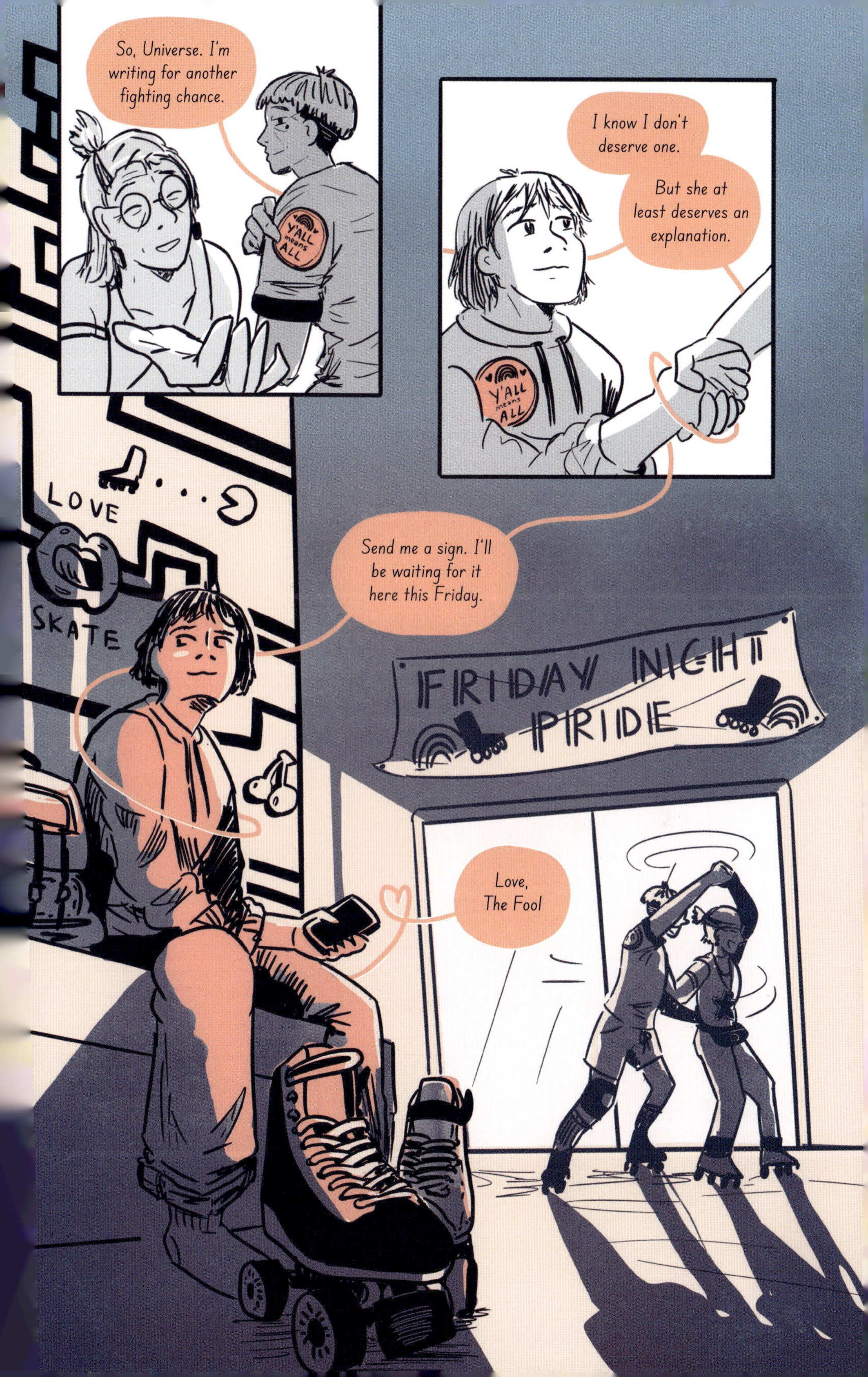
So, Universe. I'm writing for another fighting chance.
Y'ALL means ALL
I know I don't deserve one.
But she at least deserves an explanation.
Y'ALL means ALL
LOVE
SKATE
Send me a sign. I'll be waiting for it here this Friday.
FRIDAY NIGHT PRIDE
Love, The Fool

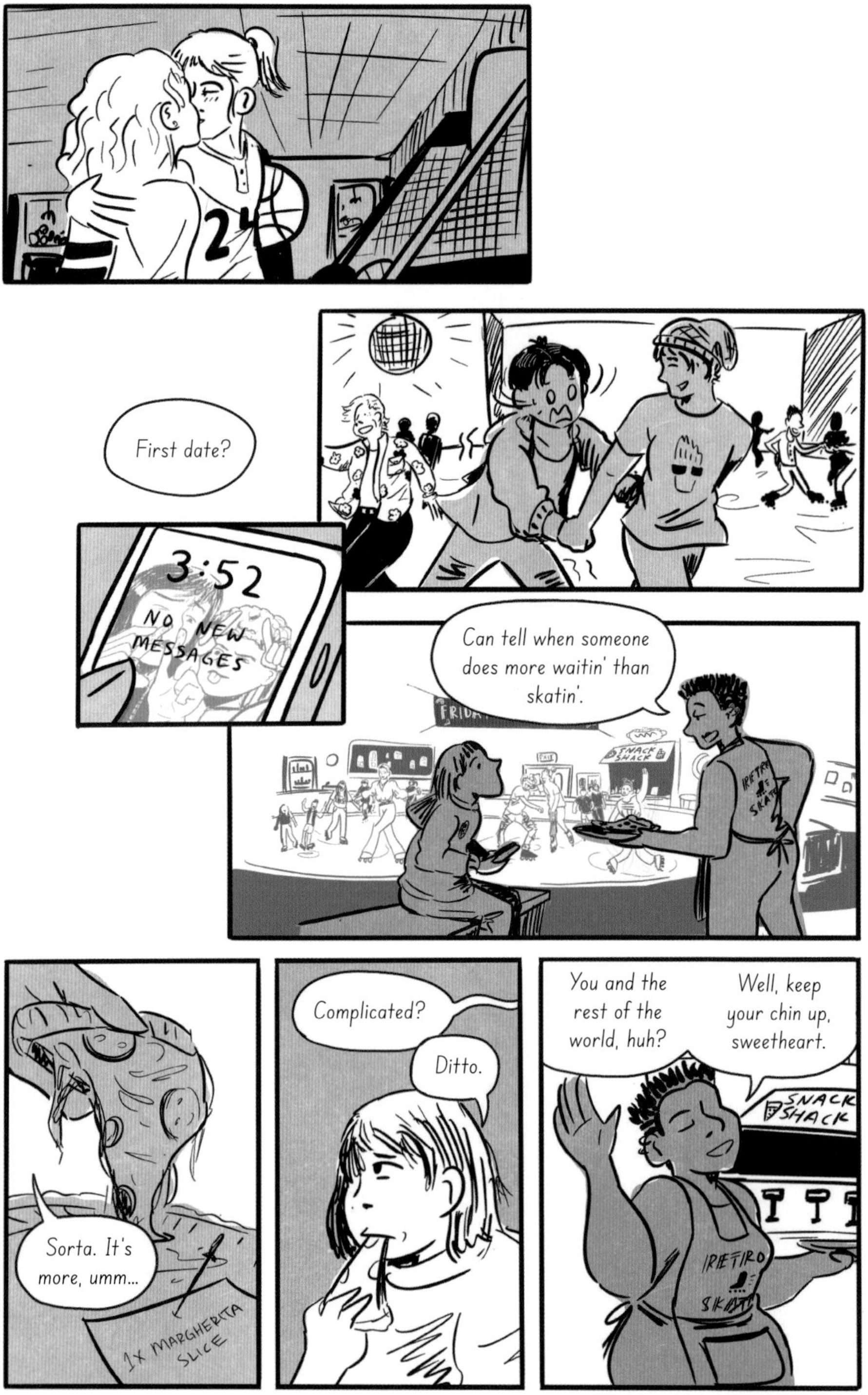
First date?
3:52
NO NEW MESSAGES
Can tell when someone does more waitin' than skatin'.
SNACK SHACK
RETRO SKATE
Sorta. It's more, umm...
1x MARGHERITA SLICE
Complicated?
Ditto.
You and the rest of the world, huh?
Well, keep your chin up, sweetheart.
SNACK SHACK
RETRO SKATE

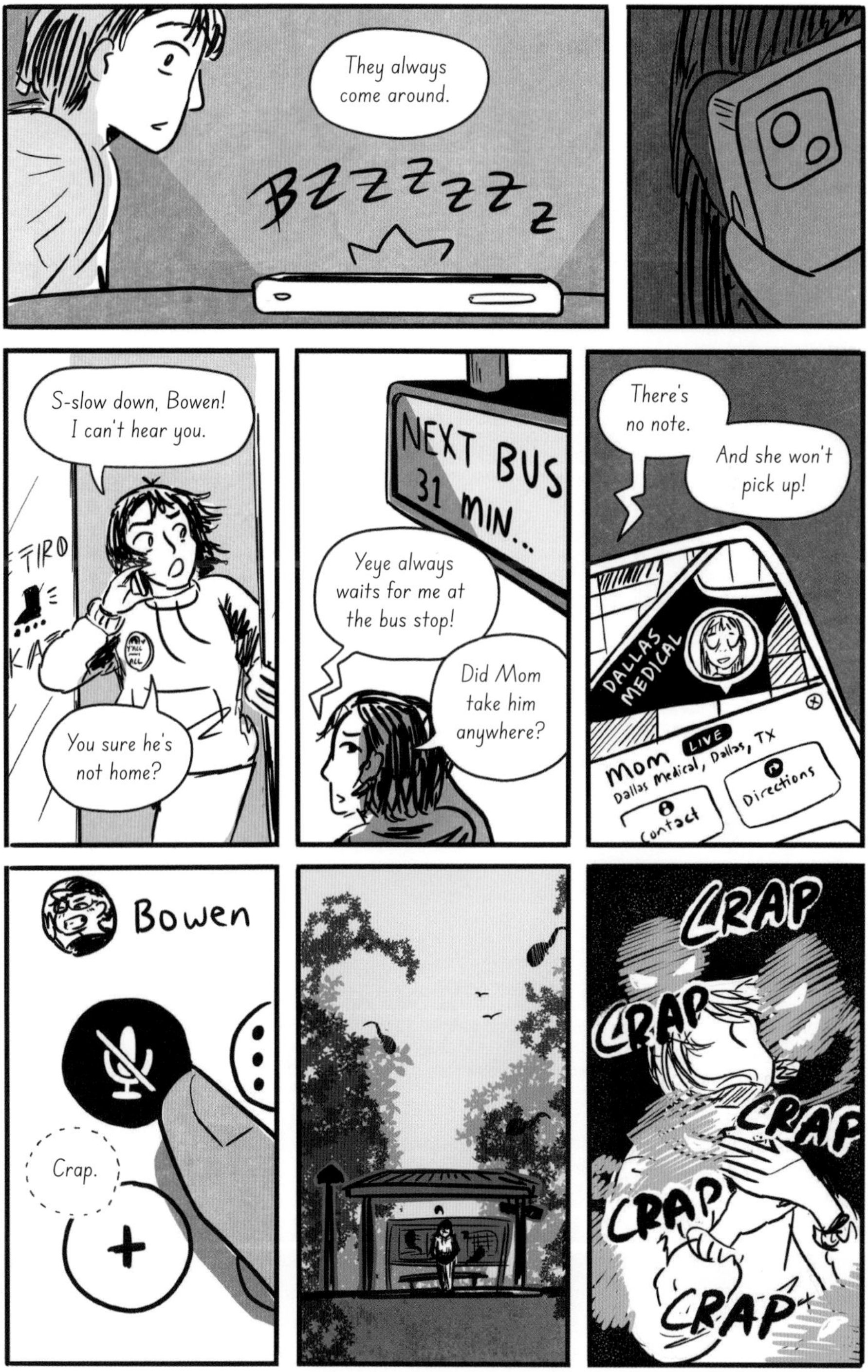
They always come around.
BZZZZZZZ
S-slow down, Bowen! I can't hear you.
You sure he's not home?
NEXT BUS 31 MIN...
Yeye always waits for me at the bus stop!
Did Mom take him anywhere?
There's no note.
And she won't pick up!
DALLAS MEDICAL
Mom LIVE
Dallas Medical, Dallas, TX
Contact
Directions
Bowen
Crap.
CRAP
CRAP
CRAP
CRAP
CRAP

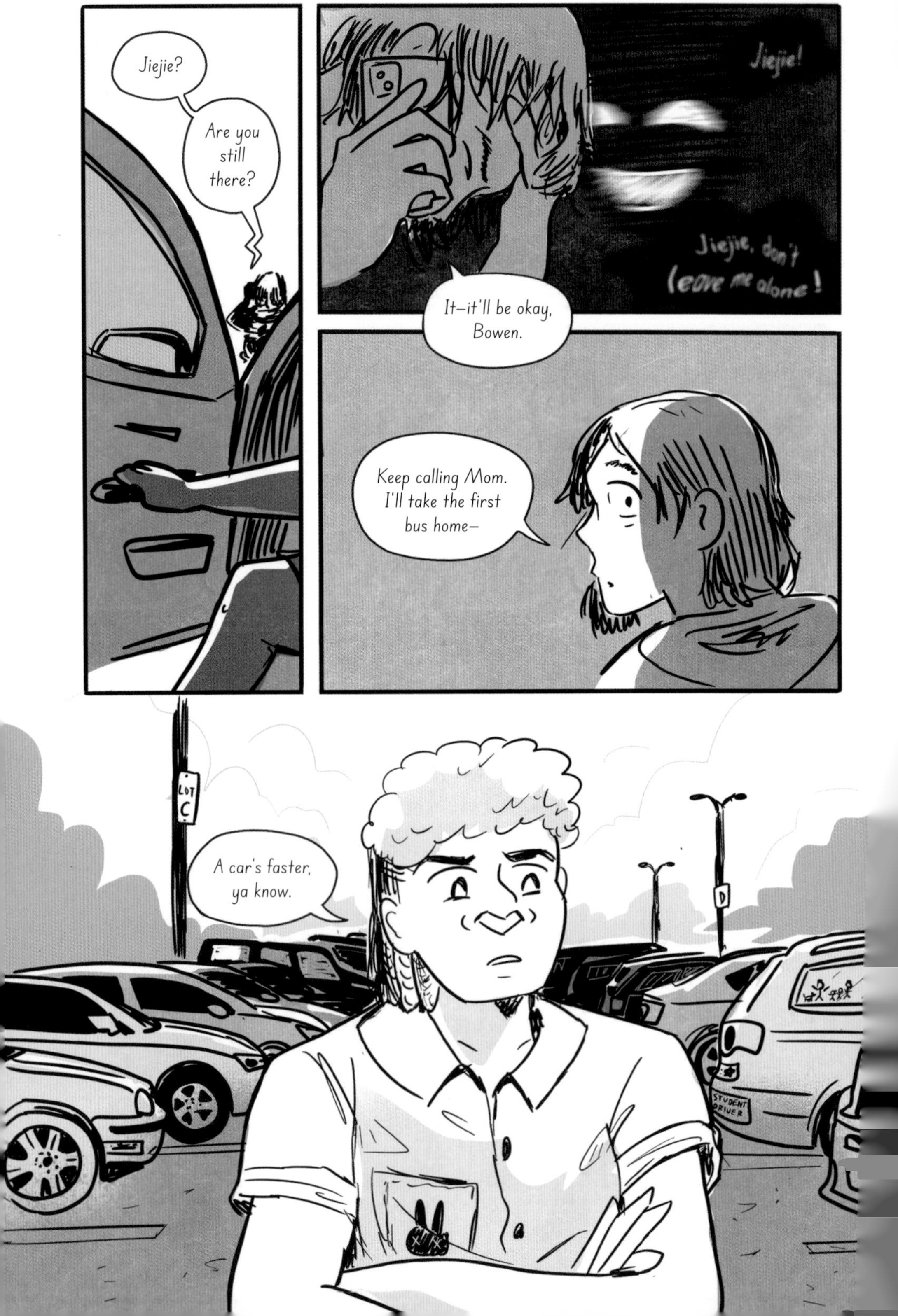
Jiejie?
Are you still there?
Jiejie!
Jiejie, don't leave me alone!
It—it'll be okay, Bowen.
Keep calling Mom. I'll take the first bus home—
LOT C
A car's faster, ya know.
D
STUDENT DRIVER

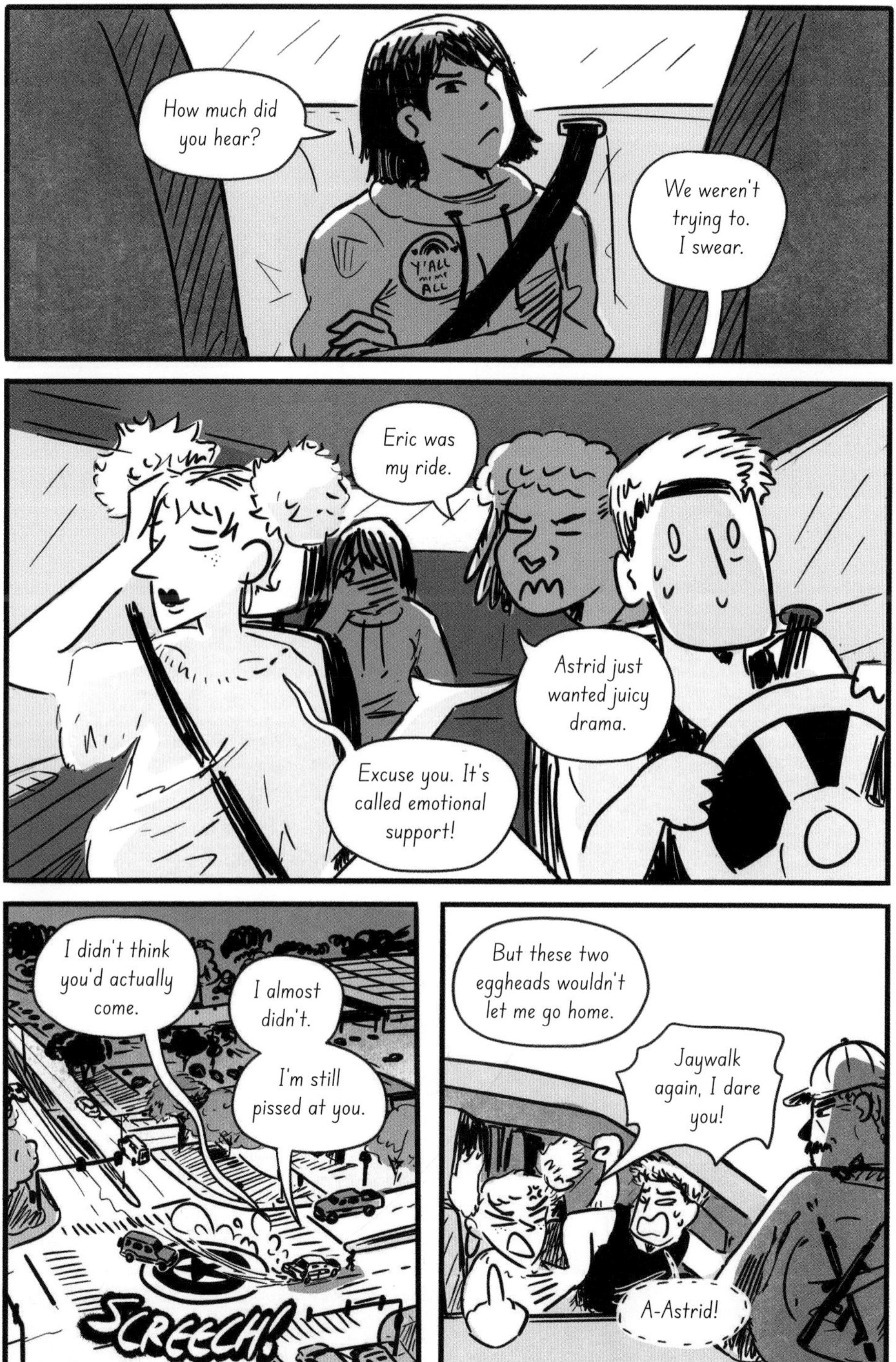
How much did you hear?
We weren't trying to. I swear.
Eric was my ride.
Astrid just wanted juicy drama.
Excuse you. It's called emotional support!
I didn't think you'd actually come.
I almost didn't.
I'm still pissed at you.
SCREECH!
But these two eggheads wouldn't let me go home.
Jaywalk again, I dare you!
A-Astrid!

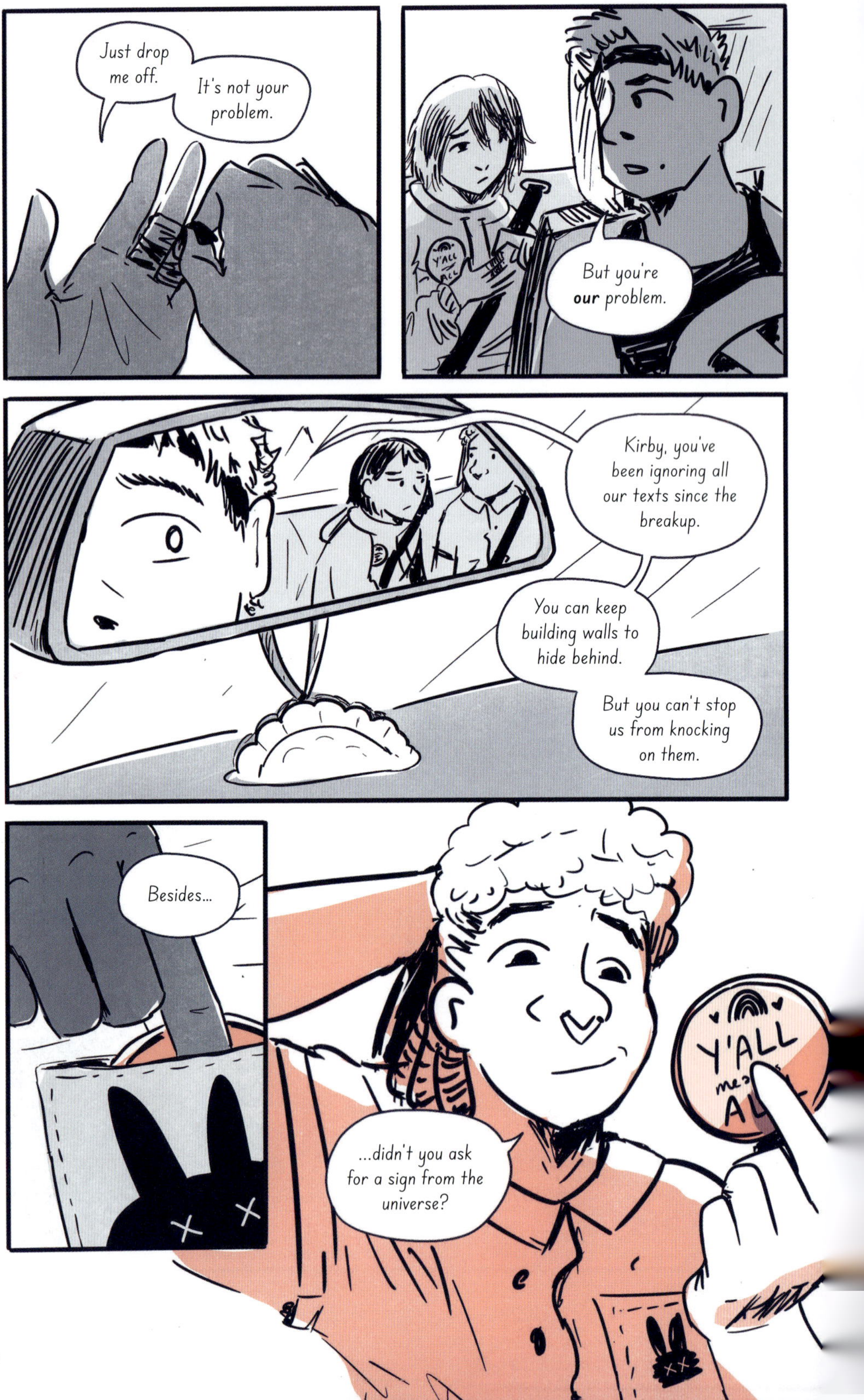

Just drop me off.
It's not your problem.
But you're **our** problem.
Y'ALL
Kirby, you've been ignoring all our texts since the breakup.
You can keep building walls to hide behind.
But you can't stop us from knocking on them.
Besides...
...didn't you ask for a sign from the universe?
Y'ALL
ALL

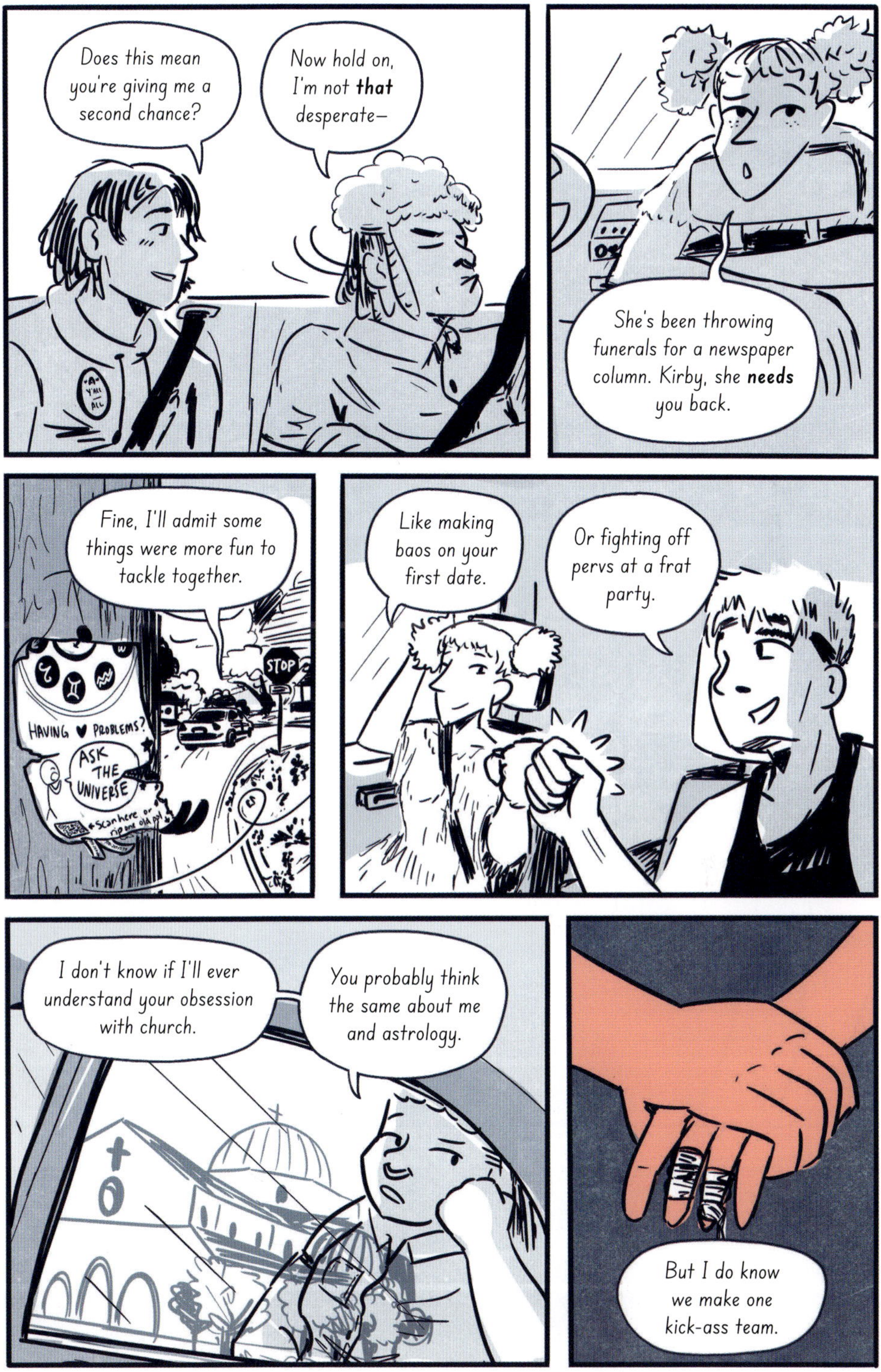
Does this mean you're giving me a second chance?
Now hold on, I'm not **that** desperate–
She's been throwing funerals for a newspaper column. Kirby, she **needs** you back.
Fine, I'll admit some things were more fun to tackle together.
HAVING ♥ PROBLEMS?
ASK THE UNIVERSE
STOP
Like making baos on your first date.
Or fighting off pervs at a frat party.
I don't know if I'll ever understand your obsession with church.
You probably think the same about me and astrology.
But I do know we make one kick-ass team.

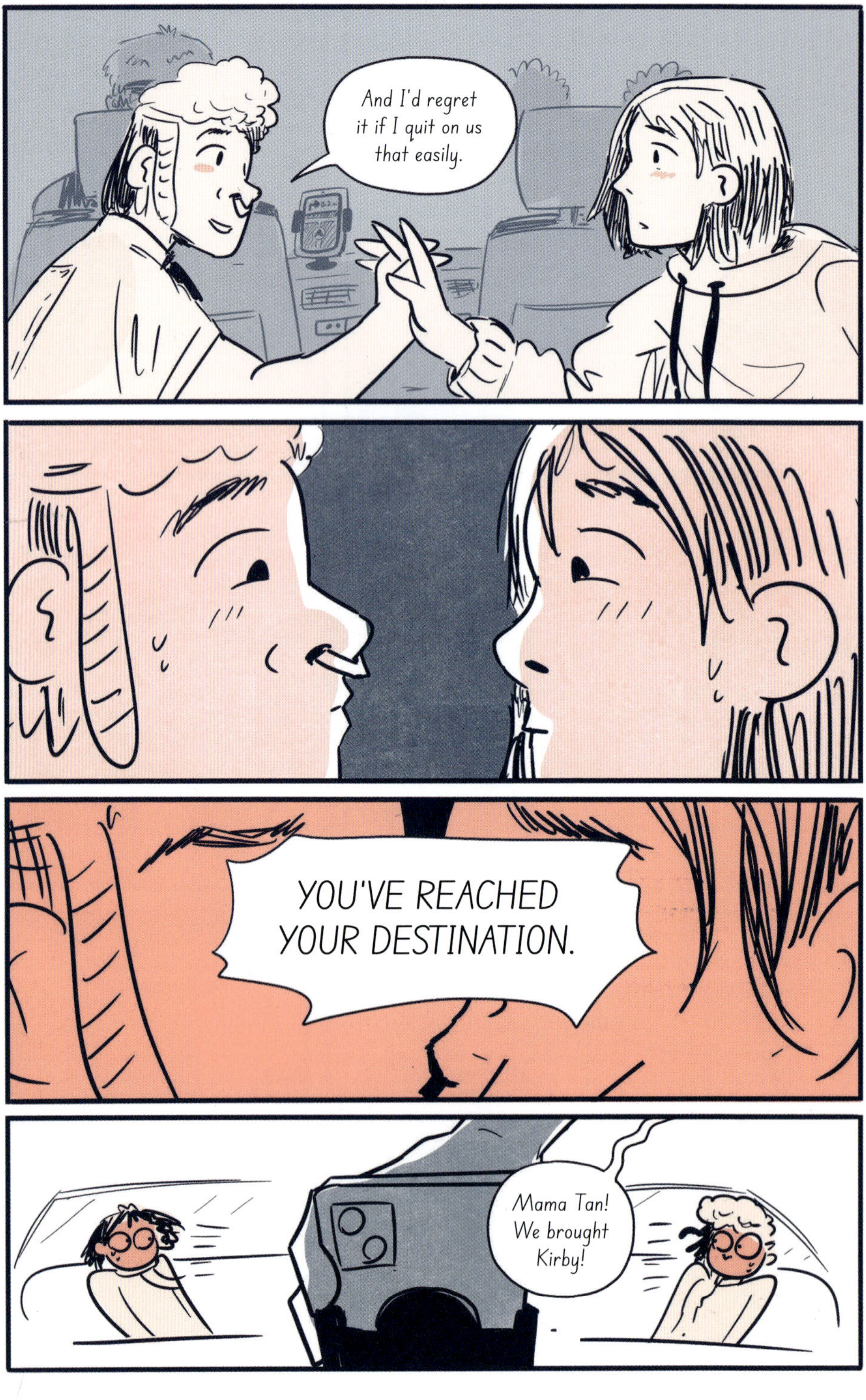
And I'd regret it if I quit on us that easily.
YOU'VE REACHED YOUR DESTINATION.
Mama Tan! We brought Kirby!

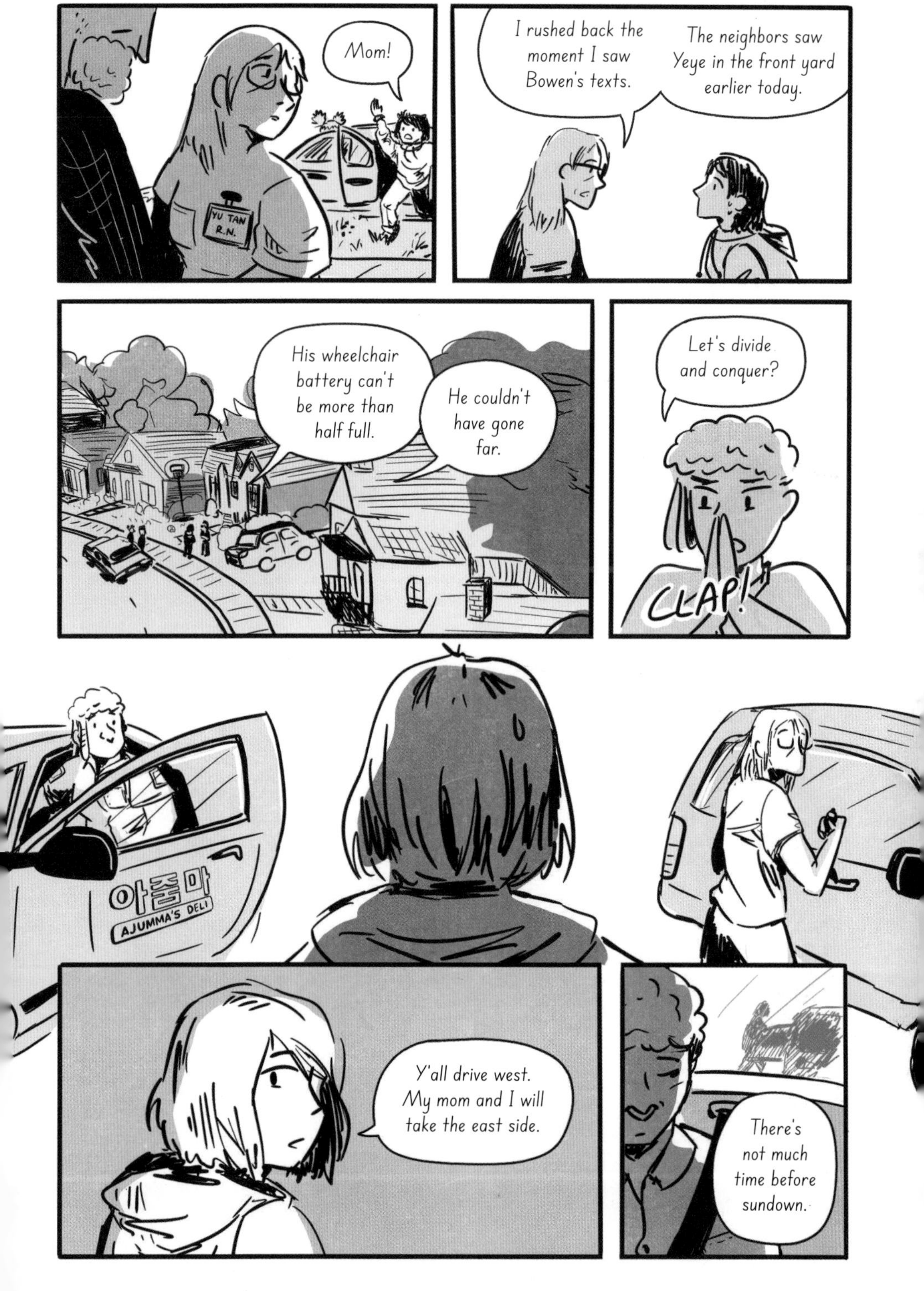

Mom!
YU TAN R.N.
I rushed back the moment I saw Bowen's texts.
The neighbors saw Yeye in the front yard earlier today.
His wheelchair battery can't be more than half full.
He couldn't have gone far.
Let's divide and conquer?
CLAP!
아줌마
AJUMMA'S DELI
Y'all drive west. My mom and I will take the east side.
There's not much time before sundown.

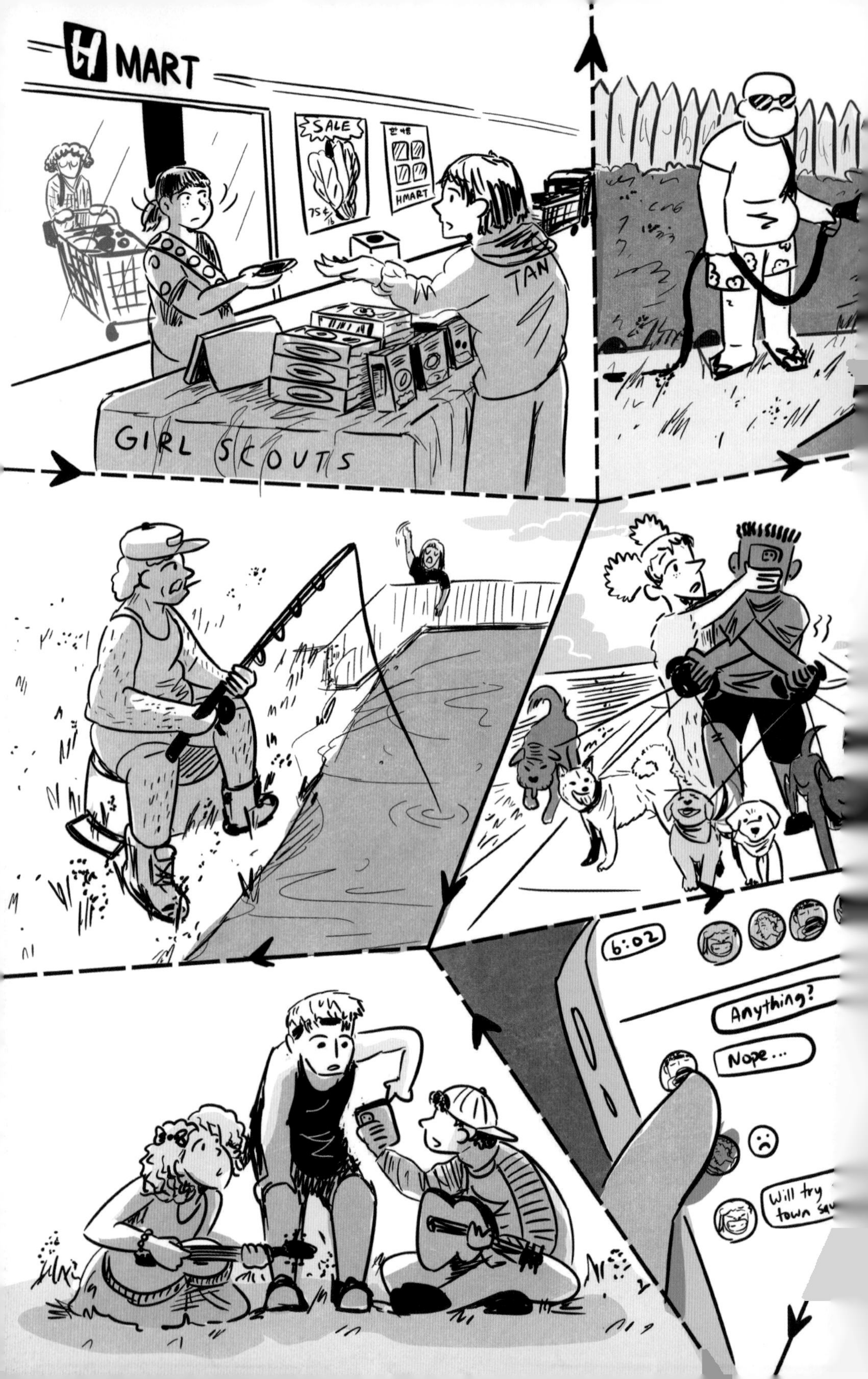
H MART
SALE
75¢/lb
HMART
TAN
GIRL SCOUTS
6:02
Anything?
Nope...
Will try
town

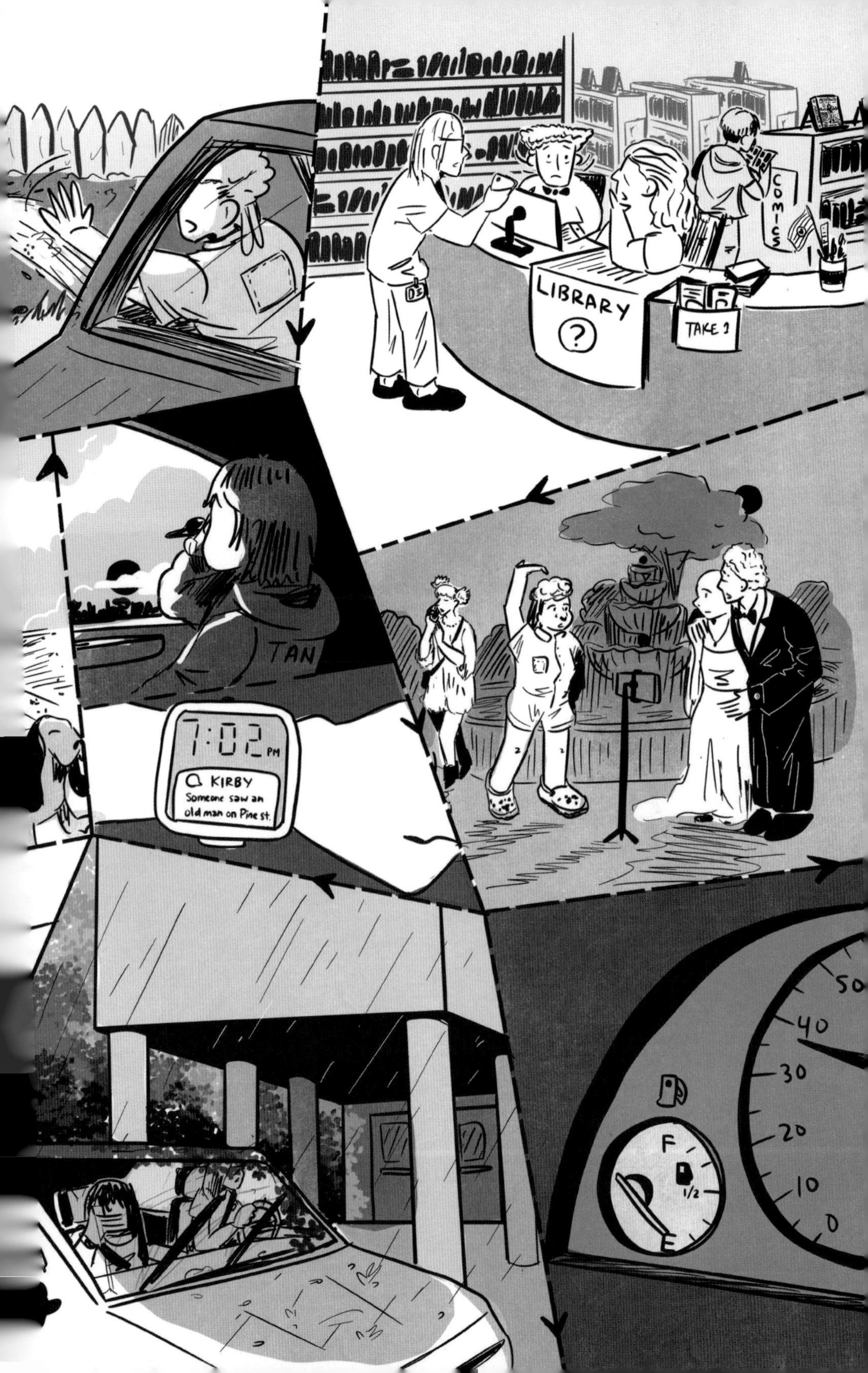
LIBRARY
?
TAKE 1
COMICS
TAN
7:02 PM
KIRBY
Someone saw an old man on Pine st.
F
1/2
E
0
10
20
30
40
50

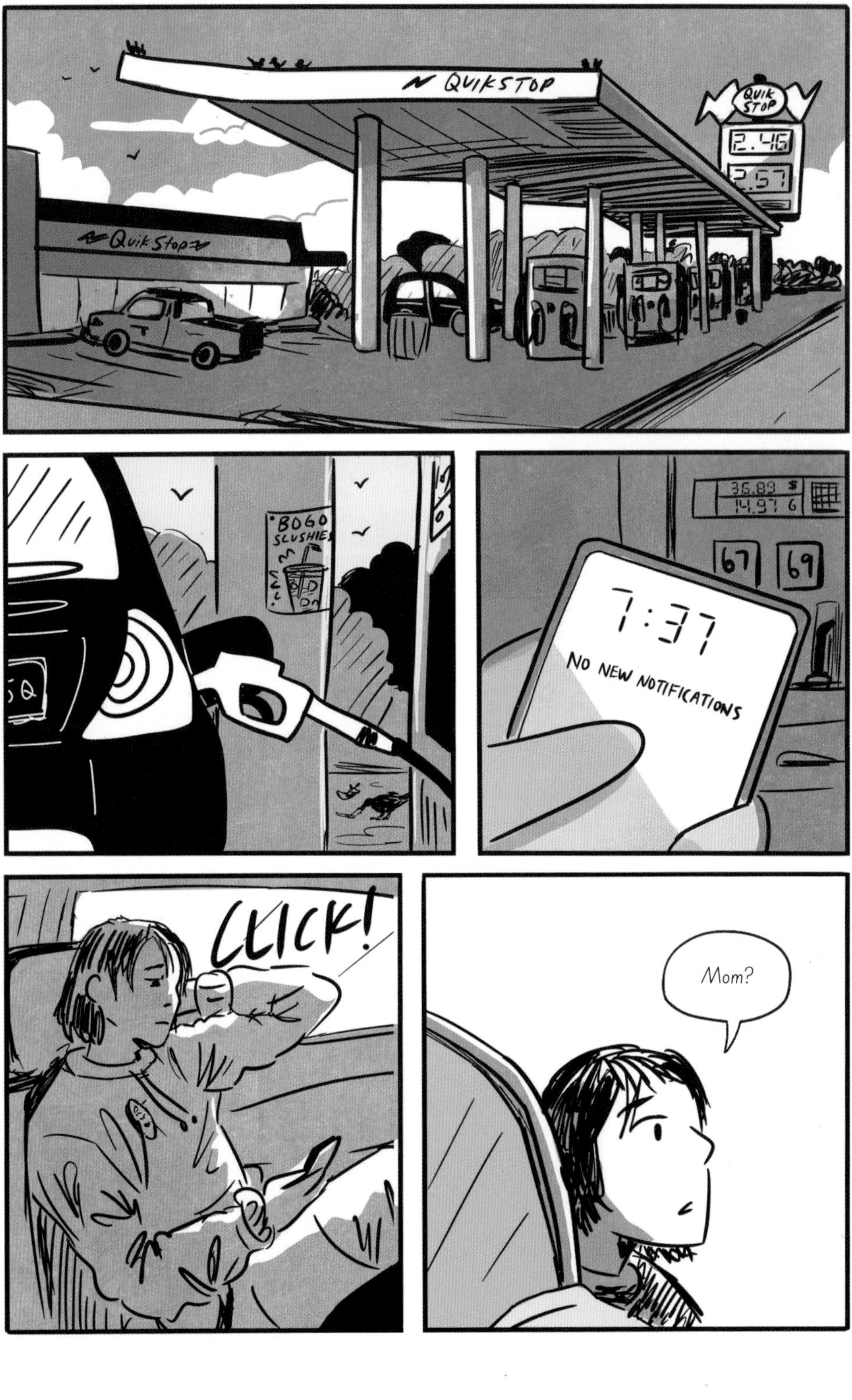
QUIKSTOP
QUIK STOP
2.46
2.57
QuikStop
BOGO SLUSHIES
36.89
14.97
67
69
7:37
NO NEW NOTIFICATIONS
CLICK!
Mom?

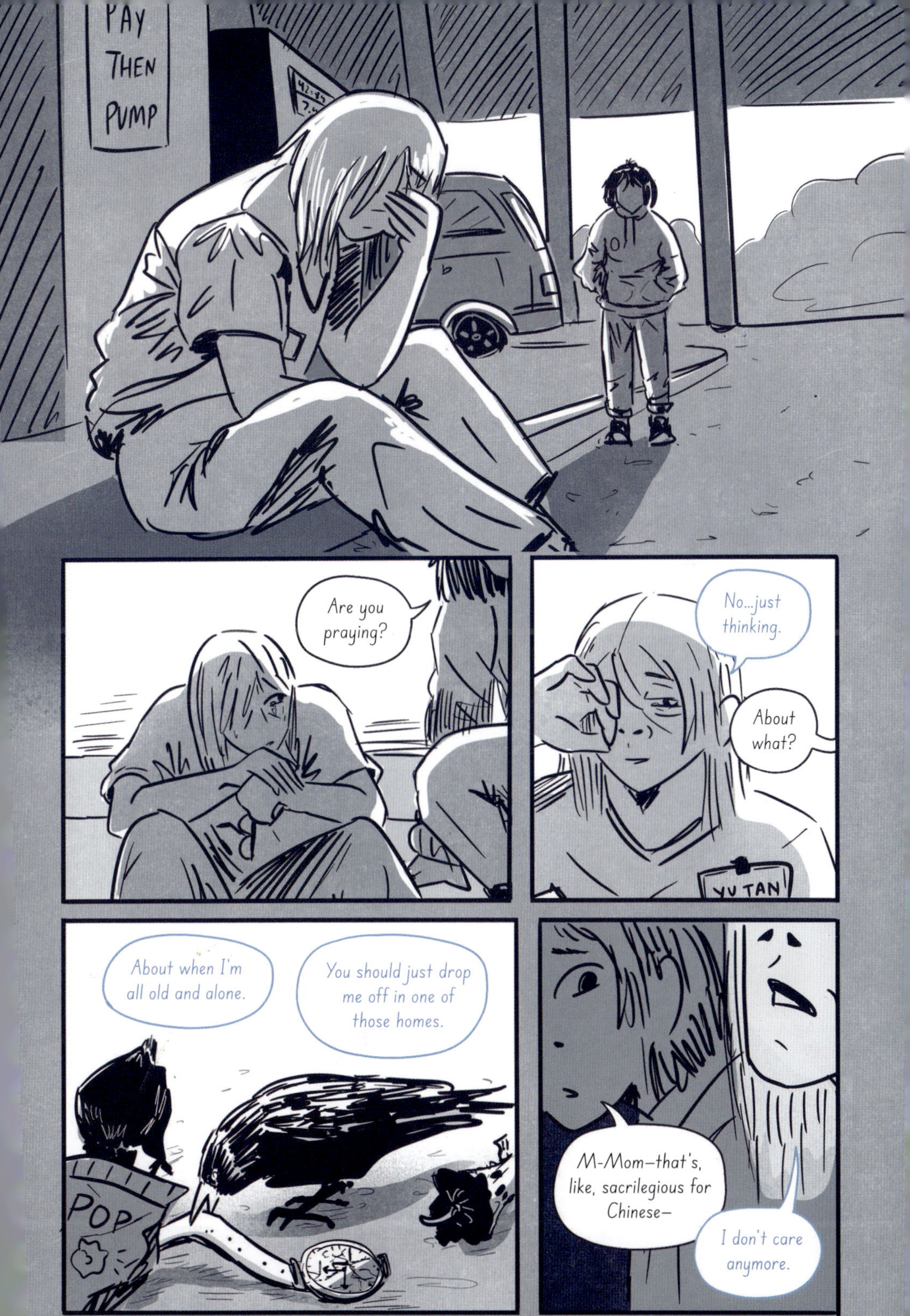
PAY THEN PUMP
Are you praying?
No...just thinking.
About what?
YU TAN
About when I'm all old and alone.
You should just drop me off in one of those homes.
POP
M-Mom—that's, like, sacrilegious for Chinese—
I don't care anymore.

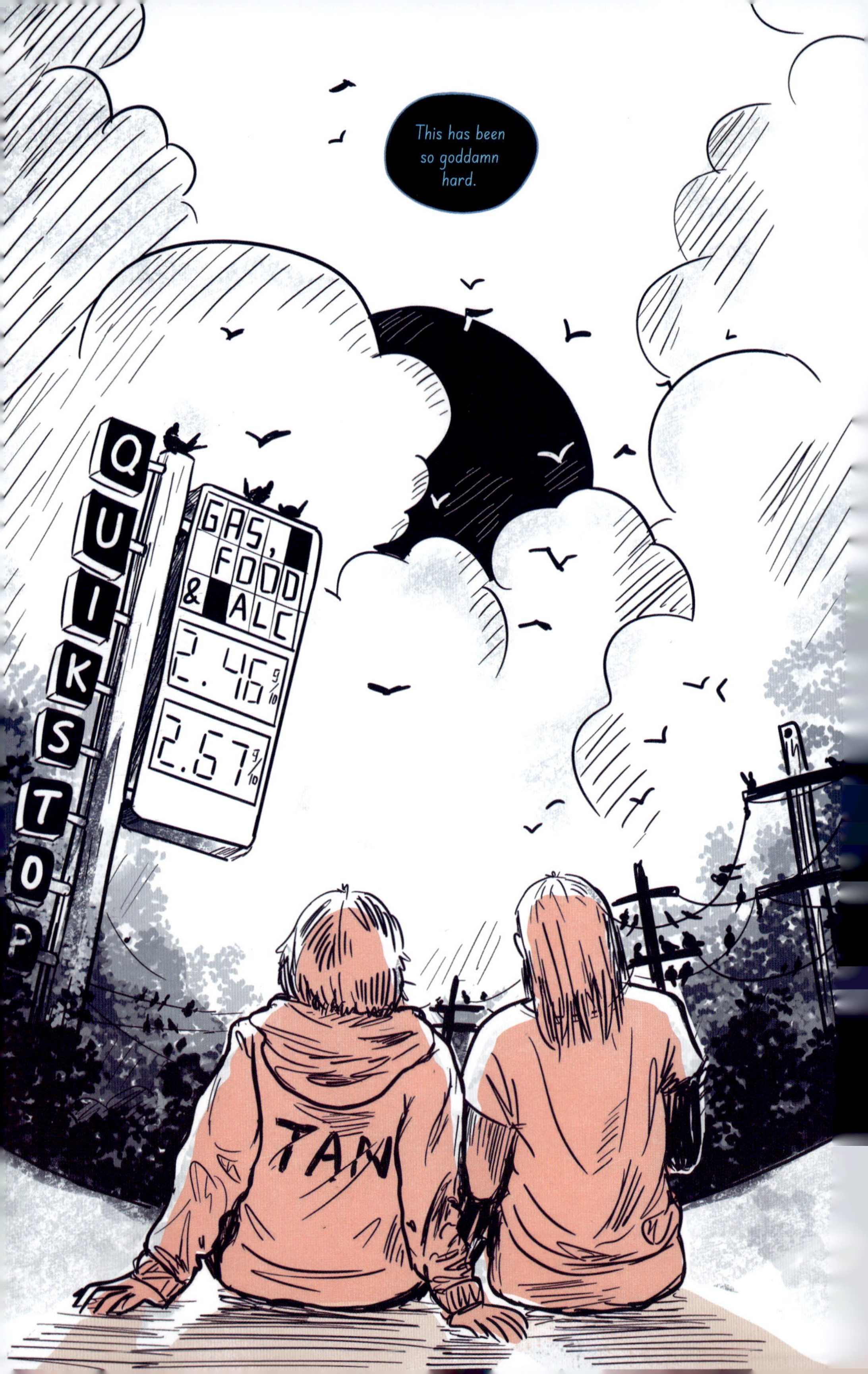
This has been so goddamn hard.
QUIKSTOP
GAS, FOOD & ALC
2.46 9/10
2.57 9/10
TAN

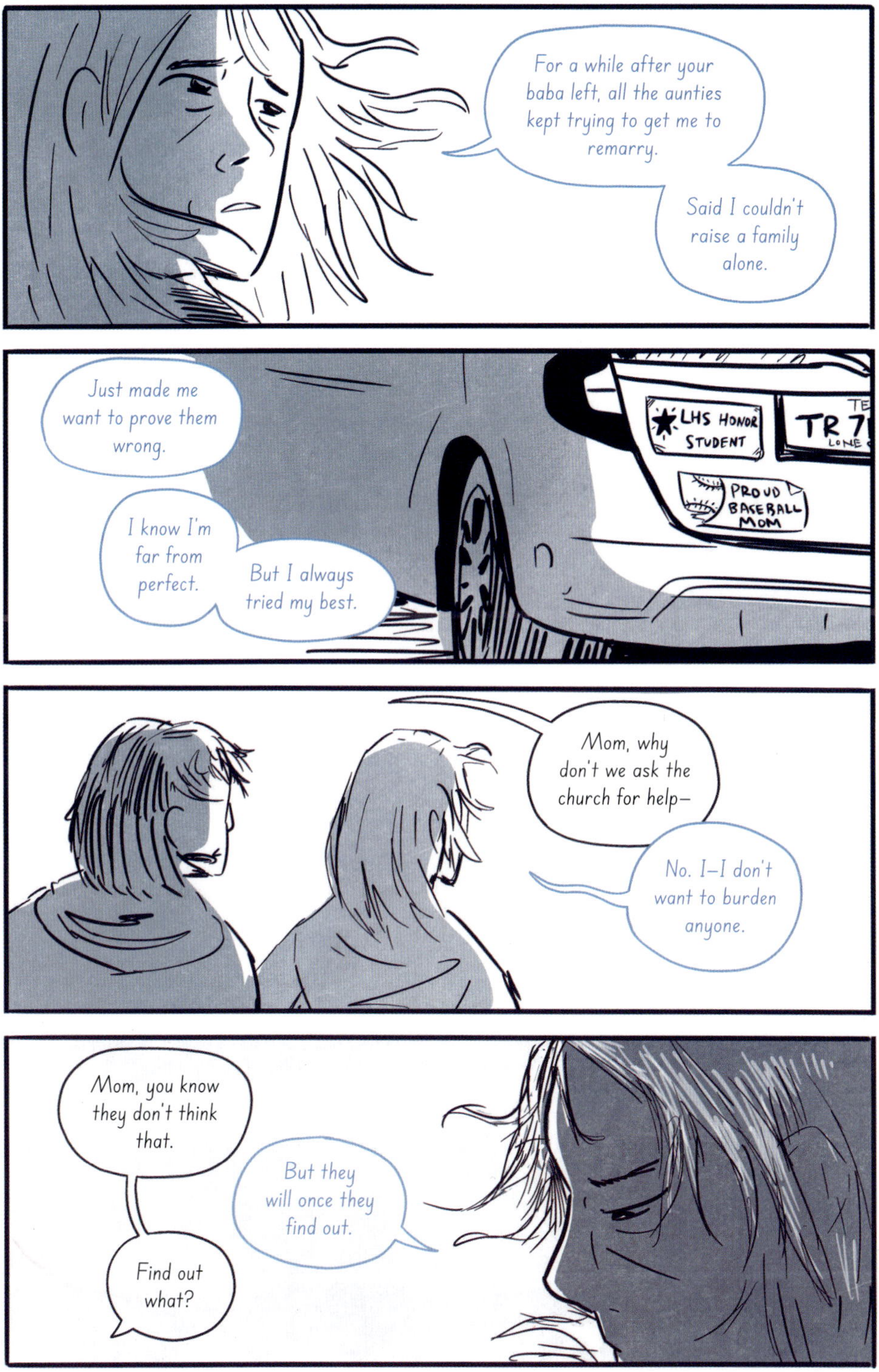
For a while after your baba left, all the aunties kept trying to get me to remarry.
Said I couldn't raise a family alone.
Just made me want to prove them wrong.
I know I'm far from perfect.
But I always tried my best.
LHS HONOR STUDENT
PROUD BASEBALL MOM
Mom, why don't we ask the church for help–
No. I–I don't want to burden anyone.
Mom, you know they don't think that.
But they will once they find out.
Find out what?

That I failed. As a mother and a daughter.

You know, you said the same exact thing when I came out.

"Who'd want anything to do with us now?"

I...I never forgot those words.

But you still went to the Suns for help...

...didn't you?

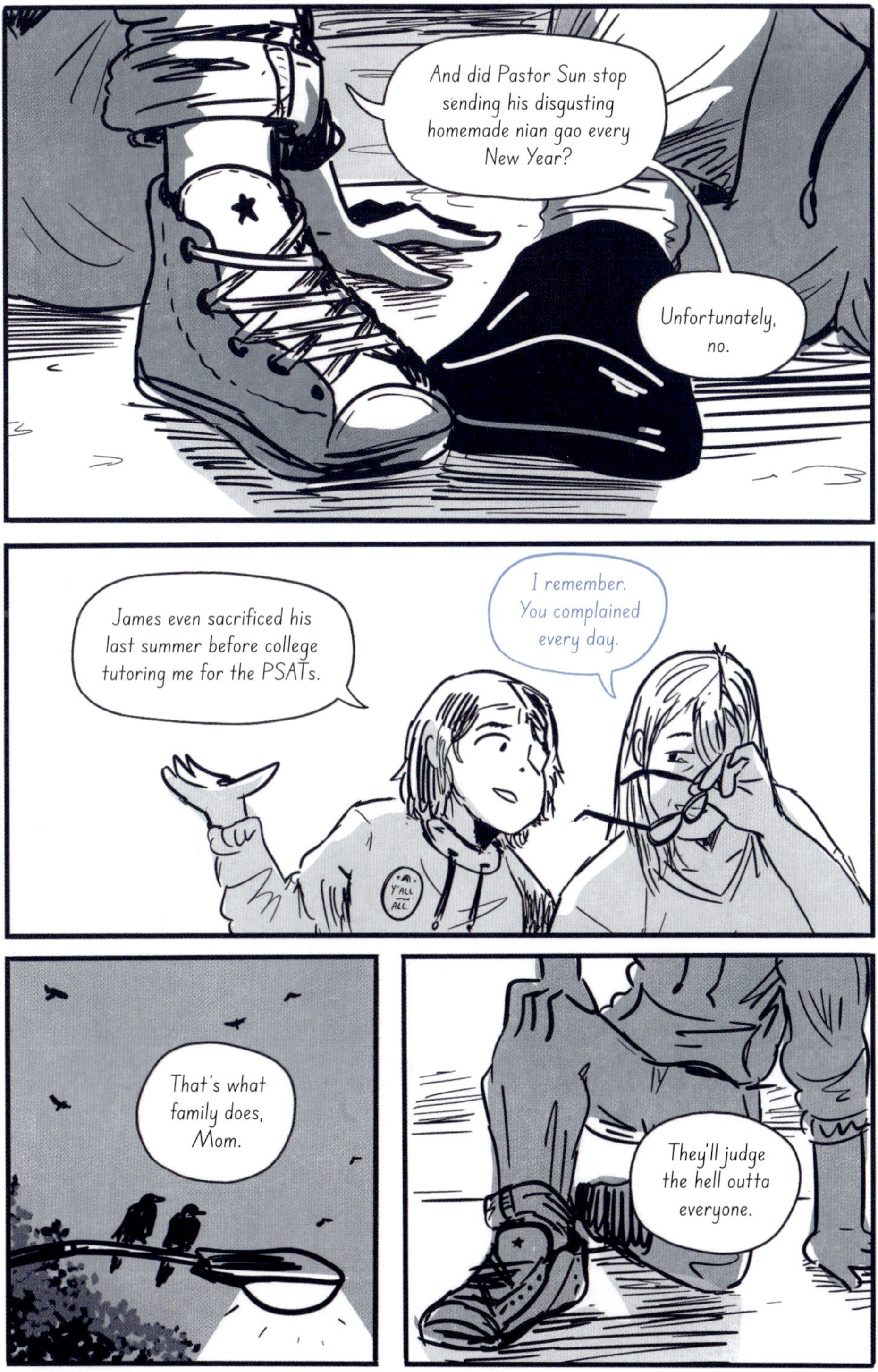
And did Pastor Sun stop sending his disgusting homemade nian gao every New Year?
Unfortunately, no.
James even sacrificed his last summer before college tutoring me for the PSATs.
I remember. You complained every day.
Y'ALL ALL
That's what family does, Mom.
They'll judge the hell outta everyone.

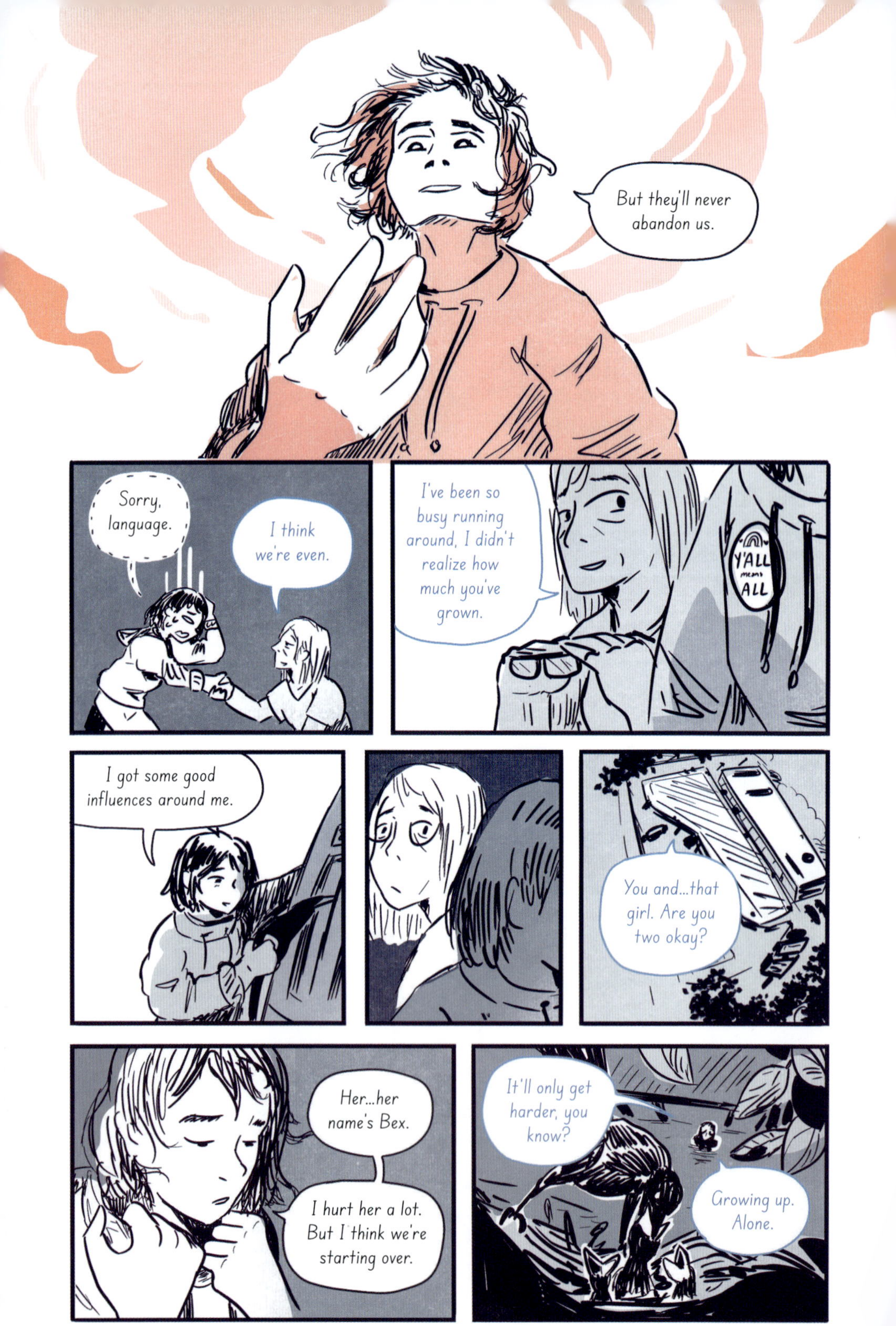
But they'll never abandon us.
Sorry, language.
I think we're even.
I've been so busy running around, I didn't realize how much you've grown.
Y'ALL means ALL
I got some good influences around me.
You and...that girl. Are you two okay?
Her...her name's Bex.
I hurt her a lot. But I think we're starting over.
It'll only get harder, you know?
Growing up. Alone.

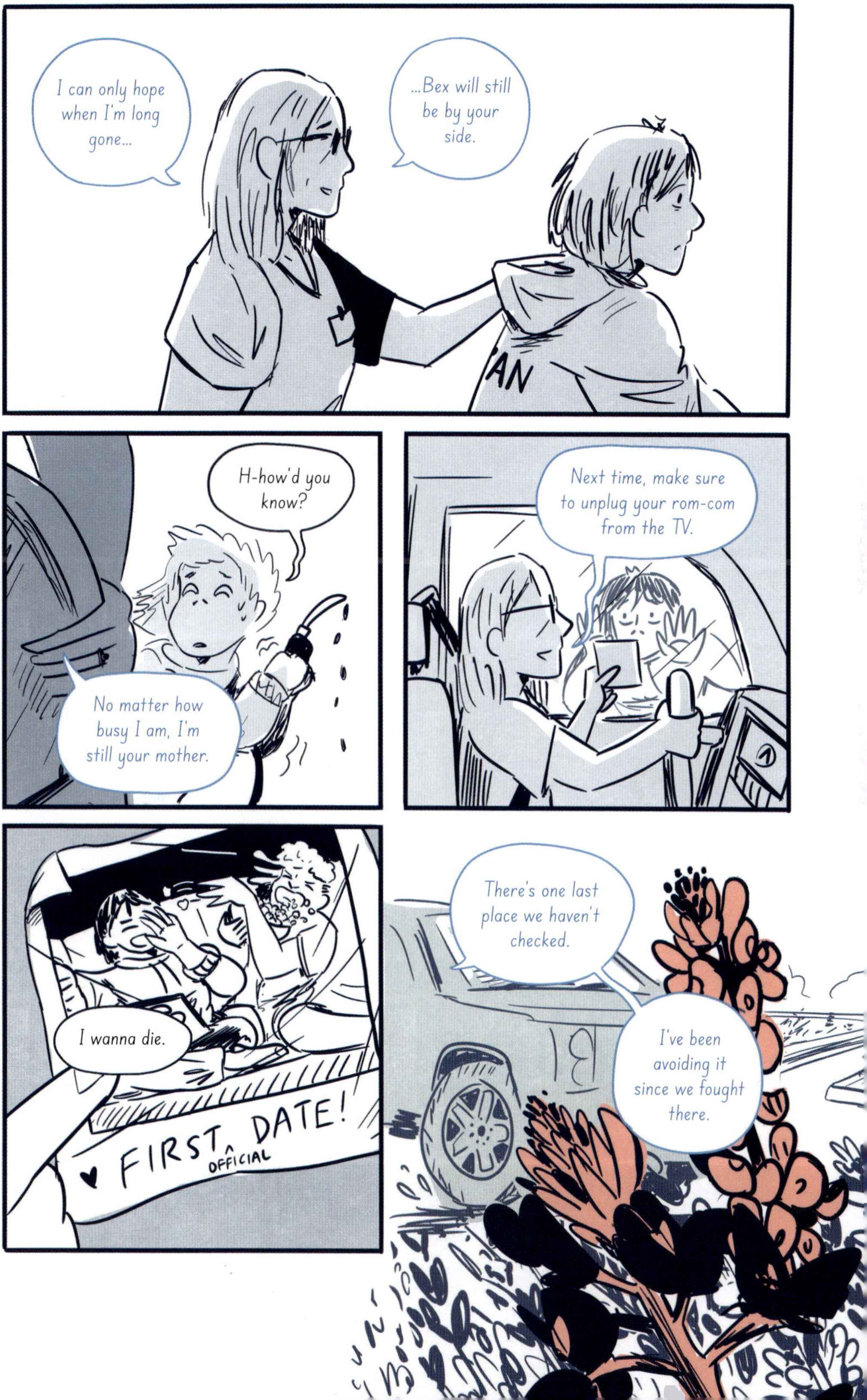

I can only hope when I'm long gone...
...Bex will still be by your side.
AN
H-how'd you know?
No matter how busy I am, I'm still your mother.
Next time, make sure to unplug your rom-com from the TV.
I wanna die.
FIRST OFFICIAL DATE!
There's one last place we haven't checked.
I've been avoiding it since we fought there.

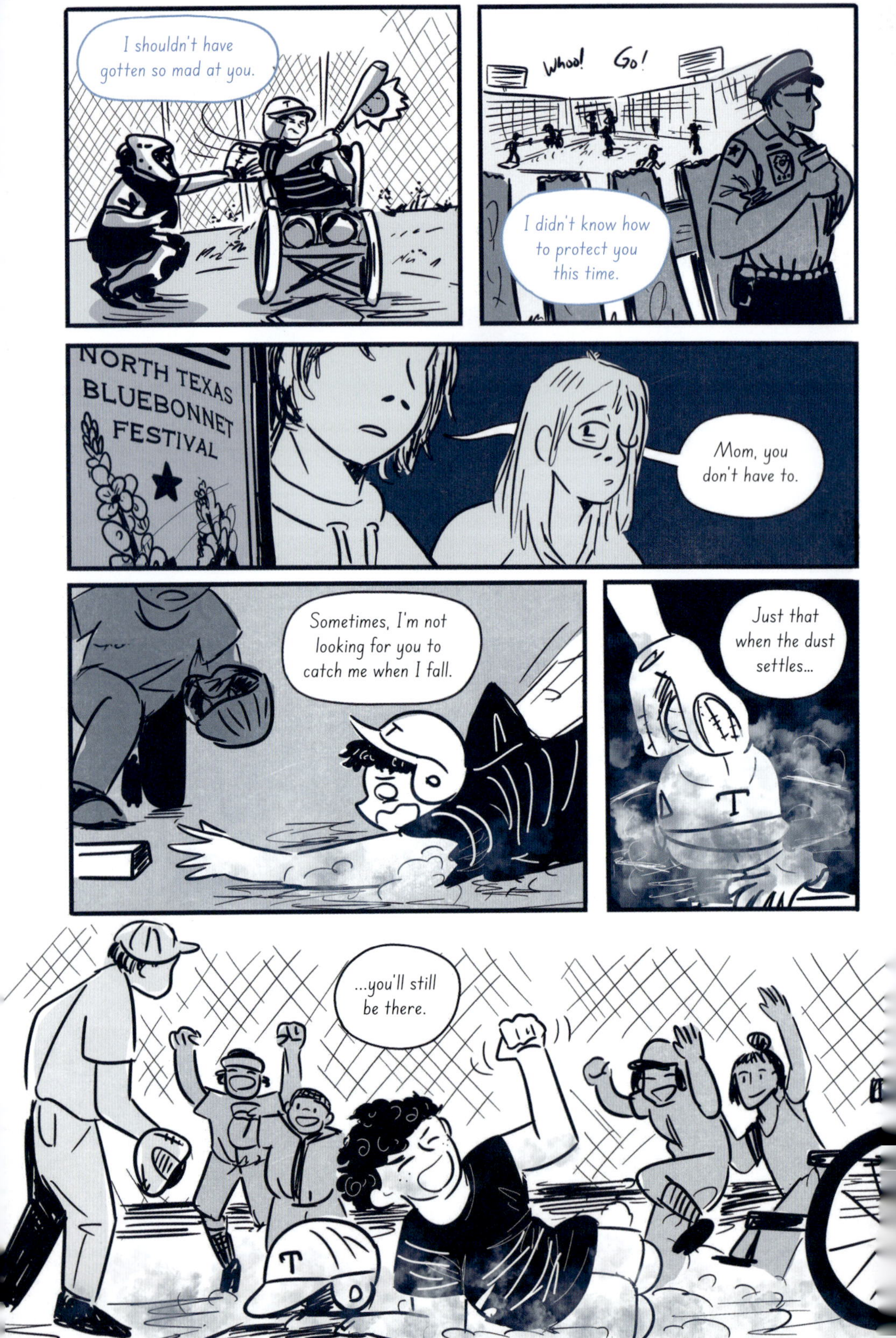
I shouldn't have gotten so mad at you.
Whoo! Go!
I didn't know how to protect you this time.
NORTH TEXAS BLUEBONNET FESTIVAL
Mom, you don't have to.
Sometimes, I'm not looking for you to catch me when I fall.
Just that when the dust settles...
...you'll still be there.

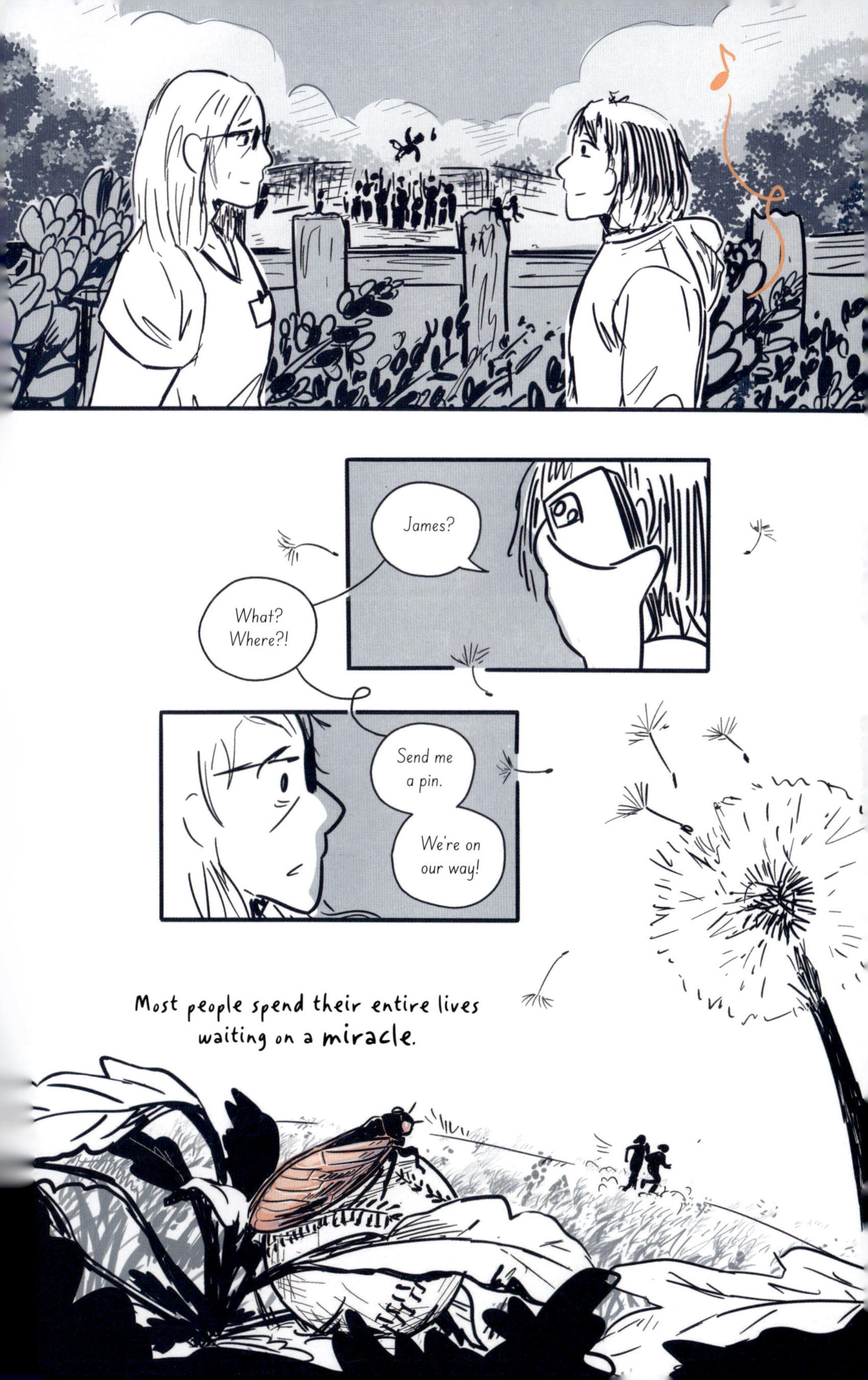
James?
What? Where?!
Send me a pin.
We're on our way!
Most people spend their entire lives waiting on a miracle.

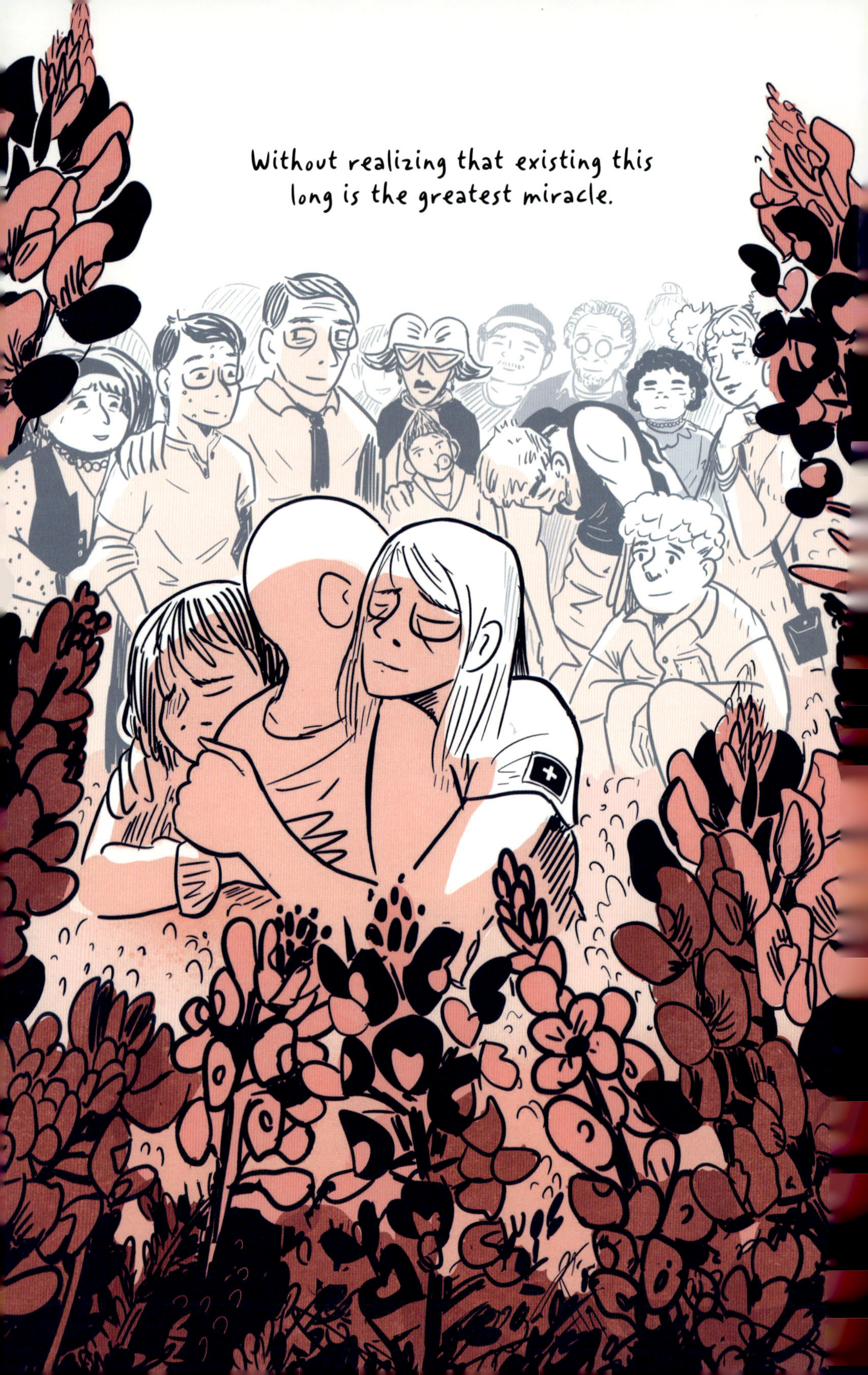
Without realizing that existing this long is the greatest miracle.

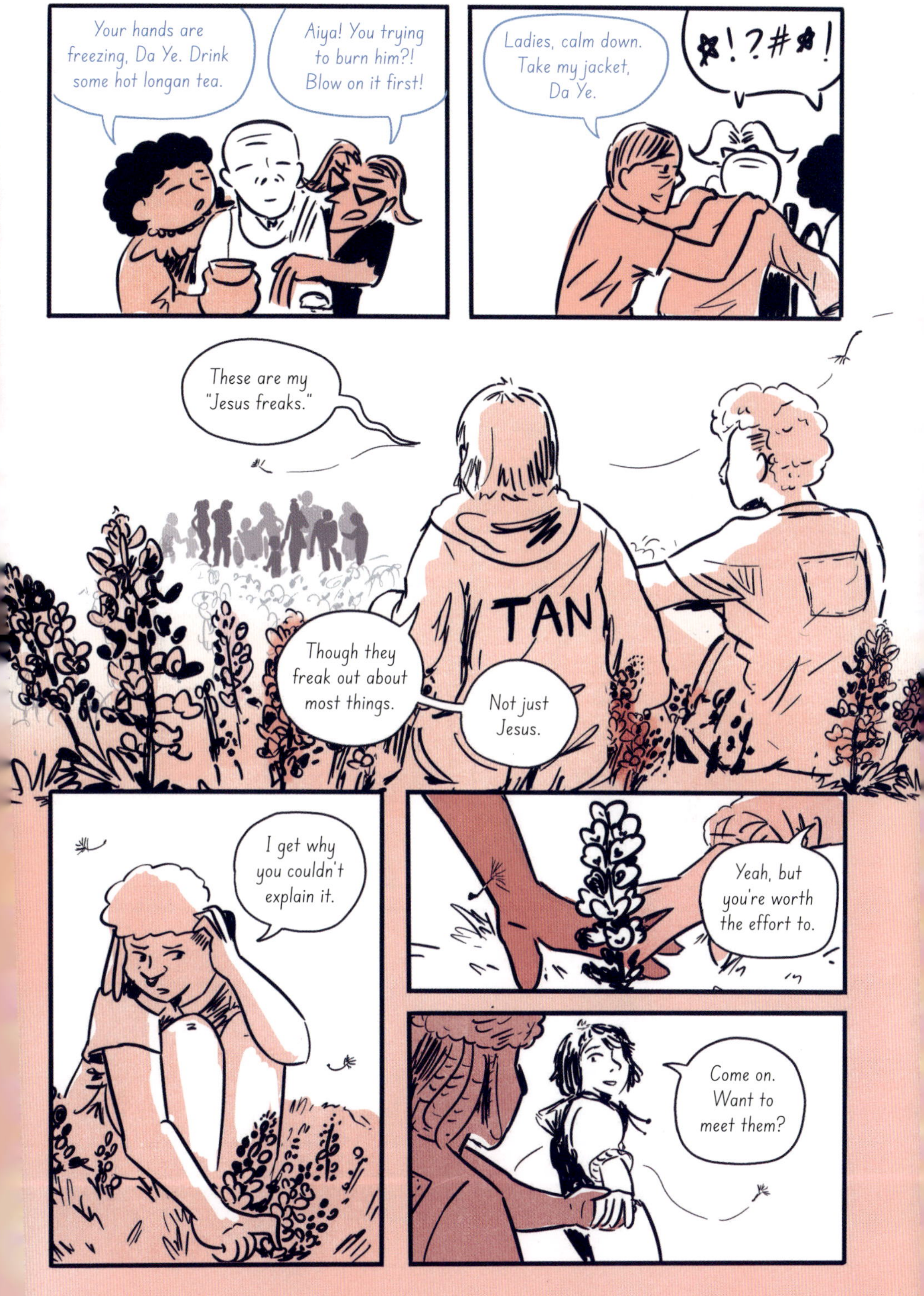

Your hands are freezing, Da Ye. Drink some hot longan tea.
Aiya! You trying to burn him?! Blow on it first!
Ladies, calm down. Take my jacket, Da Ye.
✿!?#✿!
These are my "Jesus freaks."
TAN
Though they freak out about most things.
Not just Jesus.
I get why you couldn't explain it.
Yeah, but you're worth the effort to.
Come on. Want to meet them?

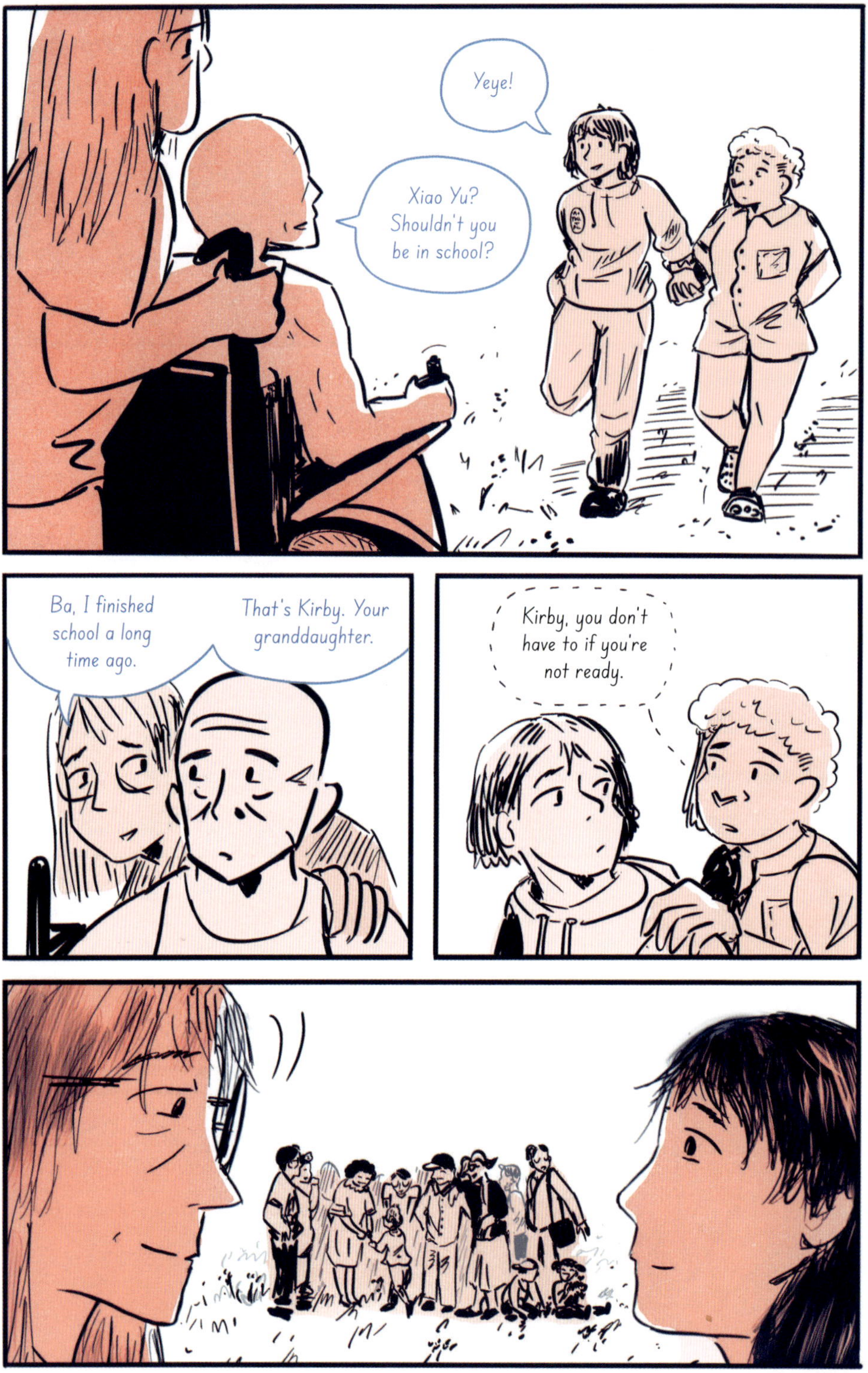
Yeye!
Xiao Yu? Shouldn't you be in school?
Ba, I finished school a long time ago.
That's Kirby. Your granddaughter.
Kirby, you don't have to if you're not ready.

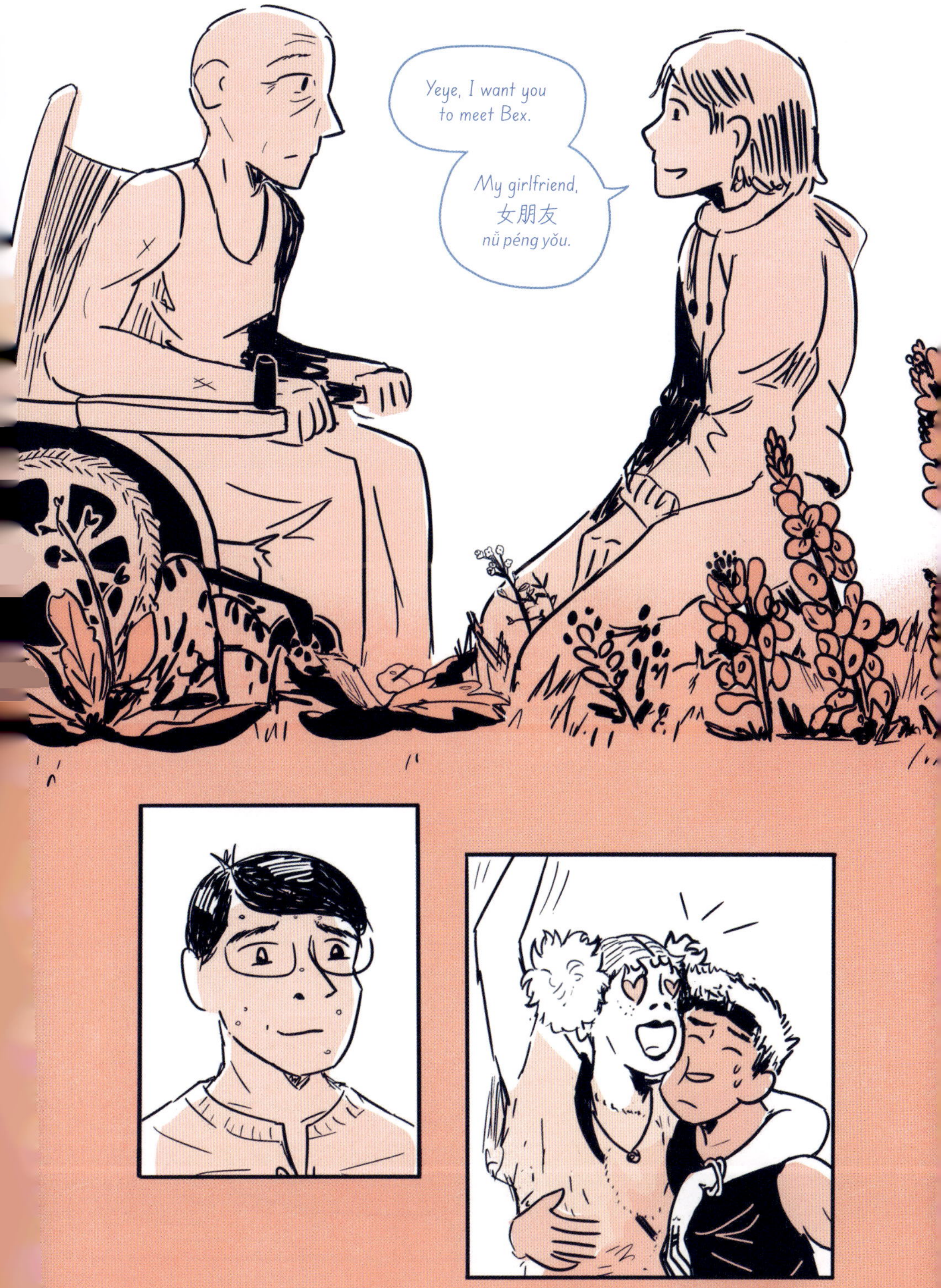
Yeye, I want you to meet Bex.
My girlfriend,
女朋友
nǚ péng yǒu.

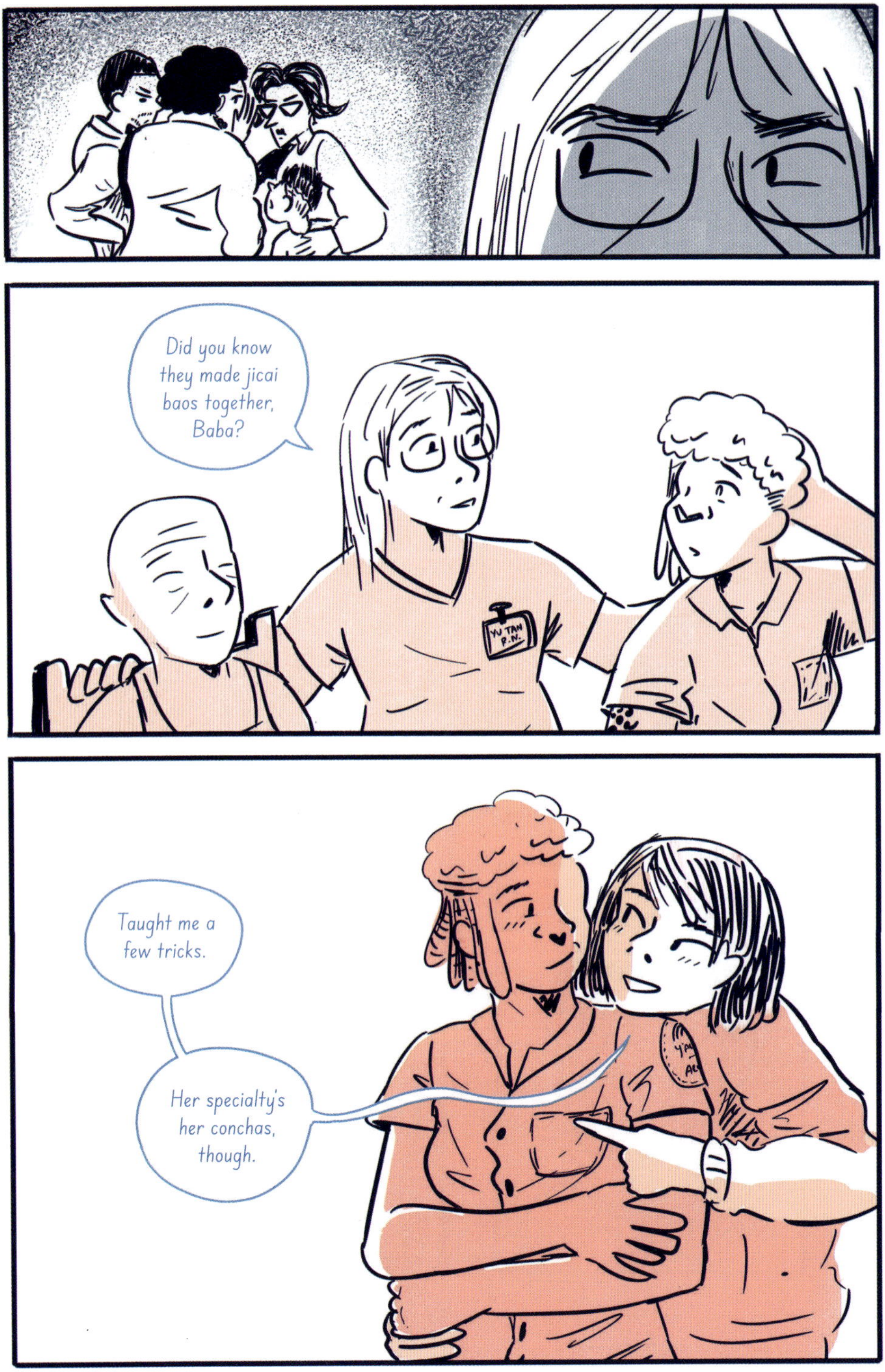
Did you know they made jicai baos together, Baba?
YU TAN R.N.
Taught me a few tricks.
Her specialty's her conchas, though.

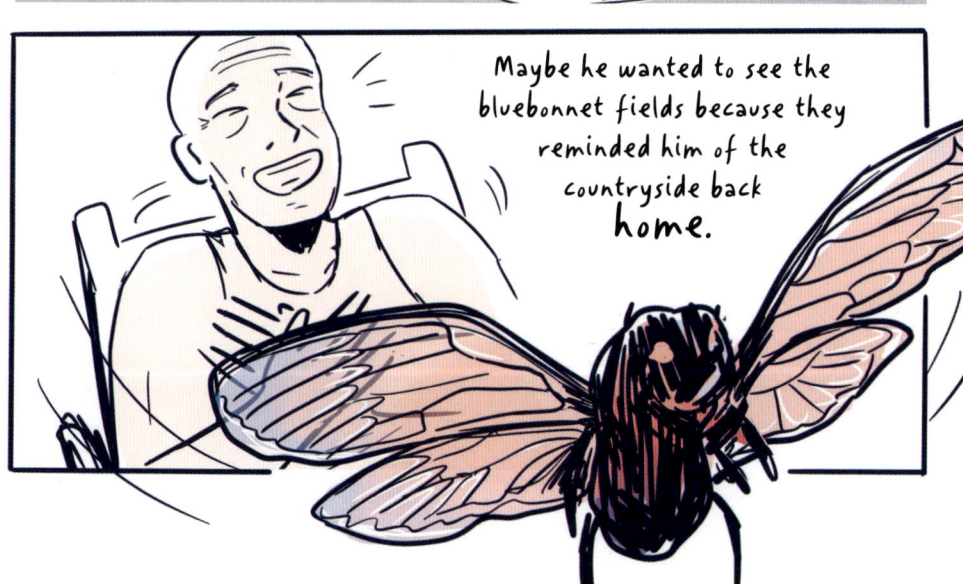

It's hard to say how much of Yeye was there that day.

Maybe he wanted to see the bluebonnet fields because they reminded him of the countryside back **home.**

291

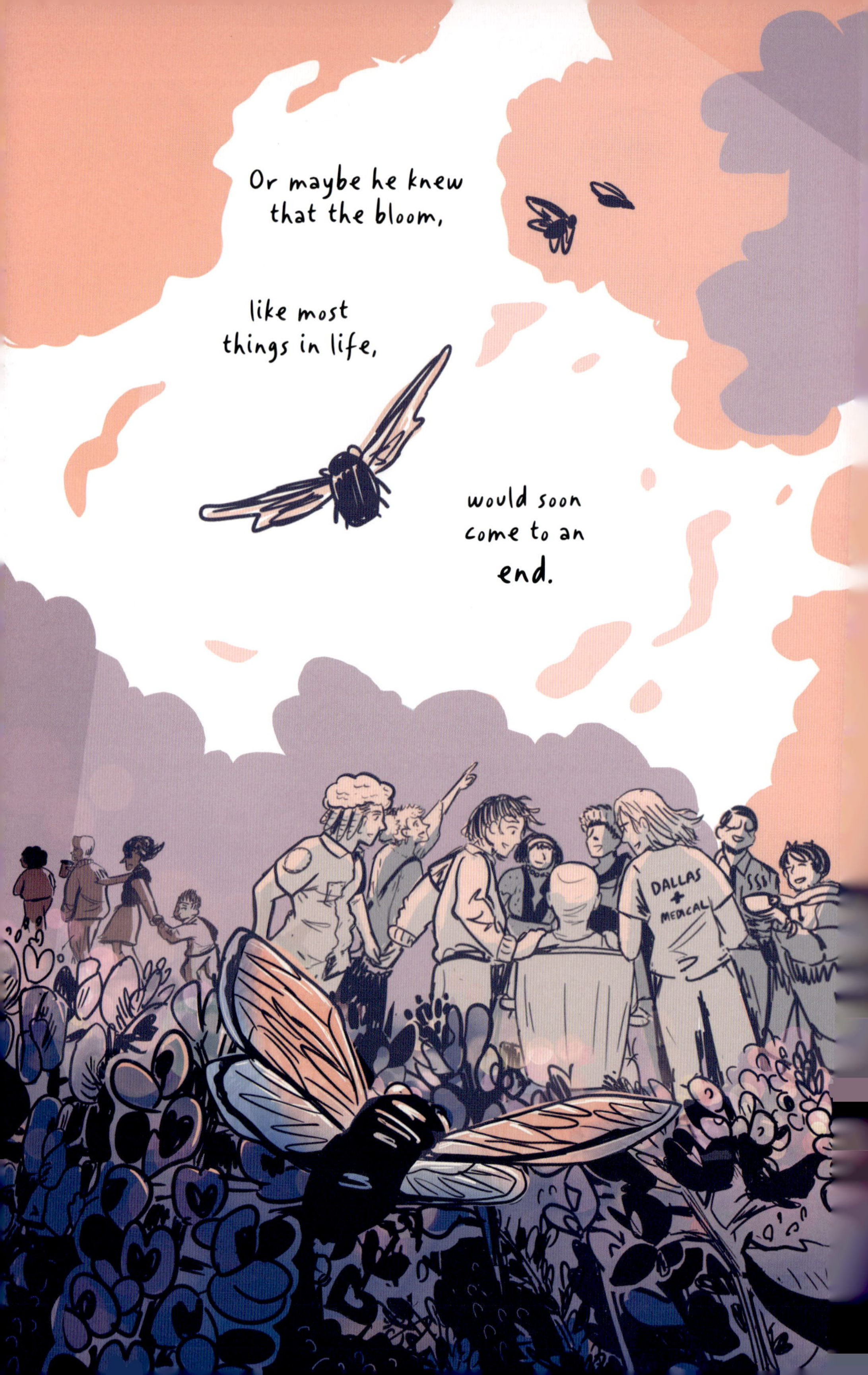
Or maybe he knew that the bloom,
like most things in life,
would soon come to an end.
DALLAS MEDICAL

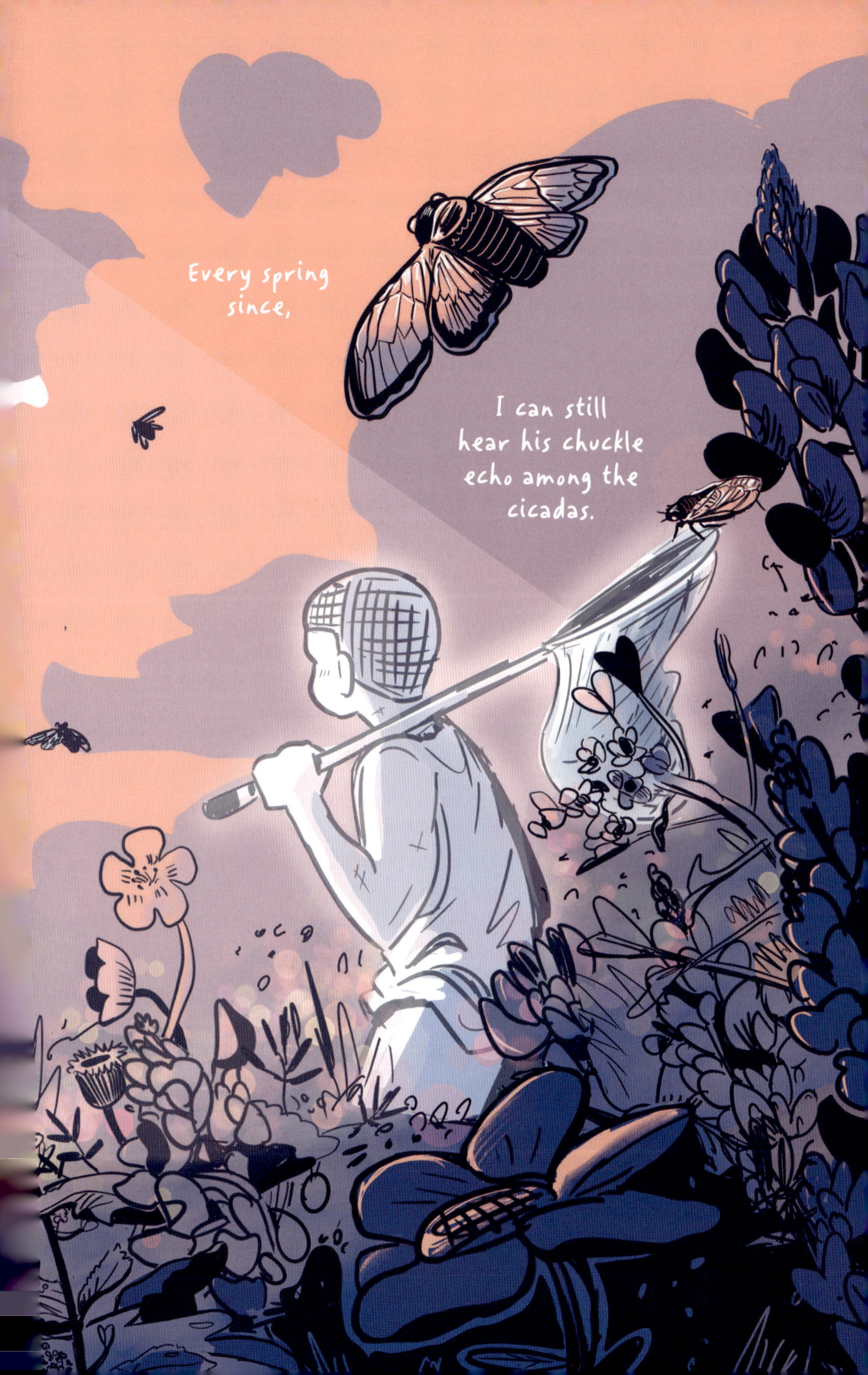
Every spring since,
I can still hear his chuckle echo among the cicadas.

epilogue

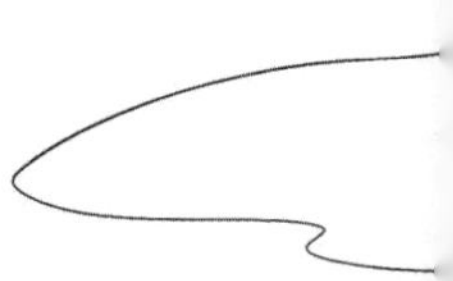

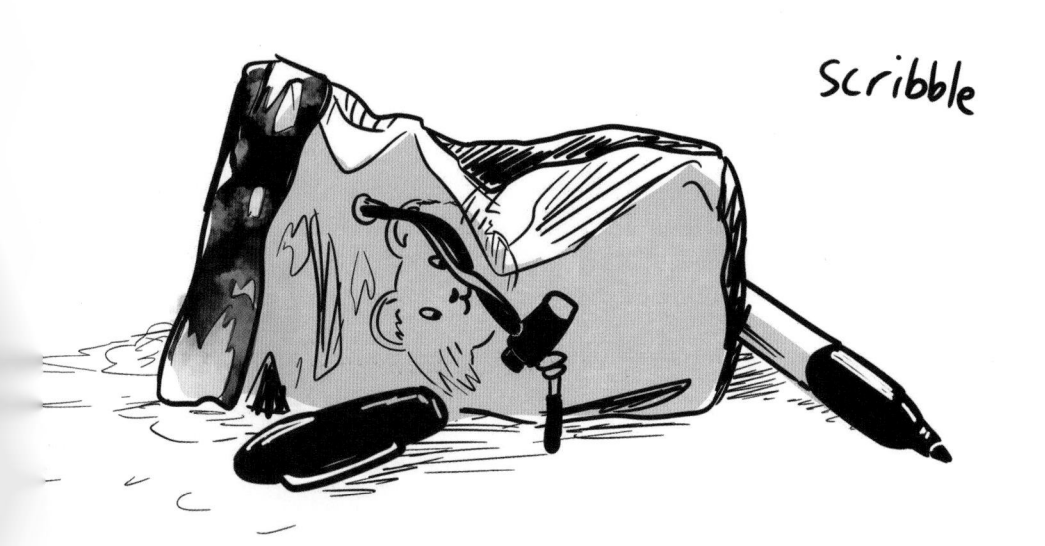

scribble

scribble

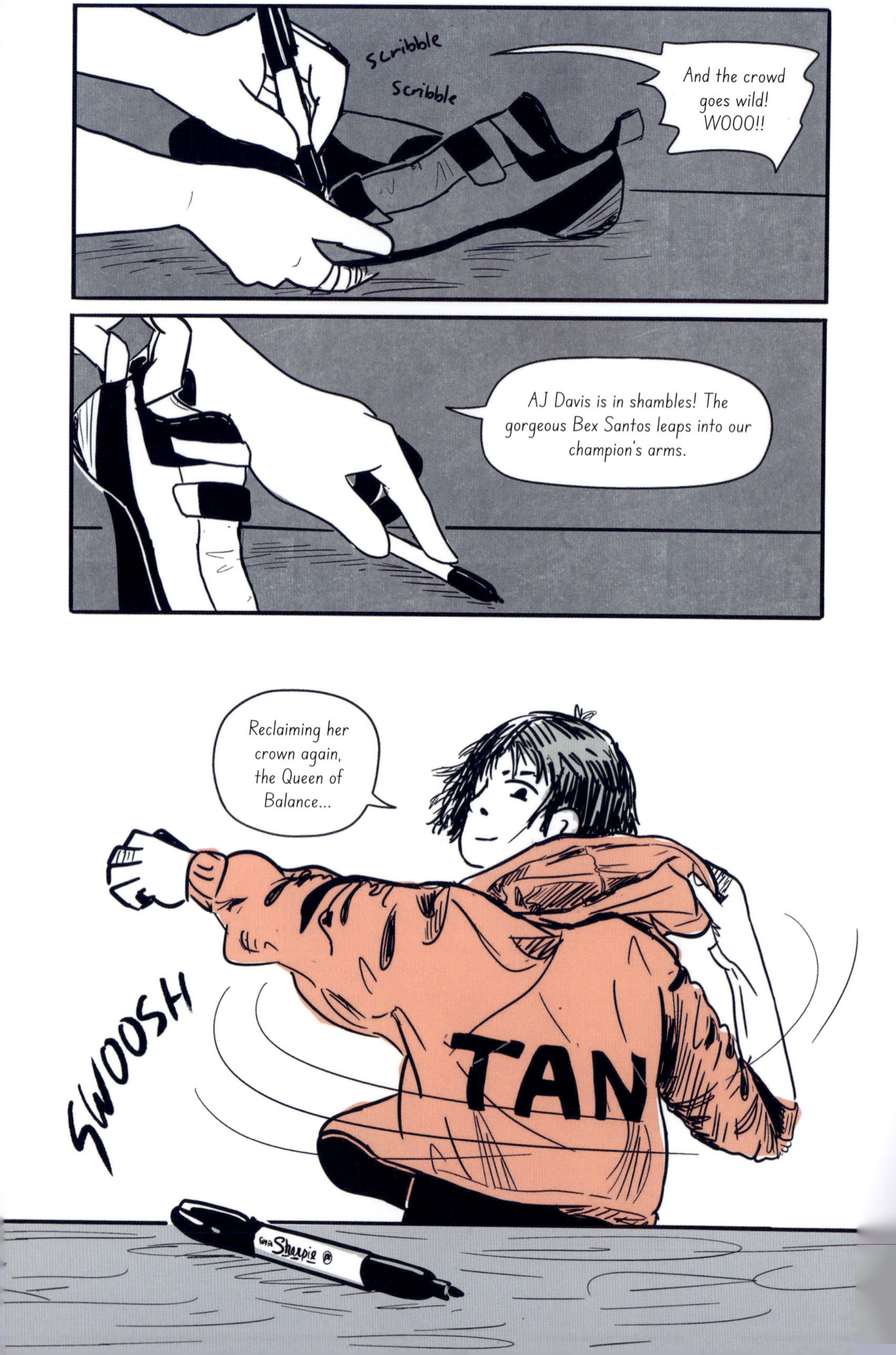
scribble
scribble
And the crowd goes wild! WOOO!!
AJ Davis is in shambles! The gorgeous Bex Santos leaps into our champion's arms.
Reclaiming her crown again, the Queen of Balance...
SWOOSH
TAN
Sharpie

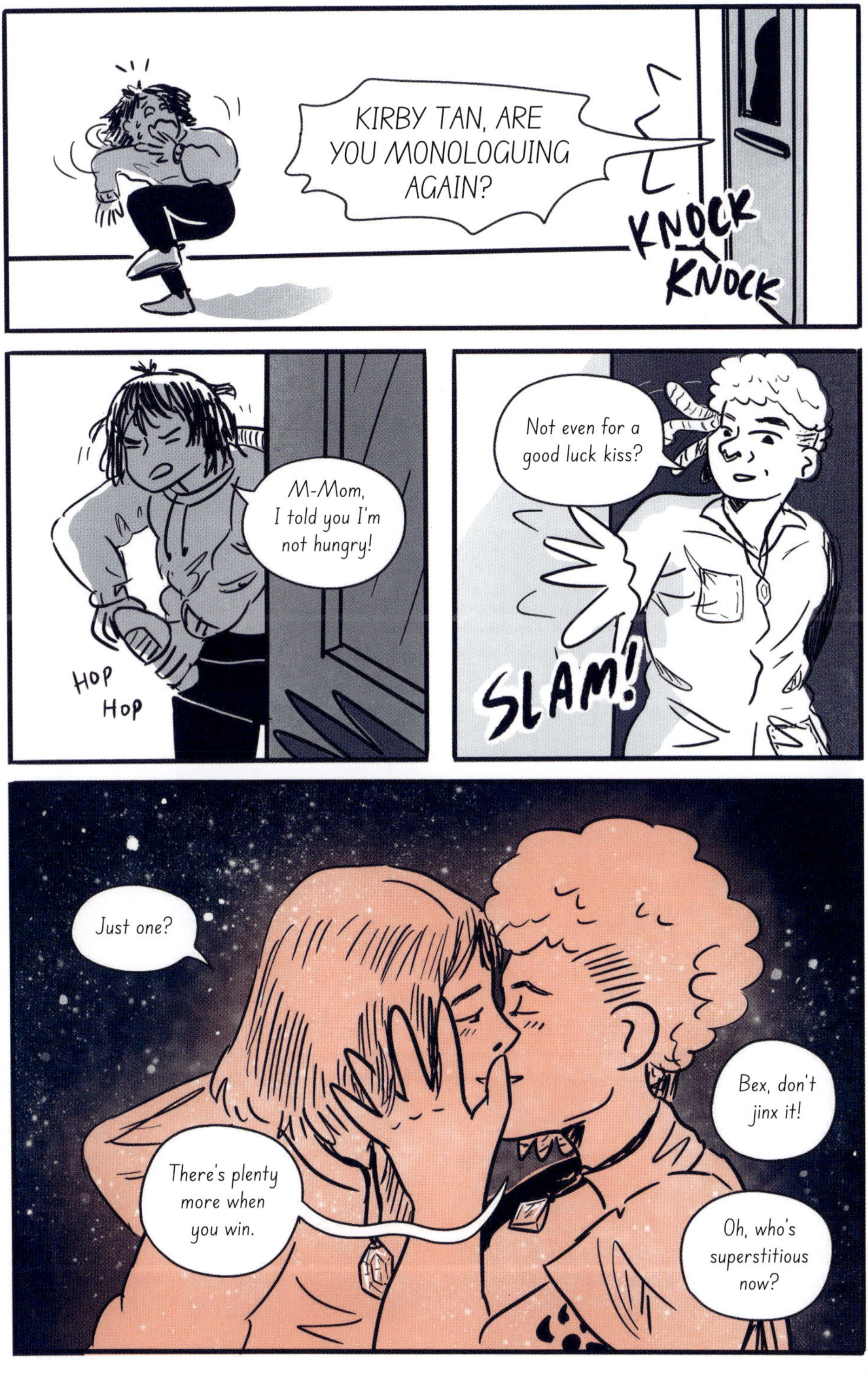
KIRBY TAN, ARE YOU MONOLOGUING AGAIN?
KNOCK KNOCK
M-Mom, I told you I'm not hungry!
HOP HOP
Not even for a good luck kiss?
SLAM!
Just one?
There's plenty more when you win.
Bex, don't jinx it!
Oh, who's superstitious now?

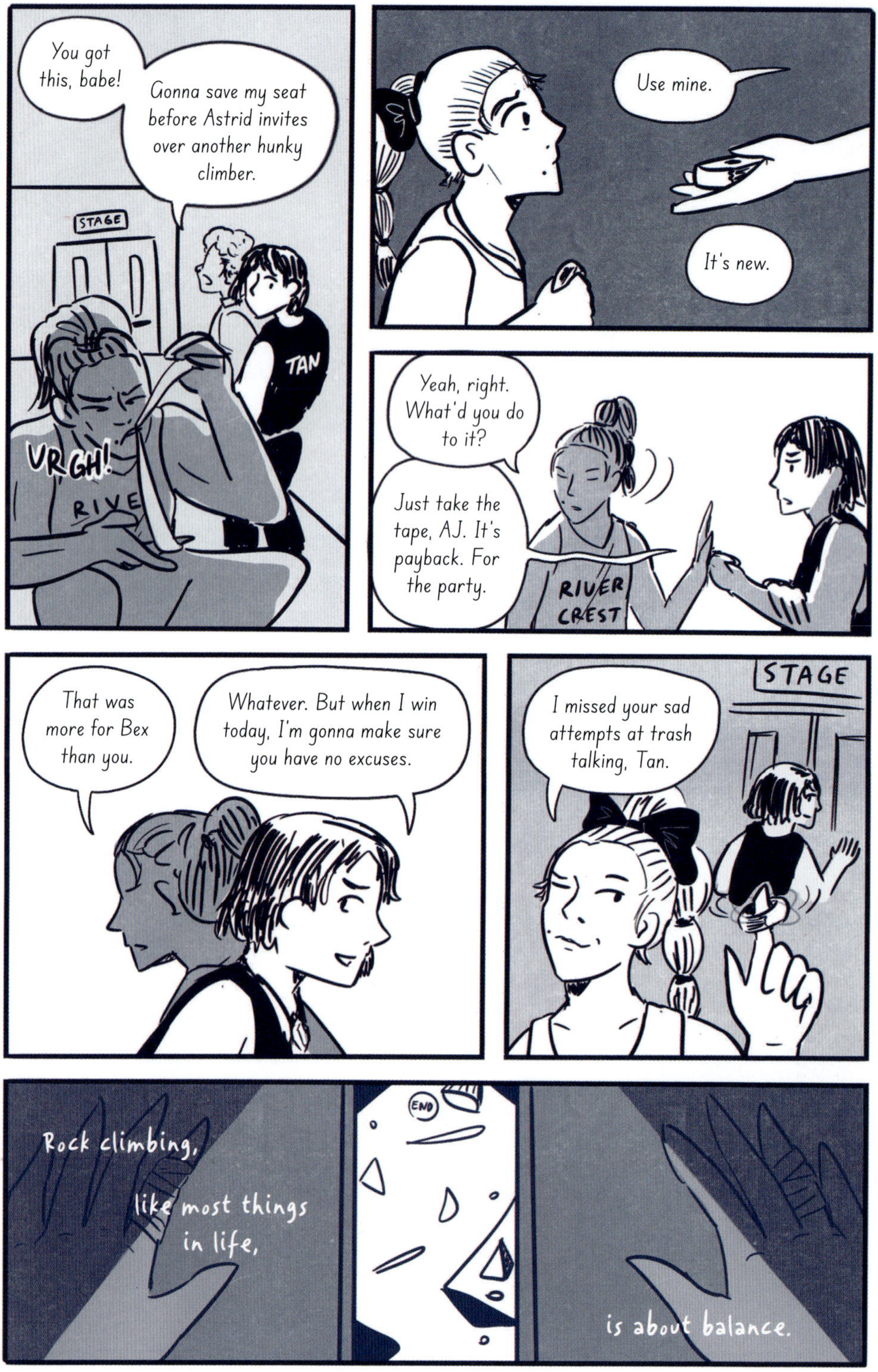
You got this, babe!
Gonna save my seat before Astrid invites over another hunky climber.
STAGE
TAN
VRGH!
RIVE
Use mine.
It's new.
Yeah, right. What'd you do to it?
Just take the tape, AJ. It's payback. For the party.
RIVER CREST
That was more for Bex than you.
Whatever. But when I win today, I'm gonna make sure you have no excuses.
STAGE
I missed your sad attempts at trash talking, Tan.
Rock climbing,
like most things in life,
END
is about balance.

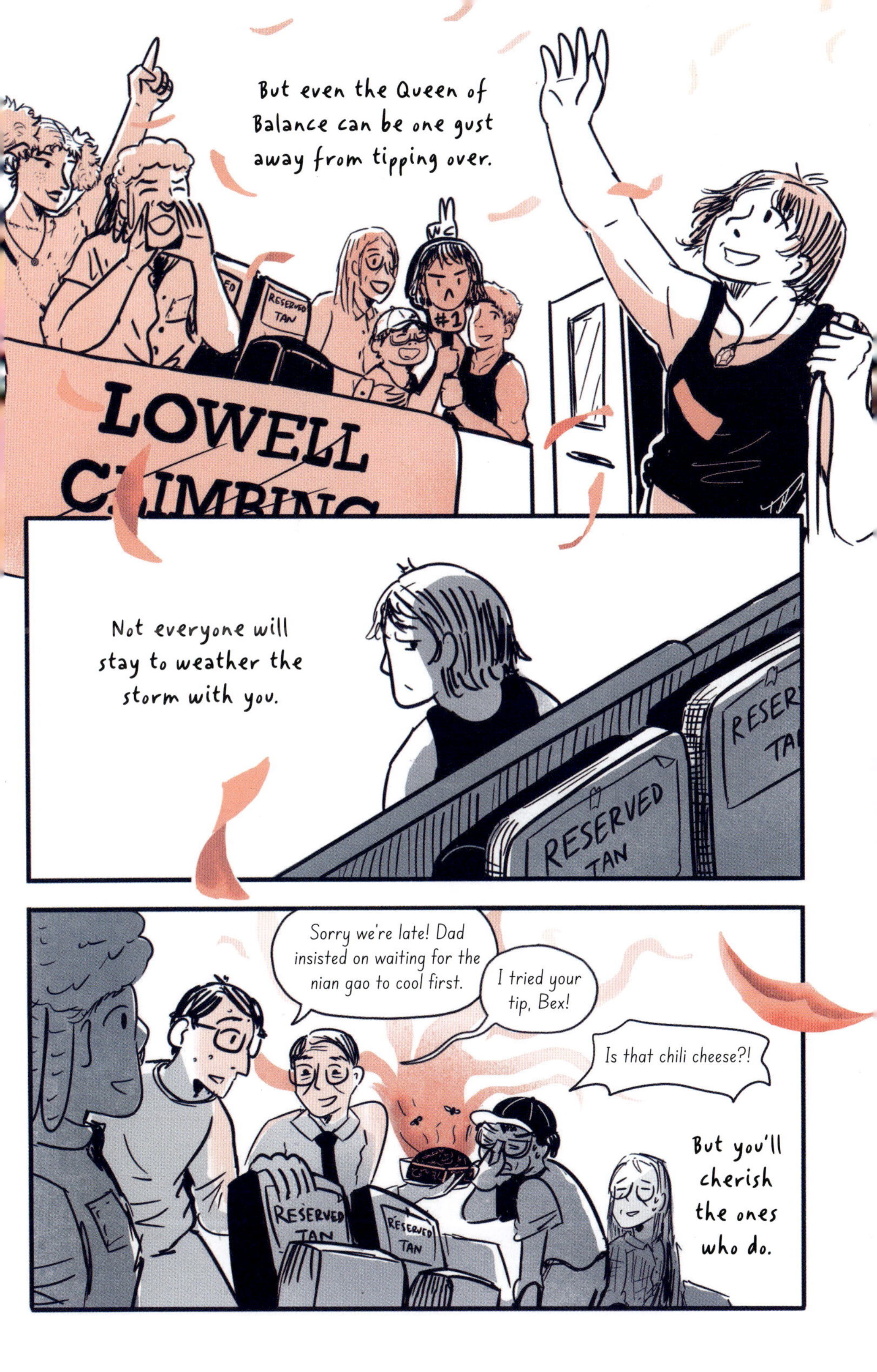

But even the Queen of Balance can be one gust away from tipping over.
LOWELL CLIMBING
RESERVED TAN
#1
Not everyone will stay to weather the storm with you.
RESERVED TAN
Sorry we're late! Dad insisted on waiting for the nian gao to cool first.
I tried your tip, Bex!
Is that chili cheese?!
RESERVED TAN
But you'll cherish the ones who do.

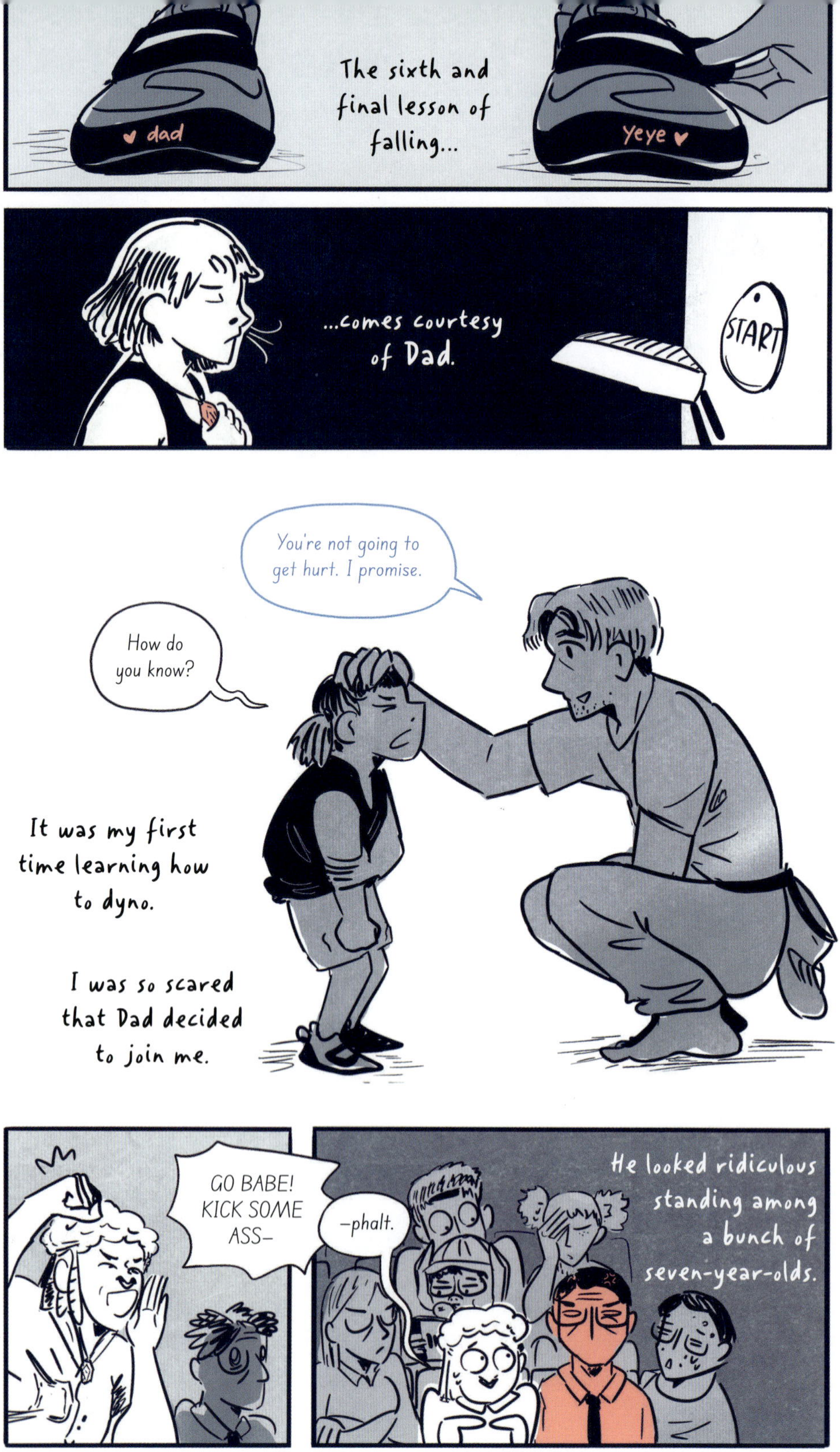

dad
The sixth and final lesson of falling...
yeye
...comes courtesy of Dad.
START
You're not going to get hurt. I promise.
How do you know?
It was my first time learning how to dyno.
I was so scared that Dad decided to join me.
GO BABE! KICK SOME ASS–
–phalt.
He looked ridiculous standing among a bunch of seven-year-olds.

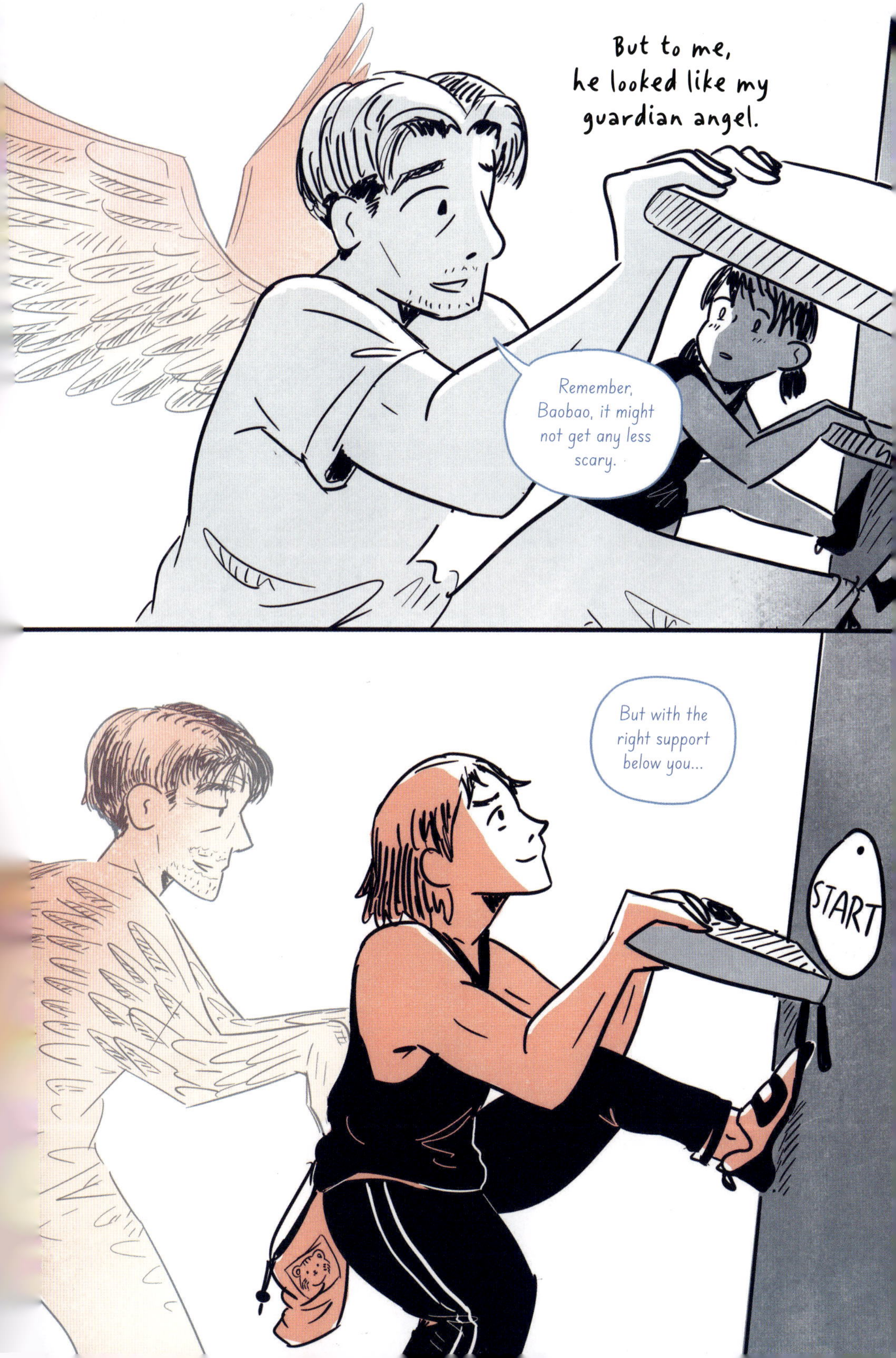
But to me, he looked like my guardian angel.
Remember, Baobao, it might not get any less scary.
But with the right support below you...
START

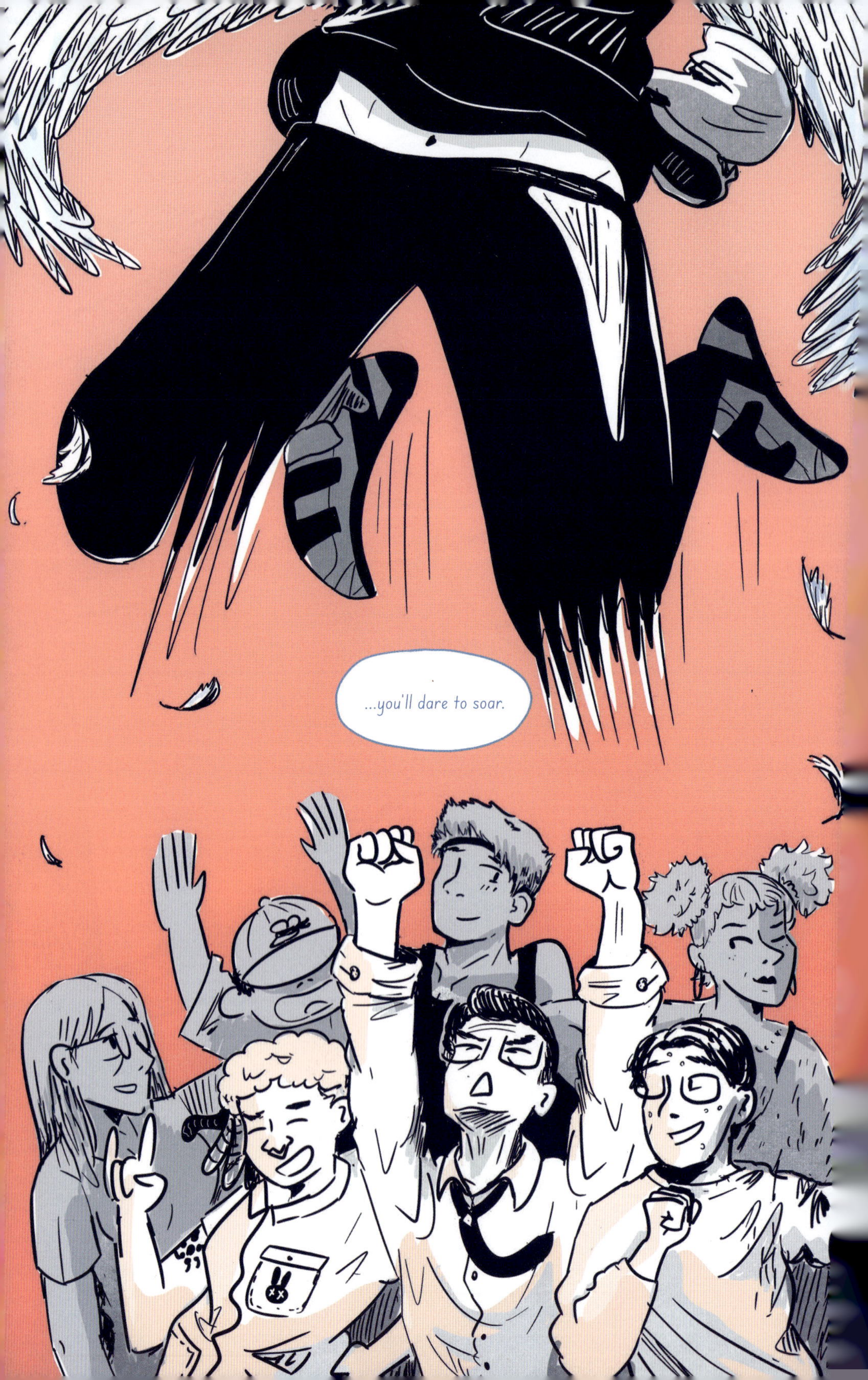
...you'll dare to soar.